THE SERRANO SUCCESSION

Baen Books By
ELIZABETH MOON

THE SERRANO SUCCESSION

BY

ELIZABETH MOON

THE SERRANO SUCCESSION

Change of Command copyright (c) 1999 Elizabeth Moon.
Against the Odds copyright (c) 2000 Elizabeth Moon.

A Baen Book

Baen Publishing Enterprises
P.O. Box 1403
Riverdale, NY 10471
www.baen.com

ISBN 13: 978-1-4391-3289-0

Cover art by Kurt Miller

First Baen printing, September 2009

Distributed by Simon & Schuster
1230 Avenue of the Americas
New York, NY 10020

Library of Congress Cataloging-in-Publication Data

Moon, Elizabeth.
  The Serrano succession / by Elizabeth Moon.
      p. cm.
    ISBN 978-1-4391-3288-3 -- ISBN 978-1-4391-3289-0 (trade pbk.)
   1. Space warfare--Fiction. I. Moon, Elizabeth. Change of command. II.
Moon, Elizabeth. Against the odds. III. Title.
   PS3563.O557S48 2009
   813'.54--dc22
                    2009018225

Printed in the United States of America

10 9 8 7 6 5 4 3 2 1

CONTENTS

CHANGE OF COMMAND

Dedication

For Susie and John Neary,
for all the years of friendship.

Acknowledgements

As always, quite a few people helped with technical bits. Certain parts of this book could not have been written without the help of the fencing group . . . I leave it to them to figure out who contributed which bit of necessary information or advice. David Watson helped choreograph some of the fights and advised on metallurgy, and Kathleen Jones did yeoman work in the structural engineering of a very complicated plot. Susan and Andrew both provided useful information on points of high finance I would never have thought of (stock parking?); Allen helped with naval procedure. Other assistance came from a panel at the Baltimore WorldCon, but unfortunately a computer crash six weeks later robbed me of all the names, email addresses, and even snail-mail addresses (I had put them in the computer, of course . . . and since it was the mail function that crashed . . .) But they have my gratitude, though I can't thank them properly unless we run into each other at another convention. Their input changed one section greatly; remaining mistakes are all mine, including having put their addresses in a computer about to lose its memory so that I couldn't thank them properly.

CHAPTER ONE

Castle Rock

Newscast: "Today the Speaker of the Table of Ministers and the Grand Council of the Familias Regnant was assassinated while en route from the shuttleport to the Palace. His close friend and legal advisor, Kevil Mahoney, was seriously injured and is now undergoing emergency treatment in a secure medical facility. Three security personnel also died. Speaker Thornbuckle's youngest daughter, travelling in a separate conveyance, was not injured, but is now in protective custody. . . ."

Breitis Medical Pavilion

Kevil was aware of disturbing dreams, and tried to fight his way to consciousness. He felt stiff, as if he'd been in the same position too long, and somewhere in the distance someone hurt quite badly. Red and pink swirls slid past his vision; when he blinked, nothing happened but the addition of ugly green smears to the swirls. He thought he heard something, but—like the vague shapes that teased his eyes—the sounds were curiously unhelpful, blunt and unformed.

He struggled harder, and finally made out a voice, speaking some arcane language he didn't know. What was a sub-cue something-or-other? What was an ivy line? His fogged mind tried to show him a picture of ivy leaves lined up in a row.

"—need complete rejuv, if he lives that long—" came suddenly, with silvery clarity.

Ice, then fire, washed through him; he never knew if it was something they did, or his body's response to what he heard. His eyes opened to see a pale blur; he struggled to get his mouth open, then realized it was open, wedged with some instrument.

"Lie still," someone said. "Close your eyes."

He was in no mood to take orders. He gagged on the thing in his mouth, and someone slid it out.

"What happened?" he croaked, in a voice he didn't recognize but felt in his painful throat.

Memory returned in that moment, even as he asked. Even as the people he could not yet see hesitated, he knew what had happened.

He and Bunny in the ground car. Bunny's face, taut and lined for so many months, finally relaxing. They had been chatting about the continuing problems resulting from the Morelline's pharmaceutical plant on Patchcock, the rising price of rejuvenations and the political implications—

And then the white flare of some weapon, and Bunny's face disappearing into a mess of red and pink and gray—

He must be dead. No one could survive that. And he, Kevil Mahoney, was alive—at least for now—because his friend's head had taken the brunt of whatever attack.

The New Texas Godfearing Militia had sworn vengeance on them. Evidently it had been no idle threat.

He needed to know what had happened. Who was in charge now? What was Fleet doing? But he felt a dark chilly fog rising over him, and slipped into that darkness unsure if it was death or a drug.

Hobart Conselline permitted none of the emotions churning inside him to show in his face or demeanor. His secretary's expression of cautious solemnity proved he'd been successful; the silly man couldn't tell how his employer was taking the news. Good.

"It's been confirmed by three separate agencies, milord," his secretary said.

"Terrible!" Hobart said, and shook his head. "I suppose it was those terrorists, in retaliation for the executions—"

"That's the speculation at this time, milord."

"How many were killed or injured?"

"Lord Thornbuckle and three security personnel killed; Ser Mahoney is alive but in critical condition. He is not expected to live."

"A terrible, terrible situation." Hobart shook his head again. Terrible for some, certainly. Bunny Thornbuckle's relatives and friends were no doubt reeling in shock and confusion. So would the whole Council be, if someone didn't take hold and give the guidance that had been so sorely needed for the past several years. If Kevil Mahoney had been uninjured, they might have turned to him, but without either Bunny or Kevil, the Familias would mill about like panicky sheep, baaing uselessly at the wolfpack around them. He knew exactly what far-sighted, strong, decisive leader should take charge.

"Send our condolences to Miranda," he told his secretary. "Inform my wife's secretary that I'm sure my wife will want to call on her." Poor, beautiful, clever Miranda, so unlucky in her choice of men and her children.

Poor Brun, for that matter. Like everyone who had met the child, he had enjoyed her scatterbrained, madcap beauty. She had needed a good husband to settle her down, but Bunny had insisted on letting her run wild, with disastrous results. Another instance of Bunny's lamentable lack of decisive, firm leadership. Nothing like that had happened to the Conselline daughters, nor ever would. Bunny's older children had turned out well enough, though young Buttons was no second Bunny. He had all his father's stuffiness and none of his father's brilliance. All the better; the last thing the Consellines needed was another Bunny Thornbuckle in that Chair.

"You have messages from several of the Families," the secretary said.

"No doubt," Hobart said. Those he had been talking to, in preparation for the Grand Council meeting this year, would want to know his plans now. For an instant, the internal vision of those plans blinded him to the room around him. With Bunny and Kevil Mahoney out of the picture—with Bunny's supporters in disarray, shocked and grieving—a man who knew what he wanted and moved quickly and decisively might go farther than he had believed possible.

He glanced over the messages as his secretary left the room. As he'd expected: shock, concern, fear, shock . . . with every passing moment, he felt more certain that he, and he alone, would have to act in this crisis. How fortunate that he had not left Castle Rock with the others. "Make a list of all the Chairholders who are still onplanet," he said. His secretary nodded. "And set up a conference call for the Conselline Sept, all chairholding members."

"Sir, I have the list—I keep a current file on all the Chairholders—"

"Excellent." He looked over it carefully while his secretary was arranging the complicated linkage of ansible and ordinary communications lines for the conference call, and realized that the opportunity would never be greater.

The Barraclough Sept, which included the lesser Aranlake and Padualenare septs, had not rallied to Bunny's side when Brun returned. The Aranlakes, with the exception of Lady Cecelia de Marktos, had supported an Aranlake candidate, Hubert Roscoe Millander, for Family head, and they'd lost. They were home sulking. The Padualenares favored Bunny's brother Harlis, who supported their claim to seniority over the Aranlakes, and their ambitions in the colonial worlds. This left only a few of the Barracloughs themselves onplanet, those closest to Bunny and therefore more likely devastated by his death.

Hobart glanced around the room, his gaze roaming from one proof of his eminence to another. Would *his* family be devastated if he were assassinated? Delphine would be; she could cry and cry until her pretty face was all swollen and splotched with ugly color. The girls would cry, but only for awhile, he was sure. They would look for another patron, another source of favor and another dispenser of luxuries. Fickle, that's what women were, unless you trained them well, as he had trained Delphine. The boys, though—if he had brought them up well, they would be planning already how to avenge him, and how to gain more power.

But he would not be assassinated. He would be more careful than Bunny, more alert to covert threats, less—not less *brave*, but less foolhardy. Brun had no doubt got her foolhardy genes from him, not from prudent Miranda.

His excitement mounted as he went on through the list. If he had had Bunny killed—and the thought had crossed his mind more than once, in the year when it seemed that nothing else would get that great fool out of an office he was unfit to fill—he could not have chosen a better time. Best of all, he hadn't done it himself; he'd had nothing to do with it. Fate had finally come over to his side. He had proven himself capable of succeeding against the worst Fate could do, and now Fate—womanlike—had chosen him for that very energy and persistence and will to triumph.

He closed his eyes a moment, allowing himself the luxury of imagining the moment when he took over as Speaker—when the faces which had ignored or turned away turned to him—*had* to turn to him—and he could finally show his true abilities. *I will make the Familias great, and everyone will know who saved it from destruction.*

R.S.S *Gyrfalcon*

"I didn't know they would take it out of *my* pay," Ensign Barin Serrano said. His voice almost squeaked, but he couldn't help it. His entire paycheck, gone . . . *nothing* in his credit cube, and he'd already ordered the traditional engagement and wedding gifts.

"Well, who did you think would pay for it? Those people have already used up the Sector discretionary fund, and most of the recreational reserve. And they're not even charging you for all of them, just the ones your pay will cover."

"Ten dependents . . ." Barin murmured. That would eat up all his pay after he was promoted, too. He supposed he should count himself lucky that Fleet regulations prohibited official indebtedness. "And I'm not even married. How could they do this to me?"

"Look at it this way, sir—it'll keep you out of trouble."

"No . . . not really. I've just sent in my order for the wedding . . ."

"Well, sir—"

"Attention all hands . . . attention all hands . . ." A pause, during which Barin tried to think how to get himself out of his present financial fix. Then the captain's voice: "It is my sad duty to announce that the Speaker of the Table of Ministers has been assassinated. Stand by . . ."

Barin stared at the chief, who stared back. The Speaker assassinated? Where? How?

And what would happen to Brun, and all those women?

R.S.S. *Shrike*

"Lieutenant Suiza, there's a flash priority message, Cobalt encryption."

"Ummm . . ." Esmay Suiza's mind had drifted, as it did often these days, to Barin. "Right—well—keep a link to the ansible and I'll get the captain." The last priority message had been medical, directing them to relieve senior NCOs with rejuv of duty, but they had none aboard. Maybe this one would be useful. What she wanted was a message from Barin, preferably with a friendly reaction from his family. Being on two different ships really hampered communication; she hoped they could meet in person for a few days. Captain Solis knew she was due leave; he had already said she could take the time off. But she'd heard nothing. . . .

Captain Solis, never talkative this early in first shift, became even more silent after the encrypted message had gone to his console. Esmay glanced over. "Sir?"

"I . . . said nothing, Lieutenant." He met her eyes. "Lord Thornbuckle is dead. Assassinated. Presumably—" his gaze dropped to the readout of the decryption device. "Presumably it's the New Texas Militia, in retaliation for our execution of their Rangers." A pause, during which Esmay did her best not to ask the question that hammered at her mind. He answered it anyway. "Lieutenant, you can count on all leaves being cancelled. I'm sorry. There are some things more urgent than a wedding."

"It won't hurt to do the paperwork," Esmay said, without thinking. Solis gave her a long look, but finally nodded.

"Good idea. Then if you get the chance . . . but in the meantime, I want a threat assessment . . . get started on that while I make the announcement to the crew."

Altiplano

Newscast: "General Casimir Suiza announced today that the Landbride Suiza is planning to marry an outlander, Barin Serrano, also an officer in the Regular Space Service. Opposition to any such outlander marriage is expected from the Landsman's Guild; questions have already been asked about the succession, in view of the fact that Landbride Suiza continues to reside offworld and serve in the Regular Space Service. In other news, the Speaker of the Table of Ministers has been assassinated on Castle Rock . . ."

**Guernese Republic
General News Service**

Newscast: " . . . of more concern is the threat of renewed violence from the New Texas Militia branches which were not destroyed by the Familias Regnant in their extravagant attempt to rescue the Speaker's daughter. Questions have been raised in Parliament about the involvement of Guernesi intelligence personnel in that attempt, and whether such cooperation with the Familias Regnant compromised Guernesi interests . . ."

Memorandum to the Chair of the Benignity:
Whatever the Familias Regnant hoped to gain by attacking the Texan Militia, and despite the successful extrication of the Speaker's daughter, they will find they have poked a hornet's nest. Although it is tempting to take advantage of this, I believe that any contact with the Militia would endanger our longstanding policy, and would risk alienating the Holy Father.

Our intelligence reports indicate continuing and widening splits between the ruling elements, however, which might well be exploited without entangling us with the New Texans. Project Dance has provided the most accurate assessments so far of the behaviors of major Familias septs. Project Retainer is showing a profit, and the latest data indicate that some 15–23% of the R.S.S. senior NCO corps will be severely affected within another 180 days, with peak incidence at 250–300 days. Three independent sources confirm early failure beginning over 300 days ago. It is somewhat surprising that the Familias have not cut back manufacture and distribution of the drugs . . .

Memorandum to the Admiral of the Fleet:
At the request of the Table of Ministers and the Grand Council, all ships not on high-alert status will maintain one minute of silence at 1200 hours on the day of Lord Thornbuckle's funeral, and no other recognition shall be given; specifically there shall be no salute of arms.

"One minute of silence in respect for the Speaker of the Grand Council."

Silence dragged on. Longer than a minute, it felt like. Esmay wondered how Brun was holding up. She had not had time to recover from her captivity, and already she had lost her father. Esmay murmured prayers she had not thought of in years.

Memorandum to the Chief of Personnel,
from the Chief, Medical Services:
Urgent you refer all enlisted personnel who received rejuvenation treatment within the past ten years to medical immediately. Make no exceptions. If necessary, refer in order of rejuvenation.

Admiral Vida Serrano, now securely in command of Sector Seven, read the memorandum in silence, very aware of the tension in Master Chief Valdos' shoulders. She herself had forwarded the concerns of Barin and Captain Escovar about mental deterioration in senior enlisted personnel, under the tightest security. She had followed the subsequent medical investigation, but the details eluded her. Rejuvenation neurobiology was not her field. She needed to be briefed on it, and so far—despite several increasingly firm requests to Fleet Headquarters—no such briefing had taken place.

How could she reassure Valdos, and others under her command, without the information she needed?

What would happen if she couldn't?

"Get me the heads of personnel and medical," she said. "We have a situation I don't fully understand, and I want to be sure we handle this with both discretion and fairness."

"Sir." A pause. "If the admiral permits—"

"Go ahead."

"Is it true they're looking for ways to bump out senior NCOs, an excuse not to offer any more rejuvenations?"

Just the kind of ideas she did not want floating around. But was it true?

"In my opinion, Chief—and it's only my opinion, but I do have some data—this may have to do with medical problems from a bad batch of rejuv drugs."

"Problems."

"Yes. I am not going to blacken anyone's name, because I don't know all the facts. I'm not a medical officer. I do know that investigation of something else revealed a source of contaminated rejuv drugs, and there was concern that they might have made it into our supply chain. Meanwhile, several senior NCOs began showing neurological symptoms within a few months to a year of each other—widely separated in their duty stations, and not all in the same branch."

"Could they—have given us bad drugs, to justify later refusal to rejuv?"

"On purpose?" He nodded. "Absolutely not. If that's what happened, I suspect it is a simple mistake—or, if not, an enemy wished to deprive us of our most valuable senior NCOs in order to make a strike easier."

"I hope you're right, sir." He went out, shaking his head.

She hoped she was right, too . . . and that he believed her. If the NCOs started worrying about whether they had been given bad drugs intentionally, the close-knit community of Fleet could unravel with fatal speed.

Internal Memorandum, MorCon Pharmaceuticals:
. . . despite the best efforts of our advertising departments to restore confidence in our product, the market share
is still severely depressed compared to the 68% dominance of
the market we enjoyed before the Patchcock scandal. Our
competitors have taken full advantage of revelations about

the inferior quality of our product, and our legal staff tells us that litigation is still increasing. This has severely affected profits, which used to make up over 20% of the total for the Conselline Sept. Non-political means of recovery have been ineffective; we need legislative relief from laws that are crippling our attempt to deal fairly and honestly with the consequences of the errors made by others. We feel it is imperative that some means be found to regain market share. Lady Venezia Morrelline continues to oppose this, and we have been unable to convince her that we cannot be held responsible for the acts of sabotage by a foreign agent. . . .

Regular Space Service
Military Prison,
Stack Islands, Copper Mountain

On a cold, windy day in local autumn, the prisoners of Stack Islands Military Prison were drawn up in ranks to witness another change of command ceremony from behind barriers of both steel and invisible force shields. In front of it, in the small enclosed parade ground, all but a few of the guards were also in formation, uneasily aware of the prisoners' gazes fixed on their backs. No matter that a force shield lay between them; nothing protected them from the malevolence.

Up in front, Iosep Tolin relinquished his command to Pilar Bacarion with relief. He had not enjoyed any moment of his stay in that exile from his former sphere of power, and he had agreed to take early retirement to get quit of it. Pilar, though—he would be very glad to put the width of the Big Ocean, and later some deepspace, between himself and one of the few women who had ever been close to Admiral Lepescu.

On her part, Commander Pilar Bacarion felt an almost physical surge of pleasure in the tension on Tolin's face. He not only disliked her, he was afraid of her. He should be. They all should be, and they *would* be, in time. She smiled at Tolin, letting him see that she recognized his fear, and saw the glisten of sweat on his forehead, even in the cold. Then she released him from her gaze, and turned it instead on her subordinates.

They did not flinch. She had not thought they would. Their gaze challenged her—the first female commander this prison had ever had. Was she tough enough, their gaze asked. Could she do the job? Others—whose identities she already knew—had no doubts about her toughness. They were well aware that Lepescu had been her mentor, that she had supported his agenda. Carefully disguised in her duffle were slivers of the ears she had taken; when it had become imprudent to keep these proofs of her status, she had sliced them thin herself and found hiding places for them.

She had Hunted, in the oldest Hunt of all; she had killed. She had survived the Hunt on Sirialis, having left to take command of a ship before the game ended with Lepescu dead and Heris Serrano once more in favor with Fleet brass. But no one knew it. They were all dead, and the prisoners she'd hunted had never seen her face. Her luck was strong, and her skills—she would match her skills against Serrano directly some day; she knew she would win.

She looked past the guards, past the force screen, to the prisoners in their drab ranks. In there she also had potential allies. In time.

Tolin left at last, in the whining aircar. She wished him a nasty storm on the way to the mainland, but it didn't really matter. Let him live—and let him realize someday just what he'd seen, in their brief exchange.

The ceremony over, Pilar summoned her staff. They were unwise enough to look surprised; she allowed herself a tight smile on the way to her office, thinking how soon they would learn what she was like.

On the mainland, at Main Base, autumn had not yet moderated a brutally hot summer. It had been a dry year, and now fine reddish dust turned the sky dirty brown as the wind lifted it high into the atmosphere.

In this kind of weather, everyone who could get offbase privileges spent hours in Q-town's bars, drinking whatever was coldest. Even combat veterans accepted the crowd in their favorite watering hole. It was too hot, and too miserable, to complain.

Margiu Pardalt, newly graduated from the Academy, and the only Xavierine in her class, had a habit of coming tops in her classes.

She had to; she had to do something to make up for her sister Masiu, killed by raiders years ago. Masiu had been the family genius: brilliant, brave, everything a family could hope for. Margiu was second-best, and knew it—a poor replacement for the fallen hero—so it was up to her to make her mark, to be Masiu's memorial. Her place in the Academy had been a gift from the Familias in memory of Masiu. Her place in the universe was to be her gift in return.

She had earned an evening's liberty by coming first in her class yet again at Copper Mountain, and she thought it fitting that her free hours came at a time when no rational person could enjoy them. She'd have stayed in her quarters, but her training CO had told her to get off the base—and orders were orders.

Another gust of wind howled down Q-town's main street and filled her nose with hot stinging dust. She sneezed, and her eyes watered. It reminded her too much of the Benignity's scorch of Xavier, when she and her family had wrapped torn sheets around their heads for weeks to filter the dust and ash.

Ahead, on the right, she spotted a doorway just opening as someone came out, and a gush of cooler air brushed her side. She turned into it.

It was only moderately crowded—less crowded than the two bars she'd glanced into and left—and smelled of food as much as drink. Margiu made her way to one of the open booths, and slid in, then looked around. The tables and seats looked a little strange, until she realized they were meant to look like ship parts. No, they *were* ship parts. Her quick glance took in the long dark bar—obviously hull material. The models—obviously military vessels. The battle honors hung on the walls, the photographs.

It was a shrine, then. Margiu felt obscurely comforted, and lowered her head to pray for the dead and the survivors alike. Her family were Synorhines; she had learned the right forms for valediction and commemoration from early childhood.

"Do you need help?" someone asked. Margiu looked up to find herself face to face with a man in a float-chair.

"No, sir—I was honoring the dead," she said.

His brows rose, crinkling the skin around the scars on his bald scalp. "You knew about this place?"

"No, sir . . . but it's obvious."

"Hmm. May I have the honor of your name?"

"Ensign Pardalt," she said. "From Xavier."

"Ah. Xavier." He looked her over carefully. "And you were at the Academy when—"

"No, sir. I was home . . . on Xavier, I mean." She knew already that to Fleet personnel, Fleet was home, and the planet of origin was just that—the planet of origin.

"And you survived the Benignity—your family as well?"

"Most of them."

"You're welcome here anytime, Ensign. You've earned it."

But she hadn't earned anything. Not yet. The way she saw it, everything she had, Masiu had earned. Still, she was not going to contradict someone like this, a combat veteran.

"Thank you," she said instead. And then, carefully, hoping she'd read the signals right, "May I offer you a drink?"

She saw a reaction, but she wasn't sure what. "As it is your first time in my establishment, I hope you will honor me by accepting one."

She dipped her head. "I would be honored." Then, as he waited, she realized he wanted her to name it. She wasn't used to that, but she glanced at the menu display and chose a dark ale spiced with ginger.

When the mug arrived, heavily frosted, it came with a bowl of raw vegetable sticks on shaved ice.

"If you like spiced ales, I thought you might like these," the man said. Margiu nibbled one; it had a refreshing bite. He sipped his own drink, watching her over the rim. She found it disconcerting.

"We had Lieutenant Suiza in here when she was on a course," he said finally.

That name she knew, of course. Suiza had been added to her family's prayers, and she had heard a lot about Suiza in the Academy and after. "I've never met her," Margiu said. "But we owe her a lot."

"You remind me of her," the man said. "She's quiet too."

"She's a real hero," Margiu said. "I'm just a very green ensign."

"You might surprise yourself," the man said.

She did fantasize about that, sometimes, but she knew it was ridiculous. She could be serious, careful, diligent, prudent—and none of those were heroic virtues, as she understood heroism.

Zenebra; *Evening Sports*
with Angh Dior,
Chauncy Network

"Lady Cecelia de Marktos, who returned to competition several years ago on one of the D'Amerosia string, has qualified for the Senior Horse Trials at Wherrin this season on a horse bred at her own stables, Seniority. With the veteran rider/owner up, Seniority won the Challenge Event for rising novices, then the Stavenge. The pair are expected to threaten the reigning champion, Liam Ardahi and the experienced champion Plantagenet, competing under the colors of Orregiemos Combine . . ."

Viewers saw Lady Cecelia's pleasant, bony, somewhat horselike face, beneath rumpled red-gold curls . . . then a shot of her exercising Seniority over fences, the horse's gleaming red coat only a shade darker than her hair, then a shot of them over the last fence of the Stavenge. The video shifted to Liam Ardahi guiding Plantagenet over the Wherrin Trials' B Course big drop-bridge combination the year before, freezing on the instant before landing, while the commentator recited their previous record.

Cecelia grimaced at the display. Like any expert rider, she could find flaws in everything she did, and would have much preferred to have the vid show her over the seventeenth fence—where she and Seniority had made neat work of a difficult combination—than that last fence, where Seniority had jumped flat, and her own hand position showed why. She'd lost concentration for a crucial few seconds.

Why had she been thinking about Pedar Orregiemos and the Rejuvenants, and not Fence Thirty?

Wherrin Equestrian Park

Two days later, Cecelia brought Seniority in from the gallops in exactly the shape she wanted—pulse and respiration had recovered beautifully, and he could have gone another mile without strain. But any more fitness now, and he would peak before the Senior Trials. No, a long hack this afternoon, then tomorrow—

"Cece! Have you heard?" Colum was waiting for her at the entrance to the gallops, as he usually did, but he spoke first.

"What?" She loosened the strap of her helmet, and pushed back under it the one lock of red hair that always managed to get loose and tickle her forehead.

"Lord Thornbuckle's been killed—it's on all the newsvids—"

She felt a heaviness in her chest as if she'd been kicked. "Bunny?" A swift montage of pictures ran through her mind—Bunny at the head of the table, Bunny on horseback on Opening Day of the hunt season, Bunny taking over from Kemtre at the Grand Council, Bunny and Kevil, heads together, discussing something . . . "It can't be—" He was younger than she by twenty-odd years; he was healthy as a horse—

"They say it might be those terrorists."

Reality came back as Seniority reached down to rub his face on his leg, and yanked the reins; Cecelia blinked, looked around, saw the subdued flurry of activity near the barns. The first acid bite of sadness seeped through the shock. If it was true, this was going to hurt a lot. Colum seemed to understand that she could say nothing; he flung a cooler over the horse's back, and put a hand to the rein. Cecelia sat there, as he led Seniority on into the aisle between the barns, where the look on the grooms' faces told her that the newsvids were playing this straight.

"You heard?" That was Roz, her head groom.

"Yes." She slid down, ran the stirrups up, automatically coordinating with the groom as they untacked the chestnut horse and began the after-workout rubdown.

"You knew him, didn't you?"

Already past tense. Cecelia shivered. "Yes. For a long time."

"It's terrible. It said on the news there wasn't even enough left for a neuroscan. No chance—"

She didn't want to hear this; she didn't want to think about this. Her rejuvenated body felt alien suddenly, the reverse of the way she had felt when her young mind lived in her old one . . . now she felt trapped in a body that could not feel what she felt emotionally.

"Do you think they'll cancel the Trials?"

Cecelia looked over at Roz, who flushed in unbecoming splotches. "I doubt it," she said. "They didn't stop the Trials when Kemtre abdicated."

But even as she said it, she felt uneasy. Whether the Trials went on or not, should *she* ride? What was the right thing to do? She paused in her strokes down Seniority's muscled haunch to calculate travel times. She could not possibly make it to Castle Rock for any memorial service, even if she gave up the competition. That being so, what good would it do Bunny for her to withdraw?

What good would it do someone else?

She stood watching as Roz and Gerry began sponging the horse down, wondering why that had come to mind . . . why, at some level, she did not believe that awful milita group had killed Bunny. But who else? And how was she going to find out?

"Cece—" Dale, her trainer, had Max in tow. "I know, it's awful, but you've got to ride this guy."

She wanted to say she couldn't, but she knew she could. And whatever happened to humans, horses needed their unbroken routine. She let a groom give her a leg up onto Max, and headed back to the gallops.

As always, just being on a horse in motion cleared her mind. Max was no Seniority, but he was maturing into a very nice ride over shorter distances, and he would bring a good price when the time came.

If the time came, with Bunny dead. Who knew what that meant politically? She didn't, though she had paid more attention than she used to. Bunny had been a good executive, except perhaps for his frenzy when Brun was taken—a frenzy no one could blame. Things had gone well—her investments had prospered, and if hers prospered then surely the economy was doing well. Except for the volatility in rejuvenation pharmaceuticals, which had pretty much smoothed out this past year. The Consellines had lost face—and market share—but they certainly weren't ruined.

And what about Miranda, and Brun? Would they move back to Sirialis? Would they—she hated the thought that forced itself to the top of her mind—would they still have foxhunting?

That wasn't the important thing, of course—the important

thing was finding out who had killed Bunny and dealing with him. Or her.

Max took advantage of his rider's wandering mind and shied at a rustle in the hedge beside the field. Cecelia caught him before he could bolt, and sent him on firmly. Best think about the horse; that was something she could control. For the rest of the two-hour hack, she managed to keep her sorrow and her worries at bay.

They returned when she handed Max over to the grooms. Roz looked almost as grim as she felt—she had worked two seasons on Sirialis, Cecelia remembered, and had a scrapbook on the Thornbuckle family. "It'll never be the same," she muttered to Cecelia. "Young Buttons is a fine man, but he's not his father."

"No . . . but Kevil will help him."

"He was hurt too, you know. Really bad—he might die."

"Kevil Mahoney?"

"That's what the newsvid said. If you can trust them. Damn those terrorists anyway; I don't know why they have to make more trouble in the world, as if there's not enough."

"Lady Cecelia—" That was Dale, more formal than usual. "You have a caller."

The last thing she wanted. She turned away, leaving Roz and the new girl working on Max, and stripped off her gloves, tucking them in her belt.

He was lounging in the stable office, flipping through the stable feed records.

"Get out of that," Cecelia said, but without much heat. She herself had sneaked a look at the hay receipts for other owners, wondering if they had a better source. Everyone snooped in stable offices.

"You're looking splendid," Pedar Orregiemos said. "Still—terrible news, terrible news."

"Yes, it is." Cecelia sat down heavily in one of the battered leather chairs. "I'm still not really grasping it."

"I came over because I knew you'd been close to both of them," Pedar said.

Cecelia looked up sharply. "Both of them?"

"Bunny and Kevil, I mean. At least, that's what the word was, the past few years. People were even twitting young George about it."

"About me and *Kevil?*"

He shrugged. "And why not?"

"Kevil and I are friends," Cecelia said, almost spitting the words out. "Friends, not lovers." Well, only twice, after which they'd both agreed it wasn't working nearly as well as they'd hoped. "Yes, I spent a lot of time with him after my rejuvenation, because I needed his legal advice to untangle my affairs. But that's all." She was aware of the heat in her face, mixed anger and shame.

"Well, a friend, then. But still . . . I was sure you'd be upset, so I came over to check on you."

Disgusting little climber. Yes, he was rich, and yes, his family was Seated, but he was, compared to her, a minor twig on the very large and ancient Conselline elm . . . her branch of the Aranlake Sept made up a much greater percentage of the even larger and older Barraclough oak.

Cecelia pushed that back down. She wasn't the sort of person who worshipped a family tree; people didn't get to choose their parentage. Pedar's mannerisms, more pronounced in old age and despite several rejuvenations, had been there from the day she first met him, at someone's birthday party. He wanted to be a protector . . . bad luck for him that she didn't need protecting.

"I'm fine, Pedar. I'll be fine—I'll grieve, and then I'll get over it."

"Why don't you let me take you to dinner?"

As so often, the kind impulse that was exactly wrong. "Not tonight, please. I just want to go back and cry a little. Another time, perhaps."

"I'll hold you to it," Pedar said, and bowed politely. *Go away*, Cecelia thought, as loudly as she could while holding a polite smile that made her face ache. He bowed again and left.

She and Bunny had laughed about Pedar, from time to time—trusting each other not to share that fact. His stiff little bows; his exaggerated courtesies; his passion for antique clothing and sports even more useless than foxhunting and eventing.

She would never have Bunny to laugh with again. She would never see that long, foolish face come alight with intelligence, with his quick wit. She would never warm herself at the glow of the love between Bunny and Miranda . . . a love she had watched grow and deepen over the many decades she'd known them both.

Tears ran down her face, and when Dale came back to the office, she was curled into the big chair, and didn't hear him step in, then quietly close the door behind him when he left again.

CHAPTER TWO

Castle Rock, the Old Palace

The day of Bunny's funeral dawned clear and cold. Miranda woke before dawn, and watched the light seep into the eastern sky. She lay still beneath the covers, feeling the weight of them, reluctant to leave that warm nest and face what would be a long and difficult day. Their room—her room—was not cold, but she had not felt warm since that first horrible moment when they'd told her Bunny was dead.

A faint click, then music so soft she could barely hear it—the music she had chosen herself. She reached over and punched up the volume—no sense in that slow crescendo if she was already awake—and threw off the covers in one angry gesture.

Bunny was dead. Nothing would change that, not the music, not the dawn, not whatever mood she was in. Beneath her feet, the carpet was still soft and thick. Around her shoulders, the fleecy jacket warmed her.

Bunny was dead. She was alive, and beautiful (she heard people whispering, and after all it was true) and very, very wealthy.

Faintly, through the closed door, she heard a lusty cry.

Wealthy, and the grandmother of bastards whose fathers were, if not dead, criminals and no doubt partners of those who had killed Bunny.

Miranda had not told Bunny how she felt about those babies. Grandmothers were supposed to have a natural love for grandchildren, but she could not see those boys as anything but vandalism perpetrated on her daughter.

24

Bunny had seen it differently. Bunny had assumed she would love them, if Brun couldn't; Bunny had assumed she would organize their care.

Bunny was dead.

She stood, unable to move for a long moment. It wasn't supposed to be like this. People their age were supposed to be adult, mature, stable . . . they were resigned to loss, said the books she'd read.

She wasn't resigned. She wanted to shake her fist and scream at the sky; she wanted to fall off a cliff and drown. The secret was that the rich had hearts too . . . she had loved Bunny the way girls in romance storycubes loved their heroes, and forty years of marriage had not changed that.

And he was dead.

And she was alive, with children and grandchildren and bastard grandchildren who were not at fault for their fathers' sins, and a daughter still healing from what had been done to her, and all Bunny's hopes and dreams for the peace of the world crashing down around them, shattered.

When her maid knocked, Miranda smiled and calmly accepted a cup of tea, which she drank with perfect composure while her maid ran her bath.

Brun Meager had wakened even earlier, when the twins cried, as they often did, in the middle of the night. They should be sleeping through the night, the nursemaids said, but they hadn't done so more than one night in four since they were taken from Our Texas. And Brun had discovered, to her annoyance, that when they woke, she also woke, even if someone else was doing the feeding and cleaning.

She used the time to exercise, the exercises she never skipped these days. By the time her maid knocked, she had already worked herself into a sweat, and showered herself back to normal. In the mirrors of the bath, her face stared back at her, strange after nearly two standard years without a mirror . . . an older face, a harder face, but—in spite of everything—a face of memorable beauty.

Something would have to be done about that . . . but not today. Today she would walk with her mother, her brothers, her older sister, in the funeral procession; today she would hold her head high in the face of the universe. They had forced her to bear their children. They could not force her to hide.

Palace Security, Castle Rock

Colonel Bai-Darlin had not slept all night. Organizing a state funeral had always been—would always be—a nightmare of protocol and endless complicated detail, but ordinarily a state funeral was not mixed with a top-level security concern. Even when a head of state was assassinated, that usually ended the threat. Only 23.87 percent of political assassinations in the past five hundred years had been followed by subsequent assassinations.

But this was different. The other branches of the New Texas Godfearing Militia had specifically threatened Lord Thornbuckle and his family, with additional threats to Hazel Takeris, the Rangers' wives and female dependents, and several members of the Regular Space Service, including Admiral Vida Serrano. Fleet, Colonel Bai-Darlin thought, could protect its own. His responsibility was the safety of the civilians, specifically those who would be present, vulnerable, in the funeral procession.

His predecessor, Colonel Harris, was even now trying to explain why they had not taken sufficient precautions, why Lord Thornbuckle had died, and no one—not one single Militia member or sympathizer—had been captured.

He would have to assume they'd try again. He would have to assume that everything Harris had done was wrong—that Harris had missed something vital.

Unless it wasn't the New Texas Godfearing Militia after all. Bai-Darlin's head lifted, as if scenting game. What if it were someone else, someone trying to use the hotheaded NewTex as a cover?

In that case, the funeral would probably go off without a hitch. Which, at the moment, was all he cared about.

Brun eyed her mother as they came out onto the porch, into the cold sunlight. Security, dark-uniformed and obviously armed, hovered around them. Five cars, all identical polished burgundy with black and gold trim, awaited them.

"Five?" Brun said.

"Security," her mother said. "Four of them are drags."

"Ah." Four would lay false trails, though since everyone knew where the funeral would be held, she didn't see how that would help.

She could at least notice who was here, and who had not been able to—or wanted to—come. No Lady Cecelia . . . well, it was the Wherrin Trials, after all, and she might not even have heard yet. Her sister Berenice, though, and her brother Abelard. No Raffa or Ronnie—absurd how she had missed them. Raffa's Aunt Marta Saenz, such a support to her father while she was missing—her mother's report of that had been just a touch acidic—had gone back to her own world as soon as Brun returned. No George—but of course the odious George had his own critically wounded father to watch over. Of their own sept, her father's younger brother Harlis, and his son Kell, who didn't look to have improved from her last memory of him. A whole raft of Consellines, most of whom she didn't know well enough to put names to, and Venezia Morrelline.

In ordinary times—not that the death of her father would ever have been ordinary—Kevil Mahoney would have given the eulogy. Instead it was her Uncle Harlis, and the eulogy slid into a subtle critique of her father's policies. A fine man, a man with strong family loyalties . . . to his children, a man of great abilities who had perhaps not quite lived up to them . . .

"Bollocks!" That low mutter was a great-great-uncle in the Barraclough main line. He took the floor next, praising Bunny the way Brun had expected him to be praised. That was the father she remembered: generous, loyal, intelligent, capable.

Others followed. Political friends, describing how Lord Thornbuckle's tactful but firm handling of the government had held it together when Kemtre abdicated. Political enemies, praising with delicate cuts at her father's occasional mistakes, and being so tactful in ignoring the obvious one that Brun found herself the target of one covert glance after another.

If it hadn't been for her—if it hadn't been for her idiot rashness—her father would still be alive, and in power, and these sly critics would be silent. She glanced down at her mother's hands, and saw the knuckles whitening the skin, though Miranda's face betrayed nothing. Guilt, sorrow, shame . . . and a deep, deep anger. It was her fault—in part—but it was not *all* her fault. Their maneuvering, their use of her misfortune and her father's death—that was *their* responsibility.

She had been determined to go away, to change herself into someone else, and break the connection with the rash young Brun who fell into captivity; but watching her father's enemies—enemies she had not known he had—at her father's funeral, that resolve weakened.

Prima Bowie sat embroidering a collar with a row of tiny green leaves, and kept a sharp eye on her household. It was hard to realize that only a short time ago she had been Prima Bowie in truth, Mitch's first wife and mother of nine children, with a real household to manage, a household with a garden and weaving shed, with court-yards for the children, and servants and tutors. Now she was Prima Bowie on her new Familias identity card, because that's what Hazel had told them, and even Hazel didn't know that wasn't a name but a title. She had been called Ruth Ann in childhood, long before she was any man's prima, but no one had called her that since her father died. And Mitch's last name wasn't Bowie—that was his title. He was really a Pardue. So her name ought to be Ruth Ann Pardue.

Should she tell someone? It would not be fitting to be called Prima Serrano, when that young woman became his first wife. She knew that, even as she hated the thought of being second or third behind such a young thing—and, what was worse, a heathen abomination who was actually in the military.

"Prima?" She looked up, to see Simplicity in the doorway. "Hazel's here, Mama . . . Prima . . ."

Simplicity had never learned not to call her *Mama.* Prima wished again that Mitch had not made such a fuss about it, but he had, and she'd had to send the child to the servant's hall even before she was out of the virgin's bower. It occurred to Prima that now she could reverse that decision.

"It's all right to call me Mama here, Simplicity," she said softly. The girl's expression relaxed.

"Mama! But the Ranger—"

"Isn't here. You may say Mama."

Simplicity ran over, just like the small child she was inside, and hugged Prima clumsily. "Love you, Mama."

"I love you, Simplicity," Prima said, greatly daring. She patted the girl on the shoulder. "There now. Go to the kitchen and bring us some lemonade."

"Yes, Mama." Simplicity had always been biddable and sweet; Prima could not help wishing Mitch had appreciated that sweetness more.

Hazel tapped at the doorframe. "Prima?"

"Yes." Prima pushed the needle through her work, and laid it aside. "Come in, have a seat. What is the news?"

Hazel looked at her. "You could turn on a vid."

"Full of nonsense," Prima said. "All that arguing, and bad language, too." She didn't mention the other things she had found there by accident. Men and women with no clothes on, doing things she had never imagined they could do.

"Lord Thornbuckle's funeral was today," Hazel said.

Prima knew that. Everyone knew that. Even with the vid turned off, there was no way to avoid knowing that the Speaker of the Table of Ministers, whose daughter had started all the troubles, had died and was being—not buried, because they didn't do that here, but . . . but whatever they called it, today.

It was all his fault, really. Prima wanted to believe that, wanted to believe that if that one arrogant blond man had not been so bad a father that his daughter had fallen into captivity, then she would still be Prima Bowie, first wife of a Ranger, safe and happy in the household she had known—had helped make—since her wedding.

That was a comfortable thought. All his fault, and Mitch the innocent dupe of heathens. Herself an innocent victim. The children . . . Prima sighed. Try as she might, she could not convince herself—quite—that it was all Lord Thornbuckle's fault. Or even his daughter's, though she loathed the tall yellow-haired woman.

"Prima—" Hazel was leaning forward. "I'm sorry, but—I really need to talk to you about your plans."

"My plans?" Prima stiffened, her fingers pausing for a moment in their busy work. "What do you mean?"

"Everyone wants to know what you are going to do—about the children's schooling, about supporting yourself—"

"Supporting myself!" Prima fastened on that; she was not about to discuss sending the children out to one of the heathen schools. "But the Serranos promised protection—"

"Protection, yes. But there are hundreds of you, all told—they can't afford to support all of you, not like this—"

Like this, in a warren of indoor rooms in a tall building, with windows that looked out on more tall buildings. Prima would have given anything for a bit of ground to walk on, sky to look at.

"And there are laws about the children, about schooling."

That she could answer. "I am not sending my children to some heathen school to be taught vileness—"

"There are religious schools," Hazel said. "I brought you a cube—"

A cube. Which she could access only with a cube reader. A machine. Machines, the parsons had always said, would make women lazy.

"I need to change my name," she said abruptly. Hazel looked surprised. "I'm not Mitch's Prima anymore," she said. "Ruth Ann was my birth name, and I should be Ruth Ann again."

"Ruth Ann," Hazel said softly, tasting it in her mouth. "It's a pretty name."

"It sounds strange to me; no one's called me that since my parents, years ago."

"Didn't they keep calling you—?"

"No, it wouldn't have been fitting. I was Prima Pardue from the day I married Mitch, and Prima Bowie from the day he became Ranger." She fidgeted a bit, wishing she didn't have to ask what she wanted to know. "Hazel . . . I never see anyone like Simplicity, even on the vid, when I do watch it. Surely your people have children that turn out . . . not quite . . . right?"

"Not many," Hazel said. She flushed; Prima knew something forbidden was in her mind. "I know you don't like to hear it, but—people do tests and medical treatment even before babies are born, to be sure nothing is wrong with them. Then, if something happens during pregnancy or birth, they fix it."

"Fix it." Like a door? But people weren't doors and shutters and shoes and . . . "How can you fix a mind?" she asked, greatly daring.

"I don't know." Hazel's flush faded. "I'm still young; I haven't finished my schooling, and I never studied any medicine."

"Could they fix . . . Simplicity . . . now?"

"I don't think so," Hazel said. "I can ask. But I think they have to be younger." She cocked her head. "But Prima—Ruth, I mean—there's no need to 'fix' Simplicity. She's a sweet, loving person the way she is."

"Your people don't value sweetness," Prima said. "They value intelligence."

Hazel paused, looking thoughtful. "There are many places in the Familias where that's true, but there are also many places that will value Simplicity for her gentleness, her kindness. I think you misjudge us. If you want to find a place—"

"No. I don't want to send her away! That's what Mitch said!" That's what Mitch had done. It still hurt her, that Simplicity had had to endure months in that nursery away from the home she loved.

"I didn't mean send her away. I meant go with her to a place where she'd be welcome."

"I can't go anywhere without my—without Ensign Serrano's permission."

"You could tell him what you want."

"Hazel—you know I can't do that. He's my—well, not husband, the way he should be, but he's our protector. It is for him to decide what to do with us."

"That's not how it works, here," Hazel said. Prima had heard that before, but it was hard to believe. Ensign Serrano was her protector, on the guarantee of his grandmother; he had the right to decide where they would live, and how. "He'd probably be delighted if you found a place where you and the others could be happy."

"I don't know how to do that," Prima said. "I don't know where to start."

"You could ask Professor Meyerson."

"Waltraude?" This had not occurred to Prima; she knew that Meyerson claimed expertise in Texan history—though a very strange version of it, from Prima's viewpoint—but what could she know about other worlds?

"She's a professor—finding things out is what she does best."

"Could you explain it?" Prima asked. She was much more comfortable with Hazel, even Hazel in men's pants, than with

Waltraude in a dress. Waltraude looked at them all as if they were carrots and beets and potatoes on the kitchen table—as if she were considering how they would fit in a stew.

"If she comes back in time. Prima—one thing I came to tell you— I'm leaving later today. I should be on my way to the ship now— clearing customs is going to take longer than usual. I'm going back to my family."

"Oh." She had known, in a way, that Hazel would leave, as the former captive women had left. Those women—she still worried about them, but they had all insisted on going, some to restorative surgery, others with voice synthesizers, back to their families if they had any, or a life of independence that Prima could not imagine wanting. "I'll miss you, Hazel," Prima said, feeling the hot tears rise.

"You were good to me," Hazel said, and came to hug her. Prima could feel the girl's young breasts now . . . Hazel was breeding age, but she would not breed. She would do—might already have done— terrible things to herself so that she would have no babies until much later. She might already be an Abomination.

Yet Hazel was a good girl—honest, kind, gentle. She had been so desperately worried about the two little girls, in the beginning; she had been so sweet to all the children. If she'd been Prima's daughter, Prima would have been proud of her. But now she'd go off to some school, or fly on a ship, or—Prima could not even imagine all the possibilities, and knew she couldn't. How could a child like this know what she wanted, what was right?

"God's blessing on you," Prima said, greatly daring in offering a blessing to a heathen. She wanted to tell Hazel not to use any abominable technology, but she knew that was futile. The girl was the product of that technology; her family used it, she would use it too. She prayed silently that God would keep Hazel safe.

Sector Seven Headquarters

"We now know what happened, Admiral." The chief medical officer touched the display controls, and blurred blots of color sharpened into focus. "The Surgeon General's office sent this out by ansible; the research labs finally figured it out. In a normal rejuvenation, on the left, the metabolites of the rejuv drugs are each involved in scavenging specific degradation products."

"In plain language?" Vida Serrano asked. She knew, and knew they knew, what was meant, but she was determined to make them say it in language that anyone could understand. She had already been briefed, very secretly, by Marta Katerina Saenz.

"The rejuv drugs break down in the body into other chemicals, and those chemicals—metabolites—bind to and remove the chemical compounds characteristic of aging."

"Very well."

"In a normal rejuvenation, that leaves only healthy, undegraded tissues as a matrix for replication, the second part of the rejuvenation process."

"So the first part throws out the old, as it were, and then the second part builds up the new?"

"Yes, Admiral. But on the right—if you'll look right here—you can see that these tissues, which stain green, are not being removed. No green on the left, and green—"

"On the right. Yes. And I presume that means that age-deteriorated tissues are left in the matrix when the rejuv proceeds."

"Exactly. Which replicate into age-deteriorated tissues, so that after some years—it depends on the amount of deterioration in the original as well as the exact kind of faulty drug—the deterioration affects brain function like any other senile dementia."

"So—how do you fix it?"

"Unfortunately, we don't know. It appears that if no actual functional degradation has occurred, then a rejuvenation with good drugs produces a fresh start. But when we tried that on one of the first patients, it didn't work. The body rejuvenated to a young age, but the mental function stayed the same. We have been observing him for months now, and while the deterioration has not progressed, it has also not improved."

"What about other treatments? Surely you had something for this kind of problem before rejuv?"

"No, not really. Admiral—I know that nobody likes to hear this, but medical miracles are rarely miracles."

Marta had told her the same thing, but she'd hoped for better news.

"How early can you detect the problem?" If they couldn't reverse it, perhaps catching it early would work.

"Within a year of a bad rejuv, which is plenty of time to correct it. But the tests take weeks—maybe we can speed it up later, but not yet—and we have a lot of people to test."

What were they going to do with those whose rejuvs had failed, who had already been damaged . . . Vida shuddered. Rejuvenate them to youthful bodies and senility of mind? Who would take care of them? For how long? Or . . . let them die? Neither horn of the dilemma seemed tenable, and for once she was glad that it wasn't her decision. Let the Grand Admiral and the Surgeon General figure it out; the mathematics of equity in this escaped her.

Zenebra, two days before the Senior Trials

For dinner, Pedar had chosen Raymond's, that year's fashionable restaurant. She steered him away from discussing the Trials—he wanted her to dissect all the other competitors for his amusement.

"It's not right," she insisted. "They're my friends as well as my fellow competitors; it's not honorable to pick them apart like that." She touched the table controls and brought up the chessboard. "Let's play."

"Don't be naive, Cecelia," Pedar said. Had he rejuved yet again? She couldn't tell. He still dressed more like an actor in some deep-historical play. Her interest in history didn't extend to clothing styles, so she wasn't sure what period. "There's no place in real life for honor. In sports, perhaps—" He picked up a black knight and a white, and made them bow to each other. "But even you know that what really matters is winning." He clashed the pieces together.

"If you break the rules," Cecelia said, trying to be reasonable, "they eliminate you."

Pedar tilted his hand. "Then you might say that Bunny broke the rules."

She could not believe what she was hearing. "You—"

"Cecelia—the rules are on a different level, when you're talking about realities . . . surely you know that." His tone indulged her, the knowledgeable adult to the ignorant adolescent. "Men like Bunny make the rules . . . until someone else displaces them." He pushed the white king along the board, knocking the other pieces askew, until it rested on the edge of the board. "Yet there are always rules beyond rules . . . the rules that keep a man in his place—or move him away." His finger touched the game piece; it teetered a moment on the edge of the table, then fell.

Her body tensed, as if she had seen an unexpected ditch looming beyond a jump she thought she knew. His expression shifted, reflecting hers; she hated that he had noticed. But he kept smiling, waiting her answer. She couldn't think what to answer. She had to say something, though; she could feel his smile beginning to stiffen in place, like overbeaten egg whites.

"I see," she said, buying time. She didn't understand about Bunny yet, what rules he had broken that brought this man and his faction to the desperate action they had taken. She didn't understand why he had hinted so broadly, or what he expected her to do about it. But she did see that none of it was accidental, not Bunny's death, or this dinner meeting, or anything else Pedar did. Perhaps as far back as the Trials several years ago, her first ride in years. He had tried then to talk to her about the politics of the Rejuvenants, and she had dismissed it as mere fashion. "I do wonder," she said after a long pause, "what, if anything, the New Texas Godfearing Militia has to do with Rejuvenants."

He relaxed just that fraction which told her she had chosen the safer alternative at that conversational fence.

"People need something to blame for their disappointments," he said. "As some opportunities are foreclosed, others must be seen to open. Or unrest might become general."

Cecelia puzzled at this. Again, he waited for her, that indulgent smile which told her he expected her to be slow to understand. She hated that patience; if this was what she would become, as a Rejuvenant, she might just as well run her horse over a cliff and be done with it. Opportunities foreclosed—that had to be because Rejuvenants could live well-nigh forever, and who was going to give up power and privilege while still young and capable? Mentally, she transferred the problem to horse breeding, where it made more sense to her. If the old horses didn't die off, and you kept breeding at the same rate . . . well, of course.

"I wonder if rejuv drugs would work on horses," she said, before she could get a lock on her tongue.

Pedar burst out laughing, and the bald man at the next table looked up. "Cecelia, my dear! Only you would think of rejuvenating a horse!"

She could feel the heat in her face. Yet—if he laughed at her like that, he was not afraid of her wits. She allowed her voice to carry a little sting. "I see what you mean, Pedar. Those who cannot afford rejuvenation, or who are simply impatient, see ahead of them a lifetime of blocked opportunities—blocked by the Rejuvenants. But the universe is large—if they are discontented and ambitious enough, there are colony worlds—"

"Theft is always more profitable, until the thief is caught," Pedar murmured.

"That's—" She was about to say ridiculous, when a tension in Pedar's face silenced her.

She had too much to think about, and she did not really want to think about any of it. Of what use were her wealth, and her skills, and her rejuvenated body, if she couldn't do what she liked without having to worry about the rest of the universe? What she had wanted—what she hoped to gain—was a long life full of her own particular pleasures . . . which began, though they did not end, in that stable block on Rotterdam. Which centered on horses and the people who had identified themselves as horse people since long before humans left Old Earth.

She reminded herself that she had time for both, now. No longer need she fear the advancing years, the aging of joints and bones that would make her slower, clumsier. She could afford to spend a few months now dealing with whatever complication Pedar meant, without losing it.

But she didn't want to.

And Pedar knew that. As she dipped the asymmetrical spoon always used with Biaristi cold soups, as she refreshed her mouth afterwards with a sip of Eran ale, and went on to the crunchy-coated strips of spiced rock grouse, she was aware that Pedar, in sounding her out, was expecting exactly the retreat she most wanted to make.

He had turned the conversation back to the Trials, to her chances, and his. She answered automatically, but watched as from a distance the subtle signals of his expressions.

What a toad the man was, after all. He would dangle some conspiracy in front of her for his own amusement, sure that she could not concentrate on anything but horses for long enough to learn anything dangerous, or do anything . . .

"I think you're quite right to ride anyway," Pedar said. "After all, it's too late to attend any ceremony."

"The horse is ready," Cecelia said, fighting back an urge to change her mind and not ride after all. "And so am I. You're staying too."

"For the same reasons," Pedar said. "I'm ready; my horse is ready, and my competition . . . is here."

And because it gave him a strong apparent alibi. While someone had plotted Bunny's assassination, Pedar had been very publicly visible a very long way away, supervising his horse in training for the Senior Trials. Cecelia knew it would have been possible to have it done—anyone knew that—but finding and proving the links would be more difficult. And dangerous.

She was, she discovered on the day, more ready than she knew for this particular event. While nothing could make the Senior Trials effortless, she was hardly aware of the effort she exerted. Seniority reacted well to her detached calmness, and put in faultless cross-country and stadium rounds . . . which, in the end, were enough to win, when the dressage leader (also faultless in cross-country) had a rail down the next day. Liam Ardahi had to withdraw during the cross-country, when Plantagenet refused the water repeatedly. Cecelia wondered if that were entirely an accident; Plantagenet had always been bold into water. But if Pedar wanted her distracted by a major win . . . he was ruthlessly competitive, but he had won a much larger competition—as he saw it.

She smiled for the press on her victory gallop, and remembered to thank all her staff, enclosing a personal note with the bonus credit each received. At the reception that evening, she wore her amber necklace carved in the likeness of Epona. Like that enigmatic goddess, she smiled and accepted congratulations, finally pleading a sore elbow in order to leave before midnight.

An hour later, wearing a groom's overall, she was hacking down the dark road to the spaceport on Max, whose alert ears and brisk movement revealed that the horse, at least, thought this was a fine idea. If anyone asked, her groundcar was parked in the stable lot, and everyone knew that she was likely to have gone to the stables to end the night's celebration there. Colum had had Max saddled for her— an extra hack would do that one no harm—but had been out of sight when she led the horse out.

Five kilometers away, where a service road met the tracks of A Course, Phase C, Dale waited with the truck and trailer, in which a horse stamped its impatience; Roz had driven her own battered little groundcar. Cecelia swung off Max, helped load him in the trailer beside Dulcy—Max could be difficult to load in an empty trailer— then struggled with the car's cranky driver-side door. Roz slammed it from outside, and climbed into the truck; Cece drove off alone to the regional airport.

The advantage of piloting her own ship was that her flight plan and her actual destination need have nothing to do with each other. She had discussed with her staff the training schedule for Seniority and Max for the rest of the season, and told them she was going to visit EquiSite's lab before returning to Rotterdam, to check on a new gene-sculpting technique only recently applied to horses.

Then she filed a flight plan for Rotterdam, knowing that her staff would not comment.

Her new planet-to-jump craft allowed her to bypass Zenebra's crowded station. She expected Pedar to check on her flight plan, and her jump vector. Fine. Let him check. The exit vector for Rotterdam actually led to the first intermediate jump point, and from there she could route to Castle Rock easily. She spared a moment to thank Heris for suggesting that she get a license and learn to pilot her own craft.

Though she did miss the luxury of *Sweet Delight*, and the deference accorded a full-size yacht. What she really wanted was another long, hot bath and a massage. She had managed to cram in a small wet-bath facility and the necessary recycling gear by eliminating any possibility of inviting someone else along. So a shower and no massage, and she would expect to wake up stiff in the morning.

Even a rejuvenated body couldn't do the Senior Trials without strain.

Still, it was worth it. *Pounce* had more speed than her old yacht, as well as the ability to land onplanet. She was past the orbital station now, following the beacons out to the system's jump point.

CHAPTER THREE

Two uneventful transits after leaving Zenebra, Cecelia was in Castle Rock's nearspace, confirming that Miranda was still onplanet and still in residence in the Old Palace. When she called, the staff person who answered reported that Miranda would indeed be willing to see her. Cecelia made her shuttle reservation while waiting for the station tug to bump her gently into the docking harness. The paperwork necessary to clear the Rockhouse Major Dockmaster and Customs seemed to take forever (had Heris really coped with this much, or was it worse because of the assassination?) but she made her shuttle with a few minutes to spare. She saw no one she knew on Rockhouse Major, and no one familiar on the down shuttle. That suited her; she was in no mood to talk to any of her acquaintances.

But when she came out of the shuttleport entryway, looking for a hirecar, she saw one of the long black official cars, with the Familias seal on the doors, and the driver clearly recognized her.

"Lady Cecelia?"

"Yes?"

"Lady Miranda sent us for you. Your luggage?"

"In the dump," Cecelia said, handing over the ID strip. The driver nodded to his second, who took the strip and went off toward the dumps. Belatedly, Cecelia wondered if she should make sure of their identity and authorization—Heris, she thought, would be scolding her if Heris were here. But the driver was now holding out a flat packet.

"Lady Miranda wanted you to have this first," he said.

Cecelia opened it. A note from Miranda, and a flatpic of the driver and assistant. "You may not be worried," the note said, "but we have learned we must all take precautions. I look forward to seeing you."

In minutes, the assistant was back with Cecelia's few pieces of luggage, all marked with the striped tape that meant they'd passed Customs. Cecelia got into the car and wondered, as it shot forward into traffic, if they were taking the same route Bunny had followed the day he was killed. She didn't ask.

At the Palace, everything seemed normal at first. The same uniforms at the gate, at the doors. The same quietly efficient staff who guided her first to her guest room overlooking a small garden, and then, when she had showered and changed, to Miranda's suite. It was hard to remember, in this quiet gracious place, that Bunny was dead, and all their peace in peril. She found herself expecting to see him coming down the corridor, his pleasantly foolish face lighting with a smile.

Until she came face to face with Miranda, and saw the devastation of that legendary beauty. Cecelia wondered how the same exquisite curves of bone, the same flawless skin, could now express a wasteland. After the rituals of greeting, when the staff had placed a tea set on the low table and withdrawn, Cecelia could wait no longer. No need, when the porcelain surface had already shattered.

"Miranda, what have they told you about it—about who did it?"

"Nothing." Miranda poured a cup of tea and handed it to Cecelia; the cup did not rattle on the saucer. "I know the news media say it was the New Texas Militia, in retaliation for the executions. I know that the former head of security is on administrative leave. But they have very gently let me know that investigations are in progress, and I will be informed when it is time. Do have a pastry; you always liked these curly ones, didn't you?"

Cecelia ignored the offered pastry. "Miranda . . . I don't think it was the NewTex Militia."

"Why?" Miranda's face had no more expression than a cameo.

"I think it was someone . . . inside."

"Family?" Her voice was cool. Why wasn't she upset? Why wasn't she frightened? Had she been through too much?

Cecelia waited a moment, then went on. "Pedar said . . . that Bunny broke rules."

Miranda's mouth twitched; it might have been grimace or grin. "He did. He was so . . . so quiet, so . . . compliant, it always seemed. But from the first time he brought me a tart he'd filched from the cook, when we were children, and showed me where we could hide from our governesses . . . he broke rules."

"More important than that," Cecelia said.

"I know." Miranda stared past Cecelia's left ear, as if she saw something a long way away, but was too tired to pay much attention.

"Miranda!" Even before Miranda turned her eyes back, Cecelia had bitten back the rest of it, all that she wanted to say. You can't give up now. You have to keep going. You have a family—

"I have a family," Miranda said, in that cool level voice. "I have responsibilities. Children. Grandchildren. You don't want me to forget that."

"Yes . . ." Cecelia had lowered her voice, and strove to sit quietly.

"I do not care." Miranda turned that cameo face full on Cecelia. "I do not care about the children—not even Brun, whom I most desperately want to care about. I do not care about the grandchildren, those bastard brats forced on my daughter—" Her breath caught in a ragged gasp, giving the lie to that *do not care.* Cecelia said nothing; there was nothing she could say. "I do not care," Miranda went on, "about anything but Branthcombe. Bunny. Whom, in this day and age, and in spite of rejuvenations and genetic selection and everything else we invented to spare us the pain of living . . . I loved. All my life, from the time he brought me that cherry tart, and we ate it in alternate bites, sitting on the back stairs . . . I loved him. It was a miracle to me that he loved me. That he survived the hunting season we still make our young people go through, that he remembered me after my years in seclusion at Cypress Hill, that he married me. And fathered my children, and no matter what stayed loyal and decent and—" Her voice broke at last, in a gasp that ended in sobs.

"My dear . . ." Cecelia reached out, uncertain. Miranda had been, for so long, another exquisite porcelain figurine in Cecelia's mental collection of beautiful women—like her sister, like all the women of that type—and she had never touched any of them for more than the rituals of class affection—the fingertips, the cheeks. But Miranda didn't recoil, and leaned into her as if Cecelia were her mother or her aunt.

The sobs went on a long time, and Cecelia had a cramp in the small of her back from twisting to accommodate Miranda's position, by the time Miranda quieted.

"Damnation," she said then. "I thought I was over it."

"I don't think you can get over it," Cecelia said.

"No. Not really. But over it enough to function. You're right, I have to do that much. But I really do not know how."

"Your advisors—"

"Are vultures." Miranda gave Cecelia a sideways glance and pulled back a little; Cecelia took that hint and stood, stretching. "You, never having married, may not realize just how complicated the situation is. Your estate is all yours, and you have the disposal of it—"

"When my ham-fisted relatives don't interfere," Cecelia said. She had tried, and failed, to put out of her mind her sister's interference in her will. The legal repercussions had dragged on for several years.

"True. But what I have is Bunny's legacy in several separate realms, some of which I stayed out of. The political—"

"Surely no one expects you to take over as Speaker—"

"No." Miranda's voice was sour. "Everyone is sure that the political realm is the one I know least about. More's the pity—since I actually do understand it, and could take over, if they'd only let me."

Cecelia managed not to gape, by a small margin. Miranda politically minded? Then she thought of Lorenza, who certainly had been, and repressed a shiver. She sat down again and poured herself a cup of tea.

"Lorenza," Miranda said, in another uncanny echo of Cecelia's thoughts. "Now there was another case of backstage expertise. She and I used to play the most delicate games of power . . . it would bore you, Cecelia, unless you could think of it in equestrian terms, but . . . if you could imagine yourself on a very, very advanced horse, which despised you but had, for some reason, agreed to obey exactly your commands."

"I had one like that," Cecelia said, hoping to divert Miranda onto a more congenial topic. Miranda's hiss of annoyance stopped her.

"We are not talking horses. Did you ever fence?"

Fence. Possible meanings ran through Cecelia's mind, the most recent out of her *Spacepilots' Glossary of Navigational Terms*; she couldn't imagine Miranda as a jump-point explorer probing into unknown routes.

"Ancient sport," Miranda said. "Derived from an ancient method of warfare. Swordfighting, also called fencing."

"No," Cecelia said, feeling grumpy. She had just spent a half hour comforting a woman in collapse, and now she was being questioned like a schoolgirl about a sport she had always considered supremely silly. For one thing, it had nothing to do with fences that horses could jump over. "I don't . . . er . . . fence."

"You should," Miranda said. She stood, and moved restlessly around the room, touching the surfaces as if she felt her way, rather than saw them with her eyes. Curtain, curtain, bureau, chair . . . "It's an excellent discipline, and apt for use aboard spaceships, for instance."

"Swords?" Cecelia could not quite keep the astonishment out of her voice. Was Miranda losing her mind? Tears, then politics, then swords?

"They do less damage to bulkheads," Miranda said. "If your only purpose is to kill people, why destroy the ship?"

She must be crazy. It must be, Cecelia thought, an effect of whatever had kept her so lovely for so long. Could she have been given bad rejuv drugs?

"Cecelia, I am not crazy. Well . . . not very crazy. Distracted with grief, and frustration, and anger, but not in the way we usually mean. Fencing—if you knew anything about it—is the ideal metaphor for what Lorenza and I did, just as Bunny and her brother Piercy—but no. You don't know the terms."

Cecelia felt her temper gathering like a boil behind her eyes. She squeezed them hard shut, and spoke with them closed. "Miranda. I know you're grieving; it was good for you to cry. But please quit treating me like a silly horse-crazy schoolgirl—"

"But you are," Miranda said, in that same flat cool voice. "You always have been; you refused to grow up—just like Brun, that way. It was ridiculous of Bunny to send Brun to *you*, of all people—"

"You—blame me? For Brun?"

"Not really . . . I mean, intellectually I know we chose her genetic type, we chose to increase the risk-taking and the responsiveness. But there you were, such a model for such a girl—every hunting season, egging her on over bigger fences, as if horses were all that mattered. And what did it get her, to take someone like you for a model? That . . . that degradation!"

Astonishment had blown out anger for the moment. "She isn't like me," Cecelia said, feeling her way.

"She's not horse-crazy, no. But that—that stubborn insouciance, that willingness to shed responsibility—"

Cecelia felt the anger gathering again just beyond her vision. "I didn't know you considered me irresponsible," she managed to say quietly.

Miranda's hand tilted quickly, a diminishing gesture. "Not in everything, of course. But no sense of family, no loyalty to the Familias—" Her head swung away; the bell of golden hair swung wide a moment, then stilled into new perfection. "And she pulled that harebrained stunt to rescue *you*—she could have been killed then—"

"I didn't ask her to," Cecelia said. Something tapped at the alarms in her brain, a tiny hammering. "I couldn't. She just—"

"Loved you," Miranda said. Under mint-green silk, her shoulders rose and fell; Cecelia could not hear the sigh but knew it had been given.

"She loved her family," Cecelia said. "And you didn't need rescuing."

"No." Miranda turned back, face composed as usual. "No, I never did." For a long moment, she stood motionless, silent. Cecelia found it hard to breathe. Miranda shrugged again. "Kata Saenz said we provided the wrong models for Brun; she told Bunny that, in the planning for Brun's rescue. I was glad of it at the time; I knew we'd done something wrong, though our other children turned out well. And the shock of being told it was partly his fault got Bunny out of his fury with the Suiza girl, and in the end she saved Brun's life. I just can't understand her, though she's my child."

"How about the rest of the family? Buttons and Sarah . . . ?"

"Are wonderfully helpful, as far as they can be. Buttons, of course, expected to take over as his father's heir. But Bunny's younger brother Harlis—you remember him?"

Cecelia nodded. Harlis had all the arrogance, all the faux-aristocratic foppery, and a third less sense, than Bunny had had. Bunny could always go in an instant from the foolish foxhunting lord of the manor to the sensible, practical, and very capable politician. Harlis was Harlis—all surface and no substance.

"Harlis is challenging the Family structure, and I'm not sure Buttons can stop him. I did tell Bunny three years ago that he ought to clarify the situation just in case, and he and Kevil were looking into it, but then Bubbles—Brun—disappeared."

"And of course Bunny wasn't thinking of it then."

"No, nor of anything else. Harlis managed to convince some of the distant relatives that Bunny's mind had gone, and that any of Bunny's children were likely to carry the trait. And some of them accepted that, and have thrown in their influence with Harlis. He's acquired an astonishing amount of stock in several of the corporations; even old Trema left him her shares—"

"Will you be all right?"

"Probably, but I'm going to lose a lot. And I wanted it for Brun—for her and the twins. She needs a safe place; Sirialis would have been perfect—"

"Harlis isn't taking Sirialis . . . !" Cecelia's first thought was that Harlis had never liked foxhunting and might end the annual hunting season; she slapped that thought down, ashamed of herself. Maybe she was as selfish and narrow-minded as Miranda thought.

"He's trying." Miranda dropped her voice, mimicking Harlis's. "'Oh, you'll always be welcome, Miranda, of course. You'll always have a place. But it was family property, not Bunny's alone.' As if I would go there to lurk in the apartment he so generously offered, while he strides about pretending to be lord of the manor!"

Cecelia forbore to say that he would be the lord, and no pretense, if he had his way. "And what are you doing about it—I assume you have some plan."

"Yes. But I haven't decided . . . it would mean tearing up much that Bunny built . . . family relationships, friendships, alliances. I can call on my family—" Of the founding Families, Miranda's had been known first for information management, and later for the development and manufacture of a variety of devices that were to the ordinary computer as a top event horse was to a child's pony.

"But it's—it was Bunny's, and it's rightfully yours—" Inheritance had been the one immutable aspect of law; concentration of assets within a Family, the foundation of Family power. Angry as Cecelia had been with her sister for questioning her will, she knew that if she had left her assets within the family, even to a distant relative, the will would not have been challenged.

"Cece—you don't understand how threadbare the fabric has become, since you exposed Kemtre and Lorenza. I suppose it had begun before, but that's when it became obvious." Miranda paused, frowning a bit in thought. "Bunny and I, and Kevil, were holding an alliance of Families by the skin of our teeth. All those years of social connections, business connections, and Kevil's legal skills and intuition. I swear he knew more about the ragged skeletons in Family closets than anyone had ever guessed. Bunny would talk them around, and I would smile and be gracious and work through the wives and mistresses. We were holding it together, just, but the crises kept knocking it out of balance. Kemtre's abdication, that Patchcock mess—the scare about bad rejuvenation drugs, and the Morelline/Conselline Family collapse, and then Brun's abduction . . ." Her voice trailed away.

"And I went back to Rotterdam to play with horses," Cecelia said.

"Yes. I understand it, in a way. Venezia Morrelline had her pottery, and you had horses, and Kata Saenz had her research. Most people do have their private interests, and that, after all, is what a good political system is supposed to do—leave you free to do what you are best at, whatever it is. People want to do the work they love, marry and have children, have some fun. But if too many people do that, Cecelia, it leaves gaps for people who want power for its own sake, and who may use it in ways that later degrade your life."

Like Bunny using Fleet resources as if they were personal, to rescue Brun. She didn't say that; she knew that Miranda knew what people thought. "How is Kevil?" she asked instead.

"Alive." From her tone, Cecelia couldn't tell if Miranda were pleased about that or not. Then she sighed. "I can't wish Kevil dead, only Bunny alive as well. Kevil was badly hurt—days in the regen tank, and then the head injury—he's still not himself. He may never be, the doctors say. And without Bunny—or me, if I could only find a way—he doesn't have the backing to do what he did for us before."

"I should visit him," Cecelia said.

"Yes, you should. You should tell him what you told me, with all the names you know. He might know something useful, something that would give us leverage."

"And Brun?"

"Brun . . . has a crazy notion of changing her identity. Going to the Guernesi and getting a rejuv and biosculpt that will make her a new person from the bones out. I think she got the idea from the prince's clones."

"She doesn't want the children," Cecelia said, not asking.

"Would you?" Miranda shivered, then sighed. "No, she doesn't want them. I don't want them myself, really. Bunny did. Bunny had some crazy idea that they could grow up to prove their existence wasn't a disaster, but it is."

"That's a lot of burden on them."

"Yes. Unfair, too. I know that. But nothing can make them other than they are: bastards, Brun's ruin, the ruin of all our hopes for the Familias. They are the lit fuse, poor little brats."

"What are they like?"

"Babies. Toddlers, really, at this point. Neither looks like anyone in our family, and they aren't identical. One has the brightest red hair I ever saw, and the other's is brown. Brun says one of the men was a redhead. . . ."

Cecelia noticed that Miranda had not used names; before she could ask, Miranda went on.

"The gene scan showed up some interesting anomalies— according to one geneticist, who's also looked at the women and other children, these people were seriously inbred, with a lot of undesirable recessives concentrated. They had noticed that children born of captured women were less likely to be disabled, but considered that as proof of their God's blessing on capturing women. Of course, we had the boys treated at once, although it was too late for a complete washout."

"What do you call them?" Cecelia finally got a word in.

Miranda blushed. "We don't actually . . . have names. Brun never did, and she refuses to talk about it. Their nurses call them Red and Brownie. I know—" She held up a hand. "Those are names for dogs or ponies, not boys. Nicknames, at best. I just don't—Bunny and I had been talking about it when he was killed." She moved her cup restlessly. "Would you like to see them?"

"Of course." Cecelia stood.

Down the hall, past several doors and now she could hear the crowing of a happy child, the chuckle of another. Miranda paused just before the open door. Cecelia looked in. Two young women in colorful smocks, a floor strewn with toys, and two sturdy toddlers. One, the redhead, was bouncing up and down, clapping his hands. The other, sitting in a scatter of blocks, looked quickly toward the door, grinning.

They were normal children, not monsters. Happy children, not monsters. Children who were more than "lit fuses"—who were potentially normal, if only they didn't grow up burdened with a past they had not made.

"You have to send them away," Cecelia said, surprising herself. "There are people who want children and don't have them; there are places where these boys will be treasured as they should be."

"Bunny said—"

"Bunny's dead. They're alive. They can have a good future—and the universe is big enough that they need not be anyone's pawns in some power game."

"And you know who—?" A tone suspended between sarcasm and hope.

"No, but I can find out. Will you let me do that? Find them homes where they'll have a chance?"

Miranda sagged. "I . . . don't know."

"Miranda. You have other grandchildren, and will have more. Children you can love naturally. Children whose political importance, if any, comes with a family commitment. You haven't even given these boys *names*—you know yourself that's wrong. Give them up; give them a chance."

"Brun wants to . . ." Miranda said. "She said . . . she doesn't want to hate them, but she can't live with them around. But neither of us can face the thought of an orphanage."

"She's right," Cecelia said. "You said we were alike—we may be, that much. If I had borne them, in her circumstances, I'd have to give them up. It's a big universe; they need never know."

She left Miranda in the doorway and went on into the room, nodding to the nurses, and sitting on the floor. Red, his hair an orange flame, put a fat thumb in his mouth, but Brownie grinned at her.

Cecelia pulled out the ring of keys from the stable and jingled it. His grin widened, and he came to her, grabbing for the keys. Though he looked little like Brun, his boldness and the sparkle in his blue eyes suggested Brun's attitudes.

Cecelia did not think of herself as a religious person, but she found herself praying to something, somewhere, to give these boys a better life than their beginning.

"Lady Cecelia!" That was Brun; Cecelia turned.

"You look well," she said. Brun looked well physically—her tall body trim and fit, her tumbled gold curls in a riot around her head. But the clear gaze was shadowed, darkening when she looked at the boys.

"I'm fine," Brun said. "Considering everything."

"I agree with you and your mother," Cecelia said. "These boys need a proper home, not to mention names."

Brun's face stiffened, then she grinned. "Still tactful, I see."

"As ever," Cecelia agreed. "My dear, I'm almost ninety, and rejuvenation did nothing to soften my personality. Why don't we do it today?"

"Today?" Both Miranda and Brun looked shocked; so did the nurses.

"They're starting to talk; they understand even more. Every day you wait makes it harder on them."

"I . . . want to be sure they have good homes . . . that they lack for nothing . . ." Brun said.

"A good home is a loving home," Cecelia said, with all the confidence of the childless. "And right now they're lacking the most basic needs of all—a name, a parent—"

"But what will you do with them?"

"Take them to a safe and loving home. Brun, you've known me all your life. Have I ever lied to you?" Brun shook her head, tears rising in her eyes. Miranda started to speak, but Cecelia waved her down. "I have told you the truth, even when it wasn't what you wanted to hear. I tell you the truth now—if you let me have these boys I will see to it that they find a good home. I will do it myself. . . ."

"But your schedule—"

"Is my own. Miranda, you were twitting me with my self-indulgence. This is what self-indulgence is good for. I can help you, right now, because I have no other obligations in the way." She softened her voice. "Please let me."

Brun looked down, then nodded. Cecelia could see the gleam of tears in her eyes.

Miranda stared at Cecelia a long moment, then said, "All right. And I still have money for them—a start in a new life—"

"Good." Cecelia tried to think what next. She had said *today* without really thinking what that would mean, but now the two nursemaids were watching her, waiting for orders. She had no idea how long it took to pack up two children, or where to take them, but she knew she must not hesitate. She spoke to the nursemaids.

"Are you full-time employees, and would you be able to travel for a month or so?"

"Yes, ma'am," said one of them. "We're from Sirialis, originally, but we thought we'd be staying for years . . ."

"Then will you please start packing—or have someone help you pack—the boys' things? I need to talk to Miranda and make some arrangements—" She would need a bigger ship—a momentary pang, when she thought of how easy it would have been with *Sweet Delight*, and Heris Serrano, to take the twins and their nursemaids anywhere. Reservations on a commercial liner? No, too much chance of publicity. She'd have to lease a ship and crew. No, to start with she'd need another room—set of rooms—in her hotel. She'd made reservations for one. Or perhaps another hotel. Ideas whirled through her head like leaves before a wind. "Miranda, let's go to your suite—we have business."

"Yes, Cecelia." Miranda nodded at the nursemaids, already beginning to gather toys. "I'll send a maid in to do the packing; just be sure the boys are clean and dressed. And I'll take care of your salaries and references."

Then she led the way to her suite. Brun came along with them, her face once more stiff with misery.

"Do you have any notion where you're going with them?" Miranda asked, when they were again in her sitting room.

"Yes." The thought had come as she walked down the passage. "I know the perfect planet, and probably the perfect couple. Do you want to know?"

"Not . . . now. Later, maybe." Brun sat hunched, her eyes on the carpet.

"Fine, then. Miranda, I'll need the use of your comset—"

"I'll just call Poisson—"

"No. I'll make the reservations myself." Only as far as the first hotel, she told herself. From there, she would arrange transportation. And she wanted no records in the Palace computers, where reporters might already have a tap.

"I have resources—"

"You said you were feuding with Bunny's brother—"

"In my own right. At least let me help."

"Of course." Cecelia turned politely to Brun as Miranda opened a line to her bank. "Brun—have you heard from that girl—Hazel, wasn't it?—lately?"

Brun looked up. "I worry about her. She seems to be doing fine, for someone who's been through so much, but she never has admitted how bad it was. She keeps wanting to get me to meet with that Ranger's wife—Prima Bowie."

"Why?"

"I don't know." Brun shifted restlessly. "Hazel liked her, I think. Says she was kind. Hazel feels sorry for her, being a stranger in our society. But she chose it; she wasn't abducted."

"Are they all still together, all those women?" asked Cecelia.

"As far as I know. I don't . . . really care."

Miranda broke in. "I've deposited a lump sum in your account, Cecelia; I can send more later if—"

"Don't worry about it," Cecelia said. "Tell me—do the maids take the boys out to play? In a park or anything?"

"Not off the grounds. The news media are bad enough as it is."

"Then—how about palace employees with children? Are there any?"

"I'm sure there are, but I don't know who. . . ."

"Perhaps the maids will. We don't want publicity when we take the children out."

The little crocodile of children from Briary Meadows Primary School being herded through the public rooms as part of their field trip acquired a short tail. They didn't pay much attention; they were tired of glass-fronted cases full of trophies, letters, gifts to this or that famous person by another famous person, the rooms of interesting furniture which they could not touch, the silken ropes on which they were not supposed to swing, the constant admonitions to pay attention, be quiet, quit straggling or crowding.

The children had been promised a stop at Ziffra's, the famous ice-cream parlor, if they were good, and only a steady murmur of commands kept them from trampling one another on the way out the door. The nursemaids, now wearing the green smocks of adult helpers in the school, complete with dangling nametags, brought up the rear, each with a toddler on her hip.

Outside, the remaining media scavengers waited for any sign of Brun or her children, but ignored the confusion of piping voices and busy adults. They had seen bright green buses with the school name arrive, and crowds of obvious schoolchildren arrive, teachers hustling them into neat lines and adult volunteers scampering to catch the inevitable escapees. At least one such field trip arrived every day; the Palace had always been a favorite tourist site, and busloads of children, retirees, and convention attendees showed up so often that no one in the press corps paid them any mind.

Now, as the chattering youngsters piled into the buses, and the harried adults counted, compared notes, and shut the doors, they ignored the confusion, keeping an eye out instead for the return of Lady Cecelia, whose limousine waited at the other end of the car park.

A half hour later, Cecelia left, smiling into the holo lens and accepting congratulations on her win in the Senior Trials. She fielded a couple of questions about her breeding program, expressed sympathy for Bunny's family, and stepped into the waiting limousine, which took her to the medical center where Kevil Mahoney was still listed in critical condition.

And later that afternoon, the two school volunteers whose green smocks and nametags had been borrowed for a time walked out the service entrance with other Palace staff who lived offsite. No one paid attention to them, either.

Miranda listened to the silence and felt something shift inside her mind. She had not really been able to hear the twins, but knowing they were not there, that she could not hear them even if she walked down the hall, tipped her toward some distant horizon. She glanced at the clock. Was it still so early? Surely Cecelia had not been able to get them offplanet yet. She could check . . . she stopped, her hand outstretched to the comunit.

No. As if it were a robotic arm she were operating, she concentrated on her hand, and brought it back to her lap.

They were gone. They were gone forever.

Lightness filled her, as if she were a transparent husk of herself. She might blow away . . . but of course that was nonsense. She was tired, very tired, and—

"Mother?"

Weight and darkness returned so suddenly she could hardly breathe. "Yes, Brun?"

"You do think they'll be all right."

"Of course." Miranda took a deep breath. "Cecelia is reliable, in her own way, and she will make sure of it."

"Good." Brun came into the room tentatively, as if she were unsure of her welcome. "I feel . . . strange."

Of course she felt strange. No one could survive what she had survived, and not feel strange, the moment life gave time to stop and notice.

"Sit down," Miranda said. "Have some tea." Cecelia had not even finished hers. Brun sat as gingerly as she had come in. They nibbled pastries in silence for awhile, then Brun set down her plate.

"What's going to happen with the family holdings?"

Not the question Miranda had expected, but one she was glad to deal with at the moment. "It's going to be very difficult," Miranda said. "When your father mobilized the Fleet to go after you, he antagonized a lot of people, his own family included."

"Too much for one person," Brun murmured.

"It wasn't their daughter," Miranda said. "And it wasn't your decision; it was his. But Harlis gained ground with the rest of the family then—he'd already been working on it, claiming that Bunny was spending too much time and energy on Council business, and neglecting the family interests. He said Buttons was too young and inexperienced; he started demanding silly, time-wasting reports, and nitpicking everything. Buttons has had a lot to learn in only a few years, but he's doing very well. It's just that Harlis promises he could do better. And now—well, he's determined to get Sirialis."

"That's stupid," Brun said, with some of her old arrogance. "That's not profit; the place has never made a profit—"

"That's partly Harlis's point. He claims it could, if it were managed properly. Which does not, of course, include foxhunting . . . or only as a commercial enterprise. He's strong on commercial enterprises. I don't know if you've kept track of the branches he manages—"

"No," Brun said.

"You can look it up later, then. He thinks Sirialis would pay as a mature colony prospect—"

"Bring in colonists!?"

"Yes. In his view, the planet is full of wasted space that ought to be put to profitable use. Buttons pointed out the agricultural areas, but he insists that this is not enough, and he's claiming that Bunny's title was only a life one. Kevil had been working on this, before the attack, but—but now he can't help either."

Brun scowled. "I wonder if dear Uncle Harlis had anything to do with the assassination."

"No, dear. It was not Harlis." That came out with more emphasis than she intended, and Brun looked at her with dawning comprehension.

"Mother—you *know* something? You know who did it?"

"I know it wasn't Harlis." Damn, she'd have to figure out something, or Brun would go charging off, straight into danger again.

"You don't believe it was the NewTex—?"

"No. Although that's still the official line, I do not."

"Then who?"

"Brun, I am not having this conversation with you. Not now, at least. We need to talk about your father's family, and their probable actions, and some of the other economic matters. These things must be dealt with now. Your father's murderers . . . can wait."

"The trail—"

"Will never be too cold. Brun, please. For once in your life listen to me—we must be careful."

Brun had blanched at that; the muscles along her jaw bunched. "I want to go to the Guernesi Republic."

"No. I need you here."

"For what, an exhibition?"

"No, for an ally. If we are to defend our position, we must all help.

Your sisters are already busy—up to their eyeballs in their family responsibilities, but trying to line up support. Buttons and Sarah are both working flat out. I need help, someone whose loyalty is undoubted—I need you."

"Oh . . ." Brun looked past her, into some distance Miranda could not imagine.

"You were willing enough to help Cecelia," she said, and hated the sharpness in her voice.

"You really need me?" Brun asked.

Miranda gave her a sharp look. "Of course—no, let me say that more precisely. Yes, I need you. No one else can do what you can; no one else in the family has the training and experience."

"You're serious . . . but you've never needed me. I'm just the troublemaker . . ." Still, an uncertain note had come into her voice.

"No. You're the one who can survive trouble. Brun, please—help me."

Brun's face twisted. "I don't know if I can . . ."

"You can if you will," Miranda said firmly. "I want to find who murdered your father, and who is trying to dismantle the Familias Regnant, and for what purpose. I am not sure they are the same person or organization, but they might well be."

Brun watched her perfect, serene, immaculate mother with amazement. For her whole life, she had seen her mother as the icon everyone thought her. Her father was the active one, the doer and maker and shaper of events. Her mother smoothed his way by smiling and standing by.

Now she saw the real person behind the label of "mother" and "Bunny Thornbuckle's wife" . . . a woman as intelligent, tough and knowledgeable as her father had ever been. As dangerous, perhaps, as Lorenza had been. From the gleam in Miranda's eye, her mother had just noticed that recognition, and was enjoying the surprise.

"I made no mistake, picking Brun *Meager* for my nom de guerre," Brun said, testing her hypothesis.

Her mother smiled. "Quite so. I'm glad you recognize it. Now—are you with me?"

"Yes. If I can . . ."

"You can. Not all at once, but—let me go on here. I warned your father, after that disgraceful affair on Patchcock, to beware of his relatives doing what that Morrelline woman did. Granted, her brothers deserved it, but others could do the same with less reason. He was sure he had it taken care of, in part because old Viktor Barraclough had always been his friend and mentor. But about the time of the Xavier invasion, he and Kevil found irregularities . . . purchases of company shares they couldn't put a name to, changes in some of the boards of directors which didn't make sense. The military crisis had to come first, of course; and after that, with proof of traitors in Fleet, they were far more concerned with that, and with Grand Council business. But what it's come down to is that Harlis has enough shares, and enough votes in various boards, that he can make a plausible case that much of your father's estate was actually not his personally. I think he'd fiddled the files, but I haven't had time to work on it. And I can't do it here."

"Could you do it at Appledale?"

"Not really . . . I need to go to Sirialis; that's where we stored the backup data. Your father thought I was paranoid, sometimes, but I insisted that we take a complete readoff every half-year, and just archive it. I think that's why Harlis is so determined to get Sirialis; he suspects that the data are there somewhere."

"Then you should go to Sirialis," Brun said. "He can't keep you away, can he?"

"Not yet. But I couldn't leave you alone here—"

Brun interrupted. "You wanted my help; let me give it. Nothing's likely to happen at the next Grand Council meeting anyway; they're probably still in shock, and they'll waffle for days."

"I'm not so sure; that Conselline fellow got himself elected interim Speaker—"

"Whatever happens can't matter as much as stopping Harlis. Go on. I'll attend the Council meeting, and let you know what happens. Promise." Brun reached over and patted her mother's arm. "We aren't going to let Harlis take everything, and we aren't going to let some idiot Conselline ruin the Familias. If that's what's happening."

Her mother gave her an appraising look. "Sometimes, Brun, you are remarkably like your father."

"Sorry . . ."

"No. Don't be. All right—first we'll clear out of this—" With a wave of her arm, she indicated the entire Palace. "Then I'll go to Sirialis."

Cecelia stopped on the way to the hospital to contact her hotel, and reassure the front staff that the two young women and two children were the individuals she had authorized to register in her name. Another two bedrooms? No problem. Cecelia grinned to herself; she had been so wise to invest in a hotel here on Castle Rock, rather than depending on the hospitality of friends.

When she got to the hospital, she was told that she had just missed George. She went upstairs, and stood in the corridor outside Special Care, looking at the motionless form in the bed.

He looked wretched, she thought; she wondered if she had looked as bad. He wasn't conscious, they told her; they were still struggling to control the pressure on his brain, and he was deeply sedated except for weekly checks of neurological function. Cecelia blinked back tears, remembering herself in that drug-induced coma . . . wondering if Kevil were more conscious than they realized . . . and silently promised him she would return and get him out of there, no matter what. She found it hard to leave, but she had something even more urgent to do.

At the Laurels, she stopped at the concierge's desk to ask for assistance in leasing a yacht. The Laurels expected such requests; it took only a moment for the concierge to connect Cecelia to the booking agent for Allsystems Leasing.

Her inspiration had been her nephew Ronnie. Ronnie and Raffaele, as newlyweds, had taken off for the frontier—to Excet-24, a world newly opened to colonization. Cecelia hoped it would have a more euphonious name before it qualified for full membership in the Familias. At last report, Ronnie and Raffa had no children yet, but were "hoping." Cecelia wasn't sure who was hoping—the young people or their parents—but she remembered Raffa's problem-solving abilities, and was sure that Raffa could find the boys a good home if she didn't want them herself.

But this meant a long trip—six weeks at least. She discussed the route with the leasing agent, and ordered the Premium Platinum package of consumables. She didn't mind doing Bunny's family this service, but why should she suffer for it? She wanted fresh food again.

On Miranda's advice, Cecelia hired three more nursemaids. One wanted to emigrate, and was glad to accept a colony share in lieu of salary. She brought along her own children, a two- and a four-year-old. Five people to care for four children might be overdoing it, Cecelia thought, but she herself didn't intend to wash a single diaper or wipe a single drippy nose.

By midnight, Cecelia had arranged everything. The yacht would not be ready immediately, of course; even with the assurance of large sums of money, it took time to prepare a large spaceship for a luxury voyage. But Cecelia had arranged for one of the nursemaids from Miranda's to take the boys to a park with the newly hired maid and her children, leaving the suite clear for at least some hours of the days. No one had seen pictures of them for months; no one, Cecelia was sure, would notice two more young women with children in a park full of young women with children. She had discussed with the nursemaids what clothes would be needed for the voyage and for six months afterward; she didn't know how easy it would be to find children's clothes on a colony world. She set up credit lines so that purchases by the nursemaids would not be traceable to her or to Miranda.

Then she fell into bed with a glow of conscious virtue. When the twins woke, bawling, at two in the morning, she pulled a pillow over her head and went back to sleep. That part of it was someone else's problem.

By the time they boosted from Rockhouse Major, Cecelia felt sure that no one had suspected anything. As far as anyone outside the Palace knew, the twins were still there. The news media had shown no more than normal interest in her doings, and seemed to accept her offhand comment that she had leased the big yacht because she was tired of doing all the work in her little one, and wanted someone else along to cook and clean.

The two boys thoroughly enjoyed the company of other children; Cecelia pored over their medical records in her stateroom, and came to the same conclusion as the doctors and psychologists. Normal children, who could expect to have normal lives. The real question was . . . should she tell Raffaele and Ronnie who they really were? In her own mind, the boys should not know—that they were adopted, yes, but not that their fathers had raped their mother and kept her captive. Of course they must have access to their medical records someday; advances in therapy might make it possible to finish cleaning up their genome.

She saw moral and emotional shoals in either direction.

CHAPTER FOUR

Excet Colony 24 looked, from space, like a paradise, sapphire seas and emerald forests, tawny drylands and olive savannas, all spatched and streaked with white water-vapor clouds. It had been seeded two hundred years before with the usual package of invader species, and closely monitored thereafter. Originally, colonization had been planned for a century later, when the introduced ecosystem would be more stable, but oxygen levels had never fallen dangerously low; the original system here had already been oxy-carbon.

The colony spaceport, in contrast, was a dirty little dump, in Cecelia's view. Her chartered yacht had its own shuttle, whose wide viewscreen gave a clear view of the mess. Discarded cargo containers lay scattered near either end of the runway. The single runway. The spaceport buildings were ugly piles, too much like the Patchcock port. The white plumes of cement factories, the lime kilns where limestone and shale were converted to cement for construction, lay gently on a background of rich green forest in the near distance.

Customs consisted of a harried young woman with a nearly impenetrable accent, whose only concern was whether the new arrivals had colony shares.

"I don't *need* a colony share," Cecelia said. "I'm not staying; I'm just here to visit—"

The young woman glared, took Cecelia's IDs, and inserted them in a machine. After a moment, she turned to give Cecelia a long look.

"Yer not stain."

"I'm not staying, no. I'm here to visit my nephew and his wife. Ronald Vandormer."

61

"Aow! Rownnie! Whyntcha sai so?"

"I tried," Cecelia said.

"He's at th' office, about naow," the woman said. "Ya kin gover." She pointed out the "office," a two-story cube of concrete.

Like most colonies, this one had been given a head start by its investors: the spaceport town had a small grid of paved streets and a larger grid of gravelled ones. The first hundred or so buildings had been put up of substantial materials—in this case concrete blocks. Beyond that were rickety constructions that Cecelia could only call shacks—crudely built of raw timber. Cecelia noticed, as she walked along, the number of people who were carrying things by hand . . . the absence of hand trucks, let alone vehicles.

The two-story building had a low wall enclosing a courtyard to one side, where a group of men were working on some piece of machinery she didn't understand. She started to speak up and ask them about Ronnie, when one of the faces in the group suddenly looked familiar. Ronnie? She blinked in the brilliant sunlight, and it still was . . . in face. The glossy young aristocrat, who had always been just one hair from a dandy—and that only because his friend George had been born with creases and a shine, as they said—stood there in tan workshirt and pants, with smears of mud or grease on both. She couldn't even tell what color his boots had been. But it was Ronnie— as handsome as ever, or more so.

Before she could call out, he turned and went inside; the men went back to doing something with machinery and wood. She followed him inside, to a rough-walled room with a concrete floor, and found him jotting something down on a deskcomp.

"Ronnie—"

He looked up, then his eyes widened. "Aunt Cecelia!"

"I sent word," Cecelia said.

"We never got it." He shrugged. "It's probably in the batch some-where but everyone's been too busy . . ." He looked out the window at the bustle in the courtyard.

"It looks like a lot of work," Cecelia said, eyeing him. This was not a change she had ever expected to see in Ronnie. And why hadn't he said anything about Bunny's death? Or asked about Brun?

"It is. It's not something I thought I'd ever be doing, to tell you the truth."

"Who's your colony governor?"

"Er . . . I am, now that Misktov ran off."

"Ran off?"

"Yes . . . it's easy enough. He stowed away on an outbound flight with most of our negotiable resources."

"But—but that's criminal."

"So it is," Ronnie said. "But I didn't see any police force around to stop him, and we don't have ansible access down here. No money, no communications."

"Oh." Perhaps he didn't know about Bunny's assassination. Cecelia took another look around the room. Not an office, exactly— she saw furniture she recognized from Raffa's mother's summer cottage. A dining room table covered with data cubes and books. A sofa piled with more books and sheets of plastic and paper that looked like construction drawings. Over everything, a layer of gritty gray dust and ash.

"But we're doing well, considering," Ronnie said, before she could organize her thoughts. "It's just . . . there's a lot I didn't know. Don't know yet. You know, Aunt Cecelia, no matter how many cubes you study, there's always something . . . ."

"For instance?"

"Well . . . the cement plants are working all right, and we've got plenty of sand and gravel, so we're fine for unreinforced construction. But my cubes said unreinforced concrete is dangerous . . . ."

"What does your colony engineering team say?"

"Engineering team? We haven't one. I know, the prospectus says we do, but we don't. Aunt Cece, ninety percent of our population are low-level workers . . . which makes sense . . . but these people are low-level workers in a high-level system. They're used to a more advanced infrastructure. They know how to do their work in a world where everything's already set up, not how to work from scratch. The farmers know how to grow crops in big fields, but they don't know how to level them. The plumbers know how to connect pipes in standard modular buildings, but they don't know how to set up a plumbing system from scratch. That's what the engineering team is supposed to do, make the connection between standard designs and standard practices, and the conditions we have locally. But we don't have one."

"If it's that bad, why don't you leave?"

Ronnie looked stubborn. "We don't want to leave, Aunt Cecelia; we want to make it work. We sank all our money in it—even the wedding presents—"

"Even your reserves?"

He flushed. "Not at first, but when Misktov ran off we had to do something. We could've bought ourselves out and run home like silly children, but . . . the colony needed help. So we blew the last on enough to keep the rest alive while we worked it out."

This was a very different Ronnie from the spoiled boy she'd known. Not a hint of petulance or whine anywhere in his voice or manner—he'd been dumped into trouble, and he was going to handle it.

"How's Raffa?" she asked.

"She's fine . . . tired, though." Ronnie grinned, but his eyes were worried. "She's trying to get a school started, but it's hard—the parents say they're too busy, they need the children at home."

"Don't these colony groups include trained teachers?"

"On paper, yes." Ronnie grimaced. "There's a lot I didn't know, in the old days. I thought every standard colony dropped with prefab housing, the five-year-contract engineering team, the education and medical backups that are on the contract."

"And they don't?"

"No—at least, right before Misktov ran off, while we still had the credit for it, I made some inquiries and found that many colonies are shorted. But they're stuck on some planet, mostly uneducated people who haven't a clue who to contact in the Colonial Office . . . no one ever knows. Even me—I sent messages out, but never got any back. We haven't heard from our families in over a year, though we've scraped up enough to piggyback messages to them three times."

"Um. Well, Ronnie, I may have added to your burdens, but—"

"Cecelia!" Raffa came through the door like a burst of spring breeze. "I'm so glad to see you! The only thing about this is that I miss my friends sometimes!"

The girl—no, young woman—looked healthy enough, and genuinely glad to see her. Cecelia braced herself for what she must do.

"Raffaele, Ronnie . . . have you heard about Bunny?"

"Bunny? No—what's wrong?"

"He was assassinated several months ago, supposedly by allies of the men executed after Brun's capture—"

"Wait—Brun was captured? By whom? Is she all right?"

How long had they been out of contact? Cecelia could hardly believe they didn't know. She gave them a quick review of what had happened, ending with, "So you see, when I started thinking of a good home for the babies, I thought of you—I was sure you could find a home for them."

"Brun's babies?"

Now she'd done it. "Yes."

"Of *course* I want them," Raffa said, almost fiercely. Then with a glance at Ronnie. "We do, don't we, Ron?"

"Of course," Ronnie said, but he sounded tired again. "I don't exactly know how, but we'll manage."

"I've brought along nursemaids, including one with two children of her own who wants to stay. And some money Miranda sent, for their education later."

"If it's enough to hire a teacher," Raffa said, "we can start that school . . ."

Cecelia had no idea if it was enough, but she would pry the necessary out of Raffa and Ronnie's parents if she had to. She would also, she thought, find out why incoming messages, including hers, weren't getting through.

"Where are the babies?" Raffa said, looking around.

"Still in the shuttle," Cecelia said. "I doubt I'd ever have gotten them past that . . . that person in the terminal."

"Oh, Ganner . . . she was Misktov's girlfriend, and he left her here, marooned her. She thought she was going to be the governor's lady, and lord it over everyone, but here she is. She hates everybody."

"Except handsome men," Raffa said, with a touch of asperity. "Lady Cecelia, you should see how she fawns on Ronnie. I know he's not susceptible, but it's a little disgusting sometimes."

"It's handy when I want something," Ronnie said. "Come on, let's get those babies out of the shuttle. If I have babies crawling all over me, I'll bet Ganner finds me less attractive."

By the time she left again, Cecelia knew that more was wrong with Excet-24 than one scoundrelly governor and a missing engineering team. She'd never paid much attention to colony worlds—why choose to live uncomfortably if you didn't have to?—or colonial policy, but surely it hadn't been intended to work like this. The nursemaids had been understandably wide-eyed at the conditions on the planet, and Cecelia had had some difficulty persuading them to stay until she returned.

"I'll find out why messages aren't getting through," she promised Ronnie. "And find you some of the experts you need. You've done wonderfully—" She didn't really believe that, but the young couple had tried, and weren't whining, and that counted for a lot in her private grade-book. "It'll be a few months, you understand—"

"That's what they all say," Ronnie said, but with no sting in it.

All the way to Sirialis, Miranda had planned what to do. If she tried to call on her family's expertise, Harlis might find out, and would certainly do his best to stop her. She had to assume he'd figure it out; she had to assume she had only a limited lead before he found some way of separating her from the data she needed to explore.

Bunny had teased her, at first, when she insisted on having her own archives, separate from the family, in machines not physically connected to anything but a solar power supply. Paranoia, he'd said, ran in the Meager family line. She pressed her lips together tightly, remembering that laugh, and her scornful reply . . . she had been so young, so sure of herself.

And so right. Not for nothing had her family been in information technology for centuries. She had insisted; Bunny had given in; her personal and very complete archives lay not at the big house—though she kept a blind copy there, as a decoy—but in a remote hunting lodge. Every hunting season—and in between, if they were in residence—she added another set of records, stripping the current logs.

It would have been easier if she could have had Kevil's help, but she could do it herself, given enough time. That was the trick, finding enough time.

The staff at Sirialis met her with the sympathy and respect she'd expected. Harlis might have local spies and supporters, but they wouldn't show themselves yet. She spent the first few days as anyone would expect, taking sympathy calls and answering what questions she could about the future of their world.

The big house felt empty, even with all the servants in it . . . knowing Bunny would never come down those stairs, never wander out of that library, never sit at the head of the long table. She missed him almost as much in the stables and kennels; although she had ridden to hounds every season, foxhunting had never been her favorite sport; she had done it because Bunny enjoyed it so, and enjoyed her company.

That first evening, alone in the big room she had once shared, her mind wandered back to Cecelia's visit. Where had she taken the twins? She had seemed to know exactly where she was going . . . well, that was Cecelia, and always had been, though it usually involved a horse.

But before the twins, what was it she'd said? About Bunny's killers, about some plot—Miranda struggled to remember, past the confusion of the last weeks, the urgency of her concern about the estate, and the travel-induced headache. Finally she shrugged, and gave up for the night.

The name didn't come to her until she was at the hunting lodge far north of the main house, where the snow still lay deep on the shadowed sides of the mountains. She'd made copies of all the critical data—astonishing herself with the number of cubes it took to hold it all—and then packed it neatly into her carryall for the flight back. It was too late that day—she didn't want to risk a night flight, as tired as she was—so she'd heated up one of the frozen lumps of soup, and settled in by the fireplace with a mug of soup and another of cocoa. She felt—not smug, exactly, but pleased with herself. She had the backups, which she could work on at the main house, and her surveillance link showed no ships in the system. That meant Harlis could not possibly get there in time to discover her hiding place.

Her mind wandered off to the twins again, and from there to Cecelia, and then—as if a cube were playing—her memory handed her the first part of their conversation. Not the NewTex Militia— well, she'd been doubtful of that herself, though they were certainly capable of killing and maiming. But . . . Pedar Orregiemos?

Cecelia hadn't mentioned it, and perhaps didn't know it, but Pedar had once wanted to marry her. She hadn't loved him; he was older than Bunny, and fussy pomposity had never attracted her—but he'd been convinced she married Bunny just for his money. He'd even said so, one afternoon in the rose garden. She hadn't quite smacked his face, but she'd been tempted.

Pedar? Could it be? She couldn't imagine him doing it himself, except perhaps with a smallsword—he had been quite a fencer in his day, and probably kept it up. And Cecelia might have misunderstood. What could be the reason? What could Pedar gain from killing Bunny, or having him killed?

She did not realize, until the handle snapped off the cocoa mug, just how agitated she was. Luckily the cocoa had cooled; she wiped up the mess, put the broken bits in the trash she'd take back to the main house, and tried to quiet the racing of her heart.

Pedar was, after all, a Rejuvenant—not merely someone who had had rejuvenations, as she and Bunny had had, but someone who felt threatened by those who hadn't. She remembered six—no, seven, at least—eight years ago, an argument about Rejuvenants and Ageists at one of Kemtre's parties, when Pedar had insisted very loudly that it would end in bloodshed. *They will kill us out of envy, or we will kill them in self-defense,* he'd said, and then some other men had hustled him away and sobered him up.

Would he have had Bunny killed for that? Was he one of a group who would have done it? And who else?

She tried to turn off these thoughts—she needed rest; she had a long flight the next morning, and a lot of work to do after it—but she lay long awake, tossing, her stomach roiled with anger.

The next day, back in the main house, she walked past the glass cases of antique weapons as she had done so often before, and paused. Bunny had fenced only because it was an expected social skill, keeping her company in the salle as she kept him company in the hunting field. But he had had a strange passion for old weapons, both blades and firearms.

It was a mixed collection, though displayed with all the organization possible: long blades in this case, short blades in that one, short-barrelled firearms here, long-barrelled ones there, glass-topped floor cabinets with helmets and breastplates and mailed gloves.

Miranda stopped in front of the wall-hung case of swords. The broadest blades below—the single broadsword, the two sabers, one straight and one curved slightly. Two schlagers, a rapier, five epees, four foils—the latter displayed in pairs, angled and opposing, their tips crossed.

On a whim, Miranda opened the case and took down the broadsword, turning its blade to the light to see the dappled pattern of refolded and beaten steel layers. When she rapped it with her knuckles, it rang a little, and its edge was still sharp enough to cut.

She wished she knew its history. Bunny had suspected it of being an ancient reproduction from the early space era, not a genuine pre-space relic. But when they'd done a forensic scan on it, there'd been human blood in the runes incising the blade. Only a trace, and the scans weren't able to date it closer than a couple of hundred years, but . . . she'd always wondered.

The sabers were easier to date. One of them had been a presentation sword made for one of Bunny's ancestors as a fiftieth wedding anniversary present, with a dated inscription. It had never been used for anything but ceremony—carried upright in processions, or laid along the top of the coffin at funerals. The other had been an officer's saber—also ceremonial, she assumed, inherited over the blanket from a family she'd never heard of, some two hundred years before.

The schlagers at least were old—one was certainly 20th Century old reckoning—but while she had drilled with such blades, they hadn't ever warmed her interest. The rapier, so seemingly similar, did. This one, with a graceful swept hilt, balanced easily when she lifted it out, and swung it around.

She put it back almost guiltily. What was she thinking? Nothing, she told herself. Nothing at all. She closed the case and locked it. These were priceless antiques, not toys; if she wanted to practice, the salle held modern weapons and equipment far better suited for her sport.

And she had no time. She headed back to the big square office that had been Bunny's estate office, and was now her workplace as she tried to figure out just what Harlis had done.

Altiplano

Luci Suiza had expected the furor over her cousin Esmay's engagement to an outlander to dispel interest in her own plans, but somehow the discussion at the dinner table spilled over onto her. She had a mouthful of corn soup when Papa Stefan opened with a volley of complaints about the quarterly accounts.

"—And that ridiculous expense for equipment we don't need, to develop a foreign market we've done very well without for centuries. We're not that sort of people, is what I say. Luci! You can't tell me this was all Esmaya's idea!"

Luci swallowed quickly, burning her throat on the soup, but managed not to choke. "No, Papa Stefan. But we were talking about the future of her herd, and I had researched—"

"Researched!" Papa Stefan in full huff would interrupt even generals; unmarried girls didn't have a chance. "You don't know what research is. You were seduced by all those outlander magazines you read. If my mother were still alive—"

Luci found that she had inherited the gene for interruption, surprising herself. "She's not. Esmay's the Landbride, and she approves. The outlanders need our stocks' genetic input, and we need theirs."

"You interrupted me!" Papa Stefan did not quite roar, but he looked as if he might.

"You interrupted me first," Luci said. She heard the shocked mutters of her parents, but ignored them in the excitement of attack. "And the genetic equipment was my idea, and is my responsibility, and I did check with the Landbride, who approved the expenses, which she thoroughly understood."

"Not like a Landbride at all," Papa Stefan growled. "A Landbride should conserve resources, not waste them on crackpot schemes—"

"Like the Barley River irrigation project?" That was Sanni, who could never resist a dig about Papa Stefan's one big mistake. As a young man, he'd been convinced that irrigation of dry coastal land with water from the Barley would be practical and profitable. His mother, then only newly Landbride, had allowed him enough money to unbalance the estancia budget for a decade.

"It's not the same thing at all," Papa Stefan said.

"It's not," Luci said. "My idea is on schedule and on budget, and in fact it's costing us less than the Landbride approved, because I got support from other breeders."

"Which is another thing," Papa Stefan said, ignoring the part about on budget and on schedule. "You went outside the family to bring in outsiders—"

"Our allies for generations," Luci said. "After all, I'm marrying Phil—" It had slipped out, not at the moment she'd planned.

"Philip? Philip who?"

"Philip Vicarios," Sanni said quietly; her quick glance admonished Luci. Papa Stefan stared a moment, then turned to look at Casimir and Berthold.

"She's marrying a Vicarios?"

Luci had not really doubted what Esmay told her, but now a chill sank through her as she saw, in their faces, additional confirmation.

Berthold shrugged. "She has Esmay's approval, I understand."

"And you, Casi?"

Casimir nodded. "The family is our ally. Paul is my friend—"

"Does she *know*—?"

"Children, you may be excused," Sanni interrupted. The younger cousins, eyes already wide, scrambled away from the table with only the briefest duck of the head to the elders. Luci's younger brother gave her a look that meant she would be ambushed later and expected to Tell All. When the door closed behind them all, Luci spoke into the silence.

"I know. Esmaya told me. She said it didn't matter, that she held no grudge against the family, and if Philip was kind—"

"Kind! Marriage is not about kindness!" Papa Stefan had turned an ugly red.

"It is," Sanni said. "Not that you would know—"

"Quiet!" Casimir rarely interrupted at these family fights, but this time he did, with all the power of command built over years of active service. "Too much is at stake here to rehash old battles or waste energy and patience yelling at each other. As the Landbride's Trustee, I know that she did in fact approve Luci's desire to marry Philip Vicarios. She did in fact approve Luci's expenditure of equipment to allow us to export genestock, and her reasons were sound enough to convince me, and the other Trustees, that this was a good idea. This is not, after all, the real issue. The real issue is, the Landbride wants to marry an outlander, and continue to live offplanet, and the other landholders would like to use this as an excuse to reduce our influence in the Guild. I see no chance of changing Esmay's mind—for all the reasons we know about—so I suggest we turn our attention to minimizing the damage to the Suiza Family, and quit inflicting more on ourselves."

Luci had not expected her uncle Casimir to be so sensible. To her surprise, Papa Stefan went back to his meal, stabbing the sliced cattlelope as if it were an enemy, but silent. Sanni sipped the rest of her soup in thoughtful silence; Berthold helped himself to a pile of potatoes in red sauce, and began eating steadily. Casimir looked at Luci.

"Have you any more bombshells to drop, Luci?"

"No, Uncle."

"Did Esmaya mention anything to you about passing on the Landbride duties?"

Luci felt herself going hot. "She did . . . in a way . . . but—"

"She spoke of you." It was not a question. Casimir tented his hands and looked over them at her. "Did you agree?"

"I told her it was too soon," Luci said. "I'm only—"

"The age that two Landbrides were invested, in the old days. A year older, in fact, than Silvia." Luci had never heard of Silvia, though she had, like all the children, memorized a hundred years of Landbrides Suiza. "It may be that having her designate you Landbride-to-be would help—that plus your marriage to a Vicarios would prove that the Suizas were not involved in interstellar politics."

CHAPTER FIVE

Hobart glared at Oskar Morrelline, former head of the Morrelline branch of his sept. "You were outmaneuvered by Venezia," he said. "That fuzzbrained sister of yours cost us market share and dropped profits twenty-eight percent—"

"It's not *my* fault," Oskar said. "If—"

"Oh yes, it is." Hobart interrupted smoothly. "Your daughter Ottala—what is it with the women in your family, anyway?—goes haring off to Patchcock and gets herself killed. That's what started it—a daughter you didn't control any better than Bunny controlled Brun—"

Oskar had flushed an ugly color; Hobart enjoyed that as he always enjoyed exercising power. "No, Oskar. I can't trust you to do it right, whatever it is. I cannot give you a Ministry. In a few years, I expect the public climate will change, and then, perhaps, we can find something for you."

"You expect my vote but you aren't giving me anything?"

"I expect your vote because you know where your advantage lies. Even if they had it to give, you would get nothing out of that clique Bunny ran. And they do not have it to give, not anymore."

Oskar glared, but subsided, as Hobart had known he would. Oskar was a blusterer, but if that didn't work he had no second weapon. Hobart always had a second weapon—and a third and a fourth, he thought to himself. He changed his tone, and went on; if Oskar could get it through his head what the problem really was, he might be useful.

"Whoever controls the rejuvenation process controls everything— as long as the public doesn't rebel against rejuvs. We must take steps against the Ageist conspiracies; the shortlifes, if they realize the danger they're in, outnumber us at this point and could be dangerous."

"But Venezia says—"

"Venezia is a fool. Yes, something had gone wrong there, something serious. A Benignity spy, if I understand the little that's been declassified. But it's not as bad as all that. Women are so excitable, not to mention sentimental, and Venezia in particular—"

Oskar nodded eagerly; Hobart smiled to himself. How the Morrelline brothers hated having Venezia in charge! "All she ever did was play with pottery—" Oskar said.

"Quite so. How could she know anything about the real world? She could not be expected to realize how many lives would be disrupted—prematurely ended, with the shortage of rejuvenation drugs—because of her finicky insistence on exact procedures."

"But Hobart—how do we get it back? How do we get her out of there?"

Exactly the opening he'd hoped for. "By doing precisely what I tell you," Hobart said. "I need your support at all the Grand Council sessions; I will let you know what I need you to say, and how to vote. With more sympathetic, more cooperative Ministers, we should be able to ease dear Venezia back into her supportive role."

"She won't like it," Oskar said, puffing out his plump cheeks.

"I don't care whether she does or not," Hobart said. "I am not going to let one woman stand in the way of progress for the Conselline Sept." He looked forward to that moment, probably more than Oskar did. Venezia had been a constant nuisance at sept board meetings, poking her nose into all sorts of inconvenient corners. He'd had to roust her out of his own offices more than once, where she chatted up the clerical staff and wheedled who knows what out of them. She seemed to think she had a moral mission to clean up the whole sept.

"Our responsibility to the whole Familias . . ." she would say, while Hobart ground his teeth. They had no responsibility to the whole Familias; they had a responsibility to Family shareholders. Period. He wasn't going to urge her to go on making faulty drugs. Bad for business, and people would be watching carefully. Beyond that, though, it wasn't their business to be saints, if that's what she had in mind.

"If Kemtre had not been a weak man, none of these disasters would have happened. He drugged his son into stupidity, and then created those damned clones."

"I don't see that cloning is such a bad thing."

"No, nor do I, except that we have a rapidly growing population anyway. We don't need clones; we need sensible strong men who know how to handle the hysterics. No offense." He eyed Oskar, but Oskar didn't mind if Hobart called his sister hysterical. "Now, Oskar, I want you to have a word with the Broderick Institute, and tell them to do their homework a little better—"

"The Broderick Institute? What have they done?"

Sometimes he wondered if Oskar had a brain. Venezia, for all her impracticality, had wit enough. "Oskar, the Broderick Institute is where Dr. Margulis works." Oskar still looked blank. "The same Dr. Margulis whose report on the so-called bad drugs coming out of Patchcock started a near panic in the market—"

"Oh—*that* Dr. Margulis. But I thought—"

"He's come up with more—the man is a closet Ageist, I'm sure, just looking for any excuse to scare people away from rejuvenation. Broderick has given him free rein for the past fifteen years, and look what that so-called independent research has led to. It's cost you, and me, and the whole Familias. He needs to be controlled; at the very least, someone needs to do *impartial* research showing how beneficial rejuv is. And since the Conselline Sept provides over two-thirds of the money to support the Broderick Institute, they need to be reminded of the importance of truly even-handed science."

"Won't they complain about academic freedom?"

"They're not a university; they're a privately funded research facility. If you're tactful, they'll get the point without blowing up. That's your job."

Oskar left, finally, and Hobart puffed air out explosively. *Idiots.* He was surrounded by idiots and incompetents, and they all wanted something from him. He glanced at his desk and told his secretary to send in Pedar Orregiemos. Another idiot. Minor family, major nuisance, but also a born bootlicker, and those could be useful.

Pedar came in looking smug about something. Hobart had no time for Pedar's self-congratulation. Besides, he would be even smugger, with more reason, very shortly.

"We have a problem coming up," he said. Pedar's expression shifted quickly from smugness to concern. "As you know, I was elected temporary Speaker at the emergency Council meeting immediately after Lord Thornbuckle's assassination." Pedar nodded. "The next meeting will be crucial. If we are not to lapse back into the ineffective vacillation of the previous administration, if we're to meet the challenges that threaten us, we need to take action quickly. Will you help me?"

"Of course," Pedar said. "What can I do?"

"In the long run, you can be my Minister of Foreign Affairs." Hobart paused, and enjoyed the sight of Pedar completely silenced, for once. He had not expected that high an honor . . . good, then he would be the more willing to earn it. "But not immediately: first there are changes in the bylaws which need to be approved. I'll give you the texts; I want your analysis of the probable response."

"Of course; right away."

"I'm calling the next meeting almost immediately; it would be unethical not to have a general meeting as quickly as possible." Pedar nodded like a child's toy. Did he even grasp the importance of that? Did he realize how critical the timing was, how this haste would work to Conselline advantage? For an instant, Hobart thought of explaining it to him, sharing some of his data on Family movements, his basis for knowing who could attend, and thus how the votes would go. No. Better not let even Pedar know how much he knew.

Hobart went on. "After that meeting, I'll be making some ministerial changes; Foreign Affairs will be high on that list, but I can't give you an exact date. What you must understand is where the real threat is." Hobart leaned closer. "It's not war, no matter what anyone says. We're large, strong, healthy, with a vigorous military—well, mostly vigorous. Anton Lepescu was more than a little crazy, but that doesn't mean all his ideas were bad. He had the right idea about the military and war, for instance. If he'd been assigned to the rescue mission, do you suppose we'd have had any problem with leftover terrorists?"

Pedar shook his head; Hobart allowed himself a smile.

"Of course not," he went on. "He'd have made sure there weren't any. None of this idiocy of bringing back hundreds of women and children—born troublemakers, every one of them. And to whom do we owe that diplomatic and political problem? Bunny Thornbuckle's friends, the Serranos. Who, as we all know, have no direct loyalty to any of the Chairholding Families."

"Well, but, Hobart, none of the Fleet families do now—"

"Not directly, not now, but they *did* in the past. That's my point. I've read history; I know what's supposed to have happened. But how do we know that the Serranos weren't involved in the massacre of their patron Family? What proof do we have?"

Pedar looked surprised, then thoughtful. "I hadn't ever considered that. But they're powerful . . ."

"Yes. Thoroughly entrenched. And I'm sure there are decent, loyal soldiers among them. But overall, their influence is questionable. We need a Fleet we can count on to crush any opponent, protect our shipping, protect the new worlds we need to open for our colonists."

After Pedar left, Hobart stared out the window, musing. His brother Guilliam had always been the pet of the family. Everyone loved Guilliam; Hobart had suspected his parents of having that easy charm built into Guilliam's genes, while he—he had been given the steel-hard core Guilliam lacked. He had been designed as the unloved workhorse, who was to stand back, walk behind, and do all the difficult tasks that were too much for Guilliam.

People still talked about Guilliam. Too bad about poor Guilliam, they said. Hobart knew what they really meant—too bad that they had to deal with him instead of his softer brother. Guilliam took no part in Family business—hadn't since their parents died, when an escalation in his addiction to starplex-tree resin resulted in permanent brain damage which even rejuv could not repair.

Guilliam would not be at the next Council meeting, any more than he'd been at the others. And on Hobart's side . . . he ran through the list again, ticking names off his mental list. The minor Families— Derringer, Hochlit, Tassi-Lioti, all that crowd, were yammering now for leadership, and would probably follow anyone strong enough. Harlis Thornbuckle, Bunny's own brother, wanted control of Bunny's estate bad enough to deal . . . though he probably wasn't trustworthy in the long run. If Kevil Mahoney had been capable, he might have talked some of the waverers into the other camp, but he was still in the medical center, and the opposition was no more than a confusion of Barracloughs, more intent on fighting over leadership within their sept than on threats from without. Since Mahoney wasn't on his side, just as well not to have him active at all. In the future, he expected to talk Mahoney over; the man needed a power base. It was purely an accident that he had been Bunny's friend; he could just as easily be Hobart's friend.

With any luck, no one from Bunny's family would attend this Grand Council meeting anyway. They would expect this one to be unimportant, with a weak Speaker elected to finish out Bunny's term. This was his window of opportunity. He could take hold of the weak, flaccid, rudderless ship of state—catch the winds of time, and take them all to a better future than anyone else saw.

And he would be taken seriously this time. Not as a substitute for Guilliam, but as the leader he knew himself to be. Young and vigorous, even without rejuv—and when it came time to rejuv, he would know exactly what source to use.

His scheduler chimed; Hobart silenced it with a snap of the fingers. He toyed with the idea of skipping his exercises for once, but habit had already brought him to his feet. Iagin, the Swordmaster who supervised his own fencing coach, was there for his twice-annual analysis of Hobart's progress.

The pine-and-sandalwood-scented changing room shifted his mood, as it was meant to, and focussed his attention on his body. Hobart stripped off his business clothes and dropped them into the hamper. His exercise clothes hung on racks . . . today, for his fencing lesson, he chose a skinsuit and the leather armor. His coach didn't approve of leather, but he was in no mood to pamper his coach.

He glanced at himself in the mirror with satisfaction. Barrel chest, flat belly, well-muscled legs, erect posture, firm mouth. Not a slack, flabby fiber in him, mind or body. A man fit to lead.

In the exercise room itself, he warmed up with the standard sets, then stretched. As he was twisting himself into a pretzel, trying not to look at himself—he hated these stretches, which were at best undignified—the door opened and the Swordmaster came in. His own coach would not have dared; Hobart had made it clear that he needed no supervision in warm-up. But the Swordmasters were an old, proud breed, and he put up with their arrogance for the sake of their skill. Bunny had never taken up fencing, and had resolutely refused to have a Swordmaster at his estate even when most Families did. Well, and who had just died?

"Lord Conselline," the Swordmaster said. "Your form needs improvement."

"Instruct me," Hobart said, proud of conquering a flash of anger.

The Swordmaster bent and twisted his own body into the stretch, and held it. "You are not keeping the knee straight," he said, from under his arm. "And you are bending the spine too much in the thoracic span, and not enough in the lumbar." He unwound, not red in the face or breathless. "Try again."

Hobart twisted and tangled himself into the required knot. He knew what it was for, but he disliked it and knew he had been skimping on it for months. The Swordmaster's hands steadied him, and then pushed and pulled . . . Hobart felt a *pop* in his spine, and the sudden ease of a cramp he had not realized he had.

"Like that," the Swordmaster said. "You really should let Orris spot you in this for several months."

"I'll consider it," Hobart said, untwisting carefully.

"Good. If you are ready . . ." The Swordmaster nodded toward the salle.

"Is it true," Hobart asked, as they passed through the archway, "that all Swordmasters must have killed with the blade?"

"It is a tradition," the Swordmaster said.

Hobart wanted to know what it felt like but could think of no polite way to ask. And which blade? The Swordmasters taught the use of all blades, had mastered all styles.

Orris held out practice masks, transparent reinforced ceram with touch-signalling circuitry embedded, and the warm-up blades. Hobart glanced at Orris, wondering what he'd told Master Iagin; he suspected Orris of reporting on more than his fencing skill. He did, after all, have to take the occasional call during a lesson, and Orris might have overheard scraps of conversation. But nothing important, he thought. Nothing that would interest a Swordmaster anyway.

Masked and gloved, with blade in hand, he faced Master Iagin on the strip. The salute—old-fashioned, formal, an utter waste of time, and yet it set the emotional tone for what followed. The initial touches . . . boring, when all Hobart wanted was to get this session out of the way so he could return to his plotting.

Master Iagin's tip smacked into his faceshield, which flared red. For an instant he could not speak for anger, and then he grunted. "Touch."

"Your mind wandered, Lord Conselline," Master Iagin said. Behind the arc of gleaming protection, his expression was unreadable—quiet, a little stern, but neither anger nor apprehension.

"My apologies," Hobart said. This was, after all, one of the reasons he had stayed with fencing, the need to concentrate utterly on what he was doing. But Orris usually gave him a few minutes to settle in. The man had never struck him so early in a session. Still . . . the Swordmaster was who he was, and probably thought fencing was the most important thing in the universe. In his, it may have been. Hobart collected these scattered thoughts, locked them away, and focussed on Master Iagin's blade.

Just in time, for it flicked toward him again, and his parry was only just enough. He missed the riposte, but by the next parry was able to riposte . . . only to meet Master Iagin's parry and a riposte so powerful it blew through his own and punched him lightly in the chest.

"Touch," he said, this time more cheerfully. He was not expected to defeat a Swordmaster, only to show that he had been working.

He had indeed, and his next attack actually achieved a touch. His spirits soared. He had never made a touch on the Swordmaster from seven before. All that work with weights must have done it. Twenty touches—sixteen to the Swordmaster and four to him—then a break to stretch out again before taking up the heavier blades.

"Your right forearm is definitely stronger, Lord Conselline," the Swordmaster said.

"Orris has me doing weight work."

"Good. But I notice that your left arm is still substantially weaker—there should be no more than five percent difference in strength, unless someone has suffered an injury. Have you?"

Hobart scowled. "It's stronger than last year."

"Indeed it is. But the imbalance affects more than your off-hand fencing, milord. It also affects the set of your spine and your gait. You need to balance them, just as you balance work and play."

Hobart's scowl deepened; he could feel the tension in his neck. "I have no time for play, Swordmaster. Surely you have heard of the terrible crisis that faces us? Lord Thornbuckle was killed by terrorists—"

"Yes, of course," Master Iagin said. "But that makes my point. You must be balanced to withstand such blows. It is the failure of balance in your society which makes it vulnerable—the undisciplined who stagger and fall when the blow falls."

"I do not intend to stagger and fall," Hobart said. He caught a glimpse of himself in the mirrors that lined the salle—flushed and truculent. Dangerous.

"Nor will you, milord, I'm sure. Your work here—the discipline needed to achieve the level you've achieved—sustains you, along with your native talents. But as each movement balances contraction of one muscle group with extension of another, so the steadfast must balance strain and relaxation."

"I find relaxation in this," Hobart said with a wave to include the entire exercise suite.

"That is good," Master Iagin said. "You have a warrior's heart, which finds ease in growing stronger."

Praise, of a sort. He would take it. A warrior's heart he knew he had, and he could feel himself growing stronger.

When the lesson ended, Hobart invited Master Iagin to dinner at the family table, but the Swordmaster declined. "With your permission, milord, I will walk in your gardens; I must take ship tomorrow, and I am not often able to stretch my legs in such beauty."

"Of course." He still did not understand Master Iagin's fascination with the garden, but he anticipated that request. Discreet surveillance had revealed that the man did not tumble a maid behind the hedges or use any sort of communications device to contact a confederate. He always did what he asked permission to do—strolled along the pebbled garden paths, stopping now and then to sniff a flower. He pretended to fence with the topiary knight, and if one of the gardener's cats appeared, he would pick it up and stroke it. At the far end of the garden, he always paused to watch the black-finned fish in the lily pond. Not what Hobart had expected of a Swordmaster, but they were known to have strange habits. Most of them, for some reason or other, liked gardens.

At dinner, Delphine asked if the Swordmaster were still there. Hobart gave her a look that shut her up instantly, but then he answered her. "He's here, but he's leaving tomorrow. Why?"

"I just wanted to meet him . . ."

"You have no reason to meet him; you do not take fencing seriously." Delphine could strike a pretty pose with foil in hand, and in fencing whites, and in the garden in front of the rose hedge, looked quite exciting that way. But her footwork was execrable, and she had never shown any determination in learning better. He would not have been too pleased if she had, but her failure to oppose him even on this was another proof of her weakness. Luckily, he had been able to choose other gene lines for his sons.

Delphine picked at her shellfish and changed the subject. "I called Miranda today, but her private secretary wouldn't put me through. I was able to make an appointment for tomorrow, when she's taking condolence calls."

"That's good," Hobart said. A quick flash of anger that a secretary prevented his wife—*his* wife, Lady Conselline—from contacting Miranda Thornbuckle flared and died. It wasn't important, after all. Miranda would find out soon enough that what power she had had through Bunny was gone, water into sand.

"Hobart—are *you* in danger?"

"Me?!" He smiled at her, surprised and pleased by her solicitude. "No, my dear. Bunny made enemies I have not made." He had others, but none that would dare have him killed. "And besides, I am more careful. We have excellent security. Do not worry about me, or about yourself and the children."

"It's all so terrible," Delphine said, putting down her fork. "Pirates capturing Brun, and then the terrorists—"

"It won't happen again," Hobart said firmly. "I'll see to that."

Her eyes widened, the periwinkle-blue eyes that he loved. "But Hobart—how? You aren't—"

If she said he wasn't important, he would kill her right there; he felt himself stiffening, and saw in her face the reaction to his expression. Her mouth snapped shut; tears filled her eyes and she looked down at her plate.

"I know it's hard for you to believe," he said quietly, through his teeth. "But I am not a nonentity—"

"Oh, Hobart, I didn't say—I didn't mean—"

"And I can and will keep you safe. And others. It's my duty, and I have never shirked my duty."

"Of course not," she said. Up came her napkin, to dab at the tears.

"We have had laxity in high places," Hobart said firmly, feeling the phrases in his mouth. "With all due respect for Lord Thornbuckle—and I have known Bunny all my life—he simply did not have the . . . the moral fiber to do what was necessary. I will not make that mistake. When I am First Speaker—and I shall be, Delphine, in a matter of days—things will be handled very differently. None of his weak deference to the entrenched bureaucracy which is always afraid to make changes lest it mean the loss of influence. I will make the decisions, and I will save the realm." He looked up, to find her staring at him, eyes still wide. He pointed his knife at her. "And you, my dear, will say nothing of this to anyone. I have no doubt that the Grand Council will be glad to elect someone who has a clear vision of what should be done, but I don't want them confused by your version of events first, is that clear?"

"Yes, Hobart."

"You will say nothing to Miranda tomorrow."

"No, Hobart."

"And you will quit messing about with that crab, and eat properly."

"Yes, Hobart."

That was better. If she would just confine herself to doing what he told her, and not argue, she would be an exemplary wife. He could imagine her in the Palace, greeting those he invited to the necessary social events. Delphine was good at social events. Decorative, tactful, soft-voiced. Like Miranda, Bunny's widow, in that respect. But his wife. His tool.

R.S.S. *Gyrfalcon*

Barin Serrano checked his appearance in the mirror yet again. Like all his class who had not actually disgraced themselves, he had his promotion to jig, and in an hour the ensigns were to appear for the promotion ceremony in the captain's office. His parents, in accordance with tradition, had sent him their old insignia—a pair from each—and a credit chip for his contribution to the celebration in the junior officers' mess. That was handy, given that his pay was now zeroed out. They'd said nothing about that, in their accompanying note. He wondered if it had been written before they found out. He wondered if they simply couldn't think of anything to say.

Luckily, these lower-level promotions didn't require dress uniforms, and he had a natural knack for looking trim. His mind strayed, as it often did, to Esmay Suiza, whose fluffy brown hair sometimes appalled her as much as it delighted him. She would never understand, he was sure, how those stray wisps made him feel.

He hadn't heard from Esmay in weeks, but they'd both been shipbound. They'd expected it. He hadn't expected to be quite so susceptible to everything that reminded him of her, but he assumed that would pass.

"C'mon, Barin!" came a call from the hatch of the ensigns' bay. With a last glance (no, hairs had not suddenly sprouted from his ears) he turned and followed the rest to the ceremony.

The ceremony itself was brief, but the aftermath wasn't. Each newly promoted jig had, by tradition, donated a dozen drink chits into the pool, and the first twelve enlisted personnel who recognized the new rank each got one. Barin, one of the last in alphabetical order on this ship, found that he was being ambushed at every crossing until his last chit was gone.

Four hours later, the first of the new ensign assignees came aboard, a ship-to-ship transfer from the *Cape Hay* which had ferried them from Sector HQ. Two were already partway through their progress from newly commissioned to jig, but three were this year's graduates, so wet they squeaked. Barin, still most junior in ship duty of the jigs, found himself assigned to escort them to the junior wardroom. He'd known the more senior ones at the Academy; Cordas Stettin was, in fact, a kind of cousin through his mother's family, and Indi Khas had been in his cadet unit. They looked incredibly young; he couldn't believe he had ever been that green. He kept almost looking behind himself when one of them called him *sir*.

The *Gyrfalcon* was on what would have been a routine patrol, if it weren't for the persistent fear that the New Texas colonies were up to something. Normally, Sector Seven was quiet; the transit points into it from Benignity space made invasion from their main enemy unlikely. Now, however, they were expecting trouble. Within the ship itself, all routines were performed under the restrictions of

Level 2 alert. A few days of this, Barin thought, and people would start slacking off: not quite dogging down the blast barriers, not remembering to close off the shower-room drains after use, forgetting one or more of the niggling little details that might—if they came under surprise attack—save lives, or waste them.

Junior officers and senior NCOs were the only defense against this natural relaxation of precautions, and they had lost eight senior NCOs to the medical restrictions on rejuv recipients. Barin took his turn at inspection with a keen understanding of its importance. He had, after all, lost an uncle to someone's failure to dog a blast barrier, and had grown up with the story.

But *Cape Hay* had brought new orders, and Captain Escovar called Barin in to discuss them.

"You remember that professor who's been staying with your wives—er, dependents?"

"Yes, sir."

"Well, we're going to stop by to pick her up, and take her with us to Sector One HQ, where we're to meet a diplomat of some sort from the Lone Star Confederation and transport her back to Castle Rock. And it might be a good idea for you to try to convince those women to do something other than sit there eating up Fleet resources. They may not listen, but they've been telling Professor Meyerson they can't do anything without your permission. Oh, and you have mail."

Barin read the message cube as soon as he had a free moment, which was hours later. His parents had recorded it, but the full weight of the Serrano dynasty lay behind it.

He was young to marry anyway, and with Fleet having already assigned him responsibility for the maximum number of dependents, how could he even think of marrying? Of course they were sure that Lieutenant Suiza would understand, and if she truly cared for him, she would see to it that she made things easier, not harder, for him. There need be no unseemly haste, assuming—

Barin argued with the message cube in resentful silence. How could he think of marrying? How could he not? Unseemly haste? They had known each other for years now; they had been through a Bloodhorde attack, the machinations of envious troublemakers, a very tricky hostage extrication, and he was not—NOT—going to be told he was too young, too inexperienced, too anything else to get married. He was a jig, not some wet-ears ensign fresh out of the Academy.

He loved her. She loved him. It was so simple, if only other people would leave them alone. Perhaps she could get leave and they could meet somewhere . . . privately . . . he toyed briefly with the idea of running away and getting married secretly, in spite of his family. That wouldn't be fair to Esmay, though. The Landbride Suiza would expect—would require—more than a hasty ceremony before some local magistrate. Still, with the ship detached for diplomatic duty, maybe—just maybe—they could manage to meet.

CHAPTER SIX

R.S.S. *Shrike*

"Mail drop, Lieutenant." Chief Conway handed Esmay the hardcopy list. Esmay managed not to sigh. All these new security procedures ate time, since every piece of incoming mail at every mail drop required her to check and initial it. Luckily, they could pick up mail only when reasonably near Fleet relays. Still, she could not believe that all these security measures were necessary on a small ship like this. She ran her eye down the list, noting that the chief had flagged three names, a pivot-major and two sergeants minor. They had received more than a sig beyond the mean number of contacts, and from multiple sources.

"No packages," Esmay murmured, checking the columns.

"No, sir, not for them. There's one for you, though. And Pivot-major Gunderson is getting married at the end of this tour. The return addresses match his next-of-kin address, his future in-laws' address, and the medical center on Rockhouse Major."

"Medical center?" Then it came to her. "Oh—of course." Gunderson was neuroenhanced, and— "Is his betrothed also a NEM?"

"No . . . civilian softsider. Gunderson's trying to get a control implant approved."

That made sense—he wouldn't want to tear his spouse apart by accident. "Still . . . a civilian marriage?"

"Security's been all over it," the chief said, correctly interpreting her scowl of concern. "The family's not Fleet, but they've been subcontractors for two generations."

Esmay let her gaze drift to the next name.

"Farley's parents have sicced the whole family on her to get her to leave Fleet and work for their shipping consortium. She says she's been hassled for years, and just trashes the notes."

A message cube from Barin. Esmay put it aside for later viewing. It bore the sticker that meant it had passed censors at Sector HQ. He must have told his family by now—his grandmother already knew; this was probably about their response to his telling them about Esmay. She still hadn't heard back from her own family, though with the long transit times the new security regs imposed, that wasn't too surprising. She hoped they'd reply promptly. She and Barin would have only a short window of opportunity for their wedding, and while they wanted it to be small and informal, she still wanted it to feel like a wedding, which meant family present.

Her other mail was all official business, addressed to her position on *Shrike* . . . all but the package, much battered after its passage through one checkpoint after another, with Brun Meager's name in the sender ID square.

A package from Brun? Esmay hadn't heard from her since she left for Castle Rock with her babies. She noticed the rumpled sealtape, where security had tried to open it, as required by the new rules. She laid her hand on the ID plate, wondering momentarily how Brun had acquired her handprint, and the sealtape flicked free. Esmay unfolded the wrapping, aware of security watching her.

The last of the paper folded back to reveal . . . a strip of embroidery so exquisite that Esmay could not repress a gasp of pleasure. As wide as her hand, a long strip—she unfolded it carefully—that was nearly as tall as she was. And every centimeter covered with white-on-white embroidery and lace. She hardly dared touch it with bare hands; she felt she should be wearing white gloves to protect it. She laid it gently across her lap and went back to the box.

Under the folded strip was a square of some sheer white fabric, more like a net, encrusted with tiny seed pearls. And under *that*, several pages of drawings, sketches of a gown—a wedding gown, Esmay realized, with long sleeves and a high collar. It was more severe than she would have expected Brun to choose; it had almost the suggestion of a uniform about the shoulders.

The data cube in the same package explained. "Barin's acquisitions need a way to support themselves, Hazel told me, and you need a wedding gown. Handwork of this quality is rare; if they're working for a good designer, they'll be paid well for it. So I took the liberty of talking to some designers. I assume you don't want to pay a year's salary on it. For the Fleet hero who rescued me, and an introduction to the craftswomen doing work of this quality, Goran Hiel is willing to design your gown. He's not considered as good as Marice Limited, but I liked the slight military flair."

It was not the first time Brun had tried to plan their life for them. This was . . . the fourth, Esmay thought, trying not to resent it. Brun had grown up expecting things to go her way; money and beauty and luck had failed her only once. No wonder she wanted to go back to running the world—or at least her friends' lives. She was only reverting to normal; she didn't mean to flaunt her power. Probably.

Esmay looked at the drawings and embroidery again. For a moment, Esmay imagined herself in that gown, made of such gorgeous stuff. She would look . . . no, she must not think about that, not now. It was far too grand a gown for her, for a plain lieutenant in Fleet who wanted a quiet family wedding.

But for the Landbride Suiza?

It was not too grand for the Landbride Suiza, but she was not marrying Barin as Landbride . . . she paused in folding the strip of embroidery to replace it in the box. Was she not, indeed?

A cascade of difficulties unfolded in her mind, beginning with her position as Landbride Suiza. What if someone thought her marrying Barin had anything to do with that? With the historical position of Suiza of Altiplano and the Regular Space Service, or Altiplano's ambiguous position within the Familias Regnant?

What if her family thought that? What if—she did not like even thinking about this, about the land link that was supposed to have been formed with the Landbride ceremony—what if the land itself, Land Suiza, thought her marriage to Barin Serrano meant something beyond love?

And she hadn't yet made formal application for a status change. Quickly, without stopping to think about any of it, she called up the relevant forms.

OFFICER APPLICATION FOR LIFE PARTNER CEREMONY: *Procedures and Requirements.*

Although she had known about the official forms in an intellectual way, having them actually loaded onto her deskcomp felt very . . . serious. First came a long, depressing series of warnings, restrictions, and discouraging statistics: she had to initial each paragraph as having been read. Formal life partnerships (also known as marriages, the text informed her prosily) failed even among individuals of long-standing Fleet background. The report cited all the possible reasons, including some Esmay hadn't thought of (Were there really people who were confused about their gender as adults? And how many people converted to a religion requiring celibacy after marrying someone?).

She read on, doggedly initialling one paragraph after another, until she came to the section warning officers against entanglements with persons of planetary importance. And right there, in a list that included governor-general of this, and assistant general secretary of that, and commander of the other, she found "Altiplano: Sector Commanders, immediate families of, and Landbride/Landgroom."

Landgroom? There wasn't any such title on Altiplano. The whole point of the Landbride was . . . her mind caught up with the warning and she glanced back at the heading. "Officers are specifically warned to avoid political entanglements, including liaisons either casual and permanent with the following classes of persons."

She could hardly avoid a liaison with herself, but—what would this mean to Barin? She was a commissioned officer of the Regular Space Service. Surely they couldn't hold her Landbride status against her . . . not her . . .

But if they did . . . she hadn't been a Landbride when she and Barin met and fell in love. She had been just another ensign . . . *just another ensign who had survived a mutiny and saved a planet* . . . but basically, a Fleet officer. She hadn't done anything wrong in falling for Barin, or he for her. What difference did it make that she was also the Landbride Suiza?

Come to think of it, had she ever *officially* informed Fleet that she was the Landbride? Lady Katerina Saenz knew, but she had been concentrating so on helping get Brun free—that was far more important—and she wasn't at all sure she'd turned in the form. Esmay called up her personnel stats. Planet of origin, family of origin, religion, local awards and decorations . . . the Starmount, she had put that in. But she hadn't mentioned Landbride.

Feeling guilty already, she hunted through the Personnel Procedures database for the right form, and didn't find one. Well . . . not that many officers became Landbride. In fact, she was the only one. But this meant discussing the lapse with Captain Solis; he would not want to be surprised by it later.

"Captain, could I speak to you?"

"Certainly." He looked up from his work, much less menacing than she had once thought him.

"It's about these forms for a change of status," Esmay began. "The warnings to personnel—"

His brows rose. "I don't imagine you're in any trouble—you and the young man are both Fleet officers. Unless you still think you're robbing cradles."

"No, sir. But the section on planetary entanglements—"

"I know your father's a prominent person, but you're a Fleet officer—"

"And a Landbride."

"Landbride? What is that?"

"A proscribed position, it says here." Esmay handed over the printout she'd made. "I don't know if it applies—I am a Fleet officer, and when we met I wasn't Landbride Suiza—"

"Umph. Landbride must be something extraordinary. What does a Landbride do, Lieutenant?"

That was not something she could explain, when she didn't half understand it herself. "It's—the Landbride represents the family's bond to the land—to the soil itself—in the family holdings. She's a symbol of the family's commitment to the land. It's . . . sort of religious."

"I didn't even know you were a Landbride," he said.

"It happened during my leave home, after my great-grandmother died," Esmay said. "When I came back, we were so busy with the rescue mission, I guess I forgot to put it in . . . I didn't think about its being important."

"Yes . . . we were all somewhat preoccupied right then. But you need to report it now. Personnel will definitely want to know, and they may have some concerns about your duties. How much time you'll need to be away from Fleet, and so on."

"I won't," Esmay said. "That's what my father said—"

"But religion . . ." He looked thoughtful. "Religious positions usually require some actual commitment of time and effort, Lieutenant. If you aren't there—"

Esmay thought suddenly of the spring and fall Eveners, when her great-grandmother had ridden out to do something—she didn't know what—in the fields. No one had mentioned that to her, but—

"It all happened so fast," she said. "And then I came back . . ." She hated the sudden pleading tone in her voice; and stopped short.

"You need to get it straightened out, whatever it is, before you marry young Serrano," he said. "Not just because of regulations, but because you both need to know what you're getting into. And I see here you're in double jeopardy, with your father being a sector commander."

"Yes, sir," Esmay said. "But they knew that when I went into the prep school."

"But you weren't then about to marry one of the oldest families in Fleet," he said. His tone held no rancor, but the very matter-of-factness of it set a barrier of steel between her and what she hoped for.

Esmay nodded, and withdrew. Master Chief Cattaro, after rummaging in the Admin database for the correct form, gnawed the corner of her lip. "There's a procedure, Lieutenant . . . there's always a procedure. Let me just check . . ." Another dive into the database. "Ah. What I think will work is a 7653, an *Application for Exception, Unspecified*, and a 78B-4, an *Incident Report, Personnel Infraction, Unspecified*, and then you'll need a 9245 . . . no, actually, two of them. One to accompany each of the others." Chief Cattaro grinned, looking happier with each additional form. "And it might be just as well to file your 8813—your application for permission for permanent bond—linked to the code tag for your pre-commissioning records, because that will have your prep-school classifications, and of course you'll need . . ."

"Chief, I'm not going to have time to do all that at once."

"Best get started then," Cattaro said. She had the quiet twinkle of the senior NCO who has just been able to dump a load of work on a junior officer. "I'll just pipe it to your desk, shall I? Or would you rather work on it in here?"

She could always fill in the blanks while working on something else.

"My desk, please, Chief."

"Yes, sir.

Filling out the forms to Chief Cattaro's satisfaction kept her busy the rest of that shift and part of the next, along with her other work. For reasons known only to the forms designers in Personnel, none of the forms asked for the information in the same order, or even the same format, which made it impossible to simply port data from one to the other. Family name first here, but last there. Middle name or names as initials in this form, but spelled out in that one. Planet of origin by a code from a table, or spelled out, or by a code from another table, which didn't agree with the first.

They really did not want Landbrides to marry into Fleet, Esmay decided.

Barin's message cube—when she finally had time to put it in the reader—was less informative than she'd hoped. He loved her—she couldn't hear that too often—and he was still waiting to hear from his parents. He was afraid they'd be upset by the administrative decision to make him responsible for the support of the women brought back from Our Texas. It was going to be hard to convince Personnel to approve the paperwork for a status change, when clearly he couldn't afford any more dependents.

Esmay wondered if someone in Admin had gone bonkers. Why were they demanding that Barin pay support for these women? He had included the data he thought she'd need—evidently he hadn't yet found the sections of the application which forbade her to exist, or him to marry her. He promised to write again, but pointed out that with his entire salary going to the support of the NewTex women, he would be limited to ship-to-ship transfers within the Fleet postal system.

Esmay added his information to her paperwork, and then completed what she could of her application, along with the belated NOTICE OF RELATIONSHIP papers. It was all so silly. They'd known she was a sector commander's daughter when they accepted her into Fleet, and Altiplano had no desire to influence the Familias Grand Council anyway. It had never even tried to get a Seat in Council. Why was it on the proscribed list? And if they were going to put Landbrides on, why hadn't they done the elementary research to find out that there was no such thing as a Landgroom? Cursing the anonymous "they" in silence, Esmay finished the forms, stamped and thumb-sealed them, and took them back to the captain's office for his clerk to make the required copies and ready them for transit.

She went back to the rest of the message cube later. The former Rangers' wives, now settled uneasily in an apartment block on Rockhouse Major, were constantly asking Barin for assurances he could not provide.

"Grandmother knows why I did it—and agrees that it was justifiable under the circumstances—but she warned me that Fleet would not be pleased, no matter what kind of report she turned in. Headquarters feels I overstepped my authority, and created a huge financial obligation for them, not to mention a publicity nightmare. They've insisted that I contribute to their maintenance, though my whole salary won't pay the grocery bills alone. Everyone—from the women to the admirals—seems to think it's my place to come up with a solution. And I'm stumped. Those women don't seem to be capable of anything but sitting around complaining, and now the civil authorities are jumping on *me* because they won't send their children to school."

Esmay thought of the women she'd seen in the shuttle during the evacuation: the long-sleeved, long-skirted dresses, the headscarves, the work-worn hands. If they were as religious as the Old Believers on Altiplano, they'd be very uncomfortable on a space station, or even one of the more—her mind struggled for awhile, looking for a different word, but finally settled on the first—*advanced* planets.

She hadn't thought much about the women and children removed—or rescued—on that mission since leaving the task force. She'd assumed the women who had been prisoners had received medical treatment, and that "someone" had done "something" about the others.

Apparently not. Though it was hardly fair to land all the responsibility on Barin, if he was going to be held accountable, then clearly she herself had to do something. What a nuisance it was, being stuck on a different ship! They couldn't just talk it over, share ideas, come up with solutions.

She prepared queries for Barin and the Fleet library-search service, and at the next downjump sent them off.

The idea woke her out of a sound sleep some nights later, and she lay there wide-eyed, amazed at herself. The women needed a place to live and raise their children, preferably on a planet. They needed a way to earn a living. Brun had suggested the latter, with her comments about their skill in handwork. And now Esmay had herself thought of a solution to the former problem. Altiplano. As the Landbride Suiza, she could settle them on Suiza lands. In their own village, if necessary, where they could follow their own customs. Their handwork could be exported, along with the genestock, to fill out their income beyond what they could produce from the land; she would be willing to give them a start of livestock from her own personal holdings. Their children could grow up as Altiplanans; in a few generations, they'd be assimilated completely.

The more she thought about it, the better it seemed. The women might even find husbands on Altiplano, if they wanted them. Since their beliefs fit somewhere on the great branching tree of religions that had grown out of Old Earth Christianity, surely they would find the tone of Altiplano's Old Believers congenial. She tried not to think of those passages in her child's history book about the religious disputes. Her great-grandmother had insisted that they were all the result of insufficient humility and excessive arrogance. And anyway, religious freedom was now part of the Altiplanan legal code, though Altiplano lacked the diversity of culture of Fleet or the more cosmopolitan planets.

Since she couldn't go back to sleep, she turned on her desk unit and recorded a cube for Barin with the gist of her idea, then one for Luci, telling her cousin all about the wedding plans, and Barin's problems, and asking about vacancies on Suiza lands. In her mind's eye, she saw them settled somewhere in the south, in a tidy little village of stone houses, with kitchen gardens. Something very like what Barin had described as the households they'd come from.

By the time she'd populated their pastures with Cateri goats and cattelopes, and imagined them all cheerful and productive, with laughing children playing in the lanes, she was sleepy again. She went back to bed sure that all problems had solutions and this one had just been solved.

Next morning she was not quite as sure—she thought she remembered that they were free-birthers, or at least their men were—but she put the cubes in the outgoing mail collection anyway, and went on with her work.

Altiplano, Estancia Suiza

Luci Suiza came through the front hall on her way in from the polo fields—she needed a shower before the Vicarios family showed up for dinner, and had let Esmay's half-brother ride her pony cool. That was one reason, and the other was that she'd seen the little red mail van driving up to the house. Philip had been sending her a note every day; when she was lucky she got to them before anyone else. She picked up his note, and a message cube from Esmay, and took them up to her room.

She read the note before she showered, stripping off her sweaty clothes and tingling all over from the phrases he'd used, as well as the cooler air wafting in through the window. Tonight—tonight the parents would have their final meeting, and after that, they would be betrothed.

After her shower, wrapped in a fluffy white robe, Luci fed Esmay's cube into the reader in her room, and brushed her hair as the message came up. Esmay was fine; she hadn't heard back from Barin about his family yet; Brun had sent her gorgeous samples of embroidery and sketches for a gown; Fleet had a lot of silly rules about who could marry whom, so she was having to fill out lots of forms . . . Luci paused, pinned up her hair, and glanced at the clock. She still had time. She made a long arm, pulled her cosmetics closer to the cube reader, and tried to do her makeup and watch the message at the same time.

Fleet didn't approve of officers marrying Landbrides. *So resign*, Luci thought to herself, and sure enough the next bit was a long, rambling apology and then the admission that Esmay thought she should resign. Was Luci interested?

Luci was interested; Luci heaved a sigh at her absent cousin, and applied lip color. No matter what anyone said, there was no way to play polo and end up with soft moist lips, without using cosmetics.

The message continued; Luci kept an eye on the clock. She liked her cousin; she admired her intensely, but Phil would be here in twenty-five minutes.

Esmay's wonderful idea of settling the women from Our Texas and their children on Suiza lands took her by surprise; the eyeliner she'd been applying so carefully swiped up and away, a dark streak across her face before she caught herself. What?! *Nineteen* women, and their children—dozens of children—all to be settled on Suiza lands? Free-birthers, from a planet with a barbarous religious cult . . . she could just imagine what the priests would say about *that*! Esmay babbled on about their handwork skills, their experience on low-tech planets. *We are not low-tech*, Luci thought angrily. *Idiot. Fool.*

Then she caught sight of her face in the mirror, and the clock, and the anger roared in her like a brushfire. Esmay had no right! Esmay was not a proper Landbride—no one who really understood, who really cared, could have considered that for an instant . . .

Luci dashed into the bathroom, nearly trampling two of the younger children.

"Luci, what happened to your—"

"Be quiet!" she snarled at them, and scrubbed the makeup off her face, leaving streaks on the facecloth. Stupid Esmay. Ridiculous Esmay. It was a good thing she'd left, and a good thing she wanted to resign as Landbride, and Luci would pluck her hair herself if she had a chance.

When she got back to her room and looked out the window to see if the Vicarios vehicle was coming yet, the alternating blue and gold of shadow and late sun streaking the grass of the polo fields stabbed her heart. It was so beautiful, so beautiful it hurt. How could Esmay not want this? How could she care so little, that she would think of violating the land for a bunch of outlanders?

She rested her forearms on the windowsill and drank in the cool air scented with early roses and apple blossom. Somewhere in the distance, horses whinnied; the grooms would be mixing evening feeds. This was what she wanted, what she had always wanted—well, this and Philip to share it with. Land to cherish and nourish and protect, beauty to nurture, the ancient cycles of the land.

Light reflected from something moving on the road, then flashed straight in her eyes when the vehicle turned into their drive. The

Vicarios, no doubt, unless it was her father returning late from the city. No time now for cosmetics, though she touched her chapped lips with color again. The blue-and-white overtunic and white skirt of the courted maiden. After tonight, she would wear the blue skirt of the bride-to-be.

Esmay, you fool! was her last thought as she closed her door and ran down the upper passage to the stairs.

The Vicarios family had gone back to their city house by midnight. At this third of the formal meetings (alternating from one family's home to the other's), the parents had been pleasantly relaxed. The exchange of gifts, the ritual speeches, the contrived—but still effective—"unexpected" visit of the priest who put her hand in Philip's, and tied a silk scarf around the pair of them—all had gone without a hitch. Luci and Philip had a few minutes alone in the rose garden as their elders watched from the lighted doorway; he kissed her respectfully on the brow, and murmured her name.

Philip went with his parents when they left, of course. From now on, no more stolen moments, let alone hours, in which to discover each other . . . from now on, they were formally betrothed, and that betrothal had its own rules. Maddening, perhaps intentionally so. Luci filched another stuffed date from the tray a sleepy maidservant was carrying back to the kitchen, and followed her father into the library. Her uncle and grandfather, already relaxed in chairs by the fireplace, looked up as she came in.

"Luci, you should be in bed."

"Papa, I'm not sleepy." He raised his eyebrows at her, but she didn't move. "Papa, I had a message cube from Esmay today."

Her uncle Casimir sighed. "Esmay . . . now there's another problem. Berthold, did you get anywhere in the Landsmen's Guild?"

"Nowhere. Oh, Vicarios won't oppose us, but that's because of Luci, and his support is half-hearted. It would be different if she hadn't left so young, I think. They don't really remember her, and even though they awarded her the Starmount, and consider her a hero, they do not want a Landbride—any Landbride but especially our Landbride—connected to an outlander family. Cosca told me frankly that even if she moved here, and also her husband, he would oppose it. *Nothing good ever came from the stars*, he insisted."

"And the votes?"

"Enough for a challenge, Casi, I'm sure of it. No, the only way out of this is for Esmaya to come and talk to them herself."

"Or resign."

"Or resign, but—will she?"

Luci spoke up. "She mentioned that in her cube."

"What—resigning? Why?"

"Her precious Fleet seems to think about us the way the Landsmen's Guild thinks about them. She says they have some kind of regulation forbidding officers to marry Landbrides."

Her father snorted. "Do they have one forbidding officers to *be* Landbrides? How ridiculous!"

"Are you serious?" Casimir asked. "They have something specific about Landbrides? How would they know?"

"I don't know," Luci said. "That's just what she said. And she said why didn't we take in all those women brought back from Our Texas—she was sure they'd fit in."

A stunned silence, satisfying by its depth and length.

"She *what?*" Casimir said finally. "Aren't those women—"

"Free-birthers and religious cultists," Luci said, with satisfaction. "Exactly."

"But—but the priests will object," Berthold said.

"Not as badly as the Landsmen's Guild, if they hear of it. Dear God, I thought she had more sense than that!"

"She is in love," Luci pointed out, willing now to be magnanimous. "Apparently Fleet is taking Barin's salary to pay for their upkeep—at least some of it—and Esmay's trying to help him out. Nineteen of them, after all, and all those children."

"At our expense." Casimir shook his head. "Well, that settles it. She'll have to resign, as soon as I can get word to her. The Trustees will certainly not approve this, if I were willing to let it be known." He gave Luci a hard look. "You didn't tell Philip, I hope."

"Of course not." Luci glared at her uncle. Esmay might not have any sense, but *she* knew what the family honor required.

"I hope she does name you Landbride, Luci," Casimir said. "You'll be a good one."

Luci had a sudden spasm of doubt. Was she being fair to Esmay, who after all had had so many bad things happen to her? But underneath the doubt, the same exultation she had felt when Esmay gave her the brown mare . . . *mine, it's mine, I can take care of it, nobody can hurt it . . .*

"I wonder if we could place an ansible call," Casimir said.

"Surely it's not that urgent," Berthold said.

"What if she just packs them up and ships them to us? Better safe than sorry."

"She won't," Luci said. "I'm sure she won't." She didn't know how she knew, but she knew—probably by now Esmay had figured out for herself why it was a bad idea, and the next mail would bring apologies.

"I hope not," her father said. He yawned. "Oh, do go to bed, Luci! I'm exhausted."

Luci gave him a kiss and went up to bed, sure she would not sleep for the warring emotions inside her. She undressed quickly, hung her clothes up, and slipped naked between the sheets, taking great lungfuls of the fragrant night air. She hoped Esmay felt this way about her Barin . . . if her poor cousin couldn't be Landbride, she at least deserved a great love.

R.S.S. *Shrike*

Esmay came onto the bridge to find Captain Solis scowling. Now what had she done or left undone?

"I was afraid I'd lose you," the captain said.

"Lose me?"

"New orders. They're sending me a new exec, and you over to line ships again. I knew they would eventually. Even though we can always use someone with your talents in SAR, they consider it a waste."

He handed over the message cube. "It's all in there; we'll be dropping you off at Topaz."

"Topaz—" A civilian station.

"In transit between ships is a good time to use a few days' leave, Lieutenant. Assuming you have a use for it."

Barin. Her heart hammered. Now if she could only figure out how . . .

"*Navarino* is in Sector Six. *Gyrfalcon*, I hear, is going to be detached from picket duty and sent back to Castle Rock, and thence to Sector One—" Solis did not crack a smile, but she did. She knew the regulations: all she had to do was show up at the right time. The route she chose from Topaz to Sector Six HQ was her own choice. There was at least a chance that she could meet Barin at some intermediate station. If she could get word to him. If she could get leave.

CHAPTER SEVEN

Benignity of the
Compassionate Hand
Nuovo Venitza, Santa Luzia

Hostite Fieddi, Swordmaster and troupe leader, bowed to the Chairman's box, then to either end of the Grande, where the notable guests of state and industry were seated, and finally, that cold chill down the spine which this required movement always brought, turned his back on the most dangerous man in his universe to salute the mortal representative of that Holy One who was even more dangerous, having dominion over all universes.

Protocol, he thought sourly, was invented by the devil, for the ensnaring of innocent hearts. Not that his was innocent; he had been debriefed by his superior in the Order, and had still to face confession. In between . . .

Trumpets blared, the old curled rams' horn trumpets, and from the corner of his eye, Hostite saw the doors open in each corner, dark mouths. In each, a gleaming figure poised in one of the Attitudes. A low drumroll . . . the first figure in each doorway stalked forward, and behind it a second.

Eight now, each demonstrating one of the Attitudes, a Full Square. The drums shifted to a subtle beat, step and step; the figures moved forward, in toward the open space where Hostite waited. Four were female, four were male. Four belonged to the Sun: pure gold, copper-red, rich bronze, and brass. Four belonged to the Moon: silver, steel, lead, platinum. And he, the dance's Shadow, gleamed obsidian in the light.

Sabre dancing had its roots in ancient days, long before the first men left Earth. More than one sword-bearing culture had its sword and knife dances, and more than one had used them as training. More than one had also the spectacle, where the rich and powerful watched as their servants danced and bled for their amusement. There had always been, for some, the heady linkage of lust and danger.

But not until the Benignity had the old threads wound into such a line of life and death as this. Hostite smiled behind his mask. Here was the imperial circus, and here were the holy warriors, and here were the dancers . . . and here he ruled.

The gleaming figures had formed the circle, with him in the center . . . the Spanish circle, he knew from his studies, with its elaborate figures. He turned slowly, enjoying as much as the Chairman, he was sure, those fine-tuned bodies beneath the gleaming paint. Unlike his mask, theirs were transparent—invisible, to all but those who knew exactly where to look. Instead, their faces—biosculpted to be as beautiful as their bodies—gazed back at him with impassivity.

Tonight's music, chosen by the Chairman, was Imetzina's "Quadrille for Evening by the Sea." The Chairman beckoned; the opening phrase began. Hostite signalled Four and Seven, brass and lead. So much was tradition, and the Dance began with what might seem dullness.

Gracefully, yet with a severity imposed by the weapons, Four and Seven stepped out of the circumference, into the circle. In practice, they danced naked but for wrist, elbow, and knee guards, but here— in formal performance, with Someone certainly watching from behind the curtain—Four wore the small, metallic-scaled breast medallions, the pleated metallic-scaled skirt that hung from her hips and swirled when she moved. Seven wore the loincloth that was hardly more than a codpiece strapped in place.

The blades were all steel, but coated to match the dancers' colors. Hostite's blade alone was not steel, but true obsidian, brittle but sharper than any other.

The traditional quadrille required each dancer to face each, first in the pairs, and then by fours. Hostite worried a little about Four—this was her first performance in the Grande, and though she had seemed completely solid in rehearsal, he knew that the excitement of a first performance could cause a fatal misstep. But Caris, who usually danced the Four, had hyperextended her knee while instructing a junior class: some careless student—not a student any longer—had left a lump of wax on the floor.

Pelinn should have had another half-year in the second company, Hostite thought, but she was very talented and very dedicated, the best of the understudies. He hoped she would not be marked badly tonight.

The music brought the dancers together, blade against blade, and whirled them apart. Four moved perfectly in time to the beat, and as the figures followed one another, including the difficult change of hand during pirouette, Hostite relaxed a little. Even though brass and lead danced the false art, a much less dangerous design than the true, they could mark each other permanently if they erred.

Eight and Two followed Four and Seven: platinum and copper, the maximum contrast of color, and the minimum of gender—both were women. Genetic twins, differentiated only by makeup and costume. Hostite smiled indulgently to himself. They were at the height of their powers now, and after all the years of training together, they always produced a spectacular show. Whirling, leaping, throwing kicks as well as rapid thrusts and sweeping strokes, it seemed they must slice one another to bits—but they never did.

Bronze and steel next, Three and Six, this time both males. Not twins, nor matched in height or style. Steel Six had four centimeters on Bronze Three, with a corresponding reach—but Three, born of a family of acrobats, matched him easily in the dance. Their corded muscles stood out; their weapons rang ever more loudly—and always on the beat.

Hostite signalled for the pairs next: One and Five would dance alone at the end, but for now joined Four and Seven. Gold and brass, lead and silver . . . the false art and the true danced both with and against each other. For many patrons, this was the best part of any dance, with its interlocking symbolism, but for the Master it was always a problem. In the finale, One and Five must be capable of the most difficult movements, which meant they must not suffer injury now—and yet they must demonstrate the True, and its superiority to the False. Hostite worried again about Four; she must be shown to be inferior, without injuring Five, or being too badly hurt.

Again he was reassured by her steady, even rhythm under the

spectacular moves required. She had the true dramatic temperament; when pressed by the true art, she grimaced, leaned back, seemed on the point of imbalance—but never quite fell. The few thin lines of red on her skin were only enhancements, not serious injuries that would take time from her training or performance.

The dance continued, with the other pairs replacing those: Two and Eight opposing Six and Three. Here, where Hostite expected no problems, Six missed his footing in a turn—perhaps the floor was sweat-slick there, or perhaps he lost concentration. Whatever the reason, his left foot slid sideways as his weight came on it, and Two— they were in the second figure by then—opened his leg across the knee from the lateral thigh to the posterior calf, exposing bone at the joint, just before the gush of brilliant blood that proved an artery had been severed. A gasp, almost a moan, came from the watching seat. Hostite ignored that, and gestured to his dancers. Three and Eight moved aside, without missing a beat; Two backed away and knelt, weapon outstretched. Hostite looked at the Chair's box. Which would it be?

A hand outstretched: the music stopped, mid-phrase. The dancers stopped, held their poses. Silence, then, but for Six's harsh breathing. He lay where he had fallen, in a widening pool of blood, struggling not to make a sound. Hostite knew already it was a crippling blow. He might live, and walk, but he would never dance again, even if the joint held.

"Steel," the Chairman said. "Our thanks for your service. It is ended."

Before anyone else could move, Hostite moved, his obsidian blade slicing through the air and Six's throat. He bowed to the Chair's box.

"Continue," the Chair said. Hostite returned to his place; the music resumed mid-phrase where it had paused. Two still knelt, having no partner. Three and Eight moved with the music, dancing, avoiding both Two and the dangerous bright blood. It honored the honorable dead, to dance before them, around them.

At the end of that figure, the Chair gestured again, and again the dance paused. Now Hostite closed the dead eyes, and made the gestures and said the words that sent Six's soul on its way. Servants came, rolled the body into a sling, and carried it out, to a soft drumbeat; others cleaned and dried the floor.

The last figures were as beautiful as anything Hostite had ever seen; the final pairing of Silver and Gold, Sun and Moon, surpassed art and entered the realm of spirit. Above death, above life, were the eternal fires, and so the dancers moved.

Afterward, in the Dancers' Hall, they all knelt to honor the memory of Steel, and with the edge of a keen blade each added a drop of his or her own blood to the winding sheet. Pelinn looked pale, and no wonder after such a first night; Hostite gave her a hug, and held her until her body quit shivering. "You did well," he whispered. "You did very well."

Caskadar, the Terakian family compound

Goonar Terakian and Basil Terakian-Junos had the combined investigative skills of any newshound in history, and more than three times the discretion. Their profits came not from revealing information, but concealing it. It had not taken them overlong to figure out that the drunk who'd accosted them back on Zenebra Main Station had been a New Texas Godfearing Militia member, and that the New Texans (as the Terakians privately referred to them, as opposed to the Texans of the Lone Star Confederation, who were perfectly respectable, if unfailingly sneaky, at "doin' bidness") were engaged in terrorism against the Familias Regnant.

Since Goonar and Basil had reported to their respective fathers as soon as they were back aboard Terakian ships, the Terakian family had a head start on the Familias Regnant's Fleet when it came to planning. They had followed, from a discreet distance, every evidence of Fleet's rescue of Brun Meager . . . and the more obvious evidence of her father's mental instability.

Now Goonar and Basil had met again, this time on the family's private resort on Caskadar. Their distant cousin Kaim, the only family member presently serving in Fleet, had taken leave due and was now sprawled on a couch on the wide veranda of Sea Breeze, glaring at the rain that poured steadily, as if from a vat overhead.

"My only leave in four years and it has to be raining!" Kaim had never been patient.

"It's autumn," Goonar said. "It's just the fall rains . . ."

"I hate planets," Kaim said. Goonar glanced at Basil, who shrugged. He looked almost as sulky as Kaim.

"You chose the time," Goonar said, with more asperity than he intended. "You know about the climate—"

"I know more than that." Kaim sighed, stretched, and beckoned to the other two. "Listen—what have you heard about rejuvenations going bad?"

"Well . . . there was always that story that the Patchcock-made stuff was tainted somehow. A Benignity plot, I heard, with a spy found right in the factory, wasn't it?"

"That's just bad drugs," Kaim said, waving aside what had been 27% of the market share, and the disgrace and financial ruin of a Family with more than a dozen Seats in Council as if it were nothing. "What I have is evidence that the primary process may be faulty. Nothing hard yet. They're still blaming it all on something wrong with that batch of drugs. But according to my sources, some of the first repeat Rejuvenants are showing mental deterioration. Lord Thornbuckle, for example."

"I don't see that," Basil said. "She was his daughter; there's nothing induced in his reaction." Basil's own daughter, just three now, had left that smear of jam on his chest. Goonar pitied her future suitors.

"I know I'm not a parent," Kaim said. "But still—risking the security of the entire Familias—"

Goonar grunted, and put out a hand automatically to tap Basil's shoulder. Kaim had been almost bragging about not fathering any children, as if he wanted the family to investigate his reasons. Basil had attitudes. That left Goonar to play peacemaker, as usual.

"Thing is," Goonar said, "if it's a matter of some drugs being bad, that's very different from the process itself being flawed. Kaim, haven't some of Fleet's senior officers been rejuved?"

"Yes, but only once. None of them have had multiples, unless one of 'em's had it done privately, not through Medical Branch. All the first ones were volunteers, done forty or more years ago, when there'd been enough civilian experience. It wasn't made standard with flag rank for another twenty years. Then they started giving senior NCOs rejuv about ten years ago."

"So . . . seen any crazy admirals lately?"

"There's always Lepescu," Kaim said. He had reported to the family about Lepescu before.

"He was born mean," Goonar said. "That kind existed before rejuv."

"I know that." Kaim shifted uneasily. "Look—this is still very, very classified."

"Yeah, right," Basil said. He crossed his heart elaborately and spat to the left.

"It's not the admirals—at least, I haven't seen any crazy admirals, not that I see that many. But there's a medical directive out on senior NCOs . . . anyone rejuved in the past ten years is being called in for immediate evaluation. And I have solid data that at least eight master chiefs have had negative performance evals in our sector alone, in the past half standard year."

"Sounds like a bad drug batch to me," Goonar said.

"Yeah—if the admirals, who've been rejuved longer, haven't gone loopy, why would you think it's anything else?" asked Basil.

"Mostly Lord Thornbuckle," Kaim said. "I just cannot fathom a man of his caliber—his supposed caliber—getting us involved in a war to save that brainless twit of a daughter."

Goonar reached out for Basil's arm again, and found it, as he expected, knotted with angry muscle. "Trust us," he said mildly. "Fathers are like that. Even yours."

"But it could also be intentional," Kaim said. "If someone wanted to ruin Fleet, making master chiefs nuts would be a good way to go."

"And who would be doing this? Who would have access?"

"Across the whole organization—if it is that widespread—it would have to be sabotage in procurement, or upstream from them. Another traitor . . ."

Goonar shrugged. Kaim's father, if not Kaim, had always had a thing about conspiracy theory, and that's why his son had had to go into Fleet, because he had ignored profit for politics too long and couldn't afford to launch his son as a family member should, with his own ship-shares.

"All organizations have some traitors," Goonar said.

"Yes, but . . . what the NCOs are worried about is that it was a plot to start with, so that they could justify not giving rejuv to enlisted personnel. I don't see that myself—admirals cost more and do less; everybody knows the senior NCOs are more valuable—but it's spooking 'em. And having 'em spooked would suit our enemies. The Benignity, I can see them doing something like this, through agents of theirs. Fleet brass is worried about more traitors in the operational end, like Garrivay and Hearne, but why wouldn't the Benignity suborn procurement as well?"

"I suppose." Goonar was much less interested in who might be a Benignity agent than in how such information could be turned for profit. "So . . . either they're going to find out it was a bad batch, and the price of any remaining Morrelline/Conselline stock will drop through the floor, and the whole combine will be bankrupt, or they'll find the basic process is flawed and all rejuv-related products will go down?"

"You lot!" Kaim glared at him. "Is profit all you care about? Doesn't it mean anything to you that if all the master chiefs go bonkers, we can't possibly stand against a Benignity or NewTex invasion?"

"New Texans are amateurs," Goonar said absently. "That silly drunk—"

"Isn't the whole story. Just as you said, any organization has traitors, and any organization also has fools that get drunk."

"Still," Basil said, with a silky tone that alerted Goonar. "Still, I do not see that finding your traitors—assuming you have them—is our responsibility. We do, on the other hand, have a responsibility to the family which, by paying taxes, pays your salary too, Kaim, so I wouldn't be so smug about your moral purity."

Goonar spread both arms. "Stop it, both of you. None of us wants to see the Familias fall to invasion, and none of us wants to see the Terakian family go broke. We're one blood." Which might, in a few minutes, be mingled on the porch floor, if the other two didn't quit posturing.

"Daddy!" Basil's daughter burst through the door from the dining room, leading her mother by a good ten feet. "Found you!" Basil scooped her up, and the child flashed a wide grin at the other men. "Lunch time!" she announced.

"Sounds good to me," Goonar said, pushing himself up. "Come here, little one, and let your father get up." The child bounced from her father's lap to Goonar and he lifted her slight weight to his shoulder, where she crowed in delight. "Don't forget to—"

"Duck," she said, leaning over his head. Inside, her mother shook her head.

"Sorry, Goonar. Lydia's Jon had put something down the toilet in the children's bathroom, and we were coping with the overflow. Jessie got away from us."

"Good timing," Goonar said in an undertone. Berish was almost as pretty as little Jessie, and he envied Basil at times like this, remembering those first years of marriage, when the children were sweet lumps of brown sugar and a wife was an inexhaustible cavern of enchantments. He'd thought of remarrying, but the pain of losing Sela and the children still stabbed; he could not risk that again. He swung Jessie down, and followed the others to the great dining table.

After lunch, the rain stopped for a while, and Goonar chivvied the men into a walk along the shore, past the orange squares of fish pens. Here, with the distractions of uneven footing and a breeze freshening into a blustery wind, Basil and Kaim were less inclined to quarrel. Kaim opened his mind, like the net of a fisherman, spilling a mixed lot of information which Goonar knew he and Basil would pick over at leisure. By dinnertime, when the wind had blown the clouds south for a time, Kaim was clearly enjoying the once-hated planet.

Goonar himself wanted nothing more than to be back aboard one of the Terakian family's ships, preferably one with the new decryption algorithms, that could intercept transmissions via the financial ansibles. He tried to settle calmly to the after-dinner word games, but he couldn't concentrate. After the third time that Kaim crossed his entry with a 10-point bonus, he gave up.

"I'm fuzzed," he said. "I'm going up to bed."

"To bed?" Basil asked. "It's not that late."

"No, but I'm that tired." Goonar yawned, and climbed the stairs to his tower room. Basil undoubtedly knew what he was going to do, and could be counted on to keep Kaim out of the way. The problem was that no security system could really keep his communications clean, not down here. He opened a line to the family headquarters on Caskadar, requested a data dump of the past two days of market reports, and told the duty operator he'd be in the next day to put something in the batch for the ansible.

"By midday, local, Ser," the operator said. "It goes off at 1300, and we have to have all the data encrypted."

"I'll be there by 1000," Goonar promised.

When Basil came up, hours later, Goonar was still picking through the data dump.

"I thought you were fuzzed," Basil said.

"I am." This time the yawn was genuine. "But I'm also worried. There's something going on with the Consellines—look at this—"

"Not now. In the morning. I had to ply Kaim with more brandy to keep him downstairs, and if I don't sleep now I'll be very sorry in the morning."

"You'll be sorry longer if you don't look at this. I'm serious, Bas. Something's going on, and it's big. Look at the fluctuations in the rejuv index."

"It's been volatile ever since the Patchcock mess," Basil said. "Took it six months to recover at all, and every little rumor shakes it like a windchime."

"So quit talking and look," Goonar said. He tapped the chart.

"Oh." Basil pushed his lips out and back in. "What about the raw—"

"Over the top," Goonar said, shuffling through the pile to find what he wanted. "There—I can't be sure without getting a hook in one of the big lines, but I'd bet that's from the Conselline plants; they're the only single source big enough to draw those resources this fast."

"And they'd lost market share, and . . . damn, cuz, I wish we could access the employment figures."

"So—we tell—"

"The Fathers," Goonar said. "And we don't tell Kaim. I'm preparing an ansible load for tomorrow."

"Today. What time does it have to be in? You want help?"

"Just keep Kaim out of my way."

Goonar's line of command ran through Basil's father, not his own—typical of the Terakian family's organization. So he was surprised when the next message came from his father.

"Goonar—tell Basil to keep Kaim onplanet another 48 hours, without fail. Then get yourself on the next shuttle up."

"As God wills," Goonar said, with both piety and practicality: the family code for "What's going on?"

"In his grace," said his father and signed off.

So he had put his finger on the lion's eyelid. Well, now to convince Basil to trap Kaim and let him run off.

The shuttle ride to the orbital station seemed to take forever, though he knew it was the standard flight time. When he arrived, he went directly to the Terakian Shipping offices, where staff were bustling around as if a ship were arriving.

"Who's coming?"

"We just got word by ansible. *Flavor* is on her way through, fast-transit, with something urgent. If you want a lift, I'm sure they'll have room for you."

Favored-of-God, nicknamed *Flavor*, was the Terakian's fast courier . . . and the family's most advanced recon vessel, loaded with the best scan equipment money or influence or trickery could obtain. "There she is—" one of the techs said, pointing to the display board. A bright splash on the screen meant something had come through the jump point at max vee, and the color shift meant she was making a dangerously fast approach.

So whatever it was, the Fathers were willing to let everyone know they had some urgent chore in hand. Usually Terakian ships moved in the same stately arcs as any other commercial carrier, never showing all their capacity unless they ran into trouble.

"What's his ETA?" Goonar asked.

"At this rate? Under twenty hours."

Twenty hours . . . so why had his father told him to leave down-side immediately?

So he would be gone before word of *Flavor*'s arrival got to the surface? So perhaps Kaim wouldn't connect the two? So there would be no transmissions to the surface which Kaim might intercept?

Goonar sighed. While the station had a perfectly comfortable lodging house for transients, and he had more than enough credit to use it, he knew—without even asking—that his father expected him to stay in the office. In the off-duty bunkroom for low-level staff, with its hard narrow beds.

"I'm going over to Spotted Lamb for lunch," Goonar said. "If anyone wants me."

He was almost through with dessert—honeyed figs stuffed with chopped bitsai nuts—when the call came. A tightbeamed packet for him from *Flavor*.

Adhem, the office manager, gave him a look, which Goonar had no trouble intepreting. He wasn't that senior in the family; he was just another of the young men moving up through the ranks . . . so why was he suddenly in the office at just the right time for the appearance of *Flavor* on a fast run, and why was he getting this packet, instead of someone more senior? He was moving up, not down or sideways, because he knew better than to give Adhem any information at all.

Flavor's commander met him at the hatch and threw her arms around him. Laisa, Basil's sister, had the same dangerous energy as her brother. As Goonar's chain of command went through his uncle, so Laisa's went through Goonar's father.

"You're coming with us," she murmured in his ear.

"That's nice," Goonar said, detaching himself. "Basil says to give you his love."

"We're fuel-and-go," Laisa said. Goonar nodded, and went through the hatch ahead of her.

In the next few hours, he briefed her on what he thought he had learned from Kaim and the more accessible data channels.

"Here's what you don't know," Laisa said, when he was through. "There was a distant family member captured with the *Elias Madero*—a young girl, Hazel Takeris. Some seventy years ago, a Terakian boy fell in love with a Chapapas girl—"

"A Greek!"

"Yes, from Delphi Duetti. Of course both families disapproved, so they changed their names—called themselves Takeris. Had lots of children, in defiance of everyone, including six boys, who continued the habit of defying parents by becoming perfectly ordinary merchant crewmen who married late and had few children. This girl is his great-granddaughter—her father was a son of the second son—and his wife died young, leaving him with one daughter. He was killed by the NewTex that boarded *Elias Madero*, and the girl captured."

Goonar listened, trying to find some connection with the news he'd brought from Kaim. Laisa went on.

"At the time we heard about the ambush, we didn't know that. The original connection's name was off our books. Then Aunt Herdion saw a news report and thought the newsie had misspelled Terakian. You know what she's like—she got on the com, all ready to chew bones. They gave her all the information they had, just to get her off their backs. Shortly after the rescue, when the newsies reported Hazel's survival, she barged into the remaining Takeris family discussion of Hazel's future, and insisted on having a say. In fact, she was all set to adopt the girl herself. They're not too happy with her, but they're also not rich, so her offer to pay for Hazel's education sweetened the deal."

"Yes, but what does this have to do with rejuvenation drugs and rejuv psychosis?"

"Not much—but you need to know that, to understand some recent decisions by the Family Council, which will affect everything from the contracts we take to the way we select crew. The Family Council hadn't paid much attention to your report from Zenebra about the NewTex saboteurs there, but now they consider that the NewTex forms a possible serious threat to Terakian Shipping specifically, because of the way we have been casual about picking up replacement crew. And because you and Basil caught that agent on Zenebra. There's also concern about spies in shipping agents' staffs. They're convinced that the raiders knew about the *Elias Madero*'s deviation from its filed flight plan."

Goonar snorted. "I'd say half the merchanters who work in that area know about that shortcut."

"No more. At least, not Terakian ships. We're restricted from anything but green-lined routes—"

"That'll put paid to our fast-courier service—"

"Yes, but we won't be subject to piracy. At least not that kind of piracy."

"So—what about this rejuvenation stuff? I still think we need to suck some data off the financial ansibles—"

"We have. I'm not sure what it all means, though." Laisa handed him several cubes. "That one's from Benedictus, and this one's Caskadar three weeks ago. We'll suck it again on the way out."

"Where are we going?"

"Where God and the Fathers will. I haven't been told yet."

Goonar settled down to data analysis. While the price of rejuv drugs had bounced up and down with every rumor of contamination or scarcity, the price of the raw materials had been growing . . . slowly at first . . . since the Patchcock mess. Somebody was buying the stuff, in quantity. Rejuv drugs used some of the same raw materials as many other pharmaceuticals, but some were unique to that process. He highlighted them—the prices rose steadily. So . . . somebody was buying, and presumably using the raw materials to make the finished drugs, for which they had—or expected to have—a market.

He kept digging, paused to eat, slept awhile, and woke to Laisa's call. "We have the new squirt."

He rubbed his eyes and groaned. "And a destination, O beauteous one?"

"Marfalk."

Marfalk. An obscure world; he'd heard the name but knew nothing about it. "How long?"

"Eight days, about."

"I'm going back to sleep."

But he didn't sleep; the new data he hadn't seen kept him awake. Finally he rolled out of the bunk, muttering curses in four languages, and punched it in.

"You didn't tell me you intercepted a memo," he said to Laisa over the shipcom.

"You were sleepy," she said.

"Not now." It had been encrypted, but *Flavor*'s systems were designed to handle all the standard commercial encryption schemata. Under the first level of encryption was another—as usual, simpler. The decryption machine made short work of that, too. Then, finally, the code. Goonar looked at it, and let his mind freewheel. Whose code was it? Something about it looked familiar . . . then it came to him. Conselline senior family branch. His breath came short. "Laisa . . . do we have a code chip for Conselline senior branch?"

"Not on board. Is that what you think you've got?"

"Looks like it. We can start running it past the other chips, but I'm betting on that one." He tipped his head one way, then the other. The Conselline memo looked almost readable as it was, but he knew that was deceptive. Nothing was ever that simple. Then the pattern popped out at him, as if someone had outlined words in red ink.

CHAPTER EIGHT

Castle Rock

Brun called the Mahoney residence and, for a wonder, George answered.

"George—it's Brun."

"Oh . . . if you want my father, he's still not—"

"No, I know that. I was after you."

"Brun, I'm sorry I didn't come to see you after your father—I mean, I've been so busy with Dad in the hospital—"

"I know, George. I'm not upset; I just need to talk to you."

"Um . . . I should tell you, I've been going out with your cousin." George, of all people, sounded embarrassed. And what did this have to do with his father's injuries, her father's assassination, or the political situation? Still, she knew what to do with that opening.

"Seriously?"

"Looks that way. We're both in law school."

"Which cousin?" Brun had a sudden cold worry that this was the leak through which Harlis had gained information.

"Not Harlis's—Jessamine's."

Her mother's sister's child. The one she had dismissed so blithely back on Sirialis, the first year the girl came for hunting. "Sydney?"

George laughed. "No, that's her older sister. This is Veronica. What did you want, Brun?"

"Information, of course. Where is everyone in our crowd, and what's going on. Since I got back . . . things have happened too fast, and you're the only one here I can ask without getting a lecture."

116

"Ronnie and Raffa are off pioneering—you knew that, didn't you?"

"Yes, though I still think they're crazy. Do you know where?"

"Some dismal colony world; I can look it up if you want. I send mail via the Development Office—rather, I did at first, but they don't answer. What with law school—"

"Never mind, George. I hope your father's better soon."

"It's—he's not like himself at all, Brun. I remember when you were getting Lady Cecelia out . . . I never realized what it's like when someone you know doesn't even seem to recognize you. And he can't talk; he just makes these noises—"

She didn't want to think about that. She couldn't, and stay reasonable.

"George, I'm so sorry. If it's all right, I'll call again—we should stay in touch."

"All right." He sounded tired, worried, miserable. Brun felt guilty for a moment, but then turned her mind to the more pressing problem of finding out what was going on in politics. She still didn't expect anything much to happen in the Grand Council meeting, but it was always better to be prepared. She checked the directory her mother had left with her, frowning as one name after another came up absent. Apparently a lot of people thought nothing much was going to happen, and had not bothered to stay on Castle Rock and find out.

Brun slipped her card into the slot, unlocking her chair's displays and communications, and settled into her chair. Aside from the formal presentation, when she became old enough to have a Seat, she had not been to any meetings, and none of her dreams in the years since had involved taking part in a routine Council meeting.

At the far end of their Family table, her uncle Harlis glowered at her, then leaned over to speak to her cousin Kell. Well, she already knew she could expect no help from him. She smiled, trying for the serenity that had always been her mother's trademark.

The Ministers straggled in, no longer in the formal robes she remembered—when had they quit wearing them? Had her father put an end to it?

Hobart Conselline stood at the Speaker's podium. Brun blinked, surprised. The Conselline family had lost ground in the wake of the Patchcock scandal, because the Morrellines were in their sept. Even though no one could prove that the Consellines had known about it, other Families had taken advantage of the opportunity to take market share from the largest and wealthiest of the septs. When had they regained their influence? And what did it mean? She skimmed the minutes of the emergency meeting after her father's death.

As she adjusted the viewer to bring each face into focus, she noticed something odd. To the Speaker's right, the Ministers' faces expressed suppressed glee mingled with impatience and even anger. To his left, the faces seemed lifeless, sodden with despair.

What was going on? She looked around for anyone she knew, who might give her a clue, but she had been away too long. The seating arrangements had rotated again; no one was where she expected. She called up the seating chart. No one—wait—Sarah's older sister Linnet had a chair one row over and four up. She entered the call-code, and her own name. The screen lit, and letters appeared. *Good to have you back, Brun.*

Thanks, she entered, then glanced at Linnet, who smiled and nodded. *Any idea what's going on today?*

Yes, but I won't put it onscreen. We'll talk at the break.

That was clear as mud. Brun glanced over; Linnet nodded again, this time without smiling. Well . . . she would have to figure it out for herself. She referred again to the desk's databank. The unhappy Ministers first . . . her father's appointees, she realized by the dates. The longest in office, Foreign Affairs, Cabby DeLancre. Minor family, but a good solid man she knew her father respected. Defense, Irion Solinari. Another minor family—her father had long promoted the view that minor families should take their turn in major roles. The Clerk-Minister, Emilie Sante-Foin, who supervised the clerical staff.

The gleeful ones were all new. Her father had appointed one, at the Council meeting just before his death: Elory Sa-Consell, Legislative Affairs. A Conselline, but one Kevil had recommended—she'd found that in her father's papers. The others had been appointed at the emergency session held immediately after her father's death. A new Minister of Internal Security, to replace Pauli de Marktos, who had obviously just failed in his duty, and whose offer to resign had been accepted so swiftly: Bristar Anston Conselline. A new Legal Advisor, replacing Kevil Mahoney: Sera Vesell. Born a Conselline, Brun noted with a quick flick of the data to the bio section. Judicial Affairs: instead of Clari Whitlow, who had held the post since before Kemtre's abdication, Norum Radsin, whom even Brun had heard of as a troublemaker in the legal profession. Colonial Affairs: Davor Vraimont.

So . . . it looked like a Conselline coup. In that case, why was her uncle looking so complacent? Did he not see it, or had he known already?

The excitement started before the meeting. Kemtre Altmann, the former king, came forward to stand in front of the Table. He had evidently rejuved again since she'd seen him last; he looked smooth and healthy, with only a decorative streak of white in his hair, though there was still the faint suggestion of a drooping eagle to his posture. Shocked murmurs followed him, and finally died away.

"I yield the floor to our beloved former king," Harlis Conselline in a voice that practically dripped butter.

"Thank you," Kemtre said. "I just want to ask you all to put the realm—the Familias—first, as you think about the issues before us. There's been a lot of dissension, a lot of anger, a lot of conflict among us—"

There had? Brun had heard nothing of it from her father in their brief time together, but perhaps he had concealed it from her.

"We need to think about the good of the whole Familias Regnant," Kemtre was saying. "In the face of all the threats to our stability, we must not fall prey to internal bickering. The welfare of all is more important than any petty personal grievances."

From somewhere behind, Brun heard an angry exclamation. Across the chamber, a man stood up and yelled "Don't *you* start, Viktor!"

Brun scrabbled at the databank controls trying to figure out who these people were, even as Kemtre bowed and made his way back up the aisle to a sprinkling of applause, clearly stronger in some areas than others. Viktor—that had to be Viktor Barraclough, a distant relative, the eldest of the elder branch of the Sept, though not the elected head of the Family—and the other man—she looked again at the seating chart. Alfred Sebastian Morelline-Contin.

Political instincts she had not known she possessed told her the whole thing was a setup . . . Hobart Conselline had pulled a coup, and Kemtre appealed for unity because he knew there was none. And her uncle Harlis was not surprised or dismayed, as he should have been when a rival Family grabbed so much power, which meant that he had known ahead of time. He had been bought, with what coin she thought she knew.

Contested inheritances were heard in the Court of Wills, and the Minister of Judicial Affairs had the right to appoint justices to that court. Hobart's new Minister had promised Harlis a deal.

Rage blurred her vision a moment, as Hobart stood up and began speaking . . . something about this sad occasion, and the need for clear direction. Hobart's voice had an unpleasant tone—monotonous and yet insistent—which made it hard to listen to the sense of what he was saying. Brun's mind drifted to the odd division of expressions on the Ministers' faces. She had never missed Kevil more. He would have known why Emilie Sante-Foin glowered and Davor Vraimont smirked. With a few low-voiced phrases, he could have made clear the relationship between Vraimont Industrial Arts and the opportunities implicit in being the Colonial Affairs Minister.

Buttons came down the long aisle to the table; Harlis glared, and Buttons nodded. Then he smiled at Brun, with the weary amity of someone who is too exhausted to fight.

"I'm sorry business kept me away—" he murmured.

"It's not your fault," Brun said. "Someone had to keep things going. I'm glad you did."

He looked surprised at that. What had he thought she'd say? Scold him for not rushing to her side?

"Have you seen the agenda?"

"No—it wasn't posted. Mother said it was, but I couldn't find it."

"What are you whispering about?" Harlis said in a harsh voice. "It's almost time for the meeting." He looked as confident as Buttons had looked worried, and his gaze passed over Brun with none of the affection he had once lavished on her younger self. She doubted she could flirt him into her camp now. His son Kell leered at her, the sneer on his face making clear what he was thinking about.

"My brother and I were exchanging greetings," Brun said. "Do you have a problem with that?"

Buttons laid a hand on her wrist; she ignored it.

"Well, he should have come earlier," Harlis said.

"You never came at all," Brun said, deliberately misinterpreting the temporal cue.

"I was at the funeral!" Harlis said, more loudly; other heads turned to look at him, and Hobart Conselline paused in his speech, glaring.

"I wasn't talking about the funeral," Brun said, her voice deliberately lower. "Before. When I first got home."

"Wasn't any need," Harlis muttered, flushing.

Brun merely looked at him, until the gavel banged on the podium and the bell rang, signalling the end of the introductory speech.

"The first order of business," Hobart said, "is to vote on the proposed changes in the Corporate Bylaws."

"I object!" That was Viktor Barraclough again. "The proposals have not been submitted to the entire Council in sufficient advance—"

"You're out of order," Hobart said. Brun could hear the gloat in his voice. "Besides, these changes are familiar to everyone; I presented them last session—"

"And they were voted down," Viktor said.

"You're out of order," Hobart said again. "If you interrupt again, I'll have you thrown out. Now sit down. If you have anything worthwhile to say, you may say it during the discussion period."

Brun felt her muscles tightening and took a deep breath. She had never seen anything like this in the Grand Council. From the shocked looks around her, no one else had, either.

"The full text is available at 34-888-16," Hobart went on. "The annotations are at 35-888-29. Please try to follow along as I go over them."

As if they were little children and Hobart Conselline their teacher. Brun called up the two files, and read quickly, with growing dismay. Proposal to limit the franchise to those presently Seated—offspring to be Seated as space allowed and in strict order of seniority. Proposal to take "suitable measures" to meet the threat of Ageists . . . what threat? Proposal to create a special commission to investigate Ageist influence in the Regular Space Service, and another to investigate the inappropriate use of Space Service resources for private purposes. With a chill, Brun realized that this was aimed at her rescue. Proposal to restrict access of news media . . . to restrict public access to records of Grand Council meetings . . . to reduce the quorum for voting on Corporate Bylaws.

Every proposal had been presented before—the links told her when, and by whom—and had been voted down before. But that had been with time for discussion, with men like her father and Kevil Mahoney to explain why the proposals were not in the best interests of the Familias as a whole. She could remember, now she was sitting here, that on the occasion of her taking her Seat, Hobart Conselline had stood up to propose limiting the franchise. On that occasion, he'd said the influence of the Grand Council was being diluted by mere fertility—that the unSeated populace had lost respect for the Grand Council because all it took to get a Seat was being born to the right parents.

She sent a private message to Buttons: *Was he always like this?*

Ever since I've had a Seat, Buttons replied.

Brun tuned back in to what Hobart was saying.

"While no one would wish such a vicious attack on anyone, it is perhaps fortunate for Lord Thornbuckle that he cannot stand before us to justify his actions."

Brun stiffened and glanced at Buttons. His expression did not change, but his stylus pushed his pad so hard that a red light came up on the margin.

"I am truly sorry," Hobart went on, "if this distresses his daughter, who has chosen this time to take her place among us—" The tone implied that her doing so was in the worst taste. "But private feelings must defer to public weal, in this case." He looked up at her Seat with an expression that made her want to wipe her face with a clean cloth. She expected the chamber to erupt in her defense—but no one moved or spoke. Hobart gave her a stiff little smile and nod, and went on.

"Since Lord Thornbuckle is dead, and cannot reply, some might consider it unnecessary to detail the charges that might have been brought against him. But I believe in full and fair disclosure. The changes I propose to the bylaws are not trivial, and you need to know why I would suggest something so drastic. The fact is, the Familias Regnant is sick, on its deathbed, and if we don't act quickly, the patient could die. Will die, I believe, without our intervention."

Buttons muttered something Brun couldn't quite hear. She glanced at him; for an instant, with his mouth compressed, he looked exactly like his father in a rage.

A light flashed on the panel: someone asking for the floor. Hobart shook his head and went on. "There's no time for discussion, we need to get this done, get it out of the way, so we can move forward."

"There's always been time for discussion—" someone yelled loudly, from a few rows over. Brun queried her panel. Minor branch of the Dakkers Sept, coded turquoise in the Family database.

"That's the trouble, all we do is talk!" yelled someone else. Conselline, minor branch, Hobart's third younger brother.

A gabble of voices rose, and lights flashed on the panel. Hobart banged the gavel repeatedly and finally the turmoil died down. Brun, looking around, saw angry, flushed faces everywhere, all glaring tight-lipped at one another.

How had Hobart Conselline become Speaker? Brun raced through the database, trying to figure out the story behind the story. It had been the emergency Grand Council meeting, held in the hours after the assassination. Emergency meetings did not require the same quorum of Seats . . . so response was limited to those attending in person, or immediately available on an ansible link. Only 23.2 percent of the Grand Council had been polled. Naturally, Lord Thornbuckle's family had not been present or available, nor had most of their friends. Hobart Conselline had received a majority of votes cast, but it amounted to only 15.8% of the whole. Yet he was acting as if he had a large majority of the entire Council.

"Look behind the obvious," one of Brun's instructors had taught her. "Who benefits?" The Consellines, clearly, but how? They were already filthy rich—as rich or richer than the Barraclough Sept—so why this grab for power? What more did they want?

"We're going to vote now," Hobart was saying. "Right now, and get it behind us, so we can move on to important external issues."

The warning chimes of Vote in Progress rang through the chamber, and Brun's screen lit with the proposals. Had Hobart really read through all of them? She struggled through the convoluted legalese, trying to figure out what they really meant. Kevil Mahoney had always said that legal language had more subtext than any fiction ever written, but she had not actually studied law. Some didn't look that bad; the reasoning as given had a plausible ring to it. She chewed on her lip, struggling to find the hidden meanings.

Safer to vote against all of them, just in case. She hoped that was safer. She entered her votes, and sat back to watch the others. Kell, tip of his tongue just showing, was marking his votes slowly, one by one. Harlis had finished. And Hobart Conselline . . . Hobart was watching *her*, she realized.

Time dragged on, as they waited for others to complete their votes. Most seemed to have had their minds made up ahead of time, but a few earnest souls were bent over their desks, clearly checking every word of every proposition, and comparing it to other texts.

The outcome of the voting was less a surprise than it might have been . . . the bylaws changes passed, and the next vote confirmed Hobart Conselline as Speaker for a normal term. The speeches had been confusing; on both sides of what was clearly becoming a deep division, speakers seemed choked with outrage, incoherent. Brun kept quiet, watching carefully and making notes. Buttons, she saw, did the same.

After the meeting ended, they went back to Appledale in the same car, by mutual consent talking only of things they could see from its windows. After supper, they settled to business, and finally Brun's big brother treated her as an equal.

"I have to say I was impressed with your performance today."

"I didn't do anything."

"You didn't pout, flounce, flirt, or storm. You sat there being attentive, intelligent, and menacing."

"Menacing?"

"Didn't you see our new Speaker watching you during the voting?"

"Yes. Made me itchy."

"As well it should. The man's odd, Brun. Well—Mother's gone to Sirialis, I hear. Are you staying here?"

"For now, yes. I'd planned to be the person on site to deal with the Grand Council, unless you want to take it over."

"Are you sure? Because if you can keep an eye on the Council, then I can concentrate on what our dear uncle was up to with the various family companies. It's hard without Kevil—"

"I'm sorry," Brun said.

He looked at her a long moment, and she knew that he knew what she meant—sorry for everything, for becoming the issue by which the Family lost ground, as well as the reason for their father's assassination.

"Don't be sorry for being yourself," Buttons said finally. "And don't be sorry for coming back—it'd be worse if you hadn't."

"I don't see how," Brun said.

"I can think of a dozen ways," Buttons said. "And so can you, if you take the trouble. But that's not what matters right now. We've got attacks on all fronts—where'd you put the babies, by the way? I don't want them used as hostages against us."

"Cecelia de Marktos took them somewhere. She's trustworthy—"

"Well, unless she puts them in a barn and tries to turn them into racehorses," Buttons said, with the first genuine grin she'd seen on his face. "Grooms, I wouldn't mind, but you never know with her."

Brun laughed aloud. "You're right—but I don't think she has them with her."

"Good. As long as they aren't going to cause us trouble—"

"Not for another ten or twelve years . . . I don't want to think about them as teenage boys. . . ."

"If we have a Familias Regnant in ten years, we can worry about it then." Brun glanced at him; his face had gone somber, and he looked far older than his age.

"Buttons—do you agree with Hobart about that?"

"That the Familias is in danger, yes. That it's in danger because of lax leadership in the past, no. It's his policies that endanger it most. This business of restricting the franchise—one way we've had of relieving strain between Families is that the small know they can enlarge by having more Seatholders. That's let them take in outsiders as clients. Dad said the movement of power from one sept to another was a major factor in keeping the Familias stable. That's why they instituted the kingship, originally."

"Why can't Hobart see it?" Brun asked.

"I don't know. Back when I was a boy of maybe ten—and you were still in the nursery—I overheard some of the adults talking about how the new rejuv methods might change things politically. But of course, I was too young to follow it. I remember Dad and Uncle Harlis arguing, though. When I asked questions in school, nobody seemed to understand them, and later, when I was in the Royals, everyone talked as if the repeating rejuvenations were just a way to stay young for a normal lifespan, not an actual extension. It was—oh, the year that Lepescu came to Sirialis, I think it was—that Charlie Windetsson got drunk at a mess dinner and pointed out that if our parents never grew old, we had no reason to grow up. There was no future for us. Everyone laughed, and drank, and—I remember a sort of cold chill. I left the party early, called Sarah, and that's when we decided to marry."

"I didn't know that."

"Well . . . you were being wild at the time. Most of our set were, and I suddenly saw it myself. Our parents had been more grown up—working in family business in some way—by the time they finished their education. Sometimes even before. But their parents barely lived past their Centuries, and retired from Family work in their eighties. The first rejuv upset that a little, but the new one . . . I came home, and talked to Dad about it. He promised that he and Mother would resign their duties while I was still young—he transferred stock to me right after that Hunt Ball, and encouraged me to be active in Council as well as business."

"And I thought you'd gone all stuffy . . ."

"So I had. But I didn't want to go from childhood to childhood—rich enough to rejuv and be twenty or thirty all my life, with nothing to do. That's no way to live—"

"But Uncle Harlis," Brun said. She wanted information, not a lecture on lifestyle. "What about him?"

"He saw multiple rejuvs as a way of maintaining Family power. He wanted rejuv restricted to the Seated Families at first. So did some others, but the proposal didn't pass. Then he tried an age restriction: no one under eighty should be eligible. That didn't pass either, of course. The Ageists, who had used the biological problems with the earlier procedure to make repeated rejuvs illegal, expected his support with the new procedure, but he didn't go along."

"So . . . you're saying the population grew?"

"Not just that. The birth rate in our set actually dropped, because people could wait to have children until they were fifty or sixty or older. It's the shape of the population that really changed, and the power structure. Age always did confer an advantage of experience, and now it could do so without losing any advantage of physical strength and energy. Younger people needed to find new opportunities because the old weren't dying—or even retiring. And of course people wanted rejuv, and especially when they found out how useful it was in some kinds of illness and injury. Everyone rich enough wanted it. And the Consellines wanted the profit."

"Ummm . . . which meant expanding, somehow . . . like Dad's proposal to open new colonies?"

"As a temporary measure. Some others wanted to annex adjacent territories, but Dad opposed spatial expansion, on the grounds that we couldn't serve all we had. And why alienate neighbors when we had planets within the Familias outline which could be settled? But he wanted more support for colonies, too—he had been pushing the Colonial Office to make allowances for the less stable ecosystems of the worlds now being opened. That translates into concessions for the companies—and families—purchasing settlement licenses."

Brun shook her head. "I don't know enough to follow this."

"Well, you can learn. Basically, the longer a world is allowed to stabilize after the terraforming treatments, the more easily it can be colonized. Until recently, this required such long-term investment that very few Families would attempt it. When the Familias Regnant came together, the Council agreed to a joint investment at one world a year. We only know how much better the old-treated planets are because of the Lost Worlds."

"Paradise, Babylon, Oasis," Brun said, to prove she was listening.

"Yes. All treated in the second wave of outreach, and all lost to the records for centuries in the Cluster Wars. So they had between seven and eight hundred years of stabilization after treatment. Nothing like the mature ecosystem of a planet in its natural state, but for human purposes vastly superior to most of the worlds we used . . . only now are others approaching the quality. The scouts who found Paradise found mature forests with 300-year-old timber . . . grasslands with deep soil, not a shallow dark layer . . . estuaries rich in shellfish rather than a few colonies that had still to be nurtured. A stable climate, reasonably predictable. Nobody had known what difference another five centuries could make. If we could let all terraformed planets have that long, colonists would have a much easier time. Not easy—it's never easy—but easier."

"But temporary, you said. Was he thinking of enforcing a limit on reproduction, or on rejuv?"

"I'm not sure. He talked about both, from time to time. But the Familias is so complicated . . . you know, we have planets populated mostly by free-birthers, and others with mostly zero-growthers, and probably eight dozen religions, not even counting the fringes. Any policy one group approves will offend someone else. And meanwhile, the percentage of the population that had been rejuved was going up every year. Every survey taken showed that Rejuvenants wanted and expected to rejuv again."

"I wonder how the Guernesi have handled it," Brun said. "They've had the process as long as we have, and they aren't falling apart."

"I don't know . . . it's a good question. Do they have our diversity of beliefs?"

"And I don't know that one." Brun shook her head. "This is seriously complicated stuff, Buttons."

"It's a seriously complicated universe, and we're right in the middle of a whirlpool if we don't figure it out." He gave her a long, steady look. "You're a grownup now, and you've volunteered for the job of being Council watchdog for our family. This is what it takes."

"Being a dizzy blonde was such *fun*," Brun said, but her heart wasn't in it.

Jessamyn Essence,
Essential Transport Ltd.

In the working passengers' mess, the men had played the newsvid cube of the assassination and aftermath three times already without more than a few muttered cusswords. Then one of them, the oldest, shut off the player.

"So we're too late and somebody got 'im first, so what do we do?" His glance challenged them.

"Git the rest of 'em. If he's dead maybe they won't be watchin' so close. I could take that yellow-haired slut."

"I keep thinkin' about the chillen, Dan . . . by rights, they should be our'n."

"Ben's right," another said. "Somebody stomps the rattler's head, no matter how it thrashes around it's not gonna attack nobody. We don't need to be goin' around killin' people like criminals. But gettin' our chillen back, that's a good thing to do."

"But how're we gonna find 'em? Sposin' they've already been sent to new homes?"

Dan held up his hand. "We don't know that yet. First thing is, we'll look for 'em in a group. Prob'ly we'll hear, if we keep our ears open. Every port we come to. Now mind—nobody gets drunk, like that idiot on Zenebra—" They all knew about that; a whole shipload had been captured. "No fights, no arguments. We have a mission—a new mission—and that's the rules. Got it?"

"Yessir."

The next day, the *Jessy* came into Goldwyn Station, and the working passengers debarked after checking off their assignments with the captain. For once, the captain thought, working passengers had actually worked—without complaint—and he added the optional minimal pay chit to their goodbye handshake. Whatever anyone said about fanatics, he always liked to hire the pious brotherhoods, because he could count on them to work hard and keep their fingers off the cargo.

The Goldwyn spacers services section, or S-3, offered a variety of cheap lodging, food, and drink. This was an all-civilian station, rarely visited by R.S.S. ships, and the diversity of Familias spacefaring cultures showed up in decor and cuisine both. The men followed their noses to something with a familiar smoky-meat odor, and settled at one long table. On one wall, a newsvid showed scenes from some business meeting, but they didn't recognize any of the faces or references. Then a face they did recognize, a blonde woman with short curly hair.

"—Any comments on the outcome of the meeting, Sera Meager-Thornbuckle?" The announcer's accent was hard to follow.

"No . . . you realize our family is still in mourning . . ." The blonde woman's accent was, if possible, worse.

"Yes, Sera, but what do you think of a Conselline as Speaker?"

"Excuse me—" She turned away, and the camera followed, showing her getting into a long dark-maroon car.

"Damn," one of the men said. "It's *her!*"

"You men are all the same." That was a waitress in red checks and blue denim, slapping menus down in front of them. "Just because she's young and rich and pretty—"

"We'll have chili," Dan said. "All of us—a bowl of chili each, and some crackers." His glance silenced the others, who looked ready to say things they must not say.

"An' some beer?" the waitress asked.

"No . . . not yet, anyway." Not until they'd found out what they wanted, where the women and children were. If they could find them and bring them home—even some of them—they'd be honored among men, maybe even more than if they'd managed to kill the Speaker themselves. That would stop the Rangers of Texas True from saying they were nothing but a bunch of wifeless drifters causing trouble.

"Look—" Ben touched Dan's arm and nodded at the newsvid. There it was again, the picture that had infuriated them all—women and children in the traditional clothes walking down a corridor from a ship's hatch, guarded by battle-armored troops of the Familias Fleet.

Dan had trouble following the accent of the newsvid announcer, but he did understand Baskar Station. Was that where the women were in the picture, or where they were now? He didn't know, but they could always go and find out. Somewhere there'd be a bar, and men talking, and someone would know, if he asked the right questions.

CHAPTER NINE

Castle Rock, Old Palace

Hobart Conselline ran his hand over the wide gleaming surface of the desk—*his* desk now, as it had been Bunny Thornbuckle's, and before that Kemtre Altmann's—and felt a glow of satisfaction. His Delphine now had the suite Miranda had occupied, and to him had come every perquisite he had once envied, from the skilled silent staff to the deference of those who had been his peers, and were now his subordinates.

He had worried, when he saw Brun and Buttons both at the Thornbuckle tables, but neither of them had offered to speak. And however they had voted, the count had gone his way. Their own uncle supported him—for a specific reason, but that didn't matter. He would have appointed new ministers for legal affairs and internal affairs anyway; he would have appointed new judges. There were certain legal actions in progress within his own sept which made that prudent. If Harlis benefitted, and assumed it was all for his own benefit, well—that was a cheap profit, and he had never scorned a cheap profit in his life.

He leaned back in the chair and gave himself up to reverie for a few minutes. He was relatively young, and with the aid of repeated rejuvenations he would remain young . . . and powerful. They had seen what happened with a succession of Speakers, generations back, and then what happened when they made leadership hereditary, with the Altmanns. Prosperity had followed prosperity, an upward trend with only minor adjustments. But no one had yet seen what he would show them: the stability and wealth that would come with one leader who would never fade into senility. Year after year, decade after decade, he would be there to serve and protect . . . to guide and lead. . . .

His desk chimed at him, and he sat up, scowling. That was the future, but now he had to deal with the problems his predecessors had left him.

"Milord, Colonel Bai-Darlin, head of the Special Security Unit, would like a meeting."

"Send him in." He would show them how hard a real leader worked. He would be tireless for the good of the realm, as he had always been tireless for the good of his Family, and his sept. And realistically speaking, given the importance of his sept in the economy of the realm, what was good for the Consellines could not help but be good for the rest—at least most of them.

Bai-Darlin came in with a crisp salute and heel-click that convinced Hobart the man was efficient. But was he smart? Was he tireless?

"Milord, I thought you might like to be brought up to date on the investigation into the death of Lord Thornbuckle—"

"It was those NewTex terrorists," Hobart said. "I can't imagine why you haven't caught them yet."

"Milord, the preliminary investigations have found no trace of anyone from any of the worlds on which they operate being on Castle Rock since the Rangers were brought to this system for trial."

"Then the investigators are incompetent! What does it take, a bright red stripe painted on someone's head? They threatened to kill the Speaker, and the Speaker was shot. What more do you want?"

Bai-Darlin looked at him in a way that made Hobart feel uncomfortable. "Evidence, for a start."

"You have evidence; Lord Thornbuckle's dead body. The damage done to Ser Mahoney, to the vehicle."

"Yes, milord, but none of that points to the New Texas Godfearing Militia. We have no indication, on travel manifests, on hotel registers, that they were here."

"If they weren't here, they must have hired someone."

"According to our best sources, they do not hire criminals to work for them, and what we know about the types of weapons used does not fit with them either. They like direct confrontation; they would be far more likely to walk up to an intended victim on the street."

"Excuses," Hobart said firmly. "Although, if it wasn't the Militia, I can think of another disruptive element it might be."

"Yes, milord? Anything you could suggest—"

"Ageists," Hobart said. "Lord Thornbuckle was a Rejuvenant, and so was his wife, a multiple." Bai-Darlin's gaze shifted to Hobart's ear. Hobart shook his head. "These are jewelry, Colonel. I support rejuvenation, of course; any sensible man does. And a man in my position must wear his colors, so to speak. I will rejuvenate when I need to, in another ten years or so; I'm quite a bit younger than Lord Thornbuckle was. In the meantime, these rings—" He touched his ear—"These rings reassure the older rejuvenants that I am serious when I support their interests."

"I see, sir. And you think it possible that Ageists assassinated Lord Thornbuckle because he was rejuvenated? Does this mean that you think they will attack you?"

"I don't think it was Ageists—I think it was the NewTex Militia, as I told you. But if I'm wrong about that, I'd look at the Ageists next."

Bai-Darlin did not look convinced. "I was hoping, milord, that you might share some insights into possible elements among the Seated Families . . . perhaps Lord Thornbuckle had aroused a particular animosity there? He seemed a popular Speaker, but there's always someone . . ."

Hobart waved his hand. "Minor resentments perhaps. Certainly there were those who felt he misused Familias resources in going after his daughter the way he did. A number of us thought so, and expressed ourselves at the time. But I'm not aware—and I wouldn't be, necessarily, since I've little to do with the internal workings of Barraclough Sept— of anything serious enough to cause someone to kill him."

"Very good, sir. Thank you, milord, for your time."

"Catch those killers, Colonel, and I'll see you get a medal." Instead of the eager grin Hobart expected, Bai-Darlin gave him a dark, brooding look before turning away. Strange fellow. Perhaps not as efficient as he had seemed.

Several days later, Hobart found himself glaring at the same desk he had coveted so much. That was the natural result of having to deal with obstructive fools, he told himself. A man had a right to have Ministers he could work with. Why should any of Bunny Thornbuckle's appointees expect to stay in office, if they were going to cause him trouble? They should have learned from his first dismissals and replacements, but they still obstructed him. They would have to go, root and branch; he was not going to deal with any more of this insubordination.

Hobart considered his options. Who should be replaced first? Defense had been making noises lately about rejuvenation in the enlisted ranks, something about aged NCOs going crazy or something. Their idiot medical branch had put a hold on all rejuvenations, and seemed to be determined to investigate thoroughly. He'd pointed out to Irion Solinari that it would be expensive and inefficient to hold a prolonged investigation into something like that, and that it would be better to cut their losses and simply discharge the affected personnel as medically unfit. But Solinari argued—Solinari did nothing *but* argue, Hobart thought, remembering that Solinari had also argued with Bunny, who had appointed him. Just a difficult personality, and not one suited to a responsible position like Minister of Defense.

If Solinari went—if he had his own choice in as Defense, then . . . he could also ease out the more difficult of the admirals. Perhaps *their* rejuvenations would fail? Those had all been done with the original Guernesi drugs, so if they failed it would take the burden of public opinion off the Patchcock connection. They didn't actually have to fail, if only Fleet could be persuaded to take them off active duty out of concern about the rejuvenations. Right now the medical branch and senior officers were being completely unreasonable, and Solinari was backing them up—or stirring them up, he wasn't sure which. Solinari definitely had to go.

He opened his private pad and began drafting a letter to Solinari, explaining his reasoning. He didn't want to be harsh, but the man had to realize that he just was not qualified. And even if he had been, his negative attitude, his contentious nature, made him unfit. More in sorrow than anger, Hobart told himself, was the tone he wanted to take. Not that Solinari had any friends worth worrying about. A bunch of backbiting, acid-tongued nonentities in the minor families, that was all. They'd soon find out what they were dealing with.

＊   ＊   ＊

Admiral Vida Serrano rarely concerned herself with civilian matters, unless they seemed likely to precipitate a war. The change from one head of state to another should have been—usually was—a matter of ceremony and speeches, which affected the Regular Space Service no more than the change from one Grand Admiral to another.

Certainly Lord Thornbuckle's assassination had been shocking, but she expected that it wouldn't make much difference in the long run. Someone else would be elected, a few Ministers might change, and the inertia of the very large organization would keep everything going very much as usual. What could be frustrating when she wanted to make a change reassured her when she wanted stability. Her business, as she saw it, was to make sure her command was ready to deal with any exterior threat, which might see the momentary confusion as an opportunity to cause trouble.

To that end, she had put herself on the list for updates on the rejuvenation problem, and had come to the same conclusion as the first blue-ribbon panel charged with investigating it. A bad batch of rejuvenation drugs, purchased because they were slightly less expensive, and almost certainly manufactured at the Patchcock plant she had seen. The solution was also clear: repeat rejuvenations with clean drugs for those who had not yet suffered significant damage, and supportive care for those who had, for whom another rejuvenation would mean prolongation of senile misery. She had cosigned the report, when it was forwarded upstairs, and had also cosigned a letter suggesting that the manufacturer bear the expense of the repeat rejuvenations and the supportive care.

And nothing had been done. The update list had disappeared; she'd asked Headquarters, and been told it was "discontinued pending investigation of security problems." She'd heard rumors that one of the big independent research labs was itself under investigation for possible falsification of evidence and misuse of public funds. Headquarters had suddenly cut off funding for repeat rejuvenations, without explaining why. Surely they understood how important it was—Fleet needed those people back at work, not to mention the individuals' own need to be saved from senility and death. Vida approved as many rejuvenations as she could out of her discretionary fund, but she didn't have the money for all of them. She thought of contacting Marta Katerina Saenz, whose pharmaceuticals she trusted. But Headquarters had put a gag order on rejuvenation; she wasn't even supposed to discuss it internally. Going outside would be grounds for court-martial, if she were found out.

She wished she knew where all this nonsense was coming from. Was it someone in Fleet? Someone in the government? The Grand Council meeting the day after the funeral had elected Hobart Merethal Conselline as the new head of government, and he had appointed some new people to various defense-related committees. But Irion Solinari was still Minister of Defense, and he'd always been solid. She toyed with the idea of contacting him directly, but admirals who got involved with Ministers went up like a rocket and down like the stick, in her experience. It was almost as bad for a career as marrying into a Seated Family.

Most of these new appointees were only names to Vida Serrano. The Consellines and Morrellines had been involved in the Patchcock mess—everyone knew that much—but she had searched the databases a long time to find Hobart Merethal Conselline, and then the only information she could get was a short official biography on the occasion of his taking his Seat in Council. Nothing in it indicated why the other Families would choose him, unless it were a general desire to repudiate Thornbuckle and all his friends.

She had reached this point in what had become an all-too-familiar reverie when her clerk called.

"Admiral—there's a courier here from Headquarters with a hand-carry."

Hand-carries were an outdated pain, in Vida's opinion, but some of the mossybacks at Headquarters believed in them. Especially the Chief of Personnel. Maybe it was the information she'd requested on the progress of other sectors in returning their rejuvenated senior NCOs to active duty.

"Send 'em in," she said.

To her surprise, Heris Serrano's acquaintance, Commander Livadhi . . . Arash? Aram? . . . came in with the case under his arm. Not commander, she realized, as the obviously new star on his collar twinkled. Admiral minor.

"Congratulations," she said. "I hadn't heard about your promotion."

She hadn't heard that a promotion board was even meeting. She should have heard. Another tiny alarm rang in her head.

"Admiral, I'm sorry to be the bearer of bad news, but thank you anyway." He looked shamefaced, almost as if he wanted to dig a guilty toe in her carpet.

"Excuse me?" He might be an admiral minor, but she was an admiral major, and she made the words a challenge.

"I don't know if you heard that we have a new Minister of Defense—"

"No! Solinari's out?" A major alarm, now.

"Yes. Out and gone—nobody had a chance to talk to him; the word is he left Castle Rock and went home, and he's not giving interviews to anyone."

"I see." What had they done to Solinari, who had never shrunk from interviews, who had spoken his mind in spite of everyone? What could send a Solinari back to—what was that world he'd come from?—and put a lock on his tongue? She felt cold, considering.

"The short of it is that the new Speaker didn't like what Solinari told him about the rejuvenation problem, and he's appointed someone who will do what he's told without question. The new Speaker does not believe that the problem with NCO rejuvenations is entirely the fault of the pharmaceuticals—"

"Of course it is," Vida said. "The data clearly show—"

"Data can be manipulated," Livadhi said. "The Speaker seems convinced that the data *were* manipulated, perhaps by special interest groups influencing scientists in the research facilities."

"He *wants* the data manipulated," Vida said, anger rising in her like a storm.

"That's not for me to say," Livadhi said. He paused, and Vida stared at him, taking in the warning she'd just been given.

"And what else, then?"

"Given the possibility, yet to be investigated, that the failure of the NCO rejuvenations was not entirely due to problems with the drugs, but to some idiosyncratic response . . . right now, they're talking about the level of inbreeding in Fleet families, I understand, though you didn't hear that from me."

"As if *their* families weren't inbred!"

"We are not Registered Embryos . . . so they said." He waited, while she seethed quietly, then went on. "Given that possibility, they say, then there is concern about the stability of rejuvenations of senior officer personnel as well. It has been decided that all rejuvenations of Fleet personnel must be investigated thoroughly, beginning with those of flag rank."

"They can't be serious!" Vida Serrano stiffened in her chair.

"Yes, sir, they are. They've extended the medical hold to all personnel—officers included, and specifically including flag officers—whose rejuvenations are more than ten years old. They're to be relieved of active duty until medical evaluations are complete."

"But—"

"Admiral, I know it's unprecedented." To his credit, Livadhi looked almost as unhappy as she felt. If he felt any triumph, he was concealing it well. "This whole mess is unprecedented. It is leave with pay—at least, full pay for those below commander, half-pay for those above."

"Which is nearly every officer involved." Vida scowled. "Besides, they *know* my rejuv is stable. I was one of the first—it's been over twenty-five years—"

"Yes, sir, but—"

"And who do they think is going to take over, all of a sudden? The losers they didn't want to waste rejuv on? Or even promote? No—don't answer that. I didn't say it; you didn't hear it. Blast!" This was how Livadhi had been promoted, and she was sure that other commanders were even at this moment pinning on the stars they had not expected to receive for another half decade or so. She wondered briefly if Heris had become the newest Admiral Serrano.

Vida swung her chair away from her desk, staring through the bulkhead into decades of memory. All lay clear to her inward sight, vista after vista, crisp images, faces, names, relationships. They were wrong—they had to be wrong. Nothing blurred her mind. She swung back. "Fine, then. I'll take myself off duty, hike down to Medical, they can take a look and put me back on."

"No, sir. Please—would the admiral look at the orders?"

"Which you didn't draft, I presume. All right." She looked at them, read them carefully, every word of every old-fashioned paper sheet.

Worse than bad. Mandatory immediate release from active duty. Immediate replacement by officers specified—in her case, Admiral minor Livadhi. Immediate surrender of all communications devices, encryption/decryption devices, data access devices . . .

"I'm not—I'm sorry, Admiral, I think it's unreasonable and ridiculous to make flag officers leave their quarters and their duty stations so fast—"

"Makes sense if someone really wants us gone, though," Vida said. She was past the first flash of anger now, and her brain had moved into combat-speed computation. "Rush us out, make sure we can't contact our friends still on active duty except by monitored channels, make sure we have no access to files—"

"I have a room in the Transient Officers' Bay," Livadhi said. "I see no reason to enforce this to the letter—"

Vida looked up and caught sympathy on his face. Heris had said he had his good points. "Don't you? Then you're more a fool than I ever thought, young man. When the wind changes, so must the sails. If you don't enforce your orders, you won't last long. I'll be out of here by the deadline."

"Yes, but—I'm not even sure what I'm supposed to do—" That was almost plaintive. Vida gave him a wide Serrano grin, full teeth, and he paled, the freckles standing out.

"You'll do your job, son, the same way I did mine—and learn it the same way too. Scary to get what you always wanted, isn't it? Now if you'll excuse me, I need to clear my desk." She punched for her clerk. "Sandy—come on in; we have a situation."

Within the hour, she had started the process that would transfer command of Sector Seven to Admiral minor Livadhi. No big change-of-command ceremony, because there was no time for it if they were to make the deadline. She called in her staff, advised them of the orders, and had them start briefing Livadhi, who had just come from Sector Five, about the peculiarities of Sector Seven. While they did so, she began peeling out her personal files from the official ones stored under her codes. She would definitely take with her the files on rejuvenation, for instance—should she offer Livadhi copies? No. If he were found to have them, he might get in trouble. What about the scant information she'd collected on the new powers in the Grand Council? Maybe. Lists of family members on active duty, people from whom she might legitimately—well, almost

legitimately—seek information . . . all the Admirals Serrano had
been rejuved, so all would be affected. From Davor, now a third-year
at the Academy, to Gossin—her nose wrinkled at the thought of
trying to work with Gossin, who was one of the rare light-skinned
Serranos (though that was only the most obvious of her problems)—
the list included nineteen—no, seventeen, because Heris's parents
had just retired. Barin's mother was still on active duty, but his father
had retired to take over as the Serrano family's agent.

Her com chimed. She punched it live. "Vida? It's Gadar Livadhi.
Have you heard this ridiculous order taking rejuved admirals off
duty?"

"Just saw the orders, Gadar," she said. "One of yours brought them
to me, in fact. Nice shiny new star young Arash has."

"Well . . . what are we going to do about it?"

"I don't know about you, but I'm going to take myself off active
duty. Were you one of the experimentals too?"

"Yes, and there's not a thing wrong with my brain but the smoke
coming off it from this nonsense."

"Gadar—this is no time—"

"—To start trouble. I know. But at a time like this, with
Thornbuckle gone, we need experienced leaders."

"If we've done our job, our juniors can take over." She knew she
didn't believe that, and Gadar's snort told her he didn't believe it
either.

"You're an optimist. By the way, what do you hear from Copper
Mountain?"

"Nothing," Vida said. "Should I?"

"Well . . . you know my brother Arkad's in the judicial division . . ."

"Yes . . ."

"He's been investigating the records of prisoners sent to Copper
Mountain's secure facilities—that Stack Islands thing—because
that's one of the places that Lepescu stashed your niece's crew."

Vida noted Livadhi's turn of phrase. Run hot, run cold, that was
Livadhi. "And . . .?"

"And he turned up something interesting. Lepescu's juniors—the
ones too far down to have been caught with their hands in the honey
jar after he was killed—have been cycling through Stack Islands. Not

as prisoners, but as guards. Not all the guards, of course, but some of them."

"Oh . . . my."

"If you wanted to recruit desperate and dangerous personnel—even those who serve their terms and aren't discharged are going to have that mark against them—you could hardly do better than to start there."

"And you think they're up to something, of course. Any idea what?"

"Another mutiny—perhaps a breakaway—"

"In service to whom? What kind of financial backing do they have?"

"I haven't been able to find out anything. I've always rather wondered if Lepescu wasn't close to the Morrellines, given his involvement in Patchcock—"

"He made things worse—the whole thing rebounded—"

"Yes—but in the long run, it cemented Morrelline control. Got the Familias as a whole bad publicity—"

"You didn't say anything about that at the time," Vida said.

"No. I didn't realize it at the time. I was all the way over in One, chatting up those Lone Star Confederation diplomats. I hate staff rotations." Vida didn't rise to that bait, and eventually Livadhi went on. "It's only recently, after your—mmm—adventure there, that I began looking into it."

"Well, there's nothing we can do now but go home like good little children," Vida said. "I hope they realize what an opportunity this is for foreign interests. Not to say anything against your family member Gadar, but your new admiral minor almost turned up his toes when he realized he was about to be responsible for the sector most likely to be attacked by the NewTex Militia, with only thirty-six hours of OJT."

"My heart bleeds," Gadar said. "I hope these are only temporary ranks, because the instant they check us out medically, I'm going to be back in my office."

"I hope it's quick," Vida said. "But if someone wanted to get rid of us—or some of us—all they'd have to do is delay the medical."

"You Serranos are so cheerful!" he said.

"You Livadhis are so lively," she said, and cut the connection.

❀   ❀   ❀

Vida could not remember a time in her adult life when she had had nothing specific to do for days on end. She'd taken leave, of course, but she'd always had plans. A trip to take, a course, a family crisis that needed her time and talents. She had money enough— she hadn't spent all her salary since she made lieutenant, and her investments had prospered. She could live quite well on half-pay. It was the idleness that bothered her, the sense of being cut off from her family.

Well . . . she'd go home, then, to the Serrano compound on Melander, that source of all—or at least many—of the Serrano family.

Making reservations on a civilian ship was annoying; she tried to laugh at herself for expecting people to jump when she said hop, but it wasn't easy. She'd so often thought of civilians as disorganized, but when you didn't have a staff . . . she grumbled at herself repeatedly, as she arranged to ship this and store that and decided what to carry on and what to stow in cargo.

She recognized other flag officers the first day on the ship; by mutual unspoken consent, they avoided each other. Though all wore uniforms at first—and of course they were entitled to do so, on leave—she and most of the others changed to civilian clothes early in the voyage.

Melander's orbital station had grown since she'd last seen it, but was still smaller than the huge combined Fleet/civilian stations she was used to. She saw plenty of people in uniform, but they ignored her—ignored *her*, just because she wasn't wearing hers, and they could not see the admiral inside the red civilian suit. She glowered at them anyway. Two of them, at least, were Serranos.

She caught a Northside shuttle, checked the arrival station weather, and pulled out a warmer jacket. Early spring on Melander would be colder than the regulated temperature on ship or station.

The Serrano family compound lay along the shore of a lake inaccurately named Serenity, since it seemed always ruffled by the breeze channeled up from the sea between the hills. A row of solid, respectable houses built of buff-and-brown stone or brick, each with its neat green lawn and floral border, rows of shade and fruit trees marking the edges of yards, neat pebbled walks from the road up to each house . . . it looked far less attractive than it had the last time she'd seen it. That had been . . . nearly thirty years ago, when the crabapple trees now in brilliant bloom above her head had been tiny sticks, her aunt's idea. They did look pretty, but she still didn't want to be here.

All the Fleet families who built compounds tended to the same organization . . . separate houses for the guardians with young children, those with older children, for the transient younger officers, for the senior officers on long leave, for those in retirement. Flag officers each had an apartment, which might be used for a special guest when its owner was not in residence. Vida had never seen hers, having qualified for it since her last visit, but she knew it would be there, furnished with the things she had sent home over the years.

It smelled of wax and wood and leather and the clean sharp scent of top-grade electronics. It was just as she'd imagined it, filled with souvenirs from all over the Familias, arranged attractively . . . and she hated it. Why had she bought that "Design in Blues" which was now, no doubt, worth four times what she paid for it? It reminded her of her first cruiser tour, and now she didn't want to be reminded. She turned on the music, Prescott's "Andante for Manamash Strings," and spent the first half hour turning pictures to the wall. If she couldn't be on a ship, a *real* ship, she wasn't going to have them staring at her from the walls. Or the caricature of the young officer's promotion dance. Or the view of Castle Rock from Rockhouse Major, with the old *Mordant*'s pods framing the continents.

Was it the rejuv going bad, or just frustration? Vida didn't know, and almost didn't care. The apartment was bigger than her quarters onstation, but it felt cramped, enclosed, in a way that ship compartments never did. She glared out the window at the lake. A walk, then, to work off this bad temper.

On the way downstairs, she saw Sabatino, the other Serrano flag officer, and her distant cousin. "I hate planets," he said by way of greeting.

"So do I," Vida said. They had never been close friends, but they were both Serrano admirals, and thus had common interests.

"I'm going up in the mountains for a week or so," Sabatino said. "Leaving tomorrow." She remembered that he had always liked wilderness camping.

"I'm going for a walk," Vida said. "Dinner?"

"Might as well." He waved and went on into his apartment.

Out of doors felt entirely too exposed. The wind, no proper ventilation current, whipped the lake surface into choppy little waves and tried to push Vida sideways. Clouds rushed by overhead, and behind the clouds was that opaque lid which groundsiders insisted was beautiful, hiding the stars.

She had liked the planet well enough growing up on it. She hadn't minded the blues and grays and mauves and pinks of the sky then, or the many shades of cloud. Vida pushed herself to walk faster, down the pebbled walk, across the road, to the footpath by the lake. Far out, bright sails glinted in red and yellow against the water. One thing about planets, you could walk a long way without retracing your steps. She walked herself breathless heading east, well past the end of the Serrano estate. There had been a small cluster of shops down here at one time, where a public boat ramp gave access to the lake for those who didn't have waterfront property.

Recovering her breath while waiting in a line of noisy children for a drink and a snack—she chose tea and a cinnamon pastry, not the sweet drinks and cream buns the children were buying—she recovered her sense of humor as well. Planets were not that bad, all things considered. She settled on a bench, protected from the wind by one of the shops, and looked at the hills behind the estates across the road. She had wandered there, as a child, splashing in the creeks and exploring little hidden valleys. She had run down here, hot and thirsty, to buy the same sweet drinks. Not bad at all, planets, if you were there by choice.

She would have to find something useful to do. With that resolve, she started back to the family compound, and by the time she arrived, she was quite ready for dinner with Sabatino. They chatted about music and art—her collection of modern prints, and his of music recordings. He invited her to come hear Malachy vu Suba's new bassoon concerto in his apartment, and she spent a pleasanter evening than she'd expected, arguing about the merits of that controversial work. Vu Suba had chosen to write for the ancient instrument, not the modern one, which limited performance to those orchestras which possessed period instruments. Sabatino argued that the tonal qualities were different enough to make this worthwhile, but Vida contended that only a very few could hear the difference.

❈ ❈ ❈

The next morning, however, he was gone and she still hadn't decided what to do. She turned her pictures face-out again, rearranged a few ornaments, checked for a third time that everything had been put away neatly. Shrieks from outside brought her to the window of the second bedroom.

The smallest Serrano children played in the garden between the houses as she had done, screaming and laughing the way children always did. Vida looked down on their playscape with its ramps and towers and bridges, and found it hard to believe she had ever been that noisy. Now that she had noticed them, the noise seemed to pierce her head with little needles.

Maybe the archives would be quieter. She went downstairs, and down again, into the underground library that housed the oldest documents the Serrano family owned.

Rows of Serrano biographies . . . Vida reread Rogier Xavier Serrano, one of her favorites (he had every attribute of a hero, including having made love to and won the heart of a beautiful heroine as brave as himself), and Millicent Serrano, born blind but gifted with extraordinary spatial abilities. She'd always meant to read about her own great-uncle Alcandor, who had managed to get thrown out of the Fleet for smuggling a tricorn vermuge onto a ship as a prank . . . and had then been readmitted, because no one else could get it off. That story in the official biography wasn't nearly as good as she remembered from his tales on the front porch of Rest House when he was a retired commander with a gimpy leg and a strange green spot on his arm. The official biography didn't mention the vermuge's lust for coffee, for instance, or the creature's curious mating behavior.

Vida spent several days browsing the family biographies before she tired of that, and looked around for something else. Battle reports . . . she'd seen all she wanted of battle reports. Service records, leave records, slim volumes of verse by Serranos who thought themselves poets . . . she opened one of these and burst into laughter. Either Amory David Serrano wasn't a very good poet, or the language had changed a lot in the past two hundred years. Mercedes Esperanza, on the other hand, had written erotic verses that should, Vida thought, have ignited the whole archive . . . but Mercedes had died young, of a typical poetic fever. What kind of space commander would she have made?

Stories, even: a few Serranos had written fiction, most of it clearly intended for children, and most of it—to Vida's taste anyway—pretty bad. *Carlo and the Starship* was nothing more than a child's tour of a passenger ship, with a biddable child asking obvious questions and a friendly puppy answering them. She passed by *Carlo and the Power Plant*, and *Carlo Goes to the Mountains*, glanced briefly at the illustrations for *Helen Is a Good Girl* (little Helen shaking hands; little Helen sitting up straight at table; little Helen offering a toy spaceship to another child with an improbably sweet smile—Serranos, even in childhood, didn't hand over ships willingly), and almost missed *Long Ago on Altiplano.*

Altiplano. Her grandson's fiancee's homeworld. She pried it out of the tightly-squeezed group of skinny children's books. Its pages had turned brown and brittle; the illustrations were not drawn in, but pasted on, ancient faded flatpics.

"Long ago, on Altiplano, a great Family ruled."

So they had, the family the Serranos had been bound to.

"A beautiful world, with magnificent snow-capped mountains, and great golden plains of grass. To this world, the Garcia-Macdonalds brought their people, who prospered there and spread across the fertile land. And their loyal guards and protectors, the brave Serranos, watched the sky above them, and kept their ships safe from piracy." That, too, she knew. The Serranos had been their space militia; someone else had been their ground militia.

"But treachery surrounded them. They were betrayed by those they trusted to guard them." Vida felt a chill. They hadn't been betrayed by Serranos . . .

"By their soldiers on the planet." That was better. Not Serranos at all, someone else.

"And they were all killed, the mothers and fathers and all the little children, because of the wickedness of the rebels and traitors. And that is why when we say our prayers, we do not ask for blessing upon the people of Altiplano."

What an odd book for a child! It was more like a diatribe, like a memoir. She looked on the other side of the gap in the row, but found only *Carlo Visits the Observatory* and *Helen Starts School,* followed by *Three Little Serranos Visit the Seashore*. Nothing else with the same faded brown binding.

Vida took her find over to the table, and paged back through it. Very, very odd. Hand-printed, of course, and the flatpics glued on with something that had bled through. They were all blurry and faded, but one appeared to show a house, and another a face. The rest might have been landscapes. The pasted-in pictures made the book fatter than its spine suggested—no wonder the whole row had been wedged tight.

Vida flipped every page, looking for any identifying mark. One of the flatpics fell off, and the paper folded behind it with it. She looked at it . . . thin, almost translucent, brown on the folds . . . it had been there for a very, very long time. Perhaps she should get the family librarian; she might damage it by unfolding it.

But she couldn't resist peeking.

CHAPTER TEN

Castle Rock

Back at Castle Rock, Cecelia was surprised to find that Miranda had left not just the Palace but the planet. She checked the net and found that Brun was the only family member onplanet. Brun had moved to Appledale, the Thornbuckle family estates on Castle Rock. Cecelia had always liked Appledale, with its pleasant view of rolling fields and orchards. She called and, as she'd expected, Brun invited her out to stay.

Brun met her at the front door, quickly directed the staff to take her luggage upstairs, and then—even on the way to the handsome downstairs morning room—frothed over with indignation about Hobart Conselline, who had gotten himself elected Speaker of the Table of Ministers.

"Hobart?" Cecela blinked. "He's not that bad, is he? He was always polite to me. I never had that much to do with him, but—"

"Hobart is a raging bully," Brun said grimly. She waved Cecelia to a comfortable chintz-covered chair and threw herself into another. "Just wait until you hear—" She took off at a conversational gallop, surprising Cecelia with her grasp of Family relationships. Had the girl been listening behind doors and actually paying attention when she seemed just a young fluffhead? It was always possible—this was, after all, the same Brun who had engineered her escape from the nursing home.

"I wouldn't have believed it," Cecelia said at last. "Are you sure . . . I mean, he's always been a bit pigheaded, but most of us are, from

148

time to time." A maid had brought in trays of pastries and sliced fruits, and pots of coffee and tea. Cecelia filled a little plate with apple slices and munched. They were just as crisp and flavorful as she remembered.

"He slapped down Great-Uncle Viktor in the meeting. Viktor! And Stefan didn't say a word. He's found excuses to get rid of most of the Ministers, replacing them with his own people—and now that he has the votes, it doesn't really matter if a few of Dad's are left." Brun was ignoring the food so far, but Cecelia took one of the ginger curls as well.

"What about Harlis?"

"He's bought Harlis, I suspect with the help of his new Minister of Judicial Affairs, Norm Radsin. You know how helpful or unhelpful the courts can be in estate cases—"

"Indeed I do." The old anger washed over her.

"Well, it's amazing how many rulings have changed in Harlis's favor since Norm took over that ministry. Without Kevil Mahoney, or access to his private files—and nobody, not even George, knows the access codes to Kevil's files—"

She did. Cecelia thought back to their last conversation, when they had discussed her own tangled legal problems in the wake of being declared incompetent. Kevil had trusted her with the voice codes for just this sort of situation.

"Has anyone tried to have Kevil declared incompetent?" she asked.

"Not that I know of. George certainly hasn't. Why?"

Why not, she thought, if Kevil was still incapacitated and unable to access his own files? Had no one in his offices tried to get access?

"I mean," Brun went on, "we could use the information, but we're not going to press for that—not after what happened to you."

"Is he conscious?"

"Yes, but he can't seem to remember much, or concentrate. His doctors don't advise rejuvenation because of the extent of the neurological damage, and the recent discoveries of what went wrong with Fleet rejuvenations." Brun finally poured herself a cup of tea, and took a pastry.

"I hadn't heard about that."

"No, it came out after you left. Some of the senior NCOs, the chiefs, started going senile—I actually saw one like that, back on

Copper Mountain, before I . . . before I left and all the rest happened. Memory loss, irrational thought processes. I mentioned it to Esmay, in fact, but then we had that fight. Anyway, there were more of them, a lot more, and when they did some research they found flaws in the process. They've put about half the flag officers on indefinite leave, because they were rejuved, just in case. None of them had shown symptoms yet, unless you count Lepescu."

Cecelia frowned. "Flaws in the process, or in the drugs themselves? Remember what happened on Patchcock . . ."

"That's what I thought of first, just a bad batch of drugs. I raised a formal Question in Council—the second meeting, that is, not the first—but Hobart claimed I was just trying to embarrass him, use it as an excuse for family rivalry, and one of his bootlickers got up and spouted a whole involved line about genetic susceptibility and the inbred genome of Fleet families."

"What did Venezia Morrelline say?"

"She wasn't there. And I can't get hold of Heris or Vida Serrano, either. Both Serrano admirals were taken off active duty; Fleet personnel offices claim not to know where they are. Heris has a ship, but it's out on patrol or something, inaccessible to civilians. Which doesn't make sense, because I've been able to contact Esmay, and she's on an SAR, way off at the remote end of Familias Space."

"How is Esmay?" Cecelia asked, to give herself time to think about the rest of this.

"Pining for Barin, worried about his NewTex wives—apparently Fleet accounting has garnished Barin's entire salary to help support them—and getting a little bored with the SAR, I gather. Also she's found out that Fleet doesn't think Landbrides should marry Fleet officers."

"But she *is* a Landbride. What do they think of that?"

"Yes—it's funny, really. She says they've got it all wrong, and she didn't want to be one anyway. But it's tied up the paperwork for her to marry Barin, even if he weren't going broke trying to support all those NewTex women. Poor Esmay." Brun gave a wry chuckle. "It's her first time in love; I remember how I pined for Tommy Rakeseller, the first time I had it bad, and thought the universe was dreadfully unfair because his parents sent him off to camp. I know this is more serious, but it's really hard on her."

"And Barin?"

"Barin's at the other end of our universe, escorting a Lone Star Confederation Ranger back here."

"What?"

"Yes. They warned me—or rather, Waltraude did, that crazy professor who's hanging around the NewTex women. It never occurred to anyone *official* that introducing me to a Ranger might upset me. Apparently, Hobart's new Minister of Foreign Affairs—he fired Cabby DeLancre for daring to contradict him—decided to shut the wrong barn door long after the horse had returned, and froze all the assets of Lone Star Confederation citizens, and closed the border."

"But Lone Star had nothing to do with it."

"You know that, my father knew that, even I know that. But all Hobart had to hear was the word 'Texas,' and the fact that they were Ageists, as he calls it. The Lone Star Confederation has been a reasonable trading partner for centuries; they were understandably annoyed, and insisted on sending someone to educate us."

Cecelia leaned back in her chair. "You know, Brun, I find it hard to believe that you, of all people, are being this politically minded."

For an instant, the old grin flashed out. "Me, too. I keep thinking, 'This is not me; this is my evil twin.' But one thing I did learn, in that hell, is what happens if you don't pay attention. So Mother's gone back to Sirialis, to dig out all of Dad's files that she can—some of them were never transferred here—and try to stave off Uncle Harlis's grab for the family properties. And here I am."

"Yes . . . I see."

"And . . . you did find a good home for the twins?" That in a tone almost wistful, and certainly pleading.

"Yes," Cecelia said firmly. "A very good home. They will be loved and cared for."

"Good. I thought, after you left, that I should have suggested Raffaele, but then she's been cleaning up my messes for far too long. I'm glad you found someone else."

Cecelia's brain tripped over that one and came up with a fresh topic. "You said a new Minister of Foreign Affairs—who would that be?"

"Minor family, major pain. Pedar Orregiemos. You probably never heard of him."

"As a matter of fact, I have. He—" She shut down that line quickly and shifted to another. "He has event horses. I beat his entry in the Wherrin this year."

"Good. I wish you'd managed to trample him at the same time. You should see him fawning on Hobart, and Hobart lapping it up. The man has *no* background in the diplomatic service, no experience in dealing with foreign entities. He thinks any political system which doesn't embrace rejuvenation is corrupt and probably about to attack us. He's already managed to insult the Crescent Worlds, and they're *ours*. Worse than that, he thinks he's the right person to comfort widows—he keeps hinting to me that he would make me a fine stepfather." Brun mimed gagging.

Cecelia grabbed for yet another topic, anything but Pedar. She had never been in a conversation with quite so many landmines. "Who's in Colonial Affairs, now?"

"Another Conselline lackey, Davor Vraimont," Brun said. "It's dawned on them—well, on everyone, I guess—that repeatable rejuvenation could cause the biggest population explosion ever, as well as locking up wealth in the very, very old. That'd mean a lot of ambitious, frustrated young people. So colonization has been speeding up for some time—I didn't know that; Buttons told me he'd talked to Dad about it. But I found out that Conselline Sept has major investments in development companies, and their projections for the rate at which excess population can be absorbed by development make no sense—unless there's a much higher failure rate than before. That bit of information I got from a clerk in Colonial who'd been fired for insubordination. Makes me suspicious."

"Ummm. You remember that Ronnie is my nephew," Cecelia said, carefully erecting bombproof partitions in her mind against a loose tongue.

"Yes, of course."

"His parents are concerned about the situation on the world he's moved to. I hear that some supplies in the contract weren't actually delivered, that there's the possibility of interference with communications. What if the Consellines are counting on a certain percentage of colonies to fail, because they get their profit from selling colony shares?"

"I could believe that. But how can we prove it?"

"I don't know. We need Kevil," Cecelia said. "I'd better go visit him."

"It's—pretty bad. You know he lost an arm, too."

"No, I didn't. When I saw him in the hospital, before I took off with the babies, he was just a shape in the bed. And I didn't have much time."

"They're trying to grow a replacement, but so far it hasn't worked—they've lost three buds. And George says his memory's still damaged, and he can't concentrate."

"Is he still in the hospital?"

"No; they moved him to a rehab center, and then George took him home. Our wonderful new Speaker decided he was a security risk at the rehab center."

"Well, then. I'll go over tomorrow. Maybe I can be of some help."

"You know," Brun said more slowly, "Uncle Harlis runs the planetary development corporations for the Barraclough Sept." She took a long swallow of tea.

"What colony are Ronnie and Raffa in?"

"Excet-24."

"Rats. I was hoping it was one of ours—that way I could pump them. Excet Environmental Group is a Conselline corporation. I wonder why they chose that one, instead of family? Not that it matters."

"I don't know," Cecelia said. "Possibly the shares cost less?"

"Could be. Anyway, I'd bet something's going on in all these new colonies . . . I wish I had Kevil's background files, because I rather suspect the data in the main computers has been fiddled as well." Brun stretched. "And now that I've talked your ears off, both of them, how about a visit to the stable? We don't have much here, as you probably remember, but there are a couple of niceish mares we can take a ride through the orchards on, if you'd like."

Cecelia shook her head. "No, thank you, my dear. Everyone thinks of me as a thoroughly horse-besotted old woman, but one prerogative of old women is to surprise young ones occasionally. I shall go stroll in your gardens, if I may."

"Well, then, I'm for the pool. See you at dinner."

❂ ❂ ❂

At the Mahoney house, a uniformed nurse met Cecelia at the door. "Ser Mahoney is in the study, madam, but he is . . . not really himself."

Cecelia thought of asking who he was instead—she had a lingering distaste for medical euphemisms—but resisted the temptation. She followed the nurse down the familiar wide passage to the double doors that led into Kevil's home office, steeling herself for what she would see. At the same time, she wondered where the security was. If Kevil was a security risk, shouldn't there be more protection around him? She had seen no guards at all.

"Ser George Mahoney is at the university," the nurse said, over his shoulder. "He won't be back until this evening."

Cecelia frowned. No security, one nurse all day . . . something wrong here.

In the study, Kevil lay awkwardly in one of the big leather chairs. His face looked strange, twisted; she realized that regen had not been able to repair all the physical damage, that part of his jaw was missing, and the skin over it rumpled oddly. In his eyes, Cecelia saw no recognition, just anxiety. Then, slowly, a spark . . . as if he were walking through a dark corridor with a candle, closer and closer.

"Cecelia . . ."

"Yes. "

"You look . . . younger. Dye your hair?"

Cecelia's heart sank. Of course she looked younger; she had rejuved several years before, to a nominal forty. He had known that. They had slept together after that. "Rejuv, Kevil," she said briskly. It was hard to look at him, but she knew she must. "I'm sorry I wasn't here when you were hurt," she said.

"Me . . . too. I can't . . . remember . . . all."

Was the slurred voice from the injury, or from drugs? Cecelia glanced around, but saw no litter of pillboxes.

"I've been to visit Ronnie and Raffaele," she said. To her delight, the spark in his eyes brightened.

"How are . . . they?"

"They're fine, except that the developer's done something foul with the colony they're on." She told him about it, gauging his attention span by his expression. For a few minutes at a time, he seemed the old Kevil—his eyes bright, his face intent. Then he would blink, and the expression slacken. She stopped, and waited, and when he seemed focussed again she went on.

"You're . . . really . . . talking to me." He smiled, a genuine smile this time.

"Yes, of course."

"You . . . understand . . ."

"Not completely, Kevil. But I know you need something to chew on."

"Yes. They keep asking me . . . questions . . . tests . . . can't remember. . . ."

"I hated those," Cecelia said, remembering her own convalescence, the idiocy of the questions in the standard tests.

"Name three vegetables, name five fruits . . ."

"Name the CEO of Excet Environmental Group," Cecelia said, as if it were another on the list.

"Silvester Conselline," Kevil said instantly, then looked blank. "What was that?"

"A reasonable question," Cecelia said. "And one I wanted the answer to. Ronnie and Raffa are, as I said, practically marooned on Excet-24, and Brun says that's an Excet Group colony planet. I want to know who's responsible for shorting the colony of its startup supplies and staff."

"Probably not Silvester," Kevil said, sounding even more awake now. "He's been spending most of his time trying to convince the universe he's a great composer. But he does tend to sign anything anyone puts in front of him."

A tap at the door. The nurse looked in, his expression exactly the one Cecelia least liked to see. "Ser Mahoney needs his rest, madam. Perhaps another time?"

"Go on—take a break," Cecelia said to the nurse. "I'm experienced with this—I've been a convalescent myself."

"But his lunch . . . his diet—"

"And I can cook. Go on now."

Finally he left, protesting and warning and muttering. Cecelia watched through the scan pickup until she had seen him go all the way down the street and board a tram.

"Officious," she said to Kevil, when she came back to him.

"You think . . . he's up to something," Kevil said.

"Nurses are always up to something," Cecelia said. "But in addition to that, yes. Now." She pulled the scrambler she carried out of her bag and turned it on. Kevil gave her a puzzled look. "Remnant of my times with Heris Serrano and those Fleet refugees she foisted on me as crew. Oblo whatever-his-name-was. Good advice, I realized after awhile. Always carry a means of tapping someone else's data, and always protect your own conversations."

Kevil grinned. "You always were smarter . . . than people thought."

"Yes, and so were you. Kevil—what's happened? Why only one nurse? Why haven't you had a proper limb replacement?"

"No money."

Cecelia stared at him, shocked. "But Kevil—you've always had money, pots of it."

"No more. It . . . isn't there."

"But—what happened?"

"I don't know. One day there, then—it wasn't. George tried—couldn't find out—"

"Someone fiddled the databases? But—people would notice—"

"Not unless it was their account. The people who normally handled my accounts would notice, unless they'd been transferred."

"And that's not hard at all . . ." Cecelia mused. "And there are new Ministers in the relevant Ministries, and a huge muddle all over . . ."

"Yes. I think . . . it happened . . . when Bunny died."

If that were true, it would mean—no, *could* mean—that it was related. That the same person or persons planned the attack on Bunny's life, and Kevil's fortunes.

"I know . . . something . . . I know it's because I know something . . . but Cece, I can't remember what it is I'm supposed to know. I can't remember. I can't think—" A muscle in his face twitched; his hand shook.

"Kevil . . . relax. Please. Let me fix you lunch—yes, you come with me into the kitchen—and we'll talk some more. I know I can help."

It took a struggle to get Kevil up, and Cecelia fought down her fury when she saw his unbalanced, lurching gait. But in the kitchen, he seemed more comfortable in the chair, his good arm propped on the wide wooden table, than he had in the study.

"I'm assuming you don't have a cook because of the money—"

"Yes."

She fixed him fruit, bread, cheese. There were custards in the refrigerator, but she didn't trust them—custards could conceal drugs. He ate, clumsily, with his left hand.

"Kevil, do you remember giving me your access codes?"

A blank look. "Access codes?"

"The second night. After we decided it wouldn't work. You said, 'If I'm ever in the state you were in, I want to know you're on my side.' And you gave them to me. You've forgotten, but I haven't."

"Cecelia—"

"When George gets home, we'll get to work. Tonight. There's no time to waste."

"I can't . . . help much."

"You did that, years ago. We'll take care of it." Somehow. Cecelia scolded herself internally—she was turning into everyone's helpful old aunt again. Well, if she was going to take her turn being civic-minded, helpful, and useful, she might as well make a thorough job of it. She'd had another brilliant idea.

Waltraude Meyerson, tenured professor of antique studies on loan to the Regular Space Service as a consultant on Texan history and culture, sat quietly in the corner of the room with her recorder on, watching the NewTex women argue about religion and education without getting involved. She hoped. This was the first conflict she'd seen among the women who had fled Our Texas, and she was fascinated.

It had been months, and only now was the rigid rank structure breaking down. The first wives of the Rangers had each run her own household without interference from the other first wives—Primas, they were all called. Prima Bowie, the one Waltraude felt she knew best, actually ranked second in the hierarchy; the Ranger Captain's first wife outranked her. That was Prima Travis, but she was older and had less vitality than Prima Bowie. Usually she let Prima Bowie make decisions, but not today.

They were arguing about schools again. Under Familias law, the children—all of them—were supposed to be in school. Parents could choose from a wide variety of schools, or school their children at home, and the requirements were—to an academic like Waltraude—minimal. All children must become literate in at least two languages, study some very basic science and mathematics, and the Code of Citizens. But these women had steadfastly resisted sending the children to school from the beginning. No one had been able to figure out why, because the women would not explain what they considered self-explanatory. Now, in the argument, Waltraude began to grasp the problem.

"Boys and girls together! I think not!" Prima Travis was holding firm on that. "They'd become Abominations!"

"There are single-sex schools," Prima Bowie said. "Most are religious—"

"Not *our* religion!" Prima Travis sniffed again. "They're heathens, or worse."

"But—"

"We should never have come," Prima Travis said. "I—I was wrong to come. We should go back." Behind her, Waltraude saw several of the junior Travis wives nodding, but one pinched her mouth up and looked stubborn. Waltraude counted—third back, that was Tertia.

"The men lied to us," Prima Bowie said. "They killed mothers—"

"*You* said," replied Prima Travis. "I never saw that picture you said you saw."

"You heard Patience—Hazel," Prima Bowie said. "She's a good girl . . ."

"She is *not* a good girl; she is one of them. Prima Bowie, has your brains run out your ears, or what? She is one of them, an Abomination. She runs around wearing men's pants, messing about with machines—"

"I'll bet she has an implant," sneered Secunda Travis. Prima Travis whirled and slapped her on the mouth.

"Don't you be saying those bad words, girl!"

"I just—"

"And don't you be arguin' with me! You see what it comes to, Prima Bowie? We left our rightful place, and now we have this—this arguin' and usin' bad language."

"We can't go back," Prima Bowie said. "They'd kill us—"

"And so they should," Prima Travis said. "Our children to grow up no proper way—"

"So you think we should just go back, die, let our children be orphans?"

"No, but we got to find a right way to live. Not hived up like bees with nowhere to gather honey." Having delivered this, Prima Travis led her family out of the common room, back to their own little hive. More stingers than honey, the way Waltraude saw it.

Waltraude shut off the recorder and waited until the remaining women were seated, back at their endless handwork.

"Prima—"

"Call me Ruth Ann," Prima said. "I'm not a first wife anymore. Mitch is dead, and that boy won't actually marry me—I see that now."

"Ruth Ann, fine. Listen—where do you think you would be happy?"

"I won't be." The woman's broad, rounded face contracted in a scowl. "Not in this kind of world."

"There are many worlds in the Familias," Waltraude said. "What sort of place, can you tell me? A city? A smaller town?"

"Hazel said there was, but how can we go there? We can't just up and ask some spaceship to take us, even if I knew. If I can't be home . . . I guess I'd like a quiet place. There's always noise here, machine noise. I'd like it where it's quiet. Open. Maybe where I could see the fields. I always missed that, after Mitch moved us to the city, not having the fields outside. The garden just wasn't the same, big as it was. Someplace where people didn't laugh at me for not being schooled, someplace where what I can do is worth something. But I doubt you got anyplace like that in your fancy confederation or whatever it is."

Waltraude grinned. "Oh, but we do, Ruth Ann. What you need first of all is to be on a planet, not on a station in space. And then you need the kind of world where the basic skills you have are desperately needed. Your gardening, weaving, sewing, cooking . . . and tell me, do your boys know anything of tools?"

"The older ones do. Boys make most of the furniture in a house— they're so rough on it, they have to learn to fix it and make it."

"Your world had trees, didn't it? Wood for manufacture?"

"Yes, of course." Ruth Ann paused, brow wrinkled. "Are there worlds without trees?"

"Nearly without, yes. Ruth Ann . . . the Familias has hundreds of populated worlds, and is opening new ones to colonization all the time. And the colony worlds need pioneers. As you pointed out so succinctly today, most of us can't boil water without a computer. You know how to build fires. You know how to make bread from wheat—and I'll bet some of your older boys know how to make a mill."

"Of course they do," Ruth Ann said. Waltraude could almost feel the slow smile working its way out of her confused heart, and just as she expected, it finally smoothed out the ridged brow. "You really believe we could get to such a place? How? We have no money. . . ."

"I know someone who does," Waltraude said. "And they owe you a lot. The only problem is making the connection. But that's what scholars do."

"Make connections?"

"Yes. It's our job, though most people don't think it is. They think of us in terms of collecting information—silly, anyone can do that. What we do is notice which bits make new connections."

"You will help us? Why? You think we're ignorant . . ."

"Of history, yes. Of life, no. And of course I'll help you. Any decent person helps others; it's one of the things people are for."

"What . . . religion are you?"

"You wouldn't recognize it, and it would only bother you." Waltraude picked up her bag. "Prima—Ruth Ann, I'm going to be gone for several weeks; I've been asked to escort a diplomat from the Lone Star Confederation back to Castle Rock. But let me just show you—" She took out some hardcopy ads for colony worlds. "See this? You might like something—"

"But what would our protector say? He'd have to say it was all right—"

Waltraude thought of the scuttlebutt she'd heard about young Barin Serrano and his problems with the women. "I think he'd be delighted if you found a place you could be happy."

"And living the right way," the woman said, the scowl returning for a moment. "Happiness isn't everything. Just because our men did wrong things doesn't mean they was wrong about everything. I want my children to grow up to be good, Godfearin' men and women."

"I'm sure there's a place, Ruth Ann," Waltraude said. "When I get back, I'll help."

Rockhouse Major had everything that two young officers in love could want, Esmay knew . . . if she could only get there. It should have been simple to get from the R.S.S. *Shrike*, over in Sector Seven, to Sector Seven HQ, and from there to the Castle Rock system. She had finally heard from Barin; Castle Rock was the one place they could reasonably meet, since *Gyrfalcon* would be there several days. Castle Rock lay on her route to her new duty station, and was admirably provided with shipping and passenger lines. But one thing after another had delayed her. She imagined Barin, on *Gyrfalcon*, making an effortless smooth transit . . . only to wait around wondering if she was even going to show up. He might even leave before she arrived, if this miserable tub of a ship didn't get a move on.

Barin saw Esmay just a moment before she saw him: saw her face with that harder edge, that warier expression. Then their eyes met, and she grinned.

"How long do you have?" she asked, as they settled at an empty table in the concourse.

"Four hours," Barin said, angry all over again. "It was supposed to be forty-eight hours on station, minimum, but all of a sudden—"

"Same with us," Esmay said. "I should have been here three days ago, but the blasted ship had a pressure-lock problem; we hung around for hours and hours at SecSev HQ, then they transferred us to old *Bowfin*, without time to send any messages, and then she couldn't generate more than seventy-two percent of her normal power, and we just came limping in . . . I was afraid you'd have left already."

"So was I. I left a message for you at the mail drop already, just in case." Barin put his head to one side and grinned. "Surely, all this scramble can't be just to keep us apart," he said. "That's an expensive abuse of Fleet resources."

"Whatever it is, it's a nuisance. Is your family still against us?"

"Yes. They think we should wait until the NewTex women are all taken care of. How am I supposed to do that? It could be years. What about you?"

Esmay handed over the message that had finally arrived, tied and stamped formally. "The Landholders are upset. Can you read Kurlik script? Basically it says that it is unacceptable for a Landbride to marry offworld at all, and particularly to marry a foreign military officer."

"But we're not *foreign*," Barin said.

"I know that. You know that. But Altiplano—"

"I don't want to take away anything you have," Barin said. "You've explained about being Landbride—it's a wonderful thing—"

"It's a nuisance," Esmay said. She straightened. "I never expected to be Landbride, and I thought I'd lost you . . . and . . . anyway, I accepted it in a time of crisis, but that's past. My father realized very early that I might resign in favor of a legitimate heir. It's not done often—" It had never been done except in cases of insanity or other permanent disability or extreme old age. She didn't like to think of marriage as equivalent to insanity or permanent disability. "But there is a ritual procedure. The hard part is going to be getting leave to go there. I can appoint a stand-in, but that's not the same thing as the next Landbride. My father says if I marry you, even though I've appointed someone, the Landmen's Guild could challenge, and intervene in our family affairs. And that would be bad."

"I can see that." Barin shook his head. "And we still haven't figured a way around the Fleet regulations; even if you do resign as Landbride, you can't quit being a sector commander's daughter. Does it seem to you that this is a lot harder than we thought it would be?"

"Yes. If it were this hard for everyone, nobody would get married."

They stared gloomily at each other for several minutes. Then Esmay sat up. "Let's not waste it. We have four hours—or rather, three hours and forty-two minutes."

"I don't suppose we could get married in three hours and forty-two minutes?" Barin said wistfully. "Maybe an hour to get married, and two hours to enjoy it?"

Esmay laughed. "It takes a lot longer; we couldn't possibly. But we can do something cheerier than sit here eating bad food in a noisy place."

"Right. But you'll have to pay. I'm flat broke." For some reason, this struck both of them as funny rather than annoying, and they thoroughly enjoyed their dinner.

CHAPTER ELEVEN

J.C. Chandler, President of the Lone Star Confederation, watched the newscube with his lower lip tucked under. This was trouble with a big T, and he didn't know how he was going to deal with it. They had had problems enough with the Familias Regnant, over the years, without *this* kind of nonsense.

"Looks bad, J.C.," Millicent said.

"There's always crazies in the world," Ramie said, leaning back with his hands folded over his belly. "It's not our fault they call themselves Texans."

The two obvious responses, J.C. thought, and neither of them useful right now. He said nothing while the newscube ran through the whole summary, then turned off the reader and put his hands on the table. Time to talk seriously.

"That new administration has closed the border to Lone Star citizens," he said without more preamble. "They say they can't guarantee our safety, and they did send this to explain why. And they haven't withdrawn their embassy staff."

"But it wasn't *us*," Millicent said. "Those idiots are all the way across Familias space—"

"More like the length of it," Ramie said, not moving. "If you look at the actual geometry—"

"What matters," J.C. said, "is that they've done it—closed the border. Frozen our assets in their banks, too—"

"They can't *do* that—" Ramie said, sitting up so suddenly that his chair rolled back. "The Treaty of Poldek clearly states—"

"They've done it." J.C. tried not to enjoy interrupting Ramie again, but it was hard—the older man was so annoyingly difficult to get a rise out of, and here he'd actually made Ramie sit up.

"But I moved most of the family's liquid capital into Goodrich & Scanlon only a year ago; it's not reasonable—"

"They claim we might be financing our 'countrymen' as they call them, even if we aren't personally involved. They want to be sure what our money's doing."

"Making more money, just like theirs." Ramie huffed his reddening cheeks out. "What do they take us for, ignorant rubes?"

Probably they did, J.C. thought, but that wasn't at issue right now. "What I want to do," J.C. said, "is tell the Cabinet and Congress that we're sending some investigators to help 'em out."

"Help them? Help them what? Steal us blind?"

"No—help them with specifically Texan issues. They seem to be blundering around not knowing the difference between those idiots and the rest of us. We could help."

"They've got a scholar, they said. That Meyerson woman."

"Milly, why do you call her 'that Meyerson woman'? That won't help our image."

"I liked Professor Lemon," Millicent said frankly. "He used to send me the nicest notes . . . all right, it's not fair. You're right. We should help them—even Meyerson—if they'll let us."

From sheer force of habit and a fondness for tradition when it didn't get in the way, the Lone Star Confederation had retained the term "Rangers" for its internal security forces. This hadn't bothered anyone—not even the Familias Regnant with their hoity-toity attitudes—in centuries, but obviously, the Familias Regnant had a reason to react badly to the title now. The abuse of the same word by the New Texas Godfearing Militia nuts made *real* Rangers wish they'd trademarked the name somewhere back down in history.

Still, it wasn't the fault of the Lone Star Confederation. Rangers had the right training to pursue an investigation—and they weren't about to change their names just to satisfy a twitchy Familias Regnant. They'd send a Ranger.

Which Ranger then became the issue . . . but not for long, because Katherine Anne Briarly was the obvious best choice. A woman like

Katie Anne, and they'd know that Lone Star's Rangers weren't like those others in any way, shape or form. Especially shape.

And besides, it would get Katie Anne out of everyone's hair for a few months. She had been getting a mite big for her britches, though not in a physical way, ever since her uncle Beau got appointed to the Supreme Court. She'd taken to being even more Texan than the Texans could stand.

Ranger Katherine Anne Briarly arrived at the Familias Regnant embassy wearing a red two-piece suit that emphasized every asset she had except brains, which—in Kate's view—couldn't be put on view anyway without making someone puke. A tumble of ash-blonde hair swirled over her shoulders; her bright blue eyes twinkled at the R.S.S. marine guards by the gate. Neither twinkled back.

"Hi," she said, holding out her ID case. "I'm Kate Briarly, and y'all are expecting me."

The gate opened behind the motionless guards, and she was facing a squad of them. The leader or whatever came out and took her ID case, then looked from the image inside to her.

"You're Ranger Katherine Anne Briarly?"

"Yup. But that's an official picture, in uniform, and I didn't see any reason to get gussied up in uniform for just a friendly visit. I figured y'all'd have an ID scan unit anyway."

"Quite so. If you'd come this way." She followed the young man toward a portable booth set up in the courtyard, ignoring the scrape of feet as the squad fell in behind her. This was going to be fun.

She was who she said she was—retinals, fingerprints, voiceprints, the whole shebang—and in another ten minutes she was upstairs waiting to meet the ambassador.

"Sera—Ranger—Briarly—"

"Oh, just call me Kate," Kate said, widening her smile. He blinked.

"It's irregular," he murmured.

"I know," Kate said. "But who's to tell on you? Not me."

"I have received permission for two Rangers to enter Familias space and help with inquiries—"

"You don't need two," Kate said. "I'll just go by myself, thanks."

"But—"

"It'll be simpler," Kate said. "Less cost to you, too, keeping track of just one. Besides, it's traditional."

She had seen the ambassador before, while running security at the Cattlemen's Association Ball three years before, but she'd been in uniform then, her hair slicked back into a neat French braid. He didn't remember her, she could tell that. All the better.

"Now I realize y'all are concerned that we might have some connection to those NewTex nuts—"

"Concern was expressed," the ambassador said. "Not by me; I've tried to reassure the Grand Council that you all . . . er . . . you . . . here, the Lone Star Confederation . . . are not part of that group."

"Heavens, no," Kate said. "I'd like to see anyone making *us* wear clothes like that! And bare feet—shoot, I was as tomboy as they come, but you don't see me shuffling around in bare feet." She pointed a long, elegant foot clad in a feminine version of the Texas style: high-heeled, but not a boot.

"It's the new government," the ambassador said. "We have a new Speaker and a new Minister of Foreign Affairs and Minister of Defense; one doesn't like to say it's inexperience, but they're just not listening to me. You've travelled in Familias space before, Sera . . . er . . . Ranger . . . ?"

"Kate," she said again. "No, not me. I've been to Bluebonnet and West and Panhandle, but not to Familias. It'll be fun."

At the border, Kate found she had an escort at the end of the docking tube.

A trim young man with a face like carved bronze. "Lieutenant Junior Grade Serrano," he said. "Ranger Briarly, your luggage will be transferred—"

"Oh, call me Kate," she said, smiling. He didn't smile back.

"You're to come aboard *Gyrfalcon*," he said. "It's the fastest route to Rockhouse Major, where the task force has reassembled—"

"Are you arresting me?" Kate asked. She glanced around the docking lobby, decorated in what struck her as bland and chilly colors, muted blues and greens, and noted two men and one woman in R.S.S. uniform lurking by the entrance.

"No, ma'am," the young man said. "Just transporting you, ma'am."

Kate cocked her head and considered him. In her experience, young men his age melted with only one smile, and he hadn't. Well, his preferences might lie elsewhere, but still . . . "Fine," she said. "Let's go." He turned as quickly as she moved, and walked beside her through the entrance, where the others lined up after them, and then guided her across the wide passage to what the sign said was a dropchute. Kate stopped short.

"I'm not going in there," she said. "I've heard about those."

"You don't have them?"

"No—we like floors in our elevators. No one's looking up *my* skirt—"

"Fine—then we'll take the cross-station tram." He led her to the station, plugged some kind of datawand into a port, and the next tram stopped, doors opening exactly opposite them. Kate was impressed, and said so. He still wasn't melting. She looked him over again. He couldn't be a mango; she had known lots of mangos and they had a certain . . . feel. So either he really hated Texans, or . . . he was resisting her because he had a girl.

Her first meal in the officers' mess gave her a chance to do more than mutter polite greetings.

"Have you ever visited Familias space before, Ranger Briarly?" asked the executive officer, on one side of her. She was not sure what an executive officer did, but she had memorized the insignia, and knew he was a lieutenant commander.

"No—and I hope I'm going to see more of it than the inside of a transfer station and this ship."

"What would you like to see?"

"Oh—all those sights the tourist brochures have. Langsdon's ice falls. Chuzillera's cloud forests. The Grand Council Chamber on Castle Rock. I'd like to have seen your king while you still had one."

"Why?"

"It's so romantic," Kate said. "All those dramacubes, set in misty Vaalonia or—what's that place where they go running around on horses chasing after a fox? We just have ordinary people doing ordinary things—" She didn't really believe that, but wanted to see their reaction.

"The storycubes you people export are extraordinary enough. Those lawnhorns . . ."

"Longhorns," Kate said. "And the stories are old—last century's revival of Wild West—"

"Annie—that woman in fringes with all those guns—?"

"Stories," Kate said firmly. "Not real history. And that's what I'm here for, to talk about real history."

"But you're a . . . Ranger . . ." No doubt about it, they were twitchy about that word. With reason, though the reason was a lie.

"I'm a Ranger," Kate said firmly. "They weren't. They were a bunch of maniacs with no legitimate connection whatsoever to real Rangers."

"So you say," said one voice down the table. Kate leaned forward.

"So I say. Are you calling me a liar?"

The air seemed to congeal around her. She smiled; the silence lengthened. The officer at the far end of the table cleared his throat.

"Mr. Chesub, that was rude; apologize."

"I'm sorry, Ranger Briarly," a young man said. "I'm not accusing you of lying." But by his tone he still wasn't convinced.

Kate let her smile soften. "We have had just as many freaks and nutcases as any other culture," she said. "But the people who stole your Chair's daughter are not ours. The Lone Star Confederation wouldn't tolerate that kind of behavior. We Lone Star *women* wouldn't tolerate that kind of behavior." Nervous chuckles. "Not that we're . . . however you say it . . . hostile to men or anything . . ."

"Well, you don't look like the pictures of their women—but you're all from Texas originally, right?"

"Not really." Kate settled into lecture mode. "The Lone Star Confederation was organized for space exploration back on Earth, and most of its members then were North Americans—many of them from the exact region then known as Texas. But most of the people in Texas came from somewhere else, all over North America. Sure, there were some hard-shell Texans among them—people whose families had been in Texas just about forever—but a lot of them weren't. And Lone Star has always welcomed immigrants who share our philosophy—"

"Which is?"

"Fear God and nobody else, ride tall, shoot straight, never tell a lie, dance with who brung you, and never renege on a handshake."

Another silence, this one slightly shocked, but responsive.

" 'Dance with who brung you?' "

"Another way of saying honor your earlier obligations—don't just look at current profit."

"Interesting."

"And your philosophy?" Kate asked.

For a long moment no one answered, then young Lt. Serrano spoke up. "If I understand yours, it's much the same. Tell the truth, keep promises, stand by friends, don't turn your back on an enemy."

"I notice you didn't mention God," Kate said. "Is that because those NewTex nutcases have you scared, or what? Any of you folks got religion?"

This time the captain spoke up. "The Familias legal codes—and those of the Regular Space Service—allow freedom of belief, and freedom of religious practices which are not directly harmful to others. Because of the wide variety of beliefs, many held strongly, we do not generally discuss religion with those we do not know."

Kate cocked her head and gave him her best mischievous kid grin. "In other words, it's bad manners to talk about God?"

"Something like that," he said.

"You people must have been descended from Anglicans," Kate said. "Well, I'm not here to make you nervous, though I don't see why a good argument about God should do anything but keep your digestion going. It's one of our favorite forms of entertainment."

"You . . . uh . . . are religious yourself?"

Kate looked him in the eye. "You bet. So far as I know, every member of my family back to Old Earth has been, and I'm not about to break tradition."

"And what, since you don't mind our asking, is your religion?"

"Baptist," Kate said. "But my mother's family was about half Anglican, and my dad's grandmother was Methodist. There's even the odd Presbyterian in there somewhere."

Glances passed back and forth.

"Y'all don't have a clue what I'm talking about, do you?"

"Not . . . exactly." That was a female officer.

"You do have Christians, right?"

"Certainly . . . many kinds, though I don't know all the names."

"Then just call me a Christian, and don't worry about it. God'll sort it out."

"Do you have any . . . uh . . . dietary or special needs we should know about?"

"No, that's somebody else. I'll eat anything I like the flavor of, any day of the week. We don't drink alcohol on the Baptist side of our family, 'cept when we're being young and sowing wild oats. Every once in awhile I sow an oat myself."

She sensed the mood warming even more.

"What do your kind of rangers do?"

"Anything that needs doin'. We're a lot like a police force, but we tend to work alone. Keep order, track down the bad guys, help the people who need it."

"How do you know who the bad guys are?" came a call from down the table.

"Same way you do, I expect," Kate said. "Liars, cheats, killers, the kind of people who'd pour gasoline on a dog—" She felt the total noncomprehension of that one, and stopped. "You have dogs, don't you?"

"Oh . . . like . . . dogs? Hounds or something?"

"Dogs, like hounds, sheepdogs, cowdogs, even those awful nippy-yippy poodley things. And do you have mean people who hurt animals?"

"Yeah . . ." That more cautiously, as if the speaker weren't entirely sure.

"Well, we don't much like people who mistreat animals, kids, or old ladies. Or old men, for that matter. They're on my list of bad guys."

By the end of that meal she sensed that most of the officers were at least neutral, if not actually friendly.

The next day, Kate met the antique historian, Professor Meyerson, and sighed to herself. So predictable, that type. The lady academic, tweedy and warty . . . not that Meyerson actually had warts, but she looked as if they should be there to complete the official look. Even on Bluebonnet, known for its beautiful women, a certain kind of academic woman looked like this, only with better tweeds.

At least Meyerson knew more about the Lone Star Confederation than the rest of the people she met. And she was finally able to clear up a question that bedeviled Kate for days.

"That young fellow, Barin Serrano?"

"Yes . . ." Meyerson, head down in a scanner as usual, didn't seem to be paying close attention.

"What do you know about him?"

"He's giving you trouble?" Meyerson's head came up, and her expression was mingled mischief and surprise.

"No, just the opposite. He's ignoring me as if I had bark like a mesquite tree, but I just can't believe he's a mango."

Meyerson laughed, a surprisingly full-throated laugh for a frowsty old professor. "He's not. He's engaged to another officer, in the first place, and in the second place he's burdened with all those NewTex women and children."

"Why him in particular?"

"They consider him their protector, and for them this means he's the only one who can make decisions about them. The Regular Space Service has taken his pay to help support them, so he can't marry until he figures out what to do with them."

"I suppose shipping them back isn't an option?"

"No, they'd kill them, at least mute them. He's stuck with them."

"That's too bad." Kate thought about it. "He's a nice boy, and if he's minded to marry, he should have the chance. You suppose those women would listen to me?"

Meyerson looked her up and down. "As a messenger of the devil, maybe. They're very serious about their religion."

"And I'm very serious about mine, Wally." They had come to first names several days before, and Kate refused to struggle with Waltraude after the first few tries. "You don't have to go barefoot and wear rags to be a believer." She cocked her head. "You ought to send those women to us—we'll make real Texans out of 'em. They had to have some gumption to get up and leave in the first place."

Day by day, the officers relaxed around her, and if she hadn't had the appetite of a healthy horse, she'd have starved, for all the talking at the table.

She talked more than she asked questions, and the information flowed her way without her having to ask. By the time they reached Rockhouse Major, she had most of them eating out of her hand, men and women, and had invited most of them to come visit sometime. She thought a few of them actually would.

All but the young lieutenant junior grade who had remained coolly distant no matter what. Well, if he wanted to sulk, let him. She had many, many other fish to fry, and others had told their own tales of Barin Serrano and Esmay Suiza. So he was in love with a hero—if the stories were true, Suiza would have made a good Ranger—and perhaps worried about whether she'd stick it out.

Security concerns kept her from touring Rockhouse Major, though she could tell it was much bigger than any of the orbital stations in the Lone Star Confederation. A Fleet shuttle took her downside, and she got her first look at Castle Rock.

Boring, she thought, but did not of course say. The government buildings, mostly gray stone, looked substantial and dull. Insides matched the outsides; the Foreign Office was all dark paneling and dark tiles and thick dark green or blue carpeting in the offices she was led to. Everyone wore dark suits—men and women both—and had a dark, muffled, hurried way of speaking.

"Sera Briarly—so pleased—" That was the Minister of Foreign Affairs, the first person she'd seen in this dismal building who looked completely awake. He wore a different style of shirt, with a tiny ruffle at the collar, and he had several blue-and-silver rings in his ear. She knew what that would mean in San Antone, but not here. "You are so . . . so *decorative*, my dear."

This she had met before, twinkling of the eyes and all. "Mister Minister," she said, putting out her hand. "I'm Ranger Briarly, but you can call me Kate."

"But I thought your . . . er . . . Rangers . . . were sort of . . . er . . . policemen?"

"That's right," Kate said cheerfully; she saw some of the man's staff wincing, and grinned at them, too. The way they acted, you'd think this solid stone building would fall over if anyone spoke louder than a murmur.

"But surely you—you're not—I mean, you're more of a . . . er . . . honorary title . . ."

That was going too far. "Mister Minister, I am a Ranger, same as any other Ranger; I qualified on the same course, and I can and will demonstrate my skills any time you or anyone else questions them." She had no weapon, of course, but she could break this fellow's neck—or any other bone—without one.

"Oh . . . certainly, certainly. Now, uh . . . we are having a reception in your honor this afternoon, in the Palace. I hope you aren't too tired . . ."

"Not at all." She was never too tired to party.

The Palace was another pile of gray stone, with outcrops on one side of a curious buff color. Inside, the formal rooms had the same sort of dull, dark look as those in the Minister's offices.

Kate was on her best behavior, smiling like a car dealer. She had been through her share of fancy events, and knew that her role, as honored guest, was to smile and tell everyone how beautiful things were. She told the new Speaker what an honor it was to meet him, and thought what piggy eyes he had. She told his wife what a lovely dress she had on, even though she longed to tell the woman that she should never in this world wear that shade of green, it made her look sick. She told the Foreign Minister, whose name was Pedar Orregiemos, that she liked his ruffled shirt, though she contemplated mentioning that a ruffled shirt plus those pretty rings in the ears would have branded him an obvious mango in the Lone Star Confederation. Then she overheard part of a conversation and learned that the local slang for the same thing was "pet."

It was all intensely boring, since she didn't know enough yet to make sense of most that she heard. Her feet hurt, and her head was beginning to throb. Then Pedar bustled up to her leading a tall blonde woman whose face Kate recognized from her briefings.

"And this is Ranger Briarly," Pedar said. "Brun Meager Thornbuckle . . ."

Kate looked at the blonde woman who had been a prisoner so long, whose father was dead, whose predicament had led directly to her own presence here—and saw a familiar shadow in those blue eyes. Automatically, she softened her approach. "Hi there—I hope you can forgive my havin' that kind of a title."

"Well—" the woman's voice was slightly husky. "You don't look much like *their* Rangers."

"Hon, they aren't Rangers; they're trash. Lower'n a groundhog's burrow. A brick can call itself a diamond—doesn't make it one."

The woman grinned, her face suddenly relaxing. "And you're the genuine diamond?"

"Pure carbon crystal, that's me," Kate said. "Cubic, but not zirconium."

"Excuse me?"

"Sorry—slang's hard to translate. Listen, my feet hurt—can we go sit down somewhere?" If she could make friends with this woman—and she liked her already—maybe she could get the embargo lifted faster than anyone had thought. Even Kate at her most optimistic hadn't thought she'd get to meet the cause of it all, or that the woman would want to meet her. But that was obvious from the satisfaction on her face: she'd come here with a purpose, and Kate was part of it.

"The reception's nearly over, Sera—Ranger—" Pedar said. "The car will soon be here to take you back to your hotel."

"Why don't you come with me?" Kate asked Brun, as much to annoy Pedar as anything else. "We could have dinner—"

Brun smiled. "Thanks—I'd like that." Pedar scowled, and Kate grinned to herself. Had he thought he was going to move in on her himself? Fat chance.

They ate in Kate's suite, which was as dull as everything else she'd seen so far. What was the good of silk on the walls if it was gray? And muted green and blue upholstery . . . cold, unwelcoming, dull.

"You people don't like bright colors much, do you?" Kate asked, halfway through a main course of some nondescript meat with a lot of fancy vegetables heaped over it. They hadn't even had steak on the menu.

Brun looked around. "This isn't very bright, is it? I'm used to it, I guess. Castle Rock is pretty conservative."

"That's what you call it? That Foreign Office is like a funeral home; the only color in it is your Minister, and he's—"

"Awful," Brun said, wrinkling her nose. "Such a little climber—"

"Climber?"

"Oh, yes. Minor family, so he pushes and climbs, trying to make himself bigger. Well, he got a Ministry, though who knows what he did for Hobart to get it."

"Hobart's your Speaker?"

"Right. But Pedar wants more . . . you wouldn't believe, he's after my mother."

"Your mother?" Kate reminded herself that this was Lord Thornbuckle's widow.

"Yes. He had the nerve to tell me, when Mother'd left for Sirialis, that he could now offer so much to a lonely widow—I nearly threw him out the window."

Kate shook her head. "I wondered if maybe he was a . . . what is it, *pet?* . . . with those rings and that shirt."

"No—the rings are Rejuvenant rings. They're actually the medical codes: they can be implanted or worn, but a lot of people like to wear them."

"How many times has he been pickled?"

"I don't know. I didn't count. Several. Why do you call it pickled?"

"Preserved, you know." Kate held up one of the wrinkled green things she hoped was a pickled cucumber. "Lasts nearly forever."

"Mmm." Brun ate silently a few minutes, then asked, "What do you make of our Speaker?"

Kate looked at her, mind on full alert. "You're asking a visitor to criticize your government?"

Brun flushed a little. "He's a Conselline, and we're in the Barraclough Sept—"

"Is that families or religions?" Kate asked.

Brun made a face. "Maybe both. Let's just say that the Consellines and the Barracloughs have been rivals for a long time, in a genteel sort of way. I don't like Hobart, but I wondered if maybe an outsider would see him more clearly."

"He's nobody I'd buy a ranch from," Kate said. "Not without walkin' over every inch of it, and checkin' the title since God made it. He's got a mean mouth, and his wife's scared of him."

"You saw that?"

"Oh, yes. Just like I saw that you didn't like Pedar with the rings and ruffles holding your hand when he led you over. But you wanted to talk to me."

"You don't miss much, do you?"

"Rangers don't. Now why don't you get down to what you really wanted to talk about, so we can enjoy dessert later and not have to tippytoe?" Kate pushed her plate away and leaned back, fixing Brun with the look that had brought confessions out of the Harkness boys.

"I hate it when everyone is smarter than I am." Brun pushed her own plate back.

"They aren't, when you leave your brain on," Kate said. "It didn't take a lot of intelligence to recognize that you wanted to meet me as much as I was glad to meet you."

"You haven't met Esmay," Brun said. "She's smarter—"

"Spare me." Kate ran her hands through her hair, fluffing it out. "I heard plenty about Miss Genius on the trip over here. Everyone says she's so wonderful, and I'll bet she is. But—she isn't you."

"No, she's—"

Kate wasn't about to let her take off down that trail, whatever it was. "Lord, girl, you sound like you haven't got a friend in the world. Didn't you ever have a best friend?"

"Yes, but she got married."

"Oh, brother. You and me both. Sally and I were closer than twins, and then she went all goopy over Carl, and that was the end of it. Two babies. She says she's still my friend, but all she wants to do is tell me about those two rugrats . . . which one put jam in the processor, and how the other one is smarter than any ten college professors. My mother told me she'll come out of it in a few years, but in the meantime I have to pretend to care what some grubby little kid is doing."

"And you don't?"

"No. If there's supposed to be some instinctive maternal drive, I missed out at the feed trough. What about you?"

"Me, neither. I don't want to hurt them, but—"

"You didn't want to care for 'em either. Makes sense to me. Where are your boys?"

"A friend of my mother's took them, and found a home for them. But I worry—"

"Don't. I mean, don't worry more than you have to. And you're evading the subject. You didn't just accept a dinner invitation because you thought a stranger might be lonesome. You just about committed the impossibility of telepathic communication, wantin' me to figure a way we could talk."

"Or to get away from Pedar; he's been wanting Mother's ansible call number. All right, all right, I'll tell you." She scratched at a spot on the tablecloth. "I want to find out who killed my father, and what kind of hold Hobart Conselline has on my Uncle Harlis, who's after my father's estate."

"Now that's smart. That's a goal we can work on."

"We?"

"Of course, *we*. Hell's bells, sweetheart, I'm not going to leave you to hunt this hog alone. And I need you, anyway, to help me find my way through this maze of protocol y'all live with. Besides, if you come out convinced that I'm not a monster, maybe you'll help me get your government to let up on Lone Star Confederation funds. You did know our citizens can't access their money in your banks, didn't you?"

"No!" Brun looked startled. "When did that happen?"

"Right after the assassination. And all our citizens expelled, and the borders closed. Even your father realized we had nothing to do with that bunch of idiots who captured you. This embargo thing has put a real crimp in our economy; the Familias is our biggest external trading partner."

"I didn't know," Brun said. "It didn't come up in the Council meeting." She scowled. "A lot of things seem to be happening without coming up before the Council . . ."

Kate glanced around the room. She had made it as secure as possible, but she didn't trust any public space.

"Maybe we ought to talk about this another time," she said. "Tell you the truth, I'm feeling the journey—" She noticed that Brun's gaze slid around the room too, as if she were also aware of the surveillance possibilities.

"Of course," Brun said. "Listen—I know some of you Lone Star people ride—"

"Ride!" Kate grinned. "Hon, I started riding afore I could sit up, in fact afore I was born. Don't tell me they have horses in this city!"

"They do, but what I had in mind was our place out in the country. It's only a small stable, but we have some lovely views."

"That's right nice of you. I don't know how busy I'll be here—I'm supposed to spend my time convincing your government that we're harmless."

"I'll introduce you to people," Brun said. "And it won't all be boring afternoon receptions like today's."

"It wasn't that bad," Kate said. "Under the circumstances." She winked at Brun.

CHAPTER TWELVE

Within a week, Kate had moved to Appledale. Brun took her to dinner with Viktor Barraclough, and hosted a garden party where she met a group of less senior Barraclough relatives. The Lone Star woman seemed unfailingly cheerful, brisk, and friendly. She persisted in wearing screamingly bright colors, and spent a long time every morning arranging her hair into its vast pouf, but aside from that, she might have been an old friend. Brun found herself explaining, over breakfast or in the intervals of their social commitments, everything she knew about the family business and her uncle's machinations.

The next time Harlis visited, Brun saw the Ranger in action for the first time. She had been coming downstairs when the bell rang; Kate waved off the maid and went to the door herself. Brun paused to see what would happen, stepping back so that she couldn't be seen from the door.

"Hi, I'm Kate Briarly," she heard Kate say to Harlis, without moving aside for him.

"I want to see Brun," Harlis snapped.

"That may be, but I don't know who you are," Kate said. Brun was fairly sure that wasn't true—she'd shown Kate ID pictures.

"Harlis Thornbuckle—now go call Brun for me."

A grunt followed, then: "Now, Mister Thornbuckle—" in Kate's coolest voice.

"That's *Lord* Thornbuckle—"

"Back where I come from it is not considered polite at all for a gentleman to push his way past a lady—"

180

"You're no lady! And you hurt me!"

"Be that as it may, you pushed at me, and that just won't do. Now you be nice, and just wait there a minute, and I'll see if Brun has time to see you—"

"She'd better, or I'll—"

"Ah-ah-ah! No threats. Y'all know Brun's still under formal guard for any threat to her safety; you'd hate to be hauled off kickin' and hollerin' to spend the night in jail." The door thudded shut softly, and Brun came down another few steps to see Kate standing with her back to it, shaking with silent laughter.

"You shut the door on Uncle Harlis," Brun said, grinning.

"I truly hope your father was a better man than that, Brun, because that man is all hat and no cattle, where brains are concerned."

"A lot better," Brun said. "But I'd better talk to him." She reached for the door, and Kate stopped her.

"No—go into the drawing room and sit down in something comfortable." Brun complied, realizing halfway there what Kate was about. She heard the door open again, and Kate's voice—all sugar now—inviting him in. Harlis stormed into the drawing room.

"Where is your mother?" he demanded.

"I'm not sure," Brun said, carefully thinking of the possibilities— her mother might be in bed, or eating, or out riding—rather than the certainty that her mother was somewhere on Sirialis.

"Dammit—she has no right to take family property while the will's in question!"

"What property, Uncle Harlis?"

"Sirialis! I'll wager that's where she is!"

"It's a large universe, Mister Thornbuckle," Kate said, before Brun could answer. "Why do you think she's there? And what difference would it make if she was? She can't take off with a whole planet."

Harlis glared at her, his face reddening. Brun tried to keep from laughing; he looked ridiculous.

"She had better not remove anything from the property," he said finally. "I have an injunction."

Brun felt cold to the marrow, but Kate spoke up again.

"An injunction—not to dispose of property? In other words, not a dismissal of the original will?"

"Not that it's any of *your* business, no. She's enjoined from disposing of any of the property under dispute, until the case has been decided."

"Suppose you just let me see that, Mister Thornbuckle—" Kate reached out an imperious hand; to Brun's surprise, her uncle put a hardcopy into it. Kate looked it over, one pencilled eyebrow elevated.

"It may be legal here, but it sure wouldn't be legal back home," she said finally. "Y'all have a really strange legal system, what with no proper constitution. But I guess you'll have to send Lady Thornbuckle a message about it."

"You don't scare me," Harlis said, and lurched out of the chair, grabbing the hardcopy from Kate on his way to the door, which he slammed.

"I don't think much of your security," Kate said after a moment. "Lettin' that man up to the door without warnin' us."

"He's my uncle," Brun said.

"And you never have family murders here? No, never mind. It's time I went to work."

Kate looked and sounded a lot less Texan when she was detecting, Brun decided. She had acquired copies of all the relevant surveillance materials, on the grounds that she needed to prove that the Lone Star Confederation had not been involved in any way. Now her room was festooned with charts and lists and flatpic blowups.

"This here is a list of every person registered in the Monos Hotel; I don't think much of your investigators for only getting the list of those on the fifth floor and above. Sure, the shot came from that high, but people can go up as well as down. They know at least one shooter was here, in room 517—"

"They didn't tell us that."

"Well, they wouldn't. I wouldn't, if you were back home and I was investigatin' there . . . I'd have rules to follow, same as they do. Now, the couple in room 517 weren't there at the time. They were attending the annual convention of the plumbing contractors, and we have good surveillance pictures of them in their booth for two hours, and another two if you don't count the one trip each made to the john. Moreover, there's witness statements, and an order book with an automatic time stamp, to show they took orders."

"They could have let someone else use their room—"

"Yup. First thing I thought of. But as it happens, the room door was forced, not unlocked. A string of DJ-8, and someone took the trouble to overpulse the mag relays so that no alarm would sound when the lock blew. They wouldn't bother with all that if they had a key. The Stringhalts might still be involved, but I doubt it. Right now I'm lookin' at eight possibles." Kate pointed them out on her list. "Two hotel employees—the assistant day manager, and the housekeeping supervisor—"

"Why them?"

"Access to files on which rooms were occupied, and which rooms were occupied at what times. I don't want to drag you through the gory parts, Brun, but look at this here—" Kate put up another screen with the plan of the hotel and street overlaid in colors. "Your security personnel did a pretty good job, even though it wasn't good enough. They'd moved all known foreigners out of rooms overlooking the route from the court to the Palace; they'd put spotters on the roofs, and the usual sort of net below. They had roving patrols, including in this hotel. My people might have made some changes, but nothing good enough to keep your dad alive, if his route was known. And his route was posted—everyone knew it.

"I can tell you this much . . . I'm convinced it wasn't even an outside job. I think it was someone in the Familias, who tried to make it look like the NewTex Militia."

"Well, I want to know who."

"D'you have any ideas? Your population's a lot bigger than ours, and we usually start with *some* idea of who's trying to kill someone."

Brun ticked them off. "There's always my Uncle Harlis, though I don't think he would—he wanted my dad's property, and he's doing his best to get it away from Mother, as you saw. His son Kell, who's meaner than a—what's your term?"

"Rattlesnake. And?"

"One of the Consellines, though I can't see Hobart Conselline doing anything that stupid on his own."

"Hmm. If it was stupid—he did end up Speaker. Well, let's go after this another way. Leaving aside the murder, for the moment, what else have we dug up?" Kate shoved one mess of papers aside, and brought up a printout that looked to Brun like rows of figures.

"Are those numbers supposed to mean something?" Brun asked.

"Quite a bit," Kate said. "If you can follow the money, you can just about always find the criminal. I got these figures off the public newsfeeds, by the way, so I can't vouch for their accuracy. But here's some things to look at . . . see this? It's your uncle's shares in companies you told me were your family holdings."

Brun recognized most of the names. Her mother had mentioned them, but had given no details.

"Brun, I need to talk to you." Lady Cecelia, sounding very upset. Brun hadn't heard from her in days, and had been so caught up in Kate's research that she'd almost forgotten about her.

"Lady Cecelia, how—"

"Now," the voice said.

"I have that Lone Star woman visiting . . ."

"I know; I heard the rumors. But can I come out for a few days?"

"Of course."

A few hours later, Cecelia erupted into the house in what Brun recognized as a fine white fury. She didn't even glance at Kate.

"Did you know that Kevil Mahoney's been robbed while he was in hospital?"

"No! George didn't say—"

"George has been trying to cope without getting them in deeper trouble. Someone swiped their accounts, the day of the assassination, though George was too busy to find out about it for a couple of weeks. And he had no way to trace it by then."

"But how? I thought the safeguards—"

"Were safe. Yes. So did I. But George is trying to take care of Kevil, and finish law school—they can't even afford a cook, and they're going to have to sell the house! The thing is, Brun, George didn't have the access codes and Kevil couldn't remember them. I have them, but I don't know how to interpret what's in the files."

"You have Kevil's access codes?"

Cecelia reddened. "Yes. And he has—had—mine."

"So what they were saying about you and Kevil—"

"Was idle gossip. Brun, I'm ashamed of you! The man's hurt, his memory's damaged, he's been robbed, and all you can think about is that?"

"Sorry," Brun said. "It did come to mind."

Cecelia looked at the papers and films spread all over the library tables, and then at Kate. "What were you looking up?"

"Goin' through the public financial records, trying to find out how Harlis was gettin' so far with a ridiculous claim, and tryin' to cross the trail of the killer. Brun's mama's over at Sirialis, doin' the same thing."

Brun looked at Cecelia.

"Kate, we need to join forces here. With the codes Cecelia has, and your ability to interpret the files, this might go a lot faster."

"If you'll keep intruders out," Kate said. "Remember what I said about your inept security—"

"I worry more about Kevil," Brun said. "Why don't I go bring him out here?"

"Excellent idea," Kate said.

"But that's all wrong, that's—"

"Somebody'd do all that, wouldn't stop at a little shootin'."

By the time Brun got back with Kevil Mahoney, Kate and Cecelia were hard at work. Brun helped Kevil into the library, and moved a pile of printouts off a chair for him.

"Looks . . . like fun . . ." he said. "You . . . must be the . . . Texan."

"Ranger Briarly," Kate said. "Just call me Kate. Somebody sure knocked a hole in your stock tank . . . but I'll get 'em."

"Kate has a healthy disrespect for thieves," Cecelia said.

"I don't like people hurtin' people, and takin' advantage, 'specially of people that's just been shot." Kate gave Kevil one of her wide smiles. "I will bet my best show saddle that there's not but one or two villains in this drama, and I aim to catch every one of 'em."

"You'd be interested in what I found at Kevil's, then," Brun said. She held up a sack and shook it. "Interesting meds to give someone with a brain injury . . ."

"I thought so," Cecelia said. "Was that nurse there? He's been harder to shake with every visit."

"Oh, yes. Very eager to give Ser Mahoney a little something to make the trip out here easier. Then very eager to clear the shelves of the meds."

"I don't suppose you have *his* access codes," Kate said, looking up.

Brun grinned. "When I got back home, and wasn't going out

much, I spent my time building some of the gadgets Koutsoudas has . . . so yes, an illegal datasuck gave me every bit of data on him. Here." She put it down on the table. "Interfaces to the cube reader or the computer, whichever you want."

Three nights later, Brun was dozing on one of the long leather couches in the library, an arm shielding her eyes from the light, when the breakthrough came.

"Gotcha!" Kate muttered. She no longer looked like the sexy blonde in red fringe; back-to-back all-night work sessions had flattened the hair, and put circles under her eyes. Instead of the tight red suit, she wore loose knit pants and shirt. But nothing could dim the grin she turned on the others. "This is it, partners—we've got what we need."

"Ummm . . ." Brun heard only the first of that, but managed to open a bleary eye for the last phrase. "Got whom?"

"Your uncle Harlis, for starters. He's been acquiring stock in ways that are illegal even here—and I have to say, Brun, that your government needs to overhaul its legal system in a big way. There's holes you could drive a herd of longhorns through, with this bylaws arrangement. All you have to have is one generation of idiots, cowards, and a few bad guys, and it'd be all over for you."

Cecelia's rumpled red head rose from the other couch. "That's all very well, but what did he *do?*"

"He extorted stock by roughing up some of your weaker relatives . . . you remember tellin' me how surprised you were that your dad's aunt Trema left her stock to Harlis? That was no accident. I've got the paper trail where Harlis got some local toughs to come in and stomp on some of her favorite china, and tell her they'd break her bones just as easy. And he had the police around there in his pocket, told 'em she was a crazy old lady who dropped things and had hallucinations."

"And they believed it?"

"Money makes a strong argument. Anyway, that's not all I've got, and the evidence ought to stand up even in a crooked court. Which is what you've got, I gather—Harlis contributed quite a bit to the education of certain judges' children. If you've got any kind of an opposition journal, this'll be meat and gravy for 'em."

"I can . . . help write . . . the appeal . . ." Kevil Mahoney said. He was standing, leaning crookedly against the doorframe.

"You're up," Cecelia said. "You're supposed to be resting."

"I've done nothing . . . but rest for . . . weeks. Enough. My memory's still as spotty as a Dalmatian dog, but if you feed me the facts, I can write. I think." His speech had already improved, but now it smoothed even more the longer he talked.

"Good," Kate said, with another of those blinding grins. "Then I think it's time for this Texas gal to go have a rest and a shower. I must look like something the barn cat dragged in."

Kevil Mahoney's name on the bottom of the petition for summary judgement upholding the late Lord Thornbuckle's will might have had little effect, but the thick stack of supporting evidence did. One of the court clerks called Brun that very afternoon.

"The judge hasn't heard of any of this before—" The clerk's voice was sharp with disapproval.

"Of course not," Brun said. "Ser Mahoney was critically injured, as you know; some of the family files were under his personal lock." She said nothing about Kevil's other problems; a clerk wouldn't have reason to know anything about them.

"Is this all the data you have, or can we expect more?" That was sarcasm, but the clerk sounded uneasy.

"No, this isn't all; this is merely the preliminary filing. My mother, Lady Thornbuckle, is on Sirialis, getting additional data from the main family archives there."

"I see. Well . . . you'll hear from us."

Two hours later, Harlis came storming up the drive, only to be stopped by Brun's new security force. After they disarmed him, and checked with Brun, they escorted him to the door. Brun met him there, backed by Kate, Cecelia, and an upright Kevil, who was leaning on George. Kate had reappeared in full Texan persona, but this time she wore her Ranger badge.

"Before you say anything," Brun said, "let me make it clear: we have all the evidence we need that you engaged in criminal activity to get control of family companies, and we are gathering more."

Her uncle glared. "I don't believe it! You can't do this to me! I didn't do anything . . . it was all perfectly legal. Hobart will take care of you—" Then he blenched.

"How very interesting," Cecelia said. "Hobart . . . Could you possibly mean Hobart *Conselline* . . . now why would someone in our sept be working with a Conselline . . ."

"I didn't say Conselline," Harlis said. But he had changed color, and his voice shook. "But it's my *right*—"

"You had no right to terrify poor old Aunt Trema," Brun said. She was startled to realize that she sounded very much like her father, and wondered if the others noticed. "And yes, we will press charges."

"I'll—I'll see you in hell!" Harlis wheeled and strode down the front walk, shadowed by the guards.

"It's not over," Brun said, as much to herself as to the others. Harlis wasn't ready to give up, and she didn't know what he might do next.

"No, but it's a good beginning," Kate said. "C'mon, hon, wait until you hear Cecelia's next good idea."

"What?"

"She's found a place for all those inconvenient women and children that Lieutenant Serrano is stuck with. She's going to take them off to a pioneer planet she knows about, where they'll be happier and their skills are needed."

"That's nice for Barin and Esmay," Brun said. "But I wanted her to go tell my mother what we've accomplished. She needs to know that we have evidence against Harlis. We can't trust that to ordinary communications—"

"You're right, but now that Harlis is on the run there's no hurry, is there? Your mother's not going to do anything rash."

Excet-24

Ruth Ann took a long look out the windows. It looked cool and green, and she didn't know if this was spring, summer, or winter. Puddles reflected the sky, patches of blue and rolls of gray cloud like unspun wool.

No towering cities, no noisy crowds. When the hatch opened, the air that swept in was cool, moist. She could smell green growing things on that air. The red-haired woman led the way; Ruth Ann followed close behind. The ground felt good to her feet, even through shoes. It held still; it didn't vibrate.

The red-haired woman with the fancy name—Cecelia whatsis, a Rejuvenant—led the way into a little square building, where they each had to show their ID. Ruth Ann felt the oddness of it, that each person handled their own cards. And hers had her own name on it, Ruth Ann Pardue.

Once they were all finished with "Customs," whatever that was, and had new purple stamps on the cards, the red-haired woman led them down the street. This was scary. The little town looked like the backwater village where she'd grown up, where she'd have been whipped till her legs bled for walking around wearing shoes and looking at people . . . but here were men and women, dressed almost decently, except that they all wore shoes, and the women didn't keep their eyes down. People looked at her, but with hope, not distaste. She recognized the admiring glances at the children.

They turned into the open doorway of a two-story building, and the red-headed woman yelled, "Ronnie! Raffaele!" Immediately, a woman yelled back. "Lady Cecelia! Just a second—I'm coming!" Then a clatter on the stairs, and a slender young woman with dark hair and eyes came running down, and gave the red-headed woman a hug. Then she looked at Ruth Ann. "I've got dinner on—we're so glad you came; I hope you'll like it here. Ronnie's out trying to see why a machine won't work or something . . . he'll be back soon."

Ruth Ann recognized, in the woman who introduced herself as Raffaele, the same signs of abomination she had seen in Brun. This woman had never lowered her eyes in respect; she had never stood back keeping silence; she had never been denied access to anything she wanted to learn.

But—from the smells coming from the kitchen—she had also never learned to do more than push buttons when she wanted something to eat.

"And we hope—" Raffaele was still talking, when Ruth Ann interrupted.

"What were you trying to cook?"

"Just some . . . some meat . . ."

"Let me take a look." Ruth Ann sailed into the kitchen on a wave of unexpected delight. Sure enough, the place was a mess, sticky implements cluttering the counter—and not a big enough counter, either, that would have to change—and a stove leaking smoke from a badly-hung oven door.

"Secunda—Shelly Marie, you get that counter cleared. Tertia—Terry, get this floor clean. Benji—" Her oldest son stared at her, wide eyed. "Benji, we need that stove fixed."

"Pri—Mama?"

"Now, Benji." She could feel her confidence coming back. "Simplicity, honey, you take the littles out into the garden—you do have a garden, don't you?" she asked Raffaele.

"Y-yes, but it's not—it's kind of a mess."

"Not for long." Messes she understood, and what to do about them. "Simplicity, just you start the littles weeding, and make sure nothing bothers them."

The dark-haired young woman was fluttering now, like a gaudy butterfly in a net. "But—but Sera—Ruth Ann—I didn't mean for you to go to work—I was making dinner for you—"

"Never you mind—why don't you go set the table or something?"

"Come on, Raffa; I'll explain about Ruth Ann." The tall lanky redhead led the younger woman away.

In a kitchen again at last, a real kitchen. Too small by far for all of them, but bigger than any of the cubbyholes called kitchens in the spaceships and space stations. Shelley had found a kettle and had water heating on the stovetop; Benji had already taken off the oven door. Inside was a lump of meat, charring on one side.

Shelley handed Ruth Ann a couple of folded towels, and she pulled out the cooking pan, wrinkling her nose at the smell. Raw inside, burnt outside; the girl had built up the fire too much too fast, trying to compensate for the ill-hung door. Probably she'd never cooked without the electric, and the electric was off.

Ruth Ann looked around for a worktable—none. It would have to be the counter, where Shelley swept aside the clutter to make room for her, then began rummaging in drawers for the knife she knew Ruth Ann would want. "We're going to need a worktable," she told Benji. "They said they had plenty of wood, so that's something to start planning."

❀   ❀   ❀

"Cecelia, I feel terrible—but the twins kept me up last night—"

"You haven't found anyone to take them—?"

"No." Raffa blushed, a becoming color, Cecelia noted. "I—we—we sort of—decided to keep them ourselves. And one of the nursemaids ran off with a farmer, and the one with children wanted to start a school, and besides she has her own children to care for . . ."

"You?" This was an unexpected complication. "Er . . . do you think that's wise?"

"You mean, will Brun mind when she finds out?" Raffa had always been too sharp. "I don't think she will, but if she does, too bad. I quite understand her not wanting to keep them. It must have been horrible, and I wish it had never happened. But I like—no, I *love* the boys, and I even love it that they're part of her. The way things are, Ronnie and I may never get off this planet again—and that's all right, but I do miss some things—"

"My dear—you don't have to stay here—"

"Yes, we do, and don't argue. We wanted a life of our own, and we're getting it. It's not anything I imagined, but—whether you believe it or not—we're happy. But the thing is, children . . . it'll be years, because . . . well . . . I don't fancy having babies without modern medical support. This way, we're helping Brun. And ourselves."

Clearly it would do no good to argue. "What did you name them?" Cecelia asked.

"The redhead's Peter, for Ronnie's great-uncle, and the brown-haired one's Salomar, for my mother's brother."

Cecelia felt her eyes stinging unexpectedly. Family names—and names she must know were in Brun's family line as well. "So—when do I see the little demons?"

"They're napping. They've had some illness—I know it's only a childhood thing, and all children do this . . . out here, I mean."

"Well, we'd better set the table then. One thing I've found out about Ruth Ann, when she makes up her mind, things get done."

"Was she one of the—one of the ones who hurt Brun?"

"No. Her husband was, but she knew nothing about it until long afterwards. Where's your table linen?"

"Used it for crib sheets," Raffa said. "All we can do is dust this off."

This had been an elegant dining table when Raffa and Ronnie brought it downside, but it had spent several years as a work surface, and looked it. Cecelia forbore to comment on the state of the floor—with no glass in the windows, let alone any household machinery, how could Raffa keep dust off the floor?—and helped wipe down the scarred tabletop.

"I still have most of the china," Raffa said. She unlocked the big cupboard in the corner, and took down stacks of plates. "Even if they look a bit silly on this bare wood."

Incongruous was the right word, but Cecelia said nothing, laying out Pierce & Samuelson's famous "Coronation" pattern, with the gold wavy rim. Partway through, she noticed that the smell from the kitchen had changed from singed meat and something sour to a delicious blend of roast and something that almost smelled like bread.

Suddenly Ruth Ann appeared in the doorway. "Oh—you don't use tablecloths?"

"We don't have any left," Raffa said. "We had to use them for the beds—"

"Deary me! And us with all more than enough in the luggage. Cecelia, where are the boxes, do you know?"

"No, but I'll find out. Which box?"

"The one with the table and chair on the side."

Cecelia headed for the shuttle and, from the piles of boxes being unloaded, located the one with the table and chair on the side. One of the crew carried it back for her; she set it on the table and opened it carefully. Inside, it was stacked full of folded linens, brilliant with hand embroidery.

Cecelia lifted out the folded cloth. "However did you have time to weave this?"

"Oh, that's not our weave," Terry said. "We had no space for looms. But Prima—Ruth—says we mustn't be idle. She got that Miss Waltraude to get us some cloth, and we embroidered it. Do you think it's good enough?"

Cecelia shook out the folds. On plain white cloth, the women had embroidered a broad band of flowers, trees, birds, stars, and what she supposed were religious symbols. "It's . . . more than good enough." It was splendid, and the Coronation pattern looked even better than it had before.

By this time the kitchen smells had attracted the twins from upstairs. The twins were much more mobile than before, and although they might have been sick the day before, they were full of life now. They made straight for the table, and Raffaele tried to intercept them. Terry grabbed Salomar just as Raffa caught Peter.

"What big boys!" Terry cooed. "Yours, ma'am?"

"Yes," Raffa said. "But I'm not ma'am—just call me Raffa. If you could help keep them out of the dinner table—"

"I'll take them out in the garden, and help Simplicity keep an eye on them."

When she'd gone, Cecelia cocked an eye at Raffa. "They'll never believe you bore those children, you know. They'll realize they're adopted."

"Yes, but not from whom," Raffa said firmly.

Cecelia dared a peek into the kitchen. The floor could not gleam, being what it was, but it had the look of a floor that would gleam if only it were smooth enough. Ruth Ann worked a great lump of dough on the counter, which did gleam except where she worked. One of the women was washing dishes; another was chopping something that smelled good. Older children were moving in and out, bringing bits of fresh greenery from the garden, carrying out trash, and—as soon as Raffa agreed—mopping the dining room floor.

The lights came back on just before Ronnie came home.

"My God," Ronnie said as he came through the door. The women bowed their heads and waited. "I mean—er—it's a surprise."

Ruth Ann looked up. "We don't take the name of the Lord in vain," she said. "I thought you were going to pray."

"I know—I just . . . what did you do? Where did all this come from?"

"It's just food," Ruth Ann said.

"It's not just food," Ronnie said. "It's a feast."

"Then you can say thanks to God for it," Ruth Ann said. She looked hard at Ronnie, who reddened and stumbled through a child's grace Cecelia was sure he had not uttered in over a decade. The NewTex women added a hearty "Amen."

The roast fell into even slices, perfectly cooked. Puffy rolls as light as clouds. Potatoes, crisp outside and mealy inside. Fresh greens that weren't bitter or too sour.

"Truly a feast," Raffa said. "I can't imagine how you got that horrid old stove to work. Ever since the electric went bad, we've all been stuck. The bread machines don't work—"

"You don't need machines to make bread," Ruth Ann said.

"I do," Raffa said, with a smile that took the sting out of the contradiction. "I don't know how to make it otherwise. I tried to put the ingredients in a bowl that the directions say to put in a bread machine, but it came out the most horrible sour lump—"

"Did you knead it enough?"

"Knead? What's that? I mixed it up, isn't that what the machine does?"

Terry snorted, and Ruth Ann shot her a look. "I don't mean to make fun," she began.

"You can make all the fun you want, if you'll teach me how to cook the way you do," Raffaele said. "If I could make an edible loaf of bread, just once—"

"You don't make good bread by making it once," Ruth Ann said, feeling more secure every moment. Cecelia had been right. Clearly this household needed her, needed the knowledge she had. "You make good bread by making a lot of bread."

"Well, here I am," Raffa said. "Ready to learn."

Ruth Ann remembered Hazel, and had her doubts. This woman was much older than Hazel, and unless she had a natural knack, she might never be very good. Still . . . she could certainly learn not to stuff too much fuel in a leaky oven, and burn a roast on one side.

After dinner, the junior wives organized cleanup without even being told, and Ruth Ann discussed with Raffaele why they'd come, and what they wanted to do.

"We can use all the instruction you give us," Raffa said. "I told Lady Cecelia last time she was here . . . we have good, hard-working people, but none of us have ever done without electricity, or running water, or all the other things that we have on developed worlds. It's not just me—it's all of us, just about. We can't learn all this out of books or teaching cubes."

"Let's start with you, then. There's room in this house; we can experiment—" She was proud of using that new word, of being able to think of it. "When we know what you need, we'll know what the others need."

※　※　※

The next day, work began in earnest. Ruth Ann had a clear picture in her mind of what the kitchen needed to be, so she and the others could work there without falling all over each other. She couldn't believe it . . . she was directing men. "Make the counter this long," she'd said, and they were making it that long. They didn't seem to mind, and she was enjoying it. So were the others. All those months of being told how backward they were, all those months of being confused by the humming machines, feeling awkward and uncertain. And now—

"If you arrange your beds so the tall plants don't shade the low ones, you'll get more yield," Becky was telling Raffaele. "See, you've got them crossways . . . if the plant rows went the other direction—"

"Oh . . . well . . . look, Becky, why don't you tell me how it should be, and I'll draw a plot of it for next season's planting."

"Fine—"

Terry had gone upstairs to work on the bedrooms—although they'd slept last night, Ruth Ann had been very aware of the clutter and dust. The boys were at work in the front courtyard on simple furniture: rope-strung bunks to get them all up off the floor. When Ruth Ann looked out the tall dining room windows, she saw a crowd of men standing watching. It was backwards, men learning from boys, but it was right that the boys and men were together. She carefully ignored the two women wearing pants in the same group.

By dinnertime that day, the shuttle had brought the rest of their things down from the spaceship, including the pop-up cots Lady Cecelia had bought. The whole house smelled different, and Ronnie had the expression Ruth Ann liked to see on the head of a household. Of course, he wasn't her husband—she kept reminding herself of that—but she did enjoy watching a man eat with relish.

Cecelia left a few days later. Ruth Ann hardly noticed; she had her worktable in the expanded kitchen, and had also set up a summer stove outside, for preserving.

"What we need is a school," Raffa said, watching the crowd around the stove as Shelley demonstrated jelly testing. "A really big kitchen, where everybody could come to learn cooking, and maybe a sewing room where they could learn sewing."

"A weaving shed," Ruth Ann said. "That fabricator cloth is too harsh. And a really big bread oven."

Raffa looked around. "This would almost work, if Ronnie and I moved into one of the smaller houses."

"No," Ruth Ann said firmly. "Your husband's the governor; you need this house. We'll build one."

More quickly than even she had hoped, the school went up. The engineering cubes Cecelia had brought, and the bundles of reinforcing whiskers, made it possible to pour solid walls quickly. One of the other colonists, who had been a hobby potter on her home world, found a lens of good clay in the riverbank, and knew how to make tiles.

"Not really good ones yet," she admitted. "We don't have a kiln hot enough. But for starters, better than plain concrete or dirt." The school was the first building to have locally made tile floors.

A proper school for proper women, with a kitchen in which they could all learn the way she had learned—from watching and doing and being knocked on the knuckles with a wooden spoon when they needed it. A big outdoor oven to handle dozens of loaves of bread at once. A weaving shed—she regretted the loss of the captive women, who had been such talented weavers, but Tertia Crockett—she used Anna now—was almost as good. Sunrooms for embroidery. Gardens for the children.

The gardens for the children produced another benefit—everyone in the colony wanted their youngest children there, under Simplicity's gentle guidance, for part of the day. Raffaele brought her twins when she came to learn cooking, and the other women copied her. As Ruth Ann had suspected, Raffaele would never be more than a middling baker. Her hand was too heavy for pastry, and not firm enough for yeast dough, though both her pie crusts and bread were now at least edible. But the other women followed her lead, and the gardens were full of busy little children.

Raffaele's twins, though—the twins gave Ruth Ann a funny feeling in the chest. Salomar, in particular, was all too familiar . . . she had seen that quirk of mouth, that shape of eyebrow and set of eye, before. She looked again and again at Raffaele and Ronnie, trying to trace in their faces the source of those details of Salomar's. What kept nagging at her had to be impossible. She had to be imagining it. Didn't she?

She put her mind firmly back on the school. A few of the other former wives were being courted by men whose wives had died, but enough of the women wanted no part of remarriage that she was sure of enough teachers for years to come. Her daughters had suitors, too, the older ones.

And her sons, about whose acceptance she had been so worried, were every one of them more expert at tool use than these city folks, for all that those men had taken courses and been passed as expert enough. They may've been, Ruth Ann thought, with the fancy electric tools they'd trained on, but few of them knew anything of unpowered tools.

Everything from beds and tables to bowls poured out of the boys' workshop. Nobody minded that it was plain stuff, though one of the other colonists began making stains out of local plants to give the wood different tones of soft red and yellow. And nobody here minded if a few girls took up woodcrafting. All through the rest of that spring, and into this new world's long summer, Ruth Ann blessed the long series of chances that had brought them here.

"I never thought nineteen women and a bunch of children could make this much difference," Ronnie said one hot afternoon. He'd taken to coming by to fetch the twins, and he often stopped to chat, leaning on one of the planters. "You've galvanized the colony, is what you've done. The extra supplies helped, but it's you, Ruth Ann, you and the rest of them, who've waked us up and gotten us moving."

She glanced sideways at him, thinking that he hadn't learned it all yet, even so. Greatly daring, but also confident, she reached to the basket of hand tools. "While you're resting," she said, handing him a weeder and nodding to the planter he leaned on.

He grinned at her. "You never do stop working, do you?"

"You don't have to rush if you don't get behind," she pointed out. "Those stickery ones are the weeds."

"Yes, ma'am." He grinned at her. "I'll learn in the end."

"By the way," she said, finding it easier to bring this up when he was bending over the tangled growth, weeding. "Those twins of yours . . . I can't believe your Raffaele bore them—she's so tiny."

Ronnie's ears turned redder. "She didn't," he said shortly. "They're adopted."

"It doesn't matter to God," Ruth Ann said. "What it is, though—and I know I'm being presumptuous, but—that Salomar. He reminds me of someone."

The back of Ronnie's neck went three shades darker, not counting the sunburn. "Who?" he asked, more coolly than Ruth Ann expected.

"I'm thinking," Ruth Ann said, folding her needle away, because her hand had started shaking. "I'm thinking he minds me of my—of Mitch. And I'm thinking, if there's any reason he should mind me of Mitch, that you might be worrying that I'd notice. You've been awful good to us, and I don't want to worry you. So if—if it is that, what I'm thinking of, then—then I want you to know that I don't mind, and I'm glad to have the boy around. Both of them."

Ronnie said nothing; his shoulders bunched, and the dirt flew.

"I won't say any more," Ruth Ann said.

"It's . . . all right." He turned around; his eyes were bright with unshed tears. "I—we didn't know you were coming, or—but— Oh, I'm making a mess of this, Raffa will kill me. But if you've guessed, you've guessed—"

"I bore nine of that man's children; I know their stamp," Ruth Ann said. She said nothing of Peter's father, though she knew exactly who that red hair reminded her of.

"Brun wanted a good home for them; she was afraid they might be stolen away and used against her."

"You don't have to defend her to me," Ruth Ann said. She still could not understand a woman not clinging to her own flesh and blood, but she wasn't going to argue that now. If their mother had been a natural mother, she herself wouldn't have this chance. "You don't know what a blessing it is, to have those children here," she said. "I've worried and worried—that's the last bit of Mitch I'll ever see; I wanted to know the children were safe. Will Raffaele mind? I'm not going to interfere, I promise you."

"She'll skin me, but she'll hug you," Ronnie said. "Ruth Ann—you are a very, very unusual lady."

"I try to be a good woman," Ruth Ann said, but a bubble of delight rose and would not be denied. She stood up, and let her head fall back. "Praise God, you aren't angry with me for seeing what I saw, and you won't keep me from him. I never thought to be happy again, and here I am happier than I've ever been."

CHAPTER THIRTEEN

**Benignity of the
Compassionate Hand
Nuovo Venitza, Santa Luzia**

Confession, for a member of the Order of Swords who had been on a mission, must always be to a priest of the Order. Even so, there were things no one confessed, not if he wanted to live; the priests had the right—ecclesiastical and legal—to mete out punishment, including death.

Hostite Fieddi knelt in silence, awaiting the priest's arrival, and thought about what he had to confess, and what he had to conceal. As a young man, he had found distinguishing between debriefing and confession very difficult, but now it was second nature.

The soft chime rang; Hostite began the old, familiar ritual, "Forgive me . . ." Even as his voice continued the opening phrases, his mind was dividing, as sheep from goats, the truths he must repent from the other truths of which he must not repent, as long as he was a Swordmaster.

"It has been a long time," the priest said.

"I was on a mission," Hostite said. "To distant worlds."

"Beyond the Church's dominion?" asked the priest.

"Nothing is beyond the Church's dominion," Hostite said. "But this was far from any priest of the Order of Swords."

"Ah. Go on then."

Category by category, he laid his soul's burden out, the temptations acted upon and those merely dwelt upon in the mind, the orders followed which ought not to have been followed, the orders not followed which ought to have been followed. He was heartily sorry for them all, for the necessities which his duty placed upon his conscience, when he would—were he other than he was—have been happy to live in peace all his days, with no more to confess than a lustful glance at someone's daughter.

"And have you any other sins . . . lust perhaps?"

They always asked about lust, though by now they should know that his conditioning had destroyed that possibility. He answered as always, and as always received his penance in true submission of spirit. When he was too old to be of service, when the Master of the Order of Swords commanded, he would confess the last of his sins, and go to his death clean-hearted, no longer the Shadow of the dancers, but filled with light. So it had been promised him, and so he believed.

There was no other life but this possible, and no other future to which he belonged.

"Hostite—!" The Master's call brought him out of the reverie which a long penance produced.

"Milord." Hostite rose smoothly from his knees and turned.

"The Chairman would like an expansion of your report on the situation in the Familias."

"Milord."

"We will be granted an audience this afternoon. I will accompany you, as will Iagin Persius." Persius, another who had recently completed a mission in the Familias. Hostite was elder by three years, but he knew Persius as a competent agent. "You will report to the Order's Clothier for a fitting now."

"Yes, milord." Hostite bowed; the Master withdrew from the chapel, and Hostite made his way to the storerooms in which the Order kept all the costumes its members might need. He did not dwell upon the afternoon's meeting. Rumor had many things to say about audiences with the Chairman, but Hostite had been there before, and in any case feared nothing, including death.

The costume appropriate for a Swordmaster in this instance was simple enough. The bodysuit of black stretch-knit fit like skin and incidentally left no space for hidden weapons. The scarlet velvet cap matched scarlet velvet slippers, and denoted his Swordmaster rank. Looped through the shoulder epaulets were cords of gold, green, and red silk—the level of experience, the number of assassinations domestic and foreign, the whole story of his career, if one knew how to read it—and the Chairman certainly did. As he was checking the fit of the slippers, Iagin Persius came in. He nodded but did not speak. Hostite nodded in return. They could not discuss their missions until after the report to the Chairman, lest they be suspected of colluding in some error.

From then until lunch, Hostite reviewed his debriefing cube, correcting minor errors in transcription with a coded datawand; four seats down, Persius was doing the same thing. At lunch, they ate at different tables in the Order mess; Hostite restricted himself, as his penance required, to clear soup and water with a lump of "sinners' bread"—a hard, sour, unleavened lump that offered just enough nourishment to ensure that the penitent could perform any necessary duty.

Outside the Chairman's office, the Master of the Order of Swords handed his red cut-velvet cloak to the gray-uniformed guards, and unbuckled his sword belt. Hostite wondered why the Master was required to wear full dress, and then relinquish the cloak and swords, but he pushed the question aside. Tradition required it, that was all. He and Persius doffed their velvet caps for inspection, then put them back on.

The Chairman sat behind his great black marble desk, his face reflected dimly in its gleaming surface. On either side, his personal guards.

"Fieddi, you were sent to see the Barracloughs . . . what, then, did you find?"

Hostite bowed, then began his recital, carefully gazing at the bronze plaque on the wall behind the Chairman's head. "This was my third visit to the Barraclough senior branch, in the persona of a sabre-dance troupe's visiting instructor. On my fourth day there, the assassination of Lord Thornbuckle was reported. The dance troupe is comprised of locals, though they have been trained by Swordmasters; their reactions indicated that they were aware of friction between Lord Thornbuckle and his younger brother, and between Thornbuckle and certain Families: the Conselline-Morrelline Sept in particular."

"Did you have speech with family members?"

"I gave private lessons to six family members while there, including Stefan, the present head of Family; Mieran, his wife; Rudolf and James, his sons; Katarin, his daughter; and Viola, his niece. Stefan spoke only of the art of fence; he is proficient in three weapons, but wishes to become expert. He asked advice on hiring a permanent master; this request had been anticipated by the Master, and I recommended Alain Detours, as instructed. Mieran expressed the opinion that Lord Thornbuckle's death was a dreadful nuisance, but that he had brought it on himself, and she hoped that the New Texan assassins would be satisfied with one death."

"How does she fence?" asked the Chairman.

"With that same wit," Hostite answered. "She answers a threat well enough, but always directly. She cannot see beyond the next thrust. Most women of the Seated Families are more astute."

"And the others?"

"Rudolf prefers parpaun; he fences only because it is done in his set, and is content with mediocrity."

"His mother's son . . ." the Chairman said. "Go on."

"James competes in school tourneys; he seeks praise from me when I visit. He may mature into a good fencer someday."

"Weapon?"

"Epee, I think, though perhaps saber later."

"Continue."

"Katarin and Viola both fence well, for women."

"You have no more to say about them?"

"No . . . they fence because it is done, as they play at nets or ball or swim."

"Are they pretty, Fieddi?"

Hostite cast his mind back; he could see the faces clearly but he had no grasp of what the Chairman's standard of beauty was. "They are young, and rich," he said. "They are not Dancers."

The Chairman laughed. "Your standards are strict, I see. Well, then . . . Iagin Persius. You were sent to the Consellines. What did you find?"

"Hobart Conselline continues in his belief that he is ill-treated. Although he is now the acknowledged head of that family and sept, he still hungers after the approval he feels was given his brother. He is ambitious for himself and his friends; he wants to ensure his secure hold on power for the rest of his life."

"And he is a Rejuvenant?"

"Yes, a multiple. He despises the short-lived who cannot afford rejuvenation."

"And does he know where the Compassionate Hand stands on rejuvenation?"

"He does, sir, and he says it is the one weakness of the Compassionate Hand."

"His religion?"

"He has no belief in any higher power than wealth and influence, sir."

"Ah. Such men are ripe for superstition. Hostite, how about the Barracloughs?"

"Some in the family are believers, but not in our faith. Theirs is debased, decadent, a descendant of those rebellious faiths of Old Earth, which broke away from Holy Church so long ago."

"Hostite! I did not know you could be eloquent." That arch surprise was dangerous; Hostite tried to empty his mind of all but his duty. "So you are passionate about the Church?"

"Sir, I am a member of the Order of Swords; I have given my life to the Order since childhood."

"I know that, Hostite. But I sense in you some deeper emotion. Have you ever had a vision or revelation of Our Lord?"

"No, sir, none that could not be explained as a child's wishful fantasy. But the contact with those unbelievers in the Familias has made me realize what a treasure the True Faith is. They play with their faith as a child with jacks and balls, putting it away in a mental box when it is not convenient. That is not real faith."

"No, of course not. But let us go back to the matters at hand. How stand the Barracloughs on rejuvenation?"

"Most of them over forty have been rejuvenated, sir, but several of the seniors have refused. The Barraclough family has an elective power structure: Stefan, the current head of family, is not actually the eldest son of eldest sons. His older brother Viktor specialized in legal theory, and he refused rejuvenation. His objection was legal—the turmoil that would be caused by multiple rejuvenations. Viktor is now in his seventies. Viktor's daughter Viviane was rejuvenated with the new process at forty; she is now forty-five, but my sources say that she is determined not to repeat the process. Stefan is fifty-seven, and has received two rejuventions, giving him an apparent age of thirty. However, he disapproves of what he calls 'frivolous' rejuvenations."

"Ummm . . . for either of you: to what extent do the non-Family citizens of the Familias regard rejuvenation as a legal or social or religious matter?"

Hostite paused, thinking, but Iagin spoke up quickly. "Because Hobart Conselline is so willing to talk—more willing to talk than almost anything else—I have data on these points. He is very concerned about opposition to serial rejuvenation. This is fuelled both by concerns about the profit margin—Conselline Sept's family investments in rejuv pharmaceuticals are large, and until the Patchcock scandal, these had formed twenty percent or more of the profits—and by concern about the social constraints that might be put on serial rejuvenants. The Consellines introduced and strongly supported the repeal of the law against repeat rejuvenations. He feels that serial rejuvenation, conferring unlimited lifespan, is the earned right of those who have shown their fitness by accumulating the wealth to afford it."

"Ah—and would he apply this same philosophy to foreign affairs?"

"In all likelihood. He follows up advantages in fencing—and, from what I've been able to gather, in other domains as well—with great vigor and intensity. I have observed him at table, and with his family, and would say that nothing is ever enough for him. If he had no access to rejuvenation and advanced medical care, he would eat and drink himself into the grave."

"Truly, the discipline of the Faith saves more than souls," the Chairman said, flashing a smile at Hostite. The Chairman, as lean and fit at sixty as he had been thirty years earlier, had not been rejuvenated and would not be: the Church forbade it. But neither would he inflict damage on his own body for selfish purposes. "So . . . Hobart Conselline, who has become the new head of government, is a man of grudges and jealousies, scheming and ruthless, a man who will not feel safe until he controls everything. What, Hostite, will the Barracloughs do when he tries to control them?"

"Viktor will fight, with all the legal knowledge he has—but the Familias Regnant has no formal Constitution. Stefan will start by hoping for the best, but if Hobart angers him sufficiently he will lead his Family in opposition. He is not a man of great vision, however. He counters the obvious attack, but does not see the oblique one that covers."

"Why, I wonder, did they elect him head of the Family?"

Hostite cleared his throat. "Of the posssibilities, he seemed least likely to interfere with the others' lives. Lord Thornbuckle was already Speaker, in any case—he did not want the Family leadership as well. His younger brother Harlis was not well-liked. Viktor didn't want it. And although the Familias is far from strict on the gender issue, few of the great Families have women at the head. None of the Barraclough women were dissatisfied enough to make a run for it."

"They have no renegade women?"

"They do, but their tastes run to inconsequentials. Lady Cecelia de Marktos, for instance, breeds horses."

"She was on Xavier," the Chairman said, with a cold contempt that almost loosened Hostite's bowels. He should have known that; he had been listening to what her family said about her. "She might be just a horse breeder, but she has been inconveniently near several disturbances in our plans. She was on Sirialis when Lepescu was destroyed—"

"Lepescu was ours?" Iagin asked. The Chairman gave him a look Hostite would not like to have received.

"No. I would not use that filth. It is one thing to kill—even to maim, as a lesson—but quite another to treat an enemy as less than human. No, what I'm remembering is that Cecelia de Marktos was the one who took the Crown Prince back to his father, and meddled. I did not authorize our agent's attack on her—women are simply not reliable, and I suspect personal jealousy of some sort—but she showed up again interfering with the Patchcock situation. It passes chance that she—a woman never previously far from a horse— should be right at the scene of problems so many times."

"Heris Serrano," Hostite murmured. "The commander was there also."

"Yes. And the Serranos have always had the reputation for neutrality in the Familias. Here they are linked to a Barraclough repeatedly . . ."

"Heris Serrano had resigned her commission; she began her association with Lady Cecelia as a hireling." That was Iagin.

"Easy enough to contrive that, if one wanted to form a duetto." A bonded pair hunting together, that meant.

"Thank you both," the Chairman said then, nodding. "Master, if you will wait a moment . . ."

Hostite backed away from the Chairman's desk until he felt the ridge in the carpet that signalled the correct distance, then turned to go.

Somewhat to his surprise, he lived to cross the threshold. He and Iagin strolled back to the vesting room, and Hostite felt the languid ease that always followed a moment of mortal danger survived.

The Chairman eyed the Master of Swords. "Hostite is our oldest Swordmaster, is he not?"

"Yes, sir."

"Unusual for a Swordmaster to live this long. And yet—extraordinary, would you say?"

"In his way, yes."

"He has a clean stroke," the Chairman said. "He never misses his mark, and I hear from all sources that he is sober and submissive."

"That is true, Chairman."

"Yet—?"

"Yet I cannot warm to him, Chairman."

"No. And that is why I insist he has not reached his end; I must have one Swordmaster whom the Master of Swords does not like."

The Master bowed. They both knew this; they had said it before.

"I find the news of Hobart Conselline disturbing, however. Such a man might do anything, if he felt endangered. We thought the discovery that their rejuvenation drugs were so easily contaminated would slow down the rate of rejuvenation . . . why would someone risk insanity, senility, just for the chance of unending life?"

"They fear death?"

"It is not just that. They do it when they are years from death, just for pleasure. I told myself it was their decadent class structure, that rejuvenation would spread to the professionals and workers only rarely and later. But no. They do not want eternal life . . . they want eternal youth. That is not the same."

"No, Chairman."

"We did not realize that at first; we had no comprehension of their desires. And without the comprehension of desires, there can be no shaping of policy. It is beyond the understanding even of Holy Father, except as another example of their sinful nature. It poses a great problem for us. The strategy which we prepared for use in one situation may be useless in another . . ." His voice trailed away, and he turned to look out the window. Children. They were aging children, who did not want to earn anything or learn anything, who abhorred the discipline of faith. How could he influence aging children? He had a terrible vision of Hobart Conselline as he appeared in the data cubes, still spoiled and smug a hundred years hence, when he himself was dead and in his grave. His successor's sucessor might be dealing with that one, and all the rest—and how many there would be by that time.

It would not do. He must find a solution, and soon. His family, his vast extended family, the entire Benignity of the Compassionate Hand, relied on him to keep them safe and prosperous and orderly. It was his duty, and he was Chairman precisely because he had never yet failed in his duty.

"I may need to speak to Hostite Fieddi again," he said. "Please inform him to remain in the compound. I also need your analysis—is there anyone in the Seated Families who has refused serial rejuvenation, and if so . . . why? Are there any sane members of their Council?"

"Yes, Chairman."

When the Master of Swords had gone, the Chairman turned to look out the window again. Aging children . . . senile children, if a merciful God limited the number of rejuvenations with even the best drugs. A terrible prospect, that great empire full of aging senile children. And in the interim, all that energy and expertise . . . their great space navy with admirals wiser than his, replenished constantly by commanders wise as admirals. But not enlisted personnel. At least they had taken care of that. Still . . . a grave, a very grave situation.

He would have to pray for Hobart Conselline. He would have to pray a very special prayer for the soul of Hobart Conselline . . . and for the soul of Hostite Fieddi, it might be.

In the Boardroom, the Chairman faced his Board, and explained what he had learned.

"So the Familias will be in even more turmoil?"

"And even more acquisitive. I have the Master of Swords looking into the possibilities of a coup d'etat, but we will need a suitable successor."

"With due respect, Chairman, I thought our policy was to promote addiction—"

"You misunderstood." A breathless silence, while everyone waited for the Chairman's next comment. "We promote no vices; we do profit from them where faulty human nature allows them to flourish. But in this case, it was my most earnest hope that they would withdraw the drugs, either voluntarily, from shame, or involuntarily, as the evidence of the danger spread. We did not object to the damage done to their military, of course, but that damage was intended to shift their policy away from that process to a safer, more limited drug which merely prolonged life a decade or so."

"Our resources—"

"Are unequal to full-scale war with the Familias. Yes. We lost an entire assault group at Xavier, and another such loss would be unprofitable. We need a way to protect ourselves, without risking ourselves."

"To eliminate Hobart Conselline?"

"That's one possibility, certainly. Especially if the right man can be found to take his place, someone who understands that unlimited expansion brings explosive decompression in the end."

His Board looked back at him. He knew what they were thinking, and knew that they knew he knew. A hundred, a thousand stalks of wheat fall before the reapers, and no one knows one from another but the Almighty . . . but the fall of a great tree brings down those around it and shakes the very ground. Perhaps God cared as much for a blade of grass as for a tall cypress . . . but mere humans noticed one more than another. It was his decision, but on them would fall the consequences.

Sirialis

Miranda walked down the hill to the stables in a chill evening drizzle that did nothing to cool her anger at the dapper little man who had been so sure of his welcome.

She had tried to be fair. She had tried to be reasonable. She had told herself that Cecelia often got things wrong, in her hot-headed enthusiasms.

But Pedar Orregiemos seemed determined to push her past her limits. He had written, expressing his delight in his Ministry. He had written again, complaining of her daughter's "interference" in foreign affairs, when Brun had invited that Texas woman to be her guest at Appledale. He had called by ansible to insist that she be "fair" to Harlis. Because, he explained, she didn't really need all that property. He could provide for her, and advance her interests himself, as Minister of Foreign Affairs.

And today, he had arrived at Sirialis, smugly certain that he was telling her what she did not already know, when he brought the results of the judgement for Bunny's will and against Harlis. Smugly certain of his welcome. Smugly certain that he could comfort a widow he was sure needed comforting.

If only he had let her alone. She glanced around, and saw only the grooms busy with the last evening chores. They nodded to her, and she to them, as she ducked into the passage between the stable offices and the vet supply storage. No one would be surprised to see her here; she often came down for evening rounds, or after, with a few sugar cubes for Bunny's favorite mounts.

If only he had left her alone, she would have done nothing. If only he had not flaunted his power, his connections, and hinted so broadly at his involvement that she could not ignore it. What did he think? That she had always loved him secretly, that she had been hoping to slough off an unwanted husband and take a lover?

Was he really such a fool?

She opened the door of the old smithy where bits and stirrups and buckles waited for repair. Above the long counter with its burners and torch tips, bottles of chemicals in neat racks. A small forge filled the end of the room, which had been built around it when the new smithy—much larger, and suited to a stable with more horses—had been built in the other courtyard.

Brun's information had been more complete than Cecelia's. Pedar was linked to the Rejuvenants and to Hobart Conselline . . . but while Hobart had refused to intervene to protect Harlis's interests, he would not cooperate in his own downfall. Neither Brun nor that

Texan Ranger thought that the evidence they had would stand up, since the Speaker could dismiss and appoint Ministers and higher-court justices at will.

"I'm sure Pedar planned it," Brun had written. "I'm sure he hired the killers, though Cecelia says he could not have done it himself; he was in Zenebra. Kate thinks she's found a money trail—a tenuous one—but in a hostile court it probably would not hold. But whether he did it on his own, as a way of currying favor with Conselline, or on Hobart's orders, we can't determine. The reward seems to indicate a payment for services rendered—why else would anyone appoint Pedar to Foreign Affairs?—but we can't prove it. Unless you've uncovered something in the archives, we're at a standstill."

The archives had thoroughly implicated Harlis Thornbuckle and his son Kell in financial chicanery, extortion, and intra-Family power plays—but not in the death of his brother, and not in connection with the Rejuvenants. At least, not that she'd found yet.

She moved about the room, then picked up a broken snaffle and sat down at the workbench. Was she sure, in her own mind, that Pedar had had Bunny killed?

Yes.

Was she sure, in her own mind, that he could not be brought to justice?

As long as Hobart Conselline was Speaker, and Pedar his Minister of Foreign Affairs, yes. Who would believe the hysterical accusations of a grieving widow?

Was she really willing to put herself at such risk, when nothing she did could bring Bunny back to life?

She thought about that, turning the bit over and over. If he would go away and leave her alone . . . no. No. He would not; it was not in his nature. He would wheedle and whine, year after year; he would act against her one way and another, to force her into his bed, as he had maneuvered when she was a young girl in love with someone else. But then she had had Bunny. Now she was alone, with no protection but her own wits.

She could do nothing about Hobart Conselline, the ultimate enemy, the one who, she was sure, had inspired Pedar to his actions, whether or not he had ordered them. But here, in her own house, she could deal with his minion.

She turned on the smaller torch, and played it over the bit in the clamps. She had first learned to work metal as a hobby, when she'd wanted a particular style of guard on her foil. Over the years, she'd learned how to make metal stronger, or weaken it; how to make it look old, how to make it look like something else entirely.

You may not approve, my love, but you will understand.

She hoped her children would.

Finally, she turned the torch off, and left the bit to cool. She had not mended it properly, but she had made a start. That was sometimes the best a person could do.

Neil waited by the outer gate.

"Goodnight, Neil," she said. "I made rather a mess in the old forge—that broken Simms bit. You were quite right; the little torch isn't hot enough."

"It'll come right in the end," he said.

She hoped it would. She would do her best to see that it did.

CHAPTER FOURTEEN

Baskar Station, Baskar System

Beatta Sorin, head teacher for the Little Lambs class of Shepherd's Glen Primary School of Baskar Station, led the way to the transit station. Every few steps, a quick glance behind showed her the neat crocodile of uniformed students, assistant teachers, and volunteer parent helpers. The adults wore an official tabard with "Shepherd's Glen Primary School" on the left and a picture of a gamboling lamb on the right; in the pockets were their official IDs, their locator chips, their emergency kits. Around each adult neck, a lanyard and whistle to supplement the earpiece and mic, and the assistant teachers wore—as she did—an adult version of the school uniform, white shirt and plaid slacks. She herself held the braided end of the organizing ribbon, to which each child was supposed to cling. So far, they all had their little hands on it . . . but they were still almost in sight of the school. They could still be sent back, to spend a boring day in the nursery class.

At the station, she handed in the school's credit cube, and the file of seventeen children and ten adults moved into the loading area. This early in the trip, the children were still behaving well, though her experienced eye recognized that Poro Orinios already needed to use the toilet, and Mercy Lavenham had something sticky in her pocket and on the fingers of her left hand. She detailed her first assistant, Uri, to deal with Poro's needs, and herself excavated the pocket, wiping Mercy's fingers carefully as she did so. Mercy's mother, it seemed, could never resist sending her youngest out without a personal treat, even when it was strictly forbidden.

Uri came back just in time, and the crocodile edged its way on board the transgrav tram that would take them on a tour all around the station. Beatta, always organized and efficient, had made prior arrangements with station transit authorities, and this tram had enough slack in its schedule to allow extra time here. They had a reserved car, and each child was properly buckled into the seat, a motion-sickness patch in place, before the tram slid away from the station, one car entirely full of Little Lambs and their keepers.

Beatta had run this same field trip eleven times before. She knew from experience how to plan the route to provide the most in thrills, education, and efficiency. First, the slow part, through the densely populated shopping and residential district. Shrill voices piped up, pointing out home blocks, or the store where Mam bought bread. The tram stopped frequently. Then, as it swung away on the first of the transgrav segments, Beatta tapped her classroom bell for quiet.

"We're going to go oopsie," she said. "Everyone remember to breathe and hold on." Safety bars swung down in front of each seat; Beatta took this opportunity to insert her earplugs. No amount of discipline would keep the children from squealing when the tram made gravity transitions, and the ear-piercing quality of Little Lambs would have rendered her deaf years ago if she hadn't taken precautions.

The tram gathered speed, rumbling a bit, and the lights blinked three times, a final warning of transition. Then the tram plunged into the dark, and Beatta's body tried to insist it had just fallen off a cliff. Even through her earplugs, the children's shrieks of mingled fright and excitement were painfully loud.

Gravity returned gradually, but not to normal. Heavy Cargo, their first stop, maintained only 0.25 G. Beatta, who had watched closely, noticed that none of her class had thrown up; this year, at least, the mothers had believed her about the need for a light breakfast. The tram emerged from a dark tunnel into a vast lighted cavern. Beatta flicked out her earplugs with a practiced twitch, and picked up her microphone.

"Attention, children! This is the cargo servicing area for most incoming shipments. Bri, your father works in Heavy Cargo, doesn't he?"

Bri, halfway down the car on the right, nodded.

"Well, this is where he works."

"I been here before—he tooked me!"

"Yes, Bri, but the others haven't. Please pay attention. When we come to the station, you'll be able to see—out Bri's side—the exit hatches of the container transport system, and the tracks of the transport system itself. If we're very lucky, you'll get to see a line of cargo containers coming through." She knew they would be lucky; she had scheduled the field trip for a time when one of the big container haulers was in, and she had checked on the transport schedule with its cargo chief. She also knew the color-coding and shape-coding for different types of containers, and was prepared to explain which carried food products and which industrial raw materials, or manufactured merchandise.

Bix and Xia were bouncing in their seats, testing the light gravity and their restraints . . . Beatta looked at them with that immemorial teacher expression, and they settled back, a little sulkily. Twins were always a problem, in her opinion, and the current fashion for twins annoyed her. Thanks to Lord Thornbuckle's daughter Brun's well-publicized pair, hundreds of thousands of parents were opting for twins on their next pregnancy, and Beatta foresaw a great deal of work for teachers in a few years.

The tram slowed for the cargo handlers' station, and Beatta reminded the children to look out the righthand windows to see the cargo containers. Sure enough, huge colored bins butted through the heavy curtains at the hatches, and bumped and rumbled along their assigned tracks. Some shunted off this way, and others that, and Beatta answered the predictable questions without really thinking about it.

"The optical sensors read the coding on the labels, and there's a cross-check by color-coding from another set of sensors . . . this allows the AI system to route each individual bin where it should go."

"Where's my daddy?" asked Bri, now looking as if he were going to cry.

"Working somewhere," Beatta said. "I really don't know for sure." She should have known; she should have made sure that Bri's father was in sight for this brief stop.

"There he is!" Bri said excitedly, patting the window in his glee. Beatta wasn't at all sure the orange-suited figure running a scanner along the markings on a cargo bin was Bri's father, but if it made him happy—her breath caught as someone in a tan shipsuit stepped out and hit the orange-suited one over the head. The top of the bin lifted, and four . . . eight . . . twelve . . . more tan-suited men crawled out. The orange-suited one lay motionless on the floor.

"Somebody hit him," Bri said. His voice rose even higher. "He's hurt, my daddy's hurt!"

"I'm sure he's not, dear," Beatta said. Experience kept her voice even, and experience made her look quickly out the other side of the car for something to distract the children. "Look!" she said, before her brain had finished processing what she saw. "Look at all the funny little cars they run around on!"

It was too late to wish she hadn't done that, because all the children except Bri had turned obediently, and had clear view of the firefight as the passengers on the funny little cars attacked first the workers on the floor, and then drove right up to the tram.

The tram gave a convulsive jerk, as if the driver had started to pull away, then stopped again. Three of the children started to cry; the other adults stared at Beatta with white faces.

"Now, children," she said, in her best teacher's voice. "There's nothing to cry about, just a little bump. Stay seated, please. Mag, would you help Bri calm down, and Sivi, you see to Crowder—" The adults responded, and by the time the man with the obvious weapon opened the car door, the children were all sitting quietly, listening to Beatta tell the story of the Brown Bunny and the Spotted Snake.

"Oh, shit!" the man said. "There's *chillen* on this tram!" He had a strong accent made all too familiar by newscasts of the previous two years.

"We don't use that sort of language," Beatta said firmly. The muzzle opening on his weapon looked big enough to swallow the tram, but she made herself look at his face. "Please do not upset the children."

"Just stay there," the man said, backing out. Beatta had no intention of doing anything else.

On the transportation board, a light blinked twice and then went red.

"Babytrain's got a problem," Kyle said. The yearly field trip had its own code name which the school knew nothing about.

"What?" His supervisor, Della Part, was trying to listen in to a conversation between an R.S.S. security advisor and her own supervisor.

"Don't know yet." Kyle hit the com button. "Transgrav 4, what's your problem?" No answer. Any problem that could pull a transgrav tram driver off his seat might really call for help. If one of the kids had been hurt—

"What compartment's Babytrain in?" Sash called across the control room.

"Heavy Cargo Two."

"I've got a slight but significant rise in pCO_2, and ambient temp's up slightly."

"Kids got loose? Running around?"

"Where's our video?"

"Blank—it's been blinky the last few days."

"Ask station security."

Kyle called down to the stationmaster. "We've got a problem in Heavy Cargo Two. What've you got on scan?"

"Lemme see." Pause. "CO_2's up a bit, O_2 consumption's up, also ambient temp . . . visual . . . the transgrav's stopped at the station. Wasn't Babytrain on for today?"

"Yeah. They've popped a red and I can't raise 'em."

"Looks normal. Cargo containers coming in from *Freedawn 24.* Cargo handlers—wait—what color's Heavy Cargo this year?"

"Orange. Changed from tan—"

"Would anyone be in the old—oh, hell!"

"What?"

"None of the Heavy Cargo crews would be carrying firearms. We have an intrusion."

"In *there*? What about the kids?"

In the appalled silence that followed, Kyle could almost hear his heart thudding. He gulped, hit the supervisor's code, and said it. "We have a Level Five emergency. Hostile intruders in Heavy Cargo Two, and a trainload of kids—that preschool field trip."

The R.S.S. officer opened his mouth and shut it again, but looked sideways at the supervisor.

"Cut out the alarms to that sector, put us on Level Five Alert. Patch to the stationmaster and the emergency response teams. Call in the second shift as backup . . ."

Then to the R.S.S. advisor. "What else?"

"How many certified emergency personnel do you have?"

"Counting security, medical, damage control—maybe five hundred."

"Find out—you need to know exactly. And I recommend you inform the picket as well; we can presume this intrusion is of foreign origin."

"Stationmaster'll have to approve—"

"I do." Kyle was relieved to hear the stationmaster's voice over the com.

"Can they help?"

"Maybe. Then recall all R.S.S. personnel on station and collect them—check MSOs . . . specialties . . . for security, demolitions, and emergency medical."

Sergeant Cavallo had chosen to finish out his present tour in mess, in part because the supply and mess personnel had more chance of a few hours on stations during otherwise boring picket duty. The weekly green run always meant 24 hours on station, and sometimes more. He liked the bustle of the markets, he had—thanks to his grandmother's gardening passion—an unusually good eye for quality produce. He knew that Purcell's Family Grocers sometimes imported fresh fruits from planetside groves, and hoped to find either cherries or cherrunes. The exec's tenth anniversary was coming up, and he liked cherries. The other part was his sense of the ridiculous: few if any neuroenhanced troops ever had the chance to indulge a harmless interest.

He was only five minutes from the station when a red light came up on the board. The shuttle pilot grimaced, and switched channels. Cavallo saw the telltale hardening of the jaw, then the pilot's hands moving to change settings on the board.

"What?" Cavallo asked.

"They've got an intrusion," the pilot said. "They don't know what, but armed hostiles in Heavy Cargo—and they've taken hostages, a whole tramload of preschool kids."

Cavallo started to ask what a tramload of preschoolers had been doing in Heavy Cargo's 0.25 G, but that wasn't the most urgent question. "Who've they got with antiterrorist experience?"

"I don't know, but they've got a Major Reichart on station, and he's ordered all Fleet personnel to assemble—that's why we're shifting docking assignment. Sorry, Sarge, but it looks like we're all part of this for the duration."

Cavallo said nothing; he was aware of the irony of his present position. He had chosen mess duty as a welcome break from the tedium of being a Special Response Team leader on a picket ship where nothing happened . . . and here he was, back in his own territory, but without any of his equipment or a trained team.

"Better let the major know I'm coming in," he told the pilot, who shot him a quick glance.

"You, Sarge? But you're a cook—" The pilot had known Cavallo only in his present duty; perhaps he thought the extra bulk was a supply sergeant's overindulgence.

"Not entirely," Cavallo said. "My primary specialty is NEM Special Response."

The pilot looked nervous, the usual reaction to someone discovering that he was sitting next to one of the few Fleet personnel trained to kill in hand-to-hand combat. "You're a NEM?"

"Yup. So call me in."

"Yessir."

Although the supply shuttle had not been fitted out with a combat mission in mind, all Fleet shuttles carried some basic emergency equipment. There was no combat armor to fit Cavallo, but he grabbed the largest p-suit and the ready pack of demolitions supplies, intended to create a small hull breach if that should be necessary in an emergency. Three bricks of LUB explosive, five standard fusing options and the components for others, detonation signallers . . . he checked it all, and by the time the shuttle docked, he had repacked it and was ready to dive out the tube.

Sarknon Philios had been celebrating the successful auction of the *Mindy Cricket II*—the old tub had sold for more than he paid for her, though not more than he'd sunk into her—and the sale of his interest in the minerals they'd towed in. His crew, equally delighted with the outcome, and the promise of a new—or at least better-quality used—ship on the next run, had joined the celebration as well. While they hadn't quite drained the *Spacer's Delight* dry, they'd made its proprietor richer, and as the morning commuters rushed past, Sarknon was finally ready for bed. Bed was two stops away on the station tram; he gathered his crew and led them across to the tram stop.

There a man in Security green demanded their IDs—even though they wore their shipsuits with patches prominent on the left shoulder, and even though it should have been clear who and what they were.

"What is, man?" asked Sarknon. "We been at the *Delight*, you musta seen us crossin' oer. We's shipcrew, we bother nobody."

"Your IDs, Ser." Station Security normally went unarmed, but this one carried an acoustic weapon slung over his shoulder. Down the platform, Sarknon could see two more Security men, now looking this way. Annoyed though he was, Sarknon didn't intend to cause trouble.

"Foodlin' shame, I say, leapin' on folks as is just shipcrew come to spend money at station." He fumbled in his shipsuit's pocket and brought out his ID folder. " 'Tisn't enough to let yon pubkeeper charge twice too much for his wares, now you have to act as if you don't know who we are."

Even when Security did ask to see ID, which happened rarely, they always just glanced at it. Not this time. Sarknon stood, swaying slightly as the man glanced from his papers to his face, again and again, and finally had had enough.

"What, you think I am not Sarknon Philios? You never heard of *Mindy Cricket*, of our strike? Or am I too ugly for you?"

"Take it easy," the man said, closing the folder and handing it back. "We've trouble—we're looking for rockhoppers with demolitions experience. Looks like you're it."

"A contract?" Sarknon blinked; he knew he was not a good negotiator when he was drunk; that's how he'd ended up paying too much for the *Mindy Cricket II*. "Can't talk contract now, m'head's fuzzled. Next shift, maybe, when the drink's left me."

"Now," the man said. The other two had come nearer, without Sarknon noticing, and now he found himself facing drawn weapons.

"Trouble, Harv?" asked one of the others.

"No—found us a demo crew, but they're soused. Help me get'm to medical."

Sarknon had paid good money for his drunk, and was not inclined to see it dispersed for nothing. "I'm not goin' to med; they'll just waste my money . . . I earned that drunk; it's mine—"

He saw the hand coming towards his face, but was too uncoordinated to evade it. When he woke again, he was on a cot in the station medical clinic, and he woke entirely, in an instant, with the unnatural clarity of the detox patient. "Dammit," he said. "An' I bought a whole jug of that Surnean ale!"

"Never you mind," said the young woman who slid the needle out of his vein. "You save those kids and I will personally buy you two jugs."

"Well, then." Sarknon sat up, not regretting the headache he didn't have, thanks to detox, and looked around for his crew. "If it's that kind of job . . ."

"It's that kind of job." He didn't recognize the man's uniform, but the tone of voice was unmistakable. Sarknon followed him along the corridor to a compartment full of people in EMS vests, and five minutes later he was explaining all he knew about demolition.

Instead of the organized, disciplined planning groups Cavallo was used to, a roomful of civilians were muttering, arguing, and even (in the case of one fat man in the corner) shouting. Cavallo spotted the major at once, and made his way over. "Sgt. Cavallo, sir; NEM Special Response Team."

"That's good news—how many of you?"

"Just me, sir. I was inbound on a supply run—I've been acting as supply sergeant for the picket boat."

"A NEM supply sergeant? No, don't tell me—later, when we have time. We have a real bad situation here." Quickly, the major laid it out—the intruders, the preschool field trip, the information he had so far on station resources. "They don't have anything equivalent to your training," he said. "Good basic emergency services, but nothing to handle large-scale terrorist actions. They'd been warned, but they didn't really know where to get the information they needed. That's why I was here. And those kids are really our problem now. The med staff has told me that they're more susceptible to sudden pressure changes than adults—they get shock lung more easily, and it's harder to treat. Same is true of chemical riot-control agents, or the acoustics.

We're going to end up hurting the kids no matter what we do, so we have to be very, very fast."

"Negotiation, sir?"

The major shrugged, with an expression Cavallo couldn't quite read. "They've got the usual complement of mental health professionals, and two of them have some experience in small-scale stuff. Man holding his ex-wife hostage and threatening the kids, that sort of thing. But nobody with this kind of experience, and I'm not sure they realize how different it is. I suspect that our bad guys wouldn't talk to a Fleet officer . . . and as you can tell I have an accent that won't quit."

"These those New Texas guys?" Cavallo asked.

"Don't know yet. So far we have no contact. The stationmaster cut all com right away; I've been unable to convince him to reopen at least one line. He's afraid they'll override the security precautions to the main computers, I think."

"We can fix that, sir," Cavallo said. "I brought the demolitions and communications kits from the shuttle."

"Good man. Let me get you to the stationmaster."

"If they want to kill the children, to make a statement or something, the kids are as good as dead—if they aren't already. We can't prevent it. What we can do is talk to them. Our sources tell us they have very strong family connections, especially to their children. We can hope they are less likely to kill children, more likely to negotiate where children are concerned."

"But they think our children are heathens—"

"Yes, but they didn't hurt the children from the *Elias Madero*. They wanted to save them. They aren't likely to have planned this for the one day a year the preschool has its field trip."

Cavallo's Irenian accent had amused his Fleet associates at first. After twentysome years he could turn it on and off like a tap—his implants helped—but at the moment it might be useful.

"Anybody there?" he asked, drawling it out.

Silence followed. Then, in a thick accent made familiar by the newsvids of Brun's captors, "Who you?"

"I'm lookin' for that teacher—Sera Sorin. We're worried about those children."

Silence again, but not so long. "What children?"

"Those children in the tram. It's time they was home, don't you think?"

"What you mean havin' chillen in a transgrav tram? Don't you care about 'em?"

"Of course we care; that's why I'm callin'. Can I talk to the teacher, please?"

"Puttin' chillen in the care of a woman like that. Boys too. Downright disgustin'. No, you cain't talk to her; she's doin' what she's tol', keeping them chillen quiet."

"But they're all right? I mean, you know kids, they need the bathroom, and they get hungry and thirsty—you got enough snacks for 'em?"

Another voice, this one older and angrier. "No, we don't got food for kids. Your kid down here, mister?"

Cavallo had considered trying to impersonate a parent, but kids that age couldn't be fooled easily. If he claimed to be some boy's father and the boy said "That's not my dad!" they'd be worse off than they were now.

"No," he said. "Not mine—but it might's well be. Children are everyone's responsibility, where I come from."

"And where's that?"

"Irene." They might or might not know anything about Irene, but if they did, that would fit—Irenians had a Familias-wide reputation for idealistic child care.

"Oh." A pause; Cavallo wished he'd been able to get a vid tap in; facial expressions would tell him a lot. But the vid pickup was still snaking its way through the utility lines, a good seventy meters from Heavy Cargo Two. "Well . . . it's too bad about the kids, but—"

"I can get you supplies for them," Cavallo interrupted. "Food and water. For you, too," he added as if this were a new thought rather than an orchestrated tactic.

"Listen, you, whoever you are—"

"Fred," Cavallo said, choosing an uncle's name at random. "Fred Vallo."

"Well, Fred, thing is, these chillen are dead if we want 'em to be."

"I understand that," Cavallo said.

"So you better give us what we want—"

"If the children die," Cavallo said, letting the steel into his voice, "none of you will get off this station alive."

"If you want 'em alive, you do what we tell you," the voice said. Behind it, another younger voice protested, "But we can't kill *children*."

Cavallo smiled to himself. Trouble in the enemy camp, and talking to a negotiator . . . they had already lost. If only small children hadn't been involved.

"I need to speak to someone who can assure me that the children are unharmed," he said. "If not the teacher, one of the other adults on the tram."

"Wait," said the older voice.

Cavallo muted his mike and turned to the major. "You heard, sir? There's at least one who's going to cause their leader trouble if he hurts the children, and so far they're willing to talk."

"Yeah . . . but how long will it last? Wonder if he'll really let you talk to one of the adults?"

"I—" The light blinked on his set, and he turned the mike back on.

"Go on—" said the voice he was used to. "Tell them the chillen aren't hurt."

"But they want to use the toilet—" came another voice, a man's.

"Tell 'em."

"Uh . . . this is Parkop Kindisson . . . with the Little Lambs field trip? . . . you know about that?"

"Yes, Ser Kindisson," Cavallo said. "Are the children unharmed?"

"Well, they aren't *hurt*, but they're scared, especially Bri because he saw his father get hit, and they need to use the toilets, and they won't let us, and they're getting hungry, and they won't let us get them anything at the tram station snack bar, and—"

"Enough!" The angry voice was back; Cavallo could just hear the distant protest of the other man. "You know this Kindisson fellow?"

"Not personally, no," Cavallo said. He had skimmed a file on all the adults with the field trip, and knew that Kindisson was a single parent, taking a day off his job as a coater for the housing authority to help chaperone the children.

"Seems kinda excitable, not like a normal man—"

"He's worried about the children. So am I. How about if we

arrange some snacks for 'em? Or carry-pots, so they can use the toilet right on the tram?"

"The tram has toilets?"

"No—that's why I said carry-pots. Families have them here, to take along with a small child, if there's not a toilet around."

"There's toilets in the tram station, though, aren't there?"

"Sure, but if you don't want to let them off the train. Little children—I'm sure you know about them, and how they run around getting into things—it's smart of you to keep them safe, in one place."

Flattery couldn't hurt, he was sure.

"We want to talk to our women," the voice said.

Cavallo felt his eyebrows going up. "Your women?" he asked cautiously.

"Don't pretend you don't know. Those Rangers' wives you stole, and their chillen—we want to tell 'em to get theirselves home."

"Just a second—" Cavallo blanked the mike and called to the stationmaster. "Are there any of those NewTex women at this station?"

"No, they left awhile back. Why?"

"Because these fellows came to take them home, that's why. Do you know where they went?"

"No. I can look on the passenger lists, but that'll only tell me which ship."

"Which we don't want to tell these lads," Cavallo said. He flipped the mike back on and spoke into it. "I just asked the stationmaster, and he says they aren't here. They were, but they left awhile back."

"Yer lying! You git us our chillen, or we'll take yours."

"I can get you a list—" Cavallo waved, and the stationmaster came back over. "We need a list or something, so these men know those women aren't here—"

"There's a directory accessible from the public dataports in Heavy Cargo, but we cut the lines—"

"Well, put in a shielded line."

"We're gonna blow up this whole place if you don't give us our women and chillen!" That was another voice, one that sounded entirely too excited. He heard a confused scuffle in the background, and a yelp. He hoped it was from an adult.

"Now just a minute," Cavallo said. "We don't none of us want children hurt. Let's see what we can figure out here—" Someone held a display screen in front of him, with the message DATA DISPLAY AT TRAM STATION ACTIVE FOR OUR USE. "It's true your children aren't here anymore—and it's true I don't know where they are. You—what'd you say your name was?"

"Dan," said the older voice. "You kin call me Dan."

"Dan, I reckon you think children should be with their parents—"

"Yeah, that's right. So if our chillen ain't here, we wanta know where they've gone."

The vid scan was in, though distorted by the wide-angle lens. Scan specialists ran tests, converting the image to a corrected 3-D version. Cavallo made himself ignore that, until they were done, and someone moved a screen close to him so he could see it.

Now when Dan spoke, he could see the computer's best guess at the face—middle-aged, as he'd guessed, the face of someone who had taken difficult responsibility before.

"How'd you plan to get 'em away?"

"Steal a ship. We done it before."

"Good plan," Cavallo said, mentally crossing his fingers. He scribbled *Find a small, cheap, simple ship* on the pad and handed it to the major.

"We kin just take these chillen instead, if ours is really gone."

"But it's not the same," Cavallo said. "And these children should be with their families."

"You offerin' to let us go?"

"Would you?"

"Might."

Cavallo watched the man put down the mike and turn away, talking to the others. He boosted the audio pickup.

"*You* said they was here!" he heard one man say; he couldn't pick out features from the fish-eye view.

"That's the best word we had."

"I tell you, I'm gettin' sick of this. We come all the way from home, workin' like dogs on that damn ship, because you didn't want to spend the money for tickets, which would've been worth it if we'd killed the old buzzard, but we didn't, on account of somebody else beat us to the draw."

"It wasn't supposed to take that long—"

"And who picked out that ship? Then you say let's go get those kids back—and they're not even our kids—and we have to work our passage again, comin' here, and when we get here they ain't. I don't know's I believe they ever have been."

"Ever'body in that bar said they was!"

"Ever'body in that bar was drunk, Dan. They ain't here, and they ain't been here, and what in Sam Hill are we gonna do now?"

"I'll think of sumpin'—just give me a minute, will you?"

"We could take these kids—"

"Hell, Arnett, I don't want these kids. These ain't *our* kids, or Ranger kids. And what'd we take 'em in, anyway?"

"Well, what d'you want to do, give up and let them kill us like they did them Rangers?"

"We ain't done nothin' yet they'd kill us for."

"I ain't surrenderin' nothin'." That was Arnett, Cavallo could tell by his voice.

"Well, I'm not killin' any chillen." That was the one who had protested in the beginning. "Why don't we trade 'em for a ship out of here?"

"A whole ship? You think godless heathens would give us a whole ship for just a bunch of chillen? They don't care about chillen."

"How's it going?" the major asked. Cavallo sat back, still watching the vid.

"They're fighting over whose fault it is. If I understand them right, this bunch wanted to assassinate Lord Thornbuckle, and when they found out someone else had, they decided to hunt up the women and children and capture them. I don't think they're NewTex Rangers; I think they're a bunch of idealistic fools that went off by themselves." He tapped the mike, and heads turned in the vid. Dan came over, almost reluctantly, to pick it up.

"Dan! Dan . . . listen. Are the children still all right?"

"Yeah, yeah, they're fine for now."

"Dan, the stationmaster tells me the women and children left eleven days ago on a passenger ship, the *Dolphin Rider*."

On the vid, two of the other men threw up their hands, and one spat on the deck.

"Now I can't change that, Dan, but here's what I could do."

"What?"

"I don't know if you'd—but if you'd—I mean, if we could get you a ship, Dan . . . and then the children wouldn't get hurt—"

"You mean trade the chillens for a ship? You'd do that?"

"Yeah, of course. It's children we're talkin' about."

"A whole ship—a ship that actually works?"

"Of course." Cavallo glanced up as someone leaned over and handed him a pad with *Mindy Cricket II* scrawled on it.

"I dunno. We'd need supplies."

Cavallo dared a grin at the major, as he flicked the mike off. "They're gonna take it," he said. "Now if they don't cross us—and there's some of them I'm pretty sure won't—where's that ship docked?"

It had taken another twelve hours of ticklish negotiation before the children were reunited with frantic parents, the NewTex terrorists were finally aboard the *Mindy Cricket II*, and the little ship lurched away from the station with her usual grace.

"You didn't really have to do anything," Sarknon said. "She's not goin' to get 'em anyplace real fast."

"Especially not now," Cavallo said. He had applied the bricks of LUB to best advantage. *Mindy Cricket II* wouldn't make it to jump distance in one piece. Two hours out, a safe distance from the station, and she'd blow. "We don't need that kind of scum wandering around causing trouble." He stretched, and grinned at the major. "Guess I'll go finish the shopping now, if it's all the same to you."

CHAPTER FIFTEEN

R.S.S. *Gyrfalcon*

"Jig Serrano to the captain's office . . ." Barin tapped his code into the wall-hung unit to signal his receipt of the message, and turned to the sergeant of the compartment.

"I'll finish this inspection later," he said. "And I expect you'll have done something about those lockers." The lockers had been unlocked, and Barin had already found three major discrepancies.

"Yes, sir!"

All the way upship, he wondered what he'd done. He couldn't think of anything, and Major Conway had actually complimented him the day before.

Captain Escobar's clerk gave him no warning glances, just smiled and waved him through. Barin came to attention and waited.

"Ah . . . I thought you'd like to know you have pay." Escobar handed a data cube across to him.

"Sir?"

"Apparently your . . . dependents . . . have found honest work somewhere. They're off Fleet's hands."

"Where are they?"

"Some colony world. Apparently Professor Meyerson and that Lone Star Confederation diplomat found them a place, and someone. paid their colony shares. Also paid off at least part of what Fleet spent on them, and HQ has forgiven the rest. So you have pay again. I suppose this means you'll be marrying?"

Barin felt himself go hot. "I—hope so, sir."

"From one fire into another. Better give your family time to get used to it. Have your parents ever met Lieutenant Suiza?"

"No, sir. But now that I'm getting pay again, if I could get a little leave—"

"You'd get married."

"No, sir, not right away. I'd get her together with my parents, though."

Escobar considered. "You have plenty of leave stacked up. Tell you what—figure out a time that will work for your parents and her, and I'll do my best."

"Thank you, sir."

R.S.S. *Navarino*

"You have mail, Lieutenant." Esmay wondered what it was this time. Her last mail had been a stiff notice from Personnel advising her that she should have informed them before accepting appointment as a Landbride, and that any request for a variance would have to work its way through the chain of command in her sector, then at Headquarters.

A cube from Barin. That had to be better than something from Personnel.

Her heart soared as she read it. Out from under the responsibility for all those women and children. Getting paid again. He'd talked to his parents; they wanted to meet her. He could get leave—what about her? He was sure he could enlist the senior Serranos to aid in bending the restrictions about Landbrides. . . .

She, too, had accumulated leave time. Surely it would be possible to meet for a few days, even a week. Somewhere private—she didn't mind meeting his parents, but she wanted at least some hours alone with Barin.

Copper Mountain

Although Fleet's Copper Mountain Training Base, named for the red-rock formation of the original landfall, had become the generic term for the entire planet, Fleet had other bases where neither mountains nor red dust were in view. Most NCO training courses, though reached by shuttle from Copper Mountain, were actually dispersed to other facilities on the same continent: Drylands, in the northern plains, Camp Engleton in the coastal swamp, Big Trees far to the west. Permanently assigned school staff had their own recreational areas which students never saw: the long sand beaches far east of Copper Mountain where the carnivorous hunters of the deep had been carefully fenced away. Eight Peaks Mountain District, which offered far more than eight peaks, though the rest of them weren't quite eight thousand meters.

Among these lesser-known bases were the Stack Islands facilities. Rising almost vertically from the cold waters of what someone had unimaginatively called Big Ocean, the old volcanic plugs of the Stacks had been engineered into even more forbidding shapes than time, wind, and water had created. The Stack Islands group had three Fleet bases altogether, two for research (biomedical and weapons) and one to supervise the confinement of its most dangerous criminals.

That proximity was no accident; although the Grand Council knew nothing about it, research into neurobiology used prisoner subjects, some of whom emerged from the program with new identities. But the proximity was on a planetary, not local, scale: though less than an hour by aircar to either of the other Stack Islands bases, the prison was distant enough to keep its prisoners secure. The research bases were only a few kilometers apart, on neighboring stacks, but the prison base lay at the east end of the group, out of sight from either and far beyond swimming distance, even if water temperature and sealife had not intervened.

The security personnel at Three Stack, as the prison base was colloquially called, made no attempt to prevent prisoners from committing suicide; it was the general feeling that suicides saved everyone a lot of trouble. So little attention was paid to preventing escape attempts that were certain to be fatal. Prisoners could jump off the cliffs into the cold water if they felt like it; if they survived the fall, and the numbing cold, they were easy prey for the native sealife, which in these latitudes was toothy and voracious. Although guards patrolled the corridors and exercise courts, and the base's aircars were carefully guarded, no regular watch was kept on the cliffs.

Commanding such a base did nothing to advance an officer's career, and most loathed brig duty. For a few, however, Stack Islands Base Three offered exactly the milieu in which they flourished.

Corporal Gelan Meharry, second-shift guard at Three Stack, wondered what it was about his new commander that bothered him. Prison COs were invariably bent in some way—Tolin had been soft, slovenly, entirely too fond of his own comfort, and easily handled by the senior NCOs—but this Bacarion person was clearly not bent that way. What had she done, to get sent here? A tour at a high-security brig was no disgrace to the enlisted security force, rather the contrary, if nothing went wrong, but . . . he had an uneasy feeling about her.

After the change-of-command ceremony, his immediate superior, Sergeant Copans, dismissed the second shift to eat and prepare for their shift. Gelan racked his ceremonial staff, and changed from his dress to his duty uniform. As always, he made sure that his gear was perfectly aligned in his locker before heading for the mess hall. Then he checked his bay in the barracks. Sure as vacuum, that new commander would pull an inspection, and he intended *his* unit to pass.

On the way to mess, he stopped by the base data center, and called up the Officers' List. At least he could find out about his new commander's official biography. Her image on the screen showed her with the insignia of a lieutenant commander—she hadn't had her image updated since her last promotion. He scanned the notes below. Top quartile in the Academy, so she wasn't stupid. Command Track with her junior duty on a series of front-line craft. As a major she'd done the usual rotation in staff, this time on a flagship, the *Dominion*. There she'd seen combat, though from the staff viewpoint.

What was it about *Dominion*? He should know that name . . . he scrolled to the flag's name. Lespescu. Bacarion had been on *Lepescu's* staff? In the engagement where Heris Serrano refused to follow Lespescu's orders, and by so doing won the battle but lost her command? Gelan clamped his jaw, hoping his expression had not changed. Thanks to Lepescu, Serrano's crew—including his oldest living sib Methlin—had been tried and imprisoned. Bacarion deserved a prison appointment, he thought sourly. She deserved to be a prisoner, really. He had not seen Methlin since her release, but he'd heard all about it. Lepescu was safely dead, but this Bacarion . . .

He switched off the unit, smiled a careful smile at the clerk in charge, and went to lunch with a gnawing pain in his belly. Partway through the meal, he stopped eating abruptly, with his fork halfway to his mouth. What if this wasn't punishment for Bacarion? What if she had wanted this assignment? What if she, like Lepescu, wanted to play games with prisoners?

He was going to have to be very careful indeed. When she noticed that she had a Meharry aboard, she was going to assume he knew . . . and knew she knew.

Gelan Meharry had not even been born when his oldest brother Gareth died in the wreck of *Forge*. He had been in school when his sister Methlin was sent to this very prison. His recruit training had been spent under the shadow of her disgrace, though his drill instructor had told him—after he passed—that he personally thought she'd been framed. He had acquired, from his family and their history, a keener awareness of social nuances than most young corporals, and the certainty that anyone keeping things from him had a bad reason for doing so.

When nothing happened during the first few weeks of Bacarion's command, Gelan did not relax his vigilance. He asked no questions; he said nothing he had not said many times before; he continued to be, to all outward signs, the same quietly competent young NCO he had been all along.

Inside, he felt himself caught in a storm. What Bacarion had done, so far, was call in each officer and NCO, in turn, from the most senior down. Each had returned from that interview looking thoughtful; a few had also looked puzzled or worried. None had had more comment than "She's one tough lady."

That in itself was slightly bothering. On such a small post, gossip about each other was the main entertainment. From short encounters came small bits of information, painstakingly assembled into the common understanding of each individual. Gelan knew that their former commander, Iosep Tolin, had an aunt who bred flat-faced long-haired cats, a cousin in the wine business, and a daughter from whom he was estranged—Tolin blamed his former wife, who had left him for a historian.

But about Bacarion, nothing. "A tough lady." His sister Methlin was tough . . . he had not known, while she was in prison, just what prison was, or how difficult, but now he did. At least from the other side of the doors. His throat closed whenever he had duty on the women's side, thinking of Meth in there, and he wondered if any of the women were like her, unfairly condemned.

His turn with Bacarion would come soon. She had access to his service record, which included a list of all relatives formerly or presently in service. What would she say? What would she ask? What should he say, since the truth—*I want you dead, like Lepescu!*— would not do.

Tolin had not been a slob, but Bacarion's offices already looked shinier, neater. Everything gleamed, smudgeless. Every paper on the clerk's desk aligned perfectly with every other.

A martinet, like Lepescu. In the inner office, Bacarion waited, sitting motionless behind her desk like a carved figurine.

"Corporal Meharry reporting as ordered, sir." It was hard not to react when her cold gaze met his.

"You don't look much like your sister," was her first comment. Then she sighed, and gave a mock smile. "Why is it the men in a family so often get the looks, I wonder?"

He felt his neck go hot, then the flush spreading up his face. Her smile warmed.

"Sorry, Corporal. Didn't mean to embarrass you."

Didn't she, indeed! Gelan hoped that looking like a silly boy was the best strategy now.

"I met her only a few times, of course," Bacarion went on smoothly, as if reading from a script. Perhaps she was. "I was shocked and surprised when I heard she'd been sentenced to prison, and delighted when her name was cleared again." A wrinkle appeared in her forehead; Gelan was sure it was intentional, intended as a sign of sincerity. "It may be hard for you to believe, Corporal, but when I was serving on Admiral Lepescu's staff, I had no idea that he was capable of any dishonesty. He seemed so . . . so focussed on defeating the enemy."

That was one way of putting it. If you ignored the way that Lepescu's allies paid the price of his focus, as well as the enemy, the fact that he liked seeing blood shed, in quantity, and didn't much care whose it was.

"I hope we can work together," Bacarion was saying, now with a little frown, as if he'd failed to carry out some order.

"Yes, sir." Gelan tried to inject some enthusiasm into the familiar phrase. Bacarion's face relaxed, but whether that was good or bad he could not tell.

"Did you request assignment here because your sister had been here?" she asked.

"No, sir." He had anticipated this question. "Personnel noticed I hadn't had a tour in my secondary specialty, and yanked me off *Flashpoint* right before deployment. I asked for Sector Three, so I'd at least be in the same sector as my—as the ship—but they sent me here."

"Do you find it difficult?"

"No, sir."

"What do you think of the general loyalty of the officers and men on this station?"

What kind of a question was that to ask a corporal? "Loyalty? I'm not sure I know what the commander is asking about."

"Don't play innocent, Meharry! Any time you have prisoners and guards, you have the possibility of collusion, even a breakout. I'm asking you if you know anything about such a situation here."

"No, sir," Gelan said. "Nothing like that."

Another searching look. "Very well. Dismissed."

The autumn evening was closing in, a fine cold mist blowing across the courtyard. Gelan shivered. It was a week yet until time to change to winter uniforms, but it wasn't the outward cold that chilled him. The ten kilometers to Stack Two and twelve to Stack One might as well have been the thousands of kilometers that stretched to the next continental mass, for all the good it did him. He could not pilot any of the aircars even if the aircars had not been kept under close guard. There were no surface watercraft; the Stacks had no beaches or harbors where such craft could land. Water met rock with brutal suddeness twenty meters below the lowest accessible path; in storms, the spray of that meeting shot upward thirty and forty meters. He could swim, but he could not swim ten kilometers in water that cold, even if the sea creatures didn't eat him.

No escape. He was trapped as surely as any of the prisoners. He had no doubt that Bacarion would try to have him killed, and in such a way that it required the least investigation. Which meant probably not shooting or stabbing or even a fatal blow to the head—any of which would require sending his body for forensic examination. She might or might not have a collaborator in the medical facility on Stack One. Though such a murder could be blamed on a prisoner, far more useful for her purposes would be a disappearance, something that would leave the blame on him. If he went AWOL—as he had been thinking of doing, he realized with a start—Bacarion would be free to make up whatever story she liked about him.

The most likely thing was a quick toss over the cliff, alive or dead. Alive, probably, because then Bacarion's agents could honestly claim not to have harmed him. She would not order an attack until she was sure it would succeed—until she was sure she had enough support. He had a little time to make his preparations, minimal though they could be.

Three Stack had fifty Personal Protective Units, Planetary, in storage. In theory, a PPU would protect its wearer from the rigors of a planetary climate, as well as a variety of traumas. Abstracting a Personal Protective Unit from stores would definitely attract attention, but they were inventoried only once a month. Would the attack come in that time? Probably, he thought.

But a PPU wouldn't be enough to keep him alive in the ocean. He needed something else.

Aircraft carried survival gear; they did occasionally come down in the ocean, and the crew did occasionally survive to use the life rafts and other gear. There was a manual—he had seen a copy once—on surviving such wrecks, modified from one written by people who liked to sail around in boats. But he had read the manual out of boredom, while waiting for a shuttle flight, and with the casual contempt of someone who would never be stupid enough to get himself in a situation where the details presented would be important.

Methlin had always said learn everything you can. Meth had survived worse.

Why did big sisters have to be right so often?

Spare survival gear for the aircraft based at Three Stack—the commander's personal aircar shuttle with a capacity of four besides the pilot, and the two mail/utility vehicles which would hold 20 in a pinch—was stored in a locked bay on the shore side of the hangar. In his first month onstation, when he was still learning where everything was, he had been part of the inventory team that preceded the annual IG inspection. He remembered clearly the fat bundles, like sausage lumps, that were stacked next to the outer wall. Heavy, awkward, and not something he could tuck under his arm.

So . . . where could he stash something like that? Before he took it, he had to have a place to hide it, and he spent the next few off shifts looking. Everywhere on the limited surface of the Stack, someone else had reason to be. The two main lava tubes were in regular use; one had a small lift tube fitted into it. Personnel were up and down several times a day, though most didn't venture beyond the stacks of reserve supplies piled at the foot, and the little nest of discarded clothing just around the corner, where those who wanted to keep their encounters private bedded down in the warmer months.

Still . . . it was the only place. The smaller of the tubes opened to the outside, above the high-tide level except in storms. Generations of guards had broken a connection between the two; he was not the only one who had stood in the sea opening watching the waves at closer range and even trying to catch one of the native sea creatures on a moly line. As long as no one saw him actually dragging a deflated life raft into the sea cave, his presence in the tubes would cause no notice. He hoped.

He felt clever about figuring out a way to get the folded raft through the buildings and into the lift tube without detection. He didn't have to take it himself; he'd stenciled it with a supply code, and simply told a pivot to take it down with other supplies when the next load came in. Supply drops were chaotic enough that no one noticed— or seemed to, he cautioned himself—when an extra container went down. Later, he found it, and—having borrowed an AG dolly—floated it down the tube, through the gap, and to his chosen hiding place.

He felt better after that, even though his chances were still, he felt sure, closer to zero than a hundred. At least he had a chance, if a small one.

※ ※ ※

Once that was done, his mind turned to Bacarion's plans, not his own. What was she up to? He was as sure as if he'd crawled into her head that she had sought this assignment. But why? She would not have come here because of him—surely revenge on Methlin's little brother wasn't profit enough for three years on Stack Three—but what was her purpose? What could she do with a prisonful of convicts and guards, isolated in the midst of the ocean?

When he put it that way, he had to wonder what she could have done with a prisonful of guards and convicts on the mainland, or in space . . . and the answer chilled him. Lepescu's protégés, he was sure, had not become exemplars of sweetness and light since Lepescu's death. Indeed, Methlin had warned the family against having anything to do with any of them. Next thing to traitors, she'd said. So involved with their own game that nothing else mattered.

What he should do was find out what Bacarion was doing, and report it. But how? He was not in Bacarion's confidence and he had no access to the administrative offices anyway. That would just get him killed faster.

As the days passed, Gelan found that acting normal stretched his nerves almost past bearing. Inspections, chores, guard duty . . . wondering which of the guards and which of the prisoners were in on the plan, and yet again what the plan was. It had to be more than just killing him. Bacarion might take pleasure in killing Methlin Meharry's little brother, but she would not have finagled an assignment here just for that. If only he knew what was going on . . . but although it became increasingly obvious that something was—that he was being left out of meetings and plans—he could not find anything out.

He had not considered himself a trusting soul, but now, trying to trust no one, he realized that he had the normal human desire to be part of a group, not a complete outsider.

Margiu Pardalt had accepted a position as junior instructor in the Schools, and discovered that she enjoyed teaching. As the weather eased, bringing the occasional cool breath from the far north, her spirits lifted. Xavier had never been quite as hot as Copper Mountain in summer, and she looked forward to winter here. Unlike some of the others, who never took to planetside life, she enjoyed learning more about the world she was on. The Regular Space Service had facilities scattered around the planet, from the frigid polar caps to the balmiest of tropical islands. Most were used for training of some kind, or testing equipment; it did not occur to Margiu to wonder why a space force would do so much training and testing on a planet. Instead, she hoped she would have a chance to see the steppes near Drylands, so much like her homeworld, and maybe climb a mountain when she had some leave coming.

Her first chance to travel came in the break between class sessions, and she didn't even have to use leave time. Priority directives of very high classification had to be hand-carried from base to base. Ensign Pardalt was the obvious choice.

So on a morning that was not quite crisp, but at least not stifling, she accepted a case full of the directives, locked it to her belt, and climbed aboard one of the regular supply aircars headed for Camp Engleton. She sat on a sack of something lumpy and uncomfortable for two hours—the supply aircars had no passenger slings—and watched the red-sand brush country give way to dirty-green coastal grasslands and then dark-green trees standing in brown water.

She had only fifteen minutes to deliver the directives to the base commander, but fifteen minutes of the sticky heat and sulfur stench of the swamp forest was more than enough to quench her curiosity. She was glad to climb back into the aircar, now headed for Drylands. The lumpy sack she'd been sitting on had been unloaded, along with others, and the crew chief now had room to rig a seat of sorts.

That flight took several hours; she fell asleep in the noisy cargo compartment, waking when the aircar came down through the late afternoon sun. This far north, a chill wind rattled the few fading leaves left on the trees planted around the base's central drill field, and the short prairie grass had turned various shades of russet and maroon. She handed the base commander his copy of the directives, and signed into the TOQ for the night. When she walked around outside, she could almost believe she was on Xavier—until dark, when the night sky looked very different. Were they really that close to the Scarf?

Next day, she was scheduled for a long-distance flight to the west coast bases, Big Trees and Dark Harbor (she wondered again who had been allowed to name these places) and then she would embark on the more dangerous journey to the Stack Islands bases.

The long distance flight was not by aircar, but in a pressurized aircraft flying much higher than the 'cars; beneath her the land faded into a dim patchwork of dun and wrinkled brown, with white tips on the tall mountains she hoped to see in person some day. Also on the flight were replacement officers and enlisted; she was crammed into her seat with only a brief glimpse through the window whenever the neuroenhanced marine beside her leaned back for some reason.

Still, it was travel. She had come to learn, and this was learning. She memorized everything she could about the inside of the aircraft.

They landed at Big Trees, the runway a long gash in the forest. She had grown up among trees, clumps and woodlots and scattered groves on the meadows, but those trees had been rounder, softer. She had seen more, and taller, trees during her years at the Academy. But the trees had always had space around and between them. Despite the pictures, she had not really imagined what this forest would be like—great spires many times the height of the buildings on base. After delivering her package to the base commandant, she found she could not get transport to Dark Harbor until the next day.

"You should see our trees," she was told. "There's nothing like them anywhere else."

So she wandered out into the afternoon light, and up to the margin of the forest. Behind her mowers buzzed, trimming the emerald grass in the quadrangle; she could hear the closer click of feet on the walkways. Looking away from all that, she faced a massive dark bole like a slightly curved wall. Ferns the height of her head grew near it, trimmed back in a straight line on the base side. Between the chinks of its bark—she thought it must be bark—other plants grew, mosses and ferns and something with bright yellow flowers like tiny fireworks.

She edged around the tree, following a vague path. Under her feet, the ground felt spongy, and when she had cleared the curve of the great tree's bole, she realized she could not hear the base . . . the great tree lay between, soaking up the sound. Uneasy in the thick growth, she went back the way she'd come, and then back across the quadrangle to base housing.

Her flight up the coast the next morning, again in an aircar, revealed how little of the land had been touched by humans—the great forest lay green and unbroken from the base to the foothills of the mountains, and almost all the way to Dark Harbor, where it eased gradually into smaller trees, and then into broken shrubland.

In Dark Harbor, she had to wait several days for a transocean flight to the Stack Islands bases. A storm system had moved in, and no one was going to risk a flight during it, not for a mere courier. In the meantime she was supposed to familiarize herself with cold water ocean survival techniques. It was already early winter in the northern Big Ocean. Margiu learned to wriggle into the PPU and fasten the hood with one hand; she went over lifeboat drill and abandon-craft drill at least four separate times.

Corporal Asele Martin-Jehore stood satellite watch at the remote Blue Islands facility. Unlike Stack Islands, the archipelago known as Blue Islands lay in warm equatorial waters. Assignment to Blue was as coveted as Stack Islands was feared: the big sea predators which lay in wait for escapees from Stack were force-netted away from the beautiful white beaches and turquoise lagoons of Blue. All the permanent personnel onplanet tried to wangle at least a week's leave time on Blue.

Martin-Jehore had worked years to earn this assignment, but help from a friend in Personnel didn't hurt. He had proven himself time and again—he had recalibrated the number four signal array after a seastorm, when his senior supervisor was out with gut flu. And—because he showed talent with recalcitrant electronics—he had been permanently assigned to MetSatIV, the weather and surveillance satellite responsible for covering the northern third of Big Ocean.

MetSatIV had been a problem since it was installed. The contractor had replaced it twice, and each time found nothing wrong. The second time, the contractor's project engineer had made the unwelcome suggestion that someone in Fleet was screwing up the software. That had been Jurowski, who held the position before Martin-Jehore. It hadn't, in fact, been anything Jurowski did which bollixed the bird, but in the interest of satisfying the contractor that all steps had been taken, Jurowski had been taken off the roster for MetSatIV.

MetSatIV was still buggy. Martin-Jehore was sure it was an AI glitch—so was Jurowski, but Martin-Jehore had one vital piece of information Jurowski lacked: the command set for MetSatIV's AI.

In theory, every transmission from Blue Islands was logged. In practice, a very good communications tech could tightbeam a satellite without detection. Not often, but occasionally. Martin-Jehore had chosen his moments carefully, gradually gaining control of MetSatIV's AI at a level no mere communications tech was expected to reach.

Now he needed only the cover of a routine test transmission to cause the desired failure.

MetSatIV's AI compared the instruction set to those previously received, and agreed that they matched in syntax and content. Then it turned off its IR scan, and tipped itself 30° around its z-axis.

In the observatory below, one of the dozen screens in satellite surveillance went from a clear visual of a seastorm in progress, a vast swirl of white, to an eye-wrenching jiggling blaze of hash.

"Blast. There goes Watchbird again." Martin-Jehore glared at the screen. "I'll bet it's a clock problem."

"Nah—it's too random." Jurowski wasn't going to agree with anything Martin-Jehore said. Eighteen months, and he was still sore about losing his place as Watchbird's senior tech.

"Well, let's see if C-28 will get it back." Sometimes command C-28 would bring Watchbird back online, and sometimes it wouldn't. This time it wouldn't, but Martin-Jehore punched in that command sequence, anyway. The hash on his screens remained. "Not this time." When C-28 didn't work, the problem usually took longer to fix, but so far he had always been able to do so.

"Try the 43-120 set," Jurowski suggested. While he could not resist the initial jibe, he was a generous-hearted man, and always willing to help. Martin-Jehore nodded, and entered it. It wouldn't work either, but it would eat up several minutes while not working. The screen hash changed to a finer grain, but nothing else happened.

"Somebody rejuved its AI," Jurowski said. The whole room chuckled appreciatively. Headquarters might not know about any connection between rejuv and mental problems, but the lower ranks had figured it out long since.

As required by regulation, Martin-Jehore reported to his superior that MetSatIV was ineffective within the hour, when the first three standard interventions didn't bring it back online. CPO Gurnach sighed, and told him to keep trying. Martin-Jehore could tell she wasn't really worried. Big Ocean was mostly empty, and the storm MetSatIV had shown was already in the model. Stack Islands already knew about it—in fact, it was just clearing them now—and it wouldn't reach the mainland for days.

MetSatIV's other capability, that of detecting small craft atmospheric penetration, didn't concern CPO Gurnach either. At last report, the only ships insystem were, as always, Regular Space Service vessels. A hostile landing would have to come from a hostile deepspace ship, and there weren't any. Why worry about a hostile landing? Besides, Polar 1, now at the south end of its orbit, carried sensor arrays designed to spot any intrusive traffic; MetSatIV was really redundant.

Martin-Jehore knew it was crucial to keep MetSatIV offline for five hours or more. He did not know why, nor did he care. He had convinced himself that it was probably a matter of smuggling something really profitable (given the size of his payoff), and he didn't think smuggling actually hurt anybody. So what if some porn cubes got past customs without paying duty?

CHAPTER SIXTEEN

Stack Islands Base Three

The attack came on a dank gray afternoon, with thin rain spitting out of a low sky and visibility just reaching from the parapet of the exercise courtyard to the administrative offices. Gelan Meharry had outside duty, and had checked the first three posts when he found that number four was missing. Even as he thumbed the control on his comunit, he felt the prickles rising on his arms. Not at night after all, but with enough daylight to see if his body caught on any of the rocks.

"Spiers here," came the answer to his call. Spiers, whom he had not seriously suspected.

"Number four outside post's empty," Gelan said. "Should be Mahdal—has he called in?"

"No, Corporal. Want me to check sickbay?"

"Request backup at this post," Gelan said. "And run a com check on the others, would you? Then check sickbay."

"Sure thing." Spiers's voice sounded normal, with only the slight concern appropriate to a missing sentry.

Gelan looked around. Number four post gave its occupant a view of the prisoners' exercise court, the entrance block beyond, the upper part of the administrative block overlooking the forecourt, which was itself out of sight, and the peak of the stack itself rising beyond that. To his left he could see the helmet of number three post; to his right and down, on the outside of the entrance block, he should have seen the bright dot that was number five.

He didn't. He leaned out over the parapet of number four, to check the path below. There, far below, a bright yellow splotch, and a white dot near it.

He used his com again. "Spiers, this is Corporal Meharry again. There's a man down on the westside path. Have you raised number five yet?"

"No, Corporal." Now Spiers did sound worried. "Sergeant says he's on the way. Want me to call Medical?"

"Better do it. I'll go on down and see . . ."

As the blow fell, he lunged forward, so that his skull took less than the intended blow. The unexpectedness of that lunge loosened his captors' grip, and he got in another good shove as he went over the edge.

For an instant, hanging in the air with the sea spread out below him, he was euphoric. They hadn't knocked him out; he'd fooled them. He was going to make it; his plan would work.

Then he was close enough to see the height of the waves—mere wrinkles from above, here taller than he was, and smashing into the sharp rocks. *And no helmet,* he thought, just as he plunged into water so cold it took his breath, with force enough to nearly knock him out.

He fought his way to the surface by blind instinct, helped by the surge of the rising tide. When he shook the water from his eyes, he saw a black wall rushing toward him, covered with sharp shells. He threw out his arms; the water slammed him into the rock with crushing force, but the PPU gloves protected his hands, and then his body, from the sharp edges of the shells, and the wrist grapples locked onto the surface. When the water dragged back, he was able to stay on the rock. In that brief second, he curled up, jamming his boots into a crack, and deployed the PPU's lower grapples.

Cold water roared over him again, smashing him into the rock, then sucking his body away . . . the grapples held; his arms and legs strained. In the next trough, he released the wrist grapples, flung himself upward, and locked the wrists again just as the next wave hit.

Minute by minute he fought his way upward, racing the tide and the limits of his own strength. Distant clamor battered his hearing, even over the roar and suck of the waves. He looked upward, only to get a faceful of cold water.

Just above high tide, well within the splash zone, he clung to the rock. Despite the PPU, he was chilled; without it, he would have been dead. He could feel his arms and legs stiffening from both cold and bruising, and out there somewhere . . . the killers were looking for him.

Gelan stripped off the last of his duty uniform, ripping it free with the grapple claws of the PPU. He hoped it would look like the damage of sea creatures if the killers spotted it. Underneath, the PPU's programmable outer surface took on the mottled dark color of the rock . . . now if they looked down, they would see only rock, not a splash of yellow. He unhooked and unrolled the hood, and pulled it over his head. At once he felt better; the hood cut the windchill. He sealed it close around his face, then pulled up the facemask. The last bite of the wind disappeared. He wasn't comfortable, but he was no longer in danger of hypothermia. Not soon, anyway.

He touched the controls on his chest, and the PPU's circuitry delivered a boosted audio signal. Another control released a fine antenna to pick up transmissions.

"—Went over right there, sir. No chance to grab him—and he went right down—may've hit his head on a rock—"

Darkness closed in early. Gelan could see lights above; he waited until they were gone, then longer: they would be scanning in infrared as well. Though his suit reflected almost all his body heat inward, to protect him from the cold, a sensitive scan could pick up a human shape in movement. But well after local midnight, he moved—stiffly at first, then more smoothly—toward the lava tube where—he hoped—his survival kit was still concealed.

Once in the mouth of the tube, he risked a brief flash of his torch. There it was.

And there was Commander Bacarion, a weapon levelled at his chest.

"I thought they might have underestimated you," she said. "I didn't."

He said nothing.

"I will be glad to take your ears," she said. "I might even send one to your family."

The thought of Methlin's reaction if she got one of her little brother's ears in the mail made him grin in spite of his fear. "Do that," he said.

Then tossed his torch aside and dove toward her dominant hand, and used the suit grapples to catch and fling himself in a tumbling arc toward her. Her weapon fired, but the needle went wide. Gelan pivoted on one suit grapple, and slammed both booted feet into her side; he felt the crunch of bone and heard her grunt, but it was dark now, and she wasn't dead. She would have more than one weapon.

He scrambled towards her, raking with the suit grapples. A thin red beam appeared, the rangefinder of her next weapon, and the sharp crack of a hunting rifle turned to the clatter of falling rock where it hit. Gelan felt something with one glove, and yanked hard; she cried out, then something slammed into his shoulder. He swung elbows, knees, feet, and took hard blows himself, barely softened by the suit. Then the blows weakened; he hit again and again. And again.

Silence, but for the sound of his own breathing, and the pounding of waves outside the tube. Was she dead, or feigning? Had she been alone? He fumbled around, trying to find the torch, but finally gave up and used the suit's headlamp.

Bile filled his mouth. His suit grapples glistened, brilliant red in the light; he had torn her face off, in that last struggle. An ear dangled from one grapple tip. He shook it free.

She took ears.

He was a Meharry.

He was a Meharry who had killed an officer, an officer who was, as far as anyone knew, his legitimate superior merely doing her duty. He couldn't just go tell the sergeant about it. Not this time.

Methlin had said there would be days like this, he'd told himself often enough. She had never told him he might have to murder his commander and then figure out how to explain it.

He needed to search Bacarion's body. Surely if she intended some serious wrongdoing—beyond having him killed—she would have some evidence on her. She would not trust everything to an office safe. But not here, not where her confederates might be on their way, alerted by some signal he knew nothing about, or simply by her failure to show up at a meeting. If she had evidence on her, he would have to take her corpse along, or they would destroy it.

A gust of icy wind curled into the tube and it resonated like a giant organ pipe. Was it a storm coming? He couldn't wait. Grunting with the effort, Gelan dragged his purloined life raft down the tube to the lip, and then considered what to do with Bacarion's body. Finally, he decided to bring it along. It was heavier than he expected, awkward to heave and tip into the raft, but he secured it carefully before shifting the raft—and himself—to the very edge of the rock.

A more violent gust of wind caught it and whirled it through the air to land hard on the water; Gelan almost lost his hold. Even through the PPU, he could feel the water's chill, and its power. He yanked the vent control, and the raft ballooned around him. Bacarion's body lurched into him as the raft whirled, tilted, whirled again, on the wild waves.

Daylight came late, and weakly; the raft was driven ahead of sleet-laden wind over tossing waves that had long since relieved Gelan of everything in his stomach. He didn't want to use his headlamp to find the medkit; it might be seen from the base. So in the dingy gray light, with Bacarion's grisly stiff corpse rolling into him with every lurch of the waves, he finally spotted the medkit on the raft's bulwark and edged over to it. He peeled back the glove of his PPU, opened the medkit, and found the antinausea patches. In a few minutes, he felt slightly better, and very hungry. First, though—he used the raft's suction pump to clear bloodstained water from the raft's interior, and dared a peek out the canopy.

Nothing but tossing waves, dimpled by sleet, receding into murky dimness. At least they were out of sight of Three Stack. He resealed the canopy and explored the rest of the raft interior.

It had been designed to hold eight crash survivors. Tucked into one compartment was a manual—the same one, he realized, which he had read so carelessly that other time. On the first page, he saw a diagram of the raft, clearly marking the location of the water purifier, the direction finder, the food stores, the repair kit . . .

Lieutenant Commander Vinet waited none too patiently for the signal he expected. Today or tomorrow, Bacarion had said, depending on weather. It had to be cloudy, so that nothing would show on a satellite scan if the scan hadn't been disabled; it had to be daylight enough that her men could be sure Meharry was safely drowned.

With the storm moving in, surely it had been cloudy on Three Stack—it had been cloudy here since before dawn, and as evening closed in an icy mix of sleet and snow pelted windows.

He ate dinner as quickly as possible. If only he could contact her— but she had forbidden it, and he knew her to be a ruthless critic of those who disobeyed. Something had caused a delay—certainly the next day would be the one, then. He fell asleep at last.

Morning brought the height of the gale, the waves below beaten down by wind, scraped by sleet into patterns that looked as dangerous as they were. Through triple insulated windows he felt the power of that gale, the chill of the wind. By noon he was unbearably restless again, pacing from desk to window and back, then down the passage to the little enclosed overlook that gave him a clear view of the entire west end of the stack, and across to several others. No more sleet and snow, now, nothing but the cold wind; the two trees in the courtyard below flailed bare limbs against the wall that protected them.

Towards evening, the storms slid off to the south, and cold green light speared under the trailing edge. Still nothing. Something had gone very wrong indeed. What should he do now? He couldn't contact any of the others; Bacarion controlled the recognition codes. He couldn't do anything with the research teams or the weapons without additional forces. Bacarion knew he had only a few reliable men. She knew that, and still . . . he made himself sit down again, but nothing could quiet his mind.

Gelan had lashed the commander's corpse to the far side of the raft, repaired the slashes he'd accidentally put in the inner hull, eaten, and slept again. The storm had eased, but he had no idea where he was in relation to the Stacks. Fear of being blown back to them warred with fear of drifting on the vast ocean until he died. Death either way—which was worse?

Surely the commander's conspiracy, whatever it was, didn't include everyone on the planet. He ought to be able to count on the people at Search and Rescue, if no one else.

He looked at Bacarion's corpse, and shuddered. He could not bring himself to look for papers or whatever else she might have had. Well, then he could write his account of what happened: the survival manual had a thick pad of water-resistant sheets and a waterproof marker. Gelan hadn't written anything by hand in years, but he decided to put down what had happened before he unlocked the beacon. That way, even if he died, there'd be some record of events from his point of view.

If someone didn't just destroy them.

No use thinking like that. He set the pad on his knee, and tried to form legible writing as the waves lifted and dropped. It was harder than he'd expected, and after three sheets, he gave up.

"Commander Bacarion's not in her offices, sir." Sergeant Copans looked worried. "The commander's not answering any call, and the locator's not lit."

"If it's not one thing it's another." CPO Slyke didn't need this. Corporal Meharry's carefully staged suicide had gone exactly as planned, along with the murder of Major Dumlin, the senior unaligned officer. But Bacarion should have been there, unless she was playing some game of her own . . . and even then, she should have been back by now. Her games were usually short ones.

CPO Slyke had been a member of the Loyal Order of Game Hunters for sixteen years, the first enlisted recruit. He had served with then-Major Lepescu, and admired the officer's grasp of the real nature of war—a test of survival, of ultimate fitness. Born and raised on Calydon by Priorists who believed that fitness in this life was determined by effort in the life previous, Slyke knew he had *earned* his superior skills and toughness.

Now, facing the implications of Bacarion's disappearance, he knew his moment had come. Although he had not been briefed on the whole mission, his part had required him to know more than any other NCO and most officers. He could—he *would*—take over.

They had been lucky. Severe weather cut off communication immediately after the commander's disappearance, giving him time to do what he could to obscure the evidence, and search the buildings. The underground storage and lava tubes were an obvious target. He insisted on leading the search party himself, with his most trusted companions, all full members.

The commander had left tagtales. Very sensible of her. What had she known about that he didn't, and why hadn't she told him? He pushed that thought aside, grunting as he squeezed into the second tube.

There. The search lights picked up the glint off the hunting rifle's barrel first, then he saw the little red dot on the far wall. The laser sight was still on, the power pack unexpended. His breath came short. Was it a trap? Her trap, to test her followers? The sea boomed outside, and filled the tube with a wash of cold wet air; the walls glistened with it.

Closer . . . and he realized that some of the glistening surface was blood, not seawater. Smears and pools of blood, a few shreds of flesh . . . and something had been dragged, something heavy, from *here* to the edge of the tube, to the sea, where a crumpled wet tarp lay, its edge flapping with every gust of wind.

That damnable, conniving, fornicating Corporal Meharry must have survived the fall . . . climbed here, hoping for refuge—no, to retrieve a life raft he'd stowed here. And the commander had figured it out, had been waiting for him, only in the struggle one of them had killed the other (such a lot of blood, and he was a man who could estimate spilled blood accurately) and escaped in the raft.

But which? Logic said Meharry; Bacarion would have come back.

Unless that was part of her plot. Unless she had planned to betray them all, and escape herself. She had, after all, come down here without telling anyone. Perhaps she had counted on Meharry's death, and the life raft was for her own use.

He chewed his lip, trying to figure it out, and finally decided it didn't matter. They were in it up to their necks, and a witness—which witness didn't matter—had escaped.

He would have to go on with it. Too many clues might remain, even though he had used a firehose to flush the lava tube of evidence. If they could get offplanet before the person in the life raft made contact with anyone, the plan could go on as originally formed.

He ran his thumb under his belt, along the strips of ears that he had taken. They were, he was sure, only the beginning.

Within the prison population, tension had risen in the past few days. Prisoners studied jailers in both their roles, as the predators they had been (and were in spirit) watch prey, and as the prey watch predators around them. Slyke knew exactly which prisoners were supposed to be released, but his own assessment suggested a few additions. First he had to find a way to contact the conspirators in orbit, and convince them of his identity.

Establishing the contact was easier than he'd feared.

"We heard." The voice contact, generated from random snips of synthetic speech, would defeat voice recognition software.

"Ready to initiate Bubblebath," Slyke said.

A long hissing silence. Then—"You?"

"Better go ahead," Slyke said, leaving out "sir" with an effort. "Investigation of the major's disappearance—"

"Affirmative. ETA stage one?"

Slyke had calculated this carefully. "Two-seven minutes plus original."

"Good."

Now he had to signal his fellows. Sergeant Copans and Sergeant Vinus looked worried, but heard him out.

"But sir—with the commander's disappearance, Fleet Security will be all over us like crushers on a broken spacer."

"Yes, and if we wait around here, chances are they'll find something the commander left that will incriminate us. Either we do it *now*, or there's a very good chance we'll be in there"—he jerked his thumb at the cell block's outer doors—"with them. Is that what you want?"

"No, but—"

"Did you earn your *ears*, Sergeant?"

"Yessir."

"Then hop to it."

R.S.S. *Bonar Tighe* requested permission from Traffic Control to practice LAC drops into the Big Ocean. Many of the warships which visited Copper Mountain took advantage of the opportunity to test their drop crews. Traffic Control approved the drop zone—200 klicks south of Stack Islands—and also advised them that the only traffic was a prop jet doing SAR to the northwest.

Bonar Tighe's crew had coalesced around the charismatic Solomon Drizh, hero of Cavinatto, and just too junior, like Bacarion, to be closely investigated as a Lepescu protégé after the admiral's demise. The conspirators had learned from the mutiny aboard *Despite*, and the proportion of those supporting Drizh and his allies was much higher in every ship, the chain of command much tighter. This time they were not acting for the Benignity, but for themselves . . . the Loyal Order of Game Hunters.

Fleet had gone soft, Drizh had declared; the whole Familias Regnant had gone soft as a rotting peach. With anyone of real vision in charge, there would have been no piracy, no incursion by the New Texas Godfearing Militia—and certainly no attempt to preserve the lives of those scum once they'd taken the Speaker's daughter. All the NewTex worlds would be taken, their vicious militia subdued . . . though Drizh had to admit that he rather admired the men who would attack big ships with little ones.

The Loyal Order of Game Hunters had survived Lepescu's death and, in the years since, had even grown. Its leaders used one political event after another to demonstrate the need for more toughness, a more realistic attitude towards war, more loyalty between brothers in arms. Weakness in high places—from the king's abdication to Lord Thornbuckle's inability to keep his daughter in line—proved the need for a stronger, more warlike, military arm.

Like Lepescu, they saw themselves as more loyal, more dedicated, than other Fleet members, and the others as wishy-washy, irresolute, and ultimately ineffective. They recruited widely, more often in the NCO levels than Lepescu had—as Drizh said, if their founder had a fault, it was his misplaced belief in high birth.

The removal of senior NCOs and flag ranking officers because of problems with rejuvenation gave them an obvious window of opportunity. The following burst of temporary promotions gave the group a flag rank member again. He might be only an admiral-minor, and only for the duration of the emergency—but that emergency would last long enough for his purposes.

Bonar Tighe's three LACs dropped into atmosphere under control of the orbital Traffic Control. Atmospheric Traffic Control on Copper Mountain was minimal except near the main training centers—and the Big Ocean had none. Once below 8000 meters, they were automatically untagged on orbital screens.

Still they stayed on course until under 2000 meters, when they angled northward, towards the Stack Islands.

❂   ❂   ❂

CPO Slyke did not know exactly how Commander Bacarion had intended to deal with the prisoners and guards who were not part of the conspiracy. For his part, he had no intention of leaving witnesses behind, even on that isolated base. When the storm passed, and the radios once more punched through with the usual demands for daily reports, he'd had to say something to divert suspicion, and had reported Meharry and Bacarion both as "missing, presumed swept away by waves." Incredulity had followed; he knew that someone would send an investigative team as soon as possible, along with a new CO. No one must be left to talk about it. Even if the mutineers gained support of the orbital station, they wouldn't have the whole planet by the time someone could get here and write a damning report.

His confederates first took care of those members of the staff who were not part of the conspiracy. Those bodies he left in place . . . he hoped later investigators would think it a prisoner breakout. Killing the uninvolved prisoners was another matter. He had them brought out into the courtyard and then turned the riot weapons on them. They had time to scream . . . and when the prisoners he'd recruited came out, they were more respectful, just as he'd hoped.

By the time the LACs were in atmosphere, he had the prisoners lined up and waiting. The most reliable had the weapons and PPUs out of the guardroom. When the first LAC screamed out of the sky, and settled on the cold stone of Three Stack's landing pad, Slyke didn't wait for the hatches to open—the men were in motion, running. The first LAC lifted, and the next settled in place. Sixty more men raced aboard, just ahead of another rain squall. Then another sixty, and another. Slyke rode the last one up.

Behind him, a driving rain battered the corpses sprawled in the courtyard, washing the blood into gutters, and finally through drains down into the sea. When the squalls moved on, the seabirds came, and for a time made a column of flickering wings above the towering stack.

Bonar Tighe's LACs screamed south, and rose from their designated drop zones back to orbit an ample twelve minutes before Martin-Lehore finally fixed MetSatIV's glitch.

MetSatIV picked them up at near-orbital level, but they were outbound, carrying Fleet beacons; the satellite's AI tagged them as friendlies.

The first LAC eased into *Bonar Tighe*'s drop bay and settled onto its marks. Pivot Anseli Markham, who always read manuals and followed them to the letter, aimed the hand-held bioscan at its fuselage.

"Put that down," growled her boss, Sergeant-minor Prinkin.

"But sir, the manual said—" Anseli goggled at the readout. The LACs had gone out empty, with flight crew only, and her instrument was showing dozens and dozens of little green blips.

"Put it down, Pivot; it's out of order."

"Oh." Anseli racked the instrument. So that's why it was showing troops aboard an empty LAC. "Should I take it to the repair bay, Sergeant Prinkin?"

He gave her a sour look. "Do that, Pivot. You're no damn use in here anyway."

Anseli unracked the bioscan and headed toward the repair bay. She was tempted to turn it on and see if it worked when it didn't have to read through hull material, but she could feel Sergeant Prinkin watching her. He'd never liked her; he was always sniping at her, and she tried so hard . . . she let her mind drift into her favorite reverie, of how much better she would treat pivots when she made sergeant-minor.

The repair bay for small scan equipment was out of sight of the LAC service bay. Once around the corner, Anseli experimented with the bioscan. When she pointed it at her foot, a green blurry foot-shaped image appeared. When she aimed at the squad coming down the passage, it showed all eight of them. When she aimed it at a bulkhead, there were two squatting shapes . . . and then a rush through the water pipes that made her blush. She hadn't *meant* to do anything like that.

Chief Stockard, in the repair bay, took the bioscan and gave her forms to fill out.

"But I think it's working now," Anseli said, trying to fit the entire thirteen-digit part number into a space only two centimeters long. Print clearly, the directions said, but how could she print clearly that small? And why did she have to fill out forms at all, when the computerized ID system would read the part number right off the bioscan itself? She did know better than to ask that one; it wasn't her first trip to the repair bay. "I tried it on people coming along here, and it always registered them."

"If your sergeant said it wasn't working, then it wasn't working," Stockard said, folding his lips under. "It may be working now, but it wasn't working then. What was he trying to do when he said it malfunctioned?"

"He wasn't using it, Chief. I was. I was taking a bioscan reading of the incoming LAC, just like it says to do in the manual, and he said put it down, it's not working right. And I guess it wasn't, because it said the LAC was full of troops."

"LACs usually are," Stockard said, the corner of his mouth twitching. "I don't see what's wrong with that."

"But they dropped empty," Anseli said. "I was there; I scanned them going out, just like the manual says, and they carried only flight crew. It was just a practice flight."

Stockard froze, his hands flat on the counter between them. "Are you saying the LACs went down empty and came up full?"

"Well . . . no, sir, not really. They couldn't have. It's just this bioscan unit, but since it's malfunctioning—"

"You just wait there a minute." Stockard turned away, and Anseli could see him talking into a comunit, though she couldn't hear him. He turned back, shaking his head, still muttering into the comunit. Then he gave her a rueful look. "I guess it malfunctioned . . . I just asked Chief Burdine if the LACs carried troops, and he said no. Oh— he says for you to take a detour up to Admin and pick up the liberty passes for the section. We'll be docking in a few hours."

"Yes, sir." No chance that her name would be on the list, given Sergeant Prinkin's animosity, but maybe he'd go, and she'd have a few hours of peace.

Chief Burdine, on the LAC service bay deck, strolled over to Sergeant Prinkin as if making his usual round of stations. "Just had a call from Stockard in repair—that idiot pivot of yours told him all about the malfunctioning bioscan showing the LAC full of troops. I think Stockard bought my assurance that they're empty, but how much chance that pivot will blab to someone else about the bioscan reading?"

"Near a hundred percent," Sergeant Prinkin said. "The girl's got no sense."

"Is she popular?"

"She's got friends. Hard worker, shows initiative, always willing to help out."

"A milk biscuit." That with contempt.

"Oh yes, all the way through."

"I wish we didn't have any of that sort aboard," Chief Burdine said. "They could have a happy life milking cows somewhere; what'd they have to join Fleet for?"

"For our sport," Sergeant Prinkin said.

"That's true." Burdine grinned at him. "Though it's little sport someone like her will give us."

Running up to Admin from the repair bay meant running up a lot of ladders, which other people seemed busy running down. Again and again Anseli had to stand aside while one or more officers or squads of NEMs clattered down. She wasn't really in a hurry, because the longer she was away from Sergeant Prinkin the better, but standing at the foot of ladders wasn't her idea of fun. Her mind wandered to the LACs and the bioscan. If LACs could drop and pick up troops . . . or drop troops off . . . why couldn't they pick troops up? Go down empty, come back full? And if you didn't bioscan the LACs, how could you tell?

"Stand clear!"

She flattened herself to the bulkhead yet again, not really seeing the uniforms flashing past her. What if there were people on the ship who weren't crew? People from down on the planet?

Of course, everyone on this planet was Fleet, so it didn't matter. Did it?

Anseli knew that pivots weren't supposed to think—well, not beyond memorizing instruction sets in manuals. But she'd always had a sort of itchy feeling in her head if she didn't get things straight. Machines either worked or they didn't, in her very clear interior universe. A bioscan which reported on real, verifiable human-sized beings behind one wall didn't turn liar and report that there were people where there weren't any. That very same bioscan unit had reported nothing in the LAC holds when the LAC left . . . when it was known to be empty. So *how* did the sergeant know the LAC was empty when the bioscan said it was loaded with troops? Sergeants knew everything, but . . . her mind itched.

A non-itchy part of her mind began its own commentary on the crew members who kept coming down the ladders. There had been no general alarm, so why were the ship's security details on their way to the LAC bays?

By the time she reached Admin, her mind was worse than a case of hives, and the only way she knew to scratch it was ask questions. The chief in Admin growled and handed her another job to do. How was she supposed to learn if no one answered her questions?

Bonar Tighe reported its LACs recovered, and requested and received permission to dock at the orbital station. This, like the request to practice LAC drops, was standard procedure, and the Traffic Control gave *Bonar Tighe* a docking priority assignment based on her ETA. The stationmaster approved station liberty at the captain's discretion, and forwarded the station newsletter. Ships of *Bonar Tighe*'s mass could not microjump so close to a planet, so the cruiser had to crawl patiently in a spiral to catch up with the station, a process which took several hours.

CHAPTER SEVENTEEN

Margiu Pardalt boarded the odd-looking aircraft before dawn. If not for the briefings, she'd have had no idea that such craft existed. On Xavier, she had seen only surface-to-station shuttles and low-flying aircars or flitters. Her years at the Academy had introduced her to high-altitude passenger aircraft like the one she'd been in from Drylands to the coast. But this uneasy compromise between aircraft and boat looked like something a mad scientist would come up with: four fat engines on the high-set wings, with whirligig propellers set into adjustable ducts; a peculiar blob hanging from the end of each wing, suspended on a thin pole. The bottom of the fuselage had the conchoidal shape, scooped and ridged, that she associated with shattered glass. She found it hard to believe it would actually fly.

This time the craft carried only three passengers besides its crew. One was a gray-haired major, with a pinched mouth and a narrow line of decorations which she recognized as efficiency awards. Admin, most likely. He went to the head of the little line waiting on the dock as by rights, boarded first, and installed himself in a seat midway down the port side, where he immediately flicked on his seat lamp and opened a handcomp.

The other passenger had waved Margiu ahead, with a flamboyant gesture that matched his flamboyant appearance. In the harsh lights of the harborage, his leather jacket blazed a garish yellow, and the metallic decorations glittered. Margiu climbed over the entrance coaming, and followed the major, almost stumbling once when the gentle motion of the seaplane on the water surprised her.

She picked out a window seat, on the starboard side. As she buckled in, she looked up to see the third passenger watching. One of those? He had pulled off his cap, revealing fine gray hair fluffed around a bald pate, and in this light she could see that his yellow jacket might be some theatrical troupe's idea of a uniform. Its shoulders were decorated with loops of green braid, and a line of stars on the upstanding collar, now open to reveal a green shirt; his dark pants were actually green.

"May I?" the man said, in a surprisingly sweet voice. "I'm really quite harmless."

She had hoped for a quiet ride, perhaps even a nap. But courtesy demanded that she say yes, so she nodded.

A crew chief checked to be sure they were all wearing the PPU, and a life vest, and that all the survival gear aboard was actually in place. Predictably, the man in yellow wasn't wearing his PPU. Unpredictably, he was quite cheerful about having to change, and quicker than she would have expected. Margiu had flown between the stars, but never over large bodies of water; she began to realize that this was serious.

Then the pilot swung the stumpy plane around, revved the engines, and Margiu felt acceleration shoving her back. The plane slammed its way across the low ripples of the harbor, spray blurring the lights outside. A few moments later they were airborne.

The headlands of Dark Harbor, edged with lights, fell away behind and below them, and then it was nothing but darkness below. Down there somewhere was water, invisible to the eye but cold and wet. Margiu shivered. To her relief, her seat companion turned a little away and started snoring almost immediately. By dawn, they were flying under high clouds, and the water below looked like a vast sheet of wrinkled silk patched with shades of blue and green and silver that she could not identify.

The man beside her woke up, and gave her a sweet smile. "I hope my snoring didn't keep you awake," he said.

"No, sir."

"I'm no sir, milady. I'm Professor Gustaf Aidersson, if you want my dull, boring, everyday name, which goes with my dull, boring, everyday profession, about which I cannot talk, or we will both be in serious trouble. Or you could call me Don Alfonso Dundee, most noble knight of the Order of Old Terra, and we could have a pleasant conversation about anything you wish."

"I'm sorry?" She had no idea what he was talking about.

"No, I'm sorry." He hit himself dramatically on the forehead. "Never accost young ladies before breakfast with strange tales out of distant mythology. You've heard of SPAL?"

"No, sir."

"Ah. Well, it's the biggest collection of galoots and misfits in the universe, and the letters stand for the Society for the Preservation of Antique Lore. Antique lunacy is more like it—I have no faith whatever in the actuality of our tomfoolery, but it is fun. We got the idea back when the rich folks in the Families first took up antique studies and arts—long before your time, milady—and we put our own interpretation on it. Let them flit about with fencing masters from the Company of Sabers, create titles for themselves, and imagine that they're re-creating scenes from Old Earth history. They're so serious about it, it takes all the fun out."

Margiu listened to the rolling flow of words and wondered if the man were entirely sane. His bright sidelong look seemed to catch her thought in midair, as if it were a ball being tossed.

"You wonder if I'm crazy. Of course you do. I'm not sure myself, and my wife tells me regularly that my pot is a little cracked. But the fact of the matter is, craziness is not necessarily a bar to genius, and my kind of craziness consists only in boring total strangers to distraction in airplanes. Or spacecraft. Or anywhere else I can trap them." He grinned at her with such obvious good humor that Margiu felt herself relaxing.

"What is that yellow jacket?" she found herself asking.

"Good question," he said promptly, in a tone that she could well believe went with a professor of something. "There was a colony world—second-order colony out of Old Earth by way of Congreve—which had successive waves of settlers. They didn't get along, so of course they started fighting. Back then fabricators were pretty basic machines—couldn't turn out any useful sort of protective garments. So the colonists started using leather from their herds of cattle. The color told what side they were on. Mine is a semiaccurate reproduction of a Missen-Asaya officer's uniform of the Third Missen-Asaya/Tangrat War. Except the insignia. I should have a little wooden bird, but I couldn't find it before I left. My wife swears I must have left it at the last awards banquet . . . so I just took the stars off a model spaceship. Not a very good model, either; Rose-class ships never had double batteries of beam weapons. I told Zachery that when he showed me the model, but he got huffy about it and threw it in the corner, the one where Kata drops her dirty boots. That's why I knew where to find stars when I wanted them. And I thought stars might be more impressive when I had to travel with Fleet officers, but of course they see that yellow canary-jacket and try not to laugh."

It was like drowning in treacle.

"But I'm talking too much about myself. Just whap me on the head when I do that; that's what my wife does. Or ignore me and look out the window if you want. I can see you're an ensign, with red hair exactly the color of my niece's, but—who are you?"

"Margiu Pardalt," Margiu said. "From Xavier."

"Xavier!" His face lit up, and her heart sank. "You know, the tactical analysis of the most recent engagement is fascinating. I was most impressed with the fire control of the Benignity ships—"

"The Benignity ships—" She couldn't help that, or the tone it popped out in.

"Yes. No disrespect to Commander . . . er . . . whoever it was—"

"Serrano," murmured Margiu.

"But the Benignity performance was markedly better than expected. And there's new data—from this very facility—well, not where we're going but where I assume you've been, the Copper Mountain base— to indicate that they upgraded one of our ships they captured. For instance, the time to recharge—no. I mustn't get onto this." Margiu could see the effort it cost him to rein that enthusiasm back. "Tell you what, let's talk about wet navies. Here we are, flying over a superb large ocean, and I'll bet you've never studied wet-navy history, have you?"

"Only a little," Margiu said. Her mind scrabbled frantically in search of some crumb of data to prove that she had studied it at all, but only the word *Trafalgar* rose up. She couldn't remember if it had been an admiral, a ship, or a battle. "Trafalgar," she said.

"Of course!" He beamed at her. "A mighty battle indeed, that was, but perhaps a little remote for our purposes. Are you familiar with the application of Nelson's sail tactics to colonial naval battles?"

"Uh . . . no, sir."

"Consider, if you will, the archipelagos of Skinner III." He spread his hands, as if touching a particular geographic area, and Margiu wondered if she ought to admit she didn't know what an archipelago was. She didn't have time. "Forty thousand islands, at least. Colonized with intent to exploit its obvious advantages for aquaculture, but, as always, underfunded and subject to piracy. Abundant timber, so—"

Margiu's com beeped; she pressed the button. Her companion watched, bright-eyed. The pilot spoke: "Ensign, Major—" She glanced back and saw the other officer sit up; he met her eyes across the plane. "There's some kind of trouble at Stack Islands. Apparently personnel are missing, believed lost at sea—"

"What personnel?" the major asked.

"Base Three commander and a guard corporal. There's also a life raft missing from the Three Base aircar hangar, and evidence of a struggle . . . they're saying the corporal may have gone crazy and kidnapped the commander. But anyway—we're to join the search; they don't have any long-range craft, and they suspect the life raft was blown west by the storm into the North Current."

Margiu started to say that her orders were to get those directives to the base commanders without delay, but decided not to. The pilot knew she was a courier, and if someone were down there in a raft, surely that had to come first. She hoped.

They were still at least an hour east of the Stacks, but Margiu could not help scanning below for the life raft. She had no idea how big it would look from whatever altitude they were flying.

Dark dots appeared on the sea. "Those are the Stacks," the pilot said. Margiu stared at them . . . a scatter of tall black rocks, whose height above the water was hard to judge in this flat light. The plane lost altitude again in a sudden lurch. "We'll be over Stack Island Three in an hour."

The Stacks looked impossibly forbidding—too tall, too narrow on top, too bleak. Why had Fleet put bases out here at all? She'd read the cubes, but it still seemed ridiculous. The plane droned on, and the Stacks rose up and sank, appearing and disappearing . . . a total of 98 visible at high tide, 117 at low, according to the cube. Some so small that not even an aircar could land vertically on top.

They left the Stacks behind, and Margiu stared at the sea from her side of the craft with more intensity.

"Signal!" the pilot said suddenly. "I've got a beacon! And confirmation from upstairs." The plane heeled on one wing, and Margiu gulped her stomach back into place. When she laid her forehead on the window, the glass felt colder than before.

The major spotted it first; Margiu heard him call out, and the pilot swung the plane around again. Now she saw the little yellow chip on the gray-green sea. Was anyone in it? Alive? She could not imagine what it must be like.

"We're going down," the pilot said. Margiu clamped her jaws shut. Going down? Was something wrong with the plane?

"It's all right, Ensign," the major said, catching her eye. "This is a seaplane, remember. It can land on the water."

Margiu drew a shaky breath. Water, yes: in a protected lagoon, shallow and calm. She hadn't known any aircraft could land on open ocean without sinking. She wasn't sure she believed it.

"Hoods on," the pilot ordered. Margiu plucked the hood of her PPU from its curl around her neck and put it on. If it was so safe, why this precaution? She put her hands into the gloves, too, and made sure the wrist and boot grapples were locked back. She peered out. They were much lower now, and she could see that the surface of the ocean heaved slowly in broad swells, reflecting the bright yellow canopy of the life raft. Through that clear, quiet water, she saw something swimming—some long, narrow shapes.

"Isn't this exciting?" asked her seatmate. "A most excellent adventure, my first water landing in an aircraft." He didn't look frightened at all. Margiu was scared, though she wasn't going to admit it. "Of course, if we come in too fast, or too steeply, we'll be killed, which would be a shame. Let me see . . . this planet's gravitational attraction is 1.012 that of Earth, and that means . . ."

Margiu closed her ears; she wanted to close her eyes, but she could not look away from the water's surface . . . the smooth water looked less smooth the closer they came. Then spray fountained past the window; the safety harness dug in as the plane lurched and swayed. The plane slowed, settling in the water; she could feel the movement of the ocean take over from the movement of the air, lifting and dropping the plane in a leisurely oscillation. The inboard engine on her side stopped, and her window cleared. She remembered the briefing, that in event of an emergency landing, the craft would keep two engines going, with the ducts adjusted to minimize blast on the escape rafts. Presumably the same technique would keep the prop blast from blowing this life raft away.

As they rose on the swell, she could see the yellow canopy of the life raft in the distance. The pilot's voice came over the roar of the engine. "We don't have current weather data—MetSatIV's down again—and although it looks dead calm now, I don't trust it. We're not going to be down one second longer than we have to be. You will all do exactly what my crew chief tells you."

The crew chief beckoned to them. The professor climbed out and let Margiu into the aisle after the major had gone past.

"Major, you and the ensign will need to hang onto this line . . . steady . . ."

Margiu wrapped her gloved hands around the rope. Line. Whatever they wanted to call it, it was rope to her, familiar from the family farm. The major, ahead of her, blocked half her view of the outside, but she could see water not that far below, and nothing but water to the horizon. She shivered in spite of her PPU.

"Why not just tie the rope to the plane?" the major asked.

"Sir, we never secure the aircraft to something like the raft. Should it capsize—"

"It's a life raft," the major said. "It's made to not capsize. I shouldn't have to stand here holding a stupid rope."

"Right, sir—just let me take that a moment." The crew chief took the rope from the major, passed the slack to Margiu, and then back to the professor, who had come along without being asked.

The canopy flap opened; a head poked out, shrouded in a PPU hood.

"Who are you?" croaked a voice.

"Chief Stivers," the chief said. "And you are . . . the missing Corporal Meharry?"

"They've reported me missing?" The voice sounded odd; Margiu could see the strain on that face. "I was supposed to be dead."

"Where's Commander Bacarion?"

"She's—her—she's here." Meharry pushed the canopy flap farther to the side. Margiu couldn't see what that revealed, but the major stiffened.

"That's—she's hurt, she's—"

"She's dead, sir," Meharry said.

"There'll have to be an investigation," the major said.

"Yes, sir. But first, sir—"

"No buts, Corporal. Chief . . . er . . . Stivers . . . you will place this man under arrest—"

"Sir, he's been on a lifeboat for days . . . he needs care . . ."

"He's a material witness, if not a murderer. Under arrest, Chief, at once—"

"We have to get him aboard first."

"And the deceased. And the raft."

"Sir, I'll have to ask Pilot Officer Galvan. It's not going to be easy to get the raft aboard safely."

"We can't leave valuable evidence at the scene—"

The pilot had other priorities. "First, we get that man aboard. He's been adrift for days, in freezing weather; it's a wonder he's alive. Major, you take that line; Professor, get back to your seat for now."

As the pilot ordered, Margiu and the major each took a line, and wrapped it around a projecting knob inside the aircraft. The pilot had a name for the knob, but Margiu ignored that and concentrated instead on the need to keep the line taut and the raft snugged up to the aircraft. The copilot and the crew chief helped Corporal Meharry clamber over the raft's inflated rim and into the plane.

He was haggard and pale; when he tried to stand, he staggered against the bulkhead. The copilot and crew chief half-carried him back to the seats, and draped him over two of them. Professor Aidersson bustled over; Margiu heard his sweet voice over the others. The major spoke to her.

"Ensign—get in that raft, and prepare the commander's body for removal."

Margiu stared at him, but swallowed the "Me, sir?" that almost came out. She glanced at the copilot, hoping he would say something, but he was doing something to the corporal's PPU.

She had never envisioned herself clambering into a blood-smeared life raft in the middle of a vast ocean to retrieve the dead body of a murder victim. Gingerly, she eased over the inflated rim and into the raft. The fabric dipped and shifted under her; she felt very insecure. She had seen dead bodies before; she had seen dead bodies days old, for that matter. But that had been on dry land, in the warm, dry climate of her homeland. She had never seen so much water in her life, and to be bobbing up and down in a raft in the middle of the ocean, with a cold stiff body, terrified her. When she looked back at the plane, it looked much smaller, entirely too small to be reassuring when everything else was water.

The next thing she noticed was the smell; cold had retarded decay, but there was a sickening odor of human filth and death both, held in by the canopy. When the raft rocked to the swell, Margiu struggled not to gag. As quickly as she could, she unfastened the canopy tabs and rolled it back. Even the aircraft fumes were better than this.

Bacarion's body . . . she tried not to look at it, especially not the ruin of the face. But it was heavy—the woman had been both taller and heavier than Margiu—and she could not get the right leverage to move it.

"Hurry *up*, Ensign," the major said.

"Sorry, sir," Margiu said, breathless, as she struggled to unlash the webbing that held Bacarion's body still. She got the last one loose, and the next swell rolled the body toward her. When she tried to lift, the additional weight pressed her knees into the raft floor, which sank, and the body rolled into the depression. It would have been hard enough on a solid support, but she had none.

"Tie a line around her and we'll haul from here," suggested the professor, who had reappeared in the aircraft's hatch.

"Don't be ridiculous!" snapped the major. "All she has to do is lift and slide the body across—"

"No—she'll need the basket. Hang on, Ensign. Be right back." The crew chief, who had come forward, now disappeared back into the plane.

"I don't think much of your initiative," the major said to Margiu; behind him, the professor winked at her. The crew chief reappeared, with a bright-orange object that looked like a long skinny basket. "Here you go, Ensign—" He slid it over the rim of the life raft to her. "Ever used one of these? No? Well, just roll the body into it, then hook those lashings over." He turned his head to look back into the plane and yelled, "Just a second, sir—"

Margiu positioned one edge of the basket thing next to the corpse.

"Now go to the other side and give it a push," said the major.

"Stay where you are," the professor said. "Your weight will make it roll toward you."

"Keep out of this," the major said, turning to glare at the professor.

"It's simple physics," the professor said. "A child could see—" He gestured. "Her weight depresses the life raft floor, and the corpse rolls—"

A gentle swell lifted her up, then dropped her, and the corpse rolled into the basket. Margiu hooked the lashings quickly, then glanced back at the plane. A line of cold green water widened between her and the plane; the two men argued in the doorway, hands waving, and the rope ran smoothly out beside them. She felt an instant of panic so strong that she couldn't even yell.

"Idiots!" The crew chief lunged past them and grabbed the trailing line. "Don't pull!" he yelled to Margiu. "We won't lose you." Even as he said it, an end of rope slipped out and splashed into the water. Panic gripped her again, until she remembered the line attached to the Berry.

Another voice yelled from forward in the plane. "What's going on, Ker? We need to get back in the air sometime this century. Swell's picking up, if you hadn't noticed."

"Loose line, sir." The crew chief did not turn his head this time, Margiu noticed. "Now, major, if you'll take hold behind me, and then you, professor. Let's bring her in . . ."

Margiu made herself look away from the plane, and recheck the lashings on the basket. Then she began hauling in the rope attached to the basket. Something yanked on it, hard, and she fetched up against the life raft's inflated rim.

"Hurry up, Ensign," the major said. "The pilot wants us to leave."

"Yes, sir . . ." Whatever it was yanked again, putting a sharp crease in the inflated rim. Then it let go, and she fell back into the smelly slime of the lifeboat floor. She reeled the line in, hand over hand, and was able to toss the dripping end into the hatch when the raft bumped the plane again.

"All right, Major—if you'll let go this line, sir, and take hold of that one—"

Margiu did her best to lift the ends of the Berry unit over the inflated rim as the major pulled, and after some minutes of breathless struggle, the corpse was aboard the plane. Margiu crawled out after it, her knees shaking. The plane might be tiny compared to the sea, but it was more solid than that life raft. She pulled herself upright, and hoped no one had noticed her fear, as the copilot came forward and slid into his seat.

The pilot peered back over his shoulder.

"Hurry it up, back there. I don't like the look of the horizon, and I'm still not getting current feed from MetSat."

"We simply must take the raft aboard," the major said.

"We're going to take off before that squall line gets here," the pilot said. "And the chief says it would take at least an hour to deflate and pack the raft, which will put us marginal on weight, since it'll be wet. Forget the raft."

"Dammit, it's *evidence*." The major visibly fumed for a few moments, then said, "Fine, then. We'll leave Ensign Pardalt in the raft to secure the evidence; another flight can pick her up later. Ensign, get back in the raft."

Margiu's heart sank. Leave her alone on the ocean with a storm coming?

"I don't think—" the professor began; the major rounded on him.

"You have no place in this discussion; you are only a civilian. You have caused enough trouble already. Go sit down and be quiet!"

The professor's eyebrows went up, and his head tipped back. "I see, sir, that you are a bigot."

"Ensign, get into that raft and prepare to cast off," the major said without looking at the professor. "We will inform Search and Rescue where you are, and they will come find you."

The pilot burst out of the cockpit. "Ensign, take your seat. You too, prof." Margiu followed the professor quickly into the cabin. "Major, if you do not shut up, I will put *you* in the raft. I'm in command of this craft—"

"What's your date of rank?" the major asked. Cold anger rolled off him in waves.

"You're a paper-pushing remf," the pilot said. "Not a line officer, and not my CO. You have a choice—you can either go sit down and be quiet, or you go out the hatch, right this instant, and I don't much care if you land in the raft or the water."

Margiu watched the little group by the hatch—did the major know that behind his back the crew chief's broad hand was poised to push him out? She doubted it; he was too angry with the pilot.

"I'll complain to your commander," the major said, turning away; Margiu could see how red he'd turned, and looked down. This was not something she wanted to witness.

"So will I," the pilot said. Already the crew chief was coiling the wet line that had held the raft to the plane. He pulled the hatch shut, dogged the latch, and secured the dripping coil of rope to the cleat on the forward bulkhead. Margiu could not see the raft from her side, but she saw the propeller of the inboard engine begin to turn, and the duct flanges move. Gouts of blue smoke, then spray, as the propeller blast whipped the surface of the sea. The plane swung in a tight circle; now she could see, through the wavering streams of water on the window, the bright yellow of the life raft rocking on the swell. The engines roared, and the plane moved jerkily at first through the water; then, with a series of shuddering slams, reached takeoff velocity and lifted away from the water. As the window cleared, Margiu looked back. A tiny yellow dot, already hard to see, and behind it, a darkening line of the oncoming storm.

She could have been down there. She could have been huddling in that miserable foul-smelling life raft, struggling to learn how to survive in a storm.

"I don't think I quite like that major," the professor said. Margiu glanced at him. His amiable face had set into an expression of cold distaste. "Not someone with the right grasp of priorities."

Safer to say nothing, especially since her stomach was leaping around with the turbulence.

"Are you all right?" he asked, then answered his own question. "No, I see that you are not. Here—" He put something chilly and wet on her cheek, the only exposed skin. "Antinausea patch. I put one on while they were still arguing. Close your eyes, and lean back—takes about thirty seconds."

Margiu counted to herself, and by twenty-seven felt that her stomach had settled. She opened her eyes. Behind, over the noise of the engines, she heard the major retching, but even the sour smell of vomit didn't make her stomach lurch. The professor leaned away from her. "Here, Major—an antinausea patch—"

The man said nothing, but the professor's hand came back empty, and he turned to wink at her. Margiu smiled uncertainly.

"Always come prepared," the professor said. "Nausea adds to no one's ability to think and act effectively. You're better now?"

"Yes," Margiu said.

Once the plane was in level flight, the pilot spoke over the intercom.

"I realize all of you have urgent orders to the various Stack Islands bases, but we have some problems to deal with. MetSatIV is offline, and has been for several hours. We do not know what our weather will be, and there's an additional concern about security at Stack Three. They can say what they like, but with the commander dead—we're heading back to Dark Harbor."

"I'm going to see what I can do for that poor lad," the professor said, unstrapping himself.

"But the major—"

"Has no authority over me—as he so rudely pointed out, I'm a civilian. And he's not any of the military officers to whom I report—he can bluster, but that's all. Besides—" He pointed, and Margiu craned her head to look. The major was sleeping, ungracefully slumped in the seat with one hand dangling to the deck. The professor winked at her again.

"There are antinausea patches and antinausea patches," he said. "He'll be out for several hours."

The rescued corporal, though swathed in blankets at the rear of the cabin, looked miserable enough. He had not thrown up, but his face had a greenish cast. Across from him, the corpse had been wrapped in another and lashed to the deck.

"How about giving him a patch?" the professor asked the crew chief.

"Fine with me—I notice our major is sleeping peacefully—"

"Nausea is so exhausting," the professor said. "Here, now—" He put a patch on the corporal's cheek. "That should help."

"He really needs fluids and calories," the crew chief said. "If he can hold 'em down."

"In a minute or two," the professor said. "What do you make of this?"

"A mess, sir. This lad's a Meharry—may not mean much to you, but it's a family with a proud history in Fleet. Meharrys are known to be a tough bunch to tangle with, but they've always been loyal."

"So—what do you think happened?"

"I don't know, sir. The major, he said no one was to talk to him—"

"And the major's authority—"

The crew chief sucked his cheeks in. "Well, sir—he outranks me. The pilot's in command here, but he's busy with the craft and I don't like to bother him. It's always a pain when one of the MetSats is out."

"How often does that happen?"

"MetSatIV's been buggy for the past two years or more. There's a new youngster at Blue Islands who's been keeping it up more often, but even he slips sometimes."

"Mmm . . . and how long has he been there?"

"Oh—eighteen months, perhaps."

"Is MetSatIV our communications link?"

"No, it's a general surveillance satellite. Outplanet, it's part of the passive sensor array for the whole planet; inplanet, it's a broad-band visual and EM scanner. If it had been up, for instance, we'd have found that life raft with less trouble."

"But the life raft's beacon—"

"Oh, it has a direct signal to GPS satellites. But they're not set up for visual scans. And the beacon has to be turned on by the occupant, after which it puts up a signal every two hours minimum. You can drift a long way in two hours."

"Tell me, Chief: if there hadn't been a life raft or a flight out here, and MetSatIV was down, would anyone have spotted a landing out here?"

"Landing, sir?"

"Landing . . . like . . . oh . . . drop shuttles from a warship?"

"On Copper Mountain? Well, Big Ocean is a training area for wet drops, but a ship couldn't get that close without the other units spotting it, even if MetSat IV were offline."

"What about the drop shuttles?"

"Once they were down below the horizon—I suppose—there aren't any ground scanners out here, of course. But—what made you think of that? And what difference would it make?"

"With all due respect for the honor of the Fleet, Chief, I've never known a society of saints. If there is a way to smuggle contraband and make a profit off it, people will do it. I can't think of a better way to smuggle than to be able to turn off the lights when you wish."

The chief flushed, but finally grinned. "Well, sir, you're right about that. I've never been on a ship that didn't have at least one unauthorized animal, person, or substance, be it what you will."

"So my question is, what might be smuggled that would involve the commander of the prison?"

"I don't know, sir."

"Nor I. But since I was headed for Stack Islands myself, I am naturally interested. Smuggling goes both ways—persons or materials can be introduced, or removed. The Weapons Research Facility naturally comes to mind—"

"Sir—" That was the corporal, his face now pale but no longer waxy greenish. His voice was weak, but clear enough.

"You need water and food," said the crew chief. "And I'll need to tell the pilot you're able to talk."

"I can give him something," Margiu said. The crew chief handed her one of the self-heating soup packets, already squeezed and warming, and went forward. When its heat stripe matched the dot at the end, Margiu put the tube to the corporal's mouth.

The professor waited until he'd finished, then said, "You had something to tell us?"

"Yes, sir. Commander Bacarion was one of Lepescu's followers," the corporal said. Margiu felt a sudden chill.

"Means nothing to me," the professor said. "You?" The crew chief shook his head. Margiu nodded.

"Admiral Lepescu was using prisoners as prey . . . he was part of a secret society that held manhunts. They used human ears as recognition symbols."

"How'd you know that?"

"I was reading up on Commander Heris Serrano—because of Xavier, it's my home planet, and she saved us—and found that after she resigned her commission, her crew had been condemned and used as prey. So I read what I could find on Lepescu. But—you're sure Bacarion's one of his followers? They were all arrested, I thought."

"Yes. She admitted it to me, when she tried to kill me the second time."

"The second time?"

"Yes. The first time she had someone push me off the cliff." Corporal Meharry coughed, then went on. "You mentioned

Commander Serrano, sir—my sister Methlin Meharry was one of Serrano's crew. She was imprisoned here, and then hunted later. She survived; she's back in Fleet now. So when I found out Bacarion had been on Lepescu's staff, I knew she'd do something. That's why I made preparations, and even so she almost got me. But that's not all—not just private vengeance, I mean. I'm sure she was up to something, but I couldn't figure out what."

"But now that we've thought of something—vague enough, still."

"The prisoners!" Meharry said. "Lepescu used prisoners before, as prey. What if she were using them a different way—as troops?"

"To do what?" the chief asked.

"Nothing good," the professor said. "Maybe she was going to sell them off to someone who wanted to hunt them, or maybe she was going to use them to hunt something . . . but whatever it was, it's bound to be bad."

"We must tell someone—" The same thought must have occurred to them all at once, from the startled glances.

"Yes, but who?" The chief shook his head. "Now our pilot, I'd trust—but you don't know him. For that matter, you don't know me."

"A bit late to worry about that now," the professor said. "And the pilot must know, you're right. And must inform as many others as possible. You do not run a major conspiracy from such a small base as Stack Three. You run a small one which you hope will become big. There must be plenty of people not involved within radio range."

"Big enough if they're behind turning off MetSatIV," the chief said. "And if it involves bringing a ship in. Using LACs means conspirators on that ship, a lot of them. The LAC flight crews, for instance, as well as a majority of bridge officers."

"What if they did embark convicts? Just the ones they'd picked? Then attacked the orbital station? They'd control access to the whole planet . . ."

"And the system defenses," the professor said. "And the weapons research labs. A fine start to a mutiny, if anyone wanted to start a mutiny."

CHAPTER EIGHTEEN

By the time Margiu and the others landed at Dark Harbor, their worst guesses had been confirmed.

"They've got the orbital station," an angry major told them, the cold wind whipping his uniform around his legs as he stood on the end of the quay. "We bounced your call up, but it was already happening. *Bonar Tighe* picked up convicts from Stack Three with its LACs, and armed them—used them as shock troops. We think—we hope—that somebody on the station got a tightbeam out and tripped the ansible alarm, but we aren't sure. The mutineers have cut off all communications from topside, and they can control the system defenses from there too. We know of six other ships insystem—anyone care to lay odds on how many of them are mutineers?" No one did.

"So what can we do?" asked the pilot.

"Damn little. Polacek over at Main has declared a state of emergency, of course, but there aren't any jump-capable ships onplanet, not even little ones. We don't have any missiles capable of taking out the station or any of the ships in space—why would we? We're stuck down a gravity well. I hate planets!"

Margiu had heard this before, from many a Fleet officer, but she was just as glad to be on something solid.

"Think they'll try to invade?" asked the professor.

"I don't know." The pilot shrugged. "Who knows what they're going to do? They're not telling us anything. Let's get all of you under cover, and see what else you might know. Does that corporal you rescued need a medical assist?"

"No, sir; I can walk." Corporal Meharry still looked pale to Margiu, but he was reasonably steady on his feet.

"Good. Chief, get this craft secured; I've arranged transport for the corpse. We'll need statements from all of you . . . where's that major?"

"Still pretty groggy, I imagine," the professor said. "I'm afraid I may have administered a stronger antinausea patch than necessary. I'd like to talk to your base commander, if I might."

Margiu looked at him. He had been calm and even cheerful until he'd thought of the mutiny, but now his face had stiffened into a grim mask. He caught her eye and managed a smile, but with none of his earlier warmth.

The little base headquarters seethed with tension and activity both. The major who had met them ushered them to the base commander's office. Lieutenant Commander Ardsan glowered at them for a long moment.

"It's not your fault, but I could wish you'd figured it out an hour earlier," he said. "Even an hour might've given those people a chance."

Margiu felt guilty, but the professor clearly didn't. "Nonsense, sir," he said. "An hour before, we were dealing with a corpse, a survivor, an oncoming squall . . . and I doubt very much that hour would have done more than prolong the carnage. The mutineers will have had accomplices on that station, as they had on Stack Three."

"You're probably right," Ardsan said. "But it's so frustrating—we don't have land lines everywhere, and with the mutineers in control topside, we can't get anything through the relay satellites." He pushed a data cube from side to side on his desk. "We have short-range ground radio, but they can interdict that from topside if they choose. They've cut off the weather information, too, which is going to make it hard to fly from one base to another. Polacek wants everyone to gather at Main, but that just makes us a handy target, the way I look at it."

"Are we sure of his loyalty?" the professor asked.

"I'm not sure of anyone right now. I never thought anything like this would happen, but then the whole Xavier mess shocked me. I don't understand it—"

"I think the point is how to handle it now," the professor said. "I have a very specific problem in mind. I'm a weapons specialist; I was on my way to Stack Two to consult on the progress of some of their research." He handed Ardsan a flake. "You'll want to check my clearance, of course."

"Of course," Ardsan murmured. He swung around and slid the flake into a slot in the cube reader. Margiu caught a glimpse of the screen before Ardsan flicked it off. "Well, that's clear enough." He looked pale. "I don't think I ever saw a—" He glanced at Margiu and away. "—Anyone with that level clearance before."

"Probably not," the professor said. "But we put our pants on one leg at a time, the same as you. Now. I happen to know that there are weapons under development there which you do not want the mutineers to have. And the fact of the matter is, if someone on that base is not part of this, I'll be very surprised."

"Why do you say that?"

"Why else would they start a mutiny here, in this system? Why not meet in some quiet out-of-the-way location, safe from discovery? I would wager that if Commander Bacarion had not been killed—if all had gone according to plan—one of those LACs would have picked up personnel and weapons from Stack Two. I suggest you check the records of the personnel stationed there very carefully."

Ardsan frowned. "We don't really have the facilities for that, Professor. I can look up who's in command, but that's about all. I'm not even sure I can get a list of personnel. With the mutineers in control of our communications, we can't access the personnel records back at Main, and we don't keep copies here at Dark Harbor."

"I see." The professor drummed his fingers on his knee for a long moment. "Well, Commander, if I were you I'd figure out a way to send some troops out there to secure the base."

"But—how?"

"We flew out there before. Can't we do it again?"

"But we have no weather data—they've cut off our feed from the weathersats."

The professor leaned forward. "Commander, I'm telling you—if you don't secure that base, and keep the mutiny from getting hold of those weapons, you'll wish you had to the end of your life, which will probably not be a long one. Now several things can happen. We can try to go back and not make it and crash in the sea. We can try to go back and—if enough of the personnel are involved—they might shoot us out of the sky, if they happen to notice us. We can get there and fail to secure the base, although I believe if you send along enough troops that won't happen. We can get there and secure the base, and the mutineers topside can land a force and drive us off . . . but if we have enough time, we'll have destroyed at least the worst of the weapons. Or we can sit here and do nothing, and be dead with no chance of helping out." He sat back. "I personally think that is the worst option."

"I—I should contact Commander Polacek."

"No, Commander, you should not. You've already said you aren't sure of his loyalty. You know communications are compromised. You know what my authority is."

"He's right," Margiu said, surprising herself by speaking up. "If we're going back out there, we have to do it before they send shuttles down."

Ardsan looked from one to the other, frowning. Finally he sighed. "All right. All right . . . let me think. We need transport that can land at Stack Two and carry troops—" He touched his desk comunit. "Chief—look up what we have on the personnel at Stack Two. And give me an estimate of our security forces here."

The professor interrupted. "Are there any heavy cargo craft based here?"

"We have the heavy-duty aircars we use along the coast, but we don't like to take them out over the open ocean. They sink like rocks if the power plant fails. That's why we use the amphibs."

"How long would it be before the mutineers could send shuttles down?"

"Depends on whether the station had any short-field shuttles ready to go. The usual shuttles require longer landing fields; there are only four long fields on the whole planet, and two of them are only used for emergencies. The LACs from *Bonar Tighe* can do it, of course, but they'll require refueling and service—at least a couple of hours of turnaround. Those other ships . . . I don't know which had LACs, and if those LACs were ready for drop. Then unless a ship did a low pass, the LACs would need several hours—I don't really know how many—to fly in. If they launched additional LACs immediately after taking the station, the mutineers could be on that island now. Or, if they're delayed, it could be tomorrow or the next day."

"And the flight times of your available craft?"

"Depends on the windspeed and direction—and we have no weathersats now. Five hours, six—I can't say exactly."

One of the enlisted men poked his head in the door. "Sir, Stack Two has thirteen civilian scientist personnel, five officers, and twenty-nine enlisted. Commander's a Lieutenant Commander Vinet. We've got fifteen NEM assault troops, and thirty ordinaries, plus the base police."

"Thank you. Carry on." Ardsan grimaced. "Enough to tempt us into trouble, and not enough to get us out—and if I strip Dark Harbor, there's no one to protect the people here—" Then he shook his head as if to clear it. "All right. It's something definite, at least. Professor, I assume you're going—"

"Absolutely," he said. "You need me to disable those weapons, and the scientists and engineers know me."

"Ensign, I'm assigning you to the professor, since he seems to have confided in you before. You are weapons-qualified, right?"

"Yes, sir." She had gone hunting as a girl; she knew she was good with firearms, and her qualifying scores had always maxed out.

"Good. I'll have the armsmaster issue you weapons; I want you to stick to the professor like glue, and watch his back. Just in case any of the people we send along aren't as loyal as we think they are."

"Yes, sir."

"Professor, it'll take some time to fuel the aircraft, brief the aircrew, and assemble the troops. You'd better eat and rest while you can. Ensign, you too—but you stick with him, you hear?"

"Yes, sir." She realized suddenly that she was very hungry, and also tired, and that she would have to go back out over that cold, wet, vast ocean . . . in the dark.

In the mess, where she and the professor ate, she overheard another conversation.

"It's that damned rejuvenation stuff," the crew chief said. "It doesn't take a grand admiral strategist to see what enormously prolonged youth will do to the career curve of anyone below rejuv age. Promotions started slowing down ten or fifteen years ago, right about when they were doing those senior NCO rejuvs . . . you don't spend all that money on rejuvenating someone and then retire 'em, now do you? And the people who might expect to step into that job see they won't have a chance. Expansion helped some, but how big a space force do we need?"

"But . . . mutiny, Chief. Can you see mutiny?"

"Not right away, no. And not for me, personally, ever. But there's been a rumor that something was wrong with the NCO rejuvenations, and some people—not me—said they were bollixed on purpose. It was one thing to have too many young-old admirals, but they didn't want the enlisted getting ideas."

"Now that makes no sense," the professor broke in. "Senior enlisted are the backbone of every successful military organization—always have been. Admirals are fine, and if you have a strategic genius you certainly want to keep him, but day to day, you need senior NCOs."

"Militaries have made that mistake before. Rank-heavy, officer dominated . . ."

"Well, I used to work in Personnel Procurement," another chief said. "Back when I was a young sergeant. I saw projections of need by rank and grade, and back then, at least, the planners knew they needed more master chiefs than admirals. So I don't think they'd deliberately sabotage a rejuvenation program for chiefs."

"Somebody sure did. Remember Chief Wang last year? We had to watch him every second, or he'd put a six-star fastener in a four-point hole, and tell everybody to do the same. I never saw anything like it, and it wasn't pretty."

"I thought they said it was some brain virus or something, from his fishing trips to the mountains."

"That's what they said then, but when we got that directive on removing rejuved chiefs from active duty until they'd been checked, that's who I thought of. 'Course, he was medically retired by then, but I asked Pauli in sickbay, and he said he thought it probably had been a bad rejuv."

"Bad rejuvs would let the people below move up . . ." a sergeant said softly. "Not that anyone would do something like that . . . I saw Chief Wang right at the end."

"Maybe they didn't know what it would do. I remember giving my mom's pet sarri a cookie once, just sharing, y'know, and it went into convulsions and died. I had no idea they couldn't eat our kind of food. But it was just as dead as if I'd poisoned it on purpose."

"That's true. Never attribute to malice what could be stupidity. It's just as likely to be a cost-containment effort by procurement or even the manufacturer."

Margiu had not even realized that some Fleet personnel had been rejuvenated; she couldn't remember anyone mentioning it in the Academy. She wondered if any of the people in that room had been rejuved. How could she tell?

When the professor finished eating, he touched her sleeve. "Ensign—we'd better get some rest while we can. Do you remember where Commander Ardsan said we could bunk?"

Margiu showed him to the assigned room—clearly an officer's quarters, now theirs for a few hours. They took turns in the shower, and changed into clean clothes. But before either of them dozed off, the commander told them that transport was ready.

This time the professor donned his PPU over street clothes, and then put his yellow leather jacket on top. "My friends out there will recognize this," he pointed out.

"You're a fine target that way." The major who had met them at the quay was in charge of the mission; Margiu now knew his name—Antony Garson. A Lieutenant Lightfoot commanded the troops.

"True, but if we have to make a hostile landing, at least *our* side will know who I am."

Margiu, who had on a clean PPU set to midnight blue, the default night-camouflage color, caught the major's eye. He shrugged, and went to check on the rest of the group. Though it was only afternoon, the heavy cloud cover and spitting rain made it seem much later.

By the time they neared the Stack Islands again, daylight had faded into murky night. They'd had clouds all the way, which was supposed to be protective, though Margiu found it dreary as the plane seemed to crawl between two layers of darkening gray. As the light failed, no lights came on in the plane—for security reasons, she was told—but she could feel, all around her, the bulky shapes of the NEMs. The professor had fallen asleep, snoring as musically as the first time, and Margiu leaned cautiously against his shoulder, letting herself doze. She couldn't lean the other way; the unfamiliar sidearm poked her. She woke when the plane slanted downward, and peered out the window into darkness.

"Umph!" That was the professor, almost choking on a final snore. "See anything?"

"No—it's all dark." How were they going to land? What if they ran into Stack Two, instead of landing on it? She could feel the plane sinking under her, and her ears popped repeatedly.

Then a sparkle of light appeared, somewhere in the gloom . . . a tiny bright line, then another line.

"Lights," she said to the professor.

As they drew closer, she could see that the lights outlined an ordinary runway, and other lights showed in buildings nearby. It looked so normal. . . .

The plane landed hard, bounced, came down firmly, and she rocked forward as the brakes caught. Instead of rolling up to one of the lighted buildings, the plane swung aside near the end of the landing strip. The NEMs were on their feet as soon as it landed. Margiu, lacking orders, stayed where she was; she and the professor had earbugs set to the same communications channel. Another plane, then another, came to a stop near them. In the dark, with only faint light from the runway lights, Margiu could just make out dark figures leaving one of the other planes.

Then someone forward opened the hatch of their plane, and a cold breath of sea air swirled into the plane, past the dark forms. Someone else muttered an order, and the troops began to move out into the night. Major Garson's voice in her earbug sounded calm: "Professor—you and the ensign come on, now." The professor heaved himself up, and Margiu scrambled out of her seat to follow him.

Outside, it was colder, but slightly less dark; Margiu could tell the professor from the others as a slightly lighter blur. She pulled up the hood of her PPU against the chill and stayed close to his side. A delicate red line pointed the way; someone had their laser guide on. She could feel the rasp of the runway surface under her boots. Was it safe? No one had fired a shot yet, and the troops seemed to know where they were going. She wasn't sure where the first troops had gone; she couldn't see them anymore.

"Looks secure for now, Professor," the major's voice spoke again in her earbug. "Come on inside."

Margiu felt more than saw the troops closing in around the them, a protective cordon, guiding them to one of the buildings near the landing strip. Ahead, a door opened, spilling out yellow light. She blinked, tried not to stare at the welcome light, but watched for any threat. She couldn't see anything but the troops who had come with them, and the dark night beyond.

Inside, Major Garson was talking to a lieutenant commander; both of them looked tense and unhappy. Armed guards stood at each exit. Margiu looked past them to the civilians—the other scientists, she supposed—in the large room.

"Oh, Lord, it *is* Gussie," one of the civilians said to the others. "Complete with that ugly yellow jacket and a cute redhead in tow..."

"She's not a cute redhead in tow, she's Ensign Pardalt." The professor nodded at her. "Show some respect; she's a very intelligent young woman—"

"Meaning he talked your ear off and you didn't object," the other man said, flashing a smile at Margiu. "I'm Helmut Swearingen, by the way." He turned back to the professor.

"When you didn't show up this morning, Gussie, and then those people took the station, we were afraid you'd been captured—"

"How far have you gotten?" the professor asked.

The other man grimaced and nodded toward the officers near the door. "Nowhere. As soon as we heard—and Ty was on the radio, trying to find out where you were, so we heard right away—I went to our base commander and told him we should start dismantling the work in progress, destroying notes. He wouldn't have it—insisted he had to wait for orders, that we were under Fleet discipline. Even said we might be mutineers ourselves. He's had us under guard, in this room—"

"What's he like?" the professor asked, in a lower voice.

"A worrier. The only good thing about him is that he's technically trained, so at least he's understood some of what we're doing. He's actually got an advanced degree, studied with Bruno at the Gradus Institute. But he's got a serious addiction to regulations, and he claims regulations won't let him make any independent decisions about what we have here."

"We don't have time to waste. What's his name?"

"Alcandor Vinet."

The two officers were glowering at each other now. Margiu looked from one to the other.

"Excuse me," the professor said. "Commander Vinet? I'm Professor Aidersson; you were expecting me this morning—"

"You're late, Professor," Vinet said. "But I suppose, under the circumstances, this is understandable."

"Yes," the professor said. "Now that I'm here, I'm taking charge of the research unit. We'll need to start clearing away files before the mutineers can capture—"

"You can't do that," Vinet said. "It's out of the question. I've had no orders from Headquarters—"

"Under the circumstances—" the professor began.

"He's got the highest level clearance and authorization," Garson said. "And I've got orders cut at Dark Harbor, directing you to give your complete cooperation."

"Dark Harbor's not in my chain of command," Vinet said. "And you don't have the rank, Major. How do I know you're not all mutineers, anyway?"

"All of us?" the professor's eyebrows rose steeply. "That's an interesting hypothesis, but do you have any data to support it? Why would mutineers want to deny other mutineers highly effective weaponry? I'm more inclined to suspect someone who tries to preserve it intact for capture."

Vinet turned red. "Are you accusing me of being a mutineer?"

"Not at all," the professor said. "I'm merely pointing out that your refusal to carry through on the very reasonable suggestions of my colleagues, or the orders I'm giving you, could be misunderstood in case of later investigation."

"That's ridiculous! This installation is extremely valuable; the equipment alone is worth—"

"Worthless to the Familias if it gets into the wrong hands. Worse than worthless. Don't you understand that?"

"Well . . . of course, but there's no proof the mutineers are after it. They may not even know about it."

"You're assuming they're stupid? That's not a good position to take. Commander, I'm afraid I must insist on your cooperation."

Margiu noticed Garson's signal to his troops. So, she saw, did Vinet. He sagged a little.

"Very well. But it's over my protest, and I will log this. If you had not barged in here with overwhelming force, you'd find yourself in the brig for such nonsense."

"Thank you," the professor said, with perfect courtesy. "I appreciate your position, and your assistance."

He led Margiu back to the cluster of civilians.

"Gussie, we had an idea—" one of them said. "Maybe we could mount the—" he lowered his voice, and Margiu heard only a mumble. "And then attack the mutineers."

"Mount it on a planet?" The professor pursed his lips. "That's interesting—that might actually work, if we have time. Do we have the supplies for adequate shielding?"

"Yes, if we dismantle a couple of other things. Oh, and Ty was working on breaking into their communications before Vinet snatched him out of the communications shack and stuck him in here with us."

The professor glanced at Margiu. "Ensign, you're going to be hearing many things you should not hear, and which I advise you to forget as quickly as possible. Do you have any specialty background in technical fields?"

"Aside from growing up making what we needed from scrap, no. Basic electronics and carpentry."

"Well, that may be useful. Come along; we're going to the labs . . ."

They began with a short meeting in what looked like a snack lounge, with a row of programmable food processors on one wall and battered chairs and couches around the others. A half-finished child's model of a space station cluttered the low table. Margiu had not suspected scientists of playing with such toys, and someone quickly moved it to a far corner.

"What have we got for communications?" the professor asked. "Ty?"

A skinny man with a bush of black hair came forward. "They've got the sats, but we can reach mainland with something I cobbled together. I want to send the specs for it over there, so they can build their own quickly. Getting into the mutineers' lines is going to be harder; they've got tight-link capability up there. But they've transmitted some outside that—I suspect to downside confederates—and that I can grab, if I have access to the equipment. I can tight-link if you give me an hour or so—it only takes reconfiguring some modules from one of the labs—but we don't have anyone to send to."

"What about scan? Can we detect anything beyond atmosphere?"

"Well—only for whatever's in our horizon. The problem's going to be tracking, not to mention what's below horizon. Knurri had a telescope with a motorized equatorial mount we could've used, but he took it with him when he went on leave. We can point something up, but we won't have an accurate fix if we do find a ship."

"Do you need anyone else to help you?"

"No, not really. There's a pretty decent enlisted tech I could use, but I'm a little worried that the mutineers had one or more agents on this base—and he'd be the logical one."

"Fine—Ensign, get Ty an escort from our group to the communications shack, would you?"

She was supposed to guard his back, but this required only going to the door. Lieutenant Lightfoot was outside, waiting; he called over two NEMs who went off with Ty.

"Now—Cole, you said you had an idea?"

"Yeah—Jen and I think it might be possible to rig the big guy for planet-to-space work. We've been trying to come up with the best way to acquire and track the target—"

"Which target?"

"Well . . . we're pretty sure we can take out the orbital station, and any ships docked there. Distant stuff, without the use of satellite-based scans, is going to be harder—"

"But I think we could do it," a woman said. "If we take out the station, then get the satellites linked to us—"

"How many hours?" the professor asked.

"Six or seven to mount the weapon, and it'll take a lot of personnel."

"We may not have six or seven hours," the professor said. "We need to know if they're coming, and how soon. Jen, what about scan within atmosphere? Is there any way to get access to the satellite data?"

"Not right now. What we have here is basically old-style radar, for spotting and guiding air traffic, and a little local-weather scanner. The range is so short that we couldn't spot incoming LACs in time to do anything useful. We haven't needed more than that; we had the satellite data for longscan. We really need those satellites, and for that we'll need to break their lock. It's not going to be easy, and it's going to take time."

"Which, again, we may not have. Bob, what about Project Zed?"

"Operational. And we really don't want them to have it."

"It actually works?"

"Oh yeah. If this were a ship, and not an island, I could flip the switch and they'd never find us. A big improvement over the earlier models. Unfortunately, as it is an island, it's easily located no matter what cloud we wrap around ourselves."

Margiu realized with a start that they were talking about new stealth gear.

"Could it be used to cover a retreat in the aircraft? If we took the data and ran for the mainland?"

"I suppose." The other man looked thoughtful. "We haven't tried it on aircraft . . . how much can those planes lift?"

"I'll ask," the professor said. He glanced at Margiu, who headed for the door again. She passed the question off to Lightfoot, and went back to the professor. In that brief interval, the discussion had already turned too technical for her understanding, but it came to an abrupt end when someone pounded on the door.

"Come in," the professor called.

Ty came in. "I've found two things—one's a datalog showing transmissions to this station from Stack Three five days ago. From Bacarion. I think someone here's on their payroll."

"Most likely," the professor said. "And?"

"And a transmission from orbit to this station, just now. Personal for Lieutenant Commander Vinet."

"For Vinet! I'd never have guessed he was part of it," Swearingen said. "He's such a fusspot. Did you answer it?"

"No, just acknowledged receipt, using the same sig code that was logged for reply to the others. But I did take a look—"

"Wasn't it encrypted?" someone asked.

"Yah, but a simple one. Not hard to break. Thing is, he's not only part of it, they were telling him they'd be coming down in a day or so, and not to worry—that they'd prevented anyone from sending word from the station. So here we are, nobody else knows what's going on."

Margiu spoke up. "We have to get word out somehow!"

The professor looked at her. "You're quite right, Ensign. And we have to keep them upstairs from finding out that we're here, if possible, to give ourselves time to work—to get word out somehow, to destroy what we can't protect."

Margiu noticed that he didn't say "to get away safely."

"We'll need the troops that came with you, Gussie, to keep the baddies out of our hair."

"Right. Ty, did your guard come back with you?"

"No, I left him there to guard the equipment."

"Ensign, we'll need Major Garson." Margiu told Lightfoot, who hurried off, and in a minute or two Garson appeared.

He listened to Ty's report, scowling. "I'll put Vinet under arrest, then. I wonder how many baddies were with him."

"And I wonder how many are with you, sir," the professor said.

"None, I hope," Garson said. "Can you people take care of the rest of it?"

"Building a tightbeam with the power to a ship insystem, yes. Building a scan to locate such a ship, yes. Destroy the more delicate research, and the records, yes. But it will take time, Major. There are only fourteen of us, and some of the work is specialized enough that only one person can do it. So we'd best get at it." He nodded to Garson, and the major withdrew. The professor turned to the group. "One thing worries me."

"Only one?" Swearingen asked, grinning.

"If they don't know we're here, they won't be in as big a hurry to get down here . . . but when the cloud cover goes, they'll be bound to take a look. And they'll see our transports sitting there like a sign in capital letters: TROUBLE HERE."

"We could send them back," Swearingen said. "But then we'd be stuck here. Besides, the latent heat would still show on a fine-grain IR scan."

"If you just want to hide the planes from scan," Bob said, "we can do that with Zed. Set it for just those parameters. It'd be a good test—"

"And if it fails, they'd not only know we were here, but they'd also know about Zed."

"It's a lot quicker to dismantle and destroy than the big guy," Bob said.

"How many more hours of darkness? And does anyone have a clue about the weather?" The professor looked around the group.

"Local sunrise is at 8:13 tomorrow; it'll be light before that, of course, if it's clear."

"And we have no weathersats . . . but we can always go outside and look."

When they opened the door, a squad waited to accompany them. The professor told Ty to get back to the communications shack; half the squad went with him. With the others he went outside to look at the weather. Outside, a cold wet wind scoured the ground. Margiu stayed close to the professor, looking up only once to see that no stars showed.

"I can't tell," the professor said finally. "Bob, go on and rig Zed to cover the planes. We'll start dismantling the other stuff—"

"Professor—" That was Major Garson. "We can't find Vinet, or several others. I want all of you back inside, until we find him."

"That could take days," Swearingen said. "Some of the labs are underground, connected by tunnels."

"Ty's at the communications shack," the professor said. "He has guards, but—"

A flare of light, followed in moments by a *whoomp*. Down the runway, one of the planes was blazing, the flames shooting up to glow on the underside of the clouds.

"Great," Garson said. "They can spot *that* right through the cloud cover. Go on now—get inside, get under cover."

"Where's Lieutenant Lightfoot?" Margiu asked.

"I don't know—he's not answering the com." Another, brighter flare of light painted one side of the major's face, and another explosion rolled through the night. The second plane. "Ensign, switch your PPU mask to enhanced, and get these civilians back under cover. That yellow jacket makes a fine target."

Margiu fumbled for the mask controls, and hit suit reflectivity by mistake. Her suit turned silver, then back to dark blue as she turned it off. Then she found the right set of buttons, and instead of dark clouds and a distant fire, she was looking at a scene painted by someone with a passion for shades of amber and orange. She could see little orange figures moving around, some with green triangles for heads; the blazing fire looked black. As her eyes adjusted, she noticed that the professor had a green triangle, and so did the NEMs around them.

Then a turquoise line stabbed across her vision, to crawl up the professor's sleeve toward his head. Margiu threw herself at him, hooked a leg behind his, and they fell together as a shot whined past and smacked into the armor of the NEM on the other side. He staggered, then all of the NEMs dropped as one.

"Target acquired," the one beside Margiu said. "Mark hostile—" Margiu turned her head and saw that one orange figure now had a red square on top. Another of the NEMs fired, and the distant figure went down. She lifted her head, and the NEM shoved it back down. "Not yet, Ensign. May not be dead, and may be others."

"Casualties?" That was Garson, on the com.

"No, sir. Small arms fire only; didn't penetrate armor. Civilians all unharmed."

"Who's on high guard?"

"Turak and Benits—report!"

"No activity on the roof—nothing, sir."

"Let's get them inside."

The NEMs formed a double row of armor, and the civilians crawled carefully between them into the building, but no more shots were fired. Margiu took a last look through her enhanced mask, and the orange figure still lay where it had fallen. Then a network of turquoise lines appeared, coming from several angles to converge on the antenna cover of the communications building. She leaned out to see, and a NEM yanked her back.

"Are you trying to get killed?" a woman's voice asked.

"No, I just—"

"Get inside, stay inside, take care of your professor!"

Margiu followed the others into the windowless break room; the professor was looking at her in a way that made her uncomfortable.

"What are they doing?" Swearingen asked.

"I think they're trying to destroy the antenna array," Margiu said. "It's under that dome on the communications building, isn't it?"

"Yes. And if they succeed, we're not going to be able to use a tight-beam, even if we construct one."

"Why a tightbeam?" Margiu asked.

"Goes farther, carries more data. We might even be able to reach the system ansible, if we can get a fix on it. That would get word out."

"But—wouldn't a regular broadcast disperse more widely, giving you more chance to warn any incoming ship that wasn't part of the mutiny?"

The professor looked thoughtful. "You mean—like old-fashioned broadcasting?"

"Yes. If you have enough power—"

"And the antenna is much easier to make. You may have saved more than my life, Ensign."

The R.S.S. *Vigor* came through the jump point in textbook fashion. Just because they knew they were coming into a secure system, just because nothing could possibly be wrong, was no reason to be careless. Captain Satir would not have paid attention if anyone had complained, and no one did: Satir was a good captain, and his fussy adherence to every little jot and tittle of the rules had saved lives before.

Now *Vigor* slowed to scan the system defenses and monitor system message traffic before proceeding insystem, even as her beacon automatically informed the system who she was. As she dumped velocity, the communications officer stripped one message after another, hardly glancing at them as they came off the printer— Captain Satir demanded hardcopy, even if that did mean plenty of recycling. He handed them to the captain's runner, who took them to Satir. Satir was already alert, peering at the system scan.

"I've been to Copper Mountain eight times, and the outer loop's never been *all* red," his scan officer was saying.

"I've been here ten times and never seen this many big ships insystem. What's going on, I wonder?"

"We're ten minutes out—twenty delay on queries."

"I don't think I want to talk to the station. Put us at battle stations, Tony, but don't light up the weapons." The alarms rang through the ship; colored lights danced across the various control boards reporting systems in operation. Satir glanced at the sheets of paper in his lap. Trouble. Major trouble.

"Sir, there's an odd signal coming in—you need to see it now."

"Odd how?"

"Not the usual frequencies, for one thing. It's surface propagated, but not a coherent signal—it's like they didn't care who picked it up. It'd dissipate to noise within this system, though."

"And it says?"

"It's in clear, and it says there's a mutiny at Copper Mountain, that the mutineers have the orbital station and control of system defenses. It's begging somebody to get the word out."

Captain Satir looked at his bridge officers. If this was a hoax, reacting as if it were real could end his career. If it was not a hoax, he had only one chance to get away.

Even as he hesitated, a bank of lights on the scan desks came alight.

"They're aiming at *us*," his scan officer said. "Tracking us—"

"Full ahead, find us a slot and take us to jump," Satir said. "We're getting out of here while we can." *Vigor* had the speed and the angle; none of the ships insystem could catch them in straight flight, and he was prepared to jump blind if necessary to put more distance between them. The system defenses were preset to defend certain arcs which he could easily avoid. "Make extra copies of all scan data, and try a squirt at the system ansible as we go by—they may have reprogrammed it, but it's worth a try."

Four days later, *Vigor* came in range of an ansible in another system, and transmitted an emergency override command set, followed by the entire load of scan data she'd collected.

CHAPTER NINETEEN

Sirialis

The long room with its high ceiling would have held twenty pairs of fencers, and had before. The walls were pale green above the mirrors, and the gilt beaded molding around the ceiling was echoed by the molding around the mirrors. The east wall, a bank of French windows, let in the natural daylight and overlooked a rose garden. This morning, bars of yellow sunlight lay across the polished wood floor. Only a few roses had opened, the early white single ones like showers of stars, but their perfume entered on the slightest movement of air. Down the middle of the polished parquet floor ran the strip, deep green.

Miranda finished her stretches, and picked up her practice foil. Facing the mirrors, she could see that Pedar, though still stretching, was watching her. She moved through the parries, smoothly but not fast, feeling for the rhythm that would best suit her needs. He finished his stretches, but made no move to pick up his own blade. He stood watching her instead. She met his eyes in the mirror, then turned.

"What? Am I doing something wrong?"

"No, my dear. I was thinking how lovely you are—and how incongruous it always is to see a beautiful woman holding a deadly weapon."

"This?" Miranda laughed, touching the button, and bending the blade with only a little pressure. "Even if it weren't so whippy, it could hardly kill anyone."

"It's the principle of the thing," Pedar said. "And I've seen you with stiffer blades."

Miranda grimaced. "I was younger, then."

"You were Ladies' Champion in epee . . . I have never forgotten your grace, that day."

"I was lucky. Berenice ran out of breath—I've always suspected she had a cold. Usually she beat me."

"But still—if you had live steel in hand, in the old days, I don't doubt you'd have been a formidable opponent."

"I'll take that as a compliment," Miranda said. "Shall we?"

Still he didn't move. "I was going to ask a favor."

"A favor? What?"

"I see you have Bunny's old collection here—in the hall. I know he never let anyone actually use it, but—do you suppose we could?"

Bait and hook, taken faster than she'd expected. She frowned a little. "The old weapons? But Pedar—they're *old*. I don't even know how old, some of them."

"If I could just hold them—just feel them."

"I don't even know if they're really mine to lend," Miranda said. "I mean, they're here because Bunny brought them along, but they are his family's heirlooms. You're the one who said I should be fair to Harlis—"

"Harlis need never know," Pedar said. "It's just—the oldest steel I've ever held was that antique Georgy has—you know."

"Oh, that old thing." Miranda allowed herself a sniff. "It's not a day over two hundred, whatever he says. These are much older—"

"I know, that's why I asked. Please?" He cocked his head and put his hands together like a polite child.

"I suppose it couldn't hurt," Miranda said. "If we're careful . . ." She could feel her heart speed up, safely hidden under her white jacket, as she led the way back to the hall.

She unlocked the case, and stood back. Pedar reached past her, and took out, as she'd expected, the big saber with the heavy, ornamented hilt. He ran his thumb down the blade, and nodded. "Still—"

"Bunny said they were still usable," Miranda said. "But he didn't want to take a chance on breakage. They're not replaceable."

"No . . ." Pedar breathed on the blade, then buffed it with his sleeve. "Derrigay work, look at that pattern! And the ring—" He rapped it with his nail, and the blade chimed softly. Miranda shivered, involuntarily. Pedar set the blade back, and took down another. "You have no idea of their age?"

"Bunny always said that one—the epee—was the oldest, and the rapier the next oldest. He said it was just possible those two were from Old Earth from an era when they might have been used." Used to kill, intentionally. Used as she would use a blade today.

"Amazing." Pedar put the rapier back, and took the broad, curved blade for which she had no name. "And this?"

"I don't know. It looks more like a chopper to me—for very large potatoes."

He chuckled. "Not a blade for artistry, no. An executioner's weapon, perhaps, from a very bloody period." His hand reached again, this time for a foil. "So—this is your weight now?" His hand stroked the blade, bent it. "Not so whippy as the one you were using, but—light enough, I'll warrant."

"Oh, probably. I still practice with heavier blades now and then." She had to be fair. She had to be scrupulously fair, and let his own folly put him in danger.

"Let's fence with these, not the modern ones."

"I don't think it's a good idea . . . I don't know what they would think—"

"They? What 'they'? Who could possibly dispute with you, now that the judgement has gone your way? What harm could it cause?"

"I don't know," Miranda said again. "What if a blade breaks? What if Harlis appeals, and then finds out I've destroyed a valuable asset?"

"He needn't know. He isn't a fencer; he's probably never paid attention to them. Besides . . . I'll explain it was all my idea." Pedar nodded at the helms. "Look—let's do it right. Use all the old gear, masks as well. It would be like fancy dress." He had always liked fancy dress; he had worn it to balls where other men wore conventional clothes.

"But—"

"Just this once. There's no one to see. Please?" Again that tip of the head, the pleading expression, then an impish grin. "I'll bet you've always wanted to. Haven't you?"

Miranda smiled. "As a matter of fact . . . I did sneak that one out once—" She nodded at the blade in his hand. "There's something about it—knowing it's old, knowing it was used by people long dead—"

"Yesss." He drew out the syllable, nodding. "I thought so. Just as you enjoy old porcelain, or jewelry. Those who appreciate such things should not be forbidden the use of them. So you will humor me this once, Miranda?"

She glanced around, as if nervous of watchers. "I suppose—and after all, if we do break one, and Harlis finds out—as you said, he's no fencer. He can hardly skewer me."

"Well, my lady—choose your weapon." Pedar set the blade he'd been holding back in the rack and waved her forward with an extravagant gesture.

Miranda reached, pulled back as if unsure, and finally took the blade he had just replaced, the longest of the foils, with a weighted hilt to balance it. He took its partner.

"Let's complete the mischief," Pedar said. "As I said, with such blades as these, our helms too should match. I've long fancied myself in one of these—had my armorer make a replica, but it's not the same." He tried on one, then another, until he found one that fit . . . the others had, as she knew well, inconvenient and uncomfortable lumps beneath the linings.

Miranda raised her brows at him. "It can't be safe, Pedar—blades last, but old metal screening—"

"Pah! It will stand up to a blunted stroke, and if I cannot defend my face at least I'm not much of a fighter. Come, my dear . . . if you are nervous, you must wear your usual mask, but permit me my conceit. The only way you will strike my eye is with your beauty."

It needed only that to erode the last grain of sympathy Miranda felt. She could have shot him where he stood, but she was not going to trial for the murder of a murderer.

Back in the salle, after they had clipped the buttons to the tips of the blades, Pedar moved out of the shadow to stand in one of the bars of sun, a glowing white figure with a shining golden-bronze head; the old helm gleamed in the light. She could not see his face through the pierced metal. From within her own mask, the world narrowed to the strip itself, and the opponent across from her. Could he see her face? She let herself smile now, with no guarding tension.

She brought her blade up in salute, as did he. Then he advanced.

They began with the formal introduction, the "Fingertips" as advocated by the fencing master Eduardo Callin, two centuries before. This allowed the fencer who wished a match to carry more meanings to suggest them by the quality of his touch, and this first contact, feeble to feeble, set up that possibility. Miranda's blade tapped crisply, to signal no particular intent, but Pedar's drew along hers, or tried to—the signal that for him, this match's metaphor was Courtship.

Miranda could feel her lip curling, within her mask, and fought down the rush of anger. Here, at the ritualized beginning, she must maintain her ruse. At the fourth touch, her tip wavered a little—someone who had recognized his offering, and was not yet rejecting it. Thinking about it perhaps. His fifth touch, the last of the right-hand touches, attempted a spiral along her blade, which she did not allow, but did not bat away. That signified Shyness, not Rejection.

They switched hands for the next five Fingertips. His tip continued its swirl, a stronger plea of Courtship; Miranda allowed hers to droop, on the ninth and next to last. Uncertainty—the last thing she felt, but an emotion she hoped he would have for one last instant. Then the tenth—a clean tap by both to signal the end of that segment. She stepped back, as did he, and switched her blade to her right hand again. Another bow and salute, and they were into the next phase.

Miranda presented a quite ordinary opening in Fourth, and Pedar accepted. In a friendly bout such as this, there was no hurry, so they crossed blades in easy parry-riposte combinations for some fifteen exchanges.

"You're so graceful," Pedar said, his voice muffled slightly by the mask.

"You're so quick," Miranda said, out of her throat so that she would sound a little breathless.

"For you, I would gladly slow," he said. His next stroke was slightly slower, and she met it just an instant late. If she could convince him to slow, if she could set a pace that lulled him into the wrong rhythm . . .

"I used to be faster," she said. "I know I did—"

"It's that blade, my dear. It's heavy for you."

"I need something—" She blocked his stroke, threw one intentionally slow which he blocked easily. "Against you, I need the extra length, and the stiffness—"

"Bah. I'm not going to press you harder than you can handle. You should know that, Miranda. When was I ever importunate?"

"You weren't. It's just—"

He stepped back and grounded his blade. "Come—let's exchange blades. That was made for a man; you can tell by the weight of the hilt."

"Besides, you want to try it," she said, chuckling.

"True. Indulge me, my dear?"

"Very well. But I'm going to do more conditioning, I swear I am. I didn't realize how out of shape I was. All those days of the funeral, and arrangements—"

"Of course." He handed her the foil hiltfirst over his arm, with a bow. If only his courtesy meant something! She handed him her weapon with equal grace, and they exchanged places on the strip, as always after an exchange of weapons.

Miranda was sure she knew which of the old weapons had actually drawn blood. She knew nothing would show on analysis; she knew her belief was irrational and indefensible, but . . . the foil conveyed to her an eagerness for blood that matched her own. It had from the moment she first handled the old weapons.

They were just poised to begin again when her comunit chimed. "Milady—Lady Cecelia de Marktos called; she has docked and taken one of the personal shuttles."

Cecelia coming? Bright anger washed over her. She had been so close; she might never have another chance. Why couldn't Cecelia mind her own business? And where was she coming from? How many minutes did she have, now, to finish Pedar?

With an effort, she regained her concentration. She would figure out something . . . as long as it was over before Cecelia walked in . . .

She found it hard, at first, to conceal the speed the foil lent her. Beat, parry, parry, beat, beat. Her heart hammered, more excitement than effort; she dared not use her own pulse for a timer. She dared not wait too long, either.

She backed a pace, then another, then, with a quick disengage, lunged and made the touch. With contact, she twisted her wrist and pushed, taking Pedar's tip on her left shoulder. Through her hand, she felt the faintest give to the tip.

"We're both dead," she said with a smile. The mask across from her gave no hint of Pedar's expression; he stepped back as she did to salute and begin again.

Was the tip gone? The foil felt no different; she parried his next stroke, and his next, and then she heard it. The tip gave way, flipped by her blade's elastic recoil into a parabolic arc; she had to drag her eyes away from it to check the break. Pedar froze an instant, then started to withdraw.

"I'm afraid a blade broke—" he said. She saw the tilt of his helm, as he looked to check his own, saw it move back.

She waited, until she knew he had time to see her blade, the sharp tip exposed by the spiral fracture.

"Miranda—?" For the first time, his voice was uncertain.

He was good; he almost parried the lightning thrust she sent at his mask—but he had dropped his arm, lost his rhythm, and responded that fractional second late. The tip of her blade—stiffer now and sharp—slammed into her target, a particular perforation in the metal of his mask. Around it, the weakened metal gave way, and she thrust on, the broken tip grating over the orbit's rim into the eye she could not see, into the brain behind it, with a wrist motion that ensured more than a single damage track. Her blade snapped again, on the back of his skull, and quickly as she withdrew it, he was already falling.

"Ohhh . . ." She sank with him, still watchful until his hand loosened and dropped his weapon. Then she dropped her own sword, grabbed at his shoulders. "Noooo. . . . ! Pedar! NO!!"

Cecelia heard the cry as she came through the door, and saw Miranda, recognizable by both form and the golden hair that spilled out the back of her helm, facing away from her, clutching at the shoulders of her opponent, who was collapsing. She moved forward quickly. Was it Pedar, or someone else?

Miranda was scrabbling at the other person's mask, trying to get it off.

"Miranda—let me help. Call medical—"

"It won't come off—it won't come off!" Miranda seemed frantic, her gloved fingers clumsily yanking at some kind of latch. Now Cecelia could see the blood trickling out where the mask had given way, and the blood on the broken short length of blade. "I told him! I told him it was dangerous! Bunny always said no one should use the old blades, or trust the old armor, but he wanted to—he insisted—"

Cecelia discovered that her mind was already working again, when she recognized all this as elements of alibi. She worked at the other side of the man's helm, wondering why the ancients had made everything so complicated. Surely this hadn't been made before the advent of pressure locks.

"What happened?"

"The blade broke—I was lunging—and it just shattered—"

Cecelia looked, but could see only the shadowed shape of Miranda's face behind her mask.

"I thought you said fencing was safe." Pedar had said that too, at the Trials. *As long as it is only steel,* he had said.

"It is. It's—he wanted to use the old blades, the ones Bunny would never use. He knew Harlis wouldn't allow it, but . . . then he said, why not the old helms. He was in one of his moods—you know how Pedar is. He'd brought me a lace scarf. He began with the Courtship, in the Ten Fingers."

Cecelia had one side of the helm loose now, and began working on the other.

"You didn't call for medical help."

"Cece—when a blade goes in the eye, there *is* no help."

"In the eye?"

"This old helm—the face mask failed. My blade went straight through, into his eye. You know how it is—well, you don't, but when you thrust, if your blade snaps, you're already moving, you can't stop. I tried—but all I did was make it worse."

"How?"

"The blade had already pierced his eye and the orbit—of course I yanked it back, but it was already in his brain. I didn't realize—it was so awful—"

She had the other side of the helm open, and lifted it away. There was Pedar's face, one eye open but dulled already with anoxia, and the other a bloody hole.

"Miranda." Cecelia looked at her, trying to see through that mask. But sunlight blazed on the metal, and behind it was only shadow. She looked down at the gloved hands, one streaked with blood . . . at

Miranda's neck, where the high collar of her fencing habit hid her pulse.

The door slammed open now, and a crowd of servants rushed in. Where had they been all this time? Was it a plot?

"Milady! What happened—"

"We were fencing, and the blade broke . . ."

Miranda took her own mask off slowly, her hands trembling. Tears had streaked her cheeks; she looked paler than usual, with red-rimmed eyes.

"You cried—" Cecelia said.

"Of course I cried!" Miranda glared at her.

"I've never seen you cry before, except for Bunny—"

"You didn't see me when I heard about Brun's capture. Or when the babies were born." She turned to the man in the gray suit; Cecelia did not recognize him. "Sammins, we'll need a doctor, though I know it's too late, and the militia. This man is—was—Minister of Foreign Affairs; we'll have to have an investigation."

All though the questions that followed, Cecelia sat quietly to one side, watching Miranda, listening to the timbre of her voice. Pedar had been coming to fence twice weekly since arriving on Sirialis. Pedar had initiated the practices; he had also come to talk business, and—she hesitated, and a faint color came into her cheeks—to propose a Familial alliance. On that day, they had begun as usual, but Pedar had asked—as he had before—about the antique weapons in the hall. Where were they going, and who would inherit them? He had wanted to handle them, fence with them. Bunny had never allowed it, but Pedar had begged—

And she had given in, agreed to fence with the old weapons, though they had not been inspected.

She must have scan data, Cecelia realized. She would not dare go into such detail if scan would not support what she said. And therefore—it could be an accident, just as Miranda said. Or she was even cleverer at arranging matters.

Slow anger churned her stomach. These had been her friends—or at least people she had known, people of her class. Wealthy, urbane, sophisticated . . . she had known them all her life. They collected fine art; they supported composers and artists and musicians; they had beautiful houses and landscaped grounds. They dabbled in this or that—china painting, horse breeding, designing exotic space stations—in between power plays in Family politics and acquiring more money and more power and more possessions. They wore beautiful clothes, and indulged in elaborate games of social intercourse.

And now they were killing each other off. Lorenza, trying to poison her. Kemtre, agreeing to poison his own son. Someone—Pedar, by his bragging—arranging to kill Bunny. Miranda killing Pedar.

Were they all crazy?

And if they were . . . why? And who benefitted?

She could not find her way through that maze, except in terms of the familiar, beloved world of equestrian sports and horse breeding. If she'd had a stable full of highbred horses, all carefully brought up, schooled . . . and if they had suddenly begun to act strange, to attack grooms and each other . . . what would she think?

Somebody got at the grooms.

Fine, but rich people didn't *have* grooms.

Her mind stopped short, like a horse overfaced by a huge, unfamiliar obstacle on the cross-country.

Yes, they did have grooms, and veterinarians. They called them maids and valets and doctors and nurses. They all depended on pharmaceuticals for rejuv. They had all been rejuved multiple times. Lorenza, Kemtre, Pedar, Miranda, even her own sister Berenice. Some had access to other illicit drugs, like the neurotoxins Lorenza had poisoned her with.

Once she'd known Lorenza was dead, she'd given no serious thought to the source of that drug. Lorenza was a mean, vicious, sadistic woman . . . that was the threat, not the drug. It's not the weapon, it's the person who misuses it.

But . . . she knew. She knew about Patchcock, though she'd put it out of her mind when Ronnie and Raffa were safely married. Bad drugs. Bad rejuvenation drugs, and who knows what else, and the fallout might be worse than anyone had thought.

Was Miranda sane? Were *any* of them sane? The Grand Council of the Familias . . . without Bunny at its head, or Kevil Mahoney to advise, with Pedar—evil as she now believed he was—dead and stiffening on the floor in the fencing salon . . . what were they going to do? Was there *anyone* she could trust?

Those who had never been rejuved. Those who had been rejuved only . . . somewhere the drugs were reliable. Marta Saenz? But just because Marta was a biochemist herself, with her own labs, did that mean her drugs were good?

No. But she could not distrust everyone. She wasn't made like that; she had to have sides, someone on hers and someone against her.

Finally the initial interviews were over, and Cecelia went up with Miranda to her suite. A white-faced maid brought them a tray of food and hot tea. Miranda stripped off her fencing whites, and took a shower while Cecelia stared out the tall windows to the hummocky country of the Blue Hunt. By the time Miranda came back in, wrapped in a thick quilted robe, Cecelia had her own questions in order.

"Miranda . . . remember when I told you what Pedar told me, shortly after Bunny died?"

"Of course," Miranda said. "You told me that you thought Pedar knew who had killed him, that it was not the NewTex Militia."

"Is . . . that . . . ?"

"Cecelia, Pedar has always been a bit of a boor, you know that."

"Yes, but—"

"He thought himself a man of power; he wanted to improve his status within the Conselline Sept. So naturally he claimed to have knowledge you didn't have."

"You didn't take him seriously."

"Not at first, no. He came courting, you see."

"Courting!"

"Yes. Hinting that if I had his protection, I need not fear Harlis's challenge to the will. That I would get to keep Sirialis—he meant *he* would get Sirialis."

"He honestly thought you would marry him?"

"Apparently. He asked if he could come here; I put him off several times, but finally consented."

"But why?"

Miranda shrugged. "I wanted to know what he knew—how he was so sure he could do what he claimed. It's not the kind of thing you can ask over a com line: 'Do you really have the power you say you have?' I thought, if he visited, I could assess his abilities and intentions better."

"But you weren't going to marry him—"

"Heavens, Cecelia, you do stick like a burr! No, I was not going to marry him. I'm not going to marry anyone. I'm going to fight Harlis, on Buttons' behalf, and save the inheritance, but I'm not going to marry. I had the best for most of my life; why would I settle for crumbs now?"

"I don't know—I just worry—"

"No need." Miranda stretched, then strolled over to the pool. Fat orange goldfish rose to the surface and swam nearer. "I'm not crazy; I didn't get my rejuv drugs from the Morrelines, and I'm not going to rejuv again. Once I get my children settled—"

"I thought I'd never get rejuved," Cecelia said. "Wouldn't have, if not for the poison. But I rather like it now."

"I understand that," Miranda said. "You have more things you want to do. But I'm nominal forty now, actual—well, you know the actuality—and have another sixty years of health without rejuv. Sixty years without Bunny is plenty."

"You might find someone else."

"And gold might drop from the sky in showers. If I do, I can rejuv then, if I want. But it's not something to plan on. End of discussion, Cece. Tell me, have you been down to the stables yet?"

"No—"

"Then you should. Just in case something happens, and Harlis ends up with Sirialis after all, you should know if there's anything here you'd like to put a bid on."

"I can't believe he'd be stupid enough to shut down the stables," Cecelia said.

"A horse broke his foot when he was a boy, and then he cracked some ribs falling off into rocks trying to keep up with Bunny. He thinks horses are large smelly abominations, a drain on the income— which they are, actually. We've never made money off the horses."

"Miranda—you're distracting me with horses, and I'm not that foolish. Did you kill Pedar on purpose?"

Miranda gave her a long, silent look. "Do you think I would do something like that?"

"I don't know anymore what people will and won't do. I didn't think Lorenza would poison me and gloat over me while I lay helpless. I didn't think Kemtre would drug his own sons, or connive at cloning. I didn't think Bunny's brother would terrorize an old lady into giving up her shares. Or that Pedar would have Bunny assassinated to get a Ministry."

"We're not answering each other's questions," Miranda said. "And I think that's probably wise. But I will remind you of that old, old rule."

"Which one?"

"A lady is never rude . . . by accident." Miranda put a dollop of honey in her cup, then sipped the tea. "I needed that."

"Sticking a blade into someone's brain and stirring goes beyond mere rudeness." Cecelia felt grumpy. She was sure she knew what had happened—or part of it—and yet Miranda wasn't reacting as she should.

"That's true," Miranda said. "But the rule applies in other situations as well. Cecelia, if you're going to make a fuss, please do so."

"You're not even asking me not to . . ."

"No. Your decisions are yours, as mine are mine."

"What are you going to tell your children?"

"That Pedar died in a fencing accident. They have brains, Cecelia, and imagination; they will put on it what construction they please."

Cecelia ate another jam-filled tart, and stared out the window again. After a long silence, she said, "I suppose it sends a message to Hobart . . ."

"I hope so," Miranda said.

CHAPTER TWENTY

Esmay scowled at the message strip the clerk handed her. They'd had it all arranged, she thought. Why meet in a private room, and not in the restaurant? She scanned the lift tubes, looking for the right range. Thirty-seven to forty . . . odd. Most tubes served at least ten floors. She tapped the access button.

"Room and name, please?"

What was this? If Barin had been there, she'd have whacked him in the head, but he wasn't. "3814," she said instead. "Lieutenant Suiza."

The lift tube access slid open, with the supporting grid glowing green for up. Esmay stepped in, and found herself in a mirrored cylinder that rose smoothly, with none of the exuberance of most lift tubes. Her ears popped once, then again. It was only thirty-eight floors—what was happening here?

She stepped out into a green-carpeted foyer, the walls striped in subtle shades of beige and cream. The pictures on the wall . . . she caught her breath at the bold geometric. Surely that was a reproduction—she stepped closer. No . . . the thick wedge of purple, that cast a shadow in every reproduction, cast a different shadow here, lit as it was by a pin spot on the opposite wall. Genuine Oskar Cramin. Then that might be a real Dessaline as well, its delicate traceries refusing to be overborne by the Cramin's almost brutal vigor. Quietly, with the confidence of greatness, the little gray and gold and black Dessaline held its place.

She shook her head and looked around. Beyond the foyer, a short hall had but four doors opening off it, and one was labelled SERVICE.

Barin must have spent a fortune . . . 3814 was the middle door. She moved into its recognition cone, and waited.

The door opened, and she was face to face with . . . a middle-aged woman she'd never seen. Before she could begin to stammer an apology, the woman spoke.

"Lieutenant Suiza! How good to meet you—I'm Podjar Serrano, Barin's mother."

Barin's mother. Panic seized her. She had been prepared for Barin, for a few stolen moments of privacy . . . a chance to talk before she met his mother.

"Come on in," Podjar was saying. "We're all dying to meet you."

We? What *we?* We *all?* She could hear a low hum of voices, and wanted nothing more than to run away. Where was Barin? How could he lead her into this?

Podjar had her by the arm—Barin's mother; she couldn't just pull away—and led her inside, to a room that seemed as big as a planet right then.

"Here she is at last," Podjar said to someone else, a short thickset man who had Barin's grin but nothing of his grace. Brother? Father? Uncle? "This is Kerin, my husband," Podjar said. Esmay hoped that meant he was Barin's father, because otherwise she hadn't a clue.

Farther into the room, her stunned wits began to register additional details. Not only was the room big, and arranged for entertaining, but it was comfortably full of people who all seemed to know each other. Barin's family?

"Esmay!" Her heart leapt. That was Barin, and he would get her out of this, whatever it was. He came toward her, clearly gleeful and full of himself. She could have killed him, and hoped he understood steel behind her fixed smile.

"I'm sorry I wasn't at the lift to meet you," he said. "I had an urgent call—"

Esmay couldn't bring herself to be polite and say it didn't matter. "What is this?" she said instead.

Barin grimaced. "It got out of hand," he said. "I wanted you to meet my parents, and they were coming through here on the way home. Then grandmother—" he waved; Esmay followed the gesture to see Admiral Vida Serrano at the far end of the room, surrounded by an earnest cluster of older people. "—Grandmother wanted to talk to you about something, and thought this would be a good opportunity. And then . . . they started precipitating, falling out of the sky . . ."

"Mmm." Esmay could not say any of what she was thinking, not with his parents standing there smiling at her a little nervously. "Are we . . . going to have a chance to talk?" By ourselves she meant.

"I don't know," Barin said. "I hope so. But—" His gaze slid to his mother, who quirked an eyebrow.

"Barin, you know it's important family business. We must confer."

Great. The only leave she'd been able to wangle, in the current crises, and it looked as if she'd be spending it conferring with his family instead of hers.

"How was your trip, Esmay?" asked Barin's father. He had lieutenant commander's insignia, with a technical flash.

"Fine, though we lost a day at Karpat for unscheduled maintenance procedures." She couldn't keep the edge out of her voice.

"Mmm. That's typical." Barin's father nodded across the room. "Let me show you to your room."

"My—"

"Of course you have your own room here. We may have descended in force, but we're not entirely uncivilized. You have to stay somewhere." Across the room, through another door, into another corridor . . . Esmay was by this time beyond astonishment when he showed her to a small suite, its sitting room wall showing a view of the station's exterior. "This is yours—and I'm sure the staff are sending up your things."

"I have only the carryon," Esmay said.

"Well, then. Come out when you're ready." With a smile, he turned away and closed the door behind him. Esmay sank down onto one of the rose-and-cream-striped chairs. What she wanted to do was put her head in her hands and scream. That wouldn't be productive, she was sure. But what was going on?

A tap on the door interrupted her uneasy thoughts. Her carryon? "Come in," she said. The door opened, and Barin stood there looking sheepish.

"May I?" he asked. Esmay nodded; he entered, shutting the door behind him, and pulled her up from the chair. She stiffened for a moment, then relaxed against him.

"Your family—" she began.

"I'm sorry. It wasn't my idea, but it is my family. They're . . . headstrong."

"And you aren't?" She wasn't ready to think it was funny; she wanted to indulge her annoyance—such justified annoyance—a little longer, but suddenly her sense of humor kicked in. She could just imagine Barin, having planned this quiet little retreat, being maneuvered by his powerful and numerous family. She stifled the giggle that tried to come out.

"Not headstrong enough," Barin said, with a rueful grin. "I tried to tell them to let us alone, but you see how well I did."

Esmay lost control of the giggle; she could feel it vibrating in her throat and then it was out.

"You aren't angry?" he asked hopefully.

"Not at you, anyway," Esmay said. "I suppose a quiet few days alone was too much to hope for."

"I didn't think so," Barin said. "You would think the entire universe was playing tricks on us—"

"Ummm . . . I've read that lovers always put themselves in the center of everything."

"I'd like to put us in the center of a bed, a long way from everywhere else," Barin said, with a hint of a growl.

"We'll get there," Esmay said. Her arms tightened around him; he felt as good as ever, and she wanted to melt right into him until their bones chimed together.

Someone knocked on the door. "Barin, if you don't let her get dressed, we'll never get to dinner—" A female voice, one she hadn't met yet.

"Oh, shut up," muttered Barin in Esmay's ear. "Why wasn't I born an orphan?"

"It would have been too simple," Esmay said. "Let me go—I want to change. And are we eating up here, or in public?" Not that the entire Serrano family wasn't public enough.

"Here. It's coming up." He let go, went to the door, and opened it. There stood a woman in her thirties, about Esmay's size, with the Serrano features.

"Esmay, I'm Dolcent. Barin—go away, I need to talk to her for a moment."

"I hate you," Barin said, but he left. Dolcent grinned.

"Listen—I gather you were expecting a quiet evening of entertainment and you have only one carryon. If I were in that situation, I'd have brought only the clothes I meant to wear, which weren't exactly family-meeting ones . . . so may I offer you something?"

Annoyance returned, a wave of it—who did they think they were?—but then she remembered the contents of her carryon. Clothes for a casual day or so with her fiance, one nice dress to meet the parents . . . blast the woman, she was right.

"Thank you," Esmay said, as graciously as she could while swallowing another lump of resentment.

"I wouldn't like having to borrow clothes, but there are times—look—"

She had to admit that Dolcent's offerings were better than anything she'd brought, and Dolcent's blue tunic over her own casual slacks met both requirements. Esmay thanked her.

"Never mind. I'll raid your wardrobe someday. If you make my little brother happy, that is."

"Otherwise you'll blow it up, eh?"

"Something like that," Dolcent said. "Or if you call me Dolly . . . just a warning." She grinned.

Dinner was less formal than she'd feared; the hotel staff brought in a buffet and left it, and people served themselves from it, sitting wherever they fancied. Esmay had a corner of a big puffy sofa with a table at her elbow, and Dolcent beside her, offering explanations. A man's voice emerged from the general babble.

"And I told him that technology wasn't mature enough, but he's determined—"

"Iones—a distant uncle. In material research; you just missed him when you were on *Koskiusko*," Dolcent said. "He's a terrible bore, but what he knows he really knows."

Then a woman, close enough to see. "—and if she *ever* takes that tone to me again, I'll rip the brass right off her—"

"And that's Bindi—never mind her; she's not as bad as she sounds."

A shrimp came flying through the air with deadly accuracy, to bounce off Dolcent's head. "Am I not, you miserable eavesdropper?"

Calmly, Dolcent picked up the shrimp and ate it. "No, you're not. Nor am I an eavesdropper, when you're talking loud enough to be heard three rooms away."

Bindi shrugged and turned away.

"Is it always like this?" Esmay asked.

"Usually worse. But I'll be accused of dire things if I try to explain Serrano family politics. You come from a large family yourself, right? You should know."

"Ummm . . ." There was, after all, some of the same flavor in the interactions. The loud ones, staking out their space and their areas of power; the quiet ones in the corners, raising a sardonic eyebrow now and then. Bindi would be an Aunt Sanni; Barin's mother, like her stepmother, seemed to be a quiet peacemaker.

Heris Serrano pulled up a chair to the other side of the end table, and sat down, and put her plate beside Esmay's. Esmay had never thought of Commander Serrano wearing anything but a uniform, but . . . here she was in silvery-green patterned silk, a loose tunic over flowing slacks.

"Esmay—I don't know if you remember me—"

"Yes, si—Commander—"

"Heris, please. This room's so full of rank otherwise, we can hardly talk to each other. I don't think I've seen you face to face to thank you for saving our skins at Xavier—and not just ours—"

"Heris, not during dinner—I know you're going to talk tactics to her sometime, but not now." Dolcent pointed with a crab leg, a gesture that would have been a deadly insult on Altiplano. "She's going to be married; you could at least choose a more suitable topic."

"And you'd talk clothes to her, 'Centa? Or flowers, or which way to fold the napkins at the reception?"

"Better than old battles during dinner." Dolcent didn't seem perturbed by Heris's intensity; Esmay watched with interest.

"Picked out a wedding outfit yet, Esmay?" Heris asked, with too much sugar in her voice.

"No, s—Heris. Brun says she's taking care of it."

"Dear . . . me. How did that happen?"

"She just . . ." Esmay waved her hands helplessly. "She found out I had no ideas, and then the next thing I knew she was sending me fabric samples and talking about designers."

"She is something, isn't she?" Heris chuckled. "You should have seen her years back, when she was really wild. If you're not careful, she'll organize the whole wedding."

Esmay was feeling reasonably relaxed and almost full when she saw Admiral Vida Serrano coming toward her, with an expression far less friendly than those around her. Like almost all the others, she wore civilian clothes, but that failed to disguise her nature. Esmay tried to get up, but the admiral waved her back.

"There's something you must know," Admiral Serrano said. "I haven't told the others because it didn't seem fair to tell them behind your back. It's not widely known—in fact, it's been safely buried for centuries. But since those idiots in Medical sent most of the flag officers off on indefinite inactive status, several of us decided to clean up the Serrano archives, and transfer them onto more modern data storage media."

"Yes, sir?" She would call Heris by her first name if she insisted, but she wasn't going to call the admiral anything but "sir," whether or not she was in uniform.

"You know the official history of the Regular Space Service—how it is an amalgam of the private spacegoing militias of the founding Families?"

"Yes . . ."

"What you may not know is that despite the effort made to eradicate the memory of which Fleet family once served which Family, these realities still influence Fleet policy. Perhaps more than they should. The Serrano legacy—to the extent that we have one—consists in the peculiar fact of our origin."

A long pause, during which Esmay tried to guess which of the great families had once had the Serranos as no-doubt-difficult bodyguards.

"Our Family was destroyed," the admiral said finally. "We were the spacegoing militia; we were, at the time of the political cataclysm that wiped out our employers, far away guarding their ships. After that, we could not go back—for obvious reasons—and when the Regular Space Service was organized some thirty T-years later, most of our family petitioned to be enrolled. We were considered, by some, safer . . . because we were unaligned."

Esmay could think of nothing to say.

"This much is well-known, at least to most of the senior members of Fleet, and it's been at the root of some resentment of the Serrano influence. Every generation or so, some smart aleck from another Fleet family tries to suggest that we were part of the rebellion against our Family, and then we have to respond. If we're lucky, it's handled at the senior level, but a couple of hundred years back, we and the Barringtons lost two jigs in a duel."

Admiral Serrano cleared her throat. Esmay noticed that the room had grown quieter; the others had come nearer, and were listening.

"The Family we served was based on a single planet—many Families were, in those days. And that planet . . ." She paused again; and Esmay felt a chill down her back. It could not be. "That planet, Esmay, was Altiplano. Your world."

She wanted to say *Are you sure?* but she knew that Admiral Serrano would not have said it if it hadn't been verifiable.

"That much the Serranos know—we all know—and there were some who argued against you on those grounds. I didn't; I felt that you'd make my grandson a fine partner, and I said so."

There were murmurs from the others. Esmay looked at Barin, trying to read his face, but she couldn't.

Vida Serrano went on. "There's more, and I think I may be the first person to see this for centuries. I was down in the family archives, bored enough to look at a row of children's books written by some *very* untalented ancestor, when I found it." She held up a dingy brown book. "I don't think it's a children's book; I think it's someone's private journal, or part of it. The conservators think it dates from the time of the events it describes, or closely after, and the pictures it had were pasted-in flatpics. The conservators couldn't find anything in the vid archives corresponding, and with maximal image-boosting, this is the best we could get . . ."

She slipped a package of flatpics out of the book, and opened it. The images were still blurry, but Esmay caught her breath. Altiplano . . . she could not mistake that pair of mountain peaks. And the building—the old part of the Landsmen's Guildhall, as shown in the oldest pictures she had seen in her history classes.

"You recognize it?" Vida asked Esmay.

"Yes . . . the mountains are the Dragon's Teeth—" And below

them, an ancient bunker . . . she didn't want to think about that now. "And the building looks like the Landsmen's Guildhall the way it was before they added onto it in my great-grandfather's time."

"I thought as much. Behind one of the flatpics, hidden by it, I found this." She held up a piece of paper that didn't look old enough. "This isn't the original, of course—that's back home, with the conservators humming over it. This is a copy. And, Esmay Suiza, it makes clear that your ancestors earned the enmity of mine, by rebelling against their patrons and slaughtering them all."

"What?"

"Your ancestors led the rebellion, Esmay. They massacred the family we were sworn to protect."

Esmay stared. "How can you know that? If no one survived—"

"Listen: *Against these our oath is laid: the sons of Simon Escandon, and the sons of Barios Suiza and the sons of Mario Vicarios, for it is they who led the rebellions against our Patron. Against their sons, and their sons' sons, to the most distant generation. May their Landbrides be barren, and their priests burn in hell, for they murdered their lawful lord and all his family, man and wife, father and mother, brother and sister, to the youngest suckling child. There is blood between their children and our children, until the stars die and the heavens fall. Signed: Miguel Serrano, Erenzia Serrano, Domingues Serrano.*"

Silence held the room; Esmay could scarcely breathe, and cold pierced her. She glanced around; the faces that had been welcoming an hour before had closed against her, stone-hard, the dark eyes cold. All but Barin, who looked stunned, but not yet rejecting.

"I never heard this," she said finally.

"I don't suppose they would brag about it," Vida said. "What story did you hear?"

Story. She was already sure that anything Esmay said would be a story, would be false. "In our history . . . there was a war, but also a plague, and a third of the population died of that, including the Founders."

"Is that what you call the Family?"

"Yes . . . I suppose, though I never knew there was one great family. I'd always thought of them as many families."

"You never heard the name Garcia-Macdonald?"

"No. Neither name."

"Ah. I've no doubt the rebels destroyed all evidence. There was nothing to show against them when Altiplano joined the Familias Regnant three hundred years later. All we could do was watch—and we did not then know which of the people on Altiplano had been involved. By then the Regular Space Service had formed around us."

"Was that the family? Garcia-Macdonald?"

"Yes. A family Serranos had served beside as far back as the wet-navy days of Old Earth. Tell me about this war, as you heard it."

"The Lifehearts and the Old Believers," Esmay said, dredging up what she remembered of those childhood lessons. "Um . . . the Founders wanted to bring in more colonists, free-birthers and Tamidians, to work the mines and develop the land. There had been a charter—a compact, they called it—promising to settle Altiplano only with those acceptable to those already in place. The Old Believers objected to the number of Tamidians the Founders wanted to import—they knew that they'd be outnumbered in two or three generations because of the free-birth policies. And the Lifehearts wanted development to proceed with due regard for the underlying ecosystem. But the Founders wanted a quick profit—they brought in shiploads of Tamidians, and the Tamidians brought diseases alien to the Altiplanans—diseases they were immune to, genetically."

It came back to her now—the accusations and counteraccusations. Infant mortality soared among the Altiplanans, as the diseases spread into an unprotected population; they would be outnumbered in decades, not generations. The Tamidians had mocked their beliefs, throwing down shrines and trampling the icons into dust. The Founders had moved people off the open land, herding them into cities, where they sickened faster. Her great-grandmother had told her about the Death Year, when no Altiplanan baby had survived a week past birth, and about the Landbride who had called a curse on the unbelievers, at the cost of her own soul.

"For Landbrides do not curse: they bless. But she was taken from her land, and her children had died, and she escaped from the city to the mountains, and there with blood and spit and the hair of her head she made a *gieeim*, and offered her soul to the land if it would destroy the invaders.

"I don't know what she actually did," Esmay said. "My great-grandmother never told me, if she even knew. In her view, the hubris of the Founders angered God and brought a just punishment upon them. But a plague came out of the mountains and the plains, and up from the sea, and in the first year the Tamidians died as our children had died, spewing blood and rotting as they fell. It was said that they begged the Founders to let them leave, but the Founders brought in more, until the cities stank of death, and the Founders themselves sickened."

"A bio-weapon?" someone said, behind the admiral.

Esmay shook her head. "No—at least, nothing I know of, and Altiplanans do not use bio-weapons today. But when the Altiplanans wanted to leave the cities, and go back to the land, the Founders denied them, and then there was war . . . but not to massacre them all, only to get back to the land from which they had been driven."

"That's not the report we have," Admiral Serrano said. "That's not what this says." She fluttered the paper.

"It's all I know," Esmay said. "Are you sure your report is reliable?"

"Why wouldn't it be? A servant . . . someone . . . escapes—"

"How? To what?"

"Atmospheric shuttle, to the orbital station. Unfortunately, he carried the disease with him, and it infected the station crew. Only three of them lived, but they passed it on . . ."

"I don't believe it!" Barin reached for Esmay's hand. "How can you believe a little scrap of paper stuck in a child's book—"

"Not a child's book—"

"Whatever kind of book. How can you believe that the real, secret truth was lost so long, and only comes to light just in time to keep me from marrying Esmay?"

Voices rose in an angry gabble, but Barin shouted over them. "I don't care! I do not care that she's from Altiplano. I do not care that this—this scrap of paper says her family were murderers hundreds of years ago. Are all Serranos saints? I love her, and I admire her and I'm going to marry her, if I have to leave the family to do it!"

"Barin, no!" Esmay grabbed for his other hand. "Wait—we have to find out—"

"I already know what I need to know," he said, looking into her eyes. "I love you, and you are faithful and true and brave—and you love me. That is what matters, not what happened then."

"There was an oath sworn . . ." Vida said.

Barin rounded on her, and this time Esmay could see the family likeness as if stamped in living bronze. "And are all oaths worthy? That's not what you told me, Grandmother, when I swore to keep Misi's secrets. There are oaths and oaths, you said, and it's a wise soul that swears rightly, which is why we swear few."

For an instant, Esmay thought Vida would scream her reply, but her voice, when she spoke, was soft.

"Then we must find the truth of this matter, Grandson—whether the story as we know it, or as the Suizas know it, is the truth. For if we know at last the names of those who killed our patrons, I see no possibility of peace between us."

"We have an oath to the Familias," Heris Serrano said. "As you keep telling the other Fleet families, when they remember who were their patrons. Would you have Serranos unravel Fleet, and possibly the Familias as well, to seek vengeance for ancient wrongs?"

Silence, an uneasy silence in which Esmay could almost hear the unspoken arguments based on rank, active service, combat experience. Barin broke it.

"It doesn't matter. I'm sticking by Esmay no matter what you say."

"The question is, will she stick by you, or will she turn traitor like her ancestors?" That was not Vida, but a male Serrano at the rear of the crush.

"Nonsense," Heris said. "The question is, does she love him?"

That set off another uproar, in which *Love is nothing but hormones!* clashed with *Love is more than just hormones!* and a dozen other comments Esmay had heard before. Through that, the shrill pipe of a communications alarm cut like a knife; the noise level dropped.

Someone across the suite picked up the com, and absolute silence spread from that focus toward the group still muttering softly about love and betrayal and honor. Heads turned; people moved away, looking in that direction.

Finally Esmay could see. A Serrano she hadn't met yet stood, one hand up for silence, listening, his face more gray than brown with some shock. He put the comunit down, finally, with exaggerated care.

"Mutiny. There's been a mutiny, on Copper Mountain, and the mutineers have ten ships already."

"What?"

"All leaves cancelled, all personnel return to their ships at once—"
His eyes sought Vida Serrano's. "They're calling the inactive flags
back, sir; you're to take the fastest possible route to Headquarters."

"Who?" Heris called. "Did you get anything on who started it?"

"*Bonar Tighe* was the first ship, Heris, but they took the Copper
Mountain orbital station with convicts from Stack Three, and the
commander there was named Bacarion."

"Bacarion." Heris thought a long moment. "Lepescu's staff—one
of his staff officers. It's that bunch again, our own little Bloodhorde.
And you know how Lepescu's crowd feels about Serranos."

Barin pulled Esmay to her feet and wrapped his arms around her.
"It's always something," he murmured. "But I do love you, and I will
marry you, and *nothing*—not Grandmother, or history, or mutinies,
or anything—is going to stop me."

She hugged him back, oblivious for a long, long delicious moment,
vaguely aware of people moving in the room, of doors opening and
closing. Finally someone coughed loudly.

"You've made your point, both of you," Vida Serrano said. "But
right now, you'd better get in uniform and get going."

Esmay lifted her head from Barin's shoulder and saw nothing but
uniforms now, Serranos with carisacks and rollerbags, one after
another emerging from the side rooms and heading for the door to
the lift tubes.

"I do love him," she said, right into Vida's face. "And I'm not a
traitor, and I won't hurt him."

Vida sighed. "There's a lot more at stake than the happiness of you
two," she said. "But for what it's worth, I hope it works out for you."

Barin turned into his own room, and Esmay went back to hers,
stripping quickly out of the borrowed clothes and putting on the
creased uniform she'd been wearing—not even time to have it
pressed. She looked at Dolcent's clothes, considered leaving them on
the bed, and then remembered having seen her, in uniform, leaving
with two others. She stuffed them into her own luggage—maybe
she'd run into Dolcent on a ship out of here—smoothed her wayward
hair, and went out to find Barin waiting for her. In the hall, the last
eight of the Serrano family were clustered at the lift tubes, waiting.

"I will never again complain about having to come to a boring
family reunion," said one, a woman who looked to be in her forties.

She gave Esmay a sidelong look. "First we find out that what had seemed to be an ordinary inspection of a potential spouse is almost the lynching of an old enemy, and then there's a mutiny." Nervous chuckles from half the others. "Is it you, my dear, or the conjunction of Heris and Vida? Those two are certainly lightning rods."

"Lightning *and* rod, I would say today." That was a bookish-looking young man. "Sparks were definitely flying."

"She knows that." Another speculative look at Esmay that made her face heat up. One of the tubes opened, and they crowded in, descending so fast that Esmay felt her stomach hovering near the back of her throat.

The hotel lobby swarmed with a crowded mass of men and women in R.S.S. uniforms, some struggling at the counters, trying to check out, and others crowding to the exits. "Don't worry about registration," the man who had spoken said. "I'll take care of it—we were last out, and that's my job."

"Cousin Andy," Barin said, in Esmay's ear. "Administration. Let's go."

The crush continued on the slidewalks and trams to the Fleet gate of the station. Every newsvid display had the story, with serious-faced commentators talking, while scenes of Copper Mountain played in the background. Esmay didn't stop to listen, but there was a clump of people near every display.

More and more people in uniform got on at every stop. Not only Serranos had been here, and Esmay wondered how they were all going to get where they were going. At the Fleet gate, she found out.

As the long line snaked through the security gate, they were divided into crew and transients: crew members of docked ships went directly to their ships, and transients were divided by speciality and rank. Within a couple of hours, Esmay and Barin both had new orders cut, sending them out on a civilian liner to join a battle group forming for Copper Mountain. They walked back down the concourse, and found eighteen other Fleet personnel in the waiting lounge for the *Cecily Marie*. Thirteen more appeared before they boarded, and a knot of angry civilian passengers were by then complaining bitterly to the gate agent.

"Welcome aboard, please take your seats, you'll be shown your cabins later—" The steward looked tense, as well he might. Thirty-three last-minute military passengers, a mutiny in Fleet, who knew what else? Esmay and Barin sat down together in the observation lounge, and she wondered if he felt as peculiar as she did. Probably not. She had come off this very ship not six hours before, and now she was back on it.

The senior Fleet officer aboard was Commander Deparre, who quickly organized the others as if the ship were Fleet and not civilian. Esmay had had a brief fantasy of spending the time with Barin—the time they had still not had, the time she had been longing for since before Brun's rescue. But Commander Deparre wanted to impress upon them the seriousness of the situation, and be sure they grasped the importance of upholding Fleet's reputation among the civilians of Familias Regnant.

The civilians aboard *Cecily Marie*, Esmay thought, were more alarmed than reassured by the way Commander Deparre controlled his little group. If they had been mutineers plotting to take over this very ship, they could not have been more ominous—always together as a group, always apart from the others. Commander Deparre, however, seemed to relish this opportunity for leadership: he was, it turned out, normally in charge of payroll processing at Sector Four HQ. He assigned Esmay responsibility for the female personnel—she was actually the senior female officer—and insisted that they should be protected from intrusion by posting a watch outside their quarters at night.

"But sir—"

"We cannot have the slightest whisper of irregularity, Lieutenant," he said firmly. Behind him, Barin rolled his eyes expressively, but Esmay felt more ready to scream than laugh. The maidens whose virtue she was supposed to guard were, all but one bright-eyed young pivot-major, older than she was, and two of the seven were senior NCOs who had been travelling with their husbands. This made no difference to Commander Deparre, who insisted that it would be "unseemly" for them to share cabins with their husbands. Why, exactly, he would not explain, and Esmay could not understand.

At least these older women understood that the vagaries of officers like Deparre should not be blamed on their subordinates, and that argument was futile. More difficult were the sergeant and corporal who had spotted civilian men they fancied, and wheedled endlessly for a chance to chat with them.

She and Barin were separated even at meals, because the commander felt that the women should dine at a different table. They could chat—cautiously—in the half-hour twice daily that Commander Deparre felt necessary for the officers to sustain their professional associations and exclusivity from the enlisted, who had the same half-hours to chat without an officer present. Lucky enlisted, Esmay thought, because they at least didn't have to have Deparre around, while she did . . . and the commander felt it his duty to have a little chat with each of "his" officers at least once a day.

"Nothing lasts forever," Barin said. "Even this voyage has to end sometime . . ." It hadn't been that many days, but it felt like years.

"With our luck, we'll end up on the same ship as Commander Deparre for the rest of our careers."

"No . . . he'll go back to his accounting, I'm sure."

"I hope so."

CHAPTER TWENTY-ONE

Old Palace, Castle Rock

"Mutiny!" Hobart Conselline glared at the face on the screen. "What do you mean, mutiny?"

"Copper Mountain, milord. Mutineers have taken it over, the whole system—"

Copper Mountain was a long way away—Hobart had no idea how far, exactly, but far enough. A training base, wasn't it? Probably a bunch of disgruntled trainees, and nothing to worry about. "Who's in charge?"

"Milord?"

He was surrounded by idiots. "Who is in charge of Copper Mountain? The base there?" A blank look, followed by a confused gabble about Main Base and Camp This and Island Something. "Never mind—just put a cordon around it."

"A cordon, milord?"

Did he have to explain everything? And these were supposed to be military personnel. "Cut them off," he said firmly. "Blockade or cordon or whatever you people call it. Just isolate them, and they'll run out of supplies soon enough."

A different face appeared, this one somewhat older. "Speaker, you do not understand. The mutiny began at Copper Mountain, but the mutineers now control the entire system—they have the orbital station, and the system defenses—we know at least ten warships are involved. That's enough to mount an attack on any other orbital station, or even one of the more lightly defended planets."

"But why would they do that?"

"We don't know, Lord Conselline, and not knowing their plans we must take what precautions we can to protect the most vulnerable population centers—"

"Damn them! I want to know who they represent! I want to know now!"

"Milord, the first thing is to secure—"

"I'll wager it's the Barracloughs—or the Serranos—"

The face on the screen seemed to stiffen. "We have no information—"

"Well, find out. I'll expect a report immediately." He shut off his unit, and swung his chair around so fast he banged his knee on his desk and caught his breath. Blast them. Smug, condescending . . . all they wanted was to feather their own nests, anyway. He sensed, as he always did, the vast sticky web of someone else's conspiracy, someone else's malice and opposition. It was unfair . . . why couldn't they see that he was only trying to make things better for the *real* Familias Regnant, that mental image of hard-working beneficent lords and ladies, and hard-working appreciative lesser families and workers, for whom he was grinding himself to nothing between two stones? Why did they always have to argue, talk back, bicker, complain? If they would only do what he told them, at once and without argument, the government could move smoothly, quickly, responding to whatever crises came up.

But no. They let personal ambition, mere selfishness and silly pride, get in the way . . . They were sabotaging his effort to save the Familias Regnant. Tears stung his eyes, and he blinked them away. It was tempting to resign, and let them find out what a muddle—what a disastrous quicksand pit—they'd be in without him. He'd certainly done his part; he'd earned respite. But no—he would do his duty, as he had always done it. He would uproot the lazy, conniving schemers who laughed at him behind his back, and save the realm in spite of itself.

He placed his own call . . . he would not work through that lemon-faced Poisson . . . and demanded of the man's secretary a word with his Minister of Defense.

"A terrible thing," he was saying even as his face slid into pickup range.

"Don't you start," Hobart said. "I'm getting no help out of the Grand Admiral's office—"

"They're upset—you know, Lord Conselline, the Grand Admiral was a mere one-star before the other flag officers were sent away—"

"Don't make excuses, Ed! Mutinies don't come out of nowhere. I want to know who's responsible for this outrage. Names, dates, the whole drill. Heads will roll, do you hear me, Ed?"

"Absolutely, Lord Conselline. As soon as I know anything, I'll report—"

"I have enemies, you know," Hobart said. "There are those who would like to embarrass me. I could name names . . ."

"In the Fleet, milord?"

"Not exactly, though I understand that the Serranos were quite close to Lord Thornbuckle and his daughter. Weren't they involved in her rescue, that flagrant misuse of government resources?"

"Yes, milord, but no Serranos have so far been identified as crew members of any of the vessels involved. In fact, a large group of them were attending a social function—"

"A flagrant alibi," Hobart said. "Suspicious by its very nature."

"Uh . . . it was a betrothal party, I understand. Milord, Fleet asked my permission to cancel the order removing rejuvenated flag officers from active duty, and of course I gave it—"

"Why?"

The man looked at him blankly. "Because we need them, milord. With part of the Fleet in mutiny, we need loyal officers, and especially the command structure—"

"How do you know they're loyal? How do you know they didn't engineer this mutiny just to be put back in the cushy jobs they had before?"

"Lord Conselline, there is no evidence—"

"If you're going to *argue*, Ed—" Hobart began, feeling himself growing hotter by the moment.

"Milord, I'm not arguing, I'm only telling you what the facts are as we know them."

"And you don't know anything worth knowing!" Hobart cut the connection, started to whirl his chair, and stopped just short of banging his leg again. He was surrounded by complete incompetents. He had *made* that man. He had taught him, shaped him, and brought him into the government, and this—*this* was his reward. Insubordination, incompetence . . .

He could fire him, of course. But whom could he appoint in his place? None of them had lived up to his hopes for them. Instead of working with him, supporting him, helping him, they all acted like spoiled prima donnas. Could he find anyone better?

"Goonar—wake up, man!" Goonar rolled over and glared at his cousin.

"It is my off watch. The ship is now in pieces. Go away."

"Goonar, listen—we just sucked a priority one report—"

"Is Laisa crazy? If we go sucking Fleet data, they'll—"

"There's a mutiny, Goonar."

"Mutiny?"

"Ten ships they know of, all in the Copper Mountain system. Who knows how many elsewhere."

"*Open* mutiny?" He was wide awake now, his stomach in a cold knot.

"That's what it said. A ship sent down LACs to a prison downside, brought up a bunch of dangerous criminals, used them to break the orbital station, got control of communications and systemwide defenses, and has declared that system to be part of the Society of Natural Men."

"And who is that when it's at home?" It sounded like nothing he'd ever heard of. Natural men? What did they do, run around naked and eat raw fish?

"My guess is it's some of those bloodthirsty lot who hung around with Admiral Lepescu. Remember the bald man who got blind drunk and wanted to show us trophies that time, after the fight in the bar? And what Kaim told us?"

"Lepescu's dead," Goonar said.

"Meanness isn't, just because one mean man dies." Basil shifted his shoulders restlessly. "I wonder if Kaim's all right, or if he's mixed up in this some way."

"He'd have told us . . . family . . ."

"Can you see real conspirators confiding in Kaim? He's so sure he can't be fooled, he's like the man holding his wallet and showing pickpockets where it is. I'd hate to have a Terakian involved, even by accident."

"I'm more concerned about the rest of the family. Mutiny in Fleet's going to play hob with shipping schedules, ours included. Things were unsettled enough before."

"Which is why I woke you up. We're playing skip-the-loop with the *Terakian Harvest*, and Laisa says we're almost in tightbeam range."

"We don't have to tube over, do we?" Goonar asked. He hated ship-to-ship transfer tubes worse than being woken out of a sound sleep.

"No. Or rather, you don't; I do. But they want to talk to you."

Goonar groaned, but rolled out of the bunk, and rubbed his head vigorously. He was not any good fresh out of sleep; he could have smacked Basil just for looking so brisk and awake.

On the bridge of *Flavor*, Laisa grinned at him. "Exciting times, Goonar."

"I never prayed for excitement," he growled. He just wanted to live his life in peace, he thought, holding the memory of dinner around the table on Caskadar ... the mellow lamplight, the smell of the food, the children's sweet piping voices. He sighed, and linked in to *Harvest*'s com officer.

"Your analysis, Goonar?"

How was he supposed to have an analysis when he was barely awake? Yet though he could barely speak, he could feel the little rolls moving in his brain, the numbers flickering past, faster and faster.

"What's your cargo?"

"Class D. Tungsten shell casings in the number four hold, conformable explosives in number three, the rest unremarkable."

"All of it." They never wanted to tell you all of it, but it was the little things which might turn a profit projection on its head.

"High-fashion software to eight destinations, plumbing supplies— plastic joints, mostly, but also some flapper valves, and a gross of solar-powered pumps, a cube of stuffed dates, and two bales of synthesilk, undyed."

Goonar knew from experience that the dates and the synthesilk wouldn't be on the manifest. Crew's personal possessions, not for sale ... except at a profit. "Fine—and your destinations and route?"

That came in a long string, directly into his deskcomp.

He looked at it and let the little gears and rollers in his head have their way. Then, just as Basil—suited up—waved at him from the bridge entrance, he had it.

"Xavier."

"What? That's not on our list at all!"

"I know . . . but I'll bet they need your Class D, and they're listed as a priority destination in the Fleet directive of last week. Nobody wants to go out there."

"Neither do I!"

"Yes, you do. It's a long way in the wrong direction from Copper Mountain. Nothing to attract mutineers: no ships to grab, no weapons factories to raid, no rich commerce to prey on. There's a Fleet presence, but after what happened, it'll be the most loyal crews they have. It's an ag world, livestock breeders, minimal hard-goods manufacturing. Also Xavier's still rebuilding—they'll take the plumbing supplies, too. They use a lot of synthesilk, and they have their own dyers. After that go to Rotterdam; they're also agricultural, and they have a little cross-trade with Xavier."

"What about the high-fashion software? It's only salable in a skinny window."

"Tube it to us, and I'll send it on by the next one we meet, when things are more settled."

"If they ever are. Fine, then. Godspeed."

Double-Sun Lines, *Cecily Marie*

At Chinglin Station, the censorious commander found orders taking him in one direction, while his very relieved companions had orders directing them to other ships. Barin and Esmay took the opportunity to stop by a dessert stand in the concourse that led from civilian docking lounges to the Fleet gate where they were to join the R.S.S. *Rosa Gloria*. They had less than two hours of time alone, with "alone" defined generously, but it was a great improvement on a suite full of Serranos or the watchful eye of the major.

"It's like Rondin and Gillian," Esmay said, swinging her feet against the counter. She felt like a child, sitting on this tall stool and spooning up ice cream. "Old family quarrels and all."

"You mean Romeo and Juliet," Barin said. "Shakespeare, very old."

"No, I don't," Esmay said. "I mean Rondin and Gillian. Who are Romeo and Juliet?"

"You must have heard of it; maybe the names changed in your version. Montagues and Capulets, traditional enemies. Duels and banishment and finally they died."

"No, they didn't."

"Yes, they did. She took a potion that made her look dead, and he thought she was dead, and killed himself, and then she found him and killed herself." Barin took another spoonful of ice cream. "Tragic but stupid. He could have asked a doctor, though my teacher said they didn't have doctors back when the story was first told."

"Not Rondin," Esmay said. "I met him."

Barin stared. "You're talking about real people?"

"Of course. Rondin Escandera and Gillian Portobello. Their fathers had quarrelled years before, and forbade them to marry."

"Why?"

"The quarrel? I don't know. I never heard, being a girl. I think my father knew, though. It was all very exciting . . . Rondin rode across our land to get to Gillian, because her father had sent her to my great-grandmother to wash Rondin out of her head, he said. That's where I met her; I was a child, and she was a young woman. Then one night Rondin came and she went out the window."

"How did he know where she'd gone?"

"Everyone knew—her father made no secret of it."

"Was she beautiful?"

"Oh, Barin, I was nine . . . ten, maybe. I knew nothing about beauty. She was a grownup who talked to me, that's all I knew."

"So what happened?"

"Oh, her father came and yelled at my father, and wanted to yell at my great-grandmother; my grandfather and uncle yelled at him— there was a lot of yelling, and I hid out in my room most of the time, so no one would ask me any awkward questions."

"Ask *you*—what did you know?"

Esmay grinned. "I was the one who'd carried the messages back and forth. Nobody paid much attention to a scrawny nine-year-old who was already known to be fond of walking the hills alone. Gillian was nice to me; I'd have done more for her than carry a note a few miles. And I knew where they'd gone. My great-grandmother tried to talk Gillian out of it, said it would be a disgrace for them both, but finally gave them permission to live far in the south, on our land, as—there is no word, in this language, but—they are under Suiza protection, but also under Suiza law. They do not own the land."

"Are they happy?"

"I don't know. After the yelling died down, I heard no more about them. But my point was that we are like that, our families opposed to our marriage, and we also must choose to lose our familes or each other."

"I don't want to lose you."

"Nor I, you."

"It's not fair to blame you for what some ancestor of yours did—"

"*If* they did," they said in unison.

"For all they know," Esmay said, "I'm actually the last living heir of that family, whatever its name was. Maybe they should be cheering me on, instead of hating me."

"They don't hate you. They're just confused. It's all Personnel's fault anyway." He reached out and touched her hair, a touch so light she could hardly feel it. Even that was risky in public; she felt her face going hot.

"Personnel's fault?"

"Well, if they hadn't put the rejuved admirals out of work, Grandmother wouldn't have been bored in the family archives. Imagine what it must have taken to get her to look at a row of children's books."

Esmay couldn't help giggling. "After she'd sat on the porch—is there a porch?"

"Oh, yes. She sat on the porch and looked at the lake, I'll bet. Then she took a walk. Then she read the newsflashes, and then she thought she should do something useful and improving . . ."

"Like read children's books." It was hard to imagine the redoubtable Admiral Serrano reading children's books. She must have been very bored indeed.

"I don't want to read children's books . . ." Barin gave her a long look.

"No . . ." She stared into the ice cream, trying not to blush again. She knew exactly what he wanted, and what she wanted.

"Esmay . . . everything's against us—both families, the mutiny, maybe a war, the whole universe doesn't want us to get married. They're so sure they know why we shouldn't, what we should do to be happy ten or twenty or fifty years from now. But I want to marry you. Do you still want to marry me?"

"Yes."

"Then let's do it. In spite of them, in spite of the mutiny, in spite of good common sense . . . let's *do* it."

A rush of warm glowing joy suffused her, banishing embarrassment. "Yes. Oh, yes! But how?"

"If nothing else we'll hold hands over a candle, but we have an hour—maybe more—before the ship gets here. If we don't waste it—"

"Let's go."

When they looked on the board, the *Rosa Gloria* was seventy-two minutes from undocking. Seventy-two minutes. Finding a magistrate with the authority to perform the ceremony took thirty-three of them. Persuading him to do it—both of them talking, proving their identification, showing all the paperwork—took another twenty-six. Thirteen minutes left . . . they stood hand in hand, and the magistrate rattled through the legal requirements as fast as possible, then added something Esmay presumed was a blessing in his religion, though not in hers. Signing and stamping and sealing the various documents took another eight minutes, and they were both racing back to the Fleet side of the station as fast as they could.

"We're crazy," Barin said, after they'd signed through Fleet Gate. His hand felt as if it were welded to hers.

"I love you," Esmay said. "I—rats, it's gone yellow—"

"Come *on*." Hand in hand, they ran for it, stride and stride, as faces turned toward them; people stared, someone yelled—she didn't care. They hit the far end of the access tube just as the light turned red, and a very disgusted petty-major held her fist on the controls to let them in.

"Welcome aboard sir . . . sirs." Her tone would have preserved fish for a century.

Behind her was a major; Esmay got her hand untangled from Barin's, and they both saluted.

"Jig Serrano and Lieutenant Suiza, I presume?"

"Yes, sir." She hadn't had time to think about whether she wanted to change her name.

"You cut it rather close, didn't you? We almost had you down as possible mutineers."

"Us?" Barin said. He sounded outraged.

"You," the major said. "We're treating no-shows that way—what did you expect?"

"Sir, we need to report a change of status."

His brows went up. "We?"

"We," Barin said firmly.

"I assume you mean a change of status that could affect billeting," the major said. He rolled his eyes. "All right. For now, we're assigning transient officers half-shift duties. You'll be on second shift, second half for now. Let's see—Lieutenant Suiza, we'll be meeting *Navarino* when the battle group is formed, and you'll be rejoining her—she's in jump transit right now. Jig Serrano, you were about to leave *Gyrfalcon*, but the ship you were assigned to has gone over to the mutineers, so your assignment's still up in the air."

"*Goshawk* went over?"

"So I hear."

"But it wasn't anywhere near Copper Mountain—"

"Serrano, I don't know any more than I've said. For now, you can wait for your chance at Admin and the captain in the junior officers' mess."

"Yes, sir."

The junior officers' mess was a buzzing hive of ensigns, jigs and lieutenants, who were much more interested in the latest news than in personal matters. Once they found that Barin and Esmay had not spent the two hours onstation watching newsvids, they went back to rehashing Fleet gossip. Barin and Esmay were able to sit together in a corner of the room, shoulder just touching shoulder, as they watched the status board for their turn to report to the captain.

"You've *what*?" Captain Atherton said.

"Got married, sir," Esmay said. As senior, she had made the announcement.

"But—but you didn't tell anyone."

"No, sir." Never mind that her CO, and Barin's, were perfectly aware of the engagement.

"Your paperwork's not even complete."

"No, sir." She didn't explain about that, either, or the unlikelihood that it would be complete any time in the foreseeable future.

"You know this could be voided by Personnel—"

"Yes, sir." She heard the stubborn tone in her own voice. Personnel could void what it wanted, but in her heart she was married, and nothing could change that.

"Why—no, never mind why. Because you're both idiots with dung for brains, pulling a stunt at a time like this."

"That's why, sir," Esmay ventured. "Things keep happening and we wanted—"

"This is not a romance storycube, Lieutenant. This is a warship in time of war. I don't care if you two are in love or if someone spiked your cocktail . . . we don't have time for this. You shouldn't even be on the same ship."

Esmay stole a glance at Barin, who stole a glance back. They hadn't been on the same ship when they weren't married, since the *Koskiusko*.

"Why couldn't you just have had mad passionate sex and gotten over it? Why did you have to get married?" Atherton turned to Barin. "Do you have any idea what your grandmother's going to do to me when she finds out?"

"It's not your fault, sir." Barin looked a little grim, and Esmay knew what he was thinking. It wasn't the captain of this ship who would bear the brunt of Admiral Serrano's anger.

"No, it's not, but she'll blame me for not stopping it. You—" He stopped in mid-bellow. "You're not laughing, are you?"

"No, sir," they said.

"Good. Because while this entire situation is so bad that laughter is the only sane response, I don't like to be laughed at, and I'm not laughing, so you can't laugh with me." He shook his head at them. "This happens in every crisis we have. I don't know what it is about youngsters—and you, Lieutenant Suiza, are really too old for that category—but every time there's a military crisis, a bunch of you decide to leap into the sack, and a few of those leap into marriage. It must be some atavistic quirk from the childhood of humankind."

"It's not like that. We didn't rush into it. We'd waited, and waited, and filled out paperwork, and argued with our families—" Esmay knew she was saying too much, but for once she couldn't stop.

"And then Grandmother came up with something really awful—" Barin added. Esmay shot him a warning look.

"And then the news of the mutiny came in, and everyone was rushing around—"

"Mmm-hmm. And you got married because your personal happiness was more important than anything else."

"As important as," Barin said. "Sir, I don't see how being miserable makes us more efficient, and right then we were miserable not being married, and being apart."

"So you'll function better if you're together?"

"I think so," Barin said.

"Good. Prove it. I see you're on second shift, second. We're certainly crowded enough to make sharing a cabin during your sleep rotation reasonable. But the first time one of you is groggy on duty, I swear I'll space you both. Clear?"

"Yes, sir."

"And you will both inform your families immediately, while we're still within range of the system ansible. We'll be in jump transit before a reply comes, no doubt, but at least you'll have told them. You have one hour."

"Yes, sir."

"You're letting them bunk together?" the exec asked. He had over-heard enough.

"It saves time. They'd get together somehow if we put them on alternating shifts with shifting bunk assignments . . . this way they don't waste any time or energy hunting each other down. My guess is, from their records, that they'll be just as efficient as anyone else."

"The Serrano family won't be happy."

"Well . . . as they said, it's not my fault. I didn't arrange it, or sanction it; it was done when I got them. Besides, I'm not a Serrano." His face relaxed for a moment into a reminiscent smile. "Back when I was an ensign on *Claremont*, and she was commanding, Vida Serrano chewed me out for spending too much time with my girlfriend. Said I'd outgrow the silly chit. Well, I've been married twenty-eight years now to that 'little chit,' and the day I outgrow Sal, I'll be dead. It's only justice that her grandson falls in love with someone she thinks is unsuitable—though how she could object to Lieutenant Suiza is beyond me. Maybe these two will be understanding of one of my kids someday."

The compartment was predictably cramped, with a second narrow bunk rigged above the first, and they would share it with four other officers. It was their space only during their assigned sleep shift. But they were alone, with a locked door between them and the rest of the universe. For now, that made all the difference.

"Sorry about the hurry," Barin said, into Esmay's ear.

"Hmmm?"

"The beautiful dress Brun was having designed for you. And the ring I'd ordered. And a ceremony you would recognize . . ."

"We can do that later, if we have the chance. I'd rather have this." *This* engaged both of them more than adequately for some time.

"Still . . ." Barin said, coming up for air at last.

Esmay poked a finger in his ribs. "Don't . . . distract me."

CHAPTER TWENTY-TWO

**The Chairman's office,
Benignity of the
Compassionate Hand**

Hostite Fieddi had always known this day would come. The Chairman sat behind his desk, and on the desk lay the knife, the ancient black-bladed knife, the hilt to the Chairman's left.

"Hostite, you have been a good and faithful servant."

"Sir."

"You have been long in our service."

"Sir."

"You are the blade I trust." The intonation suggested a pause, not a completion, and Hostite waited. "We have an enemy time will not wound for us."

"Sir."

"You are my Blade, Hostite . . ."

"To the heart, Chairman."

"To the heart, Hostite, without prejudice." A kill, a kill beyond the borders, but one only. For that he was glad, that only one kill would burden his soul in eternity.

"Come near, and I will aim my Blade."

He was already dead, though he walked; coming near could not increase his mortality. Hostite waited, and the Chairman said nothing for long moments.

Then: "It is a grave thing to order the death of one who has never been under your authority. I give this order reluctantly, Hostite, not

334

only for what it means to you and to me, but for what it means to the peoples . . . the clients. But there is no other way; the man is swollen with ambition, and would force on us all his ungodly ways."

"They are heathens, sir."

"Not all like this. Hostite, I bid you kill Hobart Conselline. None other of his family; him only."

Hostite bowed.

"The method, sir?"

"Your choice."

His last assignment. His death at the end. And the death of the Chairman, who would no longer have his personal Swordmaster, the Shadow of the Master of Swords, to ward him from that danger.

He felt the honor, and it warmed him. Death had not been a stranger to him for years, and nothing waited for him in age but someone's blade when he faltered. This—this he could do for his people and his faith, and he almost smiled, thinking of it.

"Go now," the Chairman said, and Hostite withdrew, already thinking how he would do it.

Old Palace, Castle Rock

Hobart slung his clothes into the hamper angrily. Worse every day, those damned idiots.

He put on his fencing tights, and began his exercises. When the door opened, he glanced up, expecting Iagin Persius. But he had never seen this Swordmaster. An older man, a bit stockier, in sleek black stretch with a funny-looking red cap and red slippers. In his hands he carried a sword unlike those Hobart used.

"It is time," he said, in a voice as soft as rainwater.

"All right," Hobart straightened up, and pushed past him into the salle. "Where's that other Swordmaster? I'm used to him."

"He was indisposed, Lord Conselline, and asked me to take his place, that you might not be inconvenienced awaiting his recovery."

Hobart stared at the man. "You're certainly more formal than he was. What's that blade you've got? Do I have to work out with that? I suppose you want me to learn yet another stupid archaic weapon . . ."

"Not if you don't wish it. What weapon would you prefer?"

"Rapier." Hobart looked around, and realized that his coach wasn't there either; he would have to get his own gear, since he didn't think this old man would oblige him. But to his surprise, the Swordmaster moved quickly to the racks, and brought him a rapier—his favorite, he realized—and a mask.

"You seem angry," the man said.

"I am," Hobart said. He didn't want to talk about it; he came to exercise to forget—or at least ignore—his problems for a time.

"Did someone illtreat you?" asked the Swordmaster.

"Yes—but I'm here to fence."

"Of course. My pardon, Lord Conselline. Swordmaster Iagin told me of your dedication, your seriousness."

"He did?" Hobart had never been sure the Swordmaster approved of him, though the man had always been courteous and respectful.

"Yes . . . he said you were unusual, a man who took everything seriously."

"That's true enough." Hobart adjusted the mask, and bounced a little, loosening his knees. He had skimped on stretching, and if Iagin thought him serious, then he had better be serious. "Not many are— you would not believe—no, never mind . . ."

"But if you need to stretch out, and ease your mind with talk as your sinews with the exercise, then you should, milord."

"Oh—very well." Hobart laid his blade down on the mat, carefully, and leaned over to grasp his ankle. "I hope it doesn't bore you, and you must realize it's confidential—"

"Of course. You need to turn your wrist a little more, milord."

"It's these idiots—these dung-for-brains weaklings that I sponsored to high office. I made them what they are, I led them and taught them and groomed them for office, and now that they're in power . . . they simply will not do what they're told."

"Ah. And now, milord, another centimeter of pull . . . yes. And now the other leg . . . remembering to keep the wrist rotated in . . . yes."

"I don't know what it is, Swordmaster, but no matter how smart they are, or how much initiative they show when I start working with them, no sooner do they get into a position of real responsibility than they turn on me. Insubordinate, arrogant, selfish—"

"If you can tilt the head now—yes, like that—and a little more—"

"And they're supposed to be my supporters, but do they support? No. They go off and do stupid things, like that idiot Orregiemos . . ."

"And to the other side, now, milord . . ."

"It's enough to make a saint spew rocks," Hobart said. Amazing how easy the fellow was to talk to. The combination of the warm, quiet room, and familiar scents of leather, steel, oil, sandalwood, cedar, and the quiet, patient, steady hands of the older man molding him into one shape after another that stretched out knots he hadn't even realized he had . . .

"It is difficult when subordinates are not obedient," the Swordmaster said.

"Exactly. I've tried reasoning, scolding, even threats—"

"And they resist."

"They certainly do. If they only realized, I'm trying to make things better."

Hostite had studied the files; he knew Hobart Conselline as well as anyone could, who had only files to go on. But the man in reality had shocked him. He was so miserable, so full of anger and fear and envy that the whole room stank of it. His body had been stiffened and deformed by it; the very muscles of his face were saturated with his rage and fear.

He was a skin bag of poison.

He was immortal, being a Rejuvenant, as the silver and cobalt rings in his ear boasted to the world.

So old, and yet so full of folly. He had learned nothing, Hostite saw, in all those decades of renewed vigor that rejuvenation had given him.

Pride . . . was his own pitfall, Hostite reminded himself. Yes, this man was proud, and bitter, and angry, but why? He had never yet killed without understanding *why* those he killed were as they were.

He must offer the opportunity for understanding, for contrition, for repentance, though he could not offer—must not offer—any chance of escape. He must give the soul a chance, while giving the body none.

But how to do that with unbelievers, with those who were not aware of the soul, of anything beyond the body? Hostite had studied unbelievers of all kinds, over the years, and found them all to have beliefs of a sort, just wrong ones. They believed in wealth, or security, or the kindness of strangers, or something other than the True Faith. And so what they believed in failed them, eventually, and they were brought low . . .

All that Lord Conselline was saying could be considered a confession, but in a true confession the sinner knew that what he confessed was sinful. Hobart didn't seem to grasp that at all. Everything that went wrong was someone else's fault. Hostite felt a wave of sympathy for these stupid uncooperative men who so angered Lord Conselline. They, too, were heathens, and enemies, and the Chairman might find it necessary to have them killed, but they had certainly suffered from long association with Lord Conselline.

He listened to all of it, eliciting more and more by merely being there, a neutral and unwisely trusted ear. Hobart's envy of his brother, and everyone else whose personality drew others. Envy of everyone, in fact, for he could always find something in which another had received unearned benefit. Pride—a towering pride, certainty of his own rightness, and the moral weakness of others. Anger at everyone, avarice—for nothing was ever enough, even for a day; lust, and a wide streak of cruelty that enjoyed humiliating others. And all of it, every sordid detail, drenched in self-congratulation.

A Swordmaster must know when enough was enough, and Hostite had that moment of revelation: this man would not ever realize his errors, not even in the moment of death. Poor soul, so benighted, so hopeless of a better eternity, so ignorant. But God gave each soul enough time, if it chose to use it, and Lord Conselline's soul had had the same chance—years, in fact—to come to a better understanding.

"Come now, Lord Conselline," he said finally, and stood back. "You are feeling better; it is time for your lesson."

"Yes—I am feeling better." He clambered up, rapier in hand, in body a little straighter than he had been, his mind a little clearer in the aftermath of confessing, even so inadequately, his current crop of sins.

"It is not your associates," Hostite said. "It is you." He was sure Conselline would not understand, but he had to try.

"What?" Lord Conselline's eyes widened as he saw the movement of the great dark blade, the backswing which promised such power.

"Your failure." The blade swung forward; Lord Conselline tried to parry with the rapier, and the blade sliced it short, sweeping on; Conselline jumped back, mouth open to yell, and Hostite pursued, choosing to dance the figure rather than step it. He could hear the music in his head, his favorite music, Lambert's "All On a Spring Morning, the Bright Trumpets Sing." His pursuit, and Conselline's fear, used up the man's breath, and what should have been a shout came out a series of breathless squeaks.

"No—what are . . . you doing? Help—stop—security!" Lord Conselline glanced from side to side, clearly frightened, and grabbed at another weapon off the rack.

"I am your Death, your life is over." Another swipe that parted a practice foil as if it had been a blade of dry grass. "Ask forgiveness from your God." The man had none, but again, he must offer the chance.

"I didn't do anything," Lord Conselline gasped. "It wasn't me. Don't—"

Hostite had never been one to play with a victim, past giving him a chance to repent; the great blade took Lord Conselline's head off with one stroke, and the harsh stench of death overtook the sweet spicy scent of cedar and sandalwood.

The Chairman of the Board of the Benignity of the Compassionate Hand faced away from his desk, looking out the tall windows at the formal garden. A boisterous spring breeze whipped the tops of the cypresses, and even swirled stray petals from the early roses along the pebbled walks. From here he could not see the fountains, but he could imagine the spray blowing out behind, a long damp veil that would slick the marble rim of the cascade, the seats behind it where the old ladies sat in their black dresses on fine days, watching the sea and the children playing. He lifted his gaze to the horizon, to the blue sea, its glittering tessellations flinging the sun back in his eyes.

He had had, on the whole, a successful life, and since he had just made his final confession, he was conscious of it as a whole, a story nearly complete, the defining moments as clear as if they had been painted by a fine artist. This and this he had done well, and that and that he had done less well. On occasion, the grace of the Almighty had protected him from the consequences of his own errors, and on other occasions he had taken the blame for what was not his fault. Not in God's eyes, of course, but in the eyes of the Benignity. All this was to be expected, and he regretted none of it, for regrets were useless. It had been a life of human shape and human content, and he was glad of it.

If regret had been part of his mental furniture, he might have regretted—he almost regretted—this last necessity. It was not his fault that the Familias Regnant had fallen into the hands of Hobart Conselline, and that he had been forced—he had seen no alternative— to order the man's execution. It would have taken supernatural ability to foresee all that had happened to bring Conselline to power, and to shape him into someone who could be so dangerous, and offer so little maneuvering room to the Benignity. And no one expected supernatural ability of a Chairman.

Only that if he failed, he must pay the price.

Those in the Benignity were in his power, absolutely: if the Chairman ordered that a potato farmer must die for the good of the whole, then the potato farmer would die, in the manner and time prescribed, and this was as it should be. He might pity the potato farmer, and the potato farmer's wife and squalling brats, but he would order that death without a qualm, and without a qualm it would occur. This was not even cruelty. Death ended every life; death healed the sick and the badly injured; death opened the gates to endless life.

But outside the Benignity . . . the rules changed. To compete, to convert, even to invade—that was allowable. To corrupt, and to have secret agents providing information and forwarding the interests of the Benignity—that was inevitable. But to call for the assassination of a foreign king—whatever the foreigners called their heads of state, and they called them many foolish things—that was proof that a Chairman had failed. Had not seen trouble coming, had not managed affairs in another way, had not done—by means of stealth or influence or intimidation—what needed to be done.

Still, no tool, no method, was forbidden. God in His wisdom knew that emergencies happened. If, to protect the Benignity, a foreign king must die, then the Chairman could so order, and so it would occur.

So also would occur the death of that Chairman, who had shown himself to lack the qualities of a Chairman. Whether he was stupid, or old and tired, or misled by advisors, did not matter: he had failed his people, and he must pay the price. Not unexpectedly, not cruelly, but surely and certainly and with all due ceremony.

Some Chairmen never had to make that decision, and it was the accumulation of errors which brought them to their final confession. He had expected it would be so with him, as his years advanced, until he'd realized, too late, what Hobart Conselline's leadership of the Familias Regnant would lead to. In the instant he'd seen it, he'd also seen his own folly, his own blindness: he could have recognized it years before. Whether that would have changed events or not, he could not know, nor did it matter. He had blundered; he had done what he could to fix it, but it was not enough.

No guards were in the room today. He had made his last confession, and his heart was as light and sunny as the spring breeze.

When he heard the door, he turned. Some had chosen not to look, but he had never been afraid of the man who would kill him, only of the man who would let him fail his people.

The Master of Swords stood by his desk, formally dressed, and carrying the dark blade they did not use for fencing.

"You know my reasons," the Chairman said, without meeting his eyes. It was impolite to look into the eyes; it could be intepreted as pleading.

"Yes."

"I have made my confession," the Chairman said.

"Yes." The Master of Swords stepped to one side, and raised his blade.

"Fiat—"

"Nox." The Master of Swords swung, and the blade that had taken the life of sixteen Chairmen sliced through skin and sinew and bone as easily as a hot knife through butter. Blood spurted as the head thumped onto the desk and rolled, but blood was nothing new in this place, and the servants knew how to clean it up.

"In nomine Patrem," the Master said, saluting *his* Master. He wiped the blade with a square of scarlet silk, and laid that silk over the Chairman's head. "Requiescat in pacem."

Then, as he was, naked blade in hand, with flecks of Pietro Alberto Rossa-Votari's blood on his cloak, he strode out of the office, through the anteroom—where the secretary was now already calling for servants, and would soon be notifying the family—down the hall, and into the Boardroom, where the Board had been waiting for the Chairman to appear and open the meeting.

"The Chairman has made his last confession," he said, without preamble. Faces paled, but no one spoke. "The Board will elect a new Chairman," he said. Anxious looks back and forth, and at him. Some of these men had never been through the election of a Chairman; Rossa-Votari had held that office for eighteen years. The Swordmaster stood by the door, with nothing more to say, as the low murmurs started, as they looked at him and away and back and away . . . it was nothing to him what they did, and nothing they said would he ever repeat, but they would not leave this room alive until one of them had been elected Chairman by acclamation.

R.S.S. *Rosa Gloria*

The ship had been in downtransit only a couple of hours when the captain called Barin and Esmay into his office.

"I have messages from your families," the captain said. He didn't wait for their response. "They say they have more important things to worry about than you two. They're not happy with you, and they don't approve, but in the present emergency, they're not doing anything except talking about it. To each other."

"To each other?"

"Yes. Admiral Serrano and General Suiza both signed this—" he handed over the hardcopy. "Actually, all the Admirals Serrano and Generals Suiza—I don't know what you thought you'd accomplish by running off together, but you seem to have unified a substantial number of high-ranking officers in at least one thing—you're in trouble."

"But we're married," Barin said.

"It's worth it," Esmay said.

"It better be," the captain said. "Because when everything settles down and there are no wars, mutinies, invasions, terrorist attacks, pirates, or other distractions, your families are going to come down on you like one planet hitting another."

This was, Esmay thought, a fairly accurate description of the probable interaction of Serranos and Suizas anyway, with the exception of themselves.

"Now get out of here, and go back to being the frustratingly competent officers you both are."

They did not scamper away in glee, because officers did not scamper.

"When everything settles down, eh?" Barin said, grinning. "That'll be the day."

"If they wait that long," Esmay said, thinking of her father and uncle talking to Barin's grandmother and great-uncle. If they didn't kill each other right off—and the combined message suggested they hadn't—what a dangerous combination *that* was, to have running around the universe!

"They'll get used to it," Barin said. "We aren't half as bad as we could have been—suppose I'd married Casea?"

Esmay gave him a look, and almost burst into laughter. A trail of suppressed giggles followed them down the passage to their tiny— but adequate for the immediate purpose—cabin.

AGAINST THE ODDS

Acknowledgements

As usual, I have many people to thank for help, including some who prefer not to be listed; you know who you are, and you know I appreciate it. David Watson and Kathleen Jones, for hours of brainstorming and for their collection of useful references, but most of all for wanting the story so badly that they restored my ability to tell it. The weekly fencing crowd (Allen, Andrew, Beth, Connor, Sean, Susan, Tony, Brian, etc.) for varied expertise that included such things as damage control on an aircraft carrier and the characteristics of large cables under tension, an evening of editorial comment, and especially for allowing me to work off my tension by poking them with swords. Clive Smith and Christine Joannidi for bits of physics, the history of an Anglo/Greek trading family, and the best Yorkshire pudding in central Texas. Those who hang out in my SFFnet newsgroup and provide facts, ideas, and general support (in this case, a double dose of thanks to Cecil, Howard, Julia, Rachel, Tom, and Susan.) Carrie Richerson for her ability to detect mushy spots in characterization. My husband Richard for the worst pun in the book. Our son Michael for patience with a writing parent. Michael Fossel, M.D., Ph.D., for stimulating discussions of rejuvenation. Ruta Duhon for weekly doses of sanity even when writing gets wild.

Mistakes and errors are all mine, not theirs.

Note to Readers

Readers familiar with *Change of Command* will notice a temporal overlap between the last part of that book, and the first part of this one. Here the first chapter starts between the mutiny and the second assassination.

Newcomers may wish a bit more background.

The Familias Regnant is a political assembly of great families, now spread across hundreds of solar systems. Centuries ago, they combined their individual family militias into the Regular Space Service, which has the dual mission of policing the spaceways and defending the Familias from external attack.

In the previous book, *Change of Command,* longstanding dissension and unrest in the R.S.S. came to a head and elements of the Fleet mutinied.

The mutineers first struck at the Fleet training planet, Copper Mountain, freeing some of the prisoners from a high-security brig on a remote island. The rest they massacred. Their original plan had included taking over a weapons research facility, but loyalists managed to prevent that, at least for the moment. Unfortunately, the mutineers managed to destroy their transportation: the loyalists are marooned.

CHAPTER ONE

Copper Mountain,
Fleet Weapons Research Facility

A cold wind swept the barren top of Stack Two; Ensign Margiu Pardalt's eyes ached from squinting into it. Broad daylight now; the wind had long since swept away the bitter stench of the seaplane fires. Where were the mutineers? Surely they would land, to snatch the weapons they knew had been designed here. Had the message she'd tried to send using the old technology actually reached anyone, or would the mutineers get away with their whole plan? And when would they come . . . when would they come to kill her?

"This is stupid," Professor Gustaf Aidersson said. Bundled in his yellow leather jacket over his Personal Protective Unit, with a peculiar gray furry hat on his head, he looked more like a tubby vagrant than a brilliant scientist. "When I was a boy, I used to imagine things like this, being marooned on an island and having to figure out a way to get home. I had thousands of plans, each one crazier than the one before. Make a boat out of my grandmother's porch swing, make an airplane out of the solar collector, take the juicer and a skein of yarn, two cups, and a knitting needle and make a communications device."

Margiu wondered whether to say anything; she couldn't feel her ears anymore.

"So here we are, on the perfect island, full of challenges. I should be improvising rappelling gear to go down the cliffs, and something to construct a sailboat . . . I actually have built a boat, you know, but it was with wood from a lumberyard. And I sailed it, and it didn't sink. Of course, it wouldn't hold all of us."

"Sir," Margiu said, "don't you think we should go back inside?"

"Probably." He didn't move. "And there is not one thing on this blasted island to make a boat or an airplane out of." He gave a last look at the blackened stain that had been their transport. Then he looked at Margiu and his mouth quirked in a mischievous grin. "There's only one thing to do, when the bad guys have all the transport . . ."

"Sir?"

"Make them give it to us," he said, and headed inside so abruptly that Margiu was left behind. She caught up with him as he went in the door.

"Make them—?"

"It's a desperate chance . . . but by God it'll be fun if it works," he said. He looked around the room at the scientists and military personnel who were also stranded. "Listen—I have an idea!"

"You always have an idea, Gussie," one of the scientists said. Margiu still hadn't sorted them all out by name. They all looked tired and grumpy. "You probably want us to make an airplane out of bedsprings or something . . ."

"No. I thought of that, but we don't have enough bedsprings. I want the mutineers to bring us an airplane and give it to us."

"What?"

The professor launched into an enthusiastic explanation. In the few seconds from outside to inside, his idea had already developed elaborate additions. The others looked blank.

Major Garson was the first to nod. "Yeah—the only way to get transport is to get them to give it to us. But it's not going to be easy. They've got a lot more troops topside than we have . . . they can scorch us with the shuttle weaponry, for that matter."

"So our first job is to convince them we're not that dangerous," the professor said. He had taken off his hat and shoved it into a pocket; his thinning gray fringe stuck up in untidy peaks.

"Do they even know how many of us there were?" asked Margiu. "They don't know the planes were full, do they? Vinet didn't get any messages up to them—"

"No . . . that's right. And except during the firefight last night, we've been mostly undercover. But they'd be stupid to come in carelessly," Major Garson said. "Never count on the enemy to be careless."

"But—" The professor held up his hand a moment, then nodded. "But suppose, using Margiu's radio apparatus, we give them what looks like accidental clues. We try to contact them, pretending to be mutineers fighting with scientists—"

"No, wait!" That was the skinny man with wild black hair. Ty, Margiu remembered. "Look, they know the loyalists have the radio now. Suppose we send a message, like we hope it'll bounce around to mainland, begging for help. And then break off. And then an hour or so later, there's a message to them from some of the military pretending to be mutineers, and then—"

"How would the mutineers know how to use that equipment?" Garson said. "It's nothing Fleet-trained people would know unless they happened on it somewhere else, like Ensign Pardalt. And besides, it's too fragile. It could get shot up in a firefight."

"Suppose we say the radio's the loyalists'," Margiu said. The others looked at her. "And we're begging for help from the mainland, like he said." She nodded at Ty. "But of course it doesn't come. We sound more and more desperate—we talk about being hunted by the mutineers, about the people killed in the explosions of the planes, and then the food shortages—the mutineers have all the supplies . . ."

"Yes! That's good," the professor said. "And we'll move the thing around, so when they trace the signal they'll know someone's trying to stay in hiding—and then we'll take it underground . . ."

"We'll need a visible force of baddies," the major said. "A squad'll do for that. Local uniforms . . . and PPUs can look like anything, with the right setting. We've got the suitcoms for local—have to have our people stay in character."

"So . . . what are we going to do if we get the shuttle? They can always shoot us down before we get anywhere."

"Not that easy if they come down with one of the combat troop shuttles, sir," said one of the neuro-enhanced Marines. "They're hardened and highly maneuverable."

"Which brings up—who's going to fly it?"

"I'm shuttle-qualified," said one of the pilots. "Ken's not, but Bernie is."

"If you're qualified to fly troop shuttles, why are you on seaplanes down here?"

"Fleet has a lot more shuttle pilots than seaplane pilots," the pilot said, spreading his hands. "Only a few of us mess around with the old-fashioned stuff."

"Bob . . . what about Zed?"

"On a shuttle, LAC size? No problem, Gussie. It'll fit, and we can use it. Like I said, it'd hide something the size of this island, let alone a shuttle."

The professor glanced again at Garson. "Then, Major, if you'll divide us into loyalists and mutineers—giving me the tech-trained people—and set up a scenario for us to act—"

"We'll have to do something about those bodies. . . ." Garson said, and gestured to some of the men.

Margiu had never had close contact with scientists before this, and if she'd thought about them at all, she'd had a storycube image of vast intelligence applied step-by-step to some arcane problem. They would be solitary, so they could concentrate; they would be serious, sober, abstracted.

They would not, for instance, waste any moment of their precious preparation time playing some incomprehensible game that involved a singsong chant, puns, and childish insults, dissolving into laughter every few seconds.

"Your starfish eats *dirt*," the professor finished.

"Oh, that's old, Gussie." But the others were grinning, relaxed.

"So now—we're going to get them to bring us a ship, and then let us fly away?"

"We'll have Zed on—they won't see us."

"They'll see the moving hole where we were," Swearingen said. "It's a lot harder to hide things in planetary atmospheres."

"Not with Zed," Helmut Swearingen said. "We've solved that problem, or most of it. The thing is, all they have to do is hit a line across our course—and since we have to fly to the mainland—"

"Why?" the professor asked; he had found a cache of candy and spoke around a lump of chocolate. "It's the obvious thing, of course, but being obvious won't help us now. At the very least we can zig and zag . . ."

"Not forever . . . we have to come down somewhere."

"Maybe," the professor said. "And maybe not. Suppose they think we've blown up or something. We could toss fireworks out the back—"

"Oh come on, Gussie! The fake explosion while the real vessel gets away is the oldest trick in the book." Swearingen looked disgusted.

"Because it works," the professor said. "All it has to do is distract them long enough for us to make a course change. Two points define a straight line: they have takeoff and the explosion. If we aren't at an extension of that line, they'll have no idea where we are."

"It's ridiculous! It's all straight out of storytime. I have to agree with Helmut—"

"There's a reason for stories being the way they are," the professor said.

"Yes, they're for the stupid or the ignorant, to keep them out of our way while we do the work . . ." Swearingen said.

"Can you even name one time in real life—not your pseudo-history—when someone faked an explosion and escaped in a vessel the enemy thought was blown up?"

The professor blinked rapidly, as if at a long sequence of pages. "There are plenty of ruses in military history—"

"Not just ruses, Gussie, but that hoary old cliche of faking the explosion of an engine, or a ship, or something . . ."

"Commander Heris Serrano," Margiu said, surprising herself. "When she was just a lieutenant. She trailed a weapons pod past a fixed defense point, and when it blew it blinded the sensors long enough for her to get her ship past. Or Brun Thornbuckle, during her rescue, sent the shuttle as a decoy after landing on the orbital station."

"You see?" the professor said, throwing out his hands. "A hoary old cliche still works."

"It works better if you keep them busy thinking about other things," Margiu said.

"Like what?" one of the others asked her.

"Anything. Because you're also right, if they see the shuttle taking off and then it disappears, and then something blows up, they're going to be suspicious."

"So we don't have it disappear until just at the explosion."

"We have Zed, but the controls aren't that good. Not yet."

Silence for a long moment. Then one of the pilots said, "Look—the shuttle will have a working com, right? The bad guys will want to be in touch with the shuttle crew."

"Yes . . ."

"So we continue our little charade on the shuttle. Suppose . . . suppose we talk about the weapons we've recovered. We're trying to see how they work—"

"They're not going to believe *their* people would do something that stupid."

"Wouldn't they?"

"But—" Everyone turned to look at Margiu. She could feel the ideas bubbling up in her mind like turbulence in boiling water. "Suppose the bad guys—ours, I mean—said they also had the scientists—and they were questioning them—and they found out one of the things was a stealth device. And they wanted to try it, to see if it really worked—"

"That would explain the disappearance. Good, Margiu!"

"I still think they'd be suspicious."

"Spoilsport." The professor sighed, and rubbed his balding head. "But you're probably right. Let's see. Our pseudo-bad guys question the scientists . . ." He pitched his voice into falsetto. "*Please* don't hurt me—I vill tell you effryting."

"Good lord, Gussie, what archaic accent is *that*?"

"I don't know—I heard it on a soundtrack years ago. Don't interrupt . . . so the scientists act like terrified victims and maybe that can be overheard. And then they turn Zed on, and it works—"

"And it's still as transparent as glass," Bob said.

"So I'll scratch it up—YES!" The professor leaped up and danced in a circle. "Yes, yes, yes! Brilliant. Scratchy, like old recordings, old-time radio—break-up—"

"What?! Damn it, Gussie, this is serious—"

"I am serious. I am just momentarily transported by my own brilliance. And yours, and Margiu's here." He calmed down, took a breath, and went on. "Like this: the normal takeoff, the threats of the bad guys, the terror of the scientists. But then, when they—we—turn Zed on, it doesn't *keep* working. It sort of—" he waggled his hand. "Sort of flickers. They hear an argument—more threats, more piteous pleadings, curses at some fool who—I don't know, kicks the power cable or something. The shuttle is there, then it isn't, then it is—but always on the same course. A voice shouting in the background: be careful, be careful, don't overload it, it wasn't designed for—! And *then* the explosion, and then the course change."

A long silence this time, as they all digested what the professor had said. He mopped his face, his head, and pushed the crumpled, stained handkerchief into his pocket.

"It does explain everything," Swearingen said. "It gives them more to think about, more complications."

"It seems to give them more data," said Bob. "But all the data are false. It might work."

"So what we need is something to make a big bang, that will look like a shuttle blowing up on the bad guys' scan from upstairs . . . which we can get far enough away from before it blows that we don't also blow . . ."

"Something, yes."

The group dissolved as the scientists wandered off. Margiu, used to direct orders and a clear set of directions, felt let down as she followed the professor down one passage after another. Were they ever going to go to work? And what would Major Garson think, with her just wandering around idly watching someone who seemed to have very little idea what he was doing.

But that, she soon found out, was a mistake. After a rapid tour of the ground-floor levels of the site, the professor found Major Garson and began suggesting where to put what. Garson, meanwhile, was working on his own pretense. He had divided his troops and assigned the NEMs to play mutineer.

"If they think the NEMs are mutineers," he said, "they'll believe that the loyalists are in serious trouble. Also, the NEMs are so big and bulky that it's hard to get facial detail when they're in their p-suits with the head-jacks. That means I can move them around and have them play more parts."

Margiu glanced at the NEMs sitting around, half of them sticking odd-shaped patches to their p-suits. One of them grinned at her. "The bad guys are old Lepescu cronies," he said. "They take ears from their kills. So—we thought we'd use an ear shape openly, as a recognition patch. No one else would." He slid the tube of adhesive back in one of the pockets.

"Come along, Ensign," said the professor; Margiu followed him, glancing back at the NEMs who were clustered there. She hoped they *were* all loyalists.

Twelve hours later the whole situation felt even more unreal. Periodically, Margiu and the professor joined Garson and one of the troops and scuttled rapidly from one building to another, following a plan of Garson's that had the loyalists trying to evade the "mutineers." The NEMs pretending to be mutineers, meanwhile, shot entirely too close for Margiu's comfort, and shattered all the ground-floor windows. Far underground, with doors shut against the wicked drafts from above, the scientists and remaining troops had organized the collection of boxes, cylinders, cables, and things that looked like leftovers from a junk heap onto pallets.

On one of their tours through the working areas, the professor shook his head over the tarps used to cover the loads before lashing them down. "It's too bad they destroyed those seaplanes," he said. "Look—these would have made wonderful sails, and we could have built a ship with the frames of the planes."

"No, we could *not*," Swearingen said. "I can just see us now, Gussie, setting sail in something you whipped together with stickypatch and hairs pulled from your beard. Which aren't long enough to make ropes, in case you hadn't noticed."

"Rope . . ." the professor said, his eyes going hazy in what Margiu now knew meant a moment of thought. "We're going to need one really good cable to make this work . . ."

"There was cable in the planes," one of the pilots said. "But now—"

"Spares," said the other. "They had to stock spares somewhere around here—" He looked around the room they were in, bare to the walls except for the pallets.

"I know," offered one of the scientists. "What's the cable for, Gussie?"

"Towing the explosive," Gussie said. "We don't want to just drop it . . . then we'd have to delay its explosion, and it'd be below our last visible position. We want to tow it . . ."

"Out the back of a troop shuttle," said the first pilot, blinking. "I'm beginning to wish I weren't shuttle-qualified."

"It's doable," said the other. "I did a practice equipment drop once, and they shove the stuff out the back with a static line—there's a kind of yank, and then it's gone . . ."

"Fine; you can fly that part of it," said the first.

"What bothers me," said another scientist, "is the scan analysis of the explosion. If they've got somebody good up there—and we have to assume they do—then they're going to expect shuttle components in the explosion. You've proposed that we use some of the weaponry in development, and it certainly will make a big enough bang. But it won't have any shuttle-specific ID. Once they realize that, they'll know we're still around."

"What kind of stuff would it take?" Garson asked. "Can we just throw out the life rafts or something?"

"No, it's the explosion itself. They'll expect some differences, because they'll know the shuttle has exotic new stuff on it, but the shuttle itself, when it explodes, would contribute recognizable chemical signatures. The shuttle weaponry, for instance, would be assumed to go up with it."

"Why not just add the shuttle's weapons pods to the tow load?" asked Margiu. Everyone stopped and looked at her.

"Of course!" The professor, unsurprisingly, was the first to recover speech. He beamed at her. "Didn't I say redheads were naturally brilliant?"

"But that would leave us with no weapons . . ." Garson said.

"But we weren't going to fight our way out with the shuttle anyway," said the professor. "We're just using it as transport. We know we can't take on a deepspace ship."

Garson chewed this over a long moment. Finally he nodded. "All right. It makes sense, I just . . . don't like not having them. But as you said, they'll do us more good proving we're not there, when we are. I'll add that to our list of priorities once we get aboard. Be sure we have extra tiedowns and pallets, though."

The troop shuttle made a careful circle around the island; its onboard scans could pick out details from a distance that made light weapons ineffective. The NEMS clustered on the runway with the little huddle of scientists obviously under guard and the tarp-wrapped bundles of the cargo beside them. The shuttle made another approach, this time dropping out a communications-array bundle. The NEM commander grabbed it and flicked it on. Margiu could hear what he said, but not what the shuttle crew answered.

"No—we were mainland based—at Big Tree—waiting, but we got grabbed for this mission—yeah—no. No, he died in the first firefight. Got his body, if you want it. I've got his ears. . . ."

The shuttle swung back, slower yet, and settled onto the runway. Margiu had not realized how *loud* such shuttles were, if no one bothered to baffle the exhaust. She could hear nothing but its own whining roar. The great hatch in the rear swung down, forming a ramp. Five men came out, weapons ready. Surely there weren't just five . . . no, there came another five, setting up a perimeter.

The NEMs waved; the newcomers waved back as they came forward. Margiu could sense the moment in which they decided it was all right, when their attention shifted from the "mutineers" to the scientists and their equipment. Margiu flicked through the channels on her p-suit headset, and found the active one.

"Got 'em all, did you?"

"Except the dead ones," one of the NEMs said. "Listen, we've got to get all this aboard—and there's another load packed up inside. How many personnel d'you have?"

"Eighteen. They want us to hurry it up—"

"Come on, then." Half the NEMs turned, as if to head back inside; the others were still obviously guarding the scientist-prisoners.

"Barhide—come on down—" said one of the newcomers. Eight more armed men came down the shuttle's ramp.

These were much less wary, their weapons now slung on their backs.

"We're goin' in to pick up the rest of the cargo," she heard one of them say, and someone aboard the shuttle—a pilot, she hoped—told them to hurry it up.

With her primary task still the professor's life, she had no part in the brief, violent struggle that followed, when the NEMs and the other loyalist troops jumped the mutineers and killed them, while the putative rebel NEMS chivvied the scientists toward the shuttle, talking loudly on open mikes. It took less than two minutes, and most of it had happened out of sight of scan from overhead. Margiu scrambled out of her p-suit into the gray shipsuit of the dead enemy, rolled him into her p-suit, and let one of the NEMs haul him out by the legs. She crammed the com helmet on her head, tucking the telltale red hair out of sight, and stalked out onto the runway as if she belonged there.

The cargo was moving slowly up the ramp, with the laboring scientists complaining vociferously that it was dangerous, that it could blow them all up, that they should be *careful*. The NEMs swung their weapons, threateningly; scientists cringed; Margiu found it hard to believe it wasn't real. From the unreality of those hours of waiting, when it was real, to this—the reversal confused her, but she found herself playing her part anyway.

They made it onto the shuttle, Margiu and the others working under the scientists' directions to get the cargo lashed down. Out of the corner of her eye, she saw one of the mutineer flight crew peering through from the flight deck.

"How much longer?" he called.

"They say it could blow us all to hell if it wiggles in flight," the NEM sergeant said. "And it's heavy—you don't want it to shift."

The other man grinned. "All right, all right. Just try to hurry it up. Admiral wants to boost out of this system now we've been spotted . . ."

Margiu turned her head away, afraid her expression would be too obvious. So her half-remembered design had worked, had it? And somewhere, sometime soon if not already, Fleet would find out what was going on at Copper Mountain. At least that had worked, and if she died today, she would have done something worthwhile.

When they had the last of the equipment in the shuttle, one of the NEMs signalled the shuttle pilots—Margiu couldn't hear what was said, but the sudden lurch of the shuttle made it clear they were moving. Their own pilots, wearing dead mutineers' uniforms, stood near the front, ready to take over from the mutineers when they had enough altitude and the stealth equipment was ready to use.

They had been airborne perhaps ten minutes—the wrinkled blue sea had become a hazy blue carpet far below—when Major Garson worked his way forward past the pallets and tiedowns to the front. He spoke to the NEM sergeant, and then the waiting pilots. Margiu's stomach clenched. She glanced at the professor, who was grinning. She wondered if he was ever scared, or if having a constant ferment of crazy ideas protected him from fear.

Only one NEM could fit on the flight deck, but armored as he was, the sergeant should be safe from most weapons the pilots might carry. And they'd shown no concern about their passengers.

The NEM went through onto the flight deck; the first pilot followed closely. Margiu took a good grip of the stanchion; they'd all been warned to get a good handhold, just in case. In case of what, she'd wondered.

The shuttle nosed over sickeningly, and Margiu's stomach rose to the back of her throat. What was happening up front? Weight slammed back onto her, as the shuttle pitched up, then lifted as the nose dropped once more. She gulped, swallowed, gulped, and just managed not to spew. Someone else wasn't so lucky. Her imagination raced through scenarios—the mutineer pilots trying to crash the shuttle; the loyalist pilots trying not to let them, the scan crews up on the station reacting to the shuttle's erratic movements with demands for information. The downward pitch levelled slowly, and weight returned, stabilized.

The flight deck door opened, and one of their own looked out. "He was willing to suicide—" he said shakily. "But we've got it now."

"To your places," the professor said. Margiu made her way to the rear of the shuttle, and had, from that vantage, a clear view of the actors as they went about their pretense.

Margiu found the experience very unlike watching a storycube, even though she understood the plot: knowing, as she did, that the conversation was faked on one end, she couldn't help worrying that it was faked on the other end as well.

Surely the mutineers weren't taken in by the pretense? Surely they would realize soon enough that the cross talk between the supposedly mutinous NEM and the cringing scientist was too contrived to be real? That the irregular alternation of disappearance and reappearance from scan had to be a setup? Surely they would catch on when the ship disappeared that final time, and then there was an explosion . . . She glanced at the professor, who was nodding and grimacing at the "actors."

What if the mutineers had a vid scan in here? He was enjoying himself far too much to be a real scientist captured by mutineers and forced to betray his side. They could be laughing their heads off up in the station, just waiting the best moment to blow them all away.

But the playlet went on without interruption, and the comments from above indicated that the audience had suspended any initial disbelief. Two of the scientists had uncovered the device and plugged in a control panel of some sort. At the professor's nod, they did whatever it was that turned the device on and off. Supposedly the shuttle disappeared, partially returned, disappeared, returned, repeatedly. Margiu tried to relax, as the climax neared. She had her assignment, to signal when to drop the trailer with its weapons pods and assorted junk.

"Zed's on—drop it!" Margiu tapped the crew chief at the tail and clung to the stanchion as he opened the cone and pushed the lever. The shuttle's nose bobbed up again, as the load slid out, and the marked cable unrolled in a streak.

"And Zed's on?" Garson asked.

"Zed's on," confirmed Swearingen. "We are—we should be—completely invisible, with a computer-generated scan filling the hole as we go."

Light flared behind them—the first explosion. Then, about the time the debris should hit the ocean, the second. The shock wave from that rocked the shuttle.

"That'll blur his screens for at least another thirty seconds," said one of the other scientists.

The shuttle flew on, out across the open ocean where the generated fill pattern should, the scientists thought, have its best chance to work. It had the fuel load to circle the planet, but—as Garson had pointed out—all the airfields would have crew, and might still have intact communications gear. Either loyalist or mutineer, someone would be sure to comment on the arrival of a troop shuttle, and if they tried to communicate themselves, that could be detected from topside.

"We have to assume they're using the surveillance satellites—if we drop Zed, or open a com hole in it, we're immediately visible. And vulnerable. We can land this thing anywhere, just about—that's what a combat shuttle is for, after all."

Half a world away from the main base at Copper Mountain, a loose gaggle of rocky islands rose from the blue sea. Large and small, rough and rougher, cloaked in grass and trees, they had never been used for anything but occasional shuttle landing exercises. The pilots flew low over several of them, until they spotted the bright reflection of what might be a freshwater stream. That one was much larger than any of the Stack Islands, with a shallow grassy bowl set above low cliffs. The pilots eased the shuttle in vertically, and at last it came to rest.

The broad meadow was striped with shadows from the rocky outcrops. Overhead, a wavering cloud streamed, smooth on the windward side, and ragged on the lee. Beyond it, far across the ocean they could not see from this bowl, rows of cumulus drifted slowly before the wind.

"It's a large island, but it's still an island," said the professor. "At least we're safe up here from any reasonable storm."

Now that they weren't having to fly the unfamiliar shuttle, the pilots had time to work with the instruments and see what, if anything, could penetrate Zed's stealth blanket in an outward direction.

After an hour or so, one of the pilots came out of the shuttle and shouted to the others.

"Outbound. They're outbound, the whole lot of them." The others crowded closer.

"You're sure?" Garson asked.

"Well, unless this stealth thing is creating a very weird false image that looks just like a lot of ships moving into formation toward the jump point."

"Time to jump?"

"They're hours from a safe radius for microjumping—then it'll depend on whether they choose to microjump out to the jump point or not." The pilot grinned. "But they'll be out of nearscan range in a few minutes—behind the planet."

"It occurs to me to wonder why they didn't just incinerate this planet as they left," the professor said.

"You have such cheerful ideas," Garson said. "They know they have other allies down here?"

"Perhaps," the professor said. "Though I don't know how much they care about their allies. Are there resources here they still want, even though they think the weapons research stuff is all gone? Do they want this as a base later?"

"Once they're gone, we can just fly back to the main base, can't we?" asked Swearingen.

"If we built a wooden ship," the professor said, "it'd be less detectable by conventional means, and we could sail it back—"

"Gussie, I am not going to indulge your taste for historical re-creation and try to build a sailing ship from these trees," Swearingen said. "They aren't even straight."

"That's exactly why we could do it. Look at them—they're already shaped like keels and ribs and things. I'm sure Margiu thinks it's a good idea . . ." The professor gave Margiu a wide grin; she found it hard to resist, but the thought of going out on the water in a home-made boat terrified her.

"Look at her," someone said. "You've scared her, Gussie."

"We have a perfectly good troop carrier," Garson said. "We'd be crazy not to use it."

"All right," the professor said, with a deliberate pout, "but you're taking all the fun out of this."

"We'll leave when they're out of nearscan range and then go back to the main base," Garson said. "We've done what we came for, and they may need us back there."

"I don't suppose you'd agree to stop by some tropical island for a little recreation . . . ?"

"This is as tropical as you get, professor. Enjoy it while you can," Major Garson said.

"You're no fun." But he didn't seem really annoyed. He wandered off to look at the grove of twisted trees.

"We'd better leave soon," Garson said, "or he'll decide to have us make spears and crossbows from those trees."

"Nothing that simple," said Swearingen. "He'll go for trebuchets and ballistas and a couple of hang gliders."

CHAPTER TWO

***Favored-of-God*, Terakian & Sons courier**

Goonar Terakian looked at the newsfax and found it hard to breathe. Mutinies, markets collapsing in all directions . . . and all he'd wanted to do was work his way up to become a captain of one of the Terakian ships.

"We're free traders," he said, half to himself. "We're unaligned."

"Not exactly." Basil Terakian-Junos slouched against the opposite bulkhead. "I don't fancy running off to the NewTex Militia. Hazel says—"

"And that's another thing," Goonar said. "Hazel. We're mixed up with her family, which doesn't want to be mixed up with us."

"What do we want out of all this?"

"Well, we don't want a war, that's for sure," Goonar said. "We want a chance to make a living, same as anybody else."

"Not the same . . . a good living. And wars sometimes prosper traders."

"Well . . . yes. When they don't kill them outright. Protection for our property. Opportunity. Economic stability, so we can depend on credit and currency."

" 'Profits are highest in times of trouble,' " Basil quoted.

"Yes. But so are losses."

"The question is, which side offers us the best deal?"

"The question is, how do we define the best deal?"

"It's not our decision, Goonar. Our fathers—"

"Won't have to live with the outcome. We will. I'm not going to stand by and see them ruin us."

"Kaim is one of us—"

"Kaim is crazy. We both know that. Yeah, the mutineers are strong now, but they're not the sort of people we want to do business with, not in the long run."

"What about . . ." Basil hooked his thumb and gestured to the far wall.

"The Black Scratch? You'd try dealing with the Black Scratch?"

"Very cautiously, maybe."

"Not me," Goonar blew on his finger, expressively. "The tongs aren't long enough."

"If the Familias comes apart—"

"It won't if we keep our heads."

"We?"

"All the real people—the traders, shippers, ordinary people."

It struck Goonar suddenly as ridiculous that he had described Terakian & Sons, Ltd., as "ordinary people" but he didn't let that internal chuckle show in his face. Better if Basil didn't think about that one too long.

"Right now," he said, tapping the manifest display, "we have a cargo to worry about, customers to serve. Things won't get better if we start playing doom-caller."

"Spoken like someone who wants to be a captain," said Basil, only half-joking.

"And you don't?" Goonar cocked an eye at him. Their last recommendation had resulted in a solid profit; he and Basil had their bonuses, and he'd put his in the captain's pool for the first time.

"I do, but—captains always have to think of the long term, and you know, cuz, that sometimes I'm a bit more focussed on the short."

That was true, but this was the first time Basil had admitted it.

"I'd rather be your second and stay your partner: you steady me down, and I keep you from being stodgy."

"I'm not stodgy," Goonar said, trying to sound stodgy to hide the inner glow that came from Basil's admission that they weren't in competition for the next open captaincy.

"You would be," Basil said, "if you didn't have me kicking you every now and then. I told the Fathers two days ago."

Which meant Goonar was up to number three, at least, in the pool, and sending in his bonus money had been even smarter than he thought. Captains had to have ship shares before selection; he had been saving for years for this, investing carefully.

"We'll make a good team," Goonar said, accepting Basil as formally as the Terakian family ever accepted anyone.

"We already do," Basil said.

As they turned again to the manifest display, one of the clerks knocked on the door. "Goonar—there's a message from the Fathers."

"Thanks," Goonar said. He took the sealed packet—two levels below the highest secrecy—and thumb-printed it until the seal peeled back. He stared at the first line, and felt his face flush. "Basil—!"

"What is it, your first ship?"

"You knew!"

"I didn't . . . but Uncle did hint that something nice was coming to you, and did I want to ride your coattails, or strike out on my own."

"It's the *Fortune*." Old *Fortune,* one of the real prizes of the Terakian & Sons fleet, had close to the ideal blend of cargo capacity and maneuverability, including an ample shuttle bay and two drone cargo shuttles. Goonar went on reading. "It's Miro—he's developed some neurological condition, and they don't want to rotate captains through the ships in this political crisis—they want to keep people with crews they know, and routes they know . . ."

"Miro . . ." Basil said. "Did he ever rejuv?"

"I haven't a clue. Get off that, will you? People developed shakes and bad memory long before rejuvenation. But—what a plum! What a ship!" He went on reading. "We're taking over *Fortune*'s regular routes, but I have leave to expand or contract them as I see fit . . . report acceptance/refusal by fastest secure route . . . As if anyone in his right mind would refuse this—" He stopped and looked at Basil. "Finish up that manifest check for me, Bas, and I'll go answer this."

The *Terakian Fortune* was everything Goonar had hoped for, and more. Miro's crew accepted him readily, the cargo couldn't be better—he couldn't lose money unless he flung it out the hatch—and the first two stops went so smoothly that he let Basil talk him into spending several days downside at the next, Falletta, meeting with Terakian's agents, lunching with local bankers, inspecting merchandise before it was packed up. He found a suitable thank-you gift for the Fathers and a pendant for Basil's wife. Basil came back from his own forays into the local markets to suggest an evening at the theater.

"I'm not going to sit through one of those acrobatic noise festivals," Goonar said.

"It's not that. It's something you'll like."

"Really."

"*Brides of the Mountains*. It's a really good company, too."

"Out here in the sticks?"

"Come on, Goonar; it's better than sitting in the hotel doing nothing."

The curtains opened on a stage set for the traditional drama *Brides of the Mountains* . . . a peasant village, with peasant men lounging around pretending to hold agricultural implements as if they knew what to do with them. The backdrop was painted with purple mountains that looked like nothing on any of a hundred planets.

Goonar nudged his cousin. "Even I know more about a scythe than that fellow on the left."

"Hssh." Basil gave him a brief glare. "Just wait."

The overture swelled, and the peasants drew breath. A flourish of pipes brought in the peasant women, brilliant shawls around their shoulders, and the men burst into song.

> Lovely as the morning star
> sweet girls, our brides to be

Goonar had to admit they could sing. Loudly, at least. He caught himself starting to hum along and stopped before Basil could poke him in the arm.

The women's chorus responded as the music changed keys.

> Strong as the trees that dare the heights
> brave boys, our husbands to be

Then they opened out, and revealed the most beautiful woman Goonar had seen.

And yet, my dears, we will not wed
until you prove your faithful love—

Rich red-brown hair—it might be a stage wig, of course, but it moved so naturally . . . lush figure, though of course it might be the costume. Her mellow voice filled the hall, and she seemed to be looking straight at Goonar. His breath shortened. He was too old to have this reaction—but his body paid no attention to his mind.

All through the first act, in which the men left on a dangerous quest, and the women of a neighboring village came to visit, Goonar argued with himself.

In the second act, as the women of the two villages changed places, to follow and test their respective suitors, Goonar thought he had himself in hand. Betharnya Vi Negaro—he had glanced at the program in the brief interval between acts—was a well-known actress and singer, and of course she wasn't looking at him. Not him in particular. Probably every man there felt she was flirting with him alone. Maybe she was. During the dance sequence, he tried to fault her dancing. That blonde was more nimble . . . that brunette had a wider smile.

The long interval, between the second and third acts, found him silent. He could feel Basil's gaze, but refused to meet his eyes.

"What did you think of her?"

"Who?"

Basil grabbed his elbow. "*Her*, you idiot. Bethya. Isn't she gorgeous?"

"She's an actress," Goonar said, pulling his arm away. "She's got to be. Are you thirsty?"

Basil heaved a dramatic sigh; Goonar headed for the refreshment booths. When they both had drinks in hand, Basil backed him into a corner.

"She's coming with us," Basil said. "Actually, the whole troupe is. They're worried about the borders."

"An acting troupe?"

"They'd rather perform here than there," Basil said, jerking his head to the side where, Goonar supposed, he'd already determined the Benignity to be.

"So—you pointed me out as a Terakian." Which meant she had

seen money and influence and maybe competence . . . those glances had been directed at his position, not at him.

"No. But she does know my face. Why—did you think she was looking at you?" Basil's indulgent tone stung, as perhaps it was meant to.

"No," Goonar said. And to himself, silently, *I know.*

In the third act, with the cross talk between faithful and unfaithful lovers and their various temptresses, Goonar tamed his wayward heart and put his mind to considering just how the troupe and its supplies could best be packed aboard the ship. He reached for his handcomp once, but caught himself before flipping it open. But the climax, when the mysterious stranger has won the heart of the village beauty, when her former suitor attacks the stranger, and is killed by him, and the girl must choose whether to go or stay . . . that held him fascinated by a story he had known since childhood. What would she choose? Again she seemed to be looking at him—at Basil, he reminded himself—and again he could not help responding. She was someone to fight for, to kill for if necessary.

After the show, on the street, Goonar strolled along savoring the memory of that look. He could always pretend it had been meant for him.

"Come on," Basil said. "We have to hurry."

"Why?" Goonar said. "We have two days before we lift."

"Not any more," Basil said. "I put us on the short list."

Goonar stopped short, careless of the crowd. "What! *You* put? Who's captain of this ship, anyway?"

"Goonar, please! Not here. I'll explain, but there wasn't time. Seriously." Basil for once looked more worried than truculent.

Goonar walked on, lengthening his stride to keep up with Basil. "So, just how long do we have?"

"As soon as they're loaded. I offered to help, but they said they'd rather . . . tear down, I think they said . . . themselves. Less obvious."

Goonar managed not to stop again by an act of will; he wanted to shake Basil upside down. "In other words, we're carrying fugitives." Terakian & Sons did not carry fugitives; it was a rule made long ago for good reason.

"Not . . . officially."

"Not officially carrying, or not officially fugitives?"

"Goonar . . . please, just let's get off the street."

That was beginning to sound like a really good idea. Goonar glanced up the street, at the status board for the city's spaceport tram, and moved faster.

The tram deposited them at the main terminal, where they cleared the first level of security and boarded the 'port tram, which took them to the private bays. Once they were in the Terakian compound, Goonar turned on Basil.

"Are we bringing them up on a family shuttle?"

"No, they're taking a bigger shuttle—one of the duals—but we need to prepare, I thought."

"Basil—"

"I know, I know." Basil spread his hands and tried to look contrite, an expression that sat uneasily on his face. "Terakian and Sons does not carry fugitives, does not involve itself in local politics, does not interfere in legal actions—"

"So explain." Goonar tapped out the code on the shuttle's access hatch, and the pilot's voice came over the intercom.

"Yes, sir?"

"Heading up early, Jas. Goonar and Basil—" He went on with the family codes.

"Opening up." The pilot popped the hatch, and Goonar climbed in. Basil followed, but said nothing until they were both seated and strapped in. "Five to clearance," the pilot said. "There's a Benignity diplo shuttle coming in, and that bumps the departures back a bit."

Goonar stared at Basil, who flushed.

"A *Benignity* diplomatic shuttle. Does this have any relation whatsoever to the fact that we're running off with a troupe of singers and dancers from—where are they from?"

"Various places," Basil said. "They're talent, you know—they come from all over."

"And?" Goonar said.

"Well . . . they aren't fugitives. Exactly. It's just that they don't want to be. If they're not at the theater, then . . . it won't be an issue."

"And if they are?"

"I don't know," Basil said. "None of them are citizens of the Benignity, and none of them have committed a crime. They're just . . . maybe . . . people the Benignity would rather have stay there."

"Captives?"

"Of a sort. Maybe. I don't know. I just know they wanted to be out of here before the Benignity diplomatic mission arrived and got settled."

"And they knew it was coming?" Goonar asked.

"Apparently," Basil said. He still looked embarrassed, which Goonar knew from experience meant he hadn't yet told all he knew. Goonar felt tired; dragging facts out of Basil had exhausted better men than he.

"Please, Basil," he said. "I'm the captain now; I have to know. Are we going to be pursued by Benignity warships? By Familias warships? Are we transporting stolen property? State secrets?"

Basil glanced out the window as the shuttle rolled forward slowly and pursed his lips. "I don't think we'll be pursued by anyone— certainly not before we can make it into jump." Goonar did not think that "not before we can make it into jump" was anything like "not pursued" but he waited for the rest of it. "As far as I know, there is no stolen property. I made that clear to her, and she said there was nothing," Basil said. "State secrets—I didn't ask about that, because if they are running with data, she wouldn't tell me anyway."

"So—do you think they'll be out of the theater before the Benignity gets there?"

"I think so, yes." Basil leaned forward. "If all went well, they weren't that far behind us; she said they'd be packing as the play went on."

"I assume by 'she' you mean Betharnya," Goonar said. "Is she the . . . what, the owner of the troupe or something? I thought she was just the leading lady."

"She's the manager, yes. As well as the female lead. Something happened to the manager they had before."

"When?" Goonar asked. "Where?"

"I think . . . on tour in Vorhoft."

"Which just happens to be in the Benignity—Basil, if you weren't my cousin and partner, I would cheerfully brain you."

"I know—"

"Delay," the pilot said, over the intercom. "That pigdung Benignity shuttle has asked Traffic Control for a hold for some reason."

Basil made a noise that Goonar easily interpreted, and the same thought was running through his own mind. He flicked down the seat com screen, and patched into the pilot's download of the local net. Ships at station, seven. Lucky number, seven—sometimes. But there'd been more than that when they docked four days ago. Ships insystem, incoming, three. He relaxed slightly. Ships outbound, eleven. He frowned, and checked the departure times.

"Did you notice this?" he said to Basil, pointing to the screen.

"What? No . . . wait . . . there should be more docked upstairs."

"Right. And look at the departure times . . . compared to the first scan record of the Benignity diplomatic mission."

"Ouch." Basil leaned forward. "Chickens scattering before a hawk."

"And you have us on the ground—away from the ship—a nice fat chicken, with the hawk already stooping." Goonar knew who would be blamed if Terakian & Sons lost by it—he was the captain, after all, and he was supposed to be in control. But before his uncle reduced him to mincemeat—if he survived to be minced—he could take a few chunks out of Basil.

"Sorry," Basil said, in an absent tone. "Did you know the Stationmaster up there is a Conselline agent?"

"No—and if you think that bit of information is going to distract me—"

"The ships that left—they're all Conselline Sept flags."

Goonar scolded himself for not seeing that first. "You're right. So—does that mean the Consellines are playing some game with the Benignity, or what?"

"I don't know, but Betharnya might. If we can get her safely away."

"Fat chance now," Goonar said. But at that moment, the pilot said, "Hold's unlocked. They've moved us up past a scheduled shuttle— they've got a red light on something. Ready for immediate takeoff?"

"Yes," Goonar said. The shuttle bumped over the guide strips in the taxiway, and swung onto another approach lane to the main runway. Far off to the right, he could see the main terminal, surrounded by the winking lights of other shuttles and long-haul aircraft. As they turned again, he saw something behind them. To the pilot, he said, "Something's on our tail, Jas . . ."

"I know," Jas said. Then, to Traffic Control, "Orbital shuttle outbound, Terakian and Sons, two passengers, ID 328Y. Auto shuttle outbound, Terakian and Sons, cleared cargo, manifest 235AX7."

"Check, 328Y. Cleared."

The cabin intercom clicked off. Goonar looked at Basil, who turned to look out the window.

"Basil . . . what do you know about an auto shuttle shadowing us?"

"I hope," Basil said, now studying his nails, "that it's a cargo shuttle."

"Failure to declare passengers is an offense under local and Familias law, Basil," Goonar said. Their own shuttle rolled forward, on the right-hand margin of the runway. He leaned to look out the left-hand windows. Sure enough, the other craft had come up beside them, the safest launch for an autopilot shadow. And far less visible from the main terminal.

"I know."

"Are there passengers on that shuttle, Basil?"

"I don't know. Maybe."

No use arguing until they got to the Station. If they did. Goonar leaned back as acceleration shoved him into the seat. Jas pulled both ships up into a steep climb once they were off the ground, then directed the cargo shuttle—unlit and almost invisible—to a safe distance.

They cleared atmosphere without any problems that Goonar knew about—and he had patched in to the pilot's communications. On approach to the Station, he heard Jas's bland explanation to Traffic Control.

"The boss has us on the short list, so I thought I'd just autopilot the cargo shuttle up. Otherwise I'd have to ferry Reuben down to bring it . . ."

"Some day one of you guys is going to crash one of those auto shuttles and kill us all."

"Not this day," Jas said. "I'm going to dock 'er right onto the *Fortune*. No danger to the Station at all."

"What about her papers?"

Jas reeled off the same manifest number and clearance codes.

"All right. Just be careful."

"You won't feel a thing."

❀   ❀   ❀

Once aboard *Fortune*, Goonar headed straight for the bridge. As he'd expected, Station Security wanted to inspect the autopiloted shuttle and its cargo. This was standard, and probably had nothing to do with the Benignity diplomatic mission, or even the Benignity liner docked on the far side of the station. Goonar made the predictable protests—they'd already cleared customs down below, this was costing him time and money, he might lose his launch spot. This too was standard. If he didn't protest, at least a little, they'd notice that change in behavior. When he judged the right moment had come, he gave in semi-graciously.

The Station Security team came first to the bridge, where he handed them the hardcopy of the manifest, assigned a junior officer to lead them back to the cargo shuttle, now tucked into its bay. "And no dillydalling," he said to the young woman. "We've got a slot to keep."

He spent the next hour on departure paperwork—one of the loaders had failed to clear a repair bill, and he had to authorize transfer of funds to cover it. Another loader still wasn't aboard . . . Georg, as usual. Which meant he was deep in a philosophical discussion somewhere; Georg could handle drink and women, but not the thrill of finding another person who wanted to talk about Will and the Oversoul. Goonar knew from experience that Station Security wouldn't have a clue where such a discussion might be going on; he himself had to figure it out. Universities were always a good bet, but this Station had only a technical school and a two-year arts school. Sure enough, Georg turned up in a coffee bar next door to the arts school. Goonar flagged a Station Security patrolman and asked him to get Georg on his way.

"Captain Terakian?" That was the head of the Station team, back at the bridge.

"Yes?"

"Er . . . we found nothing amiss, sir, but the Stationmaster says there's a request from the Benignity ship here to do a detailed search for some missing property." The man looked embarrassed. "I know, sir, that Terakian and Sons are reliable merchanters; I'm sure you have no Benignity property aboard. But—"

"And why is the Stationmaster kowtowing to the Benignity here in Familias Space?" Goonar asked. He would definitely throttle Basil, the first chance he got. "Or is this Benignity person, whoever he is, making a formal charge against me?"

The man flushed darker. "He's—I can't say anything, sir."

"Quite so." Goonar chewed his lip. "Then I will file a formal protest, with your Stationmaster and with Sector Three R.S.S. Headquarters and with the appropriate court." He turned to his deskcomp and called up the extensive legal files. With a few strokes of his datawand he entered the particulars, and transmitted the first file to the Stationmaster.

In only a minute or two, the com screen lit, and the Stationmaster's face glared out. "What do you think you're doing, Terakian?"

"Protecting my legal rights," Goonar said. "You're asking me to submit to an unreasonable search on behalf of a foreign power which has offered no shadow of proof that my ship or crew has anything to do with some property they *claim* they're missing. You've given me no reason to comply, but your armed men are on my bridge."

"Don't get huffy," the man said; his eyes glanced to one side, as if to someone out of line of the pickup.

"You haven't seen huffy yet," Goonar said. "We're a reputable firm; we've traded here for over forty years. We're all Familias citizens, and this is supposed to be a Familias port. If you've changed its affiliation to the Benignity, I'm sure Fleet would like to know. So would its own citizens, who are still under the impression that they have civil rights."

"I'm just trying to keep things friendly," the Stationmaster began.

"By accusing us of being thieves?" Goonar said. "That's not the way to keep Terakian and Sons friendly. And I notice all the Conselline Sept ships have left—did you fully search *them*, or are you playing favorites?"

"They left before we got the request," the Stationmaster said. "And it's not that we think you did anything. You're too defensive—"

"Of my ship, and my family's good name, I'm damned defensive, and with good reason," Goonar said.

"It's just that they wanted us to check on any ship that had cargo from downside. They said they'd help."

Alarm bells went off all the way down Goonar's spine. "The Benignity said it would help? How?"

"They've offered to lend us their own security personnel, who know exactly what they're looking for . . ."

Goonar said, "You're asking us to let *foreign troops* onto our ship to search us? What kind of traitor are you, anyway?"

"They're not troops, they're . . . more like the police."

Goonar grunted. "They're foreign, whatever you want to call them. No. No foreign personnel are going to set foot on a Terakian ship, so they can figure out how to pirate us later. Absolutely not."

"I insist."

"You can insist until the stars go cold. No. If you want your own Station Security—and I will check their Familias citizenship—to prowl around looking for God knows what, that's one thing. But the Benignity will never set foot on my decks, and that's final."

"That's unwise, Captain." Now the person the Stationmaster had been glancing to moved into pickup range. An officer of some kind, in a uniform Goonar didn't recognize. Not the usual Benignity naval uniform, which he did know. "It will save you—and us—and others—a great deal of trouble if you will only permit that search now. Otherwise—"

"Threatening civilians in the Familias?" Goonar did not have to simulate anger. "What—have you hidden an invasion fleet in the edge of the system or something?"

"We don't need such crude methods," the man said. "You will never leave this station alive if you don't let us board."

"Hey—wait a minute!" The Stationmaster reached for the man, but sagged suddenly. Goonar had seen no weapon, but he had seen enough. He glanced over his shoulder at the Security team commander, who looked as startled as he felt himself. "Sorry," he said, and gave the Terakian signal.

Even as he did, he thought of Georg, poor Georg who was about to find out if the Oversoul was any more real than his own imagination.

Terakian crew had only the usual sort of riot training, but they were more than capable of disabling the search team which had, after all, expected nothing to happen. As Goonar said, they'd seen Terakian ships before, and Terakians didn't cause trouble.

"You can't *do* this," the search team's commander said indignantly, when he was wrapped in tangletape.

"I'm sorry," Goonar said. "But I'm not about to let a Benignity team aboard this ship. They're foreigners, and it wasn't that long ago they invaded Xavier. I'm not going to let them take this ship and use it to infiltrate Familias space. Everybody knows Terakian ships—"

The commander's eyes widened. "Is that what you think they're up to?"

The excuse had come upon him like a random hit from space debris, but Goonar knew a good idea when he found one. "Why else a so-called diplomatic mission to a backwater like this? Why else would they be putting a hold on outbound traffic, wanting to search each ship? They're looking for the right one. We're an independent trading firm—we've got plenty of cubage, and they'd just dump our cargo before jumping, give themselves more room—"

"But—"

"We haven't been anywhere near Benignity space, so how could we have anything of theirs? No. They're after this ship, or one like it. They can blow me away, I don't care—" He did care, intensely, but he could see in the commander's eyes a growing belief in what he said. Embroidery in the service of truth, the family said, was not a lie. "I'm not letting them use my ship that way."

"I . . . see. I did wonder—"

"Of course you did." Basil, now that the rest of the team had been disarmed and immobilized, came to stand beside Goonar. He had waited until he heard enough of Goonar's spiel to be sure he wouldn't muddy the trail. "It's not often you get Benignity ships in here, is it? And a diplomatic one giving orders to the Stationmaster?"

"What they said was, some fugitives came in on a transport within the last four weeks, they weren't sure from where. A bunch of actors who'd been in Benignity space, fled with stolen goods, and all they knew was that all the leads led here."

"An acting troupe?" Basil frowned, as if taking this seriously. "What could an acting troupe steal that would be worth this kind of chase?"

"They didn't say. I wouldn't think actors would have access to anything that valuable, myself."

"Unless . . ." Basil said, dragging the words out. "Suppose—suppose another fugitive—a political fugitive, say—tried to take sanctuary among actors, and they smuggled the person out—or the Benignity thought they did."

"Ridiculous!" Goonar said. "Why would actors take in a political fugitive—or anyone they didn't know? That'd be like a Terakian ship picking up any riffraff off the docks. We know better; surely they do too. Besides, I don't believe there's anything behind this but the Benignity wanting a ship to use invisibly in Familias space."

"Yes, but it would make sense," Basil said. "Look at it from the Benignity point of view—"

"I am," Goonar said. "And what I see is their desire to use my ship. And I say no."

"Look," the Security commander said, "let me talk to the Stationmaster. I'm sure you don't have any contraband—and maybe he hasn't realized what the Benignity are up to . . ."

"He'd have to be an idiot," Goonar said, clashing with Basil's "He probably thought they were telling the truth, and maybe they are . . ."

"Just let me tell him. You don't really want to hijack my team—that will cause trouble."

"I don't want to take a chance on losing my ship," Goonar said. But he nodded to his crew, who cut the tangletape and let the militia leader walk up beside Goonar. The man faced the screen.

"Look . . . sir, Captain Terakian is convinced that the Benignity wants to steal his ship. He thinks this is why they've been insisting on searching ships before they leave—that they're looking for a suitable vessel in which to infiltrate the Familias."

"That's ridiculous," the Benignity commander said. "Only a guilty man could have made up a farrago of lies like that—"

Goonar leaned into pickup range. "It's not a lie that you people invaded Xavier. As far as I'm concerned, you're the guilty ones. The worst I ever did was get drunk and punch a Fleet ensign back when I was greener than grass."

The Benignity commander glared, and Goonar met his gaze glare for glare. He'd been glared at by experts in his time—his own father and Basil's among them—and he wasn't intimidated. In fact, now that he'd worked himself into believing his own story, he was able to project patriotic ferocity. Finally the Benignity commander sighed. His gaze shifted to the Security commander. "Did you actually inspect every compartment?"

"No . . . only the shuttle bays and the freight compartments adjacent."

"And they had only thirty minutes . . . What was in that auto-shuttle?"

"What was on the manifest . . . sealed containers, marked with the shipping agents' codes . . ."

"Did you open them?"

"Not all of them, no." The Security commander, who had been sounding sulkier throughout this exchange, now burst out. "Listen—you're not *my* commander, and I know the Terakians. As far as I'm concerned, they could well be right, and I see no reason why I should do your dirty work."

A long silence, during which Goonar tried to pump up his resentment of Basil for getting them into this mess into a visible rage at the Benignity. Evidently he succeeded, because the Benignity commander, after a last glare, relaxed slightly.

"All right, Captain Terakian. You may depart. I suppose you're taking those rather useless specimens of Station Security with you . . ."

"Not if they don't want to go," Goonar said. "But since you appear to be in command of a civilian Station, they might rather." He glanced at the Security commander, whose face had paled as he thought through the implications of that.

"We intend no harm to the civilian population," the Benignity commander said.

"Just like at Xavier," Goonar said.

"Can we stay?" the Security commander asked Goonar.

"I'm not going to put Familias citizens in the hands of the Benignity if they choose to avoid it," Goonar said. He sounded pompous, almost theatrical, and hoped the Benignity commander would simply think he was that way by nature. Maybe he was. His family always insisted that the real character showed in times like these. "Ask your men."

CHAPTER THREE

Merchant ships always used tugs for undocking, but Goonar didn't trust the Benignity commander; he'd signalled his crew and powered up the ship the instant the Benignity commander appeared on screen. When he realized that the only real threat could be the Station's own defenses, he knew that his insystem drive was the only viable counterthreat. Yes, the Station could blow his ship . . . but with the insystem drive up, it was suicide for the Station and every other ship docked there. Now he ordered his pilot to pull away from the Station, as slowly as *Fortune*'s attitude thrusters permitted.

As soon as possible—it seemed longer than the chronometer indicated—he increased power and set his outbound course toward the jump point. When it appeared that the Station was not, after all, going to spend any of its meagre store of missiles on him, he turned to glare at Basil.

"Come on, Bas, we need to have a chat."

In the privacy of the shielded captain's cabin, Goonar rounded on Basil. "I ought to fry your kidneys for breakfast," he said. "Of all the stupid plots to get us tangled in—"

Basil didn't even try to look innocent this time. "It was important."

"And you didn't bother to tell me—"

"We didn't have time, cousin. Truly, I would have told you—"

"But you didn't." Goonar folded his hands together, rather than around Basil's neck. "Bas, we've been partners for years. You know me, and I thought I knew you. You chose not to put yourself forward for captain; you wanted to work with me—"

"Of course, I did—!"

"Wait. You know—you must realize—that a captain needs to be able to trust his second-in-command. You should have found a way, some way, to give me warning . . ."

Basil muttered something, looking away.

Goonar could feel his own neck stiffening. "Basil," he said. "What did you just say?"

"I said, I thought you'd act the innocent better if you were." Basil had flushed. "And you did."

For some reason, this struck Goonar as funny. He was still angry, and not ready to laugh, but he couldn't help it. "I might have done even better if I had known, cousin mine . . ."

"I'm sorry," Basil said, this time seriously. "I should have found a way. I will next time."

"There's going to be a next time?" Goonar asked.

"Not that I know of, but if," Basil said.

"Well, then. What is the great secret we're hauling? Did they tell you why the Benignity wants them? Or did you just fall for a pretty woman in distress?"

"It's one of the stage hands, they said. He's not a criminal, they said, but he is a fugitive."

" 'I am innocent of all wrongdoing, but envious rumor has spread lies around my feet,' " Goonar sang. "Act Two, Scene Four. Is that it?"

"I don't know," Basil said, spreading his hands. "I did ask, but they just insisted he wasn't a thief or murderer, and begged sanctuary."

Goonar sat up straight. "Sanctuary. That's a religious word. Did you speak to the person yourself?"

"Well . . . yes. I wanted to size him up. He's a quiet fellow—older man, pleasant voice—"

"A con artist," Goonar said.

"No . . . I don't think so. Not plausible and charming—I had the sense of . . . of someone like a scholar, maybe. The quietness wasn't fear or shyness, just a habitual quiet."

"An escaping professor? Someone with technical information?"

"I don't think so," Basil said. "I know some of them are supposed to be halfwits in the real world, but this man isn't that kind of halfwit.

He doesn't seem distracted or abstracted or whatever they call it—he's right there with you when he's talking to you, and he doesn't try to drag the conversation to his pet theory."

"Odd," said Goonar. "And he used the word sanctuary, or the woman did?"

"He did. It wasn't dramatic or anything." Now that Basil was spilling all he knew, he seemed almost annoyed with himself that it was so little. "I asked if he'd committed a crime, and he paused a moment before saying no, no crime, but he had angered someone in power."

"And you asked how—" Goonar prompted.

"Yes. And he didn't say. He said he wished sanctuary, not to spread rumors."

"Right. So now we've had a Benignity diplomatic ship giving orders to a Familias Station . . . and he thinks there won't be rumors."

"I haven't talked to him since we came aboard," Basil said. "Do you want me to?"

"No, I want to see him myself," Goonar said. "But not now. Now we have other work to do. For one thing, I don't want the Security team to know the troupe is aboard. They're actors; they can pretend to be our crew. Brief them."

Basil grinned. "That's a great idea."

"Meaning, you had it first. Fine. Just be sure it's done thoroughly. At the same time, I don't want the troupe having access to any of our critical information—see that our crew know that. And when you've straightened that out, find something for the Security team to do. Not all dirty work—they didn't really ask to be here, and we don't want them angry with us."

"Right," Basil said, jotting notes on his compad.

"I'll speak to—what's his name?"

"Simon. That's all he said."

"Right. I'll speak to Simon three or four days from now. I don't want to make him obvious at this point." He sighed, and tapped his fingers on his desk. "I don't know what's wrong with Falletta Station . . . I don't think much of a security team that didn't notice a bunch of actors and actresses, plus a whole stage set . . ."

"Well . . . they didn't exactly look like actors and stage

sets . . . remember, we had the best part of two hours," Basil said. "I wouldn't be the cargomaster I am if I couldn't dismantle and reassemble big loads to fit into available space."

"So . . . the flats you broke down . . ."

"No, that wouldn't have worked. We used them as is."

"As is what?"

"Well . . . you know the crew's rec compartment?"

"Of course," Goonar said.

"It's got that little raised area—actually for the cross-connecting vent pipes, but it makes like a little stage . . ."

"Yes, I know that . . . .wait . . . you mean you made it *into* a stage?"

"Yeah . . . they had scenery for more than one play, so we put up some of it, and stored the rest in plain sight, in the crew storage area. Now that wouldn't do for the costumes, or all the props, or the lighting control panels—"

"Wait—I thought theaters had their own lighting."

"They do, sort of, but many traveling troupes bring their own extras. It's expensive stuff, and—"

"So—what did you do with the lighting?" Basil was dying to tell him, and Goonar thought he should know, just in case.

"I'll show you."

The tour that followed convinced Goonar that his cousin was wasted in the Terakian family business, as much talent as he had for it. The troupe's stage lighting panels gave the shuttle bay better lighting than it had had since old *Fortune* came out of the yards . . . and only by climbing up among the overheads would anyone discover that it was an addition.

"They did compliment us on our safe lighting," Basil said, clearly referring to the Station Security team. "Said lots of ships tried to hide things in a half-dark compartment."

The costumes, bulky and spangled, were now on the programmable mannequins shipped by a famous fashion design firm, and the data cube in the container included those images. "It's only a copy," Basil said. "We have the original, so the shippers will never know. And Security didn't know the mannequins are normally shipped neutral. They did comment that the costumes looked used, and I pointed out that they had already been through several runs—that the big shipping firms get the new stuff, and we're stuck carrying last year's trash to the smaller systems."

"I see," said Goonar. He was not surprised when Basil handed him a revised crew list that included an astonishing number of Terakian relatives he'd never heard of before.

Five days later, the *Terakian Fortune* was still accelerating toward the mapped jump point, and Goonar was still worried. They were alive. No one had shot at them. No one was following them. No one they could *detect* was following them, he reminded himself. The Security team had settled in, working their assigned shifts alongside his crew. His augmented crew.

One thing about actors, they could play a role, and they learned quickly. The Security team knew little about the crew arrangements on free traders, and had accepted that the *Fortune* had an entirely unlikely complement of Terakian family members aboard. Wives, sisters, cousins . . . all of them supposedly certified and practiced crew, except for the old costume mistress, who was thoroughly enjoying her role as an aged great-aunt with delusions of matchmaking. She had already queried the Security team about their status and prospects.

Goonar had avoided talking to the troupe's leader himself—he'd had the excuse of being busier than usual—but finally he couldn't put it off any longer. She wanted to see him, she said.

Betharnya looked as good close up as on the stage. Goonar, conscious of his role as staid merchant captain, tried to keep his gaze on her face, but he did not miss the lush shape of her, or the delicate scent.

"I wanted to thank you, Captain Terakian," she said. "It was very brave of you—"

"Basil didn't tell me anything about this until after the performance," he said. "Then it was too late—but I have to say that while I admire you as an actress, I am not happy to have been misled. You may have irreparably damaged not just my reputation, but that of our family. We do not involve ourselves in politics."

"I understand," she said. "I would be angry too, if it were my ship. But when I approached Basil—your cousin—I didn't know about all that."

"So—you are from the Benignity?"

"No, but the kind of shows we do tend to go over better there. Traditional, you know. Like *Brides*."

"I liked it," Goonar said. "I've seen it on Caskadar—"

"We've never played Caskadar, but I've heard of it. Anyway—I suppose you want to know what happened?"

"It doesn't matter now, sera. We're already breaking the laws, whether for good reason or bad. You will, I hope, help me explain to the authorities at our next port . . . ?"

"Of course, Captain. I'm very sorry to have made trouble for you. Would you like to see our passports now?"

"When we're in the next system. Um . . . I must say your people are doing a good job of being crew . . ."

"Thank you," she said. "I'd better get back to work, in that case."

He wished she could stay and talk, but he couldn't think of anything to say. If only she weren't an actress . . . He fantasized, after she'd gone, about meeting someone like her at a Terakian gathering, instead of in the theater.

"We have to tell Fleet," Goonar said, when they came out of FTL flight into the Corrigan system. The few days in FTL had been uneventful, just the way he liked it. "It's the only way to clear the family of the charges that will be levelled against us."

Basil rolled his eyes. "I can just imagine what they'll say—we'll be held up for months while they investigate us down to the rivets."

"We don't have rivets," Goonar said. "You know that."

"You know what I mean," Basil said. "Down to the monomolecular seals, if you want to get technical about it. Not that we have anything to hide . . ."

"Not other than illicit foreign nationals, a hijacked security team, and a very unhappy Benignity search team," Goonar said. "Aside from that, we're as clean as ever."

Basil looked down.

"Aren't we?"

"Well . . . there might be a little sort of private stock here and there . . ."

"Enough. We're going to turn ourselves in at the first opportunity, and explain, as best we can, how we got into this mess."

Goonar sent a message about the situation at Falletta. The Fleet picket, now three ships in this system, tightbeamed them.

"What kind of Benignity ship?"

"A diplomatic mission, they said. I never actually saw the ship—we were docked on the other side of the Station. But my scans didn't show live weaponry on it."

"Did you get any data on the captain?"

"I got a video," Goonar said. "We record incoming communications in full, and I copied it to deep storage, just in case."

"They threatened you? The Benignity or the Station?"

"Some Benignity officer was in the Stationmaster's command center, and he threatened us. Told us we'd never leave the system alive if we didn't let him search the ship. I figured he wanted a way to snatch a Familias-registered independent to go spying in."

"But he let you go in the end?"

"Yes . . . not too happily, but he did. The Station's own Security team was aboard—"

"Why?"

"Well, before I realized what was up, they'd requested a routine search of one of our auto-shuttles, and I'd agreed, of course."

"Of course. Well, we'll want that copy of the transmission—we'd prefer to get it in person, not squirted—"

"So would I," Goonar said. "Who knows what's lurking out here?"

"Nothing right now," the captain said. "But just in case."

At Corrigan Station, Goonar handed over the data cube to the uniformed officer who waited in the loading area. The security team from Falletta had come with him; they were all to be interviewed. Basil, luckily, wasn't on the list that Fleet wanted to speak with.

The Fleet interviewer asked Goonar to tell what happened, and leaned back to listen. "It all started," Goonar said, "when my cargo-master, my cousin Basil, told me he'd moved the ship up in the departure queue. I asked him why, and he didn't say at first. We were on our way back to the ship, after a night on the town, and I had been looking forward to a late morning the next day."

"A night on the town?"

"Theater. Basil's been after me, the last few voyages, to loosen up . . . he thinks I'm too morose. My wife and children died, you see, a few years ago; he keeps trying to fix me up with beautiful women."

"Ah . . ." the interviewer's face took on a sympathetic expression that Goonar trusted about as much as he expected the interviewer to trust his own.

"He cares about me," Goonar said. "We grew up together, after all; we've been partners for ten years now. His daughter's my goddaughter; he had been my children's godfather. But he doesn't understand . . . I don't *want* another wife and family. I had the best, and lost them. Why should I risk so much again, for different people, and lose them again?"

"It's a hard life, alone," the interviewer murmured.

"Not really." Goonar leaned back and scratched his head. "I'm good at what I do. I'm earning a comfortable living. I have a position in our family. I don't need a wife." But he might need Bethya, his body told him. He didn't want to think about that.

"So, your cousin had been trying to get you to loosen up, and you hadn't enjoyed it—" the interviewer prompted.

"Well, I had, actually. I like theater, especially music dramas, as much as anyone. It had been fun, but I was sleepy, and wanted to spend another night downside, in the hotel. Basil insisted we had to get back to the ship. When we were in the shuttle, on the way, he told me he'd picked up a cargo, a theatrical troupe."

The interviewer's eyelids twitched, then his face returned to its schooled neutrality. "Is this what you told the authorities on Falletta?"

"No, of course not." Goonar puffed out his cheeks. "It was like this: Basil had us in the departure queue, with certified cargo. If I raised a stink, we could be stuck there for months, and I had time-critical cargo for here, among other places, with a hefty penalty for late delivery. If we hadn't been in the queue, it wouldn't have been so bad, but we were. I could cheerfully have killed Basil, but that wouldn't have done any good."

"So you knowingly accepted illicit cargo, including passengers . . ."

"You could put it that way. Meanwhile, the Benignity pressured the local government into delaying upshuttle flights, and departures from the Station. They said something about stolen property or fugitives—they didn't specify which, or what. I noticed that a lot of ships had left the Station as soon as the Benignity diplomatic mission arrived in the system—and they shouldn't have known anything about it until it arrived at the Station, unless the Stationmaster let them know. And he's a Conselline . . . and so were the ships that left, all under sept flags. I didn't know what was going on, but it didn't look like an ordinary search for stolen property to me. I'm not that green; I know when something's gone missing across borders—what usually happens is their police contact our police."

"So what's the real story?"

"I don't know it all. I told the actors' troupe leader that I didn't want to know anything—they could tell their story to you, and I'd report it as soon as we arrived in a safe place."

"Er . . . how much of this does the Falletta security team know?"

"Nothing of our cargo," Goonar said. "It was my judgment that the fewer people who knew about whatever it was, the better."

"I see," the interviewer said. "And when are you going to deliver the fugitives—if they are fugitives?"

"Whenever you say. At any rate, I'm not leaving here with them."

"Oh, but you are," the officer said. "At least, that'll be my first rec-ommendation. Whatever they have that the Benignity wants so badly, we don't want it rattling around out here. We have enough problems already. What's your next scheduled stop?"

"Trinidad, then Zenebra, then Castle Rock . . ."

"Fine. You keep them until Castle Rock, and deliver them to Fleet HQ."

"I can't do that!" Goonar didn't have to feign dismay. "We don't—Terakian doesn't—run errands for Fleet. We're neutral."

"Nobody's neutral now." The man leaned forward. "Listen, Captain—if you were really neutral you'd have left these people there. If you didn't care who won the next war, you wouldn't have defied the Benignity. You're not neutral: you're honest. There's a difference. I'm trusting you, here. I think, as you do, that whatever the Benignity wants that badly must be of benefit to our side, and I'm trusting you to get it to Fleet HQ, because I don't think anyone else could do it better."

"But—if they really believe whatever it is got away, then they have to think it's on our ship. We'll be marked—"

"There is a way around that, more or less. They can certainly *think* you offloaded whatever it was at this point. You can debark the Falletta security team here, for instance. As long as they don't know about the others—"

"They're convinced the others are legitimate Terakian crew."

"Well, then?"

"Except for all I know, the Benignity knows how many crew a Terakian ship usually carries."

"I doubt that. I certainly don't. It's never concerned the R.S.S., or most political entities, how many crew a ship has, only the ID of any crew who enter a station or go downside."

On the transit from Corrigan to Trinidad, Goonar made time to talk to Simon, the cause of the whole problem. Simon the stagehand—or fugitive—looked exactly as Basil had described him. Late middle-aged, with short silvery-gray hair going bald on top, a nondescript face, a medium-forgettable stature . . . and very bright, very intelligent brown eyes.

"I'm Goonar Terakian," Goonar said. "Captain of this ship. Can you tell me why I shouldn't just space you for all the trouble you've caused?" He had no intention of doing it, but he thought this might startle some information out of the man who had looked altogether too self-possessed when he came in.

"It would be a sin," Simon said slowly. "Though I'm not sure what your beliefs are—do you consider spacing people wrong, or not?" He seemed utterly unconcerned about the possibility—did he think Goonar wouldn't space anyone, or did he not care if it happened to him?

Goonar blinked and changed his approach. "Wrong, of course. But I also think it's wrong to come sneaking aboard ships and get them in trouble with the authorities."

"Discourteous," the man said. "I'm not sure I'd agree on wrong, at least not at the same level as spacing someone."

This was not going to be easy. Goonar felt himself getting hot behind his ears, a bad sign. He took a slow breath, trying to stay calm and not think of what he wanted to do to Basil. "Simon, Terakian & Sons has been careful to avoid carrying fugitives—"

"Then why didn't you let them take me off at Falletta?"

"Once aboard, you became my responsibility. I was not going to let foreigners on my ship. But we simply cannot afford to have you destroying a reputation we've built over generations . . . I need to know why you're a fugitive, and I must tell you that I'm going to turn you over to the authorities when we get to Castle Rock."

"I'm a heretic," Simon said. "At least, that's what they call me. Actually . . . I prefer to call myself an enlightened theologian."

"This is . . . a religious issue?" Simon nodded. Goonar frowned. "I didn't know the Benignity cared that much about religion."

Simon's eyes widened. "You—but—but don't you know that we're the one place where the true faith has survived?"

Goonar blinked. "Which true faith? I know a dozen sects—two dozen—each claiming to be the one true faith."

"That's what is wrong with the Familias Regnant," Simon said earnestly. "Too many sects, too many different belief systems not founded on the truth."

"And there's only one in the Benignity?" Goonar asked.

"Yes, of course. Officially, at least. I suppose there are pockets of other beliefs here and there—people are so superstitious, you know."

"So . . . if they think you're a heretic, does this mean you've strayed from this truth?"

"They think I have," Simon said. "But actually I haven't. They have."

Another religious nut. Goonar had not forgotten the young drunk in the bar at Zenebra Station, and though that one had been far more obnoxious than Simon, he still considered Simon one of the same type. At least for now.

"So . . . why are they so anxious to catch a heretic?" Goonar asked, deciding that this was what he really needed to know. That and *how* anxious . . . was the *Fortune* going to be in danger after he'd delivered Simon to Castle Rock?

"Because I was the Chairman's confessor," Simon said. "His last confessor, anyway."

Goonar fished about in his mind for the term but finally had to ask: "What's a confessor?"

"A priest someone tells their sins to. In private. Under the seal of confession, which means that priest can't ever tell anyone else what the person said. Now ordinarily, I wouldn't have been the Chairman's confessor, but I was there, in the palace, and his regular confessor got sick. A priest is a priest, at times like this, so—" He spread his hands.

"A heretic . . ." Goonar said. It didn't seem reasonable to him.

"Not yet declared one. I'd gone up to the city to talk to my superiors, you see. To explain where they—or their predecessors—had misinterpreted the applicable passages—but I'd not yet done so."

"I see," said Goonar, who didn't see, but wanted Simon to finish his story.

"Well, then, I heard the Chairman's last confession, and then he was executed—"

"Wait! Executed?" Goonar hadn't meant to interrupt but he couldn't help himself.

"Yes. I can't tell you why, because he told me during his confession. Anyway, they killed him, and that was that, except that a few days later, after hearing my testimony and arguments, the church decided that I was a heretic. Had been one for at least two years, the time in which I'd been working on that thesis. Which meant the late Chairman's confession had been heard by a heretic, which was more than a little irregular. They were afraid I'd tell, you see. Because of being a heretic."

"Um. They think you know some secrets the Chairman told you, which you could be trusted not to tell if you'd not been a heretic, but now they think you'll blurt it all out?"

"Yes. They *know* I know things which no one else knows—should know—because they trust that the late Chairman made a full and complete confession, and that would naturally include many things about the internal workings of the government."

"Did he make a full and complete confession?" Goonar asked, fascinated by the whole idea. "And how would you know if he did or not?"

"God would know," Simon said. "God would know, and an experienced priest can usually tell. I certified that the Chairman had made such a confession."

Which did not exactly answer his question directly, but Goonar let it go. Something else struck him. "So . . . they didn't trust you to keep it quiet, and the first thing you do is run toward their enemy?"

"Not the first thing," Simon said. "I tried to explain that I took my vows seriously, that I would never violate the confessional. But it was clear they didn't believe me; the new Chairman, in particular, did not trust me. I—I am willing to die for my faith, Captain Terakian, but not for a misunderstanding. So I fled. As a scholar, I had traveled widely, teaching and doing research in many places, so I knew how to travel discreetly. Most of the time. I had intended to slip across to the Guerni Republic, which is shockingly liberal in its views on religion, but has a marvelous set of archives where I thought I could find more material to prove my case. But then they found my trail." He paused.

"So how did you end up with a theatrical troupe?" Goonar asked.

"God guided me," Simon said. Goonar blinked, thought about asking more, and decided it could wait for another day.

Trinidad Station

Reception at the Regular Space Service sector of Trinidad Station swarmed with hurried, anxious Fleet personnel trying to make connections to their assigned ships, and equally hurried, anxious Fleet personnel trying to keep track of them.

Esmay Suiza-Serrano stepped into the ID booth and waited for the *ping* that would mean she'd matched her reference values. Instead, she heard the door snick shut behind her, and the little flashing light that should have gone green and steady went red and frantic instead. A mechanical voice said, "Do not attempt to exit the booth; remain in place until Security personnel release the lock. Do not attempt to exit the booth; remain in place . . ."

A soft whoosh from beside her, and the voice cut off. She turned to look and found herself facing the ominous maw of a weapon, with a very tense Security guard in armor behind it.

"Hands on your head, step this way."

In the face of the weapon, Esmay didn't argue. She knew she was who she said she was; she knew she hadn't done anything criminal, but this was not the time to say so. She put her hands on her head and stepped this way.

Beyond the booth, two more guards waited, both armed, with weapons drawn. The first guard picked up her carryon from the booth, and the other two waved her ahead of them down a corridor considerably quieter than the reception hall had been.

"In here." *Here* was a small compartment where a female security officer searched her thoroughly under the watchful eyes of the guards and the very obvious scan units mounted in the corners.

"You may sit down," the security officer said finally. Esmay sat down, more disturbed than she liked to admit to herself.

"Is there something wrong with the ID scan?" she asked.

"Not a thing," the officer said. "Wait here." She left, and the guards remained. The one carrying her bag had disappeared.

Time passed. Esmay thought of all the obvious things to say—there's been some kind of mistake, what's the matter, why are you holding me—and said nothing. Whatever was wrong, she might as well wait until she found someone in authority.

More time passed. She repressed a deep sigh and wondered if her former enemies, Casea Ferradi's friends, had framed her for some crime. Finally a very angry-looking commander stalked in and slapped down a folder on the table.

"I have orders to separate you from the Regular Space Service, as of today."

"What? What's going on?"

"I think you know very well, Lieutenant Suiza." His tone made a curse of her name. "And it would be best if you simply accepted the mercy of this separation with no more protests."

Despite herself, her voice rose a tone. "Excuse me, Commander, but according to the law I have a right to know what I stand accused of and a chance to defend myself."

"In a time of war, as you very well know, summary justice can take the place of a court-martial. Though if you prefer to sit around in a Fleet brig for the next year or so until we have time to convene a court, I'll inform the admiral of your request."

"I want to see the charges," Esmay said. "I haven't done anything wrong."

"Oh? And what do you call seducing Admiral Serrano's grandson, in direct contravention of the rules prohibiting relationships between Fleet officers and Landbrides of Suiza? For that matter, you did not inform Fleet of your Landbride status until over a year after you became one—also a breach of regulations—"

"But that was because of the NewTex mess—"

"And you had concealed your family's political prominence as far back as your application to the Academy—"

"I did not!"

"And then you coerced the boy into marrying you."

So many things were wrong with that sentence that Esmay didn't know where to start. "He's not a boy—and I didn't coerce him—"

"And if you ask me, your so-called rescue of Lord Thornbuckle's daughter was an obvious ploy to gain political influence in that family—"

"What—I should have let her die?"

"You should have stayed back on your stupid dirt-ball planet and planted potatoes like the rest of your backward peasantry . . . Fleet has no place for your kind." He leaned forward, glaring straight into her eyes. "You're getting your discharge ID, more than you deserve. I don't care if you get home or not. I don't care if you live through the next hour. But if you cause the least trouble on this Station—anything at all—I will personally stuff you into an airlock and open it to vacuum. I am speaking for my CO and Admiral Serrano in this. Is that clear?"

What was clear was the uselessness of argument. Esmay took her credit cube—at least they'd given it back—and hoped she looked less shaken than she was on her way out. The looks she got from personnel were less scathing than she'd feared. Either they didn't believe it, or hadn't heard it.

Once into the civilian side of the station, she ducked into a secure combooth to give herself time to think. Admiral Serrano. It had to be Vida Serrano, but . . . but Captain Atherton on the *Rosa Gloria* had said she'd accepted the marriage. Had she changed her mind? Why? She scolded herself: she had more immediate problems than answering that. She checked her balances in the credit cube and called up current rates for a ticket home. She could just get there, on a roundabout base-rate route that would take months and give her no chance to clear herself. She looked at the rates to Castle Rock. No direct passenger travel for another three weeks. She didn't dare stay here for three weeks, not with local brass looking for an excuse to arrest her.

She scrolled through the list of ships in port, hoping inspiration would strike. The only name that looked remotely familiar was Terakian. That girl, Hazel, who'd been captured with Brun, had a name something like that. Terakian? Takeris? Even if she was wrong, they might know. She could ask, anyway.

CHAPTER FOUR

The man who answered the call had the rakish good looks of a storycube pirate. "*Terakian Fortune*, Basil Terakian-Junos here."

"I'm trying to locate the young woman named Hazel, who was rescued with Brun Meager from the NewTex Militia—I thought her last name was Terakian . . . ?"

His expression changed slightly. "Hazel—how do you know Hazel?"

"I'm—I was—in the task force."

"And you are?"

"L—" she bit off the rank she no longer held. "Esmay Suiza."

"You're Lieutenant Suiza?" Now he looked alert, and pleased. "Sorry I didn't recognize you, Lieutenant. How can we help you?"

Best get it out of the way. "I'm not a Fleet officer now."

"But I thought—well, then, sera, what can we do for you?"

"I'm trying to find transportation off this station, in the general direction of Castle Rock. I know there's a passenger ship going that way in three weeks, but I need to leave sooner, if I can."

"I hear a story in that. You're in a secure booth, right?"

"Yes."

"B Concourse?"

"Yes."

"Why don't you come along to the dockside, sera? It sounds as if we need to talk." And he didn't trust a secure combooth, that was clear. "Concourse D, level 2, number 38. We have a dockside office there; I'll meet you."

"I'll come now," Esmay said. She called up a station schematic on the combooth display and then the transportation layout.

B Concourse had a transgrav tram across to D; Esmay glanced at the schedule display and hurried out of the booth. Down there— yes—she stepped into the car marked D just as the door alarm sounded. Someone who had come up rapidly behind her tried to push past the safety barrier, but a tram guard stopped him. Esmay pulled the safety bars down around her seat and settled in. D car was half full; she could see through the windows in the end of the car that C was packed.

The tram made two more stops in B; then, after a warning whoop from the gravity alarms, slid through the G-lock barriers. Esmay's stomach insisted she was falling, but outside she could see the great bays of the heavy cargo handling section. The tram stopped, and a couple of uniformed cargo workers bounded up and into D car. At the next grav barrier, weight returned, and at the next junction, several cars turned off to other sections. D car continued through another low-grav compartment, and Esmay emerged at the second D stop.

She was on level 2. On her right, a row of shops and services for merchant crews, from bars to message services to beds-by-the-hour, with or without partners. On her left, at intervals, were the dockside facilities for ships in station. Each had space for a temporary office, decorated in as lavish a style as the ships' owners found desirable. Boros Consortium seemed to have made their occupancy permanent in 32, 33, and 34, with a continuous office: customer, service, and crew entrances, with uniformed but unarmed Boros guards watching passersby. Number 35 was bare-bones, an obvious prefab folding "office" in the middle of the bare alloted space, and a small sign that declared it was for the *Mercedes R.*, owner/captain Caleb Montoya. Number 36 was another independent, but one with more resources: Ganeshi Shipping Company had a status board displayed, which informed passersby that the office was now open.

Number 37 looked to be about the same level, simple but moderately prosperous. Clan Orange had put orange stripes on the doorframe and windows of the office, and hung out a fabric banner as well as showing a status board that included the percent of the ship still available to shippers. Passengers 0, she noticed.

Number 38 carried self-expression to an art form; Esmay didn't know whether to laugh or gasp in admiration when she came to the multicolored carpet in exuberant floral designs, the drapes hung from pipe frames, the potted palm in a vast basket. A sign declared "Terakian & Sons, Ltd., General and Express Shipping" and a very dramatic painted hand pointed to the office. Unlike the others, it was not a simple box in shape, but constructed with peaks and swooping curves, and painted in a pattern that made the carpet seem tame.

Esmay stepped under the pointed arch of the entrance, and found herself in a surprisingly quiet space before the little office. Was it just the draped fabric, or had the Terakians installed some sound shielding? She shrugged mentally and went up to the office. The door slid aside before she touched it. Inside was what looked like a luxury sitting room: another floral design on the carpet, only slightly subdued, with large, plump leather seats grouped around it. Along one wall was a counter, and behind it a bright-eyed young man.

"Sera Suiza?" he said. Esmay nodded. "I'll just tell Basil—" the young man said, and murmured into a throatmic.

At once a door opened, and two men came through. One she had seen on the screen in the combooth—he was as dramatic in person as on vid. The other was older, far less vivid to look at, but clearly in authority.

"I'm Goonar Terakian," the older man said, extending his hand. Esmay shook it. "Captain of *Terakian Fortune*, and junior partner in Terakian and Sons, Ltd. Basil here is my cousin, second in command on my ship, and the cargomaster. You're Esmay Suiza, formerly of Fleet, is that right?"

"Yes. Until this morning—" A lump rose in her throat. She hadn't let herself feel the loss yet, and she wasn't going to now. She swallowed hard.

"Sera, Basil told me that you wanted transport off this station with some urgency?"

"I wouldn't say urgency," Esmay said. "I just don't want to wait for the next direct passenger transport to Castle Rock."

"Sera, I have to tell you up front, and despite our gratitude for your part in rescuing Hazel Takeris, if you're a fugitive from Fleet, we can't help you."

"I'm not," Esmay said. She could feel the wave of heat rising up her face. "I—they discharged me this morning, and I still don't completely understand why. But they want me off this station—threatened to space me, in fact—and I want to get somewhere that I can figure out what's going on and fight it."

"Um. Yet we know you're being followed."

"I am?" Esmay thought of the man back at the tram station. "But—maybe the admiral just wants to know that I'm leaving."

"Or maybe he wants to know who you meet, and it'll put us under suspicion." That from the young man at the counter. Goonar shot him a sharp look.

"Flaci, were you asked?"

"No, I only—"

"Go make some coffee," Goonar ordered. The young man withdrew through the door behind the counter. Basil pulled out a cylinder that looked just like the ones used in Fleet to foil scans of a conversational area, twisted it, and laid it on the table.

"Have a seat, sera," Goonar offered. Esmay sank into the cushions and wondered if she would be able to climb out again. The little status light on the security cylinder glowed: they were supposedly screened from scan. Goonar took the seat to her right; Basil was across from her.

"Kids," Basil said, with a wave at the counter. "They never know when to keep quiet."

"And you do?" Goonar asked, but with a grin that took most of the sting out of it. He turned to Esmay. "Sera, do you have any idea at all why Fleet tossed you out, when there's a mutiny on and I'd think they'd want every loyal officer?"

"Well . . . sort of." Esmay felt her blush going hotter. "Admiral Serrano—Vida Serrano that is—is angry with my family, and . . . and . . . her grandson and I just got married."

"You *what*?" asked Basil. Goonar made a sort of choked noise, which Esmay recognized as suppressed laughter.

"I married her grandson—or he married me—anyway we're married. He—we—we'd been trying to talk to our families for a long time, and finally he and I had figured out a time we could meet with his parents. Only all the Serranos were there, it seemed like, and his grandmother—Admiral Vida—came out with a story about my family's history . . . and she was *wrong*." Esmay caught her breath; she was suddenly on the edge of tears. "That wasn't what happened; it can't have been. But she believed it. And she said we could never marry, and then the mutiny came, and we all had to go back to duty, and . . . and . . ."

"You and he sneaked off to get married," Basil said.

"We didn't *sneak*," Esmay said. "But we didn't—we couldn't, there wasn't time—tell anyone beforehand."

"Such as your family and his," Goonar said. He had most of his face under control, but a twitch in the corner of his mouth said he was still finding this funny.

Basil wasn't; he was scowling now. "They ditched you for marrying the Serrano kid? When you're a hero?"

"I'm also a Landbride back on Altiplano—"

"You have two husbands?" Basil looked at Goonar. "I guess that would do it. A boy in every port?"

"No, it's not like that." Esmay glared at him. "I'm not that sort of person. Landbride is a . . . a sort of family thing, and religious. It's the woman in the family who is responsible for the land—for seeing that it's cared for."

"Oh. And this bothered them? Were you going to go back there and take him with you?"

"No . . . I was going to resign as Landbride—give it to my cousin Luci—and stay in Fleet. But then things happened—"

"They always do." That was Goonar, the quiet one, not as handsome as Basil but steadier. He had sad eyes, Esmay thought.

"So—after the news of the mutiny—we were traveling together back to our assignments, and . . . we just got married. We'd waited so long, and so much was going on—"

"Without the right paperwork, I'm guessing," Goonar said. "And without family permission?"

Esmay felt herself reddening. "Definitely without."

"That would annoy them," Basil said. He leaned back and one eyebrow rose. Theatrical.

"Stop it, Bas," said Goonar. "You're learning bad habits from our passengers."

"I need to find a way home," Esmay said. "I thought maybe, if I could talk to Hazel—I thought maybe she was on this ship—she'd help me."

"Why not contact the Thornbuckle girl? She's rich enough to buy you a ship of your own."

"I don't want to bring trouble to her," Esmay said. "She doesn't deserve it."

"And you do?" Goonar's brows rose, both of them. "What we've heard of you is good, from the newsvids and Hazel both. The hero of Xavier. The hero who saved the *Kos*. And then the Speaker's daughter."

"Not by myself," Esmay said. "Any of it. And where did you hear about the *Kos*?"

"Not much we don't hear, independent merchanters," Basil said.

"Quit it, Bas. You sound like a third-rate actor in a spy thriller. Seriously, Lieutenant—sera—we do pick up a lot of dockside talk, mostly wrong. Now, I figure the family owes you, for your part in getting Hazel out. But we aren't a passenger line; we're mixed cargo."

"But you said you had passengers . . ." At the sudden change of expression, Esmay stopped.

"Well, that's done it," Basil said, this time with no expression on his face at all. "And you the cautious one."

"What?"

"Sometimes we carry passengers. Not usually. We've . . . er . . . had some recently."

"Then could I—I mean, for a fare, of course. I don't know much about it—"

"We owe you, as I said, but we really do not have passenger quarters fit for you."

"I'm not used to luxury," Esmay said.

"I suppose not." He chewed his lip. "Well . . . if you can share a small space, and sleep in rotation, we can take you. But where do you want to go?"

"Castle Rock," Esmay said. She was fairly, reasonably, almost sure that Brun would be there. She could see Brun privately, without involving Fleet. And perhaps Brun would be able to find out what, if anything, she could do to get back into Fleet even in spite of the powerful Admiral Serrano.

"Not Altiplano?"

"Not yet," Esmay said. *Not ever,* she hoped. Goonar nodded.

"Well, then—you're probably not aware of civilian regulations, but we need to list you as a passenger on the manifest. Do you have civilian ID?"

"Of sorts," Esmay said. "If discharge chips are sufficient."

"Let me see." Goonar reached out and Esmay handed over the flat cardlike discharge certification she'd been handed. Goonar reached under the low table and pulled up an ID scanner. He ran it over the card. "Yes . . . it has everything required—name, retinal and finger scan patterns, planet of origin, employment record. You left home young, didn't you?"

"Yes," Esmay said. "I was space-struck early."

"Our kids start early too—actually earlier than that, but of course their families are in space." He handed the chip back. "There. You want to travel under your own name, don't you?"

"Yes—my unmarried name; there hasn't been time to get it changed."

"Fine. I've entered you in our log. Now—about luggage—"

"I don't have much," Esmay said. "They said the rest of my things would be sent to me . . . they're somewhere between the ship I left before going on leave and the one I was supposed to be assigned to."

"Do you have what you need? We can send someone for anything missing . . ."

"I'll be all right," Esmay said. She had only a few civilian outfits, but she didn't want to go shopping here—or have someone doing it for her.

"Good. Then you can go aboard now, since you don't want to be seen on station. We're not ready to strike our tents yet; we're in the queue for two days from now and I prefer—" he paused, and looked not at Esmay but at Basil, "—not to make sudden departures from ports unless it's absolutely necessary."

"It was," muttered Basil. Esmay sensed an old quarrel.

"Will that be satisfactory, sera?"

"I'm very grateful," Esmay said. "Now about the fare—"

Goonar waved his hand. "Forget the fare. I'm telling the Stationmaster that we're not a passenger ship, but we're not about to leave the hero of Xavier in the lurch—or charge for it, either. That clears our honor, both ways."

Esmay couldn't follow all of that, but the master and second in command of *Terakian Fortune* seemed almost smug about something.

Basil, as cargomaster, took her through to another room, this one filled with electronics gear, and then through the docking tube of the ship.

A civilian merchant ship, she found, had its own ceremonies, however unlike these were to the austere formalities of the Regular Space Service. A trim youngster in a green tunic led her to the tiny compartment that she would occupy during her sleep shift, and pointed out the small cubby where she could stow a few toiletries. Her clothes would have to go across the passage, in a locker already stuffed with carryons. The boy seemed far too young to be working aboard ship, and Esmay wondered briefly about child piracy, until she remembered that Hazel, too, had been very young. Apparently civilian merchants took their children with them.

"Are you the captain's son?" she asked.

He gave her a startled look. "Me, sera? Captain Goonar's—? No, sera. Goonar, he's not got any children; they all died. I'm Kosta Terakian-Cibo, Ser Basil's aunt's son on his mother's side. It's my first trip as full crew, sera. So even though I still have classes, I'm getting paid full wage." He grinned proudly. Esmay congratulated him, and he nodded. "Only problem is, the Fathers insist that we juniors can't have all our money to spend. It's going to take me the whole voyage to save up for the new cube player I want. . . ."

"And a good thing, too." Basil emerged from a cross-corridor, and glared at the boy. "We'd just have to confiscate it to keep you from deafening everyone on the ship. Go on, now, Kosta, and let the lady alone. Have you done the rotational analysis yet?"

"Yes, Ser Basil." The boy whipped out a pocket display and flicked it on. "The sera's luggage here, and the moment here, and—"

"Good. And did you give her the ship's books?"

"No . . . I wasn't sure—"

"Yes, of course she needs them." Basil looked at Esmay. "Why don't you come along to the bursar's, and we'll get you started. Unfortunately, we don't mount cube readers in all the compartments, so you'll have to read the hardcopy—"

"Fine," said Esmay. She followed him down one corridor, then another, mapping automatically. The bursar's was a medium-sized compartment, full of desks and files, with office machines around the edges.

Basil turned to a stack of shelving and pulled out two well-thumbed manuals, one of which described the ship's layout, and the other the emergency procedures.

Terakian Fortune, she recognized, was roughly equivalent to a smallish cruiser in tonnage, but organized very differently. Unlike the big spherical container ships, *Fortune*'s cargo holds were crew-accessible—everything loaded and unloaded through the shuttle bay, though this was big enough to take the standard orbit-to-surface containers as well as the cargo shuttles themselves. The space taken up on a cruiser by weapons and ammunition storage could be stuffed with cargo here—as could the crew space required for the much larger military crews. Only twenty personnel per watch—Esmay could hardly believe anyone could run a ship with so few, and yet—as she read through the manuals—the essentials were covered, with adequate redundancy.

She hoped. The knowledge that the *Fortune* had no serious offensive armament, and shields only moderately better than a private yacht left her feeling vulnerable. The single weapon was clearly intended for scaring minimally armed raiders . . . someone had rigged duplicator lines intended to show up on inferior scans as multiple armaments.

A tap on the door; she opened it to find the same boy who had led her there. Kosta, was it? "The sera's temporarily assigned to the second rotation, which means the third seating today," the boy said. "Uncle—Captain Terakian dines ashore while we're in port. Second seating is finishing lunch now, and I'm to take you to the mess."

"Thank you—Kosta?"

"Yes, sera." His grin widened. "Terakian-Cibo, but you don't need to remember that part. Just call me Kosta; everyone else does."

The terminology of seatings and rotations meant nothing to her: was second rotation like the second watch? Instead of asking, she followed the boy to the mess hall. Mess on a civilian trader looked nothing like either enlisted mess or officers' wardroom aboard ship . . . more like a small restaurant along some shopping concourse. The compartment was just big enough for eight four-person tables: thirty-two per seating? Why, then, the need for more than one seating per rotation?

"There aren't really assigned seats," Kosta said. "You could sit with us—" He pointed to a table where two other youngsters were just sliding into their chairs and unloading trays onto the table. "If you want to," he added, in a tone that tried, and failed, to be welcoming.

She wasn't really eager to sit with a group of youngsters anyway. "Thanks, but it looks like there are plenty of empty places," Esmay said. "If you don't mind . . ."

"No, sera . . . I could use the time to review for the test this afternoon, if it's all right. Do you think you can find your way back?"

"I hope so," Esmay said. "I guess I'll just have to ask someone if I can't."

"Anyone will help you," Kosta said. "Just remember C-23, that's your number." Esmay headed for the serving line across the room. The food smelled spicy and good; she took a bowl of some stew-like dish, and a couple of warm rolls. She put her tray down on one of the empty tables, and sat down. The condiment containers in front of her held things she'd never heard of, except for the basic salt and pepper. Some of the labels were in languages she hadn't seen either.

"That goolgi is good with khungi sauce," someone said. Esmay looked up. A curvaceous woman with red-brown hair tipped her head toward the table. "May I?"

"Of course," Esmay said. "I'm Esmay Suiza."

"Ah. I'm Betharnya Vi Negaro. You must be the passenger."

"I'm a passenger, yes. And you? You're not a Terakian?"

"Not everyone is a Terakian," the woman said. She too had a bowl of the stew; she uncapped the bottle with a picture of galloping bulls on the label and shook a large dollop of a thick, slightly lumpy, brown sauce into the bowl. "You don't like khungi sauce?"

"I've never had it. I've never had this kind of stew—goolgi?— either." Esmay tried a spoonful of the goolgi and a warm glow filled her mouth. Peppers. It must have quite a bit of some pepper in it—

"Too bland, the way they make it here," the woman said. "Khungi gives it a bit of life—"

The warm glow was turning into a miniature furnace; Esmay knew that symptom of old, and reached for her water glass. "I think it's lively enough," she said, after a swallow.

"Khungi doesn't make it hotter," Betharnya said. "Just more— robust, perhaps. You ought to try at least a dab."

She might as well find out. Esmay shook out a small blob of the brown sauce and mixed it with a portion of goolgi. The resulting bite almost took the top of her head off, but after a moment the head-on collision of flavors worked. Either alone was too strong; together they set up a sort of olfactory countercurrent.

"Could you explain this rotation and seating thing?" Esmay said.

"Of course." Betharnya took a last bite of the goolgi and wiped her mouth. "Thing is, we're somewhat overcrewed right now, moving people from one place to another. So the onshift crew has first seating at each meal period—to be sure they can eat quickly and get back to work. Offshift crew has second seating—they sit the boards while the onshift crew eats. Sleepshift crew can come eat if they want to—if they're awake and hungry—but they get third seating. It's particularly important in port, when most of the crew are off duty anyway."

"Makes sense," Esmay said. "I've never been on a trader before."

"It works for us," Betharnya said. "I don't know anything about how other traders do it."

"How long are you usually away from your homeworld? Or do you live mostly in space?"

"It varies . . . I haven't seen my homeworld for three or four standard years, but some people go home every year. And we don't usually have small children out in space; our ships are too small to allow sufficient romping space." She grinned. "I sometimes wonder about the junior apprentices in that regard. They can get a bit boisterous." She cocked her head at Esmay. "Now it's your turn. Tell me about yourself."

"I was a Regular Space Service officer—left my homeworld for the prep school, then the Academy, and then went into Fleet. I've only been home twice since then."

"Are you going home now that you've left Fleet?"

"I . . . don't know." She did not want to talk about this with everyone on the ship. "Right now I'm headed for Castle Rock."

"Ah, so are we. By a roundabout route, but we'll get there." Betharnya glanced away, and her expression changed. "Ah—if you'll excuse me, sera, I should get back—"

Esmay followed her gaze and saw a handsome blonde woman and an even more handsome man at the mess hall entrance. It was amazing how many good-looking people were in this crew . . . she hadn't expected them all to look like actors.

Sirialis

Lady Cecelia de Marktos woke early and headed for the stables, even though it wasn't hunting season. The best cure for an unquiet mind—at least, her unquiet mind—was a few hours spent with animals that could not lie. She felt better with every stride away from the house where Miranda had—perhaps by accident—killed Pedar Orregiemos.

Neil, who had been running the horse operation for at least thirty years, grinned when he saw her coming through the arched gateway.

"I heard you were here, Lady Cecelia," Neil said. "How's her ladyship?"

"It was a tragedy," Cecelia said. His face didn't twitch. She hadn't expected it to.

"She'll be leaving soon?" he asked. "Going back to deal with the inheritance?"

"No, I don't think so," Cecelia said. "Harlis . . . has other problems." She wasn't sure how much to say or not say. Sirialis had its own customs, its own networks.

"That's good, then. You just tell her I said we did fix that bit she was working on."

"Bit?"

"Yes . . . she was down here a few nights ago, working on a broken bit, back in the old forge."

A chill ran down Cecelia's back. She could not imagine Miranda trying to mend a bit herself.

"I've never seen the old forge," she said casually. "Where is it?"

"Back along there," he pointed. Was that tension in his throat? "It's just a workroom now. I reckon she came down just to get some peace, like, with that fellow in the house."

Peace, thought Cecelia, was exactly what Miranda had been after.

The old forge, when she looked into it, had the tidy look of any well-maintained metal shop. Neat rows of tools, a couple of small brazing cones, a shelf of labelled bottles. She leaned forward to look at them . . . chemical labels. Most were unfamiliar. She looked along the workbench . . . someone was working on a pair of spurs, set up in a vise, and there was a can with tongueless buckles of various sizes and beside it a can of straight tongue blanks. Heavier round stock, shaped into hoofpicks, and a tub of bone and antler roughs for handles. A bowl of scrap bits of this and that . . . Cecelia stirred it with her finger, not at all sure what she'd expected to find. A rough edge caught at her finger; she looked at it . . . a small curved scrap of pierced metal that looked somehow older than the rest.

Cecelia wondered what it had been. It didn't look like any metal from horse tack. Something tickled her memory, but withdrew. It was like a fragment of shell from a very large egg, with little holes . . . a colander, for straining a mash? She put it in her pocket and wandered back to the main square, where two of the hunters were being exercised on the longe line. Neil watched, eyes narrowed at the chestnut. Cecelia watched too, and saw the same slightly uneven stretch of the off fore. He signalled the groom, and when the horse stopped, he bent over that front leg. Cecelia watched the bay, as always soothed by the sight of a good horse moving well.

"There you are!" Miranda, in spotless breeches and a pale blue shirt, came through the archway. In the cool morning, she had color in her cheeks again and looked very much the poised, elegant lady of the manor. "I should have known you'd come down here before breakfast."

"Habit," Cecelia said. "But of course it's not the season, and no one expected me to ride this early . . ."

"Ah," Miranda said. "So . . . are you just pottering around petting horses, or would you like something to eat?"

"I was . . . Neil said you'd been in the old forge a few days ago . . ."

"Oh yes?" Miranda's eyes were on the chestnut.

"I'd never seen it before," Cecelia said. She saw the sudden tension in Miranda's neck. "It's a nice little workshop."

"Yes, it is," Miranda said. "We use it for mending tack now."

"That's what Neil said. I've never done that myself . . . well, except for leather. He said you'd been working on a bit, and they finished it. All I saw was this—" She held it out.

"My . . . I wonder what that is." Miranda's voice was breathless. "Quite old, it looks like."

"Not like tack," Cecelia said. "Some kind of strainer, maybe." She put it back in her pocket. "How are you feeling this morning?"

"Shaky," Miranda said. "I can't—it's too much, too fast. I can't believe it all really happened."

Breakfast, with obligatory small talk, was excruciating. Cecelia picked at her eggs and ham; Miranda nibbled a bowl of mixed grain flakes. At last the maid took the dishes away.

"I must meet with that militia officer again," Miranda said. "I have no idea what to do, and with Kevil out of commission—"

"Miranda . . . you have to come to grips with it."

"How?" The blue eyes clouded with tears. "How am I supposed to come to grips with Bunny dying, and Harlis trying to cheat us, and Pedar . . ."

Tell the truth, Cecelia thought but did not say. She was reserving that for later. She followed Miranda down the long corridor, its walls hung with pictures, past the case from which the antique weapons had been taken—she stopped abruptly. The case was partly empty now, of course—the weapons and masks Miranda and Pedar had used had been taken away. But seeing the faint discoloration outlining where they had been, Cecelia visualized it as if it were still there.

The solid metal helm. The pierced metal mask. Pierced just like the fragment in her pocket—her hand clenched on it.

"What?" Miranda said, from two strides down the hall. "What is it?"

She had known, and not known—she had not wanted to know. She had wanted to believe it impossible, so she would have nothing to do, no responsibility.

"Miranda, I am sure that this—" she held out the metal fragment, "is from that mask. That you did something to that mask. If I had the skill, and investigated the chemicals in the old forge—"

Miranda said nothing.

"You can't expect me to let it go—"

"No." Miranda's voice was hoarse, as if she'd been crying. "I can expect you to be right in the middle of everything, with your teeth locked on the most inconvenient of truths."

It was still a shock. "You mean, you did—"

Miranda's hand smacked the table. "Of course I did. Damn and blast, Cecelia, the man had my husband killed, and his idiotic schemes as foreign minister endangered all of us—my children included. And he was putting pressure on me to marry him. He was a despicable, slimy, skirt-climbing bastard—"

"And now you're a murderer," Cecelia said.

"A killer," Miranda said. "Murder is a legal definition."

"I don't care what you call it," Cecelia said. "We both know it's not something you can live with—not in our society."

"Oh, fine. Pedar can have my husband killed, and get a ministry, but I—"

"Come off it." Cecelia linked her big hands together and didn't bother to hide the contempt in her voice. "You had the goods on Harlis; you could have waited and gotten Pedar legally—"

"I didn't think so," Miranda said. "I thought he'd get away with it."

"You can't just brazen it out. You can't. It affects your children, your grandchildren, their position in the Familias . . . there's Brun, back on Castle Rock—if you could only see her, Miranda. It's like—" She bit her tongue on *like Bunny come back*. "She's grown up, really grown up. She's got a real talent—"

"Well, of course she does," Miranda said, looking away. "She's my daughter—and Bunny's. If she'd only grown sense a little earlier, married—"

"She doesn't need to marry," Cecelia said. "She's doing very well on her own. But she does not need a murderess mother hanging around her neck, an easy target for her enemies."

"Buttons will—"

"Buttons," Cecelia said, "has his own life to live. And he's got many of your and Bunny's admirable qualities, but he doesn't have Brun's flair. And no, he can't keep people from using your act as a weapon against Brun." Miranda's stubborn expression annoyed her so much that she burst out, "By God, Miranda, I know where she got that reckless, stubborn determination to go her own way regardless, and it wasn't Bunny."

"I never—"

"You certainly did, and this wasn't the first time." Incidents she'd thought lost to memory decades before came spurting out, under the pressure of her anger. "Before you turned cool and calculating, you were hothead enough—like that birthday party where you pushed Lorrie into the fountain, and the time at school—Berenice told me about it—when you—"

"Oh, stop it." Miranda, flushed with anger, looked more alive than she had since Bunny's death. "I was like any child, hasty and unthinking. Yes. But I got over it."

"Until you stuck a sword in Pedar's eye. I wouldn't call *that* getting over it." Cecelia took a deep breath. "Listen—if you stay here, it's true they're not likely to come get you, but what about the other people here on Sirialis? What about your children? You wanted this for them, remember?"

"What, then? If you know so much, you tell me what to do."

"Exile. Leave the Familias. Go to—oh, I don't know, maybe the Guerni Republic. Get treatment for whatever it is that made you think you could kill him with impunity. Stay a long time . . ."

"And be arrested on the way—be reasonable, Cecelia."

She was going to do it again, and regret it, but she was beginning to recognize the feel of a duty she dared not shirk. "I'll take you."

"You! You hate me . . . you insist I'm a murderess. And besides, you don't have room in that little thing you fly now—"

"I don't hate you," Cecelia said. "And I'm not afraid of you—you're not going to kill me, not if you agree to go. As for the ship, I found I didn't like being completely solo all the time. It's still small, but it's adequate for two people."

"So—what are you going to tell our militia captain?"

"I will answer accurately any questions he asks me. What he makes of the answers is his business."

The interview covered much the same ground as the day before. When had she arrived, what had she seen, what had Miranda said and done. Cecelia recognized, in the militia captain, a man who did not want to think about what might have happened, if a good enough explanation appeared. Yet he would not let himself skimp the questions. Cecelia answered honestly, as far as his questions went.

"And did you know the deceased?"

"Slightly." Cecelia allowed herself a curled lip. "My horse beat his in the Wherrin Trials, right after Bunny—Lord Thornbuckle—was killed."

"Was he there?"

"Pedar? Oh, yes. He thought he could win—"

"Did he ride?"

"No, he had a rider. Pedar was never . . . particularly interested in risking himself."

"Yet Lady Thornbuckle said he asked specifically to use the old fencing gear—" The militia captain glanced at her suddenly, as if to catch her out.

Cecelia shrugged. "I don't know what he was like with fencing. I don't fence; I ride." The interviewer smiled and nodded; everyone knew this about her.

"Ser Orregiemos had been a competition fencer, milady; according to Lady Thornbuckle, he had won many championships in his younger days. She wasn't sure when his last competition was, but with his multiple rejuvenations he could have been competitive quite recently—as you yourself are." He paused. "Lady Thornbuckle said, when she came, that she was here for privacy; we were all quite surprised when Ser Orregiemos arrived."

"Well, so was I when I heard he was here. Such an appalling little tick."

"You don't—didn't—like him." It was not a question.

"No. None of us—the horse people, I mean—felt he was entirely honest."

"Ah. But you know of no reason why . . . I mean . . . there was no bad feeling between him and Lady Thornbuckle?"

"Not that I know of. He liked her rather more than she liked him, I would say, but it was Bunny—Lord Thornbuckle—who really detested him. It goes back to hunting, some twenty years ago. He insisted on having a fast horse, and then he rode over hounds—"

"Oh." He lost interest. A quarrel in the field, twenty years before, could not generate a murder by the other man's widow.

"It's difficult," he said, tapping his stylus on the recorder. "This being a private world, and all. I'm the law, but the law here has always been what the Thornbuckles wanted."

"Miranda would want you to do the right thing," Cecelia said.

"Familias investigators don't even have jurisdiction on private property—but the problem is . . . he's a Minister, you see. Somebody official. I . . . ." He cleared his throat. "May I ask what your plans are?"

"Lady Thornbuckle and I are planning to travel to the Guerni Republic. She is concerned that some medical condition impaired her ability to stop the thrust when the blade broke—that she might be in some measure responsible for Ser Orregiemos' death. There's always concern about rejuvenation failure . . . she is planning to check herself into one of their clinics."

"Ah." He tapped his chin with the stylus. "Of course. I hadn't thought of that, but we have heard rumors, even here. That might indeed be best, milady."

"But only if it's acceptable to you," Cecelia said.

"I think so. Yes. We have the scan records and your deposition. If I may, milady, I would suggest an early departure." Before the news leaked out to the rest of the Familias, before Pedar's relatives or colleagues demanded an inconvenient inquiry of their own.

CHAPTER FIVE

Sector Five HQ

Heris Serrano and her great-aunt Vida—once again an admiral on active duty—crossed paths in the Sector Five Transient Officers' Quarters, both en route to their new assignments. Heris, who had been fuming over the admiral's tirade at the family gathering, lost no time in tackling her about it.

"I want to talk to you about Barin and Esmay," she began.

"I don't want to talk to you about it. They're married now, and it's an unholy mess—"

"You're wrong," Heris said. "I don't know if it's the rejuvenation, or what, but you're acting like an idiot."

"Commander—"

"I mean it. Admiral, I've had hero worship for you since before I went to the Academy, but not any more. First you kept me from getting the support I expected when Lepescu threatened me, and now you've interfered to ruin a fine young officer, someone of proven ability and courage. I have to ask myself if Lepescu was the only traitor—"

"You! You *dare*!"

Heris folded her arms. "Yes, I dare. Do you think a Serrano is going to be intimidated by being yelled at? Do I seriously think you are a traitor? No, not really. But the way you're acting, it's a possibility that has to be considered." With the part of her mind not focussed on the older woman across from her, Heris was able to be amazed at

414

her own calm. "I realize admirals have to do things which aren't in the books, and which junior officers may not understand. But I also know that admirals go bad—Lepescu is only one example; we could both name others. I know admirals aren't perfect little gold statues up on the pinnacle of Fleet rank. They—you—are human, and they make mistakes."

"Which you think I made."

"Which I know you made. So did I." Heris took a breath. "Look—what I did at Patchcock was right, tactically. I don't regret a hair of it. Afterwards—I should have stayed for—demanded—a court-martial, whether or not any Serrano backed me up. I was wrong to resign and leave my crew to Lepescu's mercy. I was wrong to depend on family for support, to let that be my guide in what to do next. Later on, I was wrong to depend on a Fleet record to judge people—it should have been obvious to me that Sirkin wasn't the problem, Iklind was. But the habit of trusting Fleet, like the habit of trusting family, slowed my brain. My mistakes got people killed—people I cared about, and people I didn't even know. That's not a mistake I'm going to make again."

"And just what habits do you think I'm trusting, that lead to my mistakes?" The voice was deceptively mild, but Heris wasn't fooled.

"I don't know how you think," Heris said. "You alone know the basis for your decisions. But when the decisions are wrong, anyone can see them."

"And you still resent me for not coming to your aid?"

Heris waved her hand. "Resentment is not the point. We're not talking about my putative resentment or anger, we're talking about your actions. Your failure to allow even my parents to make contact before or after my resignation had dire consequences. And you have twice taken after Esmay Suiza, once when you believed rumors about her involvement in Brun's capture, and now because of some old book—fossilized rumor—about her ancestors. Look at the facts, Admiral."

Vida moved her glare to the wall, where Heris was moderately surprised not to see the paint darken immediately. "I am aware that my first displeasure with Lt. Suiza was unwarranted. I allowed myself to be distracted by other considerations. If this conversation were being held by strangers, in a story, I would have to see that someone my age would be the senile old admiral, who needs to make room at the top for the bright young officers." She looked back at Heris. "But I don't think I'm senile, whatever you think. I've taken the trouble to retest regularly, and my reflexes and cognitive markers are still where they should be. However, the tests are not designed to find areas where increasing age will change judgment on the basis of experience. Usually that's considered an advantage."

"Usually it is," Heris said. "Up to a point, anyway. But no one knows how the awareness of immortality will affect judgment—particularly risk/benefit analysis."

"Immortality! Rejuvenation isn't—oh." Vida mused over this a few moments. "I never thought of it that way. Of course, if someone keeps getting rejuv, it would be."

"Long-term planning," Heris said. "Very long term. Valuable, too, up to a point. At least in my case, I think you were operating at a time scale beyond my understanding—and with disregard of the fallout."

"I see." Vida steepled her fingers. "I suppose I may have. So much has happened since, it's hard to recall exactly what I thought I was doing. Damage control for Fleet and family, but you're right—I wasn't particularly concerned with what happened to your people."

"What I see," Heris said, "in many Rejuvenants—civilian and military—is a kind of detachment from the present, and particularly from the unrejuvenated. They're ephemerals; they don't really matter unless they interfere in a plan, in which case they're expendable."

Vida frowned. "I don't think that's how I look at them, but—I can see where it looks like that."

"If it's the effect, what matters the intent?" That old saw came easily to Heris's tongue; Vida's frown became a fixed scowl.

"You know the dangers in inferring intent from effect—"

"And also the dangers of not doing so. But this is idle fencing, and what I need to know is whether you will reexamine your bias against Suiza and recognize the asset she is to us now."

"Ignore the long view?"

"No. But prioritize. We have an ongoing mutiny; we have external enemies. We need every good officer we have, and she is one."

"Was one," Vida said. She leaned back in her chair. "Heris, she's not on the list now; she thinks she was cashiered on my orders, and she's now disappeared. The last we know is that she boarded a free trader, the *Terakian Fortune*. While that ship has a flight plan, it may or may not adhere to it."

Heris said, through clenched teeth. "You cashiered her?"

"No, she *thinks* I cashiered her. The orders were presented as from Admiral Serrano. She thinks I am that Admiral Serrano."

"And you claim you're not?" Heris said.

"I'm not. Thanks to the wholesale idiocy of Hobart Conselline, we now have a confusion of admirals Serrano: those of us who were put on the shelf, those who were promoted as a result, and the total—both older and newer admirals—when we older ones came back to active duty. We Serranos didn't pick up as many stars as other families—Conselline's never favored Serranos—but there are at least five and perhaps as many as eight. Could be even more. I had no reason to ask for a list before someone ordered Suiza out, and what with the mutiny and the chaos at headquarters, I haven't heard back from Personnel. I'm assuming one of them, hearing about my quarrel with Suiza, decided to curry favor by dumping her."

"Or someone forged the name, and it was believable because your quarrel was known," Heris said. She looked at her aunt. "Damn—I was ready to be really angry with you for a very long time."

"I know." Vida sighed. "If we hadn't been interrupted . . . if there'd been time to talk it over, Suiza could probably have convinced me to at least consider what she was talking about. I know—objectively I know—that she's not a social-climbing sneak. I realize that my rage then makes no sense now, anyway. If treachery were actually heritable, I can't think of anyone I'd trust, including myself. That's why I got in touch with her family, after she married Barin . . ."

"You did what?"

"I sent word to them about the marriage. I didn't know what she'd told them about the quarrel, so I mentioned it and said I was convinced whatever it was could be worked out."

"And?"

"And . . . that's not their view at all."

"What—that they're guilty of all those heinous things, or that it can be worked out?"

Vida took a data cube out of the rack beside her desk and put it in the cube reader. "Take a look at this. Her family sent it."

Heris looked at a picture of a young woman in a brilliantly colored costume.

"That's the Landbride," Vida said. "Look closely." She touched the controls, and zoomed in to the face.

"Esmay Suiza?" Heris said.

"Yes. And now I know what a Landbride is." Vida touched the controls again, and two fields came up, one clearly an old document—faded ink on some surface that had discolored, and one in crisp black print on white. "That's the Landbride's Charter, on the right, one of the oldest surviving documents on Altiplano. Suiza's family provided the translation and typescript. You did know that our regulations, Fleet regulations, prohibited relationships and marriages with Altiplano Landbrides, didn't you?"

"No," Heris said, skimming down the closely-typed pages. The phrasing, even in translation, seemed archaic and stilted: "—*and for the honor of the land, and the land's health, she shall not be alienated from her own, for any cause whatever . . .*"

"Before I read this, I'd have assumed it was the Altiplano mutiny . . . and maybe it was . . . but the duties of the Landbride are just not consistent with the duties of Fleet personnel."

"It's—primitive," Heris said finally. Vida pursed her lips.

"I don't think primitive's quite right, though it is old. It's far more complex than I thought, based on a sophisticated—though to me very odd—theology. And it is a theology, because they do seriously believe in the existence of one or more gods. I'm not entirely sure if the invocations imply multiples or not. They are, however, strict Ageists, though they don't use the term."

"Opposed to rejuvenation?"

"Yes. In any form, for any reason. Some of what they call the Old Believers were even opposed to regen tanks for bone fracture repair, and a few considered that no one should receive medical care past age sixty in their years—probably seventy Standard. They're also committed to population control and consider free-birthers to be immoral."

"So . . . you don't think the Suizas are villains anymore?"

"I don't think Esmay Suiza, or her father, are directly responsible for the massacre of our patrons. However, I do think there's a problem with her marrying Barin, quite apart from what happened historically. She's sworn, as a Landbride, to a religious duty that requires her to put the welfare of the land—the Suiza land, to be specific—above every other consideration."

"But she wouldn't—"

"It's a conflict, Heris, however you look at it. Her oath to the Regular Space Service, the oath she swore when she accepted a commission, requires her to put the welfare of the service ahead of everything else. It's clear to her family, and to me, that her Landbride oath conflicts. Her family is being criticized for letting their Landbride go offplanet."

"Why did she take it, then?"

"The position passes from one Landbride to another by direct appointment—her great-grandmother had chosen her, for some reason, and didn't change the appointment even after she left to join Fleet. When her great-grandmother died, she became the Landbride-elect automatically. And, since she was in some disgrace with Fleet at the time, she accepted it and went through the ritual."

"Has she appointed a successor?"

"Her father thinks she'll appoint a cousin of hers, a younger woman. But to transfer the duties from a living Landbride to another, they both have to be in the ceremony. Now she's disappeared . . . Terakian & Sons are a respectable firm, and I'm sure she'll show up somewhere, but I don't know where."

Heris thought a moment. "Wait—I can see why being Landbride is in conflict with being a Fleet officer, but not with being Barin's wife."

"The regulations," Vida said. "Remember?"

Heris choked back *Damn the fool regulations*, and nodded. "They could be changed, surely?"

"When we've beaten back the mutiny and made sure the Benignity doesn't come romping across the borders, nor the Bloodhorde pirates disrupt shipping, certainly. In the meantime . . . there's every chance that Fleet will annul the marriage, and Barin will get a black mark in his record. As for Suiza . . . she'd get one too, if she were still in the system, but she's not."

"If she were no longer Landbride?"

"If she yielded the job to this cousin, you mean? Then there'd be no bar for her marrying Barin, though if the marriage has been annulled, they'd have to do it again. As for rejoining Fleet . . . I'm not sure." Vida held up her hand, as if Heris had started to speak. "No, don't blame me. At the moment I'm not inclined to put any barriers in her path, but you have to see that others would."

"We need her. We need her now . . . can't you find out who kicked her out?"

"While I'm in transit? If you'll kindly wait until I reach my own office with my own staff, then yes, I can find out. But not here."

"It's not fair," Heris said, subsiding only slightly. "Barin's going to worry; he could get careless—"

"He won't," said his grandmother. "And I don't expect Suiza to do anything stupid, either. Nor you. I don't suppose they sent you back to your own ship—?"

"No. *Indefatigable*. In refitting, and the crew will probably be whatever they could scrape off the docks."

"Then it's a good thing they'll have you for a captain."

That was dismissal, and Heris knew it; she left her aunt admiral alone and went to see if she could get a message to Esmay or Barin, either one, to let them know Vida hadn't done it. But a mere commander in transit had no clout with communications.

R.S.S. *Rosa Maior*

Barin Serrano called up the Fleet personnel-locator database and looked up Esmay. He'd done this at every station, and kept track of her progress after they parted. He wondered if she'd done the same for him. He still didn't know why she'd been given new orders and sent all the way over to Sector Three. Luckily, Suiza was such an unusual surname that she was easy to find—

Entry not found. No personnel surnamed SUIZA located.
Check spelling and repeat search?

That made no sense. She'd been in the system only two weeks before. He ran through the available options on the system, but the searches all came up the same until he tried "Separated or Retired."

SUIZA, Esmay, most recent rank 0-3, most recent assignment, separated by order of Admiral Serrano, separation effected Trinidad—

Barin stared at the date. Nine days ago. Halfway across Familias space.

Rage blinded him to the rest of the screen. Admiral Serrano, *his own grandmother*, had taken revenge on Esmay, had kicked her out of the service she loved, and at a time when they needed every good officer. His grandmother—! She had double-crossed them, backstabbed them, and he would—would—

His thoughts steadied. He was a jig, and his grandmother was an admiral major. He could be angry; he could hate her all he wanted, but he was a Fleet officer, with a war on, and trying to quarrel with her would help none of them.

Where was Esmay? He had no idea. What was she doing? He could imagine her coming, trying to find him and let him know . . . or going somewhere—where?—to do something—what?—that he couldn't quite imagine. Rockhouse Major to protest to Fleet Headquarters? To Altiplano to settle down as Landbride? No, surely not that. Perhaps to find evidence that his grandmother's accusation about Suiza treachery was false.

In the meantime, he had his duty, and even if his grandmother could so far forget hers as to inject personal vengeance into a real emergency, he wouldn't. As a jig aboard a ship headed for combat, he had plenty of duties, more than enough to keep him busy.

In the junior officers' mess, the ensigns and other jigs looked up as he entered. They would not have heard about Esmay; that expression must mean something else.

"Have you heard anything, Barin?" That was Cossy Forlin, who had been about halfway down his class at the Academy.

"About the mutiny?" Barin said, finding his place. "No."

"I just thought—with all your relatives—"

"I wonder—" Luca Tavernos glanced at the entrance, and lowered his voice. "I wondered about the others—it's scary, nobody knowing whom to trust."

"Like *Despite*," Cossy said. "How do we know—" He stopped abruptly as three lieutenants came in, and Lt. Marcion took the head of the table.

Marcion glanced at the juniors, his expression unreadable. Then he pointed his fork at Cossy. "At least we know *you* aren't part of any conspiracy, Jig Forlin—conspirators know better than to say things with the doors open. Be glad your specialty isn't intelligence."

Cossy reddened, but applied himself to his dinner.

"So, Barin, does your family network give you anything useful?"

"No, sir," Barin said. "You know the communications aren't exactly open."

"And do you have any doubts about the loyalty of any personnel on this ship?"

"No, sir, but if I did I would report it to the proper authorities."

Marcion laughed. "I'm sure you would—you Serranos are a thorough bunch. What's your assessment of the mutineers' tactics?"

"From the little I know, sir, I suspect they concentrated on the ships they stole, to make that strike on Copper Mountain. I'd be surprised if there were many left scattered on other ships."

"You're assuming fairly small numbers to start with."

"Smaller than the loyal contingent, yes, sir."

"Interesting. I know a lot of people who were really upset with the changes Conselline imposed, starting with the new Minister of Defense."

"Yes, sir, but not mutinous," Barin said. He quoted his grandmother. "'Politicians come and go, but the Fleet remains.'"

"That was my reading, also—but I wanted the legendary Serrano opinion."

Barin ignored this jibe. "What do you think the mutineers really want?" he asked. "Do you think it was Conselline's leadership that drove them to it, or what?"

"I don't know," Marcion said. "I'm not one of them, after all, and imputing motives to enemies is a risky business. I'd be more inclined to think they took advantage of the absence of senior officers who were put on inactive status because of the rejuvenation issue. Your grandmother was caught in that, wasn't she, Barin?"

"Yes, sir."

"My guess is that in the command confusion that followed

chopping off at least half the flag rank, they were able to make moves that might have taken a lot longer otherwise. Personnel was going crazy, trying to find people to fill billets suddenly open; promotion boards were meeting round-the-clock."

"How'd you know that?" asked Cossy.

"I was on a staff rotation at Headquarters. Admiral Stearns, to start with, then when she was made inactive, it was her replacement, Admiral Rollinby. I'd be there yet, except that the mutiny shuffled assignments yet again. Did you ever know Admiral Stearns, Barin? She said she knew your grandmother."

"No sir," Barin said. "The . . . admiral had a lot of friends at Headquarters—"

"So I gathered. Apparently she'd also been poking around the rejuvenation problem on her own—she and Admiral Stearns were on a study group of some kind."

"Did you ever hear what happened with that, Lieutenant?" asked an ensign down the table.

"Conselline killed the study. It reflected badly on his sept, of course, since it's very likely it was their drugs that caused the problem. But without funding for research or treatment, a lot of our people were in a pretty hopeless situation." Marcion paused. "There are times I find it difficult to stay as apolitical as regulations demand."

That effectively ended the topic at dinner, and Barin finished his meal with nothing more than a polite request to pass the rolls. Others talked softly of sports scores or upcoming exams.

After the meal, Barin found his mind ticking over more calmly. Why had someone hounded Esmay out of the service now? The first word they'd had back from their families had been disapproving but not explosive. Had more evidence of Suiza perfidy shown up? He didn't believe it. Serrano tempers blew quickly, and—in the absence of further hostile action—subsided almost as quickly. His grandmother had all the arrogance of flag rank, but she had always been fair.

As far as he knew. And, he had to admit to himself, he didn't know her as well as he might. And the entry had said Admiral Serrano.

But his grandmother wasn't the only Admiral Serrano. Hadn't been, even before the current crisis that brought all the flag ranks back to duty. Had the entry even said which Admiral Serrano? He hadn't really paid attention . . .

And he couldn't now. Alarm sirens wailed in what he hoped was another one of the captain's drills. He double-timed through one corridor, slid down a ladder, and made it to his assigned station well within the time limit. The senior rating handed him the comp, and he started calling out names: "Ackman . . . Averre . . . Betenkin . . ." When the senior lieutenant came around, Barin had his section ready for inspection, lockers open and p-suits in hand. The lieutenant received Barin's report, and examined the p-suits as if he hadn't inspected them the day before.

Barin was halfway down the bay when another siren whooped.

Combat, from the bowels of a cruiser, was either boring or fatal. He'd been told that from the Academy on up. He hoped very hard for boring. Barin had a damage-assessment team which he was in nominal charge of, thanks to the shortage of senior NCOs—that due, of course, to the mutiny and the failed rejuvenations. Having been taught from the cradle that junior officers are inevitably less expert than the NCOs they command, he had a good relationship with the petty officer assigned to his section, a man with solid qualifications in damage assessment and damage control.

For the next three hours, his team had no damage to assess. They checked and reported compartment temperatures, flow rates in various pipes, and a host of other readings that Barin knew were important, but which offered no clue at all to what was going on outside. The artificial gravity didn't fluctuate, the lights didn't flicker, nothing at all happened.

When the stand-down came, Barin made his final report to the Damage Control Officer and returned to his regular duties. He was trying to read up on damage assessment and damage control—the junior officers' course for command track had nothing about it, and he found it heavy going.

"It's not that hard, sir," one of the few remaining master chiefs told him. "Basically you've got stuff in pipes and stuff in wires, plus of course your air and your gravity."

"It's all the different kinds of stuff in the pipes," Barin said. "And it says here that compartments may be filled with smoke or steam or—"

"Most likely's water vapor condensation, if there's a pressure loss," the chief said.

"So how are we supposed to know which pipe is which if we can't see it?"

"Well, now, that's why you're supposed to know your section from the frames out. Of course, if they need you somewhere else—"

"Chief, have you ever been in a ship that was badly damaged?"

"Once from enemy action—back in the first Patchcock mess—and once from an idiot coming back from leave and showing off. He managed to knock a hole in a hydraulic line down in the shuttle bay; he'd have been up for discipline except the leak went right through him."

"A leak?"

"High-pressure line, son. See, he'd brought back a needler his cousin gave him for some holiday or other—which was against regs, of course. And he hadn't checked the ammunition that came with it—which was, we found later, the heaviest his cousin could buy. His cousin figured somebody on a cruiser needed something that could make holes in the hull, apparently—well, not quite, but almost. Anyway, this fool had to show it to a buddy of his, and they got to playing around, and sure enough—PING. Right through the lift line. Out came a jet, drilled right through him, down came the shuttle onto the deck a good bit harder than it should, and that popped two tires; a piece of one hit another guy in the head, and another piece hit a fellow holding a torch. Couldn't blame him for dropping it, when his arm was broke, but the torch caught something—I forget what— on fire. So then we had a fire, and a hydraulic leak, and since the hydraulic fluid was vaporized by coming out at such a pressure, what do you think happened?"

"It blew up," Barin said.

"That's right, it did. Old *Harkness* that was, who'd survived two full-scale engagements with Benignity battle groups, and because of one stupid idiot, she was scrap. Explosion in shuttle maintenance. But that was only the beginning. In those cruisers—and *Harkness* is one reason they're built different now—all the maintenance functions were clustered for efficiency. That included a warren of shops and parts storage lockers and so on, and—again for efficiency, as they saw it—the main nexi for electrical. We didn't just have one fire, or one explosion—captain finally had us cut away the weapons storage—thinkin' every minute the fire would reach us and we'd go up same as others already had—and jettison the whole thing. We fought it for over twenty-eight hours, and at the end we had barely life-support for the remaining live crew. Over three hundred dead, ship completely disabled—they had to take us off in p-suits, transfer us to another ship . . ."

"Hydraulic fluid," Barin said. "I didn't know it would burn."

"They've tried and tried to get something that will work better and be less flammable, but so far—if you vaporize it, and light it, it will go up. And don't forget, it'll slice you like a laser scalpel." The master chief sucked his cheeks for a moment. "Now the other," he said. "That wasn't so bad. Hull breach, but a cold one—heavy missile got through, but it misfired. A bit ticklish getting it out, and the poor fellows in there had died, but not nearly as bad. The only real problem was a youngster who wanted a souvenir, and was workin' away at the fusing access, so's he could get it off and hide it in his locker before we got there. Old Master Chief Meharry just about took his head off then and there. Could have blown us all up, he could."

Barin wondered if that Meharry was related to his aunt's crewmember, Methlin Meharry.

"Here—this is the best data-cube course we have," the master chief said, handing it to Barin. "You learn most from the trouble you live through, but that cube'll take you a bit farther than the others."

"Thanks," Barin said, and resolved to spend every spare moment with it. He would know everything about Troop Deck, from the hull to the plumbing.

What had actually happened in the battle wasn't clear until well into the next day, when the captain made an announcement to the crew. "We came out of jump to find a couple of mutineers—the admiral expected that, so we had everything hot. They were mining the jump point, but we blew through the first cordon with no damage, and all enemy ships are destroyed. We're credited with half a kill."

Barin wondered how they knew the other ships were mutineers—if they had stopped to ask questions, the battle might have been more even, and far more dangerous for him.

The battle group would stay insystem long enough to pick up the loose mines, then mine the jump point with its own, programmed to accept the changed Fleet IDs which the mutineers shouldn't have.

CHAPTER SIX

Castle Rock, Appledale

Brun Meager stroked the length of the pool, and splashed water on the woman lounging beside it. "Kate—come on in. You're being lazy."

"The water's cold," Kate Briarley said. "I'd get cramp." The Lone Star Confederation Ranger had changed into a swimsuit, but had a towelling robe around her shoulders. Her datapad and comunit were beside her, as well as one of her many weapons, this one a black-matte needler.

"You'd get exercise," Brun said. "Your whole planet can't be warm." Kate grinned, but shook her head. Brun rolled over and swam down the pool again. The water wasn't cold; the water was just right, as long as she kept moving. On her way back, she saw Kate was sitting up, talking into a comunit. Brun ignored her and flipped into a turn for another lap. She needed to work off tension anyway. Soon—in a day or so anyway—she would have to do something about her mother. And she had no idea what. She stretched, revelling in the feel of her body's strength and agility, the flow of cool water past her shoulders, her hips, her legs.

As she came back down the pool, this time in sidestroke, she saw Kevil Mahoney come out of the house. He walked better now, without any aids, but unevenly. Would a rejuv help that? He couldn't afford it, not until they straightened out his financial problems, but she could provide it. She made a mental note to talk to the family medical advisors about it as she rolled into a crawl, and powered off the last fifteen meters, hoisting herself at the end with a rush of water.

"Breakfast out here?" she asked. Then she blinked the water out of her eyes and saw their expressions. "What now?"

"Hobart's dead."

"What?"

"Hobart Conselline is dead. At the hands of a visiting fencing master, if you can believe that."

Brun grabbed a towel from the stack and scrubbed her head with it. She dropped that one, grabbed another to wrap around her shoulders. "When did this happen?"

"Yesterday afternoon."

"And we're only finding out now—?"

"His sept put a lock on the news, to locate all the Barraclough Chairholders before it was announced."

"His sept—!" Brun clamped her teeth together for a moment. "I see." She reached out to the table already set for breakfast, and touched its pad. "Staff—change of plans; we'll be eating inside, in the library. I'll be going in to the city as soon as I've dressed and eaten."

"Are you sure that's a good idea?" Kate asked.

"I'm sure it's necessary." Brun looked at Kevil. He said nothing—he wouldn't, outside in an unsecured field—but his expression ended any doubts she might have had.

It still felt strange to her, this sense of mastery that had come during her first Grand Council meeting after her father's death. It felt strange to walk into Appledale as if she owned it, even though she did, strange to feel no guilt about leaving wet footprints on the Issai carpets as she hurried upstairs. "I'll need a secure comlink to Buttons," she said to the guard on station in the entry hall—an innovation of Kate's that she now recognized as necessary.

Upstairs, in the room she had always occupied, she toweled off, and stood a moment scowling at her wardrobe. Pregnancy had changed her body enough that many of her old clothes didn't fit. Dark mourning made her look sick; she needed to look healthy and competent. Finally she chose a tailored suit in steel gray, and tucked a blue-patterned scarf into the neckline.

When she came down, Kevil and Kate were in the library, already loading their plates from a serving table. Kate had changed from the red swimsuit into one of her less-flamboyant Lone Star suits, this one pale blue. Her high-heeled fringed boots were beside her chair; her stockinged feet looked absurd in the deep carpet.

"It's clean," Kate said, waving at the room. Brun checked the scans and fields herself anyway and saw Kate nod approvingly.

"So—a fencing master went bonkers and killed Hobart. What else?"

"His sept claims it's conspiracy. By the Barracloughs—by you, in fact."

"What, in retaliation for my father's murder?"

"Except that they don't admit having him killed." Kevil prodded a sausage and sighed. "I'm not supposed to eat these things."

"Oh, live dangerously," Kate said, around a mouthful of bacon. Brun glanced at her. Kate had never been pregnant; maybe that's why she could eat the way she did, lounge about while Brun exercised, and not gain an ounce.

"I did," Kevil said, with a grin. "That's what got me in this mess." But he forked up a bite of sausage.

"Since I know I didn't hire any fencing masters to cut Hobart's head off—" Brun got that far and noticed that the others weren't moving. "What?"

"That's how it was done. Decapitation."

Brun looked at them, one after the other. "You're serious? His head—? Yes, I see you are. And so, he had his head cut off, and I mentioned it, and now you think—"

"No," Kevil said. "I don't think that. It's not your style, hiring someone else. But there's another complication."

"Which is?"

"Your mother."

"Oh, be reasonable, Kevil. She's off on Sirialis; she can't have come back here to behead Hobart."

"No, but she is Bunny's widow, and the evidence we unearthed about your uncle's dealings with the Consellines might be construed as giving her a motive. The very fact that she's off on Sirialis could be considered suspicious."

Brun shook her head. "Not Mother. She feels deeply, of course, and if we'd caught Dad's killer, she might have slapped his face, but I can't see her conniving at assassination."

Kevil shook his head. "Nor can I, exactly, and yet—your mother's a lot more complicated than you know, Brun. Back when we were young, she and my wife were close friends, and I heard more about the young Miranda than most."

Brun wondered suddenly what had happened to Kevil's wife, but didn't ask . . . whatever it was, now was not the time. "Still, if she was going to have anyone killed, I'd bet on Uncle Harlis for the designated victim—"

"Don't joke, Brun," Kevil said. "Right now, for the sake of the sept, you must hope your uncle stays healthy."

"For all of me, he can," Brun said, scooping marmalade onto a slice of toast. "Now that we've got his sticky fingers off Dad's estate— or at least put a kink in that—" She gave Kevil a questioning look.

"A kink, certainly. I'm afraid Hobart's murder, unless the motives become clear, will weaken your case. When you talk to Buttons, be sure to tell him to be especially alert for unexplained movement in the holdings of peripheral companies, will you?"

"Of course." Brun glanced around. "Where's George? I can give him a ride into the city—"

Kevil nodded at a crumb-covered plate. "He left an hour ago."

"Your secure link to Lord Felix, milady." The security tech gestured from the doorway. Brun rose and then closed herself into the family's combooth, entered her personal codes and touched the screen with the datawand that confirmed both her ID and her codes. Buttons' face appeared, looking even more like her father's than the last time she'd seen him.

"I'm glad you called," he said. "Bad news—"

"I know," Brun said. "We just heard an hour ago—but I didn't think you'd have heard yet."

"Why not?" Buttons asked. "I'm a lot closer—"

"What? Not to Castle Rock—or are you talking about something besides Hobart Conselline's death?"

"Conselline's dead?" Buttons looked startled, then more grave than ever. "When?"

"Yesterday afternoon; they just released the news this morning, local time. You didn't know? Then what bad news did you have?"

"Pedar Orregiemos—Conselline's foreign minister. He's dead too." Buttons flushed, then paled again. "Mother. She . . . er . . . killed him. By accident, of course . . ."

"Mother killed a Crown Minister?" Brun hardly knew what she said. It came to her like a sudden rupture in the foundations of a familiar tower . . . the sagging away of the wall . . . she pulled her mind back. "Mother . . . herself?"

"Yes." Buttons chewed his lip. "Apparently this fellow had invited himself to Sirialis. The servants say he was paying court to Mother. She had been up at the snow lodge, and he announced himself while she was gone . . . she'd just come back to the main house when he arrived. Anyway . . . he wanted to fence with her. Apparently he'd fenced with her long ago, before she married Dad. He insisted on using those old weapons out of the case in the hall."

Into Brun's mind came the memory of her father, standing by that very case, leaning on the wall, and talking to Kevil Mahoney. She had been—what? eleven or so?—and her father was saying, "The thing about Miranda, Kev, is that people simply can't recognize what she is. They see the porcelain figure of elegance, the beauty, the gracious behavior . . . and fail to recognize that she's deadly as any of these blades." Her father had tipped his head toward the case. "I'm just the front for her ambitions, really . . . as a swordsman is just the means for the steel to strike. She wields me skillfully, so skillfully no one notices."

Kevil had shaken his head, but smiled, then said, "I hope to God you have the scans off, Bunny."

"Well . . . I'm not a fool either," her father had said, and then turned to Brun. "And as for you, Bubbles, it's time you fizzed away to bed."

She had argued, she remembered, and lost the argument; she'd heard the tail of one of Kevil's comments as she flounced away to the main stairs. "—your instincts? Or Miranda's?" and her father's answer, which she'd paused, just around the corner of the stair, to listen for. "Both, Kev. Though at the moment she seems nothing but fizzy bubbles, she's got a brain in her head."

"Mother killed him?" she asked Buttons now. "Herself?"

"It was an accident, apparently," Buttons said. "The old blade broke, and Pedar was wearing an antique mask as well—and the metal was brittle."

"They didn't test it before—? No, they wouldn't, of course." Brun tried to put her scrambled thoughts in order. "When did this happen, Buttons?"

"Local time on Sirialis . . . perhaps four days ago, or five. Lady

Cecelia was there, by the way. She'd come visiting—why I have no idea, it's not anywhere close to hunting season. Mother's gone off with her, to the Guerni Republic."

Lady Cecelia, who seemed to think of nothing but horses, but had the same lightning rod effect on things as she herself, Brun thought. Lady Cecelia, who could see through a brick wall at the worst possible moments. At least she was a Barraclough too.

"It's going to look bad," she told her brother. "Just Hobart alone would have looked bad, but this—"

"It was an accident," her brother insisted. "Old weapons, brittle metal . . ."

"It will still look bad," Brun said.

"But you don't think . . ." Buttons' voice trailed away; his face was taut and strained.

"I don't think our mother managed to connive at the deaths of a Speaker and one of his Ministers at the same time, and if she had, she certainly wouldn't have gone fencing with one of them with faulty equipment."

That seemed to satisfy him; his face relaxed slightly. It did not satisfy Brun.

"What are we going to do?" Buttons asked, almost plaintively. "I can't very well come back now—we're in the midst of some ticklish negotiations—and even if I did, it'd be weeks before I got back to Castle Rock."

"Stay there," Brun said. "I'll deal with whatever happens here. Did Mother ask for help?"

"No—"

"Then we'll assume she settled things on Sirialis."

"But Brun . . . can you do it alone?"

"We'll find out," Brun said, more cheerfully than she intended. "They're going to hold a Council meeting to try to ram something through. I don't know what. I have to go."

"Well . . . I guess there's nothing I can do from here. I'll contact the committee and see if they'll let you vote my proxy, but if they're convinced we did it, they won't . . ."

"That will help, Buttons. Thanks. I'd better go now."

Brun let herself out of the combooth, reset the controls, and went back to the breakfast room.

"More trouble?" asked Kevil after a quick look at her face.

"That was Buttons," she said. "You remember Pedar Orregiemos? Hobart made him a minister."

"A blot," Kevil said. "Your father disliked him very much."

"Well, my mother just killed him." She could not resist pausing a beat to see the result of that remark. The Lone Star Ranger choked on her muffin; Kevil blinked slowly, his mouth tightening. "By accident," Brun said then.

"So I would hope," Kevil said. His glance flicked sideways to the other woman. "Did Buttons give you any details?"

"Only that they were playing around with the old fencing gear and something went wrong," Brun said. She wanted to chatter; she must not chatter. In lieu of chatter, she picked up a muffin and buttered it, then spooned on a dribble of apple-blossom honey. Around a mouthful of sweetness and crumbs, she added, "Lady Cecelia was there."

"Why?" asked Kate, before Kevil, his mouth already open, could ask the same thing.

"I don't know." Brun took another bite of muffin, slowing herself down. She felt that her brain was beginning to spin out of control. "I don't think Buttons knows; he said he was surprised because it wasn't close to hunting season."

"Perhaps she wanted to look at your bloodstock," Kate said. "She's the one who's so crazy about horses, right?"

"Yes . . . I suppose that could be it." Brun was aware of a warning look from Kevil, and took another bite of muffin.

"By the way, I'm coming to the city with you."

"You don't have to," Brun began, but Kate waved her to silence.

"I'm coming, because you may be in danger. If these Consellines really believe you engineered Hobart's death—"

"I have security staff," Brun said.

"Yes, but they're just security." Kate grinned, that wide insouciant grin that made her seem so harmless. "I'm a Ranger, remember."

"I suppose you're going to wear your badge?" Kevil asked.

"On this occasion, yes."

"I think I'll come," Kevil said. "I haven't been back, since—" Since they had brought him to Appledale, out of his poverty, out of the clutches of that most suspicious male nurse.

"To the house?" Brun asked. She wiped her mouth and rang for staff, sending the first for her briefcase and the second for her car.

"No—but I'll check with the banks in person. That might loosen their memory. I can also find out when my new arm might be coming out of the bins. They said next week, but I might be lucky . . ."

"Fine, then. Let's get going."

On the drive to the city, they reviewed possibilities. Brun updated her personal comp with the whereabouts of all the Seated Family members; she was sure there would be an emergency Grand Council meeting that day or the next.

Castle Rock, Grand Council

Brun did not ever remember seeing the Benignity ambassador before. She knew they had one—she knew which building in Embassy Row belonged to the Benignity of the Compassionate Hand, a big gray stone building like so many in the city. Now, in the Grand Council chamber, she stared like everyone else at the man of middle height, dark-haired and green-eyed, who wore a perfectly conventional dark suit. She wasn't sure what she'd expected, but Sr. Vadis Unser-Marz, as his name appeared on her monitor, looked too ordinary to represent the fabulously wicked Benignity of the Compassionate Hand.

So far news of Pedar Orregiemos's death hadn't reached the news media; reporters outside the chamber had asked only for a reaction to Hobart Conselline's assassination, and she had expressed shock, and her condolences for his family. "I know what it's like to lose a father," she had said, and they had gone looking for another victim.

Brun knew the meeting would be chaired by the head of a minor family, Jon-Irene Pearsall, as neutral as anyone could be. She wondered how long he'd last; he didn't look very forceful. He tapped for order.

"On this sad day, we have only one order of business; Ambassador Unser-Marz has an urgent message from his government, which we will hear."

War. Brun could feel the tremor of apprehension across the chamber. The ambassador stepped up to the podium with ceremonious grace.

"Chairholders, it is my responsibility to read to you this urgent communication from our government and to assure you of the most sincere apologies and regrets which accompany it."

That sounded ominous, but why would anyone apologize for declaring war?

"I am having the text sent to your individual displays, but I will also read it." He began quoting; Brun glanced down at the monitor. His accent was not hard to follow, but she wanted to be sure to catch every word. "It is with sincere regret that the Benignity of the Compassionate Hand must take responsibility for the unprovoked attack by Swordmaster Hostite Fieddi on the head of state of the Familias Regnant. This attack was ordered by the former Chairman of the Board of the Benignity, without the knowledge or consent of the Board. The former Chairman has been judged guilty of political assassination and punished."

Brun realized she'd been holding her breath, and let it out. She glanced around and met startled glances. She looked down again. There it was in print—and then a sharply focussed video clip of a much older man, almost bald, with a crawler below: Pietro Rossa-Votari, the Chairman, and the charges against him. Sentenced to death, it said. Then the text flicked back up, and the ambassador started reading again.

"Although the Benignity of the Compassionate Hand did not consent to, or condone, the former Chairman's order to assassinate Hobart Conselline, it is felt that the Grand Council of the Familias Regnant should be made aware of the reasons for his decision, deplorable as that decision was."

A rising murmur, as Chairholders drew breath and looked at one another. Brun said nothing, trying to think it through. Hobart had been a power-hungry blot, but why would the Benignity want him dead?

"It is important for you to know that no one in the Familias Regnant was involved. No sept, no family, no individual. Chairman Rossa-Votari acted alone. He left the following recorded message to be transmitted to you."

"It's a fake!" blurted someone off to the right. Brun checked her display. Kasdar Morrelline, that was, Ottala's older brother.

"No, it is not a fake," the ambassador said. "I beg of your courtesy to hear this—and the text will appear on your monitors, since the Chairman's accent was stronger than mine."

The voice in the recording was pitched a little higher, and sounded older; Brun scanned the text and tried to match words to sounds. "It is with deep regret that I order the death of a head of state. This is a decision never made lightly by one in my position, for to order it is to order my own death as well. Yet I must care for my family, and it is God's will that sometimes a father sacrifice himself for his children. I am convinced that the safety of my people—perhaps of all people everywhere—requires that Hobart Conselline die.

"It became clear to me that Ser Conselline and his government favored the unrestricted use of rejuvenation technology to extend lives without limit. The implications of this, and of a free-birth policy, are clear: the Familias Regnant will inevitably seek to expand its territories at the expense of its neighbors. This will bring us into conflict, possibly into full-scale war. This we do not want.

"I urge the successors of Ser Conselline to consider the benefits of accepting the natural and legal limits of expansion. The Guerni Republic has used this technology but committed to maintaining a constant population size and has a long history of staying within its present borders. The Familias, by contrast, has been expanding slowly but steadily for the past two hundred years, and more rapidly in the past fifty."

"So have you," someone near Brun muttered. Her thought exactly. They had invaded the Xavier system.

"It is my hope that my successor and the government of the Familias Regnant can come to some permanent agreement on the border between us, and some controls to be placed on Familias expansion." The ambassador paused, then went on. "That is the end of the the former Chairman's message, Chairholders. I am at your service to answer any questions."

Brun pushed the button that signalled her request to speak.

"Ambassador, I'm not clear on something. Does your government expect us to stop using rejuvenation technology, or does it expect us to offer some guarantee that we will not expand into your territory?"

"Sera, we have many concerns about rejuvenation itself. It was our Chairman's belief that rapid population growth and the restriction of opportunities for younger persons would lead to political unrest, culminating in either civil war or expansion into the territories of neighboring states. We do not choose to be overrun by you, and we would avoid a war if possible."

"So you think repeatable rejuvenations are driving population growth and this will make us an expansionist state?" asked one of the Dunlearies across the chamber.

"Or a very volatile, unstable neighbor, at the least," the ambassador said. "It is our intent to press for some restriction on repeatable rejuvenations—"

"No!" yelled Oskar Morrelline; he was gavelled down.

"Or some other reliable, measurable means of population control," the ambassador said. "What we want is a stable border—"

"You just invaded *us* in Xavier a few years ago," someone pointed out.

The ambassador folded his lips together, shook his head, and said, "Ser . . . it is not my mission to discuss what might have motivated the late Chairman to attempt an incursion into your space. That was his responsibility, and he is no longer able to answer our questions. It is my mission to inform you of these facts; that your Speaker, Hobart Conselline, was executed on the order of the late Chairman, who has paid for that order with his life, and that the reason for the order was his concern—which the present government shares— about the instability unrestricted rejuvenation might cause in both your internal politics and our relationship."

"But it's none of your business what we do in our own space," someone else said.

"Sera, we are neighbors. A fire in your house could loose sparks to burn ours."

"But you can't expect us to just turn around and quit using a medical procedure that so many—"

"Sera, I expect nothing, but to be heard. It is not my place to tell you what to do, only to tell you what my government thinks of what you do, and what my government might do in response to what you do."

"Is that a threat?" Brun asked.

The ambassador spread his hands. "I would hope we are very far from discussing threats."

"And yet you killed Hobart Conselline."

"The late Chairman ordered his execution, yes. It is not quite the same thing. The present government deplores that decision, and wishes most heartily that the late Chairman had found it possible to convey his concern in a less . . . striking . . . way."

"By starting a mutiny, I suppose." That was Viktor Barraclough.

"No, ser. We started no mutiny. We deplore the mutiny and consider it a serious threat to peaceful interaction between our governments. Though if you want our opinion—"

"Oh, by all means . . . do give us your opinion." Viktor's sarcasm raised a nervous ripple of laughter. Even the ambassador smiled.

"It may well come back to this rejuvenation problem. The lack of opportunities for the young would naturally show up first in a stratified and disciplined segment of society. And was there not some problem with the military rejuvenations?"

Brun had the feeling that there was much more that the ambassador wasn't saying. It had been a Benignity agent on Patchcock, she remembered, who'd been involved in the production of substandard rejuv drugs, though she didn't know if it had been proved he was responsibile. Naturally . . . if the Benignity was worried about expansion, they'd try to cripple the military ahead of time, make it impossible to maintain a strong, experienced military force—the kind of force that could invade. Or protect against invasion.

"Do you have more information for us, Ser Unser-Marz?" she asked.

"Not more information, no."

"Then I move that the ambassador be thanked for his information, and that he be asked to hold himself in readiness for more questions."

"Are you trying to cut off discussion?" the ambassador asked.

"No. But I see no benefit to the Familias in discussing this in front of you, Ambassador, with all due respect."

"Agreed," said Viktor Barraclough. "I second the motion."

"If I may—" the ambassador said.

"Yes?" The Speaker looked confused.

"I would like to assure the Council that I or my staff will be available to answer questions at any time, and I quite agree that my presence is unnecessary while you conduct your business. If I might be excused?"

"Of course, Ambassador."

After he left, Brun realized that no one had asked one crucial question: had he known ahead of time? But argument swirled around her, as it had after her father's death. Although most now seemed to accept the ambassador's statement that the Benignity had been responsible for Hobart's death, the news of Pedar's death hadn't yet reached them. She was fairly sure that would change things again. One death, that the Benignity admitted to, was one thing. Two deaths, so close together, and one of them indubitably her mother's doing?

If they got out of this without a full-scale civil war, it would be a miracle.

CHAPTER SEVEN

R.S.S. *Indefatigable*

Heris Serrano came aboard her new command, the R.S.S. cruiser *Indefatigable*, and made her way to the bridge with only half her mind on the rituals of honor and response. She slid her command wand into the captain's slot and entered her codes. The computer flashed a green response, code accepted, and an array of function pads came alight. The computer, at least, was still responsive to the Fleet master codes. Now to see about the humans.

As she read herself in, the humans on the bridge looked as crew usually did during a change of command. The juniors stood stiffly at attention, focussed on her; the seniors kept one eye for the ship.

She'd had no time to check the files on her new personnel, and none of them looked familiar. Without her own crew, she felt exposed . . . but this was her crew now. And wherever Petris was, wherever Oblo and Meharry and the rest were, they would be doing their duty as she was doing hers.

When she'd read herself in, she called up the status reports on her console. Ship systems all came up as nominal, but supplies were limited. Not surprising, in the chaos of the mutiny; *Indefatigable* had been in for a major overhaul, her usual crew on long leave.

"Captain, there's a stack of messages from HQ; should I route them to your office or here?" That was a major . . . Suspiro, she read from his nametag.

"Here, please," Heris said. She would stay on the bridge, she'd decided, where she would be visible to more of the crew in this critical transition period.

"Yes, sir. The eyes-only messages will require your H-scale decryption keys, one through seven."

Heris inserted the command wand again, and reentered her authorization codes, unlocking the keys stored in her wand. From the console in front of her, a screen rose, its security wings extending to block the view of anyone else on the bridge. Eyes-only messages were a nuisance on ships like this, which didn't mount full-spec privacy booths. Heris fished in the drawer under the screen's lower edge for the visual filters that would complete the decryption for her alone and punched for the first message.

That message was time-limited; the limit had passed. Heris deleted it after a brief scan of a proposed command structure pending investigations. The second message firmed up the new command structure, and the third informed her that she would be commanding not only *Indefatigable* but a small task force: two cruisers, four patrols, three escorts, and the usual supply and service ships. The fourth gave her personnel summaries, with the most recent security information; she saved that to a secure file for later consideration. Finally she had time to meet her new officers and find out more about them.

Indefatigable had been assigned crew on the basis of first-come, first-assigned; as the designated flagship of the ships then in port, her commodore could trade off a few hands with others if necessary, but that was all. She had to have at least a few people who knew how to find their way around, or they'd have to spend a week in port.

Heris called the senior officers to a meeting in her office. Commander Seabolt, who looked as if he'd been razor-cut from a recruiting poster, folded himself carefully into the chair to her left, and Heris immediately catalogued him as a regulator. Lt. Commander Winsloe, senior Weapons officer, could have been cut from the same mold, though she had a twinkle in her eye. Major Suspiro, Communications, had the slightly rumpled, twitchy look that Heris associated with really good commtech personnel. Major Vondon, Scan, was much the same, but taller. In Engineering, she had Major Foxson, quiet and gray-haired. Her chief Environmental officer, Lt. Commander Donnehy, was a cheerful chunky woman who arrived minutes later than everyone else, to a disapproving look from Seabolt.

"Sorry, Captain," Donnehy said. "They just sent another batch of potential moles down, and I was trying to sort them out—"

"Take a seat," Heris said. She turned to Seabolt.

"Commander Seabolt, tell me about your previous assignment."

He drew himself up even stiffer if possible. "I was aide-de-camp to Admiral Markham; the admiral has been second in command of Sector Four HQ for the past four years."

"And your last ship assignment?"

"That would be eight years ago, Captain. I was on the *Picardy Rose* with Captain Graham." The names meant nothing to Heris, though she was fairly sure *Picardy Rose* was a patrol craft. "Command track? Technical?"

"Command track; I was fourth officer." Then, finally realizing what information might be most useful to her, he added, "*Picardy Rose* was a patrol craft on picket duty on the frontier."

"See any action?"

"No, sir. But Captain Graham ran a very tight ship, and we were always commended for our standards at the annual inspections."

She would much rather have had a messy combat veteran, but she nodded her thanks, and transferred her gaze to Eugenie Winsloe. "And you, Commander?"

"I was en route from the Gunnery School, where I did a round as instructor, to my new ship assignment—it would have been *Summerwine*. My last ship assignment was on *Rose of Glory*, and before that *Alerte*. We saw no action, though *Rose* did win the sector gunnery medal. I haven't been on a cruiser since I was a jig, but I assure the Captain that I'm quite familiar with cruiser weaponry."

"Very good." It wasn't good at all, but at least Winsloe seemed willing and a bit sharper than Seabolt. "Are you satisfied with your juniors' competence, Commander?"

She shook her head. "Captain, I couldn't fill a single watch with experienced weapons personnel. It's as if they just grabbed everyone within reach to fill out the numbers. However, the most experienced NCO tells me that if we're granted a few weeks for training, we should do reasonably well."

As if time would just hold still until they were ready.

"Kick 'em along faster," Heris told her. "We may not have a few weeks. And if you find someone else aboard with more weapons training, who was misassigned, come tell me about it. We may have to shift people around."

"We're short of replacement parts, too," Winsloe said. "We'd be shorter if I hadn't spotted the last load departing just as I came aboard. Contractor claimed it was his, but I took the liberty of requisitioning it."

"Good work, Commander," Heris said.

She let her gaze move on, to Lt. Commander deFries, the senior navigator.

"I've been on cruisers, most recently *Royal Reef*. But the last time I saw action was in *Clarion*, during the Patchcock mess."

"Have you had microjump weapons-track drills recently?"

"No, sir. And I was only third nav officer at Patchcock. However, I did bring aboard a full set of training sims, and four of my enlisted personnel have more recent combat experience than I have."

That was something, and he had showed initiative in the right direction. "Good . . . I'll be ordering some dry drills with other ships. Have you contacted their navigation officers?"

"No, sir. We hadn't been told that we would be traveling with other ships."

Damn secrecy. "We're to take a small group out—the ship names are now on the command board, so you'll want to liase with their navigation officers when we're done here."

"Yes, sir."

"Major Foxson . . . let's hear about you."

"Captain, all my service has been on cruisers of this class; I was on *Imperator* last and was transferred here because I'd been through the drives refitting on *Imp*, and they thought I'd be good to take over *Indy*'s new drives."

Heris had never liked the fashion of truncating ships' names, but that wasn't enough to set her against her senior engineering officer. "So what do you think of them?"

"A definite improvement over the old, Captain, but they rushed the last part of the job, what with the mutiny. Your insystem's fine, but the FTL drive isn't quite balanced. It'll get us there, but it'll leave a marked signature. And my guess is, it's going to degrade over time. We should have quite a flutter after a dozen long jumps or so."

"Why'd you accept it, then?"

"Sir, I came aboard two days after the refit crew signed off on it, or I wouldn't have. And I can't say it's not safe—there was the same modification to *Imp*, and while the trials showed our scan trace looking like a skip-jumper, the ship herself was steady as a rock, and it never failed. That was two years ago, Standard—they did take it back in and fix it, but now, with the mutiny and all, I imagine they'll refuse to delay."

He was probably right. And after all, he was coming along; if the drive failed and stranded them in some strange corner of the universe, he'd be there too.

That left Elise Donnehy, who had had cruiser duty six years before, but since then had worked with environmental systems design for deepspace repair ships. She cheerfully admitted to having forgotten which pipes ran where, though she insisted she could pick it up again fast.

Heris wanted to bang her head on the desk in sheer frustration, but she knew better. The lives of her little flotilla depended on her ability to tolerate frustration and make silk purses out of very crooked sows' ears. She could have done it with her old crew, or for that matter with any capable crew used to working together. She shook her head. No use thinking what might have been, she had the resources she had, pitiful as they were.

The other ships in the group seemed less disorganized than her own. At least that meant she had the worst problems closest at hand, where she could work on them directly.

An hour before mid-third shift, Heris's alarm went off, waking her from a pleasant dream in which she and Petris chased each other along a beach, in and out of warm, clear wavelets . . . the whole setting looked like a travel poster, in shades of blue and turquoise and white. She groaned and pushed her face back into the pillow for a moment. But she was awake . . . and now that she was awake, she remembered why she'd set the alarm. The environmental parameters at the start of first shift were always off, though the record books had been neatly initialled beside a record of perfect values all through third shift.

Heris splashed cold water on her face from the carafe of ice water she kept beside her bunk and put on a clean uniform. If one was going to appear like the wrath of gods to a slacking third-shift crew, a clean uniform enhanced the effect. Seabolt's natural knife-crease style would have worked, but Seabolt was convinced the initialled log sheets meant something was wrong with the machinery.

Heris clipped on her tagger and comunit—bridge had to know where the captain was—and pulled a pair of softies over her uniform boots. Most third-shift crew wore softies, to reduce noise, and it certainly made sneaking up on wrongdoers easier. She went aft, meeting—as she expected—no one at that hour in officer country. Down the nearest personnel ladder, one deck . . . two . . . and out into the port passage of Environmental, where the distant rhythmic thump of the pumps became audible.

She stood a moment, listening, feeling it through the soles of her feet and with one finger on the bulkhead, a trick she'd been taught as a jig by a grizzled master chief. Open the mouth . . . turn the head from side to side . . . and irregularities in the pump could be diagnosed from here. It all sounded normal, though.

She turned to her left, and saw that the hatch to the personnel lock separating the main port passage from the main starboard passage was open. She looked at the status telltales: all four green. Not good; someone had left the whole lock open, as a convenience . . . and a very definite danger. She looked at the hatch mechanisms—they should have closed the hatches automatically, but someone had stuck a stylus in the mechanism to hold them open. And . . . someone had put a stickypatch over the sensor that should have picked up the telltale lights.

Seabolt would assume sabotage and conspiracy, but Heris knew laziness was far more likely. Someone didn't want to wait while the locks cycled properly to give access from one side to the other—she'd find the forward lock jammed open too, no doubt. Instead of walking the complete round to make the required checks, someone was darting through to sign off the log at the other side.

Heris stepped back through to the port passage, pulled out the roll of tactape and laid a strip on each of the five bottom rungs of the ladder and along the underside of the handholds, just where fingers would grip. Then she went back in the lock, removed the stylus from that hatch, swung it closed, and dogged it behind her. She put a line of tactape on the wheel, very carefully. She left the stickypatch alone, went into the lock itself, closed and dogged that hatch and marked its wheel with tactape.

Coming out the starboard side of the lock, she couldn't dog the hatches behind her, but she put a line of tactape under each pull, shutting the hatches so the next user would have to pull them open.

It was pure guess which corridor the slack Environmental crew would be in, but in either case she should be able to find them before the midshift bell . . . and if she didn't, they'd respond to that with the usual report. She opened the service hatch at the end of the starboard compartment and found—as she should—nothing but the great rounded haunch of one of the settling tanks. She closed the hatch carefully, and headed back forward as quietly as possible, listening for anything but the heavy heartbeat of the pumps, the whoosh and gurgle of liquids, the hiss and bubble of gas exchange.

Outboard, on her right, were transparent tubes and containers glowing green or blue or amber with the various cultures in them . . . brightly backlit by the lights that optimized their growth. Beyond, the gleaming curves of more pipes, pumps, countercurrent exchange chambers. Beyond—invisible from here—were the honeycomb tricklebeds. Settling tanks aft, mixing tanks forward.

Inboard, the space from deck to overhead was filled with the secondary atmospheric system . . . canisters, pipes . . . and the food processing sections, neat rectangles of hydroponic beds.

Heris sniffed. Environmental was, arguably, the smelliest place on a ship. A healthy system smelled like a spring day in the country on a well-terraformed planet: a rich mix of odors from musky to astringent, but nothing actually unpleasant. The best environmental techs she'd known could diagnose a problem with just a quick sniff, recognizing at once which sludge chamber or bacterial strain was out of kilter.

Here—her nose wrinkled involuntarily—among all the yeasty, earthy, pungent odors that belonged here was an acrid one . . . a scorched smell, as if a cook had singed not just a steak, but his beard. She sniffed her way toward it, reminded incongruously of Bunny Thornbuckle's foxhounds—was this how they felt, tracking a fox?

Acrid, yes . . . and faintly metallic. Now she could hear a different sound, a hissing followed by a soft roar. Her mind rummaged through a library of smells and sounds; she could almost see it at work . . . then it came to her. Brazing? Soldering? Something with a little blowtorch and lengths of tubing. Something that was never done here on Environmental, because . . . she strained for the memory of a text she'd read . . .

Voices, now: "But, sir, the manual says—"

"Corporal, do you see these stripes?"

"Yes, sir." A very unhappy corporal. A corporal who knew the manual. "But, sir, if the metal vapor comes in contact with—"

"Just do it!" said the angry older voice.

Heris moved fast, and saw them, a cluster of figures around one of the pipes connecting two chambers. "STOP!" she said. "Don't move," she added in a quieter voice.

"Who's that?" asked the older voice. "What are you doing down here? This is a restricted area!"

"Not to me, it's not," Heris said. She had the satisfaction of seeing the man's eyes widen and his face go pale. A petty major . . . Dorson, by his nametag.

"Comman—er . . . Captain. Sorry, sir. I thought it was one of the ratings sneaking about . . ."

"Turn off that torch, Corporal Acer," Heris said, to the equally pale-faced young man. He complied, with a quick glance at the petty major.

"Now suppose you explain to me why you were about to use that torch on this equipment," Heris said to Dorson.

"Well . . ." with a poisonous glance at the corporal. "This man found a drip in the line. It dripped last shift, too, and I'd had him put some glub on it, but it was dripping again. So I told him to get the torch out and put a proper patch."

"I see. Corporal, explain your objection."

"Captain, this is a new joint, just installed at the refit. There's always a bit of a problem with new installations, a little drip, but the way Chief Kostans taught me to handle it was to glub it until the sediment has a chance to build in. That cushions it against pump surge, too, where a rigid fix wouldn't. But more than that, you don't want to put metal vapor onto this stuff—it eventually corrodes the line, and then you're in worse trouble."

"Petty Major Dorson, how long have you been in shipboard Environmental?"

"Shipboard, Captain? Never, really. My main speciality is administration, records division; I guess they put me on this list because I've been keeping the regional headquarters files on environmental issues up to date."

That figured. "And on the basis of that lack of experience, you saw fit to overrule a man who's actually been doing this job?"

Dorson flushed. "I didn't see where it could do any harm . . ."

"Petty Major Dorson, can you explain why the aft personnel lock hatches were jammed open, and the sensor blanked?"

His jaw dropped. "I—I—what's wrong with that? As long as both the aft and forward locks are fully open, then the pressure equalizes . . ."

Out of the corner of her eye, Heris could see the corporal's not quite successful attempt to hide his reaction to this.

"The point of the locks," Heris said, "is so the pressure won't equalize—so that a problem on one side does not get to the other."

"But we're not in combat—they only close the section hatches in combat—"

Heris took a deep breath, and turned to Acer. "Corporal, rack that torch where it belongs and go secure the forward personnel lock; I've secured the aft already. If you see other personnel, say nothing to them. Pick up the forward log book. Then come back."

"Yes, sir." He practically scampered away, exuding virtue.

Heris turned to the hapless petty officer. "Petty Major Dorson, you know nothing about a real environmental system. You will have to learn. But since you nearly caused a major breakdown which could have had fatal consequences, you are relieved from your duties here. You will begin studying environmental systems with the introductory course, and you will have completed the first two chapters by the end of this shift—I'll expect to see your exam scores above ninety percent, if you want to retain your stripes."

"Yes, sir." He looked more stunned than contrite, but at least he wasn't arguing.

"When you finish the introductory course, you will report to Environmental as an apprentice tech—only because we are short-handed with real techs—and you will obey the orders of anyone who has more experience. Is that clear?"

"Yes, sir."

"Good." She looked up to see Corporal Acer approaching. "Corporal, what are the most recent readings?"

Now he looked embarrassed. "Most recent? I guess that would be—"

"I don't want guesses, Corporal. Let's see that log book." She glanced at the last page. "Is that your signature, Corporal?"

"Yes, Captain."

"I see that you've recorded all values as nominal—I presume that means you checked every gauge and every readout . . ."

"Er . . . no, sir. Not all of them."

"In other words, you falsified the log?" He shot a quick glance at the petty officer, then gulped and answered. "Yes, sir; I initialled that entry, and yes, sir, I signed off on checks I hadn't made."

Heris folded the log book and tapped it against her leg. They both looked as if they would much rather be facing an open airlock than her, and that's exactly how she wanted them to feel.

"We have two problems here," she said finally. "We have incompetence attempting to rest on rank alone for authority, and we have competence choosing to be dishonest. Frankly, I have no use for either, but this is a war, and I'm stuck with you. We can deal with this at Captain's Mast, or we can deal with this here and now. It's up to you."

"Now, if the Captain wishes." That was the corporal; the petty officer just nodded.

Heris cocked her head at him. "Corporal, I don't know why you zanged that log. You may think you had a good reason—" She paused, to see if he would try to produce an excuse, but he said nothing. All the better. "But in my books, nothing—nothing at all—justifies lying to your captain, and that's what you did. I'm extremely displeased, and your competence in your specialty does not in any way change that. I'm reducing you to pivot; you'll report to the Exec at first shift and get your records changed." Again she waited.

"Yes, sir," he finally said.

"Petty Major Dorson, I will not tolerate the use of formal rank to cover up ignorance and incompetence. It is not your fault that you were assigned a job you didn't know how to do. It is your fault that you didn't listen to someone who did know. It is a form of dishonesty only slightly less flagrant than the corporal's—pivot's—when you pretend to know what you don't know. I'm reducing you to sergeant; you will also report at the start of first shift to change your records."

"Yes, sir."

"You will find that I promote as readily as I demote, if performance warrants," Heris said. "Don't throw your stripes away. Now, Dorson, go up and get busy on your lessons—use the midships ladder. Pivot, you come with me."

They passed through the forward lock in silence, and in silence walked back aft, Heris watching for the rest of the shift's crew. She found them in a circle, playing cards: three pivots, a pivot major, and another corporal. In one searing blast, she reduced everyone to pivot who wasn't already, and put them all on extra duty—which, for the ones who had no prior Environmental experience, meant shifts spent at the cube reader, getting qualified. When she was through, she turned to Pivot Acer. "You're now in command of this shift. You will see to it that first shift finds all values nominal—and you will keep an accurate log. Is that clear?"

"Yes, sir!" His eyes had light in them again.

"If I can find another qualified person, I'll send 'em down; in the meantime, it's up to you to whip this bunch into shape. I believe you can do it."

She was back in her own quarters before she remembered that she hadn't taken off the tactape which would enable her to tell if anyone had sneaked away. She looked at her chronometer . . . only two hours to sleep before she had to be bright and energetic for first-shift business. Sleepy commanders make bad decisions, she told herself, diving under the covers again. After all, tomorrow night, it was the turn of Drives to have a roaming captain in their midst. She could remove the tactape then.

R.S.S. *Bonar Tighe*

Solomon Drizh, once an admiral minor in the Regular Space Service and now commander in chief of the mutineer fleet, plotted the newest arrival on his chart. They had been unlucky at Copper Mountain; if they'd had the three weeks he'd planned for, all the mutineer ships could have assembled, with sufficient manpower to gain control of the planet and its resources. Luck of war, no use complaining. Here, at least, no accidental passerby should find them. Here he could assemble his fellow mutineers, train them, and create a force that the government could not ignore.

We are hunters, and we hunt the most dangerous of all game— others like ourselves. Lepescu had said that. *War is the best test of man, and hunting men is the next best.* That, too.

Drizh grinned to himself. Fleet had gone soft, because the government had gone soft. Always seeking peace, always looking for a way out. He'd had hopes of Thornbuckle, when Thornbuckle sent Fleet to rescue his daughter—any excuse for a war was better than no war at all—but then Thornbuckle had died, shot down by a better hunter. *The hunt proves your real nature, whether you are prey or hunter.* And the new Chairman, Hobart Conselline . . . all he cared about was profit and long life.

"He thinks like a cow," Drizh said aloud.

"Sir?" That was his flag captain, Jerard Montague.

"Conselline," Drizh said. "All belly. But he'll learn; they all will." They would bow at last; they would have to, when the loss of civilian lives rose high enough. Then he would command not just the mutineers but all of Fleet, and Fleet would command the government. No more begging humbly for the cheapest supplies: they would have the best, and no arguments.

"They still have some good commanders," Montague said. "And more ships."

"True, but they don't have our edge. Ship for ship we're superior. Survival through victory—it's the only way. Besides, there are only a few to worry about."

"Serrano?"

"Serrano, yes." For a moment, Drizh allowed himself to regret that Heris Serrano wasn't one of his people. She had the right instincts; she would have been a powerful and valuable ally. But she had destroyed his mentor, exposed Lepescu to the world as a vicious killer, denounced those who followed him. She was an enemy, and he would destroy her, rejoicing in her fall.

He looked again at his charts, and cursed the cowards who hadn't yet shown up as they'd promised. He needed more ships, now, before the loyalists had time to organize an effective defense.

In the meantime, waiting the arrival of the others, he could train this nucleus.

"Tightbeam to all ships," he said. "Close in for drill." A few days of precision drill, the ships as close as possible, would sharpen the crews' reactions immensely. Then gunnery drill, then microjump gunnery . . .

Then the war, and the victory.

CHAPTER EIGHT

R.S.S. *Rosa Maior*

Barin was in the middle of his midshift meal when the alarms whooped again. The task force was still picking up loose mines—a ticklish task even with the help of the specialty minesweeper. The diners seemed to freeze in place for a moment—waiting, he realized, for the announcement that this was another exercise—and then they all lurched into motion. Lieutenant Marcion picked up his bowl and swigged down the rest of his soup, grabbed two rolls, and bolted for the door. Barin eyed the rest of his stew with regret, grabbed rolls for himself, and a hunk of cake from the dessert table, and followed at the double.

He had almost reached his station when he staggered—the artificial gravity had wavered for an instant. That was not a good sign . . . he came around the corner to find Petty Officer O'Neil already in place. He took the list, and began calling names, glad that his voice wasn't shaky or shrill. Everyone had made it to station; Wahn came jogging up just as he got to that name. Barin reported all present up the tube and got a terse acknowledgement; he wanted to ask what was going on, but knew better.

A shrill whistle: the warning for closing the section seals.

"Must have some shield damage," a pivot said, and grinned nervously.

"Less chatter," O'Neil said.

Barin could hear the shuffle of someone's feet on the deck, the soft

454

whirr of the ventilating fans . . . and the sudden clunk-groan of the section seals as they unlocked and moved in their deep grooves. A final echoing thud cut them off from noises elsewhere in the ship. "Check the seals," Barin said. Petty Officer O'Neil told off two of the team for that task and set the others to taking initial readings of the pressure, temperature, artificial gravity, and other factors. "Suit by pairs," Barin said, when the seals had been reported secure. It seemed to take them forever, though he knew the creeping second hand on the chronometer was actually moving at normal speed, and they were suiting up well within the required time.

At last it was his turn; he stepped into the p-suit and found himself remembering a question he'd asked long, long ago. Why, he'd wanted to know, didn't ships carry escape pods for use in disasters? Everyone knew p-suits weren't really protection, not if you were blown out into a seething maelstrom of broken bits and pieces. The marines had hardened combat suits, but the rest of the crew . . . He went on fastening seals and making attachments as he remembered the instructor's answer. There was no way, on a large ship, to provide escape capsules for everyone, and the bulky space combat suits took up too much room, and besides—you shouldn't be thinking about getting out of the ship, but of saving it—keeping it working.

Barin turned so his partner could check his back—the hang of the air cylinders, the attachments of hose and cable—and then checked his partner's. For now they didn't need the suits' air supply. For now, they had air in the compartment. If all went well, they would come out of this hot, sweaty, smelly, but with fully charged tanks. If it didn't—they'd have this small additional chance. He had them all call off their air supply gauges; the only one below 100% was Pivot Ghormley, who had predictably forgotten that he was not supposed to turn the airflow on until he needed it. Barin let the petty officer chew Ghormley out and tell him to recharge his tank from the outlet.

With the section sealed off, this team was responsible for damage assessment and control in the starboard aft compartments of Troop Deck. Two open squad bays; four cramped and complicated four-man compartments for NCOs, fitted around essential ship equipment; the shower hall; the heads; a crew lounge with battered couches and cube readers; and—taking up almost half the cubage—half the gymnasium, the other half being cut off by a section seal. Barin sent his team off to take readings in each compartment; he stayed by the command console, from which he could report results, or receive orders.

He felt a lurch in his stomach—the gravity generators again?—and glanced at the gauge nearest him. Sure enough, a two percent negative spike . . . the lights dimmed, then brightened. His team reported the first set of numbers, and Barin forwarded them through his console. A vast shudder rumbled through the deck . . . missile launches. Another.

Betenkin said, "Are we taking hits, sir?" in a voice two tones higher than usual.

Barin said, "Missile launchers," almost in concert with Petty Officer O'Neil; their eyes met, and he saw that O'Neil was watching him just as he watched the others. O'Neil gave a short nod. Then the deck bucked beneath them, one great concussive blow. Barin swallowed and said, "*That* was incoming." O'Neil grinned for a moment. "Check the seals first," Barin said. Pressure had to be all right; he would have felt if it hadn't been. He glanced down at his console. Two decks down a red blaze expanded across the ship's schematic. Even as he recognized it, the loud-hailer came on. "Hull breach—hull breach—report all starboard aft teams—"

Barin pressed his code key and read off the current numbers. In his headset, the damage control officer said, "Serrano—get your team to Environmental, go down the portside access; watch the heads-up on the way down in case the aft locks don't hold."

He tried to remember what he'd been told about hull breaches. Everything tried to escape to vacuum: the air and all that could be moved by the explosive decompression. This left the damaged area clear, usually, of the noxious gases and thick smoke that endangered personnel when the ship was still whole but some system had fractured. But the next compartments, where there might be pressure loss, were likely to be cold, dark, and confusing.

In the aft portside passage, Barin and his team met up with the officer on site. The major glanced at his nametag, touched his compad, and said, "Serrano—good. We want you in SE-14. Pressure's dropping, but slow enough it must be fairly small—but big enough nothing's plugged it yet. Your report channel is eleven. Cycle through two at a time, and be careful. The pressure differential's enough to knock you off your feet. You'll go in number four, got that?"

Barin led the way into the lock. When it opened on the far side, he faced the starboard passage, now lit only by emergency lighting, and the long emergency bulkhead that separated the passage from the "plumbing works" of Environmental. Along it, several preformed partial pressure locks showed, each clearly labelled. He located #4, and, as the rest of his team cycled through, he opened the #4 emergency locker and handed out the elements of the single-person pressure lock. This was something they'd drilled in often enough: place the frame to the existing frame and seal, pop open the rest and check that the other side of the lock was closed. The first person through did not actually cycle through, but was pushed by the suction that pulled the lock into the low-pressure chamber and held it extended until the second locked the frame in place.

Barin checked that everything was ready, took another look at his suit readouts—grabbed hold of the safety bar of what would become the low-pressure side of the inner hatch, and popped the bulkhead's preformed opening.

The emergency airlock, sucked through the opening with all the force of the pressure differential, hit him in the back like a truck, and he barely kept his grip on the safety bar. All around was a dark, dense, cold, whirling wind . . . he could see nothing, but he could feel the buffeting of air currents, and the cold now rapidly falling to the freezing point of water. His feet slithered on something incredibly slippery . . . ice already?

Air screamed through the crevices as it escaped, audible even inside the suit. Barin turned on his helmet lamp, and saw swirling fog, streamers of vapor pouring away from left to right. Environmental was the wettest place on the ship, barring the water reserves or a shower in use; here the air was more humid than any-where else, and decompression chilled it below its ability to hold that water as invisible vapor.

"Lock's up, sir," he heard in his helmet com.

"Come through, but watch it—it's slippery, dark, and windy in here."

"Rig safety lines," O'Neil said.

Now why hadn't he thought of that? His suit had all the attachments ready. Barin managed to get the primary hookup out of its fitting and attached to the lock's safety bar. Now he could move away a little . . . look for other points of attachment. He tried a cautious step away from the hatch and skidded on the wet deck, slithering into something round and hard. A culture tank? His helmet light didn't show him anything identifiable but the fat shiny haunch of a metallic tank of some kind. It looked shinier than it should, and he rubbed it with his gloved hand, then wiped the glove on the chem-patch. A formula he didn't recognize came up on his suit display. Not all water, then. It had a lot of C and H and O and some Cl. Hydrocarbon, his mind reminded him, and he didn't need a laundry list to think of hydraulic fluid.

Slippery, flammable, and—if coming from a high-pressure leak— lethal to get near.

He switched his suit com to channel 11 and reported the presence of hydraulic fluid, then back to his own unit's channel.

"Sir?"

"I'm over here . . ." he rotated his head, sending his helmet light in all directions. "I slid over here—we've got hydraulic fluid as well as water vapor. Show your lamps."

Three feeble glows that could have been any distance. "Right, sir. We have five more to cycle through—three now clipped on the same safety bar. Have you found any other attachment points?"

"No," Barin said. "Not yet." He had only three meters of line on the primary attachment, and they couldn't all clip on to the same bar—there wasn't room. They could clip on each other, but they still needed other attachment points. He edged his way around the metal tank and found a handle of some sort. When he tugged, it held firm; by leaning close with his headlamp, he could see that it opened by turning, with a safety latch holding it closed. Good enough. "Found an attachment. Who's in?"

"Wahn, Telleen, Prestin."

"Wahn, clip onto my line, trail a line to the lock, and come to me."

He felt the vibration in his safety line, as someone moved—and was there beside him.

"It's only about two meters, sir, but you can't see anything in this murk."

"True enough. Let's have that line—" Barin used a running clip to attach the line Wahn had trailed to the attachment he'd found. Now anyone could come that way. "Now you clip in." Wahn did so, keeping a safety grip on Barin's line while unclipping his own and reclipping it onto the tank handle. "Telleen, find my line, and give it a tug." When he felt the tug, he said, "Now—unclip my line and put it on the trailer."

It took a tediously long time to cycle everyone through the lock safely, make sure they were all clipped in, and advance through the greasy murk toward the actual leak. Since the problem was known, at least in part, four of the last in the chain lugged a great awkward roll of bulkhead fabric, which when stretched across a gap and foamed would provide an airtight seal with some structural integrity.

Barin, in the lead, slithered and slid from one obstacle to another, barking his shins and his ribs on things he couldn't see clearly until he fell over them. This was only fair, he knew, since he had less actual experience than most of the team. He knew he was going the right way, because the wisps and tendrils of vapor blew past him—all he had to do was follow. He reported at intervals, when his helmet display prompted him to.

Suddenly his lamp threw back a bright sparkle . . . a rime of ice now outlined a line of pipe and shapes that should be a row of scrubbers. He could see past them to an irregular white shape bordering a jagged black line. Could that be the—

His boots slid on the greased icy decking again, as the strengthening current of escaping air and vapor whipped about him and sucked him toward the gap. He managed not to yelp and felt the jerk when his safety tether came up short.

"Don't worry, sir, we've got you."

He tried to think of something offhand and casual to say, but couldn't. That black crack . . . how big was it really? Not big enough for his whole body, surely . . . but an arm? A hand? "All that ice," he managed to say finally. "We're supposed to patch on a dry, clean surface."

"We can always torch it off," someone said.

"No! This vapor may be explosive," Barin said. "It's got hydraulic fluid in it, remember?"

"Well, then, we'll—" A fan of light brighter than the brightest day scythed into the compartment through the crack, giving structure and substance for a moment to the roil of vapor, striking blinding highlights off the ice.

"What was that?" yelped a frightened voice. Barin caught his breath, trying to think.

"The war's not over," the petty officer said. "The battle's still goin' on, and it's time we quit sightseeing."

He should have said that, but he was noticing the glow . . . it had not died instantly. It came again, another flash.

"Hitting the shields," the petty officer said. "Hope they hold." He sounded as unconcerned as if it made no difference either way. Maybe it didn't.

Barin reported in that they'd located a crack, and the margins were ice-covered.

"Ackman, you an' Wahn get to chippin' it off."

"Won't it just re-form?" Barin was glad someone else had asked that question. The petty officer grunted.

"Notice there's less fog? Most of the water vapor's out now, and the pressure and temp are both way down. Pretty soon it'll be clear enough to see."

It already was, Barin saw, when he flashed his lamp around. The fog was below waist level; he could shine his light all the way back to the portable airlock. Something glittered across the darkness, a fine wire . . . no . . . the hydraulic leak, still spitting a fine stream of the fluid. He reported where he thought it was coming from. Another scythe of light blazed through the crack. Barin ignored it.

They still had to fix the leak. Very carefully, in short moves each restrained by a tether, they moved toward the crack. Ackman and Wahn chipped the ice off the bulkhead. "Carefully," the petty officer warned them. "We don't want to damage it . . . lay your irons down just about horizontal to it." They chipped from the outside toward the crack; Barin and the others unrolled the patch material and cut off strips to use as supporting surfaces. As soon as they cleared ice from a strip, someone laid down a bead of adhesive and a strip of patch material.

No more ice formed on the upper surface of the patch cloth rimming the crack. Barin laid another bead of adhesive on the cloth rim, and then—turning the roll around—put the end of the roll flush with the bead at the bottom, and began unrolling upwards, sealing one side, while Averre sealed the other. The suction was less now, but still pulled the patch cloth tight against the crack. Someone—Barin couldn't tell who—pumped the foam gun and sprayed quickset foam on the cloth.

One leak down. Were there others? Barin checked the pressure in the compartment, and realized it was so low they'd have to wait quite a while to be sure. He reported in to the Damage Control Officer.

"We need you to do a check of the environmental system," he was told.

"We don't have any moles," Barin said.

"That's all right. You don't need to make it run, just report on what you find. I've got a checklist—I'm flashing it to your suit comp."

"Yes, sir." What he could see of the list in his heads-up display looked easy enough. Check each tank for leakage, check the lines, test for certain contaminants—Barin recognized some of these but not all.

"You'll report on channel six, that's the environmental officer this shift, but don't bother him unless you have to. They're trying to patch the remains of the starboard system upstream of you into the hard-chem backups."

This meant nothing to Barin, who had always considered Environmental the dullest of all specialities. Of course it was important—everyone liked to breathe—but it had none of the glamor of drives or weapons. He had passed the required courses by dint of dutiful memorization, and he'd put most of it out of his mind immediately after the exam.

The checklist was long and detailed. Every vat, chamber, pump, connection, pipe and tube . . . and the whole place was full of them. Barin looked at the time, at his own air supply, and calculated that they'd have to cycle out for air at least once. He wanted a margin of safety—he'd send half the team out when they had an hour's air left, then the other half. He set his suit alarm to remind him to check with the petty officer, and took his half-team up to the forward end of the compartment.

Here there was less ice on the deck. Barin flashed his headlamp around and wondered if it would be safe to rig lights—it would speed up their assessment. He clicked on his comunit, and heard a spirited argument about whether some unpronounceable compound could be used to do something equally hard to say to something he'd never heard of. When he clicked twice, the voices stopped, and an annoyed one said, "Yes?"

"Serrano with damage control in SE-14. Is it safe to rig lights in here?"

"What's your gas situation?"

He called Wahn over—Wahn had the chemscan—and had him read off the numbers.

"That sounds safe enough. No methane? No hydrogen sulfide? See any big leaks?"

"No methane, no hydrogen sulfide," Wahn said. "I'm not sure my chem-scan has all that stuff on the list . . ."

"No visible leaks since they cut off that hydraulic line," Barin said. "But we can't see much yet."

"All right then. Rig your lights, but watch your pressure. We're not airing up that compartment until it's secured, so any increase in pressure means you've got a leak of something coming in. Some of that stuff's nasty."

"Yes, sir." Barin clicked off, told O'Neil they were clear to rig lights, and should probably bring in something to sop up the flammable stuff on the floor.

A few minutes later, two of his team came back in, lugging strings of lights and a sack of the flocculant for the deck.

With lights strung as best they could, the damage was certainly more visible. Bulkhead material had spalled in a broad cone across the aft end of the compartment—there most of the tanks and vats were dented and one was holed, with a now-frozen mass of stringy stuff—filamentous algae? worms? Barin couldn't guess—firmly adhering to the side of the tank and the deck. Chunks of bulkhead like big flakes of obsidian lay where they'd fallen. He walked around, noting which tanks were damaged and how badly. When he got back to the forward bulkhead, he checked the pressure gauge. Seventy-eight. It was up, but very slightly.

"Wahn—what's our gas mix?"

"Oxygen's up a point, sir. But with this low pressure . . ."

Oxygen, Barin thought, was the least of his problems. He spotted the green O lines, and started checking them. Oxygen was breathable; it wasn't going to poison anyone even if it was leaking, and at very low pressure and temperature it wasn't likely to support combustion, either.

"Anything else?"

"No, sir, nothing I can identify. But most of the stuff on the list you flashed me isn't on this chemscan's selector."

"It's not?" A tiny cold finger ran down his spine. "What have you got, then?"

"Well, what you mostly need—oxygen, carbon dioxide, carbon monoxide, hydrogen sulfide, sulfur dioxide, nitrogen. But not all that special environmental stuff."

"Let's see." Barin took a look; there was oxygen, carbon dioxide, nitrogen, all at very low amounts. "What about broadscan, did you try that?"

"Yes, sir, but I don't know what all these little peaks are. None of 'em are red-marked."

So probably it was picking up traces of whatever had been in the breached vessels. Maybe some outgassing from the patch adhesive. He looked at the scan readout himself, but while whatever it was had a molecular weight of around 16, he didn't know what it might be. He tried to envision the periodic table, but most of it eluded him. Oxygen? No, that was atomic weight; the molecular weight was 32.

He looked around, and saw a tangle of green lines—the oxygen code—snaking around a series of long tanks. There was an obvious place to look for an oxygen leak. Even if you could breathe it, it still shouldn't be leaking out. He started at the nearest tank, and tested every connection with his squirt bottle. On the second, little bubbles rewarded him—sure enough, something was coming out, and the most likely thing coming out of a green-coded line was oxygen. He called up the checklist and protocol and found that he needed a special patch. Which pocket had he put it in? There. He peeled off the backing, glad that whoever made these things realized they'd have to be used by people in gloves—that long pull-tag helped.

He looked around again to see where his team was. O'Neil and his group were down at the most-damaged aft end; the rest were scattered up and down the compartment, checking every bit of tubing for leaks.

That unknown peak on the readout bothered him. He called the Environmental Officer again.

"Sir, we've got a peak our chemscan doesn't identify. Something with a molecular weight of sixteen—" He flashed the readout to the EO.

"What do you mean your chemscan doesn't—*sixteen*? Lieutenant, didn't I tell you to look out for methane? What's the readout?"

Barin went cold. Methane. That was the one that blew up when it contacted free oxygen . . ." Sir, we don't have a readout for it on our machine."

"Oh my god . . . you don't have an Environmental chemscan. Lieutenant, get your people out now. You're sitting on a bomb." He'd figured that out; terror and guilt almost strangled him. He pushed them down. Later. Right now he had to get his people to safety. "Wait—tell them to move *slowly*. If they run through a pool of the stuff, and mix it, that's when it'll blow. Turn off those lights you rigged. Can you vent to vacuum?"

"We just—" Barin bit that off, switched channels, and called his team. "Emergency—" Heads turned toward him. "We have a potentially explosive gas mix. Don't run—we don't want to move the stuff around more than we have to. Whoever's closest to the lock, douse the lights." The lock. The portable airlock . . . would it hold pressure if there was an explosion? He switched back to the EO. "Sir, we accessed SE-14 through a portable airlock; if this compartment goes, it may not hold."

"I've already alerted them, Lieutenant. Get your people out. Vent to the vacuum if you can."

Could he? If they took the patch off . . . at least it wouldn't be an explosion in a closed space. "We could try to take the patch off—" He hoped the EO would say it was impossible, not worth the risk.

"Do it," the EO said. "If there's an explosion in that compartment we could lose the whole ship—"

And it would be his fault, because he hadn't checked to see that they had a chemscan programmed for Environmental. Barin shivered, anticipating what the captain would say, or his grandmother. Again he pushed it aside. No time.

He switched back to the team channel. Who was nearest? Telleen and O'Neil.

"Petty Officer O'Neil—" He saw, down the compartment, O'Neil turn towards him. "We need to vent this compartment immediately to vacuum. The EO has authorized us to tear down that patch. You four—" He couldn't think of their names, but they were closest to the airlock. "There by the airlock. Get out now. Has anyone identified a methane line leak?"

The EO's voice came in on his other channel. "If it's from a tank, it'll be in the outboard array, about a third of the way aft in that chamber; if it's a line, it could be anywhere."

Barin glanced over and saw Pivot Ghormley standing approximately in that location, about seven meters away. "What've you got, Ghormley?"

"Dent in the fermentation chamber, sir. There's a . . . a kind of crack in this little pipe here from some sort of collection tank—I could seal it—"

"Too late," the EO said. "You're probably standing in a pool of methane—if you stir it up . . ."

"Ghormley, stay where you are. Do not move," Barin said. Then to the EO, "I'm standing by the photosynthesis chamber. And there's a crack in the oxygen line." He looked down, and at that moment someone cut the lights.

"Lieutenant?" That was O'Neil.

"I'm standing in the oxygen," Barin said. "If I don't kick it around, this explosion may not happen. You get that patch torn down. Everybody who's not with you—except Ghormley and me—get out, but don't run." He could see their headlamps moving; he could see them cycling through. Surely they'd be safer in the corridor; surely someone would get them through the blast doors to the other side of the ship. He found himself counting the disappearing lights. One safe. Two. Then a pause, and, three, four . . .

"Sir, I'm scared—" That was Ghormley. The kid, the newest of the bunch. And he, Barin, had condemned this kid to die, maybe.

"Well," Barin said, "I'm not any too happy myself, but if we don't dance a jig, we can still get out of this in one piece."

"Do you really think so?" Ghormley's voice was high and tense.

Of course he didn't think so, but what good would it do to tell the kid that? "If they get that patch off," Barin said, "the rest of the gases in here will vent to vacuum. It's cold now; it'll be colder then, and it takes heat—" But not much, he knew, not with methane and oxygen. Firedamp, miner's enemy. Anything might set it off. "And even if it blows, it won't be confined—"

"I don't like this—" Ghormley said. "I can't just stand here—"

"Sure you can," Barin said. "Smartest thing you can do." Another light, and another, vanished out the airlock. Four remained, at the aft end of the chamber, working to remove the patch they'd tried so hard to put on. "If we don't mix the two, they won't blow up."

"But sir, we was all walking around, all over; they gotta be mixed already."

What a time for Ghormley to show reasoning ability. "It hasn't blown yet," Barin said. "I promise not to kick my oxygen at you if you won't kick your methane at me . . ."

"Are you scared, sir?"

Of course he was scared, but did Ghormley need to hear it? He was saved by O'Neil's voice.

"Got a leak, Lieutenant." O'Neil's headlamp bobbed. "We'll just widen 'er out a bit—" Barin could feel through his bootsoles the impact of O'Neil's blows on the sides of the crack. "She's spalled off quite a lot—we should be able to—get—more—open—"

Barin started to ask if they had their safety lines hooked on, and realized that that was probably not a high priority at the moment. Should he bother to clip onto the tank beside him? If there was an explosion, it wouldn't help much. It might even rip his p-suit apart.

"Can you see the pressure gauge from where you are, sir?"

"No—"

"It's dropping," said the EO. "We've got you on full monitoring now. It's still dangerous." Great. They'd get to watch him get blown away.

"Do we need a bigger hole?" Barin asked.

"Wouldn't hurt," the EO said.

"Will do, sir," O'Neil said. He sounded calm enough. More shivering vibrations in the deck . . . Barin tried not to think of the effect on a puddle of cold gas of such vibrations—shaking it, dispersing it faster than it might have gone on its own, mixing it . . . he kept his eyes on the far end, where suddenly a large section of bulkhead seemed to fold back like paper, and he was looking out into blackness speckled with lights that might be stars or the worklights of the outside repair crews.

"Got it," O'Neil said.

"Get yourselves out," Barin said. "It'll start flowing your way."

"What about you?"

"Oh, I think Ghormley and I will stand here awhile and let things clear out—go on, now."

The lights moved up the compartment, toward the airlock entrance, more slowly than he wanted. Probably O'Neil was making them stay on the safety line; airflow out that size hole wouldn't be strong, but the deck down there was slick. Two reached the airlock, opened it, and went through; the others were almost there.

Barin turned his head to watch them, as they worked their way up the inboard bulkhead, the arc of his headlamp sweeping across the compartment.

"No! Don't leave me behind!" Ghormley's voice cracked; Barin looked back to see him plunge away from his position.

"No! Don't—" He knew as he said it that once in motion Ghormley wouldn't stop, that he had miscalculated again, this time in his judgment of men.

He had time for an instant of pity, for a thought of Esmay, and then the flash came, too bright to see.

CHAPTER NINE

Terakian Fortune

Esmay stared at the same page she'd read many times before. She had nothing to do; with the ship overcrewed, no one needed her help. Hours and days ran together; she tried not to think about how long it was taking to get anywhere, how much time passed in which anything might be happening. The *Fortune*'s last datafeed, before going into jump, had included nothing substantive about the mutiny, only speculation as to its effect on prices.

Barin was out there somewhere. He might be in combat, and here she was, stuck on a ship that might just as well have *TARGET* blaring from its beacon. She held a mental argument with his grandmother, in which—since she had both parts—she could win. In real life . . . in real life, admirals had the power.

In the middle of her sleep shift, Esmay rolled over, tangling her legs in the sheet yet again. She pulled it straight with a muffled oath. This would never do. What's done is done. What's over's over. She closed her eyes firmly, until speckles and smears of light rolled across the darkness, took a deep breath, and . . . she could feel Barin's touch on her face, her neck, her body. She could smell him, taste him . . . he was calling her, longing and fear both in his voice, and then, in a great flash of light, he was gone. Esmay sat up abruptly, forgetting the geometry of her compartment, and banged her head smartly on the cabinet overhead.

Would she ever see him again? Was he thinking of her? Was he even alive? She snapped on the light, blinked back hot tears, set her jaw, and grabbed a robe. She could go shower.

She opened the door to find Betharnya standing just outside.

"I heard a thud," the Betharnya woman said, in her odd accent. "I wondered if you were all right."

"I'm fine," Esmay said. "I'm going for a shower."

"No one hit you?"

"No."

"You have a lump on your head, at the hairline," Betharnya said, with professional detachment.

"No one hit me," Esmay said, suddenly angry. "You can look if you want to." She flung the door aside, but the woman caught it in midswing and took a very thorough look inside.

"Ah."

"Satisfied that I'm not hiding a lover?" asked Esmay.

"Yes. And that you are miserable." Betharnya closed the compartment door quietly.

"It's none of your business," Esmay said, and headed for the showers, but the woman kept stride with her.

"It may be my business if you endanger us. You were having nightmares?"

"You were just standing around outside my compartment spying on me?"

"No. I was not. I was walking past, I heard mutterings and then a loud noise, like someone being hit, then a curse, then the click of a light switch, then the rustle of clothing, then you came out . . ."

"You couldn't hear all that," Esmay said.

"I have very good hearing. It is a curse."

"It is a fake."

"You are not so polite as you are at meals, Sera."

"It is the middle of my sleep shift, I have had no sleep, I had a bad dream, and I whacked my head on the cabinet, and yes, you're right, I'm upset. And miserable."

"A shower is a very good idea, then," Betharnya said. They had come to the door of the shower area. She turned away. "Don't make it too hot," she said over her shoulder.

"Are you just going to walk off?" Esmay asked. The woman waved a hand, in a gesture that could have meant any of several things, and kept walking.

Esmay walked into the shower room and saw herself in the mirrors above the sinks. The rapidly purpling lump was all too obvious. And entirely too much: she burst into tears, beating her fists on the smooth, cold edge of one of the sinks. Barin, Barin, Barin! No one came in; as far as she knew no one heard. Then she went into a shower cubicle and washed off the sweat and tears of her misery. Back in her compartment, she went to sleep and slept until the alarm rang.

"Who slugged you?" asked Basil at breakfast. She already knew what she looked like; she had seen it while getting dressed.

"Nobody—I woke up too fast in the middle of the night and whacked myself on the cabinet."

"Did you put ice on it?"

"No—I didn't even think of that."

"You should always put ice on it," Basil said quite seriously. "When my daughter falls down and gets a bump, my wife puts ice on it."

Betharnya strolled in. "Ah, you have a wife?"

"You know I do." But the back of his neck slowly turned a rich crimson; Esmay watched, fascinated.

"And you, Sera—your head is better?"

"Much better," Esmay said. "If anyone needs any help, I'm quite able to stand a watch today." She offered every day.

"No, no," Goonar said, coming in with a plateful of something that smelled delicious. "You're not standing any watches—you're our guest."

"Well, I should make myself useful," Esmay said.

"Mmm. What you would be most useful for is probably not something you want to do," Goonar said. "We could use some information on this mutiny business, for instance."

"I don't have any," Esmay said. A chill ran down her back.

"Ah. Well, I didn't expect you would, or that you'd tell us if you did. Loyalty's a good thing to have, even to something you're estranged from. Families change their minds."

"I don't think Fleet will," Esmay said.

"You never know. And your sort of talent isn't limited to combat operations anyway. Tactical sense is useful in many places."

"But—" *But I loved it* was the wrong thing to say, Esmay knew.

"However," Goonar went on, "If there are unclassified things you could tell us—what we might expect, as traders, from Fleet in this mutiny situation—or what the mutineers might do—"

"I haven't been briefed," Esmay said. "I was on my way to a new duty station. I know what's on the news, that's about all. But if I had to guess, I'd say this is a serious attempt to seize power—a military coup. There are people in Fleet who think the civilian government is weak, and doesn't support the military enough."

"That sounds like our cousin Kaim," Basil said, leaning forward and giving her a look clearly meant to convey unusual trust. "Kaim's in Fleet himself, a senior NCO, but he's always been a bit odd, and on his last visit home he was extremely odd. We don't know if he's finally lost it—his father did—or what to think."

"Do you think he's part of the mutiny?"

"I don't know—I hope not—"

"He's always going on about plots and things," Basil said. "Mostly we don't pay attention to him, not that we see him that often, unless we can see how it affects trade. Last time he was talking about rejuvenation problems and how he thought Fleet was using NCOs as lab animals, he said. That's why they shut down inquiry into the rejuv failures."

Esmay shook her head. "Everybody's had some bad drug batches come out of the Patchcock plants, and from what I heard, it was Hobart Conselline who shut off research on it." It occurred to her then that if the mutiny had anything to do with rejuvenation, that probably meant it wasn't supported by the Consellines.

"Ah. That makes sense. This whole rejuvenation thing—it's going to make trouble, one way or another. Take me—the way our company's set up, the old yield place to the young as the young mature. What's to happen if the old don't—if they stay young? It wouldn't matter if it were only a few rich people, but what if my uncle and father were still ship captains? Where would I be?"

"I don't know," Esmay said.

"But do you think the mutineers will attack civilian ships, traders? Other civilian targets?"

"They might," Esmay said. "To put pressure on the government, they have to either defeat the loyal military, or show that it can't protect you. Or both. I'm afraid you can expect trouble, and soon."

Goonar shook his head and said nothing for a long moment. Then he said, "I should tell you, Sera, that we're carrying a fugitive to Castle Rock. A priest from the Benignity."

"A priest?"

"Yes. He says they think he's a heretic with some kind of secret. Fleet knows about him; they'll take charge of him at Castle Rock."

"What would Fleet want with a priest?" Esmay asked.

"I don't know," Goonar said. "I want him off our hands, anyway." He glanced at the chronometer. "I'd better be off."

R.S.S. *Rosa Maior*

He hadn't expected to wake up; he'd said sorry and goodbye and all that.

The lights scared him; he heard someone saying "Turn those off!" over and over, and didn't recognize his own voice. Then a dark shape came between him and the light, and spoke to him. For an instant he saw it flying away, silhouetted against the light, then it resolved into a person beside the bed.

"Take it easy, Serrano," the voice said.

Serrano. He blinked, and his vision cleared. He was a Serrano, though he wasn't sure which one. Serrano meant duty, meant expectations, meant . . . someone had died, and it was his fault.

"How many?" he said, around a tongue that felt like a dirty sock.

"Do you know your name?" the person said.

"Serrano," he said, repeating what he'd heard.

"Full name?"

He blinked again. He was fairly sure he wasn't one of the female Serranos, but which one of the men . . . ? "Sabado," he said.

"Still confused," the voice said. "Back to sleep, son."

Son? Was that his father? He was fairly sure it wasn't his father. Darkness closed over him while he was still puzzling about it.

The next time he woke with brutal clarity, perfectly aware of who he was—Lieutenant junior grade Barin Serrano—and what had happened: because he had screwed up, men were dead. He was no more use than he had been on *Koskiusko*, when he'd been a captive. His head felt as if someone were hitting it with a hammer, and he knew that was right and just.

"Do you know your name?" someone asked. He glanced over at the person in the green scrubs, recognized him as belonging in sickbay.

"Yes. Barin Serrano, Lieutenant junior grade . . ."

"Do you know where you are?"

"Sickbay," Barin said. "*Rosa Maior*."

"Right. Do you know what day it is?"

"No . . . was I knocked out?"

"You could put it like that. You could also say you were damn near killed—do you remember any of it?"

"No," Barin said. He didn't, really, though he had a few burning images: a dark shape flying through flame, a great black gap with stars beyond . . ." Somebody died," he said.

"Yeah, but a damn sight fewer than there'd have been without you."

"How many?"

"Two. The idiot who panicked, and somebody blown out the hole in the bulkhead, only he hit the edge. Three of you with injuries: burns, broken bones. You're the worst—you were right in the middle of it, from what I gather. But you're alive. Now answer me some more questions, son, so I can get on with my work."

"Sure," Barin said.

"Who's Chair of the Grand Council?"

"Uh . . . Hobart Conselline."

"Grand Admiral?"

"Savanche."

"Who's captain of this ship?"

"I . . . can't remember."

"That's all right. What's two plus two?"

"Four," Barin said, mildly annoyed.

"Good. Now, what hurts?"

"My head," Barin said. He tried to ask himself if anything else hurt, but his head dominated.

"Well, we can't put you in a regen tank until the concussion resolves. The pressure's down . . . we've done some surgical fixation—that's why you're mostly immobilized."

He hadn't noticed, but now he realized he wasn't able to move.

The next day his seniors descended on him in a group. He braced himself for condemnation, but instead they told him he was a credit to the service.

He couldn't understand it. Why were they praising him, when it was his fault to start with? If he'd paid more attention during his ensign rotation in Environmental, he'd have known they used a specialized chemscan. He wouldn't have ignored Wahn's complaint that his unit didn't have all those fancy names. If he'd paid more attention in chemistry, he'd have known that methane had a molecular weight of sixteen. He'd have known that even at low pressure and low temperature, oxygen and methane formed an explosive mix across a wide range of concentrations. If he'd known Ghormley better, if he'd had more persuasive ability, more command presence, the kid wouldn't have panicked and bolted like that. If he'd known what he should have known, if he'd made sure they had the right equipment, the explosion would never have happened.

Ghormley would still be alive. Betenkin would still be alive. O'Neil and Averre and Telleen wouldn't have been hurt. There wouldn't be a hole in that bulkhead, and the ship wouldn't be missing almost half its life support.

The headache subsided, but the ache in his heart did not. When O'Neil came and thanked him a few days later, that made it worse.

"I'm sorry," Barin said. "I should have—"

O'Neil shook his head. "You did the best you could, sir. Tell you the truth, when you said 'methane,' I sorta froze. Couldn't think, just wanted to run like Ghormley did. But you had a plan—"

"Not much of one," Barin said.

"That's not what the Environmental Officer said. He said it was a goddam miracle anyone got out alive, and the ship didn't blow, and he wouldn't have liked to stand there the way you did."

If he argued, they'd think he was fishing for more compliments. "I can't remember much of it, that's the truth," he said.

"Just as well, probably," O'Neil said. "Averre and Telleen were in the lock; Betenkin and I were next, and Betenkin had unclipped to go through when the flash came. The overpressure slammed the lock back through into the corridor—that's how Averre and Telleen got hurt, smacked against the bulkhead there—then it sucked back out, Betenkin with it. If I hadn't been holding onto the safety bar, I'd have gone too. I didn't see what happened to you, exactly, but they found you kind of caught in some of the piping; your leg had jammed, and they think that's what kept you from being swept out with the blast. Ghormley was dead, and you were alive, just barely."

"I couldn't stop him," Barin said, blinking back tears he hoped O'Neil didn't see. "I was too far—"

"Now, sir, you know if you'd moved it'd have done the same thing. You gave us all the best chance you could, just standing there. Nobody's blaming you."

They should, but he couldn't say that either.

"How's the ship?" he asked instead.

"Limpin' along. I doubt they'll be able to do much but scrap her. Lost a third of the FTL nodes; they're sending a DSR here to see if they can do anything."

Sending a DSR? They wouldn't send a deep-space repair ship unless *Rosa Major* couldn't make it back on her own. Barin pushed away the memory of the *Koskinska* going to the rescue, of himself as captive, that earlier humiliation.

"Got two of the mutineer ships, but three made it out of the system. The good news: Fleet's got the Copper Mountain system back. Scuttlebutt is they're sending wounded there for advanced care."

Copper Mountain . . . his last memory of Copper Mountain was that ridiculous quarrel with Esmay. Suddenly he wanted Esmay, wanted her fiercely. But what would she say? Esmay, twice and three times a hero, who always did the right thing in a crisis . . . what would she think of him? Would she be ashamed? And she wasn't even in Fleet anymore. Would he ever see her again?

Pounce II

Cecelia de Marktos, en route to the Guerni Republic with Miranda Meager-Thornbuckle, ignored the warnings about the mutiny with her usual blithe assumption that no one would interfere with *her*. She registered her flight plan with the nearest Fleet headquarters, so as not to be mistaken for a pirate or foreign spy, but refused their advice to take passage on a commercial liner.

"The mutineers aren't going to bother with two old women on a tiny little ship like *Pounce*," she told the earnest young man with the furrowed brow.

"But they might—and you're helpless if they do—"

"I think the risk of traveling on a large commercial liner with hundreds of other potential hostages is much greater," Cecelia said. She had not told them her passenger's identity; Miranda would make a fine hostage, but she didn't intend to become one.

"I can't stop you," the young man said, for the third or fourth time. "I can only advise you very strongly—"

"Not to do it. Yes, I understand. Still, it's my old bones, and I never expected to live this long anyway."

Miranda waited until they'd undocked and were well on the outbound leg before she commented. Then it was only, "And you think Brun got her reckless attitude from me?"

"She's not my daughter," Cecelia said. She had all the automatic devices available for such ships, but jump insertion was still tricky. Her course would, she hoped, take her safely past all the probable trouble zones in a series of linked jumps, popping them back into realspace on the Guernesi border.

"People tried to warn Brun, and she ended up a prisoner—"

"That was different," Cecelia said. She had the uneasy feeling that it wasn't that different, but she also knew there would be no way to conceal Miranda's identity if they took a commercial ship. Especially in the current political crisis, such ships demanded positive identification, and someone would be sure to tip off the newsvids. As far as anyone outside the immediate family knew, Miranda was still on Sirialis.

Cecelia had been regretting her bright idea for some days now—Miranda, though perfectly sane in her behavior, was not the travel companion she would have chosen for such tight quarters. Miranda belonged in a suite, with room for a maid, not in *Pounce*'s narrow passage and meagre compartments. They couldn't pass each other without bumping hips. Worse, she could not forget the sight of Miranda's lunge at Pedar, that instant's motion she'd seen before the man collapsed . . .

It had taken an act of will not to remove every sharp object from the little ship's tiny galley, but no act of will could keep her from having nightmares. She had willingly locked herself up alone with a murderer. How could she be so stupid? But Miranda wouldn't kill her . . . she had done nothing to Miranda or her children . . . of course she was the only person to whom Miranda had confessed . . .

"I don't suppose you'll ever tell me where Brun's children are," Miranda said.

"I thought you didn't want to know," Cecelia said, startled by the abrupt change of topic.

"I'd like to know if you're sure they're safe."

"Yes. Absolutely certain. They're with families who love them; they have family names to grow into. The last time I saw them, they were healthy and happy."

"That's good. I thought, after you'd gone, that perhaps we should have asked around Brun's friends . . . someone like Raffa, for instance, might have been able to place them."

Cecelia clamped her teeth together and hoped her face had betrayed nothing. "Raffa has her own life now," she said. "I very much doubt—"

"You're right," Miranda said. "I was forgetting—I'm so used to having her around to help Brun, but she's married Ronnie and they're off pioneering someplace, aren't they?"

"Berenice is still quite annoyed with Ronnie about that," Cecelia said. "She didn't mind his marrying Raffaele, but she did not approve of their decision to emigrate." If she could keep the conversation on Ronnie's mother's feelings, that might be safe ground.

"I know he's your nephew, Cecelia, but he did always seem a bit more flighty than our boys."

"According to his mother, he's not flighty now." She managed to chuckle at the memory. "The last word she had was a message cube with video of him and Raffaele, both of them sunburnt and dirty, grinning like idiots, is how she put it."

"Any grandchildren yet?"

Cecelia chose to interpret that the way her sister would have. "No . . . and she's not pleased about that, either. Apparently she and Raffaele's mother have had a set-to about it, because Raffaele's brother and Penelope Price-Lynhurst just had a baby. Berenice is claiming it's not fair. Luckily I wasn't there, but apparently it rattled the teacups."

Miranda laughed. "Berenice is so unlike you . . ."

"So I've heard all my life. I keep trying, but we are never going to get along." Cecelia leaned back in her seat. Maybe it wasn't going to be so bad. If they could talk about other peoples' children the whole trip, it would be boring, but safe. She hoped Miranda would have the sense to keep off politics.

Day by day, through the sequence of jump points, they worked their way across Familias Space. Miranda proved capable of producing edible meals from the small galley and spent quite a bit of time in her compartment. Cecelia's nightmares ceased; she no longer tensed up when Miranda came up behind her when she was in the pilot's seat. She did occasionally wonder what was going on in the world outside—how far the mutiny had progressed, where Heris Serrano was—but that was someone else's problem. She had enough to do, she told herself, keeping *Pounce* on course.

The downjump transition occurred six hours ahead of schedule, when Cecelia and Miranda were sitting down to mugs of soup. As the alarm squawked, the ship quivered like a horse shaking off flies and then lurched abruptly. Hot soup landed in Cecelia's lap; she jumped up and staggered into the cabinet as the ship lurched again. The automatic voice warning came on as Cecelia groped for an ice pack for her scalded leg. "Malfunction . . . malfunction . . . malfunction . . . proximity alarm, excessive flux . . . pilot override . . . pilot override . . ."

Clutching the ice pack to her leg, Cecelia edged carefully along, one hand on a grab bar or other handhold, until she was back in the pilot's seat. Where had she gone wrong? She'd checked and rechecked the charts; she should have been safely distant from any large mass. All the jump points she'd entered were green-coded, safe and stable . . .

Half her control panel telltales glowed red. Jump drive down, insystem drive down, shields down . . . Cecelia cut the power to emergency level; the lights dimmed. Then she made herself go through the checklist, ignoring the red lights unless they were on it.

First was hull integrity: still green. Then atmosphere: still green. She knew that already; she was alive and conscious, so there had to be air. Then environmental systems: yellow. She hesitated, but the protocol said keep going. She keyed it to the short list, and went on. When she'd worked her way through to the reds—drives, shields, longscan, the minimal weapons she carried—she came back to the yellows.

"What's the score?" Miranda asked quietly.

"We've got an intact hull, something to breathe, and some damage to environmental . . . yes . . . correctable. I need to reset the trays and a filter's come loose. Otherwise, we're not going anywhere real soon." Except they were, at their exit velocity, which was faster than she'd have chosen. But she'd deal with that later.

"What happened?"

"Don't know yet." Cecelia took the yellow list and headed back to deal with what could be fixed quickly and easily. Item after item returned to green status. They weren't leaking air; internal power was adequate for all uses at present; all environmental systems were functioning correctly. The reds . . . were beyond her capability. Beyond anyone's, in such a small ship; even if she'd known how to fix the drives, she couldn't have accessed them.

She came back to the pilot's compartment and shook her head at Miranda. "Now I have to figure out where we are, and how fast we're moving . . . we're purely ballistic at this point."

"And what happened?"

"And what happened, if I can. You never got any spacecraft ratings, did you?"

"No—I have atmospheric licenses for flitters and helos, but not spacecraft."

"Um. Well, while I'm working on position and course, suppose you take a look at this." Cecelia took a hardcopy manual out of the bin under her seat. "I don't want to use more power than necessary."

"I see. Then you'd like me to go shut down the galley, I suppose?"

"Yes, if the shift to emergency didn't cut it off automatically." She couldn't remember, at the moment, whether it would or not. Cecelia opened the cover of the Emergency Position Locator System and read the instructions graved on the inside of the cover. Supposedly this system, with its own internal powerpack, could place them accurately anywhere in Familias Space. She hoped they were still in Familias Space.

The EPLS, designed for emergency use, had only a short list of instructions. Cecelia entered their previous course data, the last jump point they should have passed, and waited for something to come up on the screen.

WAITING FOR CALCULATIONS, in glowing red letters. She stared at it for a long moment, then became aware of the pain in her leg. The burn. She'd dropped the ice pack somewhere while attending to the loose filter fitting.

"Miranda—"

"Yes?"

"See if you can find the ice pack—I put it down while I was working back near the berths—make sure I didn't leave it to melt somewhere troublesome."

"Right."

The steady red glow didn't change. Cecelia had no idea how long the calculations would take, if the device worked at all. She pulled the damp fabric of her slacks away from the painful spot on her leg, hissing at the pain. She didn't want to leave the bridge. Looking around, she remembered that she hadn't tried retrieving the automatic log.

With one eye on WAITING FOR CALCULATIONS, Cecelia tried to read the automatic log. At first, it made no sense, then she remembered that she needed to convert it to a text function. The jumble of symbols sorted themselves out into a sketchy journal. There was jump point Rvd45.7, and then (elapsed time 28.52 standard hours), jump point Tvd31.8. Two standard hours later—2.13, actually—they had passed within the e-radius of a mass sufficient to cause jump downshift.

All Cecelia really knew about e-radii and masses was that the bigger the mass, the bigger the e-radius that must be avoided. Usually this was a problem only in insertion and exit, when someone wasn't using mapped points. In a ship the size of hers, it shouldn't be a problem unless she actually ran headlong into something. But she had used mapped points, and a standard green-scored route. Nobody else had run into trouble on this route, and once in jump the very indeterminacy of position was supposed to make it safe.

The mass that they had passed too near . . . wasn't even moonlet-sized, let alone planet-sized. Cecelia tapped for interpretation, one of the options on the screen. The screen blanked. LOOKING UP DATA, it said. She glanced back at the other, which still read, WAITING FOR CALCULATIONS. The autolog screen changed first, offering a range of possibilities. All were ships.

Ships?

One (1) Very Large Container Freighter, fully loaded with high-mass cargo.

Two (2) Very Large Container Freighters, fully loaded with average cargo.

Three (3) . . . the list went on. Cecelia didn't think two or three or four container ships would be traveling in close convoy, but farther down the list, item 8 gave her pause: "Flotilla or wave of military vessels with aggregate mass as above, traveling in close convoy . . ."

In other words, she had split or nearly split a group of military ships, whose combined mass was sufficient to pop her out of jump, and disable her FTL drive.

"Oh, great," she muttered.

"What?" Miranda asked, from behind her.

"If the autolog is right, then the most probable cause of our sudden exist from FTL was that we ran into a cluster of military ships."

Miranda whistled. "I wonder what we did to them."

"Possibly nothing. Possibly we blew them away. But if we didn't . . ."

"They might be after us. I wonder if they're mutineers or loyalists."

"Me, too," Cecelia said. "Did you find that ice pack?"

"Yes—you'd dropped it in the sink. How's your leg?"

"It hurts. But not too badly." The EPLS bleeped, and she looked back at it. "Ah . . . here we are . . ." The figures it displayed made no immediate sense, but at least it had figures. Cecelia jotted them down, then called up a graphics display.

They were still in Familias Space, but that was about all the good news. They'd come out in a region of relatively sparse habitable worlds; the nearest mapped systems were two and three jump points away, respectively. Copper Mountain—she knew that, from the hoorah about Brun's abduction. It was a Fleet base. It was also—the memory jolted her like ice cubes down the spine—it was also where the mutiny had started. Cecelia muttered a string of oaths, and Miranda came forward.

"Bad news?"

"Bad news. Copper Mountain's the closest inhabited system. Want to bet the ships we almost hit were mutineers?"

Passive scan made it clear that they were a long way from anything useful . . . some 18 AU away, the nearest star glowed orange. Cecelia left the scan on, and after two minutes, it had coded six dots as possible ships based on their relative motion. Another minute, and the color shifted, confirming them as artificial and under power. They were accelerating away; the mass sensor reported an aggregate mass very close to what the autolog had postulated as the cause of dropout.

"That's what we nearly hit, I gather," Miranda said, leaning over Cecelia's shoulder.

"Yeah . . . whatever and whoever it is." The sinking feeling in her gut said they were mutineers . . . had to be.

"Are you going to try hailing them?"

"Without knowing? No. Let them think we're a dead issue." They might well be a dead issue anyway, if she couldn't get one of the drives up and running.

"Fine with me," Miranda said. "But we can listen, can't we?"

"I don't know if our communication's working at all," Cecelia said. The telltale had gone from red to yellow by itself, and she didn't trust it. "I guess we can try, though."

She turned the receivers on, and was rewarded by hisses and crackles. She ran through the settings. Then a distorted voice, quickly adjusted by the speech-recognition software.

"—could have been a ship?"

"Not likely. Got anything on scan?"

Cecelia tried to interpret the passive scan data and wished she'd paid more attention when Koutsoudas and Oblo were talking to Brun about scan technique. How far away were those ships, and whose were they?

"There it is." Cecelia flinched as that distant voice changed tone. "It's little; that's why it didn't blow itself and us to bits.

Drives are dead . . . it's ballistic . . . but there's a chance the crew are alive."

"Not our problem," said the second voice. "They're unlikely to report us . . . and without a working drive . . ."

So it was the mutineers. Cecelia looked at Miranda, who had gone white. She understood.

"We don't know the drive's dead—they might have turned it off. We can't take the chance. Too much has been going wrong—"

"Doesn't this system have a navigation beacon?" Miranda asked. "A Fleet ansible? Something?"

Cecelia looked it up. "It's uninhabited. There's a mapped jump point, but it's considered inferior—there's some big lump of metal barreling in an eccentric orbit which causes some kind of problem . . ." She put her finger on a footnote. "Wait . . . there's an ansible . . . there's been a research station here. Trouble is, I don't know if it's accessible to civilian signals . . . let's see . . ."

"Will they notice if we hail it?"

"Probably." Cecelia selected the listed frequency. "And we don't have a functioning tightbeam, or any of the other goodies I wish we had. But they already know we're here, and they're going to come after us. If we can get a signal to that ansible, we can at least let Fleet know where some mutineers are." Where they were, that is. They wouldn't stay in this system. "And maybe, if they realize we've signalled, they'll decide to run for it and leave us behind. We'll already have done all the damage we can."

"Somehow," Miranda said, eyeing the scan on which the marked icons had changed color, with lengthening cones to indicate course change and acceleration, "somehow, I don't think they'll do that."

"Probably not." Cecelia entered the pulse combination for the ansible and crossed her fingers. Six full minutes for that signal to reach the ansible, six to return . . . and she had to wait for confirmation before sending any message. She knew all too well how much could happen in twelve minutes.

Two of the distant ships disappeared from scan, and two *possible ship?* icons appeared much closer. Microjump, of course. She retuned the frequency to the one they'd eavesdropped on before.

"—got the transponder," she heard. Damn. She'd forgotten that

going to emergency power did not cut off the ship's automatic ID
signal—in fact, it boosted the power to it, on the grounds that any
ship in an emergency would want to be found. They must be lit up
like a candelabra on the military ships' scans.

"*Pounce* . . . owner Cecelia de Marktos. Isn't that the broad who's
crazy about horses . . . the one who hired Heris Serrano as a captain?"

"Yesss . . ."

Cecelia did not like the sound of that meditative hiss.

CHAPTER TEN

Sector VII Headquarters

Admiral Minor Arash Livadhi stared blindly at the wall of his office. With the star had come considerably more work than he'd anticipated, despite Admiral Serrano's honest attempt to make the changeover easy on him. Not only were all the experienced flag officers gone, but so were a startling number of the senior NCOs. Anyone who had had a rejuvenation . . . he hadn't ever noticed how many personnel had had a rejuv; he hadn't even decided what he'd do when his own number came up in a few years.

And now the mutiny, and all those personnel were coming back— the fit ones at least. The gossip mill, operating at translight speed through illicit private communications on Fleet ansibles, warned that former admirals were moving right back into their places, and the recently promoted were scrambling to find a place. He wondered what he was supposed to do. Go back to ship command? It would be easier, and he knew himself to be a good captain. But his ship—he still thought of his last command as his ship—and his crew were far away, over on the Benignity border, under a new captain.

He considered the forces available. Heris Serrano's ship was here and she'd been assigned another, halfway across Familias Space. He knew many of her crew, and they knew him. Perhaps he should volunteer to take it? Otherwise the incoming admiral he expected any day would certainly question why he hadn't assigned someone already, why it wasn't out on patrol like the others.

It made sense, in more ways than one. Arash did not like considering all the ways; there were things in his life he preferred to forget and ignore. If no one knew, no one would be hurt by the knowledge. That Heris Serrano's ship, and Heris Serrano's crew, might be insurance against that discovery, he didn't quite allow himself to recognize.

He might as well prepare the ship; he might as well make a plan that would convince the incoming admiral of his good intentions. He called in his clerk. "Please inform the officer in charge aboard *Vigilance*—"

"That'll be Lt. Commander Mackay," his clerk said.

"That I need to see him at his earliest convenience."

"I'm sure you've wondered why *Vigilance* wasn't sent out on patrol," he began.

"Yes . . . we thought at first we were waiting for Commander Serrano to return."

"Of course. But she was assigned to *Indefatigable*—I frankly thought they'd be revising the assignments as soon as people had time to recover from the first shock, so I didn't hurry to put someone into *Vigilance*. Out here on the border is the ideal place for a combat-experienced commander, and I thought she'd be back. But apparently not. Now we know another flag officer's coming to take over this headquarters, and I'm going to ask for *Vigilance* myself. I know that any ship Heris Serrano has commanded will be combat-ready, and she and I have been friends for years."

"I see, sir." The response wasn't as whole-hearted as he would have liked. "The crew will be glad to get out of dock and into space again. Does the admiral think the new admiral will agree?"

"I expect so," Arash said. "Why not? A few months behind a desk doesn't make me overqualified for ship command."

"Of course, sir."

"In any case, whoever gets her will probably use her for his flagship. We should be putting the extra communications gear aboard and making sure there's space for the admiral's staff."

The lieutenant commander grinned. "Sir, we anticipated that she might become a flagship, and most of that's in place. If the admiral has time, he might want to come aboard and look over the changes."

"I'll make the time," Arash said.

Converting any ship to flag service meant squeezing in the extra staff and their equipment as well as their supplies. Arash noted that *Vigilance*'s crew had put the flag functions some distance aft of the bridge, but in line with it, displacing the senior officers' wardroom. This was one of the two commonest configurations for large cruisers; the other put the flag space directly across the port corridor from the bridge access, but that was a busier area, and most admirals preferred the aft location. With duplication of bridge readouts and communications, it was just as convenient. Arash approved.

Not entirely to his surprise, Vida Serrano arrived to take her own office back. Arash did his best to conceal the chagrin with which he noticed her staff's burst of enthusiasm. They had worked well for him, but he had never had the kind of warm reception they showed her. The Serrano mystique, he thought sourly, and wondered for a moment if his request to take over Heris Serrano's ship was such a good idea as it had seemed before. But Admiral Serrano brought up the topic before he could sheer away. It was clear she thought admirals minor with combat experience should be out there in fighting ships.

"I'd be commanding from a ship myself if my orders didn't specifically prohibit it," she said. "You'd better take *Vigilance*— Heris's exec will make you a good flag captain, I don't doubt—"

"That'll be fine, Admiral," Arash said. "But actually, I was thinking of Commander Burleson. He's been with me quite awhile; we're used to working together. He has combat experience; he was my XO on *Firedrake* and then again on *Emperor Roy*."

"Well . . . someone you're used to could be a real help. I was hoping to keep Burleson on staff here, but you'll be the one under fire."

"Thank you, sir." Arash managed not to heave an audible sigh of relief. He was sure Heris's exec was capable, or more, but the man's coolness towards him would make it just that bit more difficult to work together. Would the man resent being displaced?

"In that case, I think I'll give Mackay a ship. You can find someone for your exec, can't you?"

"Of course, Admiral." With Burleson and . . . Keller, yes . . . he would have two people who were comfortable with him. And Mackay wouldn't see himself as shunted aside if he were given a ship. "Thank you, sir."

"You're quite welcome. I'm just sorry more of Heris's crew isn't available."

It would work out, he told himself. He told himself that again when he packed up his things and had them taken over to *Vigilance*, and when he went aboard. Heris's crew—his now—certainly gave every evidence of superb training. They rendered the honors due an admiral minor coming aboard a flagship with precision and enthusiasm.

"Welcome aboard, Admiral," Lt. Commander Mackay said. "We're looking forward to some action."

"Congratulations on your new command," Arash said. "I hear your ship's in transit, due in a few days."

"Yes, sir." Mackay grinned. "I hate to leave old *Vigilance*, but—my own ship—"

"You've earned it," Arash said. Inspiration struck. "Look here— we're all dealing with scratch crews—if you'd like to take a few people you know along with you, I'm sure we can work something out."

Mackay looked relieved. "Are you sure, sir? Admiral Serrano said they still hadn't found me an exec, and there's a fine young fourth officer aboard. He's a bit junior, but—"

"Go ahead," Arash said. "You ought to have someone you're comfortable with, on your first ship. I'll take a replacement—with the rest of this crew as experienced as they are, it's not a problem."

"Thanks, sir. When will Captain Burleson be coming aboard?"

"Tomorrow morning, I think. He had a dental checkup—tried to get out of it, but the surgeons grabbed him."

He seemed enthusiastic, and Arash—who had met the ships' officers frequently in the past few days—now felt the same warmth from all of them. He relaxed a little. Serrano mystique was one thing, but the Livadhis knew something about command as well. Admiral Serrano had already complimented him on doing a good job under difficult conditions.

The ones who worried him most, the ones who had been imprisoned on false charges when Heris left Fleet, seemed as cordial as the rest. He made a point of searching them out and greeting them, but he saw nothing in their eyes but respect. Several were now officers, and if mustangs, they were capable mustangs. Heris would have insisted on that, he knew. The ship felt good, the way a happy ship should. Burleson reported the same, once he took over.

He was waiting for the arrival of a light cruiser and some patrol craft that would form his combat group, when word came that mutineer ships had begun hitting commercial vessels as they made the long insystem crawl from jump point to orbital Station.

"Something's cut them off from their supply base," was Admiral Serrano's analysis. "They've hit ships carrying Fleet resupply, including weaponry." She looked at the group in her office. "We're going to start using convoys; I'm not waiting for HQ on this one. We need the cargos, and we don't want the mutineers to have them. Admiral Livadhi, there's a supply run heading next week. You'll direct the convoy. We're not announcing it; they'll find out soon enough."

Organizing the convoy took several days. The civilian captains of the ships involved did not like the restrictions which a convoy would place on them; they argued that Fleet should simply have enough patrols in any system to protect them. Arash wore his voice out explaining why this wouldn't work and finally had to ask Admiral Serrano to intervene. They had Fleet contracts for some of their cargo, and therefore, she said, they were under Fleet control until those cargos were delivered.

"Might as well *be* mutineers," muttered one of the captains.

"Think again," Vida Serrano said. "They take ears."

"Uh?"

"Ears cut from the bodies they leave behind. Take a look." She handed out flatpics of the carnage the mutineers had left behind on the *Saffron Dynasty* and the *Settis III*. The captains blenched and gave in.

The convoy moved out toward the jump point in a ragged formation flanked by four patrol ships and two escorts, with *Vigilance* in the lead. Arash had read that in wet navies ships could zigzag to avoid raiders, but zigzags were impractical in space, especially for ships which lacked the ability to microjump. He did insist on their practicing some maneuvers in formation, but *Eliza Garnerin* came within 1300 meters of *Haboob*, and so terrified both captains that it took all Arash's persuasive skill to keep them from dropping out altogether. "We know there aren't any mutineers in *this* system," one of them said. "We could just stay here . . ."

On that first run to the more distant pickets, they met no mutineers. Arash's force stood by while supplies were moved from the cargo ships to those keeping station. They repeated the actions in one system after another, and Arash felt a growing confidence in both *Vigilance* and the others under his command. He overheard—and knew he was meant to overhear—favorable comments on his leadership. More importantly, his staff heard even more.

Still, he worried. The mutineers' leader, supposedly, was one Solomon Drizh, and Arash had reason to wish it had been someone else. They had both served under Admiral Lepescu, as young men, and they had both fallen under the spell of his dubious charms. Arash had survived one witch-hunt for old Lepescu connections because Lepescu had made it clear that he despised the young Livadhi. The scornful phrases still rang in his ears . . . *I had thought better of a man of your family . . . there's backbone in your breeding, boy; what happened to you?*

Others had heard that scorn; it had been a permanent blot on his service record—the only one—ever since. Yet, in the long run, a good turn, for being known as an object of Lepescu's contempt was, after Lepescu's death, far better than being known as his protégé. Now, however, Drizh and the other mutineers had brought Lepescu's *Loyal Order of Game Hunters* to Fleet's attention. If Fleet mounted a search for potential mutineers among Lepescu's old associates, what else might they turn up?

He could tell, from the reactions of his staff and crew, that none of this turmoil showed on his face. It shouldn't, he thought wryly, for he had had years to perfect his calm. It was so unfair . . . he had never intended to do anything but the duty he was sworn to. He had not meant to jump from one very hot frying pan into an even hotter fire, and the displeasure of Lepescu and his supporters should have been fire enough.

But it wasn't. A scalding worm of that fire crawled through his belly as he tried not to think about it. Warned by Lepescu that members of his own family were members of the Loyal Order of Game Hunters, Arash Livadhi dared not go to them. He had turned, in the hell Lepescu made of his life, to the only friend he could count on. An outsider, from a colony world, but undaunted by the difficulties that placed in the way of a Fleet career. Jules made friends with everyone, mended quarrels, and—to Arash's relief—had never been acceptable to Lepescu because of his total disinterest in blood sports. Tubby, cheerful Jules, who always had time to listen, whose advice was so often just what one wanted to hear.

When, Arash wondered, filling in the reports he would have to file on his return, had Jules first asked him to do something he should not? And how could he have known? Young officers helped each other out—*friends* helped each other out. Everyone expected that, and always had. A little here, a little there. And only because Jules was his good friend, who had stood by him when (it seemed) the whole ship turned against him with Lepescu's disfavor. Jules had done him more than one good turn, too.

If he had known . . . but hard as he poked and prodded his reluctant memory, he could not find any unequivocal clue to Jules' real nature. Not until many years later, when it was far too late. Not until it would have meant his career, if not his life, to let the truth be known.

R.S.S. *Bonar Tighe*, now flagship of mutiny

"So," the mutineers' commander said. He wore what looked like an ordinary Regular Space Service uniform, though Cecelia wasn't sure about the rank insignia. His nametag read ADM-M DRIZH. "You're the one who killed Admiral Lepescu."

Cecelia had forgotten her close involvement with Admiral Lepescu's death. She managed not to say "Oh . . . him . . ." as if she blew away dozens of people a year. "Actually I didn't shoot him myself," she said. From the expression on the man's face, that didn't improve her situation.

"Useless old woman," the mutineers' commander said. "If it weren't for people like you, we would have our rightful place."

Six feet under and well tamped down, Cecelia thought. And it was indeed our fault that we didn't recognize you and put you where you belong.

"But you'll learn," he said. "You'll learn what we're capable of."

Wasting time making pompous speeches, Cecelia thought. The mark of a second-rate—no, make that third-rate—mind, was this tendency to pontificate.

"Take them to the brig," the commander said, with a wave of his hand. The menacing NEMs closed in.

The brig was much as she'd imagined military prisons: cramped, bare, ugly, and uncomfortable. And secure. What she hadn't expected, on a mutineers' ship, was the number of prisoners crammed into the cells. Why didn't they just kill the loyalists? Or were their own personnel so troublesome?

The guards shoved her and Miranda into a six-bunk cell with eight other women, who stared at them with sullen suspicion. One was curled up, arms clasped around her knees; she had given them only a brief glance before putting her bruised face down again.

"This is not what I had in mind," Cecelia said to Miranda, "when I suggested a trip for your health. Sorry."

Miranda looked around the cell, then at Cecelia as if she couldn't believe what she'd heard. "I scarcely think—"

"I know it's not my fault. But I feel the need to apologize. There we were, supposedly safe from all alarms until we arrived, and then— WHAM."

"What—who are you?" asked one of the women, whose pepper-and-salt hair was clipped close to her head. "Where are we?"

Cecelia gave her a direct smile. "I'm Cecelia de Marktos and this is my friend Miranda Meager. We were on our way to the Guerni Republic, and two hours into what should have been a safe jump, we were knocked loose and back into realspace."

The woman leaned closer, speaking softly. "But where—do you know where we—where the ship is?"

Could she trust this woman? Not yet, anyway.

"No," Cecelia said. "I got the course from a standard navigation package, and whatever knocked us out fouled up the drives and the navigation. When your captain picked us up, I thought we were being rescued . . ."

The other woman grimaced. "No such luck . . ."

"No. And I feel it's entirely unjustified. We're private citizens—"

"Wait—" the other woman said. "Miranda . . . Meager? Any relation to Brun Meager?"

Damn. She hadn't wanted to use the Thornbuckle name, but of course Brun had made the other just as notorious.

"I'm her mother," Miranda said softly. "Why?"

"And you're Cecelia de Marktos . . . aren't you that friend of Heris Serrano's, the one who shot Lepescu?"

"I didn't shoot Lepescu," Cecelia said. "Heris did. But I would have." If she hadn't fainted, something that still annoyed her. So she'd been in an old body at the time, that was no excuse.

"But I thought you were old," the woman said.

"I am," Cecelia said. "But I rejuved a few years ago. Someone poisoned me, and it was the only way to full recovery."

"I saw something about that," said another woman. "And it was after that you were with Commander Serrano at Xavier?"

"Yes." From the looks on their faces, they all knew about Heris Serrano. They would, of course, especially if they were loyalists. "I gather you're all loyalists?"

"Yeah," said the first woman who had spoken.

"Why didn't they just kill you?" asked Cecelia, who hadn't been able to get that off her mind.

"Cecelia!" Miranda looked as shocked as she sounded.

"It is the operative question," the first woman said. "She has to wonder if we're decoys or something, to sneak information out of you." She grinned complicitly at Cecelia and stuck out her hand. "I'm Chief Jones, by the way, milady."

"Call me Cecelia," Cecelia said. "Or 'Dammit Cece!' if you're in a hurry."

"Right, then. I'm not entirely sure why they haven't killed some of us—but some of us are serving as entertainment for their troops." She nodded at the silent young woman huddled on the bunk, who hadn't yet looked up. "Besides the obvious, they seem to get a lot of fun taunting us about how stupid we were not to join them at the beginning."

"I see. They must be pleasant to live with. . . ." Her mind raced as the words drawled out in her most ladylike manner. She saw a moment's shock, then Chief Jones grinned.

"You could say that."

Miranda spoke up. "Does this place have a . . . er . . ."

"Head, milady?" Miranda, Cece noticed, still received an honorific. But she looked utterly confused at the term. "Just over there—it's not flushable, sorry." That attempt at humor also passed Miranda by, Cecelia saw by the momentary horror on her face as she saw the stinking bucket. "They like this part best, I think."

Miranda drew herself up and managed to grin back. "Well, a fascination with excretion does define a certain kind of mind." She made no move to use the bucket, but instead held out her hand to Chief Jones. "Let's forget the whole ladyship business—I'm Miranda to my friends, and you look more like a friend than anyone I've seen on this ship yet . . . except Cece."

"Right, Miranda." Chief Jones looked around. "You might as well get to know all the crowd." She pointed them out as she gave their names. "We have Sgt. Tiraki—Gwen's our engineering specialist—" Gwen Tiraki had a small, earnest face and the calloused hands of someone who used them for something other than pushing buttons. "She can fix just about anything, or build something that works better. Then there's Sgt. Dirac—we call her Dusty because her mother named her something no one can say—who's a scan specialist."

"You worked with Koutsoudas, didn't you, Lady—uh—Cecelia?"

"Amazing man," Cecelia said. "I'm a total idiot; he taught the ones who could learn." She had recognized the enthusiast hoping for enlightenment; this was no time for it, even if she'd had the knowledge Dirac wanted.

"Petty Light Donaldson—Gerry's also a scan specialist. Petty Major Sifa—Pilar was in charge of the repair section for communications and scan. Petty Light Kouras—Jen's a drive technician; so is Petty Light Hartung." She glanced at the huddled figure. "Pivot Anseli Markham. She's here to keep us quiet." Her voice hardened. "If we do something they don't like, they torment her."

"How bad is she?" Cecelia asked, keeping her voice down.

"Physically—one day in a regen tank would help, but she's not in danger without it. Mentally, she's close to the line if not over it. She was a nice kid, but one of those who really depended on all the rules. Now they're gone, and she's . . ." Chief Jones made a wavy motion with her hand.

Cecelia glanced at Miranda, whose face was white; she realized that Miranda saw Brun in that huddled figure, Brun who had suffered alone, far away from anyone who cared. She glanced back at Cecelia, and Cecelia nodded. "Miranda can at least sit with her," Cecelia said. Chief Jones nodded.

It had not escaped Cecelia's notice that Jones had not given her first name, but she thought it was a matter of command—something she had begun to understand while traveling with Heris.

Miranda merely looked at the space next to Anseli, and Pilar Sifa stood up; Cecelia fought her stubborn mouth and managed not to grin. Miranda sat down and somehow—without seeming to move—made an inviting curve of her arm. Still without looking up, Anseli leaned into it, her shoulders beginning to shake. Miranda leaned over her.

"Mothers," Chief Jones said. She sounded more resigned than anything else. "I don't know how they do it . . . but I'm glad she's here. None of us have children."

"Nor do I," Cecelia said. "Never wanted any, myself. I have relatives enough."

Chief Jones chuckled. "One of my sisters has six, and the other four. One of 'em claims I joined Fleet just so I wouldn't have to help her diaper them . . ."

"I was the oldest of six," Sgt. Tiraki said. "I'd done all the child care I ever want to do by the time I joined Fleet."

"You're sure you don't have any idea where we are?" Chief Jones asked.

Cecelia glanced around the cell; Jones nodded. "All I know is what the emergency locator system told me." She gave the coordinates. "That's supposed to be a couple of jump points away from Copper Mountain, the closest inhabited system."

"It's the commander's bucket," Chief Jones said.

"Excuse me?"

"It's an Academy thing, sera. Officers tend to pick places—off the usual routes—where they can rendezvous with friends. They call it their bucket."

"Sounds like a recipe for conspiracies to me," Cecelia said.

Jones nodded. "It certainly can be, but in my experience young officers just like to feel they have something private, some secret. The

Academy pushes them hard, turns them inside out. Probably most of them never use their bucket once they're well into their careers. Did your locator tell you whether this system had an ansible?"

"It does." Should she tell Jones that she'd tried to get a message out, but was sure she'd failed? No. What good would that do?

"I think you fancy ladies should have the shit detail this time," the guard said. "Let's see now—Red or Blondie?"

"Oh, I think both," the other guard said. "Both of 'em need to learn a few basic skills." Cecelia looked at Miranda, but could not read her expression beyond mild distaste.

"Pick up the bucket," said the first guard, with no more humor in his voice. "Each of you—one hand. You'll both carry it."

The bucket stank and was within a few centimeters of overflowing. The round handle on the bail wasn't big enough for both their hands, having been intended for one-hand carries, and it was hard to grasp part on, part off. The thinner bail dug into her fingers; the bucket was heavier than she'd expected.

They lifted together, but Cecelia was taller, and the bucket tipped slightly; a few drops spilled.

"Messy, messy," the guard said. "You'll have to clean that up when you get back." The guards gave each other a smug grin.

It was remarkably difficult, Cecelia discovered, to carry an almost full bucket with someone of a different height, someone whose rhythm of movement you didn't know. Harder, when it was necessary to sidle through the half-open cell door . . . a trail of smelly drops followed them out of the cell, down the corridor.

"Keep going, girls," the guards said, falling in behind them. Cecelia's back crawled; she hated having people behind her like this anyway and these . . . she concentrated on the slithery movement of the liquid in the bucket, trying to compensate for Miranda's movement with her own, trying not to spill.

Another guard stepped out in front of them suddenly. "That's far enough!" he said. One of the guards bumped into Cecelia; she lurched forward, and a splash of liquid filth hit the deck.

"You're a clumsy bitch," the guard said. He sounded more pleased than angry. "Now you have more to clean up, Red."

"It's not my fault!" Cecelia said. "You pushed me!"

"Wrong answer, Red," the guard said. "Blondie—take your hand off the bucket." Miranda let go, but slowly enough that Cecelia could take the weight of the bucket without spilling any more. "Blondie, turn and face the bulkhead . . . the *wall*, you stupid civvie. Snuggle right up to it."

When Miranda stood, face to the wall, the guards surrounded Cecelia. One after another gave her a sharp nudge; she managed to stand balanced, not spilling any more.

"You're going to clean it all up, Red, by yourself. And there'll be plenty to clean—" Instead of a nudge, this was a hard shove, that sent her careening into one of the others, who pushed her back.

It took her hours to clean the floor to their satisfaction, with the single small rag they allowed. Meanwhile, Miranda struggled back and forth with the slop pails from the other cells, emptying them and scrubbing them clean. Her guards harrassed her verbally but didn't make her spill any more. Yet. Cecelia knew more harrassment would come.

Just when she thought they were finished, the guards told them both to clean the guards' latrine; they gave Miranda a little rag like hers and pushed them both into the latrine. It had two urinals, two stalls, four sinks, and a shower. That took another hour or so, because the guards swore they had missed a speck here in this corner or on top of that mirror or behind that pipe.

At the end of that first day, Cecelia hurt from her toes to the top of her head and all the way past her fingertips. Her knees were sore and her back hurt; her hands were red and raw; her bruises were darkening. Miranda looked tired too, her palms marked with the red lines of the bucket bails, but at least she hadn't had to crawl around on her knees all day.

But they were alive, she reminded herself, and alive was better than dead. So far.

Supper was a meagre bowl of some unflavored gruel, sipped without utensils from a plastic bowl which had to be handed back. Someone from another cell was brought out to wash the bowls afterward.

Then the lights dimmed, and Chief Jones explained that they were allowed to sleep only during this shift—so four of the ten had to sleep on the deck, with barely room to stretch out.

"We rotate bunk and floor assignments," she said. "You're numbers nine and ten, so I've redone the rotations. Six nights out of ten, each person gets a bunk. Four nights, the floor. What we did was put numbers in a pile, and draw them out—what was left was yours. You're four, Miranda, in the rotation, and Cecelia, you're nine. We're starting fresh, so that means Miranda has a bunk the next four days. Cecelia, you have the floor."

"But she worked harder," Miranda said. Chief Jones cocked an eye at Cecelia.

"That's all right," Cecelia said. "I'm tired enough to sleep on anything."

"Good. Pipe down, everyone."

Despite what she'd said, Cecelia found the floor hard and unforgiving, with a nasty cold draft. No matter what position she lay in, something hurt, mostly a fresh bruise. She slept, off and on, but it was nothing like a real rest.

She woke to a clangor that turned out to be the guards hammering on metal buckets.

"Rise and shine! Get off those bunks, you lazy bums!"

After some days of this, the guards abruptly handed them mops and sponges. "Use these—you've got more to clean than just this head, and the way you work, it'd take you a month with rags." After they'd cleaned the guards' latrine, they were taken out of the brig area and down the corridor. Cecelia glanced through doorways they passed and saw stacked bunks in rows. Crew housing? It must be. The guards kicked open a door into a huge tiled room . . . urinals on this wall, toilet stalls on that, rows of shower stalls, rows of sinks. "Start at that end, and don't miss anything!" one ordered.

"And you'll need these," the other said. He unlocked a cabinet in which were toilet bowl brushes and jugs of chemicals labelled for their intended use.

Cecelia headed for the far end and dipped a brush in a toilet bowl; Miranda, without saying a word, went to the urinals. Aside from choosing a urinal she'd already cleaned to use, the guards didn't harrass them that day. Cecelia scrubbed, polished, mopped, and cleaned, as if she'd been born a janitor. The guards lounged near the door, clearly bored.

Within a few days they were spending all day every day cleaning four latrines—the guards', and three others on the crew deck. Cecelia was able to describe to Chief Jones, in detail, what equipment was being stored where: exactly what chemicals were in the equipment closets where they picked up and returned mops, brooms, sweep-vacs, brushes, and sponges, exactly how many people were usually around in each corridor and head (she'd finally taken to using the military term, when the Chief kept reminding her of it).

Day by day, she brought in more information, a snippet at a time . . . and day by day, their guards became more and more bored. To amuse themselves, they occasionally dirtied an area the women had cleaned and demanded that it be cleaned again, and as they'd decided the women feigned exhausted submission. That wasn't much fun; the guards began sneaking off singly. They never actually left the women alone and unwatched, but they weren't anywhere near as alert as before. Cecelia had time to think. And one sleep shift, she told Chief Jones what had occurred to her, the answer to a question that had puzzled her since her capture.

"I know what they want you alive for," Cecelia said.

Chief Jones shrugged. "Prisoner exchange . . . ransom . . ."

"No. They want you for prey."

Chief Jones stared at her, expressionless except for the slight widening of her eyes. "Prey."

"When I was on Sirialis, when Admiral Lepescu was killed—when Heris Serrano shot him—that's what he was doing. Hunting people. As sport."

The Chief's eyes narrowed and focussed far behind Cecelia's face. "They want a hunt, do they?" Then she refocussed on Cecelia's face, and her mouth widened slowly to a feral grin. "Fine. We'll give them a hunt . . . we start now. Here."

Cecelia had been prepared for shock, for anger, but not for this almost glee. "But—" she started but Jones shook her head.

"No. There is only one answer. It must not be their hunt, but ours."

CHAPTER ELVEN

R.S.S. *Indefatigable*

Heris Serrano, having finally got her ship in order—or mostly in order—explained their mission.

"We're looking for mutineers by watching jump points and looking for out-of-range ansible transmissions. We engage and destroy mutineers, change out the recognition codes on ansibles and system defenses. If we find minefields, we'll clear them."

"What if they leapfrog us?" Seabolt asked.

"They may, but if we work our way through the jump points in between, we should pick up their trail before that happens. That was the reason for rushing crews onto ships and getting them into space, to move into this area and interdict their movement. That still gives them a lot of space, but at least it protects our most vulnerable civilians."

"Do you think they'd attack civilians, Captain?"

"I imagine they will, unless all they wanted was to run off and set up somewhere on their own. But so far no one's reported direct commmunication with them. All we have is that one report from *Vigor*, which had the sense to run like a rabbit with the distress message when it realized there was trouble. By the time we come out of jump, I expect to hear more. If they were agents of a foreign power—"

"The Black Scratch," someone muttered.

500

"The Benignity or any other," Heris corrected. "I suppose someone might even have fallen in love with the lifestyle of a NewTex
religious fanatic." There was a chuckle from the younger officers.
"My point is, it's too early to form conclusions about what these
mutineers are like, except dangerous. We know they took over the
Copper Mountain orbital station and freed prisoners from the
high-security brig. It's our job to keep them penned up until someone figures out who they are and how to deal with them."

"Captain, won't this concentration leave border defense in
jeopardy?"

"As I understand it, units are being pulled only from friendly
borders. Nobody seriously thinks the Lone Star Confederation or the
Guerni Republic or the Emerald Worlds want to invade us. There
may be more smuggling than usual, but we can stand that."

Seabolt lingered when the others left. "I'm worried about security,"
he said.

"In what way, Commander?" Heris had learned not to assume she
knew what his concerns were.

"Well, as you know—" Heris repressed a sigh. Seabolt insisted on
starting off by telling her what she knew—what anyone with a brain
knew—before finally coming to his point, and nothing she'd done
had cured him of it so far. "As you know, there's a mutiny."

"I had gathered that," Heris said. "And your point is?"

"This crew is full of people with no shipboard experience—"
Something else she already knew, and he himself was an example.
"We don't know if they're qualified," Seabolt said, and hurried on,
perhaps warned by her expression. "We don't know if they're part of
the conspiracy. Since everything's going smoothly now, I want to
start working on their dossiers. Did you know we have five people
aboard who belong to the Church of Unified Brethren, and they have
been holding meetings in a squad bay?"

Heris said, "No."

"It's true. And there was an advisory out only six months ago
about all religious groups, that they might harbor extremists—"

"I mean, no, you may not start witch-hunting. I did know about
Corporals Sennis and Solis, and Pivots Mercator, Januwitz, and
Bedar . . . they're not extremists, and the Unified Brethren have never
been any problem."

"But Captain—"

"Commander, everything is going as smoothly as it is—not nearly as smoothly as it should—because I am working very hard to find and nurture those who have competence. Among those people with competence is, for instance, Petty Major Tanira, who is also one of the Unified Brethren—there are at least fifty, not five, aboard. Tanira is the reason we didn't have a level three incident when some idiot clerk out of your former office didn't see why a valve had to be shut to three point two exactly. I will not have you upsetting him, or any of the others, on the basis of some crackpot report generated a long way from real ships or real combat."

"But Captain—"

"Is that clear, Commander?"

"Yes, but—but I must respectfully disagree."

"You can disagree all you want, but you will not—repeat *not*—go digging around making people feel that they're not trusted. We may have a would-be mutineer aboard; if we do, the best way to make that person try something is to create distrust and disaffection among everyone else. We may have a Benignity spy, or a serial killer, or a person whose idea of fun is being thrashed with dead snakes by someone wearing green paint—any of those—but in all those cases, until something definite happens, our best strategy is to build up this crew. And building up the crew starts with building their competence—which is why we're holding double shifts of training— and their confidence in their commanders."

"You're . . . you're just like they said," Seabolt blurted.

"And how was that?" Heris asked.

"Serranos," he said. "All of you. You won't listen to anybody else, you always think you know best . . ."

Heris felt the satisfaction of a cat which had the mouse firmly between its paws. "Commander, aboard a ship the captain *does* know best. By definition. Check your regulations: it's in my job description. If you act against my express orders, *that*—" she let her voice grow louder "—is mutiny, Commander. You are walking a very thin edge."

He turned pale, and sweat glistened on his forehead. "I didn't mean—of course I wasn't—I just—"

"You are dismissed," Heris said.

"I . . . ah . . . yes, sir." Seabolt left.

If only she had someone, anyone, to put in his place . . . but she didn't. She knew she wasn't at her best with his personality type—they annoyed her even when they were right—but she would have to find some way of dealing with him.

Terakian Fortune, in passage from Trinidad to Zenebra

Goonar Terakian had continued his occasional chats with Simon the priest, whenever he had time and didn't want to let himself brood about Betharnya and the impossibility of asking her to marry him. They had gone from Simon's history (which seemed unbearably dull to Goonar: a celibate life among books and scholars?) to Goonar's. Simon seemed to find the life of a merchanter captain as unattractive as Goonar found Simon's, commenting that poor Goonar never had time to think a thought all the way through. Goonar forbore to mention that thinking thoughts all the way through had led Simon to a death sentence, and turned the conversations back to religion and politics. Simon seemed convinced that the Familias Regnant's policy of religious toleration would lead straight to anarchy and immorality.

Goonar felt his neck getting hot, as it often did around Simon. "That's a nasty thing to say. Do you think I'm immoral?"

"No, Captain, not that I've seen . . ." Simon never got upset, that Goonar could tell. "But I don't see how it can work in practice."

"It's a matter of respect," Goonar said. "We respect the other beliefs—"

"How can you respect something when you know it's wrong?"

Goonar scowled. "I don't know it's wrong. I may think it's wrong—and in fact, I do think a lot of the religions I've heard about don't make sense—but that doesn't mean I can't act in a civilized way about them. If you want to believe—oh, let's say, you believe that a two-headed turtle created your planet—why should I argue with you? I think it's silly, but then most people believe some silly things. My cousin would tell you that my not wanting to marry again is silly."

"But peoples' behavior depends on their beliefs; you can't trust someone's behavior if they think it's all right to do wrong things."

"I think you're wrong—at least in part," Goonar said. "Look, a trader sees a lot—I know that some people use their beliefs, whatever they are, to make themselves better—kinder, more honest, more faithful, more responsible. Others use their beliefs as an excuse to lie, cheat, steal, and murder—all they have to do is tell themselves the other fellow isn't of their faith, and that makes it all right. So they say. Same beliefs, different people. And the good people can be found everywhere, believing all sorts of different things, and so can the bad. What I think is, religion makes a good person better and a bad person worse."

Simon sat in silence, then finally shook his head. "I can't agree, but you've posed a difficult thesis . . . it will take me awhile to work it out. I would have to say, to start with, that some beliefs would make anyone worse—"

"True. Now you take the Bloodhorde—you know about the Bloodhorde? All this thinking that only strength matters, that's going to lead to trouble. But the people who emigrate to Aethar's World are already that sort of person—people who are bullies and want to hang out with other bullies and feel good about themselves. I suppose it could be different with their children, who never know any difference. But the religions I do know about, they all hold up many of the same things as good: kindness, honesty, and so on."

"Yes. I see that. And I have to admit that even followers of the true faith have done terrible things in its name. But you're coming dangerously close to a famous old heresy, that of special election."

"Never heard of it," Goonar said. Someone tapped on his door; he said, "Come on in." Esmay Suiza stood there, looking uncertain. "Yes, Sera—do come in and join the argument. We're talking about religion."

"I don't know much about religion," Esmay said.

"That's fine—but you've met Simon, haven't you? He's a priest, from the Benignity—Simon, Sera Suiza is from Altiplano. He's just talking about special election, Sera—have you ever heard of anything like that?"

"Some of the Old Believers," Esmay said. "If you mean the idea that some are born naturally good and others naturally evil."

"Exactly," Simon said.

Goonar shrugged. "Some apples taste better than others—what's heretical about that?"

"Ahhh," Simon said, with a gleam in his eye that Goonar recognized just too late as that of an enthusiast. "Now: did God make one apple sweet and another bitter?"

"I'm not God, Simon, so I don't know," Goonar said, ducking quickly away from what promised to be a voyage-long theological exercise. "What I am is a ship captain with—up to now—a clean record in the Familias Regnant and adjoining territories. Not anymore, thanks to you. If what you say is true—"

"It is," Simon said.

"Fine, then . . . then you are just the sort of political refugee my seniors warned me about, but at least not criminal in this jurisdiction. You understand I will have to make a report—no doubt a long and tedious report—about you to both my seniors and whatever officialdom shows up at Castle Rock?"

"Of course," said Simon. "I hope it isn't too much trouble."

"It is," Goonar said, "but it has to be done. I don't suppose you know anyone in our government who could expedite this for us?"

"I'm sorry, but no," Simon said.

"Then perhaps you and Sera Suiza can thrash out the theology, while I get busy on the reports." Goonar stood up, and winked at Esmay, who was looking startled. "Only if you're willing, Sera, but he might be interested in your world's beliefs."

"Please," Simon said. "If your Old Believers are related to the Sinatians . . ." They left together, Simon talking eagerly. Goonar wondered if there was any counterbalancing profit he could show to make up for what this was going to cost.

Basil knocked. "Find out anything more?"

"Yes. I still want to wring your neck, but he's certainly no common criminal. He's a religious nut."

"He is? He seems quiet enough."

"Don't get him started on good and evil and something called special election."

"That sounds like politics."

"No . . . he was about to drag me into whether God made apples differentially sweet or they just came that way—"

Basil's eyebrows shot up. "Oh dear."

"Yes. He's a heretic to the Benignity, a nut to me, and God knows what the Patriarch would think of him, but I'm not going to keep him around to find out. We dump him on the government at Castle Rock and steal quietly away."

"Well, then. By the way—" Basil had switched to his casual voice; Goonar snorted at him, and Basil switched back. "Our hero of Xavier is making Bethya nervous."

"Why? What's she doing?"

"Bethya says she's having nightmares and won't talk about it."

"Good grief, Basil, the woman's military—of course she's not going to talk to a . . . an actress. And how does Bethya know she's having nightmares, anyway?"

"Women have their ways," Basil said. "Thing is, I was wondering if we should notify anyone."

"Who, for instance?"

"Oh . . . her family, maybe. If she needs help, they should know. And Bethya said she didn't have time to contact them back at Trinidad."

"Well . . . I suppose when we get into Zenebra we could offer to place a call for her. But I'm not going to do it behind her back. We don't have the right."

At Zenebra Station, *Terakian Fortune* crossed paths with *Terakian Favor*, with a solid fourteen hours of cargo exchange under the eyes of the Station customs officer. *Favor* had the route down the length of the Familias on that border; Goonar picked up cargo for Castle Rock, and she picked up his for Mallory, Inkman, and Takomin Roads. Goonar was glad enough to have his extra crew helping. They had removed their costumes from the fashion containers and returned the mannequins to neutral programming, so the designs could travel on to the backwoods towns awaiting them. Then both unloaded their Zenebra cargo—a matter of an hour or so for that— and Goonar, as the newer captain, invited Elias Terakian, captain of the *Favor* over for dinner.

"Well, Goonar, you're doing well, it looks like." Elias, twenty years a captain, had the assurance of that experience; in another decade he might retire to the Fathers. "You've a smart crew, the way they got that cargo shifted so fast."

"I have a message for the Fathers," Goonar said, "that needs to go by some other route."

"Ah. Well, let's hear it."

Goonar explained the whole long complicated tale, as he knew it, and Elias said nothing. When he'd finished, Elias shook his head. "You'd have done better to have a dull first run, Goonar."

"I know that," Goonar said.

"But—you've done as well as you could, I think. What about this theatrical troupe? Do you think they'll use us again?"

That hadn't occurred to Goonar. "I don't know," he said. "Bethya—their manager and star—has talked about settling somewhere and giving up touring."

"Ah. She's the redhead, isn't she?"

"Yes . . ." He knew what was coming.

"Handsome woman. Not that old. You really need to find another wife, Goonar, someone to make you comfortable between trips."

"I'm not looking for a wife," Goonar said.

"You say that now, but when you're retired . . ."

"Elias, please. Enough."

"All right, all right, I won't say any more. I'll take your message to the Fathers, and I won't mention your . . . the . . . redhead. You do know she likes you?"

"I know no such thing," Goonar said. He could feel himself reddening. "She's polite to everyone."

"None so blind . . ." Elias murmured, applying himself to his dessert.

"Do you want to meet the heretic?"

"No. What do I know about theology? Now if you'd extricated a specialist in olive genetics . . ."

Goonar laughed. "I'll tell Basil that, shall I? If you must take in fugitives, make sure they have salable information?"

Elias gave him an enigmatic look. "As a matter of fact, Goonar, that's exactly what you should do. Policy is, we don't take fugitives or mix with politics. Practically speaking . . . if you must take in a fugitive, make sure it's someone whose passage profits us."

"Um. I don't think we'll make much off this theologian—but perhaps there's a hidden treasure in the theatrical troupe. I've got that lighting in the shuttle bay now . . ."

❀   ❀   ❀

Remembering the ease with which crew got drunk and spilled secrets, Goonar didn't permit his illicit passengers to debark at Zenebra. He offered Esmay a chance to send word home to Altiplano, but she declined at first.

"But they should know," Basil said.

"They'll just worry," Esmay said.

"Of course they'll worry," Basil said. "That's what they're supposed to do. You say they knew about the marriage—"

"That's what the captain of the ship we were on told us, yes."

"And then you just disappeared. They could think you're dead. And they could help you."

"I don't think so," Esmay said. She looked stubborn.

"I'm not comfortable with this," Goonar said finally. "I feel almost like a thief, as if I'd stolen you away."

Esmay snorted, then laughed aloud. Her laughs were rare, he'd noticed. "Not likely . . . but if you insist, Captain, I'll call home and let them know I'm fine." She was not fine, he could see that—she was kilos thinner than she had been when she came aboard, despite what he knew was a good galley, but he wasn't going to argue that. Let her family take care of her.

He would have paid for the call, but Esmay insisted on paying the toll herself. The estimated delivery time, for a regular ansible relay from Zenebra to Altiplano, was surprisingly long.

"We don't have a real-time connection," Esmay said. "At least, not unless you set it up and pay in advance. Messages are batched through. And there are what—three or four relays between?"

"So we'll be in Castle Rock, nearly, when your family gets your message—"

"Unless it makes the minimum transit. But I don't see that it makes any difference. They're hardly going to come charging to the rescue—they have their own lives."

Goonar said nothing more, but when she had gone back to the ship, he placed his own. If she were his daughter, he'd want to know what had happened by priority access. And what if Fleet reported her discharged and her family had no idea how to find her?

On the passage from Zenebra to Rockhouse Major, the main commercial docking point orbiting Castle Rock, Goonar wracked his brain to find some way to make a profit from his cargo. He talked to all of them—Simon, Betharnya, the other acting troupe members, Esmay Suiza—seizing on every scrap of information that might be useful later. Talks with Simon always ended in a theological briar patch he saw no purpose in, but the actors had a unique viewpoint of all the places they'd been, and ships they'd traveled on. The difficulty of finding sound engineers on this world—the timing of theater and music festivals—Goonar filed it all away. Esmay was sure she wouldn't get back into Fleet, not for a long time, but Goonar, thinking of her as a conduit to Brun Meager and Fleet both, plied her with Terakian & Sons trade doctrine. What they wanted from Fleet, what they wanted from the government . . . just in case she might be in a position to say something useful. All this almost kept his mind off fantasies of himself and Bethya.

Esmay pored over the meagre news available at the kiosk on Zenebra. The very meagreness worried her. If the mutiny had been crushed, in these past weeks, that should surely be in the news. Instead, she noticed talk of rising prices, of concern by traders and reassurances from Fleet. She had wanted so badly to find out about Barin, but civilians had no access to the Fleet personnel databases. Would they even tell her if something had happened? She was his wife, after all. If Admiral Serrano hadn't forced an annulment.

Copper Mountain Base

The shuttle down to the surface lurched and swayed as it met a cold front, and sank through it toward the landing field. Barin tried to put his mind on something else, but every time he closed his eyes, he saw that dark chamber, the glitter of headlamps on wet metal. Then Ghormley's frightened voice, and the brilliant flash. Every bounce of the shuttle reminded him of the abrupt shifts of the artificial gravity. And that scything light . . .

The shuttle's landing gear slammed into the ground; Barin grunted and looked at the others. No one was watching him; each seemed sunk in a private reverie. He hoped theirs were better than his.

Copper Mountain's reception hall looked just the same, ugly murals and all, as the first time he'd seen it. Worse, because now he wasn't a student, come for a course—now he was a casualty, loaded into an ambulance with three others as if they were slabs of meat. Someone who still might not make it, who shouldn't be cluttering up the sickbay of a fighting ship—he'd overheard that reason for shipping some of them here, for treatment downside. On the ride to the hospital, all he could see out the back was a lowering gray sky that exactly expressed his mood. But at least it wasn't a ship; the gravity wouldn't shift, or the ground split, or the air sweep off into vacuum.

His first examination did nothing to dispel his gloom. When doctors muttered and prodded at parts of yourself you couldn't see, it never meant anything good. The phrase "the best they could" occurred several times.

"I'm sorry," one of the doctors finally said. "But we're going to have to combine surgery and regen technology. You'll be off duty quite a while." He sounded almost cheerful about it. "You'll need some rehab afterwards, because of prolonged immobilization, but you should make a full recovery."

The surgeries and regen treatments took over a week. When they were done, the surgeons came in to brag about their work, and Barin realized for the first time just how narrowly he'd missed death. Both legs, both arms, pelvis, two crushed vertebrae, and a depressed skull fracture . . . and the burns.

"You're lucky to be alive," one told him. "Your ship surgeons did a good job with what they had. But you've been immobile for several months, and your muscle mass is down—" Barin could see that, now that he wasn't encased in splints and casts. "So the next thing is to get you back in motion, so you can start getting fit again."

Several weeks later, when Barin was able to walk the length of the rehab gym without stumbling or getting out of breath, he was put on light duty. He welcomed the distraction; he was getting stronger day by day, and his mind needed something to do.

The assignment to form a support team for a forensic group investigating the Stack Islands marked his return to limited full duty. Barin looked at the information he'd been given and went to find Corporal Gelan Meharry.

Gelan Meharry didn't look much like his big sister. Barin had met Methlin Meharry only that once, on Heris's ship, back when he was trying to clear Esmay's name. She had looked every bit as dangerous as her legend, and he'd wondered at the time why she hadn't had the scar on her face removed. It was not something to ask about. Gelan had the same green eyes, but his hair was darker, and he looked more subdued than sullen.

"Lieutenant," Meharry said. Then his eyes lit up. "Excuse me, sir, but—are you related to Commander Heris Serrano?"

"That's right," Barin said. "She's my aunt. And you're Methlin Meharry's brother."

An expression Barin readily understood passed across Meharry's face. "Her baby brother, she'll tell anyone . . ."

"I know the feeling," Barin said. "But from what I hear, you're no one's baby. You nearly scotched the mutiny before it started, is how the story goes."

Now the face was closed, almost as if in pain. "Thanks, sir, but that's not quite how it went. If I'd figured out a way to do something sooner . . ." His voice trailed off; Barin knew that mental path well.

"If I had figured out sooner that there were leaks in gas lines, I wouldn't have lost two men out of my damage control team," Barin said.

Meharry looked at him.

"Hull breach," Barin said. "Cracks in adjoining compartments, in Environmental. We were trying to save the growth chambers. Spalled fragments had gone everywhere; we had leaks all over the place. I was so worried about the hydraulic lines, I didn't even think—" He shook his head, unable to go on.

"It wasn't your fault, sir," Meharry said. "You can't think of everything."

"Nor can you," Barin said. "I'll bet you were thinking as hard as you could, weren't you?"

"Yes, sir. But I couldn't find a way—"

"Sometimes there isn't one," Barin said. He didn't really believe that for himself, but telling himself that was getting him through the days. "Anyway, Corporal, what I'm actually here for is that we're both assigned to a team that's going back out there—to both the prison and the weapons research facility or what's left of it. Apparently the powers that be think the planet's secure enough now that they can afford the time and manpower to do some forensic work."

Meharry's jaw muscles clenched. "I . . . don't really want to go, Lieutenant."

"No, I imagine not."

"But we do what we have to," Meharry said. "When do we leave?"

"Tomorrow. I was hoping you'd help me out; I'm supposed to pick some people out of the pool of extras, and I just got out of hospital. I haven't a clue who's good at what. The forensic team's already assigned; they're specialists. There's a bunch of civilian scientists and technicians. But I'm supposed to come up with data transcription clerks, communications—support generally. You've been here for months; could you help me with this?"

"Of course, sir." Meharry took the thick stack of personnel sheets Barin handed him. "How many? And are we supplying food service support?"

"There's five on the forensic team, about a dozen civilians, and I was told that I could have as much for support as I wanted. The major said the more I could get out of his hair the better. And yes, I'm supposed to arrange food service. And all I've had here is hospital food." Barin put a plaintive note in that and was relieved to see Meharry smile.

"Let's see if—yes, here's a good cook on your list. And another. Clerks—hmmm. Koniston's always cheerful and doesn't make funny noises when he's working—" Meharry looked up and explained that. "Andersson's a good clerk, but he drives me nuts; he's always hissing or clicking his tongue or something. We don't need that in a small team. Koniston, Bunley, Mohash and . . . let's see, is Simi—no. Well . . . Purto, then. Four clerks ought to be enough. Communications . . . we should ask Ensign Pardalt, sir."

"She's the one who built that whatchamacallit to get a signal out?"

"Yes, sir. She was a junior instructor in history, I think it was, and after that they moved her into communications. She probably knows all the techs."

"I'll find her," Barin said. "I'm guessing we need a couple of techs—"

"Sir, I'd recommend four. If we have personnel on both Stack islands, we'll want a primary and backup for each team."

"Yes, of course. Do you think you can pick out the rest of what we need, and have a list for me when I get back from seeing Ensign Pardalt?"

"Yes, sir." Meharry paused, then went on. "Sir, am I supposed to be on your team, or with forensics?"

"They said they'd assigned you to me, because then you'd be handy to answer any questions."

"Yes, sir."

Barin found the communications building easily enough, but locating Ensign Pardalt took longer. She was not in her temporary office, or anywhere in the main control rooms. Finally a pivot said she was probably down in data analysis. Data analysis was in the basement.

At first he thought the young woman hunched over a stack of printouts was an enlisted tech; she didn't look up, which gave him a chance to notice the insignia before he blundered. He watched her a moment longer. Sleek red hair, hanging forward a little as she scanned the papers and tapped on her handcomp. Pale brows drawn together with intensity of concentration.

"Excuse me," Barin said. "I'm looking for Ensign Pardalt."

She looked up, and blinked at him a moment, then flushed and pushed back her seat to stand. "Sir, sorry . . . I'm Ensign Pardalt."

"I'm Jig Serrano," Barin said. "Sorry to interrupt you, but I need some advice."

"Advice? From me?" She looked almost scared.

"Yes," Barin said. "I'm supposed to assemble a support team for a trip out to the Stack Islands, and I need the names of some decent communications techs. Corporal Meharry suggested that you might know who on this list would work best in a situation like that." He held out the list.

"Oh . . . well, I don't know them all . . ." But she scanned down the list; he recognized total concentration and said nothing more.

"How many?" she asked.

"Four or five," Barin said.

She rattled off four names, marking them with her stylus.

"Thanks," Barin said. "May I ask what you're doing?"

"Trying to figure out who disabled the weather satellite so that no one saw the *Bonar Tighe*'s troop shuttles approaching the Stack Islands," she said. "The problem is, MetSat IV had been acting up for a couple of years. So it could have been just a random glitch—"

"Convenient, though," Barin said. "The previous acting up could have been cover for this."

"Yes. But I can't think of a way to prove or disprove that."

It sounded tedious enough to him. "I don't suppose you'd like to come along on our little jaunt?"

She looked alarmed. "Not really, sir, but of course if you need me . . ."

"No, that's all right. I'm just glad I don't have your job."

CHAPTER TWELVE

R.S.S. *Indefatigable*

Heris Serrano had a few days' peace while Seabolt thought of some other nonsense to obsess over. So far they'd been lucky; no mutineer had attacked them, and they'd detected no sign that one had passed. She was working on another drill schedule when she got a call from the bridge.

"Captain, I just wondered . . . what if an ansible transmits a pre-message alert, but then no message?" Jig Hargrove, the junior officer on communications this shift, had an earnest face that turned even the simplest question into Something Serious.

"What do you mean?" Heris asked.

"You know how—" Heris winced; all the junior officers had picked up Seabolt's habit of starting every explanation with that phrase. "—how an ansible sends out an ID and clear-channel blip before sending a message?"

"Yes," Heris said. "And the following message will be delayed by the time it takes the ansible to return a 'ready' message to the originator, and the originator's message to arrive."

"Yes, so we expect a lag, up to about four hours, between the initiation sequence and the message. But I've been waiting almost the whole shift for a message, and nothing's come through. And Commander Denehy said to report anything out of the ordinary. I just don't know if this is."

"How long, exactly?" Heris asked.

"Six hours, eighteen minutes. I guess it could be a ship that's farther than three light-hours from the ansible, but most people don't try to raise one until they're a lot closer than that."

"What's the ID? Why do you think it's a ship?"

"Well, this is the system—" Hargrove held out a description. "It's got no inhabited worlds, and no permanent settlement, though there's a research station on that eccentric planetoid. I suppose it could be that."

"I suppose," Heris said absently, looking at the system specs. "One mapped jump point, but only a yellow rating . . . oh, because of the planetoid. What are its backjump stats?"

"Sorry, Captain—I don't know. Just its com status."

"Commander de Fries—" The senior navigation officer looked up. "I need a backjump analysis of these coordinates—" Heris flicked them to his screen.

"Right away, Captain."

Heris turned back to Jig Hargrove. "Does that ansible have reversible scan capability?"

"No, Captain. The note on it in the catalog says it's just a single-channel model, for the use of the research station. It's not even very secure; its access code is in all the updated files. Anyone could have tripped it—though I suppose it could have been just damage."

"Captain—" That was de Fries.

"Yes?"

"Backjump analysis: because this isn't considered that stable a jump point, the only mapped one-jump location is CX-42-henry—"

"That's one of the one-to-go points for Copper Mountain," Heris said.

"That's right, Captain. Copper Mountain is the nearest two-jump outlet, estimated FTL time eleven days, and that's due to the short leg in from CX-42-henry. There's a notation that successful jumps were made to the vicinity of RG-773-alpha, but there weren't enough to qualify for a mapped route. Estimated FTL time on that one is nineteen days. Some of the scientists considered it a more direct route to their home systems, over in Sector Five."

"I suppose it would be," Heris said. "Do you have any data on that system which would tell us how far that planetoid is now from the ansible? How long a lag there might be between an initiating signal and the following message?"

"I'll work on it," he said.

Heris felt a prickle of excitement down her spine. What could trigger an ansible besides a signal? And why would someone start to signal and then fail to carry it out?

Because someone stopped them. They changed their minds. Someone stopped them.

"If a loyalist Fleet vessel . . . or a civilian ship . . . found itself in trouble with mutineers, they might try to signal, and be blown away before they could," Heris said softly.

"Yes, and a flying rock could have hit it," de Fries said.

"We need to go look." She was as sure of that as of two plus two.

"We're on picket duty. The admiral said we're to interdict mutineer travel, watch the jump points—" Seabolt, naturally, would take that view.

"I am watching a jump point," Heris said. "I'm watching a jump point around which suspicious activity has taken place."

"I don't think you can call a malfunctioning ansible suspicious activity."

"Commander, do you have any idea how reliable those things are? How rarely they malfunction? And when they do, it's something like sending a string of gibberish, not turning themselves on for no reason."

"But—"

"I say it's suspicious, and I'm the captain . . . and the commodore." And the great panjandrum with the little round button on top, too, she thought to herself. "I'm going to inform HQ, of course—only an idiot rushes off without leaving word behind—and the next question is whether to go in with all the force available—or send in a scout."

"A scout would be safer," Seabolt said.

"For us, right now, maybe. But just supposing there is a mutineer force in that system, and someone tried to tell us and failed. All a scout could do is alert them that someone knows their location. Similarly, if I take in one ship and it's not enough to defeat them . . . that's worse than not going at all."

"You wouldn't take all—everything—" Seabolt sounded like a supply sergeant, she decided.

"They didn't give me this many ships to just sit here being a target," Heris said. "I want a tightbeam to the ansible and a secure code for transmission to headquarters."

R.S.S. *Bonar Tighe*, now mutineer flagship

Cecelia swallowed against the rise of sour bile in her throat. It had seemed like a good plan; it *was* a good plan. It was the only plan . . . but she felt more tension than before the start of a big event. Worse than riding down to a huge fence on a headstrong horse.

It was just the same. She could be hurt, she could die, but she'd rather die doing this than live without doing it—right?

Talking firmly to her fluttering stomach, she went on mopping the guards' latrine; Miranda was behind her with the brushes, the bottles of spray cleaner. She felt for the bucket with her heel, without looking. On the next forward stroke with the mop, she pushed too hard, stumbled forward, lurched back, and knocked the bucket over.

"Nooo!" she cried, whirling around and grabbing for it. "No, I didn't mean to—I'm sorry—" The end of the mop almost hit Miranda, who fended it off by grabbing it one-handed; Cecelia scrabbled for the bucket and picked up the bottle of spray cleaner Miranda had dropped.

"You *idiot!*" the guard said, starting to laugh. "I knew you were clumsy, but—"

The end of the mop caught him in the solar plexus; Miranda's lunge with a mop was as perfect as with a foil, and he folded around it with a whoof of outrushing breath. Cecelia gave him a spray of ammonia-based cleaner in the face as he tried to gasp for his next breath. He gasped, choked, wheezed—and she had smashed his trachea with the handle of the glass scraper. Behind her, she heard sounds she interpreted as Miranda taking down the guard in the kiosk—a potent thud, another gasp and gurgle. She grabbed her guard by the arm and dragged him toward the cells—they needed his fingerprint for the cell locks—while Miranda inserted the other guard's keycard and used his fingerprint to hold the brig access open.

"That was fast," Chief Jones said, as Cecelia panted around the corner, yanking at the dead weight of the guard.

"Nothing ventured, nothing gained," Cecelia said. She pushed the body up to the bars. "Here, help me lift him—he must be wearing lead." Arms reached through the bars to lift the dead weight up, until she could insert his finger in the ID slot.

The bolts slid back with a solid clunk, and Cecelia pulled the cell door open.

"Donaldson, you and Kouras get the other cells open. Tiraki and Dirac, go help Miranda at the kiosk—see if you can set overrides. If not, we're going to have to take their fingers. Send Miranda back to help Markham."

Cecelia swallowed and tried not to look shocked. She understood the problem but the very thought of cutting parts off the dead revolted her.

"Cecelia, you brief the other cells on the chemicals stored in this section."

She almost said "yes, sir." Already, other prisoners were emerging cautiously from the other cells around the corner—men with straggly beards under their shaven heads, women whose hair was just growing out.

"This is our mission," Chief Jones said. "First, we get word out to Fleet about this ship in this location. Second, we do our best to disable this ship, by going EVA to damage or destroy its scan domes, its communications masts, and its FTL nodes. Third, we try to escape. We need an EVA party, a communications party, and a decoy/distraction party who will run around making as much noise and trouble as possible while heading for plausible targets. I've had EVA experience and so has Petty Major Sifa—who else?" Hands raised, and she nodded.

"Fine—I'll take all of you. We already have Tiraki, Dirac, and Donaldson on the communications party—any other senior com techs?" No one answered. "I want two or three good scrappers with them—who—good, you and you." She glanced around. "The rest of you, divide into two groups, one with Petty Light Kouras, and the other with Petty Light Hartung. They'll brief you on the run—we don't want to sit here jawing until they figure out something's wrong."

"What about the civs?" one of the men asked, staring at Cecelia and Miranda.

"We wouldn't be loose if it weren't for them," Jones said. "They've already chosen which party they'll be in." She grinned at Cecelia. "Cecelia here wants to see the stars from outside, and Miranda's going to keep an eye on Anseli with one of the distraction groups." She paused a moment, but no one asked another question. "All right, people. Let's move."

The brig area was at one end of the barracks area, with only one exit to the rest of Troop Deck. On their way out, the escapees emptied the shelves of the lockers available: three bottles of spray cleaner, two mops, two brooms, and a squeegee. One stuck the canister of toilet bowl cleaner in his pocket. They had the guards' weapons, the canister of riot spray from the kiosk, and the guards' gas masks and filters—a total of four. They had the little repair kit from under the desk and the damage control locker contents. Hammers, prybars with one end pointed and one flat, tubes of adhesive and dispensers that looked, to Cecelia, very much like something builders used to caulk windows. Chief Jones had explained how they'd use them—and they'd ransack every damage control locker they passed. Rope, wedges . . . soon they looked, Cecelia thought, like a combination of mountain climbers and repairmen.

At this time of day, the four nearest squad bays were always empty. Cecelia and Miranda went out to scout, carrying mops, buckets, and cleaning supplies as usual, with two of the men pretending to guard them. They made it to the first lavatory, where they could see down another empty corridor and wave the rest forward.

The men took a few minutes to depilate their faces, making them look more like the beardless mutineers; the women could do nothing about their hair, but—as Chief Jones said—"It's grown out a little, and from a distance we might be taken for men. Some of us, anyway. And you, Cecelia, if we get you into a uniform . . ."

Uniforms they could find, in the squad bay lockers, along with a variety of other useful objects: personal knives, ration bars, more gas masks, and p-suits. Miranda, in uniform, looked as perfectly groomed as in her usual expensive silks. Cecelia looked rumpled; she glowered at her mirrored image.

"How do you do it?"

"Do what?"

"Look like that. D'you have a spell you put on cloth, so it won't wrinkle when it's on you?"

"No—I don't know how it works. It just does."

Once the groups separated, Cecelia quickly lost track of the turns, the ascents and descents, through unmarked passages. She struggled to keep the coil of rope she'd been given from falling off her shoulder, and the several tubes of adhesive tucked into her "uniform" poked her uncomfortably. How did they know they were going the right way? Yet Chief Jones hardly hesitated, moving with swift silence.

They came out into a little room whose far side curved noticeably. The hull? Cecelia shivered. She had volunteered for this, but now that she saw that curve, the reality of what she was about to do struck her cold. Chief Jones was already slapping squares of stickypatch to the overhead and bulkheads. It made no sense to Cecelia, but she didn't ask—Jones always had a reason, whatever it was. After another two patches, Jones grinned at her. "Blanking the sensors. Buys us some time." One of the men had already carded the suit lockers. These EVA suits were heavy-duty models, intended for hours of use outside, with their size color-coded on the left shoulder. Jones quickly sorted them into a sequence of sizes and started them into their suits, tallest first.

Cecelia was third; she stepped into the open lower legs, and someone behind her lifted the back of the suit, until she could work her arms into it. Then it wrapped around to overlap the front section. Chief Jones checked the lower seals, helped seal the helmet, and then loaded the dual air tanks which should supply four hours of air. She attached Cecelia's load of rope, tubes, dispenser to the suit exterior, and waved Cecelia to one corner, while the rest suited up, working in pairs. Then came the tedious business of working through the small airlock, one at a time.

Cecelia had no idea how big a cruiser was, and seeing the outside didn't really help. Its surface, matte black, looked as if it had been cut out of the starry expanse or as if it were a cave, rather than an object that rounded *out*. Worse than that was the sudden loss of gravity— outside the ship's hull, the artificial gravity had no force. She felt disoriented, and was very glad of the safety line clipped to a ring on a stickypatch outside the hatch. As she'd been told to do, she followed the line from one clip to another, around a dull black plain that fell away from her in all directions. Suddenly she saw something different—something glittery.

Chief Jones' directions had been clear: if it sticks up, break it off; if there's a hole with something in it, glue it up. Cecelia stared at a transparent flattened dome with what looked like an array of daisies under it. It wasn't exactly sticking up, but she couldn't see how squirting glue at it would damage it. Something tapped her arm, and she jumped. Another figure, pointing at the dome. It held a large hammer in one hand and very slowly leaned over to put a pair of stickypatches on the hull beside the dome. Then it stepped onto the stickypatches and swung the hammer.

Cecelia had never really paid attention to gravitational effects before, and had certainly never wondered what happened when someone in zero-G performed a violent maneuver. As the person beside her swung down with the hammer and the hammer cracked the dome, its feet tore away from the stickypatches, and it rotated overhead, feet describing a broad arc, and hammer swinging away from the dome toward Cecelia. She grabbed for it automatically, and the other person's momentum rotated around this new center, wrenching her shoulder. Then the person bounced off the hull and rotated back the other way. One foot caught on a stickypatch, and the inertia rotated his body around the long axis this time.

Finally the wild gyrations damped, and the figure tapped Cecelia's arm. She presumed it was a sort of thanks. Then, very carefully, the figure knelt, and hacked at the cracked dome. This gave access to the delicate floral shapes of the sensor heads themselves. The petal shapes came away easily . . . the other figure went on to another dome, leaving Cecelia to peel them out one by one. It was ridiculous . . . it was like the childhood game of plucking petals from a sunflower and counting out the answer to some childish questions. "They find us . . . they find us not . . . .they kill us . . . they kill us not . . ." *Not*, according to the last of the petals she tossed away. She took her dispenser of adhesive and squirted globs of it over the ends of the stalks to which the flowers had been attached. According to Chief Jones, this would make repair very difficult indeed.

Cecelia wondered, if this ship were ever found, what some repair dock would say about the damage they were doing. She, a taxpayer, was costing herself a lot of money, probably. It didn't seem important enough to worry about for long. She decided that if she survived this, she would not prosecute herself for wasting taxpayers' money—she would cheerfully pay more to repair whatever damage she was doing, so long as it kept her alive.

She looked around and noticed a metallic stick protruding through the hull covering a short distance away. She started to move toward it and her tether caught her short. She almost unclipped before remembering the person she'd caught and saved. Instead of unclipping, she added a length to her tether, carefully, and made her way over to the stick. It seemed shorter, and, as she watched, it crept down past her waist toward her knees. She gave it a whack with her glue tube, and found herself hanging by her tether. That didn't work . . . she pulled herself in until she was clinging to the last attachment point. Then she thought to squirt more adhesive around the base of the rod; when it slowed, she formed a large glob on the tip. The stick didn't move; she hoped it couldn't.

Cecelia had no part in the assault on the shuttle bay—Chief Jones had put her around the hull curve and told her to lie flat. She had the pleasant task of watching her oxygen level crawl down as time passed, while she wondered what was going on a meter below her and all through the ship.

The others of the outside team, she knew, were surrounding the shuttle hatch, where they hoped the mutineers would come out to save the rest of the FTL nodes from gluey destruction. They seemed confident that they could disarm such a group and steal a shuttle of some kind, and Jones had promised to pick her up. It seemed a meagre chance to Cecelia. As she had faced reality in those long months of apparent coma, she faced it now—she would probably be dead in a few hours, her long life over.

She would like to have known if Ronnie and Raffa were doing all right . . . what Brun was up to . . . if Miranda could possibly get that girl Anseli out safely . . . but life wasn't always cooperative, and she expected to die without knowing. At least they'd had a chance and she'd bought them that. She reflected a moment on the irony of someone widely renowned as selfish having humbled herself for all those weeks just to have a chance at breaking some others out of jail.

She lay trying to rest easy and conserve her oxygen, as Chief Jones had recommended, and almost dozed off in the peaceful dark silence, when a faint vibration in the cushiony hull covering roused her. Was it over? Had they already extracted a shuttle, and was someone coming to retrieve her?

She opened her eyes to look without moving, and saw dark shapes against the starfield moving toward her. Odd. They were coming from the wrong direction. She lay very still, reviewing in her mind the exact sequence of movements that had brought her here . . . yes, *that* way lay the shortest route to the shuttle bay, and *this* way led around the circumference of the ship . . . but no one was supposed to be coming that way. All the other personnel hatches had been glued shut. Hadn't they?

The cutouts enlarged, changed shape, and finally her eyes adjusted to the perspective and she realized they were almost on her. They held weapons . . . real weapons . . . they had to be the mutineers, and they'd come up behind her friends . . .

Without even thinking, she pumped the glue gun and took careful aim at one target, then another. First the leader's rearmost foot, a half meter from her head, adhering to the hull so that he lurched forward, off balance . . . she got another's arm as it brushed past his side.

Inside the ship, Miranda watched Anseli with a satisfaction limited by the knowledge that they'd both probably be dead in a few hours. She had been able to help the girl, to bring her out of that listless, terrified submission that was worse than death . . . it was satisfying to be able to do for Anseli what she had not been able to do for Brun. Compensation, and she knew it, was fully conscious of it. That didn't make it less real, or less valuable to Anseli.

But the girl was nothing like Brun. Now that she was too far away to explain to Brun, or apologize, she saw that the daily irritations of living with a young genius had blinded her to what Brun really was. Anseli, so different, brought it home.

Brun had that reservoir of vigor, of sheer vitality . . . Anseli needed to feed on the vitality of others. Brun's mind sparkled, raced, with a thousand bright ideas—most of them impractical, many of them foolish or dangerous, but the dazzling coruscation was, in itself, entertaining and struck sparks off other people.

Anseli was not exactly stupid, but she was so rule-bound that Miranda even had to argue that it was all right for them to escape—and she had not relaxed and been truly willing until one of the petty officers reminded her of the regulation which made attempts to escape from an enemy a duty, and had led her, step by laborious step, through the reasons why the mutineers were lawful enemies.

Miranda rued all the times she had wished Brun were more down-to-earth, more persistent. When she got home—if she ever got home—she promised herself that she would take her wild, insouciant daughter into her arms and admit she'd been wrong, from the beginning. How had she ever been so stupid as to think that Brun could be put in such a harness as would suit Anseli perfectly? Why hadn't she realized where Brun's genius lay—and that it was a genius, not an aberration?

And why had she let herself ignore, for all those decades, the same genius in herself—why had she pretended to be the sedate, serene Miranda, the beautiful wife and consort, and not admitted even to herself the piratical nature, the crackling energy, which she'd inherited in full measure from her own family.

At least Brun was free to run her own life now. At least that much had been saved. She glanced at Anseli's taut, anxious little face and sighed inwardly. And she would save this one, too, if she could, to live out her own much more limited destiny. Poor thing. Free and cosseted, she would never be a tenth what Brun was . . . she taunted herself inside for that maternal burst of pride, then pushed both pride and taunt away. Her own children were fine people—she let herself linger just a moment on the memory of each face, as a child and as an adult, then locked those memories deep. In the next hour or so would come her last chance, it might be, of mothering anyone, and Anseli deserved the same fierce loyalty.

Their distraction group was headed for the engines, as if they intended to sabotage them. Miranda had no idea how that might be accomplished even if they got that far; she didn't even know what FTL and insystem engines looked like. She followed the others blindly, with a rear guard behind her, noticing that the crew—even Anseli—seemed to know how to do things that set alarms ringing and lights flashing almost every place they went. They had left a trail of broken glass, smashed cabinetry, locks pried open, lighting units darkened.

They had been attacked twice, but by gluing shut the doors behind them, their pursuers had been slowed and finally foiled.

Now they were in a maintenance passage of some sort. The crewmen had done nothing for the last ten minutes but now paused where another passage joined theirs. One of them had opened a hatch in the overhead, and pulled down a folding ladder.

"Where *is* this?" Miranda asked.

"Aft communications nexus," Petty Light Kouras said. "Another one of those things they could rebuild to communicate with, if we left it untouched. Pivot, pass up that tool kit." Anseli passed it forward. Kouras led the way up the ladder into a dark crowded space full of more incomprehensible shapes. When they were all jammed in, she turned on her headlight. "Miranda—glue us up." Miranda and Anseli pulled up the ladder, then the hatch, and sealed its edges with a glue gun.

Under Kouras's direction, they clipped lengths out of all wires and cables, making them too short to rejoin, and then turned the ends back and glued them into knobbly masses. "Some of this is probably also navigation stuff," Kouras said. "Doesn't matter . . . whack it all out." A few minutes later, she led them between long cylindrical shapes to another folded ladder. But when she tried to open the hatch, it wouldn't move.

"Locked?" asked one of the men.

"No." Kouras pointed her headlamp at the seam between hatch and deck, where the telltale bubbles of yellow sealant were still glistening. "They're using our tricks now."

"We have solvent," one of the others reminded her.

"Sure. And we can walk right into a trap that way. Let me think a minute."

Miranda sat back against one of the long shapes—rejuv or no rejuv, her back was aching from the crawling and stooping and she would like to have had a long nap. Suddenly Kouras moved again.

"They've got the shuttle bay open . . . let's go!" Kouras urged them faster. Miranda wondered if the mutineers knew that the groups aboard would try to get to the shuttle bay—surely they would—and where they might try to intercept them. She still didn't understand the ship's layout well enough to predict that, but she trusted that Kouras took that into account. Certainly their route seemed circuitous enough. In this hatch and out of that, up into the space between decks, then back down . . . she was completely confused, and would not have been overly surprised to find herself dropping cleverly back into their cell in the brig.

But at last she saw the warning signs on the bulkheads: SHUTTLE BAY AIRLOCKS: EXTREME CAUTION topped by a row of red status lights. To either side were personnel airlocks, one with a green light and one with red.

Then she saw the bodies lying sprawled like piles of old clothes being sorted for the wash . . . except for the blood, bright as Pedar's blood, on the polished deck. And the men and women in uniform, with weapons, across the compartment from them . . . but surely that was Hartung . . . ?

"Hurry up, we've got to get suited up!" It was Hartung; Miranda's heartbeat steadied again.

"Perimeter?"

"Holding for now. Come on!"

The EVA suit lockers inside the shuttle bay held most of the suits; normally anyone using the shuttles would be aboard before the hatch opened to vacuum. Three of Hartung's people had suited up in the only suits left inside, and gone through the locks to bring back enough for the others. Each could fit only four of the bulky suits at a time through the personnel locks, and fewer than half of Hartung's group were now out in the shuttle bay helping the outside group break into and activate a shuttle. The red light on one lock turned green, as the one on the other turned red, the hatch opened, and four more pressure suits tumbled out, to be grabbed and donned as fast as possible by the crew nearest the lock. Then they crammed into the lock and cycled through. The second lock disgorged another four suits.

"Go on," said Kouras. "I'm senior."

"Good luck," said Hartung, struggling into a suit along with the last of her group.

"Vallance, get that suit on," Hartung directed one of her people. She waved as the others pushed into the lock, and sent four of her group to the other lock, which would cycle next.

"Comm crew coming!" yelled someone from the left-hand corridor. "Open up for 'em."

But only two remained, dragging one wounded who turned out to be dead. Kouras's first four suited and exited, then the first lock opened again. She put the comm crew into suits, then—as she turned to point to the next to go—they heard screams from the corridors, hardly understandable but clear enough even without words. "Too many—perimeter's gone! Go!!"

Kouras's heartfelt expletive was calmer than that. Then she nodded to the two men who had already volunteered to be rear guard. "Give us every second you can, and thanks."

That left her, and Anseli, and Miranda. "You and you," Kouras said. "I'm staying."

Miranda's head cleared. "No," she said. "I'm staying."

Kouras's face twisted. "I don't have time to argue with any idiot civ—get in that suit."

"I got you out—I earned this," Miranda said. "You know I can kill—" She wrenched Kouras's weapon away and shoved her toward the suits. "Take care of that kid."

"Miranda . . ." That was Anseli. Miranda gave her a look she hoped mirrored the petty officer's.

"Do what you're told, Pivot. Don't waste this."

She had the weapon, she had the target . . . she had the chance to be someone she had never allowed herself to be. Flattened to the bulkhead, waiting for the enemy, she felt supremely happy, and very much in touch with her lost children and the love of her life.

Cecelia's luck ran out before she had completely immobilized the patrol. A flechette holed her suit; the automatic setfoam shut off the vacuum leak, but before she could do anything, another mutineer's riot weapon wrapped her in tangletape. He held the trigger down until she was entirely covered and motionless, then she judged by the nauseating rotation that they were using her for cover as they advanced on the loyalists by the shuttle bay.

The rotation went on and on; she willed herself not to vomit in the suit and tried to pretend she was jumping a series of no-strides with her eyes closed for some reason. It seemed an eternity before the rotation stopped.

Cecelia woke up to find herself being yelled at by someone from a great distance.

"CAN YOU HEAR ME?"

"I can hear you," she said, not in the mood to shout back.

"She's awake," came more quietly. "Get the rest of that stuff off her suit . . ."

"What stuff?" asked Cecelia, then she began to remember. The fall out of FTL, then the capture, then the mutineers' ship, then the attempt to escape. "I hope you're the good guys," she said. Someone chuckled, and it was a nice chuckle.

"Well, we think so." Definitely Chief Jones. "We're in a troop shuttle, off the ship . . . but we have a little problem."

"Oh . . . ? Is Miranda all right?"

A silence that lasted a beat too long, then Jones' voice again. "No. She refused . . . they were one suit short."

"She got Anseli out, didn't she?" asked Cecelia. She could just see a blur of light swiping back and forth across her suit's faceplate, as if someone were cleaning it of the opaque glue.

"Yes. And told Kouras to get out, and Kouras did."

"Good decision," Cecelia said. "Can you get me out of this suit?"

"Once we get the tangle stuff off it."

Cecelia emerged from the confines of the suit feeling as sweaty and dirty as if she'd just ridden a major event. The troop shuttle's interior looked stark and unpromising—a long open space with racks along the sides for weapons and suits and other equipment she didn't recognize.

Several of the survivors of the breakout were wounded, propped on pieces of suit, being tended by their fellows. Chief Jones beckoned Cecelia forward.

"The problem we have, sera, is that not one of us is qualified to pilot this thing. Or any other ship. We were hoping you could, but you were so tangled up when we found you, that we didn't dare wait. We had one sergeant who had a license for a surface-to-orbit before he joined Fleet, but he hadn't passed the Fleet aptitude test and hadn't handled anything like this . . . He got us out the door, but he's unfamiliar with the navigation system and hasn't a clue what to do next. You're qualified, right?"

"For a ship like my own, yes. For this one . . ." Cecelia looked around, and bit back the suggestion that they should have asked her what she could pilot before picking a ship. "I suppose you took the one nearest the hatch," she said finally.

"Yes. There's an automatic launch, that sort of throws them out . . . this was sitting on it. So what I was hoping—"

"Was that I had somehow acquired proficiency in flying Fleet combat troop shuttles. Well . . . I suppose I can try."

"Are you sure you weren't ever military?" The unspoken *sir* hovered just off the end of that question. Cecelia grinned.

"Not me. But it wouldn't do me or any of us any good for me to sit here howling, now would it?"

CHAPTER THIRTEEN

R.S.S. *Indefatigable*

Despite Heris's sense of urgency, she took her flotilla through the intermediate jump points with all due caution, checking ansible activity along the way. Nothing more from the ansible at CX-42-h and the only word from HQ was "Proceed with caution." Heris would like to have arrived at CX-42-h in an off-axis insertion, but the erratic planetoid made that too risky. So she ordered a textbook insertion and hoped the mutineers—if they were there—hadn't had time to mine the entrance.

She missed Koutsoudas most at times like these, when insertion blur robbed her of eyes at the moment they were most vulnerable. But the scan finally cleared—it had been only a couple of minutes after all—and the navigation board came up with a perfect match for the chart, except that the erratic planetoid was a degree off from where it should have been.

"Ship?" she asked.

"One . . . masses a cruiser . . . no ID yet."

"Mutineers could have disabled the ID." No Fleet cruiser should be here; the last ansible download had given her all cruiser locations in this sector, and this wasn't one of them. "What's its course?"

"It's . . . zero acceleration relative to system, Captain." A worried note in that voice. "Drives appear to be shut down. They may be trying to lie doggo."

Thank the gods for small mercies. "Weapons?"

"Nothing lit, Captain."

"Is that the only vessel insystem?"

"The only thing that size—the search program's on . . ."

Indefatigable continued its own deceleration, in company with its companions.

"Captain, I have a tentative ID—"

"Go ahead."

"It's based on just the mass data—"

"Go ahead!"

"Well . . . it's the same class as the *Bonar Tighe*. We have to get a lot closer before I can be sure."

"Our beacon's transmitting, isn't it?"

"Yes, sir."

"So unless they're all dead over there, they know we're here, and who we are."

"If their scan's working . . ."

"Why wouldn't it be? You want to bet our lives on the notion that they have even their passive scan shut down for some reason? I don't. When will we be in tightbeam distance, Chief?"

"Forty minutes, Captain. There'll still be lightlag, of course."

"That's all right." Heris considered. If she blew them away without hailing them—which she was inclined to do—she would have to pick up debris proving they were a mutineer ship, or she'd be in worse trouble. Officially at least; being caught by surprise would be the worst. If she hailed them by tightbeam . . .

"Captain! Ansible flash!"

Here? Now what had happened at HQ?

"What is it?"

"Local origin—this ansible—and it's . . . omigod!"

"The message, please."

"Sorry—yes, Captain. It's to be transmitted to any Fleet unit querying any ansible . . . it's on a two-hour repeat. Danger Blue, Danger Blue, Danger Blue, mutineer fleet this location on 23/4— that's today, Captain—ship names include *Bonar Tighe*, *Wingate*, *Metai*, *Saracen*, *Endeavor* . . . attempting to disable mutineer flagship, execute code zero, repeat execute code zero."

Heris let herself breathe again. Someone on that ship—several someones, it would have to be—had just committed suicide, but their deaths would save many. "Weapons," she said. "Lock on to that ship—give me a solution."

"We're still too far out," the weapons officer said.

"I know. But there's some urgency. We're going to microjump closer. Any other ships in the system yet?"

"There might be—nothing as big as the other named ships—"

"They've left," Heris said. "But the loyalists don't have that information—"

"There's this little something—yes—it's really little, about the size of a troop shuttle."

Mutineers escaping a disabled cruiser, or loyalists who had managed to escape the mutineers? Either way, she'd prefer not to destroy it.

"Weapons, we want to take out the cruiser and not the troop carrier. Where's the best location? Nav, heads up on this, and prepare to microjump."

While they calculated, Heris tightbeamed her captains on the other ships and sent them out on search.

"Here, Captain," the Weapons officer and Navigations officer presented their plot.

"Do it," Heris said. "And I want a firing solution the instant we come out, and then immediate fire."

A split-second later, the screens blurred and cleared again as they microjumped. There was the blunt ovoid of the cruiser, showing no activity in drives or weapons or active scan. From this distance, they could get a positive ID: it was the *Bonar Tighe*, last reported on Copper Mountain.

Troop Shuttle Two

The combat troop shuttle was larger than the shuttle she'd taken up from the surface of Xavier that time, but the cockpit, when she reached it, looked much the same. The sergeant had chosen the right-hand seat. He gave her an anxious look as she edged past a console covered with knobs she didn't recognize and took the pilot's seat.

"You can fly this, right, sera?"

"We don't know yet. I certainly never trained in it, or anything nearly as big." At first glance the screens, buttons, dials, and controls were a confusing blur; she forced herself to look at them one by one. She recognized the rate-of-climb indicator, and then the roll-and-bank next to it, where it should be. "We're under power?"

"Yes, sera, just five percent. I didn't dare go faster . . ."

Percent power, percent fuel remaining, flying time at this fuel usage . . . all in the right relation, which meant that here—yes—would be the onboard power supply, and there would be the artificial gravity indicators and controls. Something in the right place looked like a scan screen, but it was dark. "Did you try scan?"

"No, sera—I don't know anything about scan."

So they were under power flying blind . . ."You have scan experts," she said to Chief Jones. "Get someone up here to handle scan, while I figure out the rest of this." She ignored the scan screens, found the attitude controls, and then the primary navigation system. It was off; she flicked it on, and a screen came on, showing much the same display she'd seen from her own ship . . . from a different angle, but she recognized it. There was the mass of the system's star . . . a label popped up giving its ID number in the catalog. Then another mass, then another, appeared, each with a descriptor.

Dusty Dirac spoke up from behind her. "Hey—need some help with scan?"

"We need to know who else, if anyone, is in the system," Cecelia said. "And I've got enough to do learning the rest of these controls."

"Gotcha. Do you need Pete right now, or can I switch places with him?"

Cecelia glanced over at her copilot. "Do you mind?"

"Not me. I'm way over my depth." He struggled out of his seat.

"See if you can find a manual while you're up," Cecelia said. Heris had finally convinced her of the utility of hardcopy manuals, and she hoped the rest of the military had Heris's habit of stashing useful manuals near the places they might be needed.

Dusty slid into the copilot's seat and started tabbing systems on. Cecelia ignored the results for the moment; she had to decide if she could really get this craft to go where she wanted it to.

"Uh-oh," Dusty said.

"What?" Chief Jones leaned into the cockpit.

"Something big just jumped into the system."

"Whose side, I wonder?"

"Theirs, most likely. We only just got our message out. This is probably one of their people coming to rendezvous."

Cecelia shut her ears to this distraction and located all the controls she was used to from her own runabout. Unfortunately, this craft was missing some she expected—it had no FTL drive, for instance—and had some she'd never seen before. Intended as it was for near-space work, mostly shuttling from orbit to surface and back, its fuel load was far less than she could have hoped. They certainly weren't going to leave the system in it.

"How far are we from the ship we left?" she asked.

"Oh . . . about ten kilometers. Why?"

"How far away should we be for safety if that ship blows up?"

"Blows up . . . why would it blow up?"

"Because if that's one of their allies coming in, and they can't answer—and they can't, because we destroyed their ability—it'll probably shoot them preemptively, won't it?"

Jones looked at her and shook her head. "Cecelia, you continue to amaze me. Let's see—a cruiser under fire, not returning fire, shields down . . . the fireball will be . . . we need to be a *lot* farther away."

"Their scans will still be foxed by downjump turbulence," Dusty said. "We can move *now* and they may not notice us . . ."

"Tell everybody to hang on," Cecelia said. "In case the artificial gravity does something I don't know how to fix. I'm going to go insystem . . ." She changed the ship's attitude, then advanced what she hoped was the throttle. The delta vee changed abruptly, and then increased.

"We're going *somewhere* fast," Dusty said. "Or faster, I should say."

"It's the *Indefatigable*," Dusty said suddenly.

"Can you tell if they're loyalists or mutineers?"

"They just blew up *Bonar Tighe*. I'd say that makes them loyalists."

"That could be a mistake," Jones said. "Or they may think like you, Cecelia."

"Whoever it is, they'll have scan that can pick us up, right?"

"Well . . . maybe. There's a lot of noise from the ship blowing up. If we hailed them—"

"And if they're the wrong ship, then we're in worse trouble."

"We can at least be listening," Cecelia said. Dusty turned on the receivers and the automatic tuners.

"—Shuttlecraft, identify yourself or we will fire upon you."

"Don't fire!" Dusty said quickly. "Who are you?"

"R.S.S. *Indefatigable*, Serrano commanding. Stand down your weapons."

"Weapons . . . what weapons?" Cecelia asked. "Do we have weapons?"

"Combat shuttles do, but I don't know anything about them. Maybe it's these switches—"

"Don't touch that!" Chief Jones said. "Tell them our problem."

"We don't have a real pilot aboard," Dusty said. "We don't know which switches are which."

"What do you have?"

"Well . . . a civilian who holds a surface-to-orbit license for a small civilian craft—we used the automatic launch to get out with."

"Just stay where you are—don't touch *anything*. We'll match course."

Cecelia sat back and took a deep breath. Against all odds, they'd escaped the mutineers, escaped the destruction of the ship they'd been on for . . . however many days . . . and she was still alive. Miranda . . . she did not want to let the others know how merciful Miranda's death had been.

It took hours for the *Indefatigable* to match courses and for one of the shuttle pilots aboard it to make an EVA trip across to take over and maneuver the shuttle into the other cruiser's bay. Then at last they could debark and work their way, one at a time, through the airlocks into the ship proper.

Cecelia, rumpled and dirty, saw across the compartment the compact dark woman she knew better than perhaps any other . . . Heris Serrano.

"I might have known," Heris said. The corner of her mouth twitched.

"What?"

"You . . . of course . . ."

Chief Jones looked from one to the other, alert and almost suspicious. Heris transferred her gaze to the Chief. "Chief Jones? I'm Commander Serrano . . . welcome aboard. I understand you're the ranking NCO?"

"Ranking survivor, yes, sir. Master Chief Bigalow was senior to me, but he was killed during the escape."

"Let's get your wounded to sickbay and get you all something to eat, then we'll need to hear the whole story.

* * *

The captain's office into which Heris ushered Cecelia looked nothing like she'd imagined. Blonde, fake wood, soft-focus pictures of desert scenery in peaches and tans . . .

"It's not my ship, really—I inherited it during the mutiny. This is what her former captain wanted."

"So who has your ship?" Cecelia asked.

"I don't know. Haven't had time to find out. There is a war on, you know."

"I know," Cecelia said, rubbing her bruised shoulder. "I was in it."

"Just what *were* you doing on a mutineers' ship, and how did you get from there to a combat shuttle? The last I heard, you were clear across Familias Space, having just won that horse trials thing."

"It's a long story." Cecelia sank into the soft cushions with a sigh. "It started with finding a home for Brun's children—"

"The family's not keeping them?"

"No. I took them away because Miranda and Brun were immobilized after Bunny's death—they couldn't think. They hadn't even named the boys. Anyway, I took them off to Ronnie and Raffa, who were out on this colony—" She launched into the whole story, and Heris listened without interruption, until Cecelia came to that last bit of the voyage. "So I tried to signal the ansible, but they got to me before there was time to get confirmation that it had accepted my signal . . ."

Heris nodded. "It did accept your signal—and Fleet's been watching out for ansible activity not associated with normal message traffic."

"Took you long enough," Cecelia said, not quite grumbling. Heris shrugged.

"So—then they captured you. Then what?"

Cecelia would have preferred not to give the details of everything that had happened—it wasn't so much humiliating as simply unpleasant—but Heris insisted on extracting every bit of information.

"I don't see why you need all this from me," Cecelia said at last. "You've got the others—"

"Yes, and I'll talk to them," Heris said. "But your viewpoint is unique. You were in at the beginning, with the Lepescu mess; you were involved with the crown prince and the clones; you were at Xavier. And you saw it from a civilian viewpoint—from an *old* civilian's viewpoint."

"Well, this old civilian is hungry and thirsty and tired and could really use a shower."

"I know. I'm sorry. It was imperative that I hear your story first, before talking to the others. Remember at Xavier that you had that lieutenant—what was his name?—convinced that you were some sort of covert ops person?"

"Well, you'd put me in an odd position—"

"Don't blame me—you were the one who insisted on coming up to the Station. But my point—I'd like you to do that again. I'm burdened by an Executive Officer of surpassing pedantry—no combat experience at all, very little ship experience, a born paper-pusher. But senior to everyone else, and he's driving me insane. If you could keep him busy—"

"Why not let Petris take care of him?" Cecelia asked. "He's an officer now, right?"

Heris grimaced. "Petris isn't here. This isn't my ship—I mean, not the ship I'd been on, with my crew. In the turmoil right after the mutiny, they were assigning officers to command the nearest ships, and this one was just finishing a refit. The crew is a mixed bag from a dozen other ships and the sweepings of regional headquarters. That's where I got Seabolt."

"But I'm not covert ops," Cecelia said. "I'm not military at all."

"So you say . . ." Heris said, grinning. "I'm willing to bet that even the women in that cell with you will accept the story that your life as a self-indulgent rich horsewoman is just cover. Everyone knows, you see, that self-indulgent rich women are all fools. What did they think of Miranda's trick with the mop?"

"They were impressed," Cecelia said. "But it was only fencing—"

"It was lethal," Heris said. "We stuffed-shirt military types recognize lethality as proof of competence. I will bet you that during their own debriefing, at least two of them ask if Miranda wasn't undercover military at some time in her life."

"So . . . what would I have to do?"

"Just be yourself, but drop some hints, and come confer with me from time to time."

"They'll catch me out—there's a lot I don't know . . ."

"Of course—you've been undercover. And you do know my Aunt Vida, and many useful facts about the square of the hypotenuse—"

"What?"

"Old verse, I don't know how old. It's a spoof on the education of a complete military officer. Play it by ear, Cecelia. You did before, and I'm sure you can now."

"It sounds crazy—"

"Please. If it will loosen Seabolt's tenacious grip on regulations even a little, it'll be a help."

"All right. I'll try. Anything for a shower and a meal and a long, peaceful sleep."

"Right away," Heris said.

Cecelia's first sight of Seabolt came at once; he was waiting outside the captain's office. As soon as the door opened, he gave her a cursory look and spoke to Heris. "Captain, I simply must insist that you file a Signal 42 at once."

"Commander Seabolt," Heris said, "you must meet Admiral de Marktos. She goes by the name of Lady Cecelia de Marktos usually."

Seabolt blinked. "Admiral? I don't remember that name on the admiral's list."

Cecelia drew herself up and gave him the look she would have given an impertinent groom. "Naturally not, Commander. It would not do for my name to appear on any list *you* would have access to."

Seabolt spluttered an instant, then paled. "Admiral—excuse me, sir, I didn't think—"

"Obviously." Cecelia turned to Heris. "Captain, if you'll excuse me, I'd like to get cleaned up—"

"Of course, sir." Heris touched a button on her desk, and one of the marines stationed outside her door saluted. "Take this officer to her quarters, and be sure someone has arranged clean uniforms."

"Yes, sir. What insignia, sir?"

Heris tilted her head at Cecelia, who considered quickly the pros and cons of demanding insignia to fit her newly acquired rank. "For the time being," she said, "let's leave off all rank insignia. There are advantages . . ."

Seabolt's face was a study; Cecelia repressed a giggle at the combination of indignation and avid curiosity.

"Yes, sir," the guard said.

Chief Jones, in a crisp clean uniform, looked entirely recovered from what must have been a considerable ordeal. She came to attention in front of Heris's desk; Heris waved her to a seat. "Chief, I'm amazed that you managed to hold together an effective group and get out of that brig. I'm recommending you for a commendation."

"Thank you, sir. But they're all good people, including the ones who didn't make it off. We weren't going to let a lot of mutineers get us down."

"Were all of you from the same ship, or did they combine loyalists from several ships?"

"From *Saracen* and *Endeavor* that were docked at Copper Mountain's orbital station at the same time. And two personnel were from the Station itself, but they didn't make it out."

"I'm surprised they didn't just kill you," Heris said.

"So was I. Cecelia said they were probably saving us for prey—for a hunt like that Admiral Lepescu had." Her brow wrinkled slightly. "She did say to call her Cecelia—but I suppose now I should call her Lady Cecelia?"

"It might be better," Heris said. "You may hear other things about her, Chief; she and I have been involved in a few bits of excitement before."

"Yes, sir. She said you shot Lepescu—"

"Yes. But she got one of his lieutenants on that trip."

The chief's expression was knowing. "She's not just a rich-bitch playgirl, is she, Captain?"

"Explain," Heris said.

"Well . . . she and Miranda, who was supposed to be Lord Thornbuckle's widow . . . they both *looked* like rich aristocrats. The clothes they were wearing when they were brought in must've cost a year's pay. And the way they talked, that accent. But there was something—I caught on to it that first day, and then later, when they'd come back from cleaning latrines and pass on things they'd seen . . . that's not what ordinary society ladies are like, as far as I know."

"They're not exactly ordinary," Heris said. "Go on, Chief."

"Well, the way they got us out—I already told it on tape, but I don't think I can make it as clear as I see it. You know, most of us, back when we first join, it's hard to get most of us to actually hurt someone, let alone land a killing blow. An' I didn't really expect they could do it, just hoped . . . and then both of 'em did it, no problems. We couldn't really see, from the cell, anything but Miranda with the end of the mop, but she lunged. I guess she was a fencer . . ."

"Yes. She'd won competitions as a young woman."

"She must have kept in practice. I didn't see the blow hit, but I could hear it. One of the men saw it, said it was as neat a strike as he'd ever seen. And the guards were dead, just like that, and Cecelia—Lady Cecelia, I mean—came dragging one of 'em, so we could use his finger in the cell door ID slot. No fuss, no tears . . . and Miranda, too, and besides, she had that command presence."

"Chief, you have to realize that this is not something I can talk about. You may think what you think, but you're not going to know the whole story. Just know that you've made a very good friend, someone who doesn't forget her friends."

Jones' face relaxed. "That's all right, Captain. She did more for us than we did for her, and I'm glad to be part of whatever it is, so long as it's for the service."

"It is." Heris paused for any more questions, but Jones said nothing, just sat there looking alert and professional as she was. "Now," Heris said, "we need to get all you people back to duty. This ship's got a scratch crew, some of whom have little or no shipboard experience, let alone cruiser experience, and combat. Most of the petty officers were yanked out of regional headquarters. I'd like your assessment of which of your people would be best where. If you could get that to me by this afternoon—"

"Yes, Captain. I'll get right on it."

"We have particular need of expertise in drives; I'm not satisfied with the tuning of the FTL drive, but our FTL tech is just out of school."

"Petty Major Forrester and Petty Light Kouras, Captain—both have FTL drives certification. And there's a sergeant—Forrester would know."

"That's a relief. Look, write this up—I need something in the record ASAP."

Cecelia scrubbed until even her fastidious nose couldn't detect the faintest trace of the slop bucket contents, then opened the shower door to find a complete uniform hanging in the dressing cubicle. The automatic underwear dispenser saved her from having to wear someone else's used garments, and the uniform fit well enough. She glanced at herself in the mirror, where the midnight blue made her face paler and her hair flame out against it. She looked—striking, was perhaps the best word for it.

An escort was waiting for her when she came out into the corridor.

"And you are?" she asked, unwilling to admit she didn't have a clue which of the various bits of braid and metal meant which.

"Corporal Baluchi, sir." The young woman saluted smartly. "I'm to be your escort for now."

"They have explained that we don't talk about my . . . exact position?"

"Oh, yes, sir." Baluchi's eyes sparkled. "We're not to say a word, or repeat anything you say to *anyone*."

"Very good," Cecelia said, and tried to remember if she was supposed to say anything else.

"If the . . ." there was a pause, as Baluchi tried to think of a way to address a person whose rank must not be mentioned. Cecelia came to her aid.

"For the time being," she said, "you may address me as if I were a civilian, Lady Cecelia de Marktos. That, and the fact that I'm wearing a uniform without insignia, should prevent many problems."

"Yes, sir!" Baluchi almost quivered with enthusiasm at being on the inside. "If the lady would care for a meal first—or rest?"

"Food," Cecelia said. "And I hope the others have already eaten," she added, remembering a commander's responsibility for the troops.

"Yes, sir, they have. I'm to take the . . . the lady to the junior officers' wardroom, because the senior officers' wardroom is occupied right now, though if—"

"That's fine, Corporal," Cecelia said. She felt as if she were stepping blindfolded over a pattern of trip wires.

"The junior officers' midday mess starts at 1100 hours, and it's only 1000, so you won't have any interruptions—but I'm sure they'll wait until you're through."

"Corporal, if I eat for more than an hour, I'll explode." Even as she said it, Cecelia remembered the long, leisurely, gourmet dinners of her past, including that one with Heris, early in their acquaintance. She gulped down the food put in front of her and was more than ready for the promised rest.

"Down here, sir." The corporal led her to a row of compartment doors. "Right now, we're moving things around, but you'll have this to yourself for the first twenty-four hours anyway, and one of us will be outside the door if you need anything. Right across here is the head; the showers are two down."

"Thank you, Corporal Baluchi."

Inside was a double-bunked compartment with clothes lockers. One of the bunks had a set of pajamas in her size laid out on it. Cecelia pulled off the uniform, put on the pajamas, and then realized that she'd better act the part and hang the uniform up. She found little labels pasted in the locker, making it clear which part went where.

The bed was narrower than she liked, but after the cell she found it easy to sleep . . . and when she woke she knew she'd slept too long—she felt logy and uncomfortable.

And she had no idea if military personnel ran across the hall to the head—at least she knew what that meant now—in their pajamas or dressed first. She had to have help. Heris was far too busy to tutor her, but she knew where to go.

Chief Jones gave her a careful smile. "Lady Cecelia—"

Cecelia sighed. "I suppose now we're not in jail we have to be formal? And here I was hoping you'd finally gift me with your full name."

"Gwenllian Gwalch-aeaf Jones—my parents had a passion for genealogy and kept telling me to remember my Welsh heritage—which I don't, because I don't even know what planet they were talking about. They died when I was eight."

"There was a Wales on Old Earth," Cecelia said. "It's in some of the books I've read. Then there's New Wales on Caratea. I don't know anything about it, though, except a lot of the names have double *d* and double *l*."

"Hills and castles is all I remember, and something about music. Anyway, I changed my name legally when I entered Fleet, because the recruiter had such a time with my original names, just as all my teachers and the orphanage staff had done. Parents should think of things like that when they name children. I picked my new name out of a book I'd read, with a girl hero who wasn't always fainting or cooking things for the others. Katrina; they called her Kat."

"Ah. And my parents gifted me with not only Cecelia but a string of other fancy names—I think you're right, parents should pick something nice and boring and ordinary."

"Anyway, the captain said it'd be better to call you Lady Cecelia, not just Cecelia, so—"

"That would be fine," Cecelia said, "except for one little complication."

"And what's that?"

"Heris Serrano and I have known each other for years; we've been through some difficult times." This was harder than she'd thought it would be. "At times, it's been handy to pretend that I was actually in the military." Jones just looked at her. Cecelia went on. "In covert ops, you see."

"And you're not?"

"It's . . . hard to explain."

"You don't have to explain; the captain gave me a hint."

"I need to explain this much. Heris is having a little problem with someone and needs me to be an admiral."

Jones' mouth twitched. "Naturally . . ."

"It wasn't my idea," Cecelia said. "The thing is, I don't know how to be an admiral. I mean, I know Vida—Admiral Serrano—"

"You're on first-name terms with an admiral, but you're not an admiral and you don't know how to pretend to be one?" There was a definite twinkle in Kat Jones' eyes.

"Yes. Exactly. I need a coach. For the . . . er . . . shipboard sorts of things. That I would have learned if—"

"If you hadn't been busy doing other things. Of course, sir, I'll be glad to help."

※　※　※

Cecelia caught Seabolt just outside Heris's office. Did he live there? No matter . . ."Ah, Commander Seabolt. Just the officer I wanted to see—"

"Sir!" Seabolt came to attention. "Admiral . . . er . . . de Marktos, I was wondering—"

"Commander, please. I'd like to see your JS-135s."

"The . . . er . . . JS-135s? For the whole ship?" His voice almost squeaked.

Cecelia gave him her best admiral look. Chief Jones had explained that the JS-135 was the history of each item assigned a ship: its date of service, its maintenance record, and so on. A cruiser had tens of thousands of JS-135s in the computer file, and invariably some of them were not complete.

"You are the executive officer of this vessel, are you not?"

"Yes, Admiral, of course, but—"

"Then I want to see the JS-135s. It should not have escaped you that this would be an ideal time for pilferage and misappropriation of materiel."

"Er . . . of course, Admiral. Er . . . now?"

"Commander, did someone put a sedative in your cereal? Of course, now."

Cecelia's approach to checking JS-135s was to drag Seabolt from one end of the ship to the other, pointing out items and demanding to see the file on each one. He made a couple of abortive attempts to escape her clutches, but Cecelia imagined the cruiser as a badly run training stable, and was having fun finding the mice in the feed room—or the Fleet equivalent. Thanks to Chief Jones, she had enough of the administrative vocabulary down to convince Seabolt that she was, after all, a real admiral, though a capricious and difficult one.

When she felt hungry again, she insisted that he eat with her. "I can see," she said, "that I have a lot of work to do here, Commander, and I will require your personal assistance."

"But, Admiral, I have other—"

"I'm sure Commodore Serrano can cope without you for a while," Cecelia said, invoking an admiral's right to interrupt. "And you are, as you know, responsible for the disposition of all furnishings and munitions . . ."

"Yes, Admiral." Seabolt looked harried, as well he might, but still knife-creased. Cecelia eyed him as she ate, and wondered if she could make him crawl through some grimy tunnel—if she could find anything grimy on Heris's ship. She had not missed the glances some of the crew sent their way, wicked delight in seeing Seabolt being harrassed by someone else.

After the meal, she kept him busy again—he was, despite his trim appearance, not as fit as she, and he was puffing long before she felt tired. She paused, between decks, and gave him a minatory look. "Commander, it's important for officers to maintain physical fitness. You shouldn't be out of breath just from running up a few ladders—"

"Sorry, sir—"

"I'll try to moderate my pace—" Cecelia set off sedately, scolding herself inwardly for taking such delight in making him miserable. Was she as bad as the mutineer guards? She hoped not. In the spirit of reform, she inquired seriously into his diet and most recent health checkups. "I'm sure it's hard," she said, "with all the work you do, but you won't be much use in combat if you're sick or unfit. You must learn to take care of yourself."

"It's my bad ankle, sir," Seabolt said. "I broke it a few years ago—"

"Oh, ankles," said Cecelia, who had broken both at one time or another. "The best thing's exercise, and lots of it." She explained, at length, everything her physical therapists had told her. "Now if you ever blow a shoulder—"

Seabolt looked green; she took pity on him.

"Never mind; you can worry about that if it happens. Now tomorrow, we'll finish up the JS-135s and make a start on correlating those to the ship's table of organization—"

"Yes, Admiral. What time?"

"I should be ready to start by 0700," Cecelia said. "We have a lot of work to do."

She slept well that night, and woke full of more ideas for things Seabolt could do for her.

Heris had plenty to do without worrying about Seabolt, and noticed his absence only occasionally, with mild relief. She had actually been able to organize a search for useful debris from the *Bonar Tighe* without his interference. She had prepared a packet for the ansible, and had the patrol craft out mining the jump point; the next mutineers to pop in had a nasty surprise coming. Major O'Connor, the third officer, had taken over the executive officer's functions so seamlessly that Heris didn't notice.

Ten days later, Seabolt was in her office again. Heris noticed that he looked pale and uncomfortable.

"What is it, Commander?" she asked.

"I'd like to request a transfer, sir."

"A transfer? In the middle of a war?"

"I know, sir—it's most inappropriate, but—I think I'm losing my mind."

"Seabolt, if this is some kind of joke—"

"No, sir; I swear it's not. It's—I just can't keep up—she always has something else, every second—"

A glimmer crossed Heris's mind. "She?"

"The admiral—Admiral de Marktos."

"She's bothering you?"

"Not bothering—not exactly. But she's on me every second, question after question, and you know, Captain, when we got this ship we didn't have time to check it out completely. My stomach's burning, my eyes—"

"Go down to sickbay and get some antacid, Commander. You have your stresses in this war and I have mine."

"But sir—"

"Tell you what, Commander; if you want off the ship at the next station, I'll find a way to reassign you. But all I can do now is ask the admiral to let up on you a little. And if I do that, she'll be down on *me*. I have a flotilla to command and mutineers to find. I'm afraid you'll just have to stick it out."

"Yes, sir." Seabolt, Heris noticed, wasn't nearly as knife-edged as he had been.

"You might ask the admiral if she has time to see me," Heris added as he went out the door.

"You are a wicked woman," Heris said to Cecelia, handing her a cup of tea.

"Yes," Cecelia said. "I believe I am. But it's keeping him out of your hair, isn't it?"

"Just don't drive him into a heart attack," Heris said. "That would be another set of forms to fill out."

"I'll give him time to work out in the gym," Cecelia said. "But I'll want real stars at the end of this."

"If we all survive, I'll come to your promotion party," Heris said.

CHAPTER FOURTEEN

Copper Mountain, Stack Islands Three

Barin had never seen anything like the bleak dark rock that jutted from an angry green sea. It was almost enough—almost—to make him want to be back in space. The craft settled onto the landing space with a soft bump.

The wind was icy; Barin pulled the hood of his PPU up and sealed it around his face. The prison buildings looked as grim as the rock itself. Had people really lived here? Been confined here?

"I thought it was bad before," Corporal Meharry said. "But this is ridiculous. I want back in space."

"How'd you get assigned here, anyway?" Barin asked.

"I asked for it, fool that I am. You know my sister was here once. Lepescu put her in. I wanted to know what it was like, what she'd been through." He shivered, and Barin suspected it was from more than the cold wind. "Better get set up, sir, if you'll excuse me."

As the one person who had served here, Meharry knew where everything was, and went with forensics to find them quarters that wouldn't interfere with the investigation. Barin had the others unload their supplies off the transport; the scientists would fly on to the weapons research station in the same craft. Margiu, he'd noticed, was with them, and a bearded fat man talked to her the whole trip. When the transport had left, he looked around the courtyard. It looked like a nightmare setting: the cold, dark, stone walls, the barred

549

gates to the prisoner block.

He'd heard about the massacre of the prisoners who didn't mutiny, and wondered which dark streaks on the rocks might be blood.

Meharry came back out and spoke to the other troops, who started carrying the supplies inside. Barin followed. Inside the staff block, dark stone walls gave way to ordinary paint and plaster. "They're keeping us out of the officers' quarters, sir," Meharry said. "But we can use the kitchen over here; it's a better size for this small a group." Barin avoided the warning tape the forensic team were already stretching.

Organizing the outpost and making sure support ran smoothly occupied him for the first few days. The forensic team went about their business, whatever it was—Barin saw them collecting scrapings from various parts of the courtyard, and assumed that they were doing the same in cells and other buildings. Meharry disappeared for hours at a time, coming back white-faced and tense. Barin didn't want to add to his discomfort by asking more questions, and tried to find solvable problems for Meharry to work on. He ventured into the prisoners' block once himself, and came out more shaken than he wanted to admit. He'd imagined things like that in the Benignity, not here in the Familias. Not in *his* Fleet. He couldn't imagine anyone in his family putting people in those holes, no matter what they'd done.

Then Corporal Meharry asked if he'd come along while Meharry pointed out details of his escape for the forensic team.

"They threw me off from up there—" Meharry pointed. "It's a guardpost, with a good view of the inner exercise yard, and also out to sea."

"I don't know how you survived a fall like that into icewater," Barin said.

"I wasn't worried about the water," Meharry said. "Not that much, anyway. The rocks, now . . . that and the surge. But you see, sir, I knew something was coming. I'd been telling myself, if they push, jump. Use their help, get out as far as possible. I had the PPU on, y'see."

The forensic team wanted Meharry to reenact everything but that last leap. Barin felt almost sick just sitting in the first guardpost. The whole island seemed to shrink below him, leaving him teetering on a tiny pinhead. Meharry pointed out the rough path to the one from which he'd been thrown, scarcely protected from the seawind by a low row of stones on the seaward side. Despite his previous experience, Meharry started down the path as if he'd known it all his life. Barin forced himself up and followed, more slowly. He felt exposed and unbalanced, as if the great open space to his right and below were pulling at him, tugging him away from the safe path.

He slid into the lower guardpost with relief, and hoped it didn't show too much. One of the forensic team had come with him; the others were back at the high post with the recorders.

"And this is where you'd seen someone down?"

"Yes—over there." Meharry sounded a little breathless, but that could be the icy wind. Barin hoped no one would ask *him* a question.

"And the drop is—" The forensic tech leaned out, stiffened, and jerked back. "My God . . . it's . . . there are *rocks* sticking out down there. You could've been killed—"

"That was the idea," Meharry said; Barin glanced at him, and caught a flash of satisfaction on his face. He was not entirely displeased that the other man had reacted so strongly.

"Yes, but—I guess I'd better record it—" The other man brought his recorder up to his eye.

"We'd better hang on," Meharry said. "Just in case of a wind gust." He glanced at Barin. Barin did not want to get up and hold on to someone who might overbalance and drag him along. He knew that wasn't likely, intellectually, but his body—

"Good idea, Corporal," he heard himself say. He got up and took a good handful of the other man's PPU. Meharry, beside him, did the same on the other side. Sure enough, the man leaned out, shooting downward. Wind whipped at him, shaking him; Barin and Meharry leaned back. Meharry, Barin saw, was as white as he himself felt. He was the one with the right to have the shakes here, and he was doing his job.

From there, they went back to the high post, and then back across the courtyard to the main building. Down the elevator, into the storage levels. Meharry pointed out to the forensic team where he'd hidden his own supplies, where the entrance to the lava tubes was. They clambered over the broken shards of black rock, now lit by a string of lights. It looked depressing and dangerous, but after the guardposts, Barin felt much safer inside the rock than precariously balanced on its surface.

They came around a turn, through another broken segment, into the opening where Meharry had stored his raft. It faced south; thin winter sunlight speared into the sea entrance, revealing every texture of the lava—here glassy, and there scuffed and roughened. It was curiously beautiful—the black rock, the green sea beyond. The place was full of sound—the growling boom of the sea, the hiss of foam and spray, the screech of seabirds, all echoing back and forth, side to side . . . Barin couldn't really hear what the forensic team were asking Meharry.

He walked nearer the entrance. Out of the north wind, with the sun on him, it wasn't nearly as cold. He saw something on the floor and squatted to look at it. Something stringy and green, and in it, a tiny many-legged thing with a scarlet shell. He had no idea what he was looking at. Closer to the opening the noise was less confusing; now he could distinguish the originals from the echoes. The outer part of the tube slanted downward a little; he stopped there, staring out into the morning.

"If it had been daylight, she'd have nailed me," Meharry said. Barin jumped; he hadn't heard the corporal come up behind him. "I'd have been an easy target, dragging myself over that edge."

"How did you?" Barin asked. "It's slippery—"

"Suit wrist and leg grapples," Meharry said. "Push the studs there—with your thumbs—" Barin obeyed, and the bright steel sprang free.

"Some kind of special tip," Meharry said. "Supposed to stick into most anything. This rock's brittle, but I went slow."

"And in the dark," Barin said. "Did you have enhanced night vision?" He pressed the studs again and the wrist grapples retracted.

"No—guards on night duty were issued goggles, but they weren't built into the suits. And I wasn't on night duty when I went over."

Barin glanced at him. Meharry spoke in a flat tone unlike his usual voice.

"Does the water ever come up this far?" Barin asked.

"Yes, sir. This planet has a solar tide, of course, and then in storms the wind can pile it up around here. Spray gets in all the time; you probably saw that seaweed back there."

"I didn't know what it was," Barin said.

"Some kind of plant. There's lots of it out there, on the rocks right at the water line."

"It reminds me of the ship," Barin said, almost to himself.

"Sir?"

"When the bulkhead opened—standing in the dark looking out. Then it was stars, and not a sea, but . . . never mind that. How long do you think they're going to be?"

"Looks like they're through," Meharry said, looking behind them. Barin started up the tube, but Meharry didn't follow. Barin turned and went back to him; the man's face was taut with misery and some determination.

"Corporal, I know you said you didn't want to come back here— let's go back up."

"Just—just a few minutes, sir."

Barin's instincts told him not to leave; he found a smooth bit of floor and sat down. "Come on over here, then; I don't want to have to squint against the sunlight to see you."

The sunlight that flashed off the waves almost like the sparkle of an enemy's attack on shields, the brightness in the sky that was too much like the flare of the explosion.

Meharry came and sat near him, and began talking as if Barin had asked a question. "Thing is, sir—I can't trust myself—"

"Trust yourself?"

"They told you I killed Commander Bacarion, right?"

"Yes."

"Well . . . they probably didn't tell you how."

"No, they didn't." Barin wondered what was coming now.

"Sir, I—" Meharry gulped and looked away. "Being back here, it— it brings it back. It's like—it's like it's still happening. Over and over."

Barin knew that feeling, too. Meharry needed a psychnanny. Had needed one for months, most likely. But here they were, right at the site of whatever happened, with no psychnanny available and no transport out for the next several days.

"Tell me," he said.

"I . . . don't . . . know if I can," Meharry said. "And anyway, you'll—"

"I'll listen," Barin said. "I'll hear you."

"I killed her, but I never meant to. Not at first. She tried to kill me—she had the weapon—" It sounded almost impossible to Barin, that desperate struggle in the dark. "And then when I got my headlamp on, after she quit moving, I saw . . . so much blood . . . and her face . . ."

"Her face—?"

"I . . . my wrist grapples were still out, sir, and when we came to hand to hand, I just hit—and—it was all gone, sir. I—the grapples . . . just tore it off . . ." Meharry was shaking now, eyes squeezed shut, hands clenched under his armpits.

Barin reached out and gripped Meharry's arm. He wanted to say something, but he knew he had to wait.

"It's—I never thought of myself like that, sir. Someone who'd attack like that. An officer. A woman. But I did it. I can't pretend I didn't, and if I did it once . . . and then I thought of my sister, when she was in prison here. What had Methi done, what did she have to do to survive? I mean, she's my *sister*, and she . . . and I . . ."

"I met your sister once," Barin said. "On my aunt's ship. She's a fine person." She was also a dangerous killer, he was sure, but that wasn't what Meharry needed to hear right now.

"I thought of asking for a psych-out, sir. When I realized what I'd done, how evil it was. That I was just like Bacarion. But right then they needed everyone, and I thought—I hoped—I could keep it under control. Only now, coming back here, it's all right now again, just like I was afraid of. I can't—what if I do it again?"

Barin choked back the first easy reassurances, the *Of course you won't* and *You'll be fine, don't worry* that sprang automatically to his lips. Would he believe that if someone told him? Would he never again make the mistakes he'd made? He wished someone else were here, someone with more experience. Heris would know how to talk to this good man, or his grandmother. Or Esmay, what would she say?

"I guess—you understand, sir, why I'm going to have to leave—" Meharry opened his eyes, staring straight out to sea. "It's all right, Lieutenant. Just go on back up and let me sit here and think things out awhile."

"No," Barin said, putting all the command into it he could. He had lost Ghormley; he was not going to lose Meharry. "No, I'm not going to go back upstairs and let you throw yourself into the sea to die."

Meharry turned toward him, eyes wide with shock.

"If you're ever faced with another murderous mutineer commander trying to kill you in the dark, Gelan—" He saw the effect of that use of the first name. "If you ever have to fight hand-to-hand like that again, I hope you will do *exactly* what you did. If she had killed you, and completed her plans, we'd all have been a lot worse off. You didn't rip her face off"—he used the brutal term intentionally—"for any of the reasons she'd have done it. If you'd had a weapon, you'd have shot her dead, clean and quick. But you didn't."

"But—"

"And if you ever have to do it again, which we both hope you won't, I trust you will feel the same anguish you've felt since, *because* you aren't like her—like any of them. You don't take pleasure in cruelty. It was a horrible situation, and what you had to do to survive is something no decent person could be proud of—but the survival mattered. It matters now. I'm not going to let you destroy it."

Meharry still trembled, but it felt different under Barin's hand, a definite change.

"I . . . have nightmares."

"Yeah, I'm not surprised. Have you talked to the psychnannies about it?"

"No—I didn't think it was their kind of problem. I mean, it's a moral thing."

"When I was captured," Barin said, "it wasn't nearly as bad as this, but I had a rough time afterwards. Nightmares, seeing those men—"

"You were captured, sir?"

"Yeah. I was on a deepspace repair vessel, *Koskiusko*—"

"The one the Bloodhorde tried for?"

"That very one. They got some personnel aboard, impersonating Fleet personnel from a damaged ship. By the time our people realized they were imposters, they were loose in the ship. They got me when I went to inventory for some parts my boss wanted . . ." He stopped, remembering more than he wanted of the next hours and days.

"What did they—? I mean, if you want to say, sir."

"I think the worst," Barin said, "was feeling so damned helpless. They had me trussed up, dragged me around like a parcel. They killed three people in front of me, one of them a woman they raped first. And I couldn't do a thing . . . me, a Fleet officer, a blinkin' *Serrano*. I'd always thought, if something happened, I'd react well, solve the problem. And here they'd knocked me cold before I realized anything was wrong, and . . ."

"But you couldn't help it—"

"No, but that didn't keep me from feeling guilty and thinking I *should* have done something. Thing is, I got some help with all that afterwards. Didn't want to go; was sure it wouldn't work, just be a black mark on my record. Thought the nightmares and so on were just punishment for being an incompetent young twit."

"It really helped?"

"It really helped. Took awhile. Involved going into all sorts of other stuff I thought was totally irrelevant. But it did help."

"Maybe I should . . ."

"I think so. At least give it a try before you quit on it. There are always ways to die, if it doesn't work."

"There is that, sir." Meharry sat up straighter, stretched his arms. "Sorry—I shouldn't have—"

"What, bothered me? What else are jigs for?" Barin let his tone go lighter. "Of course you're supposed to bother me. It's part of my training. If you want to make master chief someday, you'll have to recognize your duty to bother young officers."

Meharry managed a shaky laugh. "I . . . can't imagine making master chief right now, sir."

"Well, I can't imagine making admiral, but given the way your family and mine tend to mature, maybe we'd better start working on it."

"Do you think . . . they all have this kind of thing to deal with?"

"Bad memories, times they feel they screwed up? I guess . . . I never really thought about it, but . . . I know my aunt does. She doesn't talk about it to me."

"No, nor Methi with me." Meharry took a long breath, then another. "Sir, thanks. I was . . . just purely desperate."

"I know. And it may come back, at least until you get some treatment. But you're a lot more than one blow in the dark, Gelan Meharry."

"And you're a lot more than one mistake in damage control,"

Meharry said, with an accuracy that took Barin's breath away. "I'll bet you did the best you could—and you were tryin' to save lives— maybe you'd have lost people anyway."

"It's still my responsibility."

Meharry cocked his head. "So tell me about it. You listened to me; I'll listen to you."

This wasn't in any leadership manual, and he was dead sure his aunt had never been in a situation like this. But he had demanded trust; now he had to give it. That much he knew, bone-deep.

"All right. There was the hull breach, aft of the compartment I was working in . . ."

"Don't they usually have a chief running that?"

"The rejuv problem," Barin said. "Not enough chiefs, too many jigs. Actually our station was up on Troop Deck, but they needed all of us. So there I was, with my team. Enough of the bulkhead between us and the hull breach had spalled off to send shrapnel through the compartment, causing a lot of damage, plus there was a leak to vacuum. When we went in, it was dark, cold, wet, slippery, and you couldn't see more'n a meter at first."

"Sounds like a bad stormy night here," Meharry said.

"What I worried most about was a hydraulic leak," Barin said. "I'd been warned about those, and sure enough, there was one. And then, whether the bulkhead would hold—it was strained, and that's where the air was going." He told the next part quickly— how they'd put up the big patch, how they'd been told to go on and check the environmental tanks.

"Did you have moles in your unit?" Meharry asked.

"No; they were sending us some moles, they said, but in the meantime we could look at gauges and read them off. We had one guy with a chemscan . . ." He stopped, swallowed. "So we rigged emergency lighting. The deck was wet, of course, and part of it was icy as well. Pressure was way down, and the temperature."

"Was the fight still going on?"

"Yeah. But we were too busy to pay much attention. What I should have known was that we had the wrong kind of chemscan; the one we had was fine for the rest of the ship, but didn't identify organics. There was a spike . . ." He went on with the rest, gesturing to show where everyone had been, and what he'd tried to do. "I couldn't move, you see. Not without moving the oxygen around—it's dispersing all the time, of course, but moving would make it happen faster. And Ghormley, he was the youngest, the newest. I didn't realize—I thought I'd convinced him to stand still, but he thought I was moving—"

"He triggered it?" Meharry said.

"He was scared," Barin said. "I guess when I turned my head away from him, he thought we were leaving him alone, but I wouldn't have—"

"Of course not," Meharry said. "If you were that kind you'd have bolted for the airlock first thing, and blown them all up." He pursed his lips. "Kid should have listened to you."

"I said the wrong things," Barin said.

"I doubt it. You kept him there longer than he'd have stayed on his own, right? An' then he panicked. In the dark and cold, knowing he was standing in something that could blow him to bits . . . I can understand that, though he was wrong."

"I couldn't stop him," Barin said. "And if I'd known what I should have about the chemscan, it wouldn't have happened anyway—we'd have known it was a methane leak right off. Two people dead, several injured, because I thought Environmental was boring. . . ."

"I guess you do know about guilt," Meharry said. "So how did you survive, standing in the oxygen?"

"Blind luck," Barin said. "I don't know, really—I was knocked cold—but they said the explosion jammed me in between a couple of tanks. I came out fine." The bitterness in his own voice surprised him.

Meharry's eyebrows went up. "Fine? A medical evacuation here, and how many hours in the regen tanks?" He blew out a long breath. "With all due respect, sir, I think if I need the psychnannies, maybe you do too."

"Maybe I do," Barin said. Now he'd let it out, he could see the resemblance to his earlier experience, when he'd felt so inadequate because he couldn't save them all. "Sauce for the goose, eh? So neither of us gets to jump into the ocean. It's a deal, is it?"

"Deal, sir." They shook hands on it; Barin had the sense that he was shaking hands on another deal, one he didn't quite understand yet.

Rockhouse Major

Captain Terakian offered to let Esmay stay aboard, but she felt she had abused their hospitality enough.

"You will stay in touch?" he said. "I feel responsible—"

"I'll be fine," Esmay said. "Whether they let me back in or not, I'll be fine. And yes, I'll let you know."

Rockhouse Major had hostelries in every style and price range; Esmay checked into a modest hotel where she could afford to stay for weeks, if need be. She put her few clothes away, grimaced at the thought of having to shop for more, and went out to find a communications nexus. There she looked up "Brun Meager" in the Rockhouse Major database, and found long strings of news stories about her, but no address. She found the address subdirectory and tried again. Restricted. Well, that made sense. She entered "Brun Meager, agent of record" and got a name she'd never heard of: "Katherine Anne Briarly." A search on that returned only a comunit number. Esmay copied it to her handcomp, moved to a secure combooth, and entered the number. A screen came up with a message: "Sorry, it's the middle of the night here. If this is an emergency, please press 0; otherwise press 1 and put a message in my morning bin."

Option 1 gave her more choices: voice, text, video. Esmay chose voice and waited until the return signal came. "This is Esmay Suiza, formerly of the Regular Space Service," she said. "I need to contact Brun Meager; I'm presently at Rockhouse Major, at the Stellar Inn, room 1503."

She wasn't even sure which time zone Brun was in—assuming she was in this system at all. She walked back to the Stellar Inn, wondering if she should have stayed aboard the *Fortune*—was she really wasting money, as Goonar had said? But the very anonymity and blandness of the hotel's rooms—the dull colors and plain sur-faces, so different from the Terakians' decor—helped her think through what it was she wanted to tell Brun, and what she thought Brun might be able to do. It seemed less practical here and now.

She stretched out on the beige-and-cream bedspread, and turned down the light. She might as well try to sleep. . . .

❈   ❈   ❈

The comunit's beep woke her from a dream about Altiplano—not Barin for once—where she had been, for some dream-logical reason, sitting in an apple tree plaiting multicolored ribbons while children sang jingles down below. She reached for the comunit and eyed the time display. Six hours after she'd come back to the room—she'd had more than enough sleep.

"Esmay Suiza?" a woman's voice said. It didn't sound like Brun, but her voice had still been hoarse and scratchy when Esmay heard it last.

"Yes," she said.

"This is Kate Briarley. Does your room have a secure comunit?"

"No—there's one in the lobby."

"Here's my day number—"

In the secure booth, Esmay entered the number she'd been given. The screen lit almost at once, and the video pickup showed both Brun—still unmistakeably Brun—and another blonde woman who looked to be a few years older.

"Esmay—what's this I hear about you leaving Fleet? Did you quit, or did they boot you out?"

"Booted me out," Esmay said, unaccountably cheered by Brun's matter-of-fact tone. "You wouldn't have heard—Barin and I got married—"

"Good for you! Is that why?"

"Yes . . . it's all rather complicated. I wanted to talk to you, if I could."

"Ah—you haven't met Kate—" Brun nodded at the other woman. "Kate Briarly's from the Lone Star Confederation, and she's been helping me out, including with security. What with the assassinations and all, we're being careful."

"That's good," Esmay said.

"But you need to come on down, so we can talk. There's a twice-daily shuttle to Rockhouse Minor, which is all civilian; lots of people take it just to sightsee, and there are excursions to the planet from there, too. When you get to Rockhouse Minor, go to section B, give the guard at the private entrance your name, and say you're expected. You'll be passed through to a departure lounge for private shuttles. No one will bother you." She turned to Kate. "Should we go up and meet her?"

"I'd let your staff handle it," Kate said.

"Fine, then. A steward will tell you when the shuttle's ready . . . let me see . . . you can catch the Rockhouse Minor shuttle in about three hours—"

"If it's not full," Esmay said. "Is it usually booked in advance?"

"Yes, but it's usually half-empty anyway. Tell the concierge—they have some pull with the transit companies. Anyway, if you catch that one, then it'll be about two hours after you arrive before someone will be there to pick you up."

Rockhouse Minor was quieter than Rockhouse Major . . . less bustling. Esmay strolled down carpeted corridors bordered by exclusive shops with window displays arranged like works of art: small, jeweled, entrancing. Here a single shoe, draped with ropes of pearls. There a scarf, behind a diamond necklace. An antique chronometer, a crystal decanter.

Section B turned out to be even more luxurious—the carpet, deeper piled, curved halfway up the bulkheads, and padded seats faced a series of aquaria, each housing a collection of rare marine life. The Lassaferan snailfish, with its elongated purple fin, looked as improbable as its name.

Ahead was a barrier in the form of a huge work of fabric art, with a guard kiosk in front of a gap in the fabric. The guard appeared to be alone and unarmed, but Esmay doubted this was the case.

"May I help you, sera?" the guard asked as she walked up.

"Yes, thank you. I'm Esmay Suiza. I'm expected." She felt silly saying this, even though it was true.

"Ah . . . yes. Excuse me, Sera Suiza, but may I see your identification?"

Esmay handed over the folder, and he checked it over. "If you would just put the fingers of both hands here . . ." She did so. "Thank you, sera; sorry to have delayed you. Go right on through."

As she passed through the opening, Esmay saw that immediately behind the tapestry was a large, efficiently-laid-out guardroom where a half-dozen uniformed personnel manned scan equipment, including a full-spec scan of the corridor she had just come down.

Ahead, in the lounge area, were more clusters of padded chairs as well as an area with tables and desks. She saw a couple of people chatting at a table . . . an older man lounging in one of the chairs . . . and no one else. She chose a chair, and sank into it. Almost at once, a green-vested steward came to her. "Would the sera care for any refreshments?"

"No, thank you," Esmay said. Whatever they served here would no doubt cost four times as much as the same food and drink somewhere else.

"Sera Meager wanted to be sure you were comfortable," the steward said. "This is the Barraclough private lounge, sera, and all refreshment is complimentary. There has been a slight delay in the shuttle; it will be several hours . . ."

She'd eaten at Rockhouse Major before she left, but that was now hours ago. "I don't suppose you have soup . . ." she said.

"Indeed we do, sera," said the steward, now looking more cheerful. By the time the shuttle arrived, Esmay decided that if she couldn't get back into Fleet, she wanted to work for someone who had this kind of life. She could easily get used to such luxuries.

The shuttle came in low over rolling hills, green fields and orchards . . . .much greener than her part of Altiplano, with no soaring mountains nearby. As the shuttle eased down, she saw a small stone building and a few groundcars, then—as it rolled to a stop—she saw two blonde women waving. Esmay braced herself for the impact of Brun's personality as the steward opened the shuttle door. Brun would have her own agenda for Esmay's visit; she needed Brun's help, but staying on track might be a problem. *I'm not here to talk about fashion,* she rehearsed mentally. *I'm here to get into Fleet.*

CHAPTER FIFTEEN

Terakian Fortune's Rockhouse Major docking space wasn't quite roomy enough for the entire pavilion, so Basil had put up only the sign and half the office segment. With the extra "crew" now helping Fleet with their inquiries, and all the Rockhouse cargo unloaded, he tried to estimate what their cubage and mass allowances were. Would any of the troupe come back? He hoped so; Goonar was grumpier than he'd been for years, muttering about lost time and wasted space—

"Hey there!" Basil looked up to see a tall, lean, square-shouldered man at the door of the office. Basil didn't like his tone. That man had been in authority somewhere, though he didn't look like the businessman his suit made him out to be. Military. Ex-Fleet? Not very ex by that settled air of command.

"Yes?" he said.

"How many passenger spaces have you?"

Basil's neck hairs stood up; he could feel the roughness on the back of his shirt collar. "Five, usually," he said. "But I'll have to check with the captain; we have a tentative reservation." He wanted Bethya back on this ship, if he had to drag her by the leg and shove her into Goonar's cabin.

"I'll take them," the man said. "Cash on the deck—isn't that what you free traders say?"

"Have a seat and I'll get the captain," Basil said.

"I'll just wait here," the man said. Basil noticed how he stood, half-concealed from the busy concourse beyond, but in position to jump either way. Basil had taken that same position himself more than once when dockside trouble threatened. He retreated to the inner door, stepped through, thumbed the call button for Goonar and came back out at once. The man had not moved, but gave him a sardonic look.

"The captain's on his way," Basil said.

Goonar, when he arrived, looked tired and depressed, but greeted the man politely, as he always did.

"Passenger space? Five cabins, but they're simple. This isn't a passenger liner."

The man gave Basil a sour look and turned back to Goonar. "Your . . . man . . . said you had a tentative reservation tying up one of those cabins. I'd like to pay cash for all of them, now."

"There was a deposit," Goonar said. Basil relaxed slightly; Goonar was going to stand behind him. "We don't renege on deposits."

"You said five," the man said.

"Total, yes. There may be five, if the person who reserved that place doesn't show up, but otherwise, there are four available. Where are you bound?"

"That's no concern of yours," the man said. "I want passage with you as far as Millicent."

"Umm. I presume your papers are in order, yours and the other passengers?"

"Of course; what do you take me for?" the man said, and Basil was suddenly sure he was lying.

"Because we don't transport fugitives," Goonar said stolidly, "or involve ourselves in politics of any kind. We list passengers on the manifest, which we provide to the Stationmaster prior to departure, just like the regular passenger lines. This is the policy of Terakian & Sons, and it is my duty as captain of a Terakian & Sons vessel to so inform anyone seeking passage with us."

The man sneered. "I'll wager you don't bother with that if it's a pretty girl."

"On the contrary, ser. The company is most particular, no matter the passenger's age or sex, to avoid any entanglements." Basil, knowing Goonar's every mood and tone, caught the tinge of study now forcing that flat, bland, almost boring voice. So Goonar had caught on to something as well.

"Well, it's no problem to me," the man said. He stretched, as if quite at his ease, but Basil knew that stretch was as studied and intentional as Goonar's bland tone. And as the man's arms went over his head to stretch, Basil caught a shadow that bespoke something under his jacket which ought not to be in the armpit of an ordinary businessman.

"Good," Goonar said. "Now our run from here to Millicent is sixteen days . . ."

"Sixteen days—! Isn't that rather leisurely?"

"We're not a fast passenger packet, ser; we're a cargo ship primarily."

"Hmmph. I've spent some time in ships myself, Captain; I . . . er . . . lost my ship when the company lost a court action—that's why I'm on Rockhouse. Sold her, they did, to pay the fines."

Basil grunted. That was a stupid lie, if it was a lie, which he was sure of: court actions were public information, and he could check it. And would.

"I know that route, Captain," the man said. "There's a way to knock several days off it . . . it'd increase your profit."

"There's a flux-bight in there," Goonar said, "if you're talking about that yellow route."

"Oh, that—that's what they tell you," the man said. "You'd never even notice it; Fleet just yellow-tagged it because they want the fast routes for themselves." Then, as if he felt it needed explanation, he spread his hands. "My wife's cousin's in Fleet," he said. "He told me."

"Well, I'm not taking old *Fortune* on a yellow route, just to save a couple of days," Goonar said. "My company'd have my ears."

Basil saw the man's hand twitch, an involuntary movement quickly controlled.

"Not even if I offered a bonus? We really need to get to Millicent faster than sixteen days."

"What can a couple of days matter?" Goonar asked. "Millicent's a bore anyway."

The man's face hardened. "It matters to me," he said. "Why isn't your concern. I'll pay extra for you to take the fast route, and I assure you the flux-bight is of no concern—I've gone that way many times myself. Not the slightest bobble."

A reddish tinge crept up Goonar's neck. "I'm not taking my ship through on the say-so of some stranger."

"Not for half again the fares? Man, that'd make your profit on the voyage by itself—"

"It wouldn't pay me for the ship if something did go wrong. You're maybe hazarding your own life; I'm hazarding my ship and my kin. No."

"Your *ship*." The man's lip curled, and Basil noticed that his knuckles had whitened as his fists clenched. Basil shifted his own weight, ready just in case. "Your ship is nothing but a fat-bellied old tramp—"

White patches stood out around Goonar's mouth. "Then I gather you won't want passage with us," he said. "Kindly clear the space."

"You—you fool!" The man turned on his heel and strode away; Basil leaned out the door to watch, as he headed on down Traders' Row.

"I reckon we should've gotten his name before we cut him loose," Goonar said. His normal color was returning. "Did he really think I'd let him send us into a trap?"

"What kind of trap?"

"You saw as well as I did that he was military. Could have been a mutineer, or just a bad 'un turned out years ago and turned pirate."

"I wonder what he wanted at Millicent."

"I wonder what he wanted on that yellow route." Goonar scowled. "If I remember correctly, there's an extra jump point in there, with about a two-hour transit. You have to make a low-vee downjump, reorient the ship . . . in other words, it's the perfect place for an attack. But that would require another ship."

"Huh. If we knew about it, maybe we could trap the other ship and get a reward."

"What we could get is dead, Basil." Goonar shook his head. "I don't like this a bit. He'll find someone to take him on that route, him and whoever he's got with him. Did you notice anything else?"

Basil poured it all out, every detail he'd noticed, from the way the man stood in the door and wouldn't sit down to the twitch at Goonar's mention of the Fathers taking his ears—

"Ears?" Goonar said. "Now I wonder . . ."

"What?"

"Basil . . . remember what Esmay said? Rumors that the mutineers were followers of Lepescu and took ears as battle prizes?"

"So . . . he *is* a mutineer."

"Might be. I suppose pirates might take ears, too. But I wish we'd gotten his name."

"We have some of his ID, anyway," Basil said. He could have laughed at the shock on Goonar's face.

"How? He didn't come all the way in, or sit down."

"No—but he did put his hands on the doorframe, and I don't think he was wearing gloves. And—since he conveniently stood in one place—I was able to reconfigure the office scans to pick him up. If you're thinking of making points with the Stationmaster, we can call up—"

"Not the Stationmaster," Goonar said. "Fleet. But do something, Bas, to protect those prints on the door . . . that fellow just might come back and smear them himself, if he thinks of it."

"Right." Basil moved to the door and glanced out. There he was again, headed their way, but stopping short when Basil appeared. Basil lounged there, putting his own hand on the doorframe, but a handspan higher than the other man's, and stared him down. This was fun. This was almost as much fun as rearranging the man's face, which he hoped to have the chance for later. If he was smashing up a mutineer, no one could object too much. Finally the man shrugged, and turned away, ducking into one of the little shopping arcades that opened onto the main concourse.

"Call now," Basil said over his shoulder to Goonar. "Your instincts were right; he was on his way back."

"I'm assuming you didn't put your hand in the same place," Goonar said.

"Not me. I've been in enough rows to know better."

"Trust you to know . . . I wonder if it fooled him. I'm putting on full security," Goonar added, and then nothing more. Basil assumed he was on the com, talking to Fleet, but no sound came through the security screen. Basil busied himself in the little waiting area outside the office, bustling in and out, carrying and stacking cartons. Assuming he was under surveillance, he managed to bump or touch the doorframe repeatedly, each time avoiding the area where the other man's hands had—he hoped—left their prints.

He was running out of ways to rearrange the same few cartons, when someone hailed him from outside the line. "*Terakian Fortune!*"

"Yes?" Basil said, turning around. Two men in Fleet uniform. Great. Now the mysterious stranger would know they'd snitched.

"Did you transport a former Fleet officer named Esmay Suiza?" the taller of the two asked loudly.

"Suiza? Why?" asked Basil, feeling as surly as he sounded.

"We're trying to find her," the man said. "I'm Commander Tavard. You know there's a mutiny on?"

"Yes."

"Well, Fleet's recalling all former officers, and offering them commissions again. Anyway—we were told Esmay Suiza was a passenger of yours—is that right?"

"Suiza of Altiplano?" That from a dockside idler. "The hero of Xavier?"

Commander Tavard's eyes rolled, and the corner of his mouth twitched. "The very same," he said. Then, to Basil, "Could we come aboard and talk to your captain? Or Suiza, if she's here?"

"She's not here at the moment, but our captain is. He may know where she's gone. Follow me." Basil flicked on the perimeter security, which wasn't by any means as good as that in the office, but would foil the idlers.

"Anything we shouldn't touch?" Commander Tavard asked, in a quieter voice.

Basil grinned to himself. So this wasn't about Esmay . . . it was the answer to Goonar's call. "Right through here," he said, opening the office door with an extravagant gesture and waving them in—the waving arm happening to protect the side of the doorframe with the prints.

"Captain," Basil said, though Goonar was already on his feet, alert. "This is Commander Tavard, come to ask us about Esmay Suiza. He says they want her back in Fleet."

"Glad to meet you, Commander," Goonar said. Basil noticed at once that the office security screen was off, and raised an eyebrow at Goonar, who shook his head. "Sera Suiza's a fine young woman; it beat me why she was discharged."

"A misunderstanding," Commander Tavard said. He nodded to the other man, without introducing him, and the man opened his case and removed the sort of equipment Basil had seen Station security use to gather evidence. "It should never have happened. But we couldn't trace her, at first. I know you listed her on your departure manifest, but quite frankly no one thought to check the manifests for general cargo vessels. The local command was sure she'd rented a yacht under an assumed name, or something."

Basil watched the shorter man apply a strip of some translucent material to the entire doorpost on the correct side, without revealing anything that could be seen from dockside. He himself stood where he could see through the narrow opening he'd left. He had to admire the cover story the commander had come up with. When the second man had peeled the strip away, sprayed it with a fixative, and coiled it neatly into an evidence pouch, Basil handed him the data cube that Goonar pointed out—a copy, no doubt, of their original scan data.

"I can understand why you'd want her back," Goonar said, "But she's not here."

"Is she coming back? Did she leave any luggage?"

"No—she told us she was going downside, to Fleet Headquarters on Castle Rock itself. I think she was hoping to get back in, somehow."

"If so, they haven't informed us yet. But I'll make a few calls and see. Oh, by the way, you might want to be on your guard for mutineers trying to make contact with civilian ships; we've had some reports of attacks that might be piracy or might be mutineer activity. You'll be getting a Fleet advisory in the next day or so, when we've refined the data, but I strongly advise you to stick to only green routes, even if you normally use a few yellows to save time. And if anyone approaches you, wanting a fast or secret passage, I hope you'll let us know."

"Of course," Goonar said, grinning at the commander. "But—I don't suppose there's a reward in it . . . ?"

"No," the commander, grinning back, managed to sound prim and disapproving anyway. "I would think your own self-interest would lead you to do the right thing. If these mutineers start robbing ships because of information they get from you civilian captains, you'll wish you hadn't been so greedy."

Goonar nodded his appreciation of that speech and launched into a suitable reply. "I don't call it greedy," he said. "I call it making a decent profit from risk, which you people don't have to worry about, with all your expenses paid for you, by taxes on me."

"I'm not going to argue with you," the commander said. "I just hope you'll do the right thing . . . or you'll regret it someday."

The two men left, trailed by Basil and Goonar; the commander turned at dockside. "If you see Suiza, please let us know. And remember what I said—"

"I'll remember," Goonar said. "You take care of your precious Fleet, and let us get on with our trading." When the two men had walked out of sight, he turned to Basil. "What a lot of pompous twits they are," he said. "As if I didn't know how to spot troublemakers myself." He led the way back into the office, and Basil followed, wondering who had been in the audience for that little playlet, and how they'd taken it.

Castle Rock, Appledale private shuttle field

"Sorry to be so secretive," Brun said. "But this second assassination has every conspiracy theorist going crazy. Even though the Benignity's claimed responsibility—"

"They have?"

"Oh, yes. Very formally, in the Grand Council. Apparently they inserted an assassin by having him impersonate a fencing instructor."

"A fencing instructor?" Esmay's mind raced, wondering why the head of the Grand Council would have wanted to learn how to build fences.

"Swordfighting," Kate said. "That kind of fencing." She grinned at Esmay. "Fooled me, too, the first time I heard it."

"So anyway, that was fantastic enough, so of course a lot of people didn't believe it," Brun said. "They thought maybe our family had done it to get back at Hobart for having my father killed."

"He did?" Esmay felt she'd somehow missed more than a month or so of time and was being yanked into the future at high speed. "I didn't hear anything about that—"

"Actually, he didn't. Not directly. It was one of his hangers-on, who hoped to curry favor with him."

"Wait—" Esmay held up her hand. "Your father was shot, wasn't he? Or was he stabbed with a sword, too?"

"Shot, yes. And everyone thought it was the NewTex Militia, only it wasn't. But Pedar—the man who had it done—gave enough hints to Lady Cecelia—do you know Lady Cecelia?"

Esmay said, "No, but I've heard of her. Who is Pedar?"

"An idiot," Brun said. "A distant relative of Hobart Conselline's and a pain in the rear. Hobart made him Minister of Foreign Affairs."

"So—if you know he did it, what have you done about him?"

Brun and Kate exchanged glances. "That's another of the difficult bits," Brun said. "My mother killed him—by accident—during a fencing match."

Esmay took a deep breath and let it out slowly. "Your mother killed her husband's murderer by *accident*?"

"That's what the report said," Brun said. "Mother's foil broke, leaving a sharp point, and Pedar's mask failed. Of course, there are people who don't believe that, either. The timing couldn't have been worse, from the family's point of view."

One failure might be accident . . . two failures made a suspicious coincidence. Esmay said nothing and waited.

"It was an old foil," Brun went on. "An antique. I don't know why they were fencing with antiques. Probably Pedar; he was like that. He thought old meant stylish."

"And then it broke," Esmay prompted.

"Yes. As near as we can tell, Pedar died several days before Hobart was assassinated—you know how it is with relative time between systems. Lady Cecelia arrived just after it happened."

Another handy coincidence. Esmay thought of her one glimpse of Lady Thornbuckle, the day Brun had come back to Rockhouse Major . . . the slim, elegant woman who had seemed far too tame a mother for someone like Brun. Maybe not . . .

"So some people blame your family because both this Pedar and the Speaker were killed with swords?"

"It's more than that," Brun said. "We're in the Barraclough Sept, you know, and Hobart was a Conselline." Esmay didn't interrupt to explain that she had no idea what a sept was. "There used to be five septs, but now there are just two. All the Families—the Seated Families—have aggregated into these two. They're rivals economically and politically. The Consellines lost prestige and also profit when the Morrelline mess on Patchcock came out—about the rejuvenation drugs."

"Rejuvenation drugs?"

"Yes—it was right after the battle at Xavier. I guess you'd have been tied up in legal matters. But—to make a long story short—the Morrelline pharmaceutical plants on Patchcock were making rejuv drugs and using a cut-rate process that produced inferior product. There was a lot of other stuff involved—a Benignity agent, abuse of workers—but it meant that the Morrelline brothers lost control of the family company to their sister Venezia, and profits dropped like a stone. Rejuvenation pharmacology had been their main cash cow, and the reason they had so much influence in the Conselline Sept."

Esmay's mind grabbed at the fact relevant to her experience. "Wait—bad rejuvenation drugs? Do you know if any of them were bought for Fleet?"

"As a matter of fact, yes. Apparently Fleet had noticed some problem with rejuvenation of senior NCOs—"

"Yes," Esmay said. "We certainly did."

"Hobart wanted market share back; when he became Speaker, he stifled the discussion and research, and started pushing rejuvenation in the open market again. The Benignity claims that's why they killed him."

"And in the meantime," Kate put in, "Brun's uncle was trying to grab her father's inheritance, on the grounds that he was not of sound mind, because he sent Fleet to get Brun away from the NewTex Militia."

"We thought we finally had things under control," Brun said. "Before the two deaths, we'd found evidence that my uncle had intimidated other family members into giving him their proxy or leaving him their shares. The court upheld my father's will, and Harlis is under investigation. But now—"

"It's a mess," Kate said.

"I can see why," Esmay said. "And then the mutiny."

"Yes. The Consellines would probably declare open war on the Barracloughs if they had the military to do it with, but so far the loyalists in Fleet are holding firm." Kate paused. "The mutineers . . . we hear rumors that some of them have offered their services to various families, including the Consellines."

"Mercenaries," Esmay said.

"Yup." Kate sounded oddly cheerful; Esmay reminded herself that this was not Kate's home. "Here's the house."

Appledale reminded Esmay a little of the big house on the Suiza estancia: large, surrounded by gardens and orchards and outbuildings. Inside, Brun led the way to a room that overlooked a walled garden and swimming pool.

"Now, Esmay, let's hear your news," she said, settling into a chintz-covered easy chair.

Esmay made the story as brief as she could: the quarrel with Admiral Serrano, the emergency call announcing the mutiny, her hasty marriage to Barin while in transit to their new assignments, her abrupt dismissal from Fleet.

"That doesn't sound like her," Brun said, frowning. "She's a Serrano, yes—the temper and all that—but I found her fair. She has to know that whatever happened hundreds of years ago isn't your fault."

Esmay shrugged. "It's a matter of honor, she said."

"Honor," Brun said, "is highly overrated. At least when it makes people do stupid things."

"We think a lot of honor on Altiplano," Esmay said. "And in Fleet."

Brun waved her hand. "There's honor and honor. I'm thinking of the stupid kind, like children taking dares. Not that I didn't—but I wasn't using my head when I did."

"Leaving honor out of it," Kate said, obviously determined to head off an impasse, "why do you think Admiral Serrano changed her mind and kicked you out?"

"Because I was told Admiral Serrano had signed the order," Esmay said.

Brun shrugged. "There's lots of admirals Serrano. Maybe it wasn't Barin's grandmother after all. I liked her, even if she was a bit scary."

"A bit—!" Esmay thought of the cold eyes that had been so full of enmity. "But it must have been Vida Serrano . . . who else would do it if she didn't want it done?"

"Stupidity and confusion," Kate said. "Happens all the time in big organizations. Someone thought he could make Barin's grandmother happy by canning you, not knowing that she'd changed her mind. Who else was at this family meeting?"

"I didn't even get to meet them all," Esmay said.

"What you need," Brun said, "is a good lawyer. I can use my influence, but we need help. Kevil Mahoney's the obvious one. I think he's still getting his new arm grown in, but if he can't do it, he still has contacts who can help us. And perhaps we should move into town for a while. I don't think it'll be that much harder to secure the town house than Appledale. I'll call George."

Breitis Rehabilitation Pavilion, Limb Unit

Kevil Mahoney grinned as Brun and Esmay came in to his room at the rehab center. "I was wondering if that was your cheerful voice I heard coming down the hall," he said to Brun. "And this is the redoubtable Lt. Suiza, no doubt."

"Not a lieutenant any more, sir," Esmay said.

"What'd you do, Brun, poison her mind with your anti-discipline nonsense?"

"Uncle Kevil!" Brun sounded only half amused. "She was kicked out unfairly. We have to do something."

He raised an eyebrow. "You mean you want *me* to do something."

"To start with, to listen to the whole story. Go ahead, Esmay."

This seemed brusque at best, but Kevil nodded to Esmay. "Go on, then."

Esmay retold the story, beginning with Admiral Serrano's attack on her. Kevil listened with his eyes closed—she wondered if he were dozing off—but when she finished, he opened them, and began asking questions. The same questions as Brun and Kate, at first, and then more and more, questions that had never occurred to her. Altiplano's trade policy? She knew nothing about it. Altiplano's association with the Crescent Worlds? Nothing, so far as she knew. The Emeralds? Esmay felt that he was dragging out of her everything she knew, had assumed, or even imagined, about her home world. Finally he stopped.

"Interesting." He closed his eyes again. Esmay took the chance to get a drink of water. "Very interesting indeed," he said when he opened his eyes again. "I was talking to Bunny about this sort of thing, before he died. We were both aware that the underlying structure of the Familias Regnant had not kept pace with the spatial and population growth."

"In what way?" Brun asked.

"Well . . . when you come right down to it, the Familias began as a commercial consortium dedicated to profit . . . a consortium that agreed to pool resources to control space piracy, which was cutting into everyone's profits. And if that sounds like a government to you, Brun, it's because your very expensive finishing school taught you more about social graces than social sciences."

"But aren't governments always designed for the profit of the citizens?" Esmay asked.

"Good gracious, no! Where'd you get that idea? Altiplano, of course, one of the grand social experiments of history . . . sorry, didn't mean to be sarcastic." Kevil hitched himself around in bed, grunting. "Blast this thing—I want to move my shoulder, and I know I can't, not for another twenty-three hours and sixteen minutes."

"That soon?"

"That *long*. It feels like forever—but this is an interesting distraction. It's certainly not often that two beautiful young women have come to me to listen to a lecture on legal history."

"Don't be silly, Uncle Kevil," Brun said.

"I'm not. I'm quite serious, and I hope you will be, you young scamp. It's time to grow up, Charlotte Brunhilde—you, and me, and the entire Familias. We're like a child who's been playing games in a large walled garden. Now we're outside, and it's not make-believe."

"I think I've seen a bit of the real world," Brun said, scowling.

"Yes. And Lt. Suiza here has seen more. But there's a lot neither of you knows about. Remember when Ottala Morreline disappeared, and there was all that trouble on Patchcock? That's when your father and I began to realize how deep the chasm was, just on the topic of rejuvenation therapy alone. The Familias isn't like the other multistar organizations we know of . . . there's no . . . no coherence to it. It just sort of grew, absorbing anything that lay in its sphere of influence."

Brun looked thoughtful. "Kate says something like that, but she keeps harping on a constitution."

"Yes, well, the Lone Star Confederation is a constitutional government. Until we moved in, the Crescent Worlds were a religious one. Most governments start with either a common culture or a common political theory. We didn't. This laissez-faire approach worked very well for a long time, because the founding septs were rich, and the worlds they gathered in brought them even more profits. But it couldn't go on forever. Especially not when most of the people who actually had power started acting like dilettantes."

"Excuse me—" A brisk woman in a flowered jumper came in. "It's time to turn the tank, Ser Mahoney." Esmay and Brun stepped back as she came to the bed. "Visitors out, please. This'll take about a half hour, to rotate and reposition."

CHAPTER SIXTEEN

**Castle Rock: Breitis Rehabilitation Pavilion,
Limb Unit**

Esmay thought about what Kevil Mahoney had said, and the others had said, but none of it satisfied her, and when the nurse told them they could go back into Kevil's room, she spoke up.

"I think your priorities are all off," Esmay said. Brun and Kate both looked startled.

"What d'you mean? What could be more important than getting the government straightened out?"

"Putting down this mutiny," Esmay said. "Look—if you don't have a loyal military, you're easy prey. The mutineers may be trying for a military coup. The Benignity says it won't invade right now . . . but why would you believe them? They admit to murdering one head of state; they say they've done it before. They tried to take Xavier just a few years ago. I'll bet they still want it. And the Bloodhorde—"

"They're just ignorant barbarians," Brun said. "They're not a real threat."

"Tell that to the people who died on *Koskiusko*," Esmay said. "Or the people they've hit on planets and stations with their piracy. They're not as serious a threat to the entire Familias as the Benignity, but I wouldn't call them negligible, either. They could certainly disrupt trade. And if they got hold of some of our front-line ships and weapons—"

"You think like an admiral," Kevil said. "That's not a criticism; we need that input too."

"I was looking up some history, last night," Esmay said. "All the way back to Old Earth, political entities had to start with security first, and then worry about organization. Even the old kingships, it said."

"People gather to a government that makes them feel safe?" Brun asked. "That sounds kind of dull."

Esmay grinned at her. "Which way would you rather get your thrills, in a sport you chose, or in a war?"

"Point taken. So, the Fleet officer—"

"Former officer—"

"And soon to be again. The officer says look to our security first, which means get the mutiny settled."

"And then—?"

"And then we see what we have to work with. There's no way to hold all this together by force, even with the full strength of Fleet."

"If you're right, Esmay—and I have to say you may be—then we need to get you back in Fleet as fast as possible."

"I have no idea how a discharged officer gets back in service," Esmay said.

"Heris Serrano did it," Brun said.

"With the help of the Serrano family I don't doubt," Esmay said drily, "which I don't have."

"You have me on your side, that counts for something. I could tackle Admiral Serrano on your behalf."

Another ally appeared almost as soon as they were back at the Thornbuckle town house. A servant announced, "General Casimir Suiza." Brun stared at Esmay, and Esmay, stunned, could not speak for a moment. Then she went to the door.

Esmay's father, out of uniform, looked just as impressive. "Esmaya . . . I hope you'll let me in . . ."

"I . . . of course." She opened the door wider. She could feel Brun's curiosity at her back and quickly introduced them.

"You'll want to be alone," Brun said, standing up.

"Not at all," General Suiza said. "Please stay—at least until I've explained why I'm here."

Brun sat back down, but gave Esmay a glance.

"Yes," Esmay said. "Please stay." Her heart was pounding; her mouth felt dry.

"Esmay—I know I've failed you in the past, but I couldn't sit home and see you in trouble again without at least trying to help."

"Sit down," Esmay said, waving to the couch. He sat, and clasped his hands. "How did you get here so fast?"

"Someone sent word when you were discharged—to your home of record, apparently that's standard procedure—but you'll understand, it took quite a while for news of that to get to Altiplano. Then I heard you'd gotten on a merchant ship."

"The *Terakian Fortune*."

"Yes. There were delays in contacting Admiral Serrano, because she was in transit and because Fleet wasn't too cooperative with me in granting ansible access to what they called 'foreign military.' The thing you need to know first, Esmaya, is that Admiral *Vida* Serrano had nothing to do with your discharge."

"She didn't?"

"No. She was angry, and so was I, that you young people chose to get married without anyone's consent. She was angry about what she thought our family had done to the Serrano patrons. But we agreed that history can wait while we deal with the present crisis."

The thought of her father and Admiral Serrano concentrating their formidable executive powers on her career gave Esmay a shiver of apprehension.

"Then the captain of the trader ship sent me a priority message from Zenebra, so I knew where you'd be next . . . and here I am. And don't tell me you don't need help," her father said. He glanced at Brun. "Everyone needs help sometimes. You've proven your ability and independence."

"Thanks," Esmay said, feeling very trapped.

"But I can ask you what Admiral Serrano can't. Do you want to get back in Fleet and command ships, or would you rather go back to Altiplano? Or settle in the Familias as a civilian?"

"Space," Esmay said without hesitation. "But what about—"

"First things first," her father said. "That was first—finding out what you wanted. They weren't going to draft you against your will. Then the next complication is, your status as Landbride.

Their regulations and our Landsmen's Guild are both clear and unequivocal. I've argued the Landsmen's Guild into the grudging agreement that you can resign in absentia, and Luci can be invested without delay—we will need several locks of your hair—" He looked at it. "If you could manage even a short braid—"

"Of course. And do I need to sign anything?"

"I brought the Order of Renunciation . . ." He gave her a long look. "Esmaya . . . I want you to know that you will always be welcome at home; Luci says that too. She's still managing your herd; your Starmount award grant will always be yours. Your children— should you and Barin have children, which I hope you do—will be welcome there, as well, and considered legitimate heirs to the estancia."

Her eyes stung with sudden tears. "Father—I do love the land . . . and Altiplano . . ."

"I know that. And Altiplano is very proud of its hero." He took a big breath and sighed. "Thank God you're not shutting me out—I was so afraid—"

From the distance of several years her anger now looked more like a local storm than a planet-circling cataclysm. He had been wrong; he was trying to make amends. A last niggling voice in her mind pointed out that he faced considerable difficulty in securing the Suiza place in the Landsmen's Guild if she hadn't cooperated, but she suppressed it. He did love her; his convenience wasn't the only measure of worth.

"I'm glad you're here," she said, surprising herself because it was true. She had been baffled, and now she had an ally of no mean ability, one who was not trapped in a hospital bed. "Are you going to send the braid and certificate back to Altiplano, or carry them?"

"Carry them. Both Luci and the Landsmen's Guild believe the Landbride's Hair must not be consigned to the post like any ordinary object. I will need to make an ansible call back, to tell them you're willing, and then I can stay long enough to be sure you get back into Fleet without trouble."

Esmay was suddenly struck with another problem. "I don't have but one uniform—the others were in transit when they discharged me, and who knows where they are now?"

"Surely this place has some military tailors who can fit you out?"

"Yes—" She wasn't used to spending the kind of money it would take to replace all her uniforms.

"Don't worry," her father said. "Consider it my belated gift to you. Now if you don't mind, I should make that call as soon as possible. Luci's wedding is being held up pending—"

"Of course. There's a terminal over in the banking center—"

While her father went to make his call, Esmay showered and washed her hair. She didn't cut it, having a vague memory that the hair must be cut in front of official witnesses. "Do you want us to go or stay, Esmay?" Brun asked.

"Stay, please. I don't know if he'll need additional witnesses or not. That is, if you're willing."

"I wouldn't miss this for the world," Brun said. "This whole Landbride thing fascinates me, and it's not just the fancy dress. I remember my mother telling me about something she'd heard from her grandmother, about customs somewhere . . . can't think where. Anyway, there it was the man who married the land."

That sounded obscene to Esmay, but she told herself it was just a different culture. When her father returned, he had brought along the Altiplano docent, the representative who had no Seat on Council, but was allowed to submit minutes on Altiplano's behalf. Esmay had never met him.

The man bowed. "Landbride Suiza. It is an honor."

"Docent Faiza."

"It is my understanding that you intend to renounce your position, in favor of a younger relative. Is this true?"

"It is," Esmay said.

"In accordance with law and custom, belief and practice, it is my duty to be sure that this is indeed your will. If you will excuse us—" His gaze swept the room; Esmay's father, Brun, and Kate retired into the hall.

Esmay noticed now that he held the paper which must be the Order of Renunciation. Her stomach clenched. Now that it came to it . . . the very feel of the earth beneath her bare feet that morning when she had sworn to protect the land forever came back to her. Could she renounce that? Tears stung her eyes again.

"Do you swear, Landbride Suiza, that you desire this of your own will, that no one has threatened you, or done you harm, or coerced you in any way to renounce your status?" He gazed at her solemnly; Esmay could hear the wind of Altiplano blowing through the summer grass, smell the rich fragrance of the summer pastures. Yet . . . much as she loved it, she did not love it enough.

"I so swear," she said.

"Do you swear, Landbride Suiza, that your reason for this renunciation is your sincere care for the land of Suiza, and that your chosen successor will, in your unquestioning belief, protect this land better than you yourself could?" Was she sure Luci would be a better Landbride? Yes, for Luci had the undivided heart, as well as the intelligence and the character. The land would be better for having Luci as its guardian.

"I so swear."

He lowered the paper. "I'm sorry, Landbride . . . though I am not a Suiza, and it has been years since I was home, I had been so proud of you—you made Altiplano famous in a good way."

"I can't do both," Esmay said. "And I was away too long—I wanted to do the best for the land, but I don't know enough about it. My cousin does. She's been my agent."

"Very well." He picked up the paper again. "Now, I'll need three witnesses to shearing your hair and your signature."

Esmay called the others, and they came back. Docent Faiza spread the document on the table, and said, "Now you sign, and then your witnesses—and, Landbride, you must add a drop of blood."

"Here, Esmay," her father said. He took a small sheathed knife from his vest pocket. "This is the knife that has been used in the family for generations."

"Most correct," Docent Faiza said. "Landbride?"

Esmay slipped the small knife from the tooled leather sheath. She remembered seeing it on her great-grandmother's desk; she'd always thought it was just a letter opener. She pricked her left ring finger with the sharp tip and squeezed a drop of blood onto the parchment. Then she took the pen the docent offered her and signed her name. Her father handed her the Landbride's Seal, and she stamped it in blood . . . the most solemn of all seals. Then her father signed, and Brun, and Kate—the oddest collection of witnesses, Esmay thought, which could ever have witnessed a Landbride's renunciation.

"In the old days," the docent said, "a Landbride renouncing her position would cut off all her hair, that it might go into the Wind's Offering. But since you're going to have to live here, in the Familias . . ."

"They've seen bald women before," Esmay said. "Besides, I can get a wig. If you think it's best . . ."

"If you're willing, it would certainly please the older members of the Landsmen's Guild."

What Barin would think of a bald wife, if she saw him again before her hair grew out, she didn't know. But the ache below her breast-bone told her this was the right thing to do.

"According to my researches," the docent said, "they did not shave their heads—merely cut their hair as short as they could. Then they went into exile from their former lands until it grew long enough to touch the shoulders." A very practical way, Esmay thought, to ensure that the new Landbride had time to gain control without interference from the former Landbride.

"I expect I'll be away longer than that," Esmay said.

"It'll be easier if we braid it," Brun said. "Here, sit down."

"Good grief, it's fluffy," she said, as she tried to coax the first strands into a braid.

"I just washed it," Esmay said. "You know that."

"Well, we'll have to wet it again, or we'll have wisps instead of braids. Kate, bring me a bowl of water."

Docent Faiza was disposed to be solemn about it, but even his solemnity was no match for the cheerfully irreverent banter of Brun and Kate as they struggled with Esmay's recalcitrant hair. "I know I told you to get a layered cut next time," Brun said, "but this is ridiculous. Nothing's the same length as anything else . . ."

When they were done, Esmay had little tufts standing up where the braids had been, and even her father and the docent couldn't keep a straight face.

"You should be glad we're your friends, Esmay," Brun said. "If we wanted to blackmail you—"

"I've been teased about my hair all my life," Esmay said. "You can't embarrass me that way. And now that I know what a good hairdresser can do—"

"Now," the docent said, getting formal again, "I wish you the best of luck in your military career, Esmay Suiza. You have brought honor to Altiplano, and I'm sure you will bring more." He rolled up the document, tied a black ribbon around it, and handed it to Esmay's father.

"You'll join us for some refreshment?" General Suiza said.

"Forgive me, General, but I cannot at this time. Later perhaps?"

"Of course. I expect to be here several days."

The planetside headquarters of the Regular Space Service comprised a warren of buildings that radiated from the back of the Ministry of Defense, tunneling under and bridging over streets and tramways and throwing out subsidiary departments into odd corners of other governmental offices. Esmay, her father, Brun, and the docent of Altiplano began at the front end, at the Ministry of Defense, where a harrassed staff immediately announced they were in the wrong place. "Try recruiting," one receptionist said. "It's in the Michet Building."

"It's a personnel matter, not a recruiting matter," General Suiza said.

"Oh—that would be the Corvey Building, but you have to go through security first. That way—" She pointed.

"That way" led down a long hall that wound to the right, then back to the left, and finally led them up a ramp to an elevated walkway along one side of a courtyard; down below, two people were talking, leaning on some kind of ornamental column. At the far end of the walkway, they came to the first set of guards.

"We're looking for the Corvey Building," General Suiza said. "They said it was this way."

"You don't have any ID tags," the guard said.

"Do we need ID tags?"

"Visitors are supposed to get ID tags at the kiosk by the entrance."

"There wasn't one," Brun said.

"Right by the State Street entrance—"

"We didn't come in the State Street entrance; we came in the Lowe Street entrance."

The guard frowned. "You're supposed to have ID tags to come in that entrance at all. Wait here." He stepped back and spoke into his comunit; they couldn't hear what he said; his eyes never left them. Then he stepped forward again. "Which sept are you?"

"Barraclough," Brun said without hesitation. "Why?"

The guard changed expression. "You're—you're the old speaker's daughter . . . .you're Brun Meager!"

"Yes," Brun said. She sounded slightly truculent.

He beamed at her as if she'd just handed him a fortune. "I never thought I'd get to meet you. You look different in that suit; I'm sorry I didn't recognize you right away. And these are friends of yours?"

"Yes," Brun said.

"Oh, well, then, I'm sure it's all right. If I could just see your ID, to have it on the records . . ."

Brun handed it over; Esmay was appalled. If they called this security—! She was glad Kate had decided not to come with them.

"That's fine, sera . . . milady?"

"Thank you," Brun said, without clarifying her status. "Are you sure it's all right? We don't want to get you in any trouble."

"No, sera, that's quite all right. It's an honor to be of service. If your friends don't mind, I'd like to put their names on the roster . . . will they need independent access? If so, we should get them some tags made up."

"Certainly," Brun said. "This is General Suiza, from Altiplano— his daughter Esmay Suiza—you may remember that she saved my life—"

The guard's gaze rested briefly on Esmay, then slid quickly back to Brun. "Yes—of course—the hero of Xavier."

"And the Docent of Altiplano, Ser Faiza."

"Docent?"

"Diplomatic status," Brun said, as if she'd always known it.

"Ah . . . yes, thank you, sers and seras. Sera Meager, I know it's an imposition, but if you wouldn't mind—my wife's a big fan—" He fumbled in his pockets and pulled out a crumpled shopping list. "Would you sign it?"

"Of course," Brun said, and scrawled her name with the stylus he offered.

The man said, clearly as an afterthought, "And you, Sera Suiza? My wife bought a cube of Sera Meager's rescue—"

Esmay fitted in her signature under Brun's—she couldn't think of a gracious way to refuse—and wondered if the 2 p. crts. on the list under her name was crates, carrots, or something illegal.

The guard waved them through double doors into another corridor—a bridge over a street—and at the far end another guard opened the matching doors for them. "Sera Meager? It's an honor—I'm calling ahead so you shouldn't be stopped again, just go down this ramp, turn left, take the first corridor to the right and keep going . . ."

Brun, in what Esmay considered an excess of honesty, said, "But weren't we supposed to go through security?"

"Oh, you don't want to bother with them," the man said. "They're backed up at least three hours processing recruit clearances from that new intake that came in overnight. My wife works in catalog over there; she called to tell me she had to work overtime tonight. You'd be sitting on a bench until dark, most likely, and besides—they're just not very helpful."

Esmay closed her mouth on the comment that security was not supposed to be helpful, but thorough. She had no more desire to sit on a bench for hours than anyone else.

"What you do," the man said, "is just go along here, and then out the door at the end, and straight across the Sif Memorial Garden to the side door of Corvey. Don't go in the front; they'll make you go back through security. Go in that side door; I'm calling Bev, and she'll be expecting you."

"Thank you," Brun said.

The Sif Memorial Garden was only a small courtyard with a plinth in the middle, two straggly trees, four flowerbeds, and two benches. Straight across—with a detour around the plinth—brought them to the side door of the Corvey Building, where a woman let them in.

"Sera Meager! I'm so glad to meet you! And you, of course, Sera Suiza. Although I should know your rank; I just don't remember—"

"Sera's fine," Esmay said. She could see, in the corridor ahead, figures moving about in the familiar uniform.

"I have temporary tags for all of you," the woman said. She pulled out four violently pink tags, with little clips attached. "These are only day passes; I believe your permanent passes will be ready this evening or tomorrow."

After all this confusion, Esmay was prepared for almost anything, she thought. Except for the discovery that her discharge hadn't yet been transmitted to Headquarters and therefore they couldn't reinstate her.

"Why not?" she asked. "Can't you at least take my application, and the proof that I'm no longer a Landbride, so when it comes in—"

"Well, we *could*, if it weren't for the mutiny. See, we have to run everything like that past the Judge Advocate General's office, and right now they're having some kind of snitfit because the admiral in charge disappeared, and they think he's part of the mutiny."

"And that means—?"

"It means they won't take anything from us without a complete file. For the complete file, we'd need a copy of the discharge order, with the file number an' everything, and your PR-S-87, your personnel file—"

"Isn't there a copy of that here?"

"Yes, of course. But it may not be complete, because your most recent evaluations may not have been forwarded yet. I can't think why the discharge wasn't, unless it was cancelled—"

"Cancelled?"

"Well—if someone overruled whoever signed it, when they got it, then they might have sat on it until you showed up and they could tell you. Let's see, where were you discharged?"

"Trinidad Station," Esmay said.

"Oh, dear."

"What?"

"You haven't heard? Trinidad was sacked by the mutineers several weeks ago. We can't get any records out of *them*. Do you have a discharge order?"

"Yes . . ." Esmay took it out and handed it over.

"Umph. Some people can't even sign their names legibly . . . I'll call up your file, and we'll see how out-of-date it is . . ."

Her file was up-to-date only as far as the ill-fated leave to visit Barin and his family. "Nothing here about a discharge," the clerk said. "The emergency orders that sent you from there to your next ship are here, but no more." He paused, looked thoughtful, then said. "If the discharge hasn't gone through, Lieutenant, you may actually be down as AWOL. You'd better go check with Personnel Assignment; I can't access their server from this station. That's in 2345. In the meantime, I'll ask what we'd better do about clearing this discharge up when we don't actually have it. Our CO's in a meeting, but he'll be back in the office any time now."

Trailed by her support group, Esmay headed off for 2345—up a lift and down another long corridor. Once in Personnel Assignment, she gave her name to the clerk and explained briefly that she was trying to straighten out her records. He called up her name, and let out a long whistle.

"You're in trouble, Lieutenant. You overstayed your leave, and we have you listed as a deserter. I'm going to have to call this in to the Judge Advocate General's office; please do not try to leave. Here— you were notified twice—" He turned the screen so she could read it. First there was a message addressed to her on the transport *Rosa Gloria*, pointing out that she had not reported for duty as ordered at Harrican and warning that she would be considered AWOL if she did not report in within 24 hours and a deserter if she had not reported within seven (7) days. A second message to the same address informed her that she was now considered a deserter and should turn herself in to the nearest Fleet facility or face pursuit and arrest. Both time limits had long since expired.

"Great," Esmay muttered as she read it. "Now I can be prosecuted for desertion after being thrown out on my ear . . ." Then, to the clerk, "I never got those notices; I wasn't on that ship because I'd been discharged."

"Do you have proof of discharge that predates this notice?" the clerk asked, as if he were sure she did not. "We should have had any such discharge in our records, which would have automatically cancelled this notice."

"Good thing we made those certified copies of your discharge certificate," Brun said. "Maybe we should have made more."

Esmay handed over one of the copies, and the clerk compared the dates and consulted a graphic of relative dates. Sure enough, she had been discharged at Trinidad well before she was supposed to have reported at Harrican. The clerk nodded. "Well, then, you're cleared of these charges presumptively, but I'll have to get it signed off . . . just wait right here. If you leave, I'll have to assume you're deserting again." He disappeared with all the documentation.

"I didn't desert the first time," Esmay muttered to the floor.

"This is stupid!" Brun said.

"No, it's the military," General Suiza said. "I hate to admit it, but even in Altiplano, we have mixups like this. Of course, there I can usually cut through it in less time, but even generals—and admirals, obviously—are at the mercy of clerks at times." He looked around the office. "I'm going to get us some chairs; we may be here awhile." He left before Esmay could say anything.

"He reminds me of my father in some ways," Brun said. "Pretty much unflappable."

Esmay did not mention that Brun's father had been capable of flapping quite a lot when Brun was in danger. In a few minutes, her father returned with two chairs.

"Here. Have a seat. This is actually a magic trick, because if we get at all comfortable, they'll be back to tell us to go somewhere else."

Sure enough, Esmay and Brun had only just relaxed with a sigh when the clerk bustled back in.

"There you are—where'd you get those chairs? There aren't supposed to be any chairs in here—"

"I brought them," General Suiza said. "I'll take them back."

"You shouldn't have," the clerk said. "Lieutenant—or Sera, since you're not a lieutenant now—Major Tenerif is trying to access your personnel record to see if that discharge certificate is genuine—it's not the original, you know."

"They have the original down in 1118," Esmay said. "I left it with them, because they hadn't received anything on the discharge yet." She wondered just how soon after she'd left the mutineers had hit Trinidad Station.

"It's most irregular," the clerk said. "You'll need to speak to Major Tenerif."

"Is he free?"

"Well, not now—he's on the horn trying to get your records."

But at that moment, a major emerged from behind a screen. "Suiza?"

"I'm Esmay Suiza," Esmay said.

"Damnedest thing I ever heard of," the major said. "I've called JAG, and they're willing to agree that you are not, at present, a deserter, but that still leaves a mess. Either the discharge was valid or it wasn't. If it was, you're completely clear of charges of desertion, and you're a civilian. You'd have to apply to enter Fleet as a civilian, with a lapse in service and a considerable blot on your record. If the discharge wasn't valid, or was cancelled somewhere in the process of completion, then it's worse. You could be reinstated, of course. If you're reinstated as of the date of discharge, which would be normal if the discharge were shown to be a fake, then you were actually on active duty when the notices of AWOL and desertion were sent, and the defense that you'd been discharged prior to that is no longer valid. You'd have to stand at least a judicial inquiry to ensure that you were not at fault, that you had reason to believe you'd been legitimately discharged, that it wasn't some plot you'd cooked up to avoid duty in time of war."

"The discharge certificate—"

"Well, yes, you have one, but it would still be a matter for a formal inquiry. If you're reinstated as of this date, that means something has to explain the gap, besides the loss of time for pay and promotion consideration. And it's messed up the assignment process. Someone else took over your slot; we can't bump them out just because you showed up." He shook his head. "We need you combat-experienced people, but we do not need a mess like this. And you need a friend in high places. You don't happen to know Grand Admiral Savanche, do you?"

"No, sir," Esmay said. "The only admiral I know is Admiral Serrano—Vida Serrano."

"Ah. Her. Well, if the Serranos are behind you, that might help. But scuttlebutt has it they're peeved with you."

"Some of them," Esmay said. She was not about to say more about her relationship to Barin unless she had to.

"You'd better hope she's not one of the peeved ones," the major said.

Fleet Headquarters planetside had access to Fleet ansible communications, but it took the combined efforts of Esmay, Brun, and General Suiza to convince someone to try to reach Admiral Vida Serrano, who had just taken over at Sector VII. When they finally did, her response was terse: "Reinstate her at once and get her out here where we need her. Mutineers attacking civilian ships . . ."

It took more than that one message, but by afternoon the next day, Major Tenerif was much more cheerful about the situation. "JAG's dropped the desertion charge; apparently it's been decided the discharge was a valid order when you got it, but a mistake at a higher level, and it didn't get here because of the mess at Trinidad. Someone's probably in a lot of trouble, but not—at this point—you. However, we do have some urgency in getting you back to duty. When can you be ready to travel?"

"Pay and allowances?" murmured General Suiza.

"Oh. Of course. I guess, if you haven't been paid since—that would be before you went on leave, right?—and did your luggage catch up with you? No? Then you'll need some things, I imagine. Well, we don't issue pay here, but over in the Bursar's division, you can get any monies owed. But can you be ready to travel in—let's see, it's already 1500—two days? That will put you aboard our next transport to Sector VII."

"Yes, sir," Esmay said. She would find a way, she told herself.

"Good. We already cut your orders—you're going out to Sector VII to command *Rascal*, an upgraded patrol class."

"*Command* a ship? Me?" Esmay's voice almost squeaked.

"I don't see why not," Brun said.

The major shrugged. "We're short-handed, Lieutenant. You're the next qualified person on the list. And you *are* command track—"

"Yes, sir. Sorry, sir. It's just—a surprise."

"That's all right." The major allowed himself a small smile. "We've had similar reactions from some other younger officers who weren't aware they now qualified for ship command." He turned to the clerk. "Get those orders cut for shuttle transport day after tomorrow." Then to Esmay. "You'll want to get your credit updated before you leave. I've already told the Bursar's office to expect you. . . ."

"Thank you, sir."

On the way to that office, new orders in hand, Esmay couldn't feel that this was real. From utter disgrace to ship command in one day?

"I still can't believe they gave me a ship. I'm only a lieutenant—"

"Who has commanded ships in battle . . . What do you want, Es, an engraved invitation?" Brun asked. Then she mimed shock. "This *is* an engraved invitation."

"Protocol . . . I don't know all the protocol for it . . ." The memory of that hasty and scrambled assumption of command on *Despite* did not reassure her.

"That's what fast-tapes are for. What about uniforms?"

"Right. Bursar's office, then the tailor's . . ."

CHAPTER SEVENTEEN

Swainson & Triggett, Officers' Outfitters (All Services), greeted the new captain of a patrol ship with suitably restrained delight, and the presence of a distinguished-looking father only increased the respectful hush in the room. Lieutenant Suiza, the hero of Xavier, yes of course. An honor. And newly made captain? Congratulations. Luggage lost in transit, in the confusion of the mutiny? What a shame. Complete set of uniforms, as quickly as possible, money no object? They purred over her, the younger Ser Swainson, and the elder Ser Triggett. The senior women's fitter was summoned; she led Esmay away to a booth large enough to host a small party, where an entire team of fitters measured her from tip to toe, then had her move . . . sit, stand, walk, raise and lower her arms . . .

"We have items in stock, of course, which can be altered—that might do for everyday uniforms, since you're in a hurry—" The old lady sent a young one off to the racks. "But your dress uniforms must of course be custom-fitted. You're lucky; you have a nice shape for uniforms."

Esmay assumed that was simple flattery, until the woman said, "Now you take Sera Meager—lovely woman she is, but if you tried to fit a uniform on her it would be quite difficult. She looks good in many kinds of clothes, and she knows how to dress, but it's the ratios, you see. The ratio of upper to lower arm, of thigh to lower leg, of torso length to leg length." Esmay was glad Brun had stayed out front and hadn't heard this.

The girl came back with a uniform that fit better than any of her own ever had. Esmay said so, but the old lady sniffed as she began marking and pinning for alterations. "That may be, Lieutenant, but I daresay you didn't order your wardrobe *here*."

"No—this is my first time on Castle Rock."

"Ah. Well, we have several branch offices. There are other good firms—Hatan Meior does quite nice work—but we do feel that we have a little something extra."

"I'd agree," said Esmay, watching her image in the mirror as the pins subtly changed what had already seemed like a smarter silhouette.

"Is that the way you usually wear your hair?" the old lady asked, with a swift glance at the mirrored image.

"No—I had to cut it off for a religious ceremony," Esmay said. "I usually wear it short, but not this short. I was thinking of getting a wig or something."

"It's the cap, you see. If we size it to your head now, it may not fit when your hair grows out, depending on how you style it. A wig would certainly change the size, but if you don't mind my advice—"

"Not at all."

"It's our experience that those officers who try wigs find them inconvenient aboard ship. We've had to replace quite a few caps for that reason. And they don't work well with the command helmets, either."

"Thank you," Esmay said. "I'd only thought, because it's so much shorter than usual—"

"You might consider a hair booster; it'll grow out about twice as fast, for thirty days. Then it slows back down. Any good salon can do the treatment, and I understand it doesn't affect the ID process. Many of our officers use Dorn's, down the street."

"Thanks," Esmay said again.

"They'll be ready tomorrow," the elder Ser Triggett told them, when the fitters had done with her. "And do you have a list of your decorations? You'll need the ribbon and the miniature and full-size dress medals." Esmay handed over the list feeling more and more that she was in some fantasy world . . . she was suddenly back in Fleet . . . she was to command a ship . . . she had just ordered a full set of uniforms from what had to be the most expensive tailors in the universe . . . it was as if she'd fallen into one of the tales in which the despised outcast sister is transformed into a beautiful princess by magical hands.

She did notice that Ser Triggett passed the bill discreetly to her father, who scanned it closely before handing over his credit cube. "You're sure you don't need a second pair of ship boots?" her father asked. "If those are really comfortable . . ." Ser Triggett paused on his way to the credit desk.

They were comfortable; they felt like walking on pillows. Her father could afford it, and he wanted to treat her. "Yes," Esmay said. "I would like a second pair."

She walked out in uniform—the first of the working uniforms, quickly but perfectly altered to fit her, with the insignia of a ship's captain embroidered on epaulets and cap, and the rank insignia gleaming on her shoulders. The day itself seemed brighter, though in fact it was almost dark: Swainson & Triggett appeared not to mind that outfitting her had kept them busy until well after the stated closing hour.

That night, they all had dinner at the Thornbuckle town house— she, her father, Brun, Kate, and Kevil Mahoney, who was finally out of rehab with his new arm. After the meal, the talk turned to Familias politics.

"You young ladies will most likely not agree with me," General Suiza said, "but I see the Familias facing more and more trouble unless it reconstitutes its government on more rational lines."

"That's what I keep saying," Kate said. "They need a constitution . . ."

"They need clear thinking," the general said. "A bad constitution would not help."

"But the first thing," Esmay said, "must be the mutiny. Without security, they won't have time to think clearly."

He smiled at her. "You are definitely my daughter, Esmaya. Of course they must put down the mutiny first and repel any invaders. That's the job of the Fleet. But while you are out there blowing up mutineers, someone here must be thinking clearly about the reasons for the assassinations and mutinies, and the other unrest that troubles the realm." He cocked an eye at Kevil Mahoney. "Is that not so, Ser Mahoney?"

"Yes, of course," Kevil said. "But I don't quite see how we're to do that. Bunny and I were working on it, but without Bunny's influence I'm small potatoes and few in the hill, as the saying is. I rode his coattails . . ."

"Or drove him with them," Brun said. "I know you influenced his thinking a lot."

"Well . . . it became clear to me when I was a young man that something was stifling opportunity for talent of all kinds. It took me a long time to figure it out—you'd think with colony worlds opening all around, with hundreds of populated worlds all linked by trade and expanding almost visibly, that there'd be plenty of chance to rise."

"Some worlds are more conservative," Brun said. "Look at the Crescents, for instance."

"Yes, that's what my professors said. And there was a lot of scoffing, of the 'That's just what they're like, what do you expect' from senior men of law who were content that it should be so. But I had the advantage of my grandfather's library—he had a passion for old books that went far beyond having rows of attractive bindings to show on a library wall, or a few reproduction books on foxhunting or military history to lay out for display on a fancy table. By the time I was in law school, he'd long retired, and nothing pleased him so much as arguing over history with me—and not just legal history. One thing he convinced me of—and all the evidence I've seen since confirms this—is that any system which does not give ample opportunity for talent to displace unearned rank will, in the end, come to grief."

"What do you mean by unearned rank?" Brun asked.

"What you have, for instance," Kevil said, with a smile that took most of the sting out of his words. "Or for that matter, my son George. This is not to say you and others like you don't have talent— you do. But your talent is displayed, as it were, on velvet, like a precious jewel. Think of those women in the NewTex culture, Brun: were they all stupid, lazy, incompetent?"

"No . . ."

"No. Given your advantages, some of them would have been quite able to act the lady, don't you think?" He didn't wait for an answer. "Not that acting the lady is the best goal for a woman, in my opinion, any more than acting the lord is the best goal for a man. My point is that every time society has given it a chance, it's been shown that talent exists in previously despised populations. For instance, in the early days of space colonies, there are multiple instances where the supposedly necessary leadership was killed by some disaster, and it was presumed the colony would fail—but it didn't. Over and over again, it's been shown that an ordinary sampling of the population, including those considered inferior or hopeless, contains men and women of rare intelligence, wit, and ability. Just as ponds turn over their water yearly, revitalizing the pond's life, so a good stirring of the human pot brings new blood to the top, and we're all the better for it."

"But—" Brun struggled to express what she felt. She was a Registered Embryo—specially chosen genes for excellence. Maybe they'd had to depend on talent from below in the past, but now people like her parents could select it even before birth.

"We had that happen in Altiplano," the general said. "Our patrons thought their colonists were just stupid peasants, born and bred to be inferior and ruled by themselves. But we did quite well without our natural leaders."

"And yet you have rich and poor, don't you?"

"Of course we do. But I like to think, with a smaller population and our educational system, we give the children of poor families more chance to show what they can do."

"Boys, at least," Esmay said. "And all the Landbrides are from wealthy families."

"That's so," General Suiza said, frowning. "Our system is not perfect. But since we don't have rejuvenation, our young people know they will have a place in society at a reasonably young age."

"Now there you've touched it," Kevil said, leaning forward. "Even the old forms of rejuvenation, each pretty much limited to a single application because of side effects, widened the opportunity gap at the top end of society. Repeated rejuvenations made things worse— much worse. It would have been bad enough if it been available only to the richest families, forcing youngsters like you to sit idly waiting for a chance to take responsibility in the family that never came. You, from your perspective, may not be able to see how much the education and lives of rich young people changed in the ten years before you were born. But I did. And rich young people, kept out of the family business, can amuse themselves in all sorts of ways."

"Then rejuvenation spread," General Suiza said.

"Yes. Take a professional man like myself, who has accumulated forty years of experience in his field, and can return to a vigorous younger body . . . why would he retire? So why would he take on a younger partner, when he himself felt young again? It's like crystallization, spreading and freezing through society, making brittle what had been fluid."

"But people want to live," Brun said. "That's natural."

"Yes, it's natural. It's as natural as wanting to find the perfect love that lasts forever, or peace without disturbance . . . it's the old natural infant desire to have what you want, when you want it, forever. Up to now, the human race has been blessed by having such wishes impossible to fulfill: harsh as it seems, the young have been able to count on their elders losing first strength, and then dying . . . making room. All human societies have been built on that awareness that everyone dies."

"So we have to figure out how to live if they don't?"

"Exactly. Much as I dislike the Benignity, their Chairman's comment on endless adolescence hit the target. We need a range of maturity—if we're going to live for hundreds of years, we need to be grownups, not perpetual children. We need opportunities for the young, a chance for them to mature as well. We need to do something to include more of the population, to tie it together."

"Can it be done?" General Suiza asked.

"I don't know, but we have to try, or we'll have a bloodbath, with the young and hopeless attacking the old and rejuvenated directly," Kevil said. "We already have foreign enemies who tell us—who are adamant—that our use of unrestricted rejuvenation frightens them so much they will assassinate our head of state and consider invasion."

"The Terakians," Esmay said, "talked about this a little. They said the free traders weren't as affected, because they could always go somewhere else, but they saw a lot of unrest that made them uneasy."

"We've got to get people like that into the government," Kevil said. "As long as the only people with power are the rich rejuvenated oldsters, something's going to blow. There are a lot more people—including intelligent, thoughtful, decent people—who aren't rich or able to get rejuvenation. The last time I went over this with Bunny, we noticed that there are more unrejuvenated young people with a right to Seats in Council than rejuvenated ones with Seats. That might give us a wedge, for as long as that majority lasts. But we still have to go outside the old Families. However much inconvenience and trouble it may take to widen the franchise, a revolution would be far, far worse."

The hours ran out like water down a drain . . . a restless night's sleep . . . the salon appointment . . . a day spent in final fitting of the new uniforms (the sight of herself in the cape and long skirt of the mess dress startled her—she looked almost regal), in buying the luggage in which to pack them—she couldn't have crammed them into the carryon even if she'd been willing to, in finding out what she could about the crew she would have on her ship (her ship!). A last flurry of other shopping when the old lady reminded her that a captain would be expected to pay calls on civilians and would need a civilian wardrobe as well—she took Brun along for that. Her father left for home that second night; she was surprised at how she missed him in the few hours left before her own departure.

Then Brun and Kate took her to the shuttle terminal, and after a last round of good-byes, she joined the stream of travelers in uniform heading for the Fleet shuttle access. This time the ID booth recognized her at once; she had only a moment's claustrophobia from the memory of her earlier arrest before the light turned green.

"Welcome home, Lieutenant," said the guard at the gate when she arrived at Rockhouse Major. "Your transport to Sector VII HQ leaves in four hours, sir."

"Thanks, Sergeant," Esmay said. She hoped that was enough time for luggage transfer. She didn't want to lose her new finery. Meanwhile, she could look Barin up in the Fleet database now that she had access again. Two hours later, she turned away from the display in confusion.

Copper Mountain? What was Barin doing on Copper Mountain?

Rockhouse Major, 0900 local time

Harlis Thornbuckle eyed the gray-haired man across the table. Tall, trim, square-shouldered, erect, with a look on his face that came— Harlis knew—from command of a ship in the Regular Space Service.

A ship no longer in the Regular Space Service. A ship now at the service of anyone who could hire it.

"But why would you want to go to Sirialis, the first place they'll look?"

"They won't, because they aren't looking for me, and no Family member is there." Never mind that they would be looking for him as soon as they knew he'd slipped his surveillance cuff. That discovery was hours away, thanks to his dentist. If he could finish his business with this fellow, make that quick run back to Castle Rock and return, get off this damnable Station quickly enough, it wouldn't be a problem. The messages on his comunit at home should make it clear he was actually headed for his own estates. Besides, it was none of his hireling's business. "You can cut off communications, can't you?"

"Yes, or control them. But it's an out-of-the-way system . . ."

"All the better, isn't it? Low population, high productivity, not on regular trade routes. It's known as a Family Seat, so why would anyone look there?"

The gray-haired man frowned. "We'd need more information."

"I can get that for you. But can you do it?"

"Probably. Yes. But it will cost you."

"That's not a problem. I have plenty of money."

"Fine. Then suppose you get us off this station."

"Off—?"

"You don't suppose I brought my ships in here and docked them alongside a bunch of traders, do you? That would be walking into the lion's mouth indeed."

Harlis had assumed that a faked ID beacon would do the trick, but if they needed transport, that was no problem. "We can hire a yacht," he said.

"Just like that?"

Harlis drew himself up. "I am Seated Family," he said. "Whatever else happens, they can't take that away, and I have more than ample funds to hire any yacht up here. What do we need?"

"Let me check what's listed." The man, who still hadn't given his name, pulled out his comunit and called up the list available from Allsystems Leasing. "Get us the *Lillian C.*," he said after scrolling through it. "Passenger capacity's fifteen. Bare. We've got crew. If they won't lease it bare, ask to speak to Denny, and when you get Denny, say 'Little ships have big ears.' That should take care of it." He sat back, tucked the comunit in his pocket, and nodded at Harlis.

"Now?"

"How fast did you want to leave?" the man asked.

"All right." Harlis called Allsystems, where his name got him past the first two levels of reception and onto a personal sales officer. "I need to lease a yacht," he said. "What's available?" The man began describing yachts, transmitting the data. Harlis made disparaging comments until he mentioned the *Lillian C.*, then he said, "That's not so bad." He listened to a few more, then said, "That *Lillian* yacht— that sounds like what I'm looking for. How soon can she be ready?"

"Six hours, Ser Thornbuckle, but obtaining a crew—"

"Never mind about the crew," Harlis said. "I'll take care of that."

"Ah . . . family retainers, I suppose?"

"Qualified crew," Harlis said.

"We really prefer to have at least one Allsystems—"

"If it's a matter of cost," Harlis said, "I'm prepared to pay your crewed rate."

"Oh . . . well, then, how long do you need her for?"

"Sixty days . . . no, better make it ninety. I've got to visit several systems . . . Burkholdt, then Celeste. If I remember rightly, the transit time will eat up forty days, and then there's my business onplanet . . ."

"How about ninety with an option for another ninety? You can contact any Allsystems office to extend your lease; we have agents in both Burkholdt and Celeste . . ."

"That will do very well," Harlis said. "What are your provisioning options?"

"Well, there's the basic package, but for a gentleman of your rank we usually recommend at least the gold level—"

"Fine. I'll be over shortly to sign and make the deposit. Put us down for the departure queue, would you?"

"Of course, Ser Thornbuckle."

Now it was Harlis's turn to sit back and look at his new employee. "Six hours, and she'll be ready," he said.

"Good," the man said. "By the way, my name's Taylor. I'll go get the crew together; you get that information you said you could find, and meet me at the Allsystems office at—" He looked at his watch. "At 2100."

It occurred to Harlis that his employee was giving him orders and very little information.

Castle Rock, 0930 local time

Brun turned away from the shuttle terminal with a sigh. "Well . . . I'm glad she's going back where she belongs, but we sure have a mess to deal with here. And I don't really have a clue where to start."

Kate grinned that brassy grin, and said, "You might want to start by helping me finish up my mission, so's I can get home. With that Conselline out of the way, and a new foreign minister, we ought to be able to get those trade restrictions lifted, and those assets unfrozen, don't you think? And this would be a real smart time for the Familias to make nice to its neighbors."

"You're leaving too?"

"Well, hon, I can't stay here forever, and I figure I've given you folks about all the advice I can, without asking for a salary."

Brun laughed. "I'll miss you. But yes, we should be able to get your government's needs attended to. Though since my mother killed the former foreign minister, you might do better without my help."

"Let's just see," Kate said. "I'll meet you for lunch, why don't I, and let you know how it went. The town house?"

"Fine," Brun said. Kate waved, and turned away. Brun started to offer her a ride, but realized that the Ranger was more than capable of finding her own way. Brun glanced aside, to be sure her security detail was in place, and then walked tamely to her own transport.

At the town house, she kicked off her shoes as she entered the small but comfortable library. It had been her father's . . . his father's, too, she presumed. Now it was hers—at least, when she was here alone. She sank into one of the big armchairs, propped her feet on the hassock, and closed her eyes. She couldn't hear street traffic from here, but she could hear a gardener complaining to another about a shipment of bedding plants.

She heard the distant burr of an incoming call and ignored it, closing her eyes a moment. But the soft swish of footsteps coming down the hall brought her upright. "For me?" she said, as the housekeeper came to the door.

"Yes, sera. Viktor Barraclough." Viktor! What could he want? "I'll take it in here," she said.

"It's on the secure line," the housekeeper said.

Which meant using the privacy booth in the hall. Brun fitted herself into the booth, put her hands on the ID plate and looked into the scan mask. When the light turned green, she sealed the unit, then spoke.

"Viktor? It's Brun—how may I help you?"

"Brun, Stepan wants to meet with you."

The head of the Barraclough sept wanted to meet with her? Her heart started pounding, and questions raced through her mind. She asked the only useful ones. "Where and when?"

"He would prefer that you come to his attorney's office—and is Kevil Mahoney well enough to come along?" What was going on?

"I have a lunch meeting," Brun said. "But I'll contact Kevil and see—I'm assuming he wants to meet today?"

"If possible, this afternoon at three—if not, tomorrow."

"I see."

"And—it's Family and sept business, which we would prefer to be kept private. I know you have that woman from the Lone Star Confederation with you—some kind of law officer?"

"A Ranger, they call it. Yes—she was helpful when Harlis was fighting Dad's will."

"So I understood. If you believe her to be discreet, Stepan would not object to your letting her know where you are, but not anyone else."

"Fine, then."

She called Kevil, now home from the rehab center, from the same booth and waited while he made the secure connection.

"What are you up to now?" he asked.

"Viktor Barraclough," Brun said. "He called to tell me Stepan wants to see me—and you, if you're up to it—on Family and sept business, this afternoon or tomorrow afternoon."

Kevil pursed his lips a moment. "That's . . . very interesting. Have you been following the news the past couple of days?"

"No—we've been getting Esmay back to Fleet and off to her new command. Why?"

"The Consellines are bruiting it about that your family colluded with the Benignity to arrange the deaths on Patchcock, Hobart's assassination and Pedar's death."

"My," said Brun. "That's ingenious—how do they think we did it?"

"Well . . . apparently Oskar Morrelline came up with the idea that the Benignity spy in their Patchcock pharmaceutical facility was planted there by your family—to ruin the Morrellines' reputation, you see."

"But that's ridiculous," Brun said.

"Paranoid in high degree," Kevil agreed. "Unfortunately, however, Ottala, Oskar's daughter, must have told her father unflattering things about you, from your school days together, because he's convinced that you all had a grudge against the Morrellines."

Memories of schoolgirl pranks rose in Brun's mind—the time she had . . . the time Ottala had . . .

"She was fairly poisonous," Brun said, "but I didn't do anything worse than she did."

"That's not how he heard it. He's almost got himself convinced that this spy was not only planted by your family, but that Ottala was on the spy's trail and about to expose him when he killed her."

"Ottala couldn't have trailed a paint-dipped cat across a white carpet," Brun said, the old resentments flaring up. "She was impenetrably self-centered." Kevil said nothing, and she felt herself going hot. "Of course, so was I—so were we all, except maybe Raffaele—but Ottala wasn't just spoiled and rich and selfish . . . she wasn't overbright, besides."

"Whatever the facts," Kevil said, "what people believe is something else. Oskar got a little of his influence back under Hobart, and he's making the most he can of Hobart's death. He's convinced the Benignity ambassador is lying—that the Benignity wouldn't really have someone killed just because of their beliefs about rejuvenation—and besides, Hobart wasn't a rejuvenant."

"So the Consellines are painting us black," Brun said. "Our immediate family, or the whole sept?"

"The whole sept."

"I suppose Stepan wants me to be the sacrificial lamb," Brun said. "In Council, in front of everyone."

"I doubt it," Kevil said. "Stepan respected and liked your father—he's very old, you know, and he's never rejuved. I suspect he wants you to do something, and we'd better find out what."

"Can you make it this afternoon?"

"Of course. Three? I'll be there. And I would bet you, if you were a gambler, that if I call his attorneys right now, someone will ask me to lunch, and then we'll go back to their offices around two, chatting about how to get my business back in shape . . . and I just might still be there at three, when you arrive."

"Deviousness," Brun said.

"Yes. And if you think you and Stepan will be pulling up to the door at the same time, think again. Three this afternoon gives him plenty of time to arrange staggered arrivals for everyone he wants to have come and not much time for leaks. Look worried, Brun, when you arrive—look like someone who's expecting a scolding or even to be denied her Seat. And it wouldn't hurt if you called Buttons and asked what he thought of the Morrelline rumor mill, without mentioning Stepan."

"More deviousness," Brun said. "I can do that."

Shortly after that, Kate arrived for lunch, kicking off her high heels as she stepped onto the patterned carpet of the hall.

"I don't see why you wear those things if they hurt your feet," Brun said.

"For the sheer pleasure of taking them off and wiggling my toes in this," Kate said. She looked triumphant. "I've almost got the Foreign Ministry to agree to cancel the trade embargo, and I have appointments with two other ministers this afternoon. When I get those assets unfrozen, then it's over and done and I can take off for home. With maybe just a bit of sightseeing along the way."

"Sightseeing?"

"Well, like I told that young man on the ship that brought me here, I wouldn't mind a bit seeing the famous sights of the Familias. When else am I going to have time?"

"What's on your list?" Brun asked. "You know it could take a year or more . . ." They discussed tourist destinations over lunch, then Kate put her shoes on and headed out to do battle with the bureaucrats.

CHAPTER EIGHTEEN

Brun arrived at the offices of Spurling, Taklin, DeVries, and Bolton with what she hoped was a worried scowl. She had considered, and discarded, the idea of a disguise, but she wore another conservative dress.

"Ah . . . Sera Meager," the receptionist said. "Please come through," and unlocked the interior door. Brun stepped through, to be met by a glossy young man whom she realized, after a moment, was George Mahoney in formal business attire with an expression so different from his usual that he didn't look like himself.

"Fooled you, didn't I?" he said. As he grinned, the old George reappeared. "Passed my exams. I'm here to interview—"

Brun almost asked if he weren't going to work with his father, but the thought occurred that that was probably the best excuse any of them had.

"Dad had lunch with a senior partner today," he went on, for the benefit of anyone in any of the small offices they were passing. "They have an opening—he called and said to get myself over here. So here I am, and I think they're checking out my willingness to do as I'm told by asking me to escort visitors."

"How were the exams?" Brun asked, the least dangerous of the questions she was thinking.

"I did pretty well," George said. A flush reddened his cheekbones. "Actually—I did very well, and Dad was pleased, and I think that's why he wangled a lunch invitation, though he said Ser Spurling had been asking before if they could help."

"Come tops in the exams?"

The flush deepened. "As a matter of fact, not quite. You know that cousin of yours? Veronica?"

Brun remembered the slightly gawky girl at the Hunt Ball long ago, when the Crown Prince had ridden a horse into the dining hall.

"She came first; I came second. And—we're getting married." Before she could say anything, he said, "And here you are, Sera Meager—Ser Spurling's office."

Ser Spurling, who looked to be about sixty, led her into his spacious office and suggested to George that he might go downstairs and bring some files which the library clerk would have ready for him. In the office were Kevil, looking far more comfortable now with his new arm, Viktor, and Stepan Barraclough.

"Brun, my dear, how good to see you again." Stepan stood and came to her. He was an old man, though not so old as Viktor, and looked it, his face furrowed and sagging with age, showing the bones underneath, his eyes sunken beneath heavy lids. "Thank you for coming."

"Thank you—you're quite welcome."

"You will have wondered why I asked you to come, and you must have heard what Oskar Morrelline's come up with."

"Yes to both," Brun said.

"Good. Brun, I don't know if you ever heard why I refused rejuvenation—" She shook her head. "It was the price Kostan—my grandfather—demanded for ensuring that I would be in succession for the position I now hold. It was his opinion that in the transitional period, as the scope and effects of rejuvenation spread, the sept must have someone in the power structure who had not rejuvenated. Who would be a reality check for the rest, reminding them of the passage of time, and the needs of the whole."

"Long life or power, not both," Viktor put in.

"Exactly." Stepan grinned. "And also, the experience of longing for long life, and the experience of dealing with those who had it. At twenty, I had no difficulty choosing power. At forty and fifty, moving up the power structure of our sept, I first felt the longing, as my friends rejuvenated, and regained their youth. My wife wanted me to rejuv—she had, and when I wouldn't join her, she left me. It was hard, then, to stick to the bargain I'd made, but I am nothing if not stubborn." He chuckled. "Besides, he'd extracted the same promise from one of my uncles, who was then the new head of our sept, so if I'd reneged, my uncle would have found someone else. And I was, as my grandfather had foreseen, good at the kind of work it takes to be a good head of the sept."

"I chose long life," Viktor said. "But then I always had too much temper to be a candidate for the job."

"Ah, but you make a very good stalking horse, Viktor. I can count on you to draw the enemy's fire and reveal their ambushes."

"That's why he's so good at it," Viktor said to Brun, grinning. "He always finds a way to flatter you into doing what he wants."

"Not always. I never found Harlis very cooperative and blessed Bunny for being born first." Stepan looked at Brun, now. "I know what you were bred for, but not entirely what you've made of it," he said. "I need your talents, my dear. I had hoped to wait another ten years or so, but events turned against me. You are young, but you've been through an experience that would mature most people; I'm hoping it's matured you."

"I hope so too," Brun said. She began to have an inkling of where he was going, and the excitement of the possible challenge warred in her mind with the fear that she wasn't ready.

"I need an heir," Stepan said. "And I am offering you the same bargain that was offered me." He paused; Brun said nothing . . . she could not. "The government is at a crisis; even without the Morrelline accusations, the economic problems resulting from this rejuvenation issue, and the threat from the Benignity, would have brought it to the same crossroads. The woman who would have succeeded me first—Carlotta Bellinveau—developed intractible renal failure after treatment for a routine infection. Only rejuvenation would save her life, and she was only forty-five. She opted to risk it, but despite auto-transplants, she died last year. If I were paranoid, I'd suspect the Consellines of doing this by means of the drugs she took for the original infection, but frankly I think it was just one of those things."

"Was that . . . all? You had just one?"

"Not originally, no. But it's the combination of leadership talent and a willingness to forego rejuvenation that makes such people hard to find. Back when I was young and repeatable rejuvenation was new, there were plenty of cautious people my age who didn't rejuv at forty or fifty—but that number dwindled. Now, many of the wealthy are doing their first rejuv at thirty; your own older sister and her husband, Brun, just rejuved and thought nothing of it. They're in their thirties."

Brun wondered if he knew that she had wanted to rejuv to change her appearance and identity, to wipe herself out . . . now that seemed a macabre idea, clearly the thought of someone mentally unbalanced.

"So if I agree not to rejuv, you will support me for head of the sept? I thought it was elective . . ."

"It is elective, but like nearly all elections, it's somewhat rigged," he said. "And just agreeing not to rejuv is only the first step in the selection process. If you're going to say yes, please do so, so we can get on with the rest of it."

After a moment of startled silence, Brun said, "Yes. I will agree to that. A short life and a merry one."

Stepan smiled. "Good—that's the first step. I've found it a good bargain, by the way. Hard to hold in the middle, but I have no regrets at this point. Now. I haven't had time to get to know you since your return, but I've had my feelers out. Viktor, hand her the cube—" Brun took the data cube. "You'll want to view that in private—it's your complete dossier. If there's anything not on it, especially anything that could affect your political effectiveness, I need to know. How many Grand Council meetings have you been to now?"

"Five," Brun said.

"Good. You're over the awe of taking part, I hope."

"Oh, yes," Brun said.

"I'm going to ask you to address the Grand Council on behalf of our sept, at the next session. That is, as you might expect, coming up very shortly; the Consellines are demanding it to discuss Pedar's death. It is a critical session, and I'm hoping that you'll come as a startling surprise."

Brun managed not to gulp audibly.

"What would you say," Stepan said, "if you were going to speak now—knowing no more than you do?"

Brun gave Kevil a quick glance, but he was watching Stepan, not her. Ideas raced through her mind . . . which was the priority? Defend her Family and sept against the accusations of the Morrellines?

Tackle the difficult and complicated subject of legal reform and its relation to rejuvenation? Attack the Rejuvenants? No . . . in a flash she saw that what was needed now—at this moment—was a common goal, something to bring the almost-warring Families into alignment, as the sight of running prey would pull bickering hounds into a line of cooperation. Was this how her father had done it? She couldn't ask him; she'd have to figure it out for herself.

"Sirs and ladies," she said, as if this were actually the Grand Council, "whatever other problems face our realm, we have one clear priority—for to solve the difficult and intricate problems, we need time and security, and the one thing which most threatens our security, at this time, is the mutiny within our Regular Space Service. First, let us give all support to the suppression of this mutiny, the maintenance of security to our population and our trade, so that we can have the time and peace we need to discuss other issues."

Stepan nodded. "Good. Excellent, in fact." He looked at Kevil. "You were right; she has the instincts and she's learned to use them. You will want to flesh that out, polish it—but I like the spirit of it. How will you deal with questions about your family?"

Brun said, "With the truth, sir. And then tell them they can tear me and eat me later, if they want, but right now they must support the loyalists in Fleet."

"One thing about a foxhunting background," Kevil put in, "is that it provides a wealth of colorful metaphor and language."

"Yes . . . as long as you have a fox for them to chase, and I'll admit the mutiny is a very laudable fox which I hope we catch, cast, and tear before it gets to earth."

Thornbuckle town house, 1730

Brun heard Kate coming down the hall and blanked the cube reader's screen. She was breathing fast, more than a little astounded at the contents of Stepan's dossier on her. That he could readily find out about many semipublic scrapes—the ones that had appeared in various newsvid shows—didn't surprise her. But how had he dug up that mess at school when she was thirteen—and how had he found out that it wasn't her fault, when even her own parents had always believed it was? How did he know Brigdis Sirkin had refused her?

"Only one more official appointment," Kate said, throwing herself into a chair. "Then I'm free—" She looked at Brun, and her expression changed. "What's happened to you, this afternoon? You look like someone ran over you with a herd of longhorns."

"Old family stuff," Brun said. "Did you ever come across something that let you know exactly what someone thought about you when you were a kid?"

"You mean like old letters or school records or something? Yes . . . I guess I know what you mean. Even if they say something nice, it's never the kind of nice you expected or wanted. And usually it's not. I remember when my mother showed me what old Miss Pennyfield had written on the bottom of my report: 'Katharine Anne would be an excellent student if she would spend her energies on her studies instead of attempting to evade honest work.' And I'd thought the old prune liked me; I could always make her laugh. She'd seen right through my clowning—I could hardly laugh for a month."

"Exactly," Brun said.

"'Course," Kate said meditatively, "I did start workin' harder, and I did learn a lot more about somethin' other than making prune-faced teachers laugh. But then she had to spoil it by adding a note to the final report about how Katharine Anne was finally applying herself. That's why I wrote 'Old Prune-Face' on her front porch floor with nail polish . . . and spent half the summer doin' yard work for her to make up for it."

"She caught you?"

"Not her—she'd left the day after school let out to go on vacation. That's why I thought I was safe. It was her friend Miss Anson, who came by once a day—usually in the afternoons, but that day in the morning—who caught me in the act." She grinned at the memory, then looked at Brun again. "So what did you find out?"

Brun told her about the mess in school.

"Well, what do they expect with a lot of girls that age locked up together? Ottala—was that the same Ottala Morrelline that Oskar Morrelline's going on about?"

"The very same," Brun said. "But I didn't do anything that bad back to her."

"No, I wouldn't think you would. But—I hate to be self-serving about this—what effect is all this going to have on the stability of your government? It's not going to do me much good to have things going well, go home, and then have it all come unravelled again. Rangers are supposed to settle a problem once and for all."

"It's our problem, not yours, to solve," Brun said. Kate raised her eyebrows, but Brun was getting tired of the Ranger's attitude. "But I'm arguing for Esmay's approach. First we deal with the mutiny—get ourselves some secure breathing space—and then we can work on the rest. In the long run, we've got to make big changes, as you've said—as a lot of people recognize—but in the short run we need to get Fleet back on sound footing."

"That sounds reasonable," Kate said. "Have you had supper yet?"

"No," Brun said. "You?"

"Just a snack. But you're looking a bit peaked. We blondes need to keep our strength up for the roses in the cheeks; I could manage to keep you company in a snack . . ."

"All right . . ." Brun shut off the cube reader, and got up. "Now that you mention it, it's odd that no one's asked me. It's not the staff's day off, and they knew I'd be in this evening."

At that, Kate's eyes narrowed. "Where's your security?" she asked softly.

"Outside the house, I assume. Why?"

"Weren't when I got here. Not visibly."

Brun felt a chill run down her back. Here, in the family house, she had no weapon to hand. She hadn't thought she'd need one.

Kate gave her a long look, and said, quite clearly, "Well, never mind. Let's have dinner out somewhere. Didn't you tell me about a place Lady Cecelia liked?"

"Why not? This place is too quiet anyway." Brun felt prickles all over her skin as she stood up, stretched, fished around under the desk for her shoes. She slipped the cube from the cube reader and put it in her pocket. She looked at Kate. Now what? An attack in the hall? Outside the door?

"I'm in the mood for fish," Kate said. "That Lassaferan snailfish you people have—I wonder if we could import some eggs or larvae or whatever a snailfish has."

"No fish for me," Brun said. "I'm thinking rabbit fillets stuffed with herbed cheese."

They were in the hall. She could see the front door, and light spilling into the hall from the front rooms. No odd shadows. She glanced back toward the service door. Shut. Quiet. The wide carpeted hall, with its umbrella stand, where her father's walking stick still stood . . . Brun slid it out of the stand as she passed, without missing a stride, as if she always took a man's walking stick out to dinner.

Nobody lunged at them as they walked past the open door of the study, the front room. They paused before the door; Kate's eyebrows went up and she shrugged. "How cold was it out?" Brun asked. "Are you going to need a wrap?"

"I might," Kate conceded. "Your so-called spring is colder than ours, but you'd probably call it balmy." She reached for the door of the cloakroom; Brun held the walking stick poised.

The door opened and the interior light came on, revealing nothing more sinister than a rack of hangers, mostly empty. Her father's old smoking jacket, which she'd looked for at Appledale and not found, her mother's moss-green cashmere scarf, a tweed jacket of her own, an assortment of raincoats, dark blue and tan and gray. Kate chose a dark blue raincoat and wrapped the green scarf around her throat. Brun took another like it.

Still nothing. She flicked off the lights in the front of the house, waited a moment for her eyes to adjust to the darkness, and opened the front door. Cool damp air washed in.

Kate moved past her, staying close to the entrance; Brun left the door slightly ajar, in case they needed to bolt back inside, though she didn't think that was a good idea anyway.

"Leave it wide open and come on," Kate murmured, close again. Brun jumped. Then she pushed the door open, and followed Kate along the house wall to the corner. Outside, the distant streetlights gave enough glow that she could see rough shapes. A light in the study shone out and gilded the top of the hedge she had heard the gardener trimming that morning. At the back of the house, another bar of light lay dimly on the lawn. "Let's go," Kate said.

They struck out across the lawn; Brun had remembered to bring the lockout, so the perimeter security—if whoever had removed her staff hadn't disabled it already—wouldn't start the alarms and let the bad guys know where they were. Of course, if they had the right gear, none of this sneaking around would work . . . she sidled through a row of camellia bushes, then peered through the shoulder-high evergreen hedge beyond . . . nothing but the gleam of pavement reflecting distant streetlights. Not that she could see anything to either side. Brun pulled the raincoat up over her head to keep the needly foliage from catching in her hair and pushed the branches of one bush aside with the cane. Kate was right behind her.

Still nothing. There they were, on the sidewalk, with no obvious threat anywhere. Brun jammed her hands in the pocket of the coat and found an old scarf, which she tied over her head as they walked along.

"That was interesting," Kate said. "I think I'll report a house with an open front door when we get a little away from here."

"Mmm. I was thinking of calling the security agency and mentioning that their employees had disappeared."

"Two strings to your bow. Are you going to carry that cane all the way into town?"

"I think so," Brun said, shifting it in her hand. "Since everything else I might carry is upstairs in the bedroom."

As they came to a busier street, they joined a stream of pedestrians headed for a transit stop, and paused in the sheltered kiosk where the public comunits were. Brun called the security company, then Kevil to report where she was so he wouldn't panic. Kate called the police. They boarded a tram, got off at the next stop, dove down a subway entrance, and—three transfers and a call for reservations later—were ushered into the ladies' retiring room at Celeste. They grinned at each other in the mirrors, handed over the raincoats and scarves to the attendant, and strolled out to be seated in one of the bay-window alcoves overlooking the stone garden. This early the restaurant wasn't crowded.

"You people go in for strange gardens," Kate said. She turned her attention to the menu. "Ah . . . they do have Lassaferan snailfish. Now why is the fin twice as expensive as the whole fish?"

"You complain about everything," Brun said. "And it's because it's decorative, and nobody's been able to fake one yet. Also there's a piquant flavor to the spine of the fin. Not worth it, though, if you ask me."

"I'll have the whole fish, then. Baked, or broiled?"

"Broiled is better, and ask for a garnish of roast garlic. Some people say lemongrass, but I think garlic. Or both. Drat. They don't have rabbit—many apologies, supplier failed to deliver. If I'd known I'd have told the people at Appledale to send in some of the nuisances that ravage the kitchen garden out there."

"So what are you going to have?"

"Mmmm . . . I don't know; my mouth was really set on rabbit. Lamb maybe. Cattlelope is just too . . . too."

"Start with soup," Kate said. "So will I. We both need it."

They were most of the way through the soup, when a stir near the entrance caught Brun's attention. Someone was talking urgently to the maitre d', trying to get past him.

"She's my *niece*, dammit!" Uncle Harlis. Brun swallowed. Uncle Harlis was supposed to be under detention or surveillance or something—she hadn't paid much attention, beyond being assured he wouldn't bother her—pending investigation of his felonious actions in the various family businesses, and his attempt on Bunny's inheritance. "I have a right to see her; I'm worried . . ." At that, Kate turned around.

"The wicked uncle returns?"

"Something like that," Brun said. A colored light had come on at their table, discreetly signalling that someone wanted to speak with her. She pressed the response. Kate raised an eyebrow. "Might as well," Brun said. "He'll just make more of a scene if we don't, and he's not likely to try a physical assault here, in public." Now the maitre d' was leading Harlis over to their table.

"Brun, I've been so worried," Harlis said. He looked more flustered than worried, Brun thought, but she didn't argue the point. "After all, your mother—and I tried to call you but no one answered, and when I went by, there were police all over the house."

"Really?" Brun said. "Why?"

"They wouldn't say. Are you all right?"

"Fine," Brun said. "Is that all you wanted? Or is there something else?" She couldn't imagine he'd come to the restaurant just to find out if she was all right.

"Look . . . Brun . . . I know this may be a bad time, but . . . I want to go to Sirialis."

"Sirialis? Why on earth—you know the court upheld Dad's bequests."

"Yes, I know. But there're things of mine there—you know, my room in the east wing—and I want them."

"I can have them sent to you," Brun offered.

"I need to go there myself," Harlis said. His voice was louder again; Brun could see others giving them sidelong glances. Was he drunk?

"I don't think that's a good idea," Brun said. "There's no one in the family in residence—"

"I'm in the family!" Harlis said. "It's as much my home as yours—it should be—it's not fair—" He faltered.

"Harlis, you would have had the same access you always had, if you hadn't tried to cheat us. *That* wasn't fair."

"Neither is making the daughter of a murderer the Barraclough heir," Harlis snarled. Brun could almost feel the tense fascination of the other diners.

"Is that what this is about?" Brun said, wondering where he'd heard it.

"What'd you do, diddle the old man?" Harlis's voice rang through the room, and the maitre d' and one of the larger waiters started toward them.

Kate laughed, and leaned back in her chair. "What's the matter, Harlis, did you give it away?"

Brun felt her face heating—Kate's taste in humor belonged in a barn—but managed to hold her neutral expression. When the maitre d' was near enough, she spoke in a low but clear voice. "I believe my uncle is not feeling well. Perhaps you could help him to some assistance?"

"Of course, sera," the maitre d' said.

"You'll regret this," Harlis said. "Spoiled, bratty, stupid little bitch—"

The other diners applied themselves to their food with commendable delicacy until Harlis had disappeared from the room.

"I will say this about your uncle," Kate said. "He doesn't let an occasion for stupidity pass him by."

Brun snorted and almost choked on her water. "I needed that. But I have to call someone, a secured call. Can I leave you a few minutes?"

"Of course. I will amuse myself by flirting with that handsome young fellow who just walked in and is standing by the wall over there. Could it be our George?"

Brun glanced that way. "Oh. I don't need to make the call."

"You don't have to be so mysterious with me," Kate said.

"Actually I do," Brun said. "Excuse me a moment." She walked across the room and stepped out into the foyer with George Mahoney.

"I'm glad you're all right," he said, bowing formally.

"Things . . . happened."

"Yes. Dad's taken care of it."

"Harlis was here," Brun said.

"Here?"

"Yes. You must've just missed him—he was . . . asked to leave."

"Did you talk to him?"

"Yes. He wants to go to Sirialis."

"Let me call Dad—then can I join you for dinner?"

"Of course. I'll tell Kate and snag a waiter."

When George exerted himself to be charming, he could be very charming indeed. Kate, who had only seen him worried about his father, or being casual at Appledale, had not experienced the glossy splendor of George in full feather. Brun sat back and watched them banter and flirt and chat, as she worked her way through her saddle of venison without saying much. The food revived her, and by the time they were ready for dessert, she was ready to ask questions.

"The house staff?"

"All safe. Variously disposed of, but safe. Your security was less fortunate, but they're all alive. Stepan has assigned Barraclough senior security to you; the house will be safe tonight, but he recommends that you spend the night elsewhere. You can always stay with us, you know."

"Do you know who, or what?"

"Not for sure, but Harlis's name was mentioned."

"He started out saying he was worried about Brun," Kate put in. "Said he'd been by the house, seen the police . . . as if he thought something might have happened. Seemed put out that she was safe and unworried."

"Hm. Nobody told me he'd been to the house. I'd have thought they'd hold him if he'd shown up . . . where'd he go?"

"I have no idea," Brun said. "All I know is, he wants to go to Sirialis, and when I didn't agree that he could, he said I'd be sorry."

"I think we need to call that in right now," George said. "With any luck we can find him, but—" He looked at the time. "He could have caught the up-shuttle already."

"If we'd been there . . . if he'd had backup," Kate said, "Brun could be dead and he could be on that shuttle."

"Well, I'm not," Brun said, eyeing the pastry cart coming toward them. "I'm alive, and I want something with chocolate all over it."

CHAPTER NINETEEN

Rockhouse Major, 1800 local time

Goonar was just getting ready to head up to the main restaurant block in this section of the Station for dinner when his comunit buzzed. "It's Commander Tavard," a voice said. "Those fingerprints and video were very interesting."

"Oh? Are—uh—this isn't a secure link at this end, Commander."

"Not a problem. Just wanted to tell you how glad I am you aren't heading out with that particular passenger. And to keep a close eye on your area, in case he decides to retaliate for your inhospitality." Tavard sounded almost smug.

"Believe me, I shall. We were going out to dinner, Basil and I, but we could stay aboard, if you think that's wise."

"No, dinner out sounds fine, as long as you have someone reliable aboard. If we should happen to meet, I presume you're still annoyed with Fleet for its ungenerous attitude towards informers?"

"Of course. Shall I snub you, or you snub me?"

"Both a little cool, I'd say. Oh, and thanks for your information about Suiza. She's turned up—she was visiting a private residence and that's why we couldn't find her."

"You mean you really—?" Goonar had not considered that this interest might be real.

"Two strings to my bow, and two arrows nocked . . . though if I understand bows at all, that's not how it could work. But you grasp my meaning."

619

"Indeed." He thought of asking about Betharnya and her troupe, but decided better not complicate an already complicated situation. "I'm taking my comunit along, if you need to contact me."

With a last warning to the ship's crew, he and Basil headed up to the main levels. Rockhouse always made him feel he was in the thick of things; Zenebra might be as crowded just before the Trials, but that was all horse people, all one sort. Here it was the variety, the sense that everyone, at one time or another, might turn up on business. Shops, news kiosks with screens flickering and hardcopies racked below, more shops, the bustle of the evening traffic, mostly well-dressed at this hour: the soberly dressed businessmen and women who were still working, the gaudily dressed young out for an evening.

He watched an old woman in a brilliant red and purple caftan, her thick gray hair in a braid piled on her head, swing along as if she owned the entire station. She wasn't particularly tall, but people moved out of her way as if by some arcane force. Basil nudged him. "Reminds me of Aunt Herdion."

"She's somebody's aunt, I'd say," Goonar said. She cheered him up, for reasons he couldn't grasp. In a universe with brisk old ladies like this, old ladies who could mend quarrels between families for the sake of a lost child, he could almost believe that Betharnya would consider giving up the stage for a nice house at the family compound, next door to Basil's.

As a Terakian captain, Goonar now had a membership in the Captains' Guild; he had booked a table for himself and Basil. He'd been here before, as a junior guest of his uncle's, but this was his first time in the door as a member in his own right.

"Captain Terakian, of course." The maitre d' smiled at him. "We're always delighted to see captains of Terakian and Sons here. Please—follow me."

Then, he had been awed by the decor, unused to the style of the inner worlds of the Familias. Now . . . he could almost feel he belonged here.

Once the first course was on the table, Basil leaned across. "You aren't going to leave here without talking to Bethya, are you?"

Goonar almost choked on his soup and glared at Basil. "How can I talk to her when she disappeared into the Fleet side of the Station, and I've heard nothing?"

"You could ask. You could have asked that commander."

"He came to ask about the Suiza woman," Goonar said, mindful of listeners. "Why would he know anything about Bethya?"

"Goonar . . . she likes you, and you like her. I can tell."

"You cannot. Last year you thought I was falling for that blonde—"

"I was hoping. I knew better, truly I did. But don't try to tell me Bethya doesn't stir you—"

"Don't be vulgar, Bas." Goonar leaned over his soup, the rising steam an excuse for the heat in his cheeks. "Besides, if she wants to talk to me, she knows where I am. Anyway, she's an actress. Why would she be interested in a plain old ship captain?" Other than the reasons he didn't want to hear.

"She's ready to settle down, maybe."

"I doubt it," Goonar said. The soup lay heavy in his stomach, and he wished dinner over already. Basil went on spooning his in—his appetite hadn't suffered.

His comunit buzzed. Goonar flicked it on. "Captain? This is Bethya—" His pulse raced. "We're . . . um . . . finished here." He could hear the careful phrasing. "We're contacting agents to see about a booking . . . I know we need to get our equipment off your ship and into storage or something. Could I come talk to you about that and about settling up?"

"Don't worry," he said automatically. Then, with a feeling like plunging over a cliff, he said, "Actually—Basil and I are having dinner at the Captains' Guild. Would you like to join us?"

"I don't know if I . . . yes, Captain, I'd like that. Where is it?"

Goonar gave her directions and looked up to find Basil grinning like a boy who had just pulled the prize ring out of the barrel. "What!"

"It was Bethya, wasn't it?"

"Yes, it was Bethya, and yes, she's coming over here to have dinner." He signalled a waiter and explained that he had another guest coming.

"You're grinning all over your face," Basil observed. "Some of our competitors are going to think you just made a deal."

"Let them," Goonar said. His appetite had returned with a rush; he could have eaten an entire cattlelope.

Bethya arrived a few minutes later, and Goonar would have

sworn every male in the place perked up. She knew it, too, he saw, and enjoyed it. But her smile was for him alone when he seated her.

"I didn't want to call you until they were completely through," she said. "And then Dougie started up—insisting that he knew just what we should do, and how, and when. I had to get them all back to the hotel, and call two agents, before he'd leave off."

"That's all right," Goonar said. "What will you have?"

"That looks good," she said, glancing at his plate. "Cattlelope?"

"Yes—soup to start, clear or cream—"

"Cream," she said. "I need something soothing."

Goonar ordered dinner for her and waited.

"Go on," she said. "Don't wait for me."

"I'd rather," he said. "It's been one of those days, and I don't need indigestion tonight."

"I wanted to thank you again . . . both of you." She looked at Basil, then back to Goonar. "I know it caused you trouble and worry, and perhaps your company will be angry—"

"It's all right," Goonar said.

"I've been trying to think how to make it work for you, make it pay—"

"Your presence, sera, was all we needed," Basil said. He widened his eyes at her; she grinned at him.

"You are married, my fine young cockerel; don't pretend to offer what you don't have. And I'm talking business here. I thought, Goonar, you might want a share in the company."

"In an acting company?"

"Yes. It wouldn't amount to much, most likely, but we've talked it over, and we're all willing to split off another share for you. We know what could have happened if you hadn't taken us in. And if miracles happened and we had a long run in some major theater . . ."

Her soup arrived, saving Goonar the need to answer. Basil, who had not slowed down, pushed his plate aside. "Goonar, I'm going back to the ship; I'm just not comfortable with none of us aboard. My vote's to take the share, if it comes to that."

As transparent an excuse as any he'd seen, but he, too, thought having Basil aboard was a good idea. Goonar toyed with his vegetables, and watched Bethya covertly.

"Bethya . . . would you ever consider—" He cleared his throat. It was hopeless, why was he even trying? "Er . . . settling down?"

"Settling down? You mean in one place? Goonar, I'm talented, but not that talented."

"No, I meant as—with a family. Live in a house on a planet, raise children."

"Goonar, are you asking me to marry you?"

"I would if I thought it would do any good."

She laughed, not unkindly. "Goonar, that has to be the most depressed proposal I ever got. But I don't want to give up travel. Someday I'll have to give up the stage, yes: as I said, I know the limits of my talent, and it won't survive my forties. And though I'm a reasonably good manager, there's been grumbling in my company that I'm too old to have the lead roles. Dougie thinks he could run the company as well, and Lisa is sure she'd be a better village belle."

"She's wrong," Goonar said. "She looks like a village idiot and sounds like a goose with a bone in its throat."

Bethya laughed again. "Not quite that bad, but I'll agree she's not as good as she thinks. Anyway, I'd like to have children. But stay in one place? No." She gave him another of those looks that had raised his hopes. "I confess I've been selfish, Goonar . . . traveling on the *Fortune* was such fun, and I thought maybe trader captains took their wives along. I like you—we can laugh together, that's important, and you're honest and kind. But not even for you will I go sit in a house on a rotating mudball."

"Some captains take their wives along," Goonar said. "I mean, it's not against the rules."

"Many are fooled by glamour," Bethya said. "But wives and husbands see behind the stage makeup."

"I'm not in love with your stage makeup," Goonar said. "I'm not some callow boy."

"Then who are you in love with?" Bethya asked.

"The woman who took in a fugitive when she didn't have a clue how she was going to get him out. The woman who sang and danced and stole my heart, while she was scheming to evade the Benignity. The woman who could act two parts and never scramble them, and who in all those weeks, doubled up in bunk space, never said a cross word. Was kind to Esmay Suiza—"

"All right, all right." She had gone red, and as the blush faded he saw that her eyes were bright with unshed tears. "I . . . this is utterly crazy. I have had suitors—"

"I'm sure you have," said Goonar. His heart pounded until he was sure it would fly out of his chest. Would she?

"I'm—I can't just—" But the look on her face said she could, and suddenly she opened to him like a rose in midsummer. "All right— yes—I've been taken with you since I saw you sitting there beside Basil, sad and worried and tired. I told myself it was just a performer's pride, to make you laugh, make you smile, make you . . . think . . . you wanted me. But . . . it's ridiculous, you and me, we aren't the lad and lass in the story."

"That's true," Goonar said, pulling her to him gently and inexorably. "We're not that lad and lass . . . but we are this man and this woman." He buried his face in her hair. "You are so beautiful."

Rockhouse Major, 2130 local time

Harlis arrived at the Allsystems dock area thirty minutes late.

"What happened?" asked Taylor.

"A slight inconvenience," Harlis said, breathing hard. "Let's go aboard and get out of here."

"Our departure slot isn't for another hour."

Harlis went aboard, to find that the owner's suite was full of duffel and four men were asleep there.

"What's this?" he asked Taylor.

"You're down here," Taylor said, showing him to the smallest cabin—meant, Harlis could see, for a cook or valet or something like that. "My people need to be together."

"But—"

"Don't worry," Taylor said. "We'll get you to Sirialis." Harlis settled himself into the narrow bunk and wondered how far behind his pursuers were. Could they find him in the next hour? He cursed himself for letting Brun know he wanted to go to Sirialis.

Rockhouse Major, Captains' Guild

How long they might have sat there, to the amusement of other captains and the waiters, Goonar was later unable to guess, but their time of bliss was interrupted by a waiter bearing a note.

"Drat," Goonar said. "It's that fellow from Fleet who was looking for Esmay. I thought they'd found her. I wonder what he wants now."

"I should get back to the hotel," Bethya said. "I'll have to tell the others and endure Dougie's lectures and Lisa's gloating." She pushed back her chair.

"I don't want to rush you," Goonar began, standing up.

"Yes, you do," Bethya said. She came around the table, and in full view of everyone gave him a kiss that made his ears catch fire. Yes, he wanted to rush her, straight back to his quarters on the ship. "I'm not a sweet little virgin, you know," she said into his ear.

"I should hope not," Goonar said. "All right—go settle 'em and let me know when you want to come back."

He had walked her to the foyer, aware that Terakian & Sons' newest captain had just furnished juicy gossip that would be all over the intership coms just as soon as those captains made it back to their ships.

As Bethya left, Commander Tavard stepped out of an alcove. "Handsome woman," he said.

"Yes," Goonar said. "We're getting married."

"Um. I thought she was that actress—"

"She was."

"I see." For a moment, the commander looked confused, but then he said, "Come outside with me, will you? We have a bit of acting to do ourselves."

Goonar grinned. "Maybe you should have asked Bethya."

"No—I think you'll do."

Outside, the commander walked Goonar along the concourse in the direction of the slideways. "You had a visitor this morning you didn't tell us about," he said, quietly but clearly. His tone was intentionally antagonistic and, even though Goonar understood what was going on, he could still feel his neck getting hot.

"I don't see why I should tell you about every possible customer who comes by," Goonar said. "And you were asking about Sera Suiza."

"I told you we were interested in possible mutineers and pirates—and you sat there and didn't say one word about this man—" The commander pulled out a flatpic of the man who'd been at the ship that morning. "He's a former commander in Fleet, a mutineer, the very sort of man I talked to you about—"

"I'm not your spy," Goonar said. "Why didn't you show me that picture before and ask if I'd seen him?"

"Would you have answered?"

"Of course," Goonar said. "What kind of an idiot do you think I am?"

"Idiot enough not to tell me about this man when he came by—and now he's escaped."

"He's not on the Station?"

"No." The commander sounded very disgruntled. "If you'd only used your head, we might have caught him. I want to come check out your office area, see if he left any clues—"

"All right," Goonar said. "But I can tell you he didn't. He walked in, wanted passage, and we didn't have enough cabins and weren't fast enough. Yes, it's true he wanted me to take a yellow route, but old *Fortune*'s not mine to risk, and he didn't want to wait while I asked the company."

"Did he say where he was going?"

"No—he said he wanted passage to Millicent."

"Well, I hope you'll act more responsibly next time," the commander said. "And encourage other captains to do the same. We don't want you people being hijacked."

In the *Fortune*'s dockside office, the commander handed Goonar a data cube. "Good acting, Captain. Now—that really is a mutineer, and his name really is Taylor, and we do consider him extremely dangerous. We don't know if he left anyone behind to spy on this Station—I wouldn't be surprised if he did. He did get away—in a yacht leased by one of the Seated Families."

"What? The Families are in league with the mutineers?"

"Not all of them. But the mutineers—some of them—have tried to make contact with the Families they worked for, before Fleet was organized. And a disaffected Family member, looking for some muscle to impose on the rest of his Family, would make exactly the right employer. They have their quarrels, same as anyone else."

"So this was . . . who? One of the Consellines?"

"Captain—this is not something you need to know. But it wasn't a Conselline."

"And you don't know where this person wanted to go?"

"No. Or where the mutineers wanted to go. This man may have bought his way into a mysterious death . . . I wouldn't trust my life to these cutthroats."

"I hope, Commander, that if my routes are taking me into dangerous territory, you'll let me know."

"Yes. You may be at special risk, since he knows you've seen his face. I'm hoping that this evening's little charade convinced anyone he left on guard, but once you're in space again—what's your route?"

"It depends—I told the Fathers that we'd be delayed here because of the troupe—as we have been. And if Bethya wants to be married here, we might well be delayed longer. *Terakian Princess* is bound this way; if she arrives before we leave, we may switch routes—I'd head out towards Xavier, Rotterdam, Corian and—that loop."

"I'd recommend that. Now if we could only figure out for sure where that yacht is going. They told the leasing company one thing, which almost certainly isn't true, but there's a lot of space in the Familias. If they even stay in the Familias."

Basil, when Goonar went aboard, wanted to know all about Bethya; Goonar put him off by telling him about the commander. "He interrupted us," Goonar said. "Wanted to talk about that fellow who came this morning."

"A criminal?"

"A mutineer. Very dangerous, he says, and worst of all he got away—he's already off the Station."

"That's good."

"Is it? That commander says he has a warship somewhere— probably somewhere along that yellow route to Millicent. On top of that he's linked up with a rogue Family member—someone rich enough to walk in and hire a fully-stocked yacht at the drop of a hat.

They don't know where he's gone, but they know he has money enough at his command as long as this Family member is with him."

"So—do they think he caught on to us?"

"He doesn't know. He suspects the man might have left a spy here on the Station, and that he might be watching us—we played quite a little drama for any watchers, with me as the selfish captain who had been stupid enough not to tell him about this mutineer earlier."

"But what about Bethya?" Basil said, returning to his earlier topic.

"She'll call before they leave, she said," Goonar said. "Probably tomorrow."

"You're blushing, Goonar."

"Well . . . I do like her, Bas, you're right about that. But there's a lot to think about."

"You're not getting any younger . . ."

"I'm not doddering along with one foot in the grave, either," Goonar said. "I don't have to rush into things." But the memory that he had done just that made him grin; Basil gave him a suspicious look.

"What? What did you say to her?"

"Basil, go to bed. I am."

Castle Rock, 2030 local time

Brun Meager sank into the worn tapestry upholstery of the couch in the Mahoneys' living room. "Kevil, are you sure this is all right? You've only just gotten the house back . . ."

"Stepan suggested it," Kevil said. "I see you've got your father's stick—"

"So I have." Brun leaned it against the couch. "Do you—does anyone—have the slightest idea what was going on, and who did it?"

"The present idea is that Harlis wanted to talk to you in private, he and your cousin Kell. There's no real evidence, except that Harlis found you at dinner and told you he'd been to the house looking for you and found police there. That didn't happen. My guess would be that he wasn't actually planning to kill you, just trying to bully you into doing something he wanted."

"He wanted to go to Sirialis, he said," Brun said. "I can't imagine why."

"To find out what your mother found?" asked Kate, from an armchair across the room.

"Possibly," Kevil said. "If he thought it was your mother's evidence that landed him in trouble."

"Has anyone located him?" Brun asked.

"No. He didn't go up on a scheduled shuttle, but you know there are other ways . . . does he own a shuttle?"

"He might've taken the family one—"

"Not the one at Appledale; we checked on that. But with the Grand Council meeting coming up, there are Family shuttles of all sizes coming and going. He might have caught a ride with someone. We're trying to find out. And of course he may not have tried to get offworld at all—he could be on his way back to his own place, or somewhere else—"

"And there are a few more things for the police to do than chase one suspect, I'll bet," said Kate.

"Yes." Kevil sighed. "Brun, we've made up the spare bedroom for you and Kate. Stepan's having his senior security staff check over the town house; he expects you can move back in tomorrow morning. We're covered, of course."

"Of course," Brun murmured. She felt both very tired and very alert.

"Have you told Kate about the meeting today?"

"No," Brun said. "I wasn't planning to—"

"Stepan said it wouldn't hurt, and might take the strain off you, not to be keeping more secrets than you have to." He turned to Kate. "Stepan's head of our sept—the Barracloughs—and he asked Brun to become his designated heir."

Kate frowned. "The sept—I've never quite understood. Families I understand . . . is this like a sort of super-family of families?"

"Yes, in a way."

Kate whistled. "Well—quite a step up, then."

"You'll like this," Brun said. "One thing I had to do was agree not to be rejuved."

"My . . ."

"Yes. Power versus longevity. Take your pick. And I'm being dropped in at the deep end: he wants me to address the Grand Council formally at the next meeting. So I think I'd better toddle off to bed and get my beauty sleep."

❧ ❧ ❧

She woke with a start in the unfamiliar bed, with Kate snoring lightly across the room. She could just make out the green and cream stripes of the wallpaper. What had woken her? She heard voices in the distance, muffled by the closed door, then footsteps coming closer. A tap.

"Yes," she said softly. Kate's snore stopped in the middle.

"It's me," George said. "Can you come out?"

Brun looked at the time and sighed. She could have used another hour's sleep, but she was, after all, wide awake. "Coming," she said.

She wrapped the borrowed robe—one of Kevil's she thought—around her, and went out to find Kevil waiting for her in his study. "We just heard—Harlis rented a yacht from Allsystems Leasing yesterday. He's with a mutineer commander, and apparently rented the yacht bare. Probably crewed by Fleet personnel, in other words. They requested and got a fast-transit exit route and went into jump two hours ago."

"Did they say where they were going?"

"Harlis told Allsystems Burkholdt and Celeste, but the same mutineer had tried to get passage on a civilian ship to Millicent. I think the question at this point is, who's in command of that yacht?"

"They don't get up this early on ranches," Kate said from the doorway. She yawned. "Found Harlis, did they?"

"And lost him," Kevil said. "Case of the right hand not having told the left what was going on." He explained what they knew.

Kate frowned. "It doesn't make sense," she said.

"What doesn't?"

"The timing. He was at the restaurant when we were eating dinner—what time was that?"

"I don't know . . . it wasn't late . . . 1900 maybe?"

"And the yacht left the Station at 2230. So he must have run for a shuttle and then gone immediately . . ."

"Yes . . . that makes sense."

"Except that he leased the yacht earlier. He'd have to have been on the Station, then come down to the surface, then gone back up . . . Why? Is that even possible?" Kate looked from face to face.

"With good private shuttles, of course," Brun said.

"He came down to pick you up," George said suddenly. "He

arranged to hire the ship, he leased the shuttle, and while the ship was being provisioned, he came down to get you."

"He was going to take her away? Where?" Kate looked at Brun; Brun felt a chill that struck through her like a spear of ice.

"I . . . don't want to know," she said, struggling to keep herself from showing the panic she felt. Had she really come so close to another captivity? But her mind went on working. "Sirialis. If he took me to Sirialis, the people there would think it was me. I mean, they'd think it was all right, at first, and then—"

"A hostage." Kevil said. "Against your sept, certainly against anything the people on Sirialis might do. And—Brun, you have the family codes for the communications and data storage systems on Sirialis, don't you?"

"Yes, of course. Everything but Mother's private ciphers."

"Would he know about hers? About your not having them?"

"I don't know." Brun felt a wave of panic, and shoved it down.

"Our files on him are at Appledale," Kate said. "We didn't bring them into town—didn't see a reason to. He was detained, we thought." She sounded annoyed.

"Gentleman's detention—he wore a scan bracelet," Kevil said. "His attorneys argued that he wasn't going to bolt, and he'd posted a huge bond. Anyway, he claimed to have a toothache; apparently his dentist took the bracelet off for him early yesterday morning. Nobody realized he'd slipped away for hours: the dentist claimed he had an emergency ahead of Harlis, and the bracelet returned a signal. The dentist's now in detention himself; they found the bracelet tucked under the cushion of one of the chairs."

"Did Harlis go to Appledale?" Brun asked.

"No. We've called out there; no intrusion."

"*He* has the family codes," Brun said suddenly.

"What?"

"Harlis. He has the codes. Some of them, anyway, the general ones. I'm sure—unless Mother changed them, when she left, but she would have thought he was in detention. No reason to change them. And nobody's there."

"The staff are," Kevil said. "The others . . ."

"No *family*," Brun said. "No one who can change the codes, and lock him out."

"If that's where he's going, with a Fleet warship, just changing the codes wouldn't help."

"I'll bet that's how they got in, in the first place," Brun said.

Kevil looked blank, and so did George. "Who got in? When?"

"Lepescu and his . . . hunters. I'll bet it was Harlis, or my cousin Kell."

"You could be right. Your father never did figure out why that fellow who was Stationmaster of the Pinecone let him in. If Harlis had pressured him, it makes more sense."

"But now—we have to stop him getting there. I'll have to go—"

"Brun—you can't. You have to be here."

"But Kevil—we can't just let him go in there and terrorize people . . ."

"What could you do if you were there?"

"Warn them. Try to help." But she knew it would be futile; she wasn't a battle group of Fleet ships, all in herself. No. She had to give that up, and do what she could for the Familias as a whole. She could warn them, that was all.

She suspected that Fleet would not do anything, but she had to make the attempt. Sure enough, after taking her report, the admiral minor on the screen shook her head.

"I'm sorry, sera, but in the present situation we can't detach troops to protect one world." One rich family's playground world was the implication.

"I understand that," Brun said. After the expense of her rescue, she knew she could not ask Fleet for favors. "But you needed to know that we suspect one of the mutineers' ships—or maybe more—is headed there."

"Yes, I understand that. But that's a fairly isolated world with a small population. Better they should go there than attack a more populous planet. It has no manufacturing capacity, has it?"

"No—only light industry."

"It would take them five years to build up a shipyard capable of producing FTL ships, and that's with stolen parts, not from scratch. That gives us time to cut them off. I doubt very much they have the resources to mount a proper systemwide defense. In the meantime, we have urgent concerns elsewhere. As soon as possible, we'll go get them."

"I've already warned the population that Harlis may be coming with an armed ship. I don't want to interfere with your dispositions, but may I at least tell them you *won't* be coming?"

"Of course, sera. In fact, if the mutineers go there, and find that out, perhaps they'll stay in what they think is a safe haven until we can get there. Quite frankly, sera, we have no resources that could reach Sirialis before the mutineers can, if you're right about when they might have started."

"Thank you," Brun said. She wanted to rage, to kick desks and stamp the polished floor and scream . . . but that wasn't the way to get things done, not now. "Do you have any idea what force of ships that man Taylor might have?"

"I'm sorry, sera, I don't have that information."

After Miranda and Cecelia left, Sirialis subsided into summer somnolence, with Opening Day a safe hundred or more days away. Not that its inhabitants were idle, not on an agricultural and recreational world. Sirialis fed itself and the guests who descended on it yearly. The early crops of grain were in; the first cutting of hay lay open to the sun, drying before baling. Truck farms were in full production and so were the food processing facilities that took the surplus and preserved it for the season. For most of the planet's population, life went on as usual: the schools and stores and other services for the locals didn't change much with the activities of the owners. The changing seasons and the vagaries of local weather were more important. Dredges grumbled away at the entrance to Hospitality Bay where unusually severe winter storms had raised a sandbar and caused problems for the fishing fleet. In the other hemisphere, scattered settlements—timber camps, mining camps—prepared for the depths of winter. Many people migrated with the seasons, but a few chose to stay in one place.

Whenever family members weren't in residence, the big house went to a skeleton staff except for maintenance. This spring, plumbers worked on the balky pipes of the east wing, which had given trouble off and on for over fifty years, and the engineering consultant prodded at timbers in the attics in the triennial structural inspection. Stables and gardens, of course, were fully staffed year round. Horses and roses needed constant care; grooms and gardeners both preferred the quiet seasons.

System defense, at Sirialis, had been minimal for over a century. There was the communications ansible, by which the family alerted the system to their arrival. The landing fields at the main residence and Hospitality Bay had longscan capability, but system defense and traffic control was handled mostly by the Stationmaster at the largest orbital station. All three orbital stations had longscan and there were a few batteries of anti-ship missiles from the old days, which no one had tested in at least five years.

Brun's first ansible message set off a flurry of activity. There were not enough shuttles and ships within the system to evacuate everyone from the surface; Sirialis' population was small only by comparison with more developed worlds. They had no weapons that would stand up to a military invasion, and Brun had not been able to say how many ships might show up. She had been able to get Fleet to transmit the specs of various kinds so they'd have a clue.

CHAPTER TWENTY

Rockhouse Major

Goonar heard nothing from Bethya the next morning—or afternoon. Had she changed her mind? Was she trying to think of a way to let him down easily?

When the call finally came, he'd immersed himself in a study of the shipping figures for a colony Terakian & Sons was thinking of offering regular service to. He picked up the buzzing comunit absently. "Captain Terakian—how may I help you?"

"Goonar—" It was Bethya. His heart started to pound. "It's done. I'm still at the hotel, and I'm really too tired to move tonight. But I'd like to have dinner—would you mind coming here?"

"Of course not," Goonar said, dragging his mind away from the profitability analysis of the colony. "How formal?"

"Not very."

Bethya looked very tired, almost wan in fact. He wondered if the execrable Dougie had been nagging at her and felt a strong urge to hunt Dougie up and push his face in.

"Are you up to this?" he asked.

"Yes," she said. "Don't be fooled by theatrics, Goonar. I—came up with something.

"The problem," she said, over the salad, "was money. It usually is, in theater. Money or jealousy, or both. In this case, both."

Money Goonar understood. "They owed you?"

"They owe both of us," she said. "We still—*they* still—haven't paid for the passage, beyond the first segment. And when we founded the company, the four of us—Merlay, Dion, Sarin and I—all contributed equal shares. Merlay died five years ago—the most ravishing tenor you ever heard, and it was just a stupid traffic accident. Dion got an offer from his homeworld's most prestigious school of the arts a year later, and we bought out his share. We being Sarin—who's our set and costume designer—and me. Well, we were short two males, and Sarin and I decided to look for more partners. What we really wanted was another good male lead and a business manager, but the people you want don't necessarily have the money when they're available. Usually, in fact."

"So . . ."

"So Lisa, already in the company, wanted to buy in. She had the money—an inheritance, she said. We couldn't reasonably refuse. Dougie was working for the Greenfield Players—he'd pulled them out of a financial hole, and he said he wanted to travel. We still didn't have enough capital, so we talked to the rest of the troupe, and most of them scraped up enough to buy a share when we restructured."

"Is it equal shares now?"

"No . . . the way it was, Sarin and I each had four, and everyone else had one. I thought it was fair, as long as we were all together. But when I leave, I'll want to take out my shares in cash, and they won't want to pay it."

"What did you do?"

"I went to a clinic, and came back looking the way I look now, and explained I'd had a shock."

"A shock."

"Yes. I reminded Lisa that she'd been saying my voice was not what it had been—I could have smacked her for smirking at me— and that I hadn't wanted to tell them where I was going ahead of time. And the doctors had found a problem—that I was going to have to give up singing, and have surgery, and it might never be as good after. That it would be months—it was something difficult, which regen wouldn't fix."

"Is that true?" Goonar asked. "When Brun Meager's voice was lost—"

"Goonar, what Lisa and Dougie know about medicine would fit in a single pill. They want to believe I'm over the hill, that my voice is going; they ate this up like whipped cream with honey in it. I said I'd decided to leave the troupe and wanted to buy out my shares. That's when the haggling started, but since I was leaving for reasons of sickness, I had the high ground."

"Did you . . . ?"

"Goonar, there's truth and truth. I've known since before Lisa started carping at me that my voice isn't as good as it was. I've pushed it to the limit in some of the theaters we've played. It's time and past time for me to quit. This is a reason they can accept, and still fork over my share; if I told them it was to marry you, they'd say 'Oh, he's a rich trader, you don't need the money.'" Her trained voice conveyed both the whine in theirs, and the scorn she felt for that whine.

"I'm not shocked, Bethya," Goonar said. "We traders know about creative explanations."

"Good. I'd hate to have burned all my bridges and then found I'd alienated you."

"What about a wedding? Do we have to wait until they go away?"

"No. They saw us on the ship; they know I think you're a fine man, and that you admired me. Lisa even had the gall to suggest that perhaps I should console myself with the nice Captain Terakian, if he didn't mind the fact I wasn't the same offstage as on."

"So . . . this dinner . . ."

"Lets them think I'm working their suggestion. In the meantime, I have the bank draft."

"You are a wicked woman, Betharnya," Goonar said. "You might have been a trader born."

"My grandparents were, in a minor way," Bethya said. "If you count wholesalers in kitchenware and restaurant supply."

"So . . . what about a wedding?"

"There are some I'd like to invite, including Sarin—we've known each other fifteen years—which means there's no way to exclude the others without causing trouble."

"Fine with me," Goonar said. "At this point, we might as well wait for the *Princess* to come in—" He explained the crisscross of routes. "She's insystem now. It will make the Fathers happier if we have another Terakian witness. What kind of wedding party do you want?"

They dove into wedding planning, and when Goonar came back to the ship that night, Basil looked at his face. "Did you ask her?"

"Yes, cuz, I did," Goonar said, and grinned. "And she accepted, too. We'll have the wedding when *Princess* gets here."

"I don't suppose she's brought much dowry," Basil said. "Not that it matters, really."

"As a matter of fact, she has," Goonar said. She had shown him the bank draft. "Or rather, she has some money of her own."

"That's what I meant," Basil said. "I didn't expect her to turn it over or anything."

"That's good, because she won't. She's investing it."

"Trust you," Basil said, "to find a second wife who is beautiful, talented, *and* rich."

Sirialis

"She said we're on our own." The militia captain from Hospitality Bay glared at the militia captain from the home village. "Fleet can't come, and we sure can't fight off an invasion. My men know what to do with drunks, thieves, and stupid younglings who think it's funny to cut the nets of fishing boats . . . not NEMs in battle armor."

"So what are you saying, we should all take to the woods? Or just stand around to be beaten up or shot?"

"No—but I can't see wasting any time on fancy stuff—pictures and books and that."

"I'd like to save as much as we can. The Thornbuckles'll be back some day."

"Maybe. Maybe not. You heard what she said. What if she meant it? Then it's our choice."

"If it's my choice, there's things in there I'd save," the other man said.

"I don't want to see war here," said another. "I served in the first Patchcock mess, you know."

"We know, Gordy."

"You don't realize what they can do from space. If we go hide out in the bush, if they don't have time to bring us in, it's a lot safer."

"We can't possibly move everything—that house is stuffed with treasures—art, books, furniture—"

"And the stables with horses—"

"Horses can move themselves, house furnishings can't."

"People first, then the animals, then things . . ."

"Yes, but—"

"We don't have time for anything else."

Much of the main landmass had been kept a hunting preserve, dotted with small camps and lodges here and there. Every flitter and aircar on the planet was pressed into service, moving family groups and neighborhoods out to the remote areas. When everyone who would go had gone, the same flitters and aircars descended on the home village. Already the staff had prepared what they could of the furnishings—the jewels, the old plate, the oldest and rarest books in the library, the pictures known to be family favorites. The heaviest went down the service lifts into the basements . . . maybe it would be enough protection. The rest went into the vehicles, to be dispersed as far as possible.

Meanwhile, Neil had organized the stable staff—first to move feed and supplies, then horses. The staff tacked up every rideable animal and set off with the others in a long, uneven string across the hayfields and grainfields that spread for kilometers south and east. Almost all the mares had foaled; Neil assigned the lightest riders to the mares, and the foals romped alongside. That group necessarily lagged, as they had to stop for the foal to nurse every hour or so. Lumbering along with them were the village's milk cows and their calves; the sheep and goats skittered along in their own flocks, chivvied by excited dogs that had never had this much fun. The foxhounds trotted along in their couples, obedient to the huntsman's horn.

The only animals Neil didn't take were those that couldn't travel; it broke his heart to leave them behind, but they would be all right in the home paddocks if the mutineers didn't specifically attack them. He'd left his log—or what looked like his log—in his office, with the comment that he had sprayed for graylice, and evacuated the stable for 60 days. If the attackers believed that, they might not come looking. At least, not if they were in a hurry.

Former R.S.S. patrol *Gaura Secundus*

Harlis had interacted with Fleet only at the higher levels, when, as Seated Family and younger brother of the Speaker, he had been treated with great courtesy. He had gone aboard ships, certainly—ships docked at Stations, whose crews stood for inspection. He had been impressed with the crisp salutes, the obvious discipline, the spotless cleanliness, the deference accorded superiors. He had imagined himself as another admiral alongside Lepescu, commanding ships in battle . . . cool, imperturbable. Let Bunny play with politics: he would have real power, he had thought often, remembering the racks of missiles, the orderly arrays of power coils for the beam weapons. Of course, he couldn't actually join Fleet, not with his Family responsibilities. But he could befriend admirals, and know that he, under his civilian exterior, was at heart a warrior.

The reality aboard *Gaura Secundus* was very different from his earlier brief experiences. Order, discipline, efficiency—yes. The crew, still in Fleet uniforms, with the Familias insignia removed, saluted crisply and moved briskly to their work. But the deference due him, as a Family member, as a Seat in Council, as the brother of the former Speaker . . . that was missing. They were coolly polite—they addressed him as Ser Thornbuckle—but they did not consider him one of them.

He had never realized before just how closed a community the military might be. True, Captain Sigind had never warmed to him, but he'd assumed that was Bunny's fault. By the time the *Lillian C.* was partway to Millicent, he was wondering if he might have made a mistake. When his "hirelings" bundled him into a p-suit and pushed him through a docking tube from the yacht to their warship—to his eyes a vast black blot on the starfield—he was uneasily aware that he was alone in a crowd of men and women who had killed before, who enjoyed killing, who would kill him if he stood in their way. Right now, as the source of funds, he was useful to them. They respected money, in a way, as another form of power. But if they decided he wasn't useful? If Brun or Stepan managed to cut off his access to the banks?

Harlis shivered in his little cabin, and realized that he did not want to die. He found himself rubbing his ears, and yanked his hands down.

He had never really liked the staff at Sirialis. They were Bunny's people, and though they treated Family members with due courtesy, he knew they were not *his*. He had always wanted an empire of his own—his estates were not enough. He had thought hiring his own military force was a good idea. His private space navy, his private army—then he could have what he deserved, and forget about Bunny.

He had his meals with the officers, with Taylor always at one end of the table and himself at the other. It was here, even more than in the working parts of the ship, that the difference between himself and these men showed up most. He had grown up in a sea of politics, playing at power even as boy—he'd thought he knew all about it. When he'd pressured old Trema into leaving him her shares, he'd been, he was convinced, as straightforward and pragmatic as any admiral planning a war.

No. He had been held back, he now realized, by his own shrinking flesh. He had not himself gone to Trema's house; he had not himself risked injury or discovery by any of the acts he'd hired. These people had no such scruples. They were as direct as a blow. The uniformity of their dress, which also excluded him (his best-cut suits looked slovenly next to their uniforms), proclaimed them.

Finally one day, Taylor commented, "I fear we alarm Ser Thornbuckle."

"Alarm me?" Harlis said. He could feel his pulse speeding up. "In what way?"

"You're looking at us like a deer at a hunter," Taylor said, grinning. "Wondering what's going to happen." He licked his lips. "The difference between us, Ser Thornbuckle, is that I don't worry about what will happen, because I intend to make it happen . . . my way."

"It's not always that easy," Harlis said.

"No . . . war is not easy. Nor is hunting. But it's that or letting the human race degenerate to a lot of parlor ornaments, unfit for anything but eating and breeding. Something has to clean the genome, Ser Thornbuckle, and we can't all be Registered Embryos. But I don't expect much trouble at Sirialis. If you've told us the truth, they have no system defenses worth speaking of, and no defense against armored shuttles. Morever, the shuttles stored at the three orbital stations will increase our transport capacity."

"Unless someone back at Castle Rock thought to tell them we might be on the way," Harlis said.

"And who would do that?" Taylor asked.

"It's just possible someone figured it out," Harlis said. He could feel himself starting to sweat. "My niece—Brun Meager—she was just named the Barraclough Sept heir. Stepan chose her. I was going to . . . to persuade her to come along. She has all the codes. But she and that disgusting woman from the Lone Star Confederation went out to dinner before we could—"

"You *idiot*," Taylor said. "You said you weren't a fugitive."

"I'm not. I wasn't, anyway, when I said that. And I don't think I am now. She doesn't know who—"

Taylor gave him a look that stopped the words in his throat. "Even if she's too stupid to figure it out, someone will. And you left tracks all over the place—with Allsystems—"

"I told them I was going to Burkholdt and Celeste."

"And you think they'll believe that? After you made a grab for the girl and didn't get her?" His face hardened. "You lied to me, Thornbuckle, and I don't like being lied to."

"It wasn't a lie—" Harlis said. "At the time, it was true—"

At some signal Harlis didn't catch, the two officers nearest him slid out of their seats, and before he could push back from the table they had his arms twisted behind him.

"I don't like liars, Thornbuckle. And I don't accept excuses. Is that clear?"

Harlis remembered the pain from childhood, when boys were forever tormenting each other, but this was worse . . . boys knew about twisting arms but not about the nerves more subtly available to skilled fingers. The pressure increased steadily, hot flares of pain in shoulders, neck, elbows, wrists; his mouth opened involuntarily, and he gasped.

"I asked you a question," Taylor said, and someone grabbed Harlis's hair and pulled his head back. Through the tears of pain in his eyes he could see Taylor and the others, sitting there calmly and enjoying his pain.

"Yes," Harlis said finally, in a sort of grunt.

"Yes, *what*?" Taylor prompted. Harlis glared at him.

"I said yes," he said. "I'm the one who hired *you*!"

A hard punch from behind rammed him into the edge of the table.

"You're the one who lied to me," Taylor said. "I'm not your servant, or your peasant. When you hire troops, you don't lie to them. Not if you want to live long. Now, again: is that clear?"

"Yes . . . sir." The *sir* was wrung out of him by a last twist of the arms that made it clear his shoulders would come loose if he didn't say it. At a nod from Taylor, they released him, and he fell back into his chair. His shoulders hurt; his arms hurt . . . most of all, his pride hurt.

"Here's how it's going to be," Taylor said. "You're going to tell me everything you did, and planned, and thought, and heard . . . everything . . . and you're going to do exactly as you're told by me or by any of these officers. We will continue to treat you well, as long as you do not disobey us, or lie to us. But withholding information, or lying, or disobedience, will be punished."

Harlis nodded, speechless, hoping he wouldn't be made to say "yes, sir" again.

"Finish your dinner. We'll talk afterwards."

Taylor said, "We need money, and we need a secure base. You promised us both, and now you can't deliver—"

"I can—I have the money, all I have to do is get it. I have the access codes for the family ansible, at Sirialis—that's communication with anyone you want, free. I have the access codes for family accounts, as well as my own. There's information—stuff Bunny's wife had—about family businesses and things. And the place itself has money."

"You're sure you have the codes."

"Of course I'm sure. Bunny was my brother; I've had the codes since I was in my twenties. Look, you're worried about pursuit, but is there really any way Fleet could get there before we do?"

"No . . ."

"And even if they do, you could just hide. It's a whole system—"

"That's why we couldn't. It's too empty. But we could make a fast passage, see if your codes work, get some money, and head out."

"You won't need to," Harlis said. "I keep telling you, I'm Bunny's brother. Everyone on the planet knows who I am. They're not going to give you any trouble."

Over the course of the next several days, Harlis answered hundreds of questions about himself, his family, his fortune, and Sirialis. Taylor recorded all of it. Harlis knew how that would look to his family if they got hold of the cube. He'd heard that in storycubes the hero always managed to find some way of showing that he was being coerced. He couldn't think of anything that Taylor wouldn't recognize and punish.

When they arrived at Sirialis, Taylor called him in. "We need the ansible access code."

Harlis handed it over. Taylor handed it on to one of his communications techs. "Strip the records and check our control," he said.

"Sir." The man turned away and fiddled with controls Harlis couldn't see. "Someone did think we might come here. It's a voice message from Brun Meager—warning the population Harlis might show up, and then that she couldn't get Fleet to respond."

"A trap?"

"Could be," Taylor said. "We won't stay that long. We can resupply anyway—it's an ag world. With money on it, all concentrated in one place, right, Harlis?"

It still stung that Taylor had quit calling him Ser Thornbuckle, or even Thornbuckle. "Yes," he said slowly. "The main banking outlet's in the home village."

"Just how fancy is that house?" Taylor asked. "Got a lot of things in it? Jewelry those women left behind?"

"I doubt it," Harlis said. "They take it with them, or put it in the bank."

"We might just take a look," the man said. "Admiral Lepescu said this was a showplace. Gardens, lawns, stables—you ride, don't you, Harlis?"

"I can, yes. I'm not that fond of it."

"Not that fond of it." Lately they'd taken to mocking him, repeating his phrases.

"Captain, I can't get past the lockout. His password got us into the incoming queue, but there's a traplink on the outgoing, and I can't budge it."

"That might make it difficult to get your funds, mightn't it, Harlis?"

"Maybe it wants an ID check—sometimes it does—and I have to go to the terminal."

"Well, then, I think we'll take a shuttle down and see for ourselves . . ."

Harlis felt naked without even a p-suit when the others in the shuttle wore PPUs and armor. Six of them were neuro-enhanced marines, huge and bulky in their battle armor. At their order, he called down to the shuttle field. Someone answered—he didn't know the name—and turned on the field's electronic guidance system. He couldn't see it himself; this shuttle had no windows. He felt the BUMP-bump-bump of the shuttle's landing and roll in, then the hatch opened and the scent of Sirialis rushed in, the smell taking him back to a childhood that now seemed very far away.

In the midst of them, feeling small and vulnerable, Harlis walked across the field wondering why no one had come to meet them. The men looked this way and that, assessing, cataloguing.

"Piece of cake," someone said.

"Find us transport," said Taylor. But the hangars and shelters were empty. In the office, the only sign of occupation was the main control board, powered up and humming faintly. Taylor grinned. "They're playing hard to get, are they? Want a hunt?" The other men grinned too, and nodded.

"We'll see. Looks like we'll have to walk—where's this bank, Harlis?"

The village street, in early summer, looked like a travel poster: the neat stone buildings, the planters full of flowers, more flowers on the vines that clambered here and there. A marmalade cat raised its head from a doorstep, then slid down and into a flowerbed between cottages.

"Where is everybody?" Taylor asked. "Did they just run off in the fields?" One of the NEMs kicked open the door to the bank. "Some security," Taylor sneered.

They herded Harlis inside. No one was there, but the autobank was on, just as the shuttle field power had been on. Harlis entered his access codes, and his credit cube, and waited for the light to come on. The autobank transferred the contents of his accounts to the cube.

He strained to remember Bunny's code—the bank would lock out for two hours if he made a mistake—but his first try worked. Bunny's account balance, however, was zero.

"Get your offworld accounts," Taylor said. Harlis entered the complete access codes for financial ansible transfers, and waited.

ANSIBLE ACCESS DENIED. ENTER CORRECT CODE.

"They changed the codes," Taylor said. "They changed the *codes*." With the word he backhanded Harlis across the face. "And all you had here was a lousy two hundred thousand—" He jerked his head at the others. "Let's go."

"I can get more," Harlis said. "I know I can, if—"

"Shut him up," Taylor said. One of the NEMs flipped his weapon over and tapped Harlis on the shoulder. It looked like a tap, but it felt like his shoulder was broken.

"Stuff at the house, Captain?" asked one of the men.

"Knickknacks," Taylor said. "Probably all that's left—the civs have run out, like the rabbits they are; they'd have taken the good stuff that was easy to move. Unless you want sheets and pillowcases and things they wouldn't bother with—"

The man laughed. "Not me, sir."

Harlis looked up the street, where the top stories of the house rose above the trees that edged the gardens.

"Want a last look, Harlis?" asked Taylor. "Think there's something worthwhile they won't have taken away, or locked up so you can't get at it?"

"Pictures," Harlis said hoarsely. "Books, tableware, furniture, weapons . . ."

"Weapons?"

"Hunting weapons, and old ones, antiques."

"Worthless trash," Taylor said. "I'm not getting blisters going up there for souvenirs."

He led the way back to the shuttle; Harlis looked around, hoping against hope that someone would come to rescue him. There were only twenty mutineers in the landing party; he knew the militia could muster more than that. Couldn't they see he was a prisoner?

No one came, and the NEMs shoved him back aboard the shuttle for its return journey.

When they got back aboard, Taylor had two men bring Harlis to the bridge. "I think this smug little world needs a lesson," he said. "As does Harlis here. We're going to break a few windows, knock down a few chimneys." He looked at Harlis. "We'll start with your house, *Ser* Thornbuckle." He turned to his weapons officer. "You have the coordinates—drop one down the middle."

"Harlis felt his mouth drying. "No—don't do that. Why destroy it?"

"Because I want to," Taylor said. "Because I can."

"But—they didn't do anything to you . . ."

"They didn't," Taylor said. "You did. You lied to me. And it annoyed me, and when I'm annoyed I sometimes take it out on things."

"But—but it's *mine*," Harlis said. "It's mine, it always should have been, and besides, it's beautiful."

"Not anymore," Taylor said. He grinned. "Show us, Leon," he said. Up on the screen, the great house appeared, serene and lovely in its encircling gardens and lawns, glowing in the early summer morning light, as beautiful as Harlis had ever seen. He could almost smell the roses. Then the missile struck; the house bulged, as if swelling with outrage, and was hidden in a boiling cloud of explosive debris. "Good shot," Taylor said. "So much for that one."

The expanding cloud from the first explosion obscured the view of the stable, but not the second billow, the thicker, more boiling cloud. Harlis felt sick; his stomach churned. He had never liked horses that much, but he had never wished them harm, either, and he could imagine the terrified animals that weren't killed at once, the shattered legs, the blood . . .

"We got what we came for," Taylor said. "Now that we have the money."

"Lob a few more at 'em?" asked another man.

"No. We may need our weapons for something else. But it makes a statement. Nobody's going to think we're playing a game." His voice changed, turning soft and sweet and rotten. "Ser Thornbuckle seems unwell, Smithers. Take him to his cabin."

Harlis lay staring at the overhead, unable to sleep, his mind running the sequence over and over and over. The house—*his* house—gone, utterly gone. Destroyed. The grand staircase, the ballroom, the fencing salon, the billiard room, the library, the morning

room, the sunroom, his own suite with his personal treasures
. . . gone, in a moment of time, a puff of smoke and surge of flame.
Horror and grief and fear circled around the memory of what he'd
seen, dread furies that screamed his name. Bunny would kill him for
this—Bunny was dead—so many were dead—so much destruction—
how could he? How had he? And what could he do? His body shivered, long shuddering quakes, as he remembered the hard hands that
had hurt him, the cold eyes that had examined him and found him
soft, contemptible, the feral smiles that had delighted in his pain, in
his fear, in his horror at their capacity to destroy.

R.S.S. *Fremantle*

"Would you look at that, now," Lt. Commander Coston said to
nobody in particular. A patrol ship . . . two patrol ships . . . or
something with that mass and drive signature . . . had just down-
jumped into the system. "Were we expecting anything?" he asked his
exec.

"No, sir." His exec, also a lieutenant commander, grinned. "Some
excitement at last," he said.

"Definitely." At the angle the ships had entered, scan had picked
up their location only eight light minutes away, with a rapidly
lengthening "tail" aiming toward their entry point as the data
streamed in. "Beacon data?"

"No beacons," reported his scan tech. "Running hot—"

"And so are we—" Their orders were to prevent mutineers from
reaching Aethar's World—futile orders, he'd thought, since space
was far to big to barricade. But sure enough, someone had come right
past his picket, and the only ships that would run without beacons
were those up to no good. He reminded himself that mutiny did not
make people stupid, that these ships would know every trick he did.
But he had something up his sleeve: *Gorgon* and *Matchless*, plus a
tactical plan designed for exactly this situation.

"If they haven't got a trailing heavy cruiser, they're meat," Coston
said.

"All signatures confirm Fleet patrol craft," his scan tech said. "No
beacon, but everything—the weapons lit and all—"

"Fine, Kris. That just makes it easier." He nodded to his Exec. "Put us on the plan. I'll hail 'em."

The hail was more for the record than anything else. Those could not be innocent merchanters out there, and only the largest private yachts had near that mass.

Before his message would have had time to reach the vessels, one of them fired at him.

"Good," Coston said. "That makes it simple. No need to wait—"

Fremantle microjumped, halving the distance to the mutineers, then jumped again to only five seconds away. When they came out, the mutineers had fired a salvo at where they'd been. *Fremantle* microjumped ahead, to less than a second ahead of the mutineers' computed course. Her own course, warped by the successive microjumps, gave only the smallest window for firing down the mutineers' throats—but this was only the first such attack. *Fremantle* hopped out, to be replaced by *Gorgon*, and then *Matchless*, in a precisely timed dance that ensured they didn't hit each other with their weapons. On the screens, hit after hit ablated the mutineers' shields, degraded their ability to fight back. One of the two mutineer ships attempted to break away, microjumping five minutes out. But at that moment the first blew, and soon the trio of loyalists had caught and destroyed the other.

Coston grinned at his Exec. "This'll make the admiral happy. Now if we can just get some ID on those ships . . ."

Headquarters, Sector VII

When Arash Livadhi returned to Sector VII HQ from the first convoy, and made his report to Admiral Serrano, she nodded. "Good work. I'm sure you have ideas now on training for the ships in convoy; I'd like you to brief the captains waiting for the next convoy as soon as you have them organized."

"Of course, sir." Arash explained his observations.

"Have you heard the good news?"

"Haven't heard a thing, sir," Livadhi said. "Somebody get a mutineer ship back?"

"Not back, no. But Heris located the mutineer flagship, *Bonar*

Tighe, and destroyed it. We have confirmation that Solomon Drizh—he was bumped up to admiral minor, just like you—was the actual spearhead." Livadhi's stomach did a slow turn. He had avoided Drizh for years. "Apparently he was one of Lepescu's proteges that we missed, and he'd reconstituted the Loyal Order of Game Hunters . . ." Admiral Serrano looked sharply at him. "You did know about that, didn't you?"

"Heris told me," he said quickly, feeling the sweat slicking his hands.

"That bastard poisoned everyone he touched," she said, shaking her head. "Lepescu, I mean. But apparently Drizh was just as bad."

Livadhi swallowed. He had to say it; he had to know what she knew. "I . . . served with Admiral—then Commander—Lepescu once, you know. I was pretty young."

"I know," she said. "You may be the exception to the rule. You're lucky he took a dislike to you. He hated Heris, too. The youngsters he thought had promise—"

The youngsters he thought had promise he invited into his circle. Flattered them. Taught them. Urged them to become the elite, the best they could be. And then . . .

"He ruined them," Admiral Serrano went on.

"It's a shame," Livadhi said, unable to think of anything else.

"If he were still alive, I'd strangle him myself," Admiral Serrano said.

"Me, too," Livadhi said, and meant it. He had been so young, so naive, so willing to be flattered, so honored to be singled out by a commander already known for his dash, his fighting ability, his high standards. He had admired Lepescu, had tried to copy him, even to what he preferred in music and food.

"It's amazing," Admiral Serrano went on, "how many people one bad apple comes in contact with. And yet there must be others, like you, who were around him and not part of his coterie, and what we don't need right now is another witch hunt aimed at everyone who served under him, however far back."

"I agree," said Livadhi. He agreed with every fiber in him.

"Heris seems to be doing well with old *Indy*," Admiral Serrano said. "How are you getting along with *Vigilance*?"

"Fine, sir. Though I'm sure Heris's old crew would like to be with her—" Was this the time to suggest that they could transfer away?

"No need to worry about that. Not with a war on." She went on. "Besides, she's not coming back here; she's over at Copper Mountain, with the debris she picked up. Chances are none of it is a complete personnel list of the mutiny, but the analysts there might find something."

"Copper Mountain's ours, then?"

"For the time being. The bad news is bad indeed. Mutineers hit a battle group over in Sector V, blew one ship and badly damaged a cruiser. They're trying to blackmail some of the Families into hiring them—the old protection racket. There've been sporadic attacks on orbital stations and even planets. We just don't have enough ships to guard everywhere, not and protect the borders. I expect any minute to hear that the Benignity has mounted an invasion; I can't think why they haven't."

CHAPTER TWENTY-ONE

**R.S.S. *Turbot*, en route from
Castle Rockto Sector VII**

Esmay Suiza found herself in a crowd of officers heading out to take command of their ships: a couple of lieutenants, like Esmay, the rest majors and one lieutenant commander. Like her, most of them spent hours studying the specs of their new commands.

Her ship, *Rascal*, had been upgraded from an ordinary patrol craft—she had been on picket duty in a sector where nothing was expected to happen for years—with the new weapons suites which made her almost a mini-cruiser. To power this weaponry, she'd been given new drives, and despite all the additions and changes, she was still not overly cramped in her personnel compartments, so she had a full complement of crew. Esmay had studied the specs all the way out from Castle Rock, until she was sure she could recognize and name everything. Those months she'd spent on *Koskiusko* learning about hulls and drives made it much easier; she actually understood exactly which modification supported which of the new additions.

Now she was about to see her ship—*her* ship—for the first time. She had checked in when she arrived, so if her crew were alert, they'd know she was on the way, and she had taken a few moments in one of the lounges to make sure that her fringe of hair was as neat as it could be. The several weeks of accelerated growth had produced a surprising amount of hair, but it wasn't what she was used to. Up ahead she saw the docking number and the name *Rascal*.

She squared her shoulders, felt in her pocket one more time for the command wand that would make the ship's electronics accept her as the commander, and approached the smart-looking corporal standing guard at the docking tube hatch. He saw her, recognized the captain's patch on cap and sleeve, and came to attention.

"Captain Suiza! Welcome, sir!" He sounded as if he meant it, and his salute was crisp. She returned it. "Is the captain coming aboard now?"

"Yes," Esmay said. Why else would she have come along, just to see if they knew who she was?

"Very well, Captain; I've just notified the bridge. We have no officers aboard at present; Master Chief Humberly is in charge. The captain's luggage?"

"They're sending it when they've unloaded the transport," Esmay said.

"Captain Suiza—welcome!" That was Master Chief Humberly, a lean older man whose hair was cropped so short Esmay couldn't be sure if he was also balding or not. He had the same brisk, competent, cheerful look as the corporal. Esmay liked him at once, and noted that he had none of the blurry look that had signalled the older NCOs whose rejuvenation was failing. "I'm sorry Jig Turner isn't aboard— he'd wanted to meet you, but he was called to the admiral's office."

"That's all right," Esmay said. She already knew that the formalities of coming aboard were minimal for captains below the rank of commander. But Humberly surprised her; he'd turned out the crew in *Rascal*'s rather narrow main corridor, and Esmay walked to the bridge to read herself in, feeling very honored indeed.

When that was over, and the status board lit with "Captain: Esmay Suiza" and "Captain Aboard," she felt simultaneously fully happy and fully anxious. As on *Despite*—once she was captain, it was all her responsibility, every bit of it. But she'd wanted it. She would make good of it. She started at once, turning to Humberly.

"What's our readiness, Chief?"

"Did they tell you about the refit and upgrades?"

"Yes—new drives, new weapons suites. I looked them over—we have thirty-four percent more firepower, half of it in beam weapons, and the drives to power that without dropping shields. But they didn't say what that did to our microjump ability, if anything."

"Ah. We haven't tried it—haven't had the chance. My best guess is that it may knock a few percents off our response time. Not good but—"

"Worth the trade, if that's all there is," Esmay said. "What about crew? I know that a lot of ships are being crewed with people just thrown together—"

"We were lucky," Humberly said. "Because of the need for training with the upgrades, most of Drives and Weapons have been here throughout. We were between captains anyway, and about half of Environmental is new, but being as we have such a small complement, we were able to do a bit of weeding." He looked smug; Esmay grinned at him.

"You went scavenging, didn't you?" she said. "Good for you."

"Patrols don't have much in the way of clerical—mostly it's the captain's own staff," he said, eyeing her to see if she knew that already. Esmay nodded. "We've got a couple of bean counters from supply that haven't been out in a fighting ship before, but they should be all right."

"Provisions?"

He frowned. "There we've had some problems—small ship, busy Station, and no captain aboard. Jig Turner . . . he's a fine young officer, you understand, but a jig just doesn't have the clout of someone more senior, and he's not the type to presume on his position as officer in charge."

"How bad is it?" Esmay said.

"Nothing we can't fix in a few shifts with the captain aboard, I'm sure, sir. Nobody's going to give *you* that much trouble."

Esmay doubted that, but she knew she'd fight back if they did. Her ship wasn't going into action on outdated rations or medical supplies. "What've we got in spareables?" she asked, using the polite term for items used in illicit trade.

"Not much—just a few bits and pieces from the refitting. I was saving some of those back for last-minute problems."

"Good idea."

Esmay found, to her surprise, that her name and image on the screen worked wonders with Supply, which promptly disgorged containers of fresh ration packs whose contents actually matched the lists on the containers. She had a little more trouble with Munitions, who tried to insist that patrol craft had no need to stuff themselves with missiles, multiple fusing options, and alternative warheads. Esmay finally had to go in person, with copies of the refit details, and argue her way up the chain of command to the admiral minor in charge.

"If they didn't think we'd see serious fighting," she pointed out, "they wouldn't have upgraded the weapons suite. There's no reason to have weapons and no ammunition—"

"Do you have any idea how much a 347-Xa warhead costs?" he asked.

"Yes—" Esmay quoted the figure. "And I know how much a patrol ship costs, and how much the cargo of the next convoy is worth to the mutineers. Do you want them to get that shipload of weapons going out to Sector VIII, just because I don't have the weapons to protect them?"

He glared at her and she glared back. In the back of her mind was the rebellious thought that this was actually fun, in its own way. He had to resist, she had to demand . . . it was like a dance of sorts.

"All right," he said finally. "But don't tell the other patrol captains— I'm not giving out everything we have or there won't *be* anything to ship to Sector VIII."

"They don't have our upgrades," Esmay said. "Why would I arouse their greed?"

He chuckled, and shook his head. "Lieutenant, I'm glad you're not any more senior than you are . . . that was worthy of a Serrano. Which I guess you are, now, eh?"

"I'm not sure they'd agree," Esmay said. She didn't want to get into that.

She had presented her name to the admiral's staff, only to be told that for the duration the normal protocol of paying calls had been suspended. At first she wondered if this was aimed at her, but the few brief conversations she had with other captains made it clear it wasn't.

"We've got—what, four admirals?—serving as convoy commanders, and who knows how many ships and captains coming and going. Way too many to hold formal calls. What she's doing is holding a get-together before each convoy leaves, counts as calls from every- one."

❀   ❀   ❀

Rascal eased away from the Station with permission to proceed to the system's practice sector for four days of maneuver practice. Esmay, on the bridge, watched as her crew ran through the sequences . . . no mistakes so far. Behind them, she knew one of the ships which had just finished its practice was nosing in for a last bit of supply.

Rascal's insystem drives, upgraded to the power of a small cruiser, nudged her out of Station space efficiently, and made short work of the run out to the first maneuver site. Most patrol class took 18 hours . . . *Rascal* made it in fifteen and a half, on the same power setting.

"Makes me wonder if some of those supply crates are empty." Esmay's executive officer, Jig Turner, had a dry sense of humor she already enjoyed.

"Hope not," she said now. "I was planning on feeding everyone regularly for the next several months."

Commander Kessler, on the supply ship *Plexus*, ran the maneuver region with an iron hand, not hampered at all by being in a fat, slow, cargo vessel. Esmay reported in promptly: "R.S.S. *Rascal*, Suiza commanding, permission to engage in maneuver . . ."

"*Rascal*, note traffic in Sector Yellow: patrol craft *Sitra*, *Scamp*, and *Salute*. Confirm ID match, return signal." Esmay's senior scan highlighted the blips on his screen; the beacon IDs came up correctly, and he transmitted his match to *Plexus* for confirmation. "Traffic IDs confirmed. No microjumping in Sector Yellow. You will proceed as follows . . ." Up on the main screen came the course they were to match. The first part of maneuver practice was simply designed to ensure that the ships could follow a designated course solo. Then they'd begin to practice in formation.

The first day's work went well; Esmay's crew knew their business, and *Rascal* answered the helm neatly, once they'd figured out the corrective function for their velocity under the new engines. Esmay forced herself to go to bed, but woke up at least once an hour.

The next day, they were assigned to microjump practice, in the far reaches of the system, light hours from anyone else. Esmay found it less nerve-wracking than she expected, with a navigational computer that wasn't shot full of holes, as *Despite*'s had been. She could feel the rising morale of the bridge crew, as *Rascal* hit one designated set of coordinates after another. When they had finished the set of sixteen jumps, and recalibrated all the instruments, she grinned at them. "Well done, people! I don't have to wait for our scores to know we aced that test."

That ship's night, with *Rascal* on insystem drive working its way back to the area for the next day's formation maneuvers, she slept well. Formation maneuvers tested the bridge crew almost as much as microjumping practice. Fleet had not used formal convoys in decades, with the result that no one was familiar with the formations needed. Commodore Admiral Minor Livadhi, who would command their convoy, wanted to try out first one, then another, formation. Should the escorts be farther away? Closer in? Should the patrols be alternated with escorts, or bunched together?

When they finally finished (and the commodore still hadn't made up his mind, apparently), and headed back for the Station for a final resupply, Esmay felt that only one thing was certain: She had a good crew which was rapidly getting better.

Admiral Livadhi invited the captains of all the ships that would be in his convoy to dinner aboard his flagship. Esmay, who had last seen *Vigilance* under Heris Serrano's command, wondered how many of Heris's crew were aboard. Livadhi himself impressed her as a competent officer much like her own father; he had a pleasant comment for each officer as he shook hands.

"You're the most recent arrival from Castle Rock," Livadhi said, after they were seated. "Tell us, Lt. Suiza, about the latest gossip."

"I'm sure you know all the Fleet news, sir, but had you heard about the fugitive from the Benignity?"

"A fugitive? No, tell us."

"He was on the ship I took from Trinidad to Castle Rock," Esmay said. "A merchanter. He told the strangest story—" She paused. "I don't think there's anything wrong with telling you—not now that he's reached Castle Rock."

"Don't torture us, Lieutenant," Livadhi said. He sipped his wine.

"Yes, sir—well, I don't know the whole story, but he claimed to be a priest in the Benignity, who had to flee. He said they claimed he was a heretic, and he wasn't—"

"Do they kill heretics in the Benignity?" someone else asked.

"I'd believe it," said another.

"It wasn't just being a heretic. I'm not sure I understand it—it's his religion anyway—but he claimed he was the last confessor for someone important, and his government was afraid—because he was a heretic—that he'd reveal what he heard."

"Did you believe him?" Livadhi asked.

Esmay considered, remembering her conversations with the colorless but nonetheless passionate little man. "I think *he* believed what he said. He wanted to talk to me because I'm from Altiplano, and he thought maybe we had useful religious archives."

"But do you think he had any state secrets to reveal?" Livadhi said it lightly, and several people chuckled.

"I don't know," Esmay said. "He said he wouldn't tell what he knew anyway, because—heretic or not—he still considered himself bound by his oath not to."

"But he's at Castle Rock, you said. Surely Fleet Intelligence will get it out of him?"

Esmay shrugged. "He's a civilian, a priest with a monomania about some cult or something they have in the Benignity, something to do with swords or something. Why would they be that interested in him? And anyway, they were shipping him out to the Guernesi on a diplomatic ship; he may be gone by now."

"They did assassinate our Speaker . . ." someone else said thoughtfully. "Maybe that was his big secret."

"When did you meet up with him, Lieutenant?" Livadhi asked. Esmay tried to calculate and failed.

"Sir, I've been hopping around so, I really don't know. I didn't really notice him aboard the merchant ship for some time after I came aboard . . . and then we stopped at Zenebra . . . I'm sorry, sir, but I can't remember whether it was before or after that."

"It doesn't matter, I suppose," Livadhi said. "But just supposing he were the confessor for their head of state, and bolted immediately for our borders, he might have reached Familias Space before the assassination took place."

"But they've said they did it," Esmay said. "It's not a secret now."

"Not now . . . but it could have been *then*. And who knows what other bombshells he has to drop?"

"Well . . . I had to have my security clearances reinstated, so I was stuck at HQ for a couple of hours, and I did hear somebody speculating about whether he might have a complete list of Benignity agents or something, but I can't imagine that. Having planted spies might be a sin, but a list of names wouldn't be."

"Are they concerned about Benignity penetration, do you think?"

Esmay nodded. "Under the circumstances, with the mutiny and the assassination coming so close, I'd say they have reason to worry. The combination certainly made things easier for the Benignity. They deny having anything to do with the mutiny, but someone's come forward to say that Bacarion and Drizh had said favorable things about discipline in the Benignity Space Forces." She chuckled. "Of course, there were people saying that I had expressed treasonous ideas when it was to their benefit."

"So you don't believe it?"

"Sir, I haven't the data on which to form an opinion. I know that, unfortunately, gossip and rumor can be taken as truth—with dire consequences for the subjects of it. On the other hand, what I learned about the Benignity while talking to Simon—to the priest—certainly makes a connection sound more possible. The mutineers say the rest of us are undisciplined, soft, self-indulgent: that's what the Benignity says about the Familias, too. I haven't heard of the mutineers being religious, particularly, and Simon says the Benignity would not sanction anything like that hunting business, but—the mutineers might think it did."

"You're fair-minded, for someone who's been burnt twice now on the basis of rumor, Lieutenant. It does you credit. What do the rest of you think?"

Esmay listened to the rest, trying to discern from their conversation what kind of commanders they would be if the convoy saw trouble. Collingwood, with a sidelong glance at Esmay, said, "Where there's smoke, there's usually fire, sir. I mean, I know rumor isn't always true, but on something this important, it probably is. If the Benignity's behind the mutiny, they don't even have to like the mutineers; they could just be supporting it from a distance."

"But we don't want to be conspiracy theorists," said Bondi. "I mean, what if they started looking for everyone who'd ever served under Lepescu or any of the people now leading the mutiny, and then for everyone who ever had a friend or relative from the Benignity, for two generations back or so? My grandfather stowed away and came to Familias Space as a boy: how do you know he wasn't some deep agent or something, instead of just a scared teenager who wanted a better life somewhere else?"

"So *that's* where you got your weird ideas, Pete?" asked Collingwood, putting on a thick accent.

"It's not funny—!" Bondi said; his face flushed.

"Gentlemen." Livadhi intervened smoothly. "I hardly think Fleet's going to start another witch hunt. Reasonable caution, yes, but Lieutenant Bondi has a fine record, which I'm sure will overwhelm any trifling concern about his grandfather—it certainly does with me."

"Thank you, sir," Bondi said. "I'm sorry I brought it up."

"No, it's a reasonable question. And it's not something to joke about, especially not now."

"No, sir. My apologies, sir, and Pete—I'm really sorry. I didn't mean to torque you at a time like this. Misplaced sense of humor."

"It's all right." But to Esmay the apology seemed a bit glib, and Bondi's color was still higher than usual.

"Let me show you the ship," Livadhi said. "You can meet the personnel you'll be communicating with—and for those of you who haven't had cruiser duty, here's a chance to familiarize yourselves—"

Livadhi started at the bottom, perhaps to give tempers and tensions time to dissipate as they clattered down the many ladders. Esmay admired this way of handling a difficult interaction; riding down in the officers' lift they would have been immobile and staring at one another's backs or the grill. Environmental first, then up to Engineering, where almost the first person they saw was Petris Kenvinnard, who recognized Esmay.

"Lieutenant Suiza—good to see you again."

"You know Suiza?" Livadhi asked.

"Yes, sir; we've met before. She's one of my—Heris's—favorite young officers."

"With reason, no doubt," Livadhi murmured. "Lieutenant, you've had cruiser duty; if you'd like to stop and chat with Mr. Kenvinnard—"

"Don't let me slow you down, Lieutenant. But I heard you'd

gotten *Rascal*—congratulations. Tell Rudy—Master Chief Humberly—I said hello."

"Thanks," Esmay said. "And I will." She went on, cheered more than she would have liked to admit to know Heris Serrano's good opinion of her from someone else. Heris had stood up for her at the family gathering, but this was proof of a longer-standing opinion.

When they came to the great generators that powered the beam weapons, and Livadhi rattled off the specs, Esmay realized again just how big an upgrade *Rascal* had. *Vigilance* still had more firepower, but the gap had narrowed appreciably. She trailed behind, trying to calculate exactly the size of the remaining gap.

"Lieutenant Suiza!" That was Methlin Meharry, another of Heris Serrano's "old" crew. "I hear you shook 'em up, the Serranos."

"Rumor flies," Esmay said. "I hope it's settled now."

"Nothing's ever settled for good," Meharry said, falling in step beside her. "Did you hear about my baby brother?"

"I didn't know you had a baby brother." Esmay would have expected Meharry to have been hatched from some piece of ordnance, except for the impossibility. She could imagine a string of identical Meharrys, but not one that could be called "baby" in any form.

"He was stationed at the high security brig, on Copper Mountain. Same one where Lepescu stuck me an' the others." She shook her head. "Idiot fool. I s'pose he wanted to see if he could understand his big sister better. Anyway, he figured out that bitch Bacarion was up to no good, and he killed her, and escaped—and nobody escapes that place, I still don't know how he did it, he's gonna have to tell me all the details—an' then he told them about the mutiny. Too late; it was starting, but he tried. Little scamp."

"He's your brother," was all Esmay could think to say.

"Yah. He is. Meharry all the way through." She grinned. "I am really, really proud of that kid, but I better not let him find out, or he'll get sassy with me." She nodded, then, to the end of the passage, where the others had disappeared around a corner. "Better catch up, Lieutenant. Don't forget to say hello to Koutsoudas if he's on the bridge."

Esmay lengthened her stride, but was delayed again by Oblo Vissisuan, coming down the ladder.

"Hoped I'd catch you, Lieutenant, just to say congratulations on your new command and your marriage."

"Thanks," Esmay said.

"That's a really tidy weapons upgrade you've got on *Rascal*," he went on. "I went over and took a look when she got in. And by the stats, she handles well, too."

"She does," Esmay said.

"Though nothing like *Vigilance*," Oblo added. "I hear you got your supply problems straightened out—you know, Lieutenant, if you ever have a problem, maybe I could give you a hand. Nothin' against your supply officer, but Heris—Commander Serrano—she says I have a real talent—"

Esmay had heard Oblo's talent for obtaining the unobtainable described as something else, but she knew it was valuable. "Thank you—I think we're fine now, but if I run into trouble—"

"You just give me a call. Any friend of our—of Commander Serrano's—is a friend of ours. And a member of the family, I guess I should say."

"I don't suppose you know why Barin's on Copper Mountain, do you? I found him on the database."

"They didn't tell you about that? Hell, Lieutenant, he damn near died in the explosion—no! It's all right, he's out of the hospital; he'll be fine when he gets his strength back. I got that from a friend on the admiral's staff. I'd've thought they'd tell you, you bein' his wife and all."

Esmay could have clobbered him for scaring her like that—her heart had seemed to stop for an instant—but clobbering Oblo would be like clobbering a draft horse. It wouldn't hurt him, and he might hit back.

"I'd better catch up," she said instead, and fled up the ladder, working off her fear and anger with every step.

She caught up with the others; no one commented on her absence, and she hoped it hadn't been noticed. They moved on in stately procession through section after section, and finally came to the bridge. Here, docked at the Station, only a skeleton crew manned the bridge. Esmay looked around, but did not see Koutsoudas.

When she got back to *Rascal*, she called up whatever she could find about Barin's ship and its combat. Nothing useful, except that it was listed as out of action. Not destroyed, just out of action.

The next day, Admiral Serrano hosted the farewell gathering. Esmay wore one of her new dress uniforms, astonished all over again by the difference in fit. It looked as if she'd been sewn into it and yet it was comfortable and didn't hinder her movement. She joined the line of officers that snaked in to shake hands with Vida Serrano. For a moment, her stomach churned as she saw the admiral's glance pass over her, but the thought of her ship steadied her. She was here; she was a captain; *Rascal* was a ship to be proud of.

When her turn came, Vida greeted her with a smile. "Lieutenant— I see you found a really good tailor. Congratulations on your return, and on your scores from the exercise. I'm expecting you to live up to your reputation."

"Thank you, sir." Esmay moved on, bemused and wondering which part of her reputation the admiral expected her to live up to.

Later, as she contemplated a towering display of canapes, and considered whether the little brown things with a green fringe or the green paste on crackers would sit best, she realized Admiral Serrano had come up beside her.

"I'm sure you realize by now that I'm not the one who cashiered you—" The admiral took two of the brown things, and one of the crackers.

"Yes, sir; they told me."

"This is not something we want to discuss now, but let me just say that I am genuinely glad to have you back on active duty and a member of the family."

"Thank you, sir."

"Those things on the second tier are deep-fried gengineered locusts with frillik; if I understood your father correctly, it's something you're not supposed to eat."

"No, sir. What about the green paste?"

"Puree of Caskadar neosquid liver with dill. Something else you're not supposed to eat."

"Yes, sir." There was something bizarre about an admiral advising her on the food laws she'd grown up with as applied to alien cuisine.

"The devilled quails' eggs, on the other hand, should be all right."

"Is that what they are?" Esmay had not recognized the elaborate little sculptures as originating with eggs.

"Yes . . . it's this strange little man in food service. I've had him for years, but have never convinced him to let anything look like what it is." She gave Esmay a mischievous sidelong look. "In my wicked moments, I enjoy watching ensigns trying to figure it out, and then choking when they find out what they've just consumed. A low pleasure, I admit."

Esmay said nothing, since her mouth was full of devilled quails' eggs.

"What do you think of Commodore Livadhi?" Admiral Serrano asked, having waited politely for the swallow.

Esmay felt like a quail beneath a stooping falcon. "Well, Admiral, he's . . . he's—" An admiral, and lieutenants who wanted to avoid causing trouble didn't gossip to one admiral about another.

"I know, it's unfair. What I really want to know, if you have a clue, is how my great-niece's crew is getting along with him. They can be a handful, and there's no way I can talk to them without stepping on his toes."

"He had us to dinner," Esmay said. "I happened to see a few of them that I recognized. Petris, Meharry, Oblo—"

"Just the trio that concerned me," Admiral Serrano said. "I doubt it was happenstance you saw them. How did they seem?"

"Fine, sir. They congratulated me on getting a ship—" And on her marriage, but this didn't seem like a good moment to mention that. "Meharry told me about her younger brother—" The term *baby brother* was not one to be used with admirals. "And Oblo told me Barin had been wounded." She couldn't keep a sharp note out of her voice at that.

Admiral Serrano closed her eyes a moment. "Damn! I should have thought—it was while you were out of touch and we didn't know where you were, and then I just assumed you'd hear about it at Headquarters. I'm sorry—I should have made sure you knew. His ship sustained a hull breach; he was working damage control, and there was an explosion—it's a long story; I'll flash it over to your console later tonight. Anyway, he was badly injured; we were all worried until they got him to Copper Mountain. The latest report is that he's come through treatment well and is in rehab now. Expected to make a full recovery. He's been written up for an award. If you want to send him a message, flash it to my office before you leave tomorrow; I'll forward it priority."

"Thank you, sir," Esmay said.

"I'm just sorry I didn't think to tell you myself before now. But I'd better go circulate, or Arash will wonder why I'm chatting you up. He did a good job while he was running this place, but he's just a wee bit sensitive. Old family rivalry, probably." Admiral Serrano moved away, to startle another young officer, Esmay noticed, when she eased up beside him.

Esmay ate two more devilled quails' eggs, allowing herself to feel relief that Barin was no longer in danger.

"Ah, Lieutenant Suiza," That was Commodore Livadhi. "This is certainly more elaborate than my dinner." Was there an edge to that? She couldn't be sure.

"But not so . . ." She paused, trying to think of the best word.

"Comfortable, perhaps?" Comfortable was not the word she'd been thinking of, but one did not argue with admirals. He smiled down at her, and she was aware once more of his charm. "I saw that Admiral Serrano had buttonholed you, and came to the rescue—but I see you need no rescue."

"No, sir. The admiral—Admiral Serrano was just telling me that my—that Barin—her grandson—was safe and recovering well."

"Ah . . . of course. You've been in transit, and the full details aren't being made available." Livadhi took three of the gengineered locusts onto his plate and popped one into his mouth. Now that Esmay knew what they were, the little crunch as he bit into it struck her as obscene. She knew that was ridiculous. "I was just going to ask if you remembered more about that fellow—priest, I think you said?—from the Benignity."

Esmay dragged her mind away from the recitation of *Barin is safe, Barin is safe* to Livadhi's question. "The priest, sir? Mostly we talked about religion. He was curious about me, because he thought Altiplanans had a branch of his religion, and might have some old texts he could study."

"And do you?"

"Sir, I don't know. I left home as a youngster, really, and the history of our beliefs wasn't ever my interest. I told him he should contact the Docent for Altiplano, there on Castle Rock, who could tell him more."

"Mmm. Well, I'll see you at the final briefing." Livadhi walked off. Esmay looked after him with the feeling that she had missed something, perhaps disappointed him in some way.

CHAPTER TWENTY-TWO

Copper Mountain

"I hate these islands," Gelan Meharry said. "If I have to be stuck on a planet, it should at least be somewhere you can do something." He was standing hunch-shouldered in the courtyard; the winter sun slanted in, but a razor-edged wind took all the warmth from its rays.

"I wish someone would invent one of those transporter rays," Barin said. "Straight from this to a nice tropical island would be nice."

"You're right there, sir. But I've put my name in for ship duty. What about you?"

"Dunno yet. I'm still on a medical hold. If they hold it long enough, I might as well take my next required course while I'm here."

"I was kind of hoping, sir, we might end up on the same ship."

Barin gave him a quick look. "Oh? On the grounds that you already know the worst about me?"

"Something like that, yes, sir." Meharry's voice was placid, but his green eyes had a wicked glint. "My sister always said, if you find a Serrano you can stand, hook up with 'em."

"Oh," Barin said again, obscurely pleased. "Well, what kind of ship did you have in mind?"

They discussed the relative merits of the different classes until the transport came.

The flight to the weapons research facility was, despite the clear day, rough enough to make Barin wish he hadn't eaten breakfast.

Here were no walls and towers, just low buildings on a flat windswept space. Barin noticed that all the windows had been broken out, and some replaced with clearfilm and tape. He could see the black scars of fires and other destruction. But bleak as it was, it wasn't as depressing as the prison island; he didn't mind that they'd spend the next few days here.

"Who is that?" Barin asked. The stout man in the funny-looking jacket and fuzzy hat that he'd noticed on the flight from the mainland stumped around the blackened soil where the aircraft had been.

"That's the professor." Meharry grinned. "He was there when they pulled me out of the water. I think he's crazy, the way geniuses usually are."

"He's a genius?"

"They all seem to think so."

"Well . . . the beard's right," Barin said.

"He's the reason Ensign Pardalt came along," Meharry said. "She was his bodyguard when he went out to keep the mutineers from taking over the lab. I heard he asked for her again."

"She didn't want to come when I asked her," Barin said.

The next morning, Barin came into the mess hall—its shattered windows now covered with clearfilm—and looked around. One table was all civilians, talking faster than they were eating. At another, the man in the yellow leather jacket—did he ever take it off?—was sitting next to Ensign Pardalt and leaning towards her.

Barin didn't like the look the professor gave Margiu. She didn't seem to mind it, but . . . she was young. Inexperienced. Geniuses probably thought they could do whatever they wanted, just because they were geniuses. He was determined not to make the mistake he'd made before, and fail to understand his people.

For a moment he remembered the annoying major on the ship he and Esmay had taken from the family reunion, but he pushed that aside. That had been different, if for nothing else than he and Esmay were the same age.

He went over and sat down beside Margiu. "Morning, Ensign."

"Good morning, sir."

"Young Serrano comes down like a wolf on the fold—or at least the spring lamb . . ." the professor said.

"Excuse me?" Barin suspected it was a quotation, but he didn't know the source.

"I only meant that you, like me, chose to sit beside the most ravishing young creature here."

"That's not why I—"

"Tut-tut, my boy. Never suggest anything less to a lady. Whatever your real motive, such as, perhaps, that she's got the only saltshaker on the table, it's only gallant to tell her you came in pursuit of her beauty."

"Professor—" Margiu looked embarrassed; Barin thought she should. What a wordy old flatterer the professor was, after all, and old enough to be her father. Even her grandfather.

"My dear, this is not about you. Unless Lieutenant Serrano thinks I'm a danger to your heart or your safety—" The professor looked at him, and Barin was suddenly aware of a very bright, very piercing glance from those gray eyes, a directness that reminded him of his grandmother. Then the professor looked down, and stabbed his waffle.

"I—thought Ensign Pardalt might not mind some—younger company."

"She might, if you were single," the professor said. "But rumor has it you're married. To Esmay Suiza, in fact. Or is rumor mistaken?"

He was playing dirty, Barin decided. He wrapped himself in Serrano dignity. "Yes, I'm married," he said. "And no, I'm not trying to express any interest in Ensign Pardalt which is inappropriate to . . ." He was floundering and he knew it; there was a wicked glint in the professor's eye which said he was enjoying Barin's difficulty. "As the senior present—"

"He's not bothering me, Lieutenant," Margiu said softly. "He's sort of . . . crazy . . . but he's harmless."

The professor raised his eyebrows dramatically. "Harmless! And this is what I come to, after a life of dedication to the sweet beauties . . . to be called *harmless*."

Barin's anger evaporated, for no reason he could name. He grinned. "You don't look harmless."

"Thanks be for small mercies. And you, young woman, don't ruin my reputation. My colleagues would tease me unmercifully if they thought I was losing my appeal." He looked at Barin again. "Actually, you've done me a favor. They'll see your challenge as proof of my performance, not my feathers. Now I'll take myself off, as if you'd threatened me, and you two young people can enjoy breakfast."

After the professor had gone, Margiu said nothing more, eating steadily.

"I'm sorry if I interrupted," Barin said, finally.

"No . . . it's just . . . he's fun sometimes. He reminds me of home, in a way."

"Xavier?" Barin asked.

"Yes. It's just an ag world, but we do have a university. My parents are farmers, but they're not stupid—" She said this as if expecting an argument. When Barin said nothing, she went on. "Before the— before the Benignity came, we had a house with wide porches, and every week my parents would invite people over. We kids would play games, and the grownups would talk and talk."

"Did you lose your home?" Barin asked.

"Oh, yes. But we rebuilt, just not as big. In time, it will be. Dad says he can't do without a porch to sit on and watch the sky over the fields. Anyway, the professor's a lot smarter and more educated, but some of his talk reminds me of home. The teasing kind of thing." She sounded wistful.

"Do you miss it?"

"Xavier? Sometimes. But I like Fleet, too. Sir—if you don't mind— would you introduce me to Lieutenant Suiza sometime? I'd like to thank her personally."

"Of course," Barin said automatically. He didn't feel like explaining that Esmay wasn't in Fleet anymore. He wondered if everyone was going to think of him as Esmay Suiza's appendage for the rest of his life, the way the family spoke of his aunt's engineer as "Heris's Petris."

His deskcomp informed him he had downloaded messages waiting. Barin sighed. His parents had been sending him jaunty little get-well messages every week or so, but that was not what he wanted. What he wanted . . . was right there in front of him. PERSONAL on the header, and Esmay Suiza-Serrano down below.

His breath caught in his throat. She was back—it had all been a mistake, not his grandmother's fault. She wasn't Landbride anymore.

She had a ship of her own. She loved him. She hoped he was better, and she was sending a cube.

He looked away, and blinked back tears. She was all right. She wasn't dead, or hurt, or lost; she hadn't gone back to Altiplano. He should have known she'd manage. Esmay always managed. Things always worked out for her in the end.

Whereas he . . . he shook his head hard. She loved him; he loved her. He was glad she was back in—of course he was. He was glad she had a ship—she deserved to have a ship. His mind automatically calculated how long it would be before he could hope for a ship, and he swatted it down. That didn't matter . . . did it?

He looked at his reflection in the bureau mirror and grimaced. All the scars were gone—the visible ones—but he still looked gaunt and older than he had.

Because you've grown up.

Had he? Was this restlessness, this dissatisfaction, part of growing up?

He fled from that question and decided to follow his doctors' recommendation to walk at least five kilometers a day. Around the training field, around the main buildings . . . and down to Q-town would just about finish the distance. His legs ached by the time he got to Q-town, and he was glad to stop and rest. Now which? He could eat supper here, just as well. He knew the name and reputation of each bar and restaurant, and shied away from Diamond Sim's, where someone would be sure to comment on experiences. Mama Zee's, on the other hand, served hearty food in its small crowded dining room.

He had finished his salad and was waiting on the main course when the door opened, letting in a cold gust of wind. He glanced up and met the professor's inquisitive gaze.

"Lieutenant Serrano—what a pleasant surprise. May I sit with you?"

Barin had been in the mood to brood alone, but the professor was an older man, distinguished. "Of course," he said.

"I wanted to apologize," the professor said. "I should not have embarrassed you with Ensign Pardalt that way. It's my instinct for mischief."

"That's all right," Barin said. "It doesn't matter."

"Of course it matters," the professor said. "You were only trying to protect one of your people from danger—albeit an imaginary danger."

"Get you something?" That was the waitress, an older woman with gray hair. She handed the professor a menu.

"Ah yes." He ordered quickly. When the waitress left again, he cocked his head at Barin. "Something's troubling you, young man. Have you fallen for the fair Margiu instead of your own illustrious Esmay Suiza?"

"No, it's not that." Barin pushed the saltshaker back and forth. "She's got a ship now, Esmay. She's back in. And she should be."

"Mmm?" The professor busied himself with his napkin, folding it into a precise triangle before putting it in his lap.

"You're married, professor, aren't you?"

"Yes." The professor's face softened. "Kata. Wonderful woman . . . I'll tell you what, young Serrano, they get better as they get older. Softer. Mellower. When she was young, she was like a green peach, but now . . ." He smacked his lips. Barin found it a little disgusting. Esmay was not a peach at all. And yet . . . this was maybe the only married man he could talk to.

"We only had those few days," Barin said. "And I don't even know where she is . . ."

"I'm sorry, I'm not following this." The professor leaned back against the rock. "Why don't you start at the beginning?"

Barin started instead with Esmay's disgrace as a result of the quarrel with Brun Meager, and worked his way to the family reunion, and their hasty clandestine marriage.

"You just ran off to a magistrate? How . . . charming."

"We just couldn't stand it," Barin said. "What with the mutiny and my family and everything—we wanted to have some kind of link—"

"And then things hit the fan—"

"Not really. We made the ship by a hair, the captain chewed us out a bit but not much, and—it was so wonderful, those days."

"Those nights, I suspect you mean, unless you were on third shift," the professor said dryly.

"Well . . . yes. Both, really. Working together, at least part of the time, and then—"

"You found you could get along with half the sleep you thought you needed. Yes. Youth is wonderful that way. So what happened?"

"Esmay got new orders; she was to leave and tranfer at Sector V to another ship, and then on across to her final assignment. The next thing I knew, she wasn't in the Fleet database. She'd been separated, and I didn't know where she was." Barin chewed his lip, remembering how frantic he had felt. Had she felt the same way?

"Did you think she'd gone back to Altiplano?"

"I didn't know. And I was on a warship, a cruiser; I had no chance to start looking. I kept thinking . . . worrying . . . and then we were in combat and then—"

"I heard," the professor said. The waitress reappeared, with a loaf of fresh warm bread and a bowl of butter. The professor pulled off a hunk and started eating. Around a mouthful of bread, he said, "They were determined to save your life, because you'd saved the ship, is what I heard."

"All I did was stand still," Barin said.

"Yes, well, sometimes standing still is the right thing to do. But you're waffling, young man. Get to the point."

Barin found himself blurting it out, more than he'd meant to say, and finished with, "And she's older, and she's got a ship, and I'll always be behind . . ."

The professor stopped, folded his hands on the table and said, "It's not a race."

"Sir?"

"It's not a race. Marriage. There is no 'behind' or 'ahead.' You're not in competition; you're a partnership." He cocked his head. "Do you love this woman?"

"Esmay? Of course—"

"Not 'of course' . . . I mean really love her, heart and soul and body?"

"Yes . . . I do."

"But right now you're jealous, aren't you? You think she's the famous one, the hero twice over, the captain of a fine ship—because if she's the captain, it will be a fine ship. You don't want to be a bauble on her necklace, a trophy husband."

Barin felt himself flushing. "It's not jealousy, exactly."

"Yes, it is—exactly. Barin, I'm going to talk to you as if you were one of my sons or grandsons. It's probably going to upset you, too, just as it upsets them. Now it's obvious to me that you're a fine young officer, a proper Serrano. But your whole life has been Fleet, and one particular segment of Fleet. Here you're a prince; you've inherited a name and all that goes with it. That's fine, so far as it goes. But your wife's not just Fleet; your wife's a Landbride—or she was—and she's got connections that go far beyond Fleet."

"I know that," Barin said.

"Yes, intellectually, you do. Emotionally—you haven't begun to cope with it yet. I will bet that when you first met her, you thought you were doing her a favor."

Barin felt his face going hot again. "I admired her," he said, a little too firmly.

"Yes, but you knew more about Fleet, I daresay, and you were glad to show your expertise."

"I suppose," Barin said, and reached for the bread himself. "She did ask me things."

"Yes. And you generously instructed her. And that's fine, so far as it goes. Tell me how much you've learned about Altiplano."

"Er . . . not much." It occurred to Barin that he hadn't even considered learning more about Altiplano.

"Tell me—what about those women the news media called your NewTex wives? What does your Esmay think of them?"

"Oh, them . . . they're not a problem anymore." He hadn't thought of them in months, since his pay was no longer being garnished for their support. The professor's eyebrows went up, and he explained. "Someone Brun Meager knows found them a home on a colony world someplace . . ."

"Someone . . . someplace . . . ? That's not very specific. Do you feel any responsibility for them, these women who left their native world because they trusted your word?"

Put like that, it sounded as if he were an irresponsible selfish wretch. "I hadn't really thought about it, not since they left. They seemed happy enough to go there."

"Umm. Out of Fleet, out of mind? Only the standards here in Fleet are real to you? I suppose that's why you're so worried about being always junior to her."

"I hadn't thought of it like that," Barin said. He didn't want to think of it like that, and he was relieved when the waitress returned with their food. He dug into his food and hoped the professor would forget what they'd been talking about. But the professor, halfway through his steak, returned to the topic.

"If you worry about her rank, Barin, you'll make yourself miserable—and her, too. You can't grow by cutting her down. This is what I meant by your needing a wider base. If you see everything through the narrow filter of Fleet, date-of-commission and all that, then you can only regret being born later. But if you see that both of you can grow in all dimensions . . . then what will it matter? What kind of person cares, in twenty years, if you were commissioned a year or two after her? Who's wearing which insignia?"

"But that's how we . . ." His voice trailed off.

The professor hammered another nail in that coffin. "Rank isn't merit. Age isn't merit. Neither young nor old, high nor low, but only the action, honorable or not."

"You're quoting again," Barin said.

"Guilty as charged," the professor said, grinning. "It's part of my job, preserving ancient culture. Barin, there are dozens—probably hundreds—of ranking systems. Academic degrees . . . intellectual pedigrees, who you trained with . . . publications. Every organization in the universe has some kind of pecking order, and people who make themselves miserable because someone is ranked higher."

"You think competition is wrong?"

"Of course not! Ask my colleagues—they'll tell you I'm cutthroat when it comes to my career. But that's not all my life—and your profession of arms shouldn't be all of your life. A man who is just a scientist, or just a soldier, or just a woodcutter isn't a whole man. I'll tell you what I think a man is—and by man I don't mean a featherless biped or something who just happens to have human DNA and a Y chromosome. A man is a person who has learned—is learning, is willing to learn—to know himself. Who can face the truth about himself and go on living, who makes the right kind of difference in the world.

"Truth's not always easy," Barin muttered into his potatoes.

"Truth is never easy," the professor said. "Truth about yourself is the hardest. But men love, men protect those they love, men walk with honor. So can women—Kata would smack me with one of her carving tools if she thought I didn't know that—but right now, because we're both men, we're talking about men."

"What if you . . . make bad mistakes?" Barin asked.

"You fix them, as best you can," the professor said. "Admit

them, make amends, try again. I've certainly made them. Lots. It's how you learn."

"But other people can pay the price of your learning," Barin said.

"Yes, absolutely. And that's terrible, a burden you have to shoulder the rest of your life. It's happened to you, has it?" The professor didn't wait for an answer—he rarely did, Barin had noticed—but went right on. "Your Esmay's had that experience, or she will. If you have, then you'll understand her, and she'll understand you, those nights you wake up at 0300 and see it all happen again." The professor's voice had a steely edge now, like someone who had been there.

"You, sir?"

"Oh, yes. Smartass young scientists can make deadly mistakes too, Barin. Think we know more than we know, forget that between the theory and the device, between the equations and the engineering, things . . . change." He shook his head and applied himself to his food. Barin didn't know whether to ask more or just wait, and chose the easy way of finishing his own food.

As they waited for dessert, the professor started in again. "Kata and I have been married forty-two years, and I can tell you there were some stormy times. Weapons scientists don't get recognition, not even from peers, not early on. She had a name as a sculptor before I was through my first post-doc. She'd go off to some gallery show, where I could imagine all those rich men fawning on her. She loves shows; she'd come back all flushed and happy, and there I'd be with a sour taste in my mouth and a pile of tests I'd graded or some-thing equally unglamorous."

"So what did you do?" Barin asked, fascinated.

"I drank too much for a while," the professor said. "Then I tried to boss her around, which is always bad, but particularly bad for a creative person's spouse, because they can lose their gift, at least for a while. Kata tried to be what she thought was a good wife, and the gallery owner came over and screamed at me for two hours one day about how I was a patriarchal retrograde mastodon who didn't deserve her and belonged in a history museum with a spear up my butt."

"So?"

"So I threatened to demonstrate to the gallery owner just how retrograde I was, which cost me a fine later, but it was good in the long run. I thought about it, and joined the Society for the Preservation of Antique Lore with my friend Barry. Met a lot of fascinating people, learned a lot about historical weaponry which turned out to be useful, though I can't tell you why, and worked off my frustrations on the field. Worked my way up to Knight-Commander of the White Brigade, which meant a lot of people fawned on me when they weren't trying to crack my skull in tournaments. Did wonders for my ego."

"And you're still married," Barin said.

"More to the point, we still *want* to be married. Yes, I ogle the girls, especially the shy ones who need it more than you might think, and yes, Kata still purrs and preens when some rich old fart tells her how talented she is . . . but the fact of the matter is, we're each other's best friend, and partner, and that's how it is, was, and will be."

"It sounds . . . good."

"It's better than good. And what it takes is character, commitment, and time. You have to find a partner who's honest—because lying, even to yourself, will kill it. You have to find one who's brave, because let's face it, life is scary. Someone who's openhearted, not grasping. And then make the commitment—both of you. And if you find that person of character, and stick with it, you'll get the honey in the comb."

"Esmay has character . . ."

"That's what attracted you, probably, besides your hormones. You come from a heritage of character. And you know she has courage."

"Yes . . . but I'm not sure I'm a match for her."

"Ah. So we're back to matching again. It's not a race; it's not a contest. All you have to do is be honest, brave, and true—something you were bred for, if I'm any judge. If that's too much, you can always change your mind, decide that the marriage was a mistake. You can walk away. You can walk away from those NewTex women and never give them another thought, too. But if you walk away from too many of your responsibilities, you aren't a man anymore; you're a parasite. It's addictive, walking out on things."

"I don't want to walk out on her," Barin said. "But I don't know how to be what I need to be."

"You already are," the professor said. "You're just barely old enough to grasp this point, but I'll try anyway. You're comparing yourself to Esmay and your Serrano relatives. You don't need to be anyone else, Barin. You need to be you, because you are enough. Anyone—anyone at all—can be enough. Smart enough, brave enough, good enough."

"You sound so sure."

"I'm not exactly a spring chicken; I've seen a lot of military men. I've seen Meharry around you. He's not a fool; he's not going to give his loyalty to an idiot, a coward, a dolt." That bright eye speared him again. "The fact is, you're revealed by your creation, and a military commander's creation is the way his people act. You determine their bond, their morale. If your people get better, then you're a good commander; if your people get worse . . . look to yourself. Meharry was nearly a wreck when we picked him up; I don't know what hurt him so badly, but I do know what got him back: you did."

"Oh." Barin digested as they ate dessert. "So . . . if I'm not competing with Esmay, then . . . we sort of grow in parallel?"

"Exactly." The professor beamed at him. "It'll be easier if you'll broaden your base. Something that will help you—in your career, and as your wife's husband—is getting comfortable with more kinds of people. How many civilian friends do you have?"

"Civilian friends?"

"Yes. We're not all dolts, you know. There are a lot of us. The more you know about civilians—all kinds of civilians—the more perspective you'll have. The higher you go, the more you'll have to interact politically as well as militarily."

"I never thought of that." Barin thought now. Civilians as something other than more or less docile sheep in serious need of shepherding had never crossed his mind. He was startled to realize that he didn't know any . . . that his closest approach to civilians had been those depressed and frightened women and children from Our Texas. They had needed his help, his guidance, his support . . . that's what he expected from them.

"Militaries always rest on the foundation of a civilian population," the professor said. "They don't feed themselves, or supply themselves . . . someone grows the food you eat, makes the cloth for your clothes, builds the ships, manufactures the weapons . . . and that's not counting trade, entertainment and the arts. Start now building your networks in all these areas."

"I guess I can use you for the sciences," Barin said.

"You could indeed."

"But . . ." Barin drew lines on the table with his dessert fork. "I still don't know if I want to go back into space."

"After being blown up, I don't wonder. And you don't have to. Not a race, remember. Not a contest. You can be an honorable, decent man and a good husband to Esmay if you never go out on a ship again."

"Mmm." That was a new thought, and a hard one. Unaccountably, just thinking it made him less afraid. Did he really want to stay on a planet the rest of his life? Not really. He had one reason to be scared and many reasons to go back to ships.

"Not that I think that's your path; personally I think you'll go out there and command a cruiser yourself someday. But what I think doesn't matter. It's your life."

"It is." Barin saw it then, a wavering vision that split and recombined like reflections on water . . . but lives—more than one life—in which he was someone he could respect. Someone Esmay could respect.

"If I were you, I'd check up on those women," the professor said, pushing back his chair. "You'll feel better for it."

Barin nodded, but his thoughts were on Esmay. Now he could feel for her the joy he should feel—she had a ship, her own ship. She would be magnificent.

They would be magnificent.

CHAPTER TWENTY-THREE

Castle Rock

With Kevil and Stepan's help, Brun studied the structure of the Grand Council, Seat by Seat. Unsurprisingly, Stepan had a file on every member old enough to be Seated, similar to the dossier they'd had on her. Brun began to see the Council as a vast overgrown sprawling tree of complicated relationships. Out at the ends were the individuals—some shiny green leaves, others spotted with mold or half eaten away by insects . . . some healthy green, others yellowing or even brown, about to fall. Behind them were histories—their own, those of parents and grandparents and great-grandparents, aunts and uncles and cousins. She felt a constant bubbling amazement at the number of mysteries cleared up: why this uncle and that great-aunt refused to sit at the same table, why this minor family had bolted to the Conselline Sept seventy years before.

"We've made a lot of mistakes," Stepan told her. "We're a sept, not a collection of mythical saints. Individuals, families, all restless and twitchy about our place in the whole, just as individuals and families have always been." He pushed over another data cube. "Be sure you don't misplace this one. It's our analysis of Conselline Sept."

It was, though not quite as detailed, fascinating. Brun hadn't even known Hobart Conselline had an older brother, let alone that he was an addict incapable of acting on his own, whose proxy Hobart had held since reaching his own majority. She hadn't known about Oskar Morrelline's personal proclivities and wondered if that had anything to do with Ottala's behavior in school.

It was far too much to absorb completely in only a few days; her brain felt stuffed. But when Stepan began talking strategy with her, she found she had retained more than she'd thought possible.

"I will make my own analysis available to you, via the deskcom, but necessarily in brief. However, you'll be using your own judgment; where the younger members are concerned, you may have insights that are better than mine."

"I see," Brun said.

"Do you think you also need Kevil Mahoney there? He certainly has valuable experience, though he isn't Seated himself. If he sits with you, that makes a statement. . . ."

Kevil was a link to her comfortable past, but she was leaping into an unknown future. Still . . . even on a journey into the unknown, wise people took with them supplies and tools from their past.

"Could he sit with you? Would that be too conspicuous?"

"No, but it would place a limit on the communication, you understand."

"Yes. But I don't need him for every little detail—I'd like to be able to ask for clarification on points of law and order."

"That's reasonable. I can certainly ask him as a guest for my own purposes. But, Brun, that leaves you alone—your brothers and sister aren't coming, are they?"

"No. Cousins might."

"Harlis's son, yes. I'm going to move to have him unSeated, on the grounds that his father is a fugitive who's taken up with mutineers. And you will be guarded, Brun."

Brun shook her head. "Don't keep him out, Stepan. It'll look vindictive and weak. Let him come; he has a right to a vote, and we have no proof he was involved in his father's activities. Do we?"

"No, but—you've read his dossier, Brun. He's explosive, like his father, and he's shaped by his father as well. We know he acted as messenger from his father to Hobart Conselline on more than one occasion."

"Even so. I'd rather have him sitting right there glaring at me than sitting at home brooding about how he was treated unfairly."

Stepan thought a long moment. "Hmm. I shouldn't ask for an opinion and ignore it. I said your insight might be different from mine and yet valuable," he said. "I chose you for your abilities; it's only fair to let you demonstrate them. All right, I'll withdraw my motion. But be careful; I consider him dangerous."

She started to say she wasn't afraid of Kell and then realized that was stupid. In present circumstances, she should be at least concerned. "I don't think he'll do anything violent in the Council chamber," she said instead.

"Probably not, but we don't take chances on his mood." He paused, sipped from his glass, then said, "Have you heard anything about Sirialis? How are you dealing with that?"

"There's nothing I can do from here, and here is where I need to be," Brun said. "I hope—I hope they didn't go there, or if they do, that they don't hurt anyone. That's naive, I know, but—I told the people there to get everyone out, dispersed, as best they can, and not worry about the property. Maybe, if the mutineers don't have time to settle in, the damage will be minimal."

"I know you love the place," Stepan said. "It was a paradise for you children."

"It was beautiful," Brun said, and hated herself for using past tense as soon as she heard it. "Is beautiful," she corrected. "But it's too much for one person, or one family."

At the surprise on his face, she went on. "Look at the situation now, ser. Our people, those who looked to us for protection and care, are in danger—and we can't do anything. Not all our money, not all our political influence. Should we claim control of something we can't protect? I don't think so."

"Hm. And to whom would you give it? Or would you sell it?"

"Those who live there, who will have to survive our failure."

"That's an option, certainly. But we don't even know yet that Sirialis will be under attack. When—if the mutineers did go there— would they arrive?"

Brun said, "I'm not sure. Fleet might know. It depends where they picked up the mutineers' warships, for one thing. My guess is, in another five to ten days by our time, but that's very uncertain."

"Hmm. And Fleet could do nothing."

"I wouldn't say *nothing*, but in the present crisis, they can't afford to keep a force in the Sirialis system for any length of time. They're quite reasonably concerned about mutineers attacking more populated worlds, a major shipping nexus—even here, at

Castle Rock—or hopping the border to the Benignity, or the Bloodhorde."

"You did remind them Sirialis is only one jump away from the Bloodhorde, I hope?"

"They knew that already. I think they're watching the jump point."

"Makes sense, I suppose." Stepan sighed. "I didn't get there as often as I liked, but it was a beautiful place, and your mother's hand made it better. Speaking of your mother, do you know where she and Lady Cecelia were going?"

"I have no idea," Brun said. "By the time I found out, they were already gone, and I haven't heard anything."

"Brun, my dear—I know you loved both your parents dearly, and you've already lost one to violence. Have you considered that they might be lost in this turmoil, Miranda and Cecelia?"

"Of course . . . but it doesn't do any good to think about it."

"Perhaps not, but to be prepared for bad news, if it comes, that can be important." Stepan watched her steadily.

"What—have you heard something?" Brun felt her heart contract.

"Not directly, no. But I do know something's caused a flurry in Defense. I don't know if it's just a space battle somewhere—and that's a terrible thing to say, I'm sorry—or if it could involve your mother. The Consellines have been badgering Fleet to take time to look for her; that's why I thought I should prepare you."

"Thank you," Brun said. She had thought she was prepared, but now that she let herself really think about it, her face felt stiff, her mouth dry. Her mother dead? Lady Cecelia? On top of everything else—it was like a vast weight of sand landing on her, squeezing her . . .

"It may not be anything," Stepan said.

Brun forced her mind back to the practical. "I presume we'll find out," she said. "Thanks for the warning."

"If there is bad news, and if it is too much for you, let me know at once; we can do something else this Council meeting—"

"Not really," Brun said. "You've already explained the problems, and why my speaking will give us the best leverage we have. I'll do it."

Stepan's warning could not entirely prepare her for the news, she found, when the message came from Grand Admiral Savanche the afternoon before the next Grand Council session. She and her mother had never been close until after her father's death; she had always felt reproved by her mother's cool composure. And now—there was no more time. Her mother was dead. Had been dead days, or weeks . . . she couldn't concentrate on the time adjustments.

She took a long breath, as she folded a scarf into the neckline of her suit. She could not cry now. She could not afford to be red-eyed and puffy-faced for this. She took more slow deep breaths, watching herself in the mirror, watching the outward signs of inward turmoil fade, until it was almost her mother's serenity that looked back at her.

Another pang: had this been how Miranda did it? Had she hidden, beneath that serenity, such anguish? Probably. Brun probed that reaction, testing her own composure. Could she trust herself to stay this calm under the certain pressures of the Council meeting? She let her mind throw up images of her mother, her father, Sirialis. The face in the mirror did not change.

The great starry-roofed chamber might have imposed its own serenity on the anthill of scurrying humans below its dome, but familiarity had dulled their responses. Intent on their own concerns, their own worries and ambitions, most of them didn't even glance at the painted stars, or the Family mottoes blazoned around the rim of the dome. Brun, arriving early, had the time, and the inclination, to look around. Now, watching the other Seated Members coming in, she ran over the points she must make. How would her words affect these people, most of them so wealthy they had no idea how much they owned—how many worlds, how many people, how many things? Would they shrug and say it had nothing to do with them, what happened ten or twenty light-years away?

The Consellines, bereft of Hobart Conselline, were in as much disarray as the Barracloughs had been when Bunny died. Hobart had systematically destroyed a dozen able Conselline politicians on his own climb to power. Would this consolidate their vote, making them cling harder to any perceived Conselline interest, or would it open them up, make them more receptive to the interest of the Familias as a whole?

She couldn't know that for sure, she could only know what Stepan told her of the Barraclough Sept's situation. She watched as her cousin Kell came down the steps and hesitated at the Family Table. She hoped she was right that mercy here would not be misplaced and gave him a steady look as she nodded towards his Seat. He looked grumpy, but then he usually did.

"I don't know where my father is," he said. "So don't ask."

"I do," Brun said.

His expression changed to alarm. "Where? Did you have him thrown in prison, or what?"

"He hired a mutineer to take him to Sirialis," Brun said.

"What?! You're lying!"

"No," Brun said, amazed at her own calm. She felt almost as Miranda had always looked, and from the look on Kell's face that's what he was seeing in her. "I'm not lying, and that's what he did. It was really quite foolish. It makes us look bad—"

"Huh?"

"To the other septs," Brun went on. "To have a Thornbuckle, a Barraclough, making deals with mutineers for private business. Very bad."

"Then why'd Uncle Stepan let me take my Seat?"

"He didn't want to," Brun said. She gave him another long look. "I insisted. I'm not feuding with you. This is no time for intrafamily feuds."

"You're . . . different," Kell said.

"Yes. Being a captive, having children, and losing your parents does that to you," Brun said. "Danger, they say, has a wonderful ability to concentrate attention."

"Dad never had a chance, did he?" Kell asked suddenly.

"Not really, not in the long run," Brun said. "Why?"

"He always said your father was soft underneath—that he got the prestige just because of his smooth manner and his connections." He hesitated then plunged on. "He said that's why he sent Fleet after you . . . that anyone stupid enough to get picked up like that deserved what she got."

"Then I trust he won't be upset to realize that we're not going to rescue him from the mutineers," Brun said crisply. Kell stared. "Kell, your father's hired some of the most dangerous men in our universe—he's gone off with them alone. Do you think they'll respect his noble birth and take his orders if they don't like them?"

"But—but he's rich—"

"And wealth buys *things*, Kell. Things. People's loyalty has a higher price, which your father has never learned to pay. He's chosen men who have no respect for riches—oh, they want riches, but that's different. They respect strength, personal courage, personal fitness. They will take his riches and—if he's lucky—kill him quickly."

Kell paled. "Are you serious? You really think—"

"I've seen the dossier on the man he hired, and some of his crew."

"Can't you do something?"

"Like what? Beg Fleet to go after him? Listen to my speech, Kell, and you'll understand why not."

Kell looked around. "Are any of the others coming? Buttons? Dot?"

"No. They've registered their proxies."

The great chamber was less than two-thirds full; many members had been unable to return for another session and had registered proxies with their Family representative. Brun compared the Seats taken with her display. Stepan, to her left and two levels higher, smiled and nodded when she glanced his way; she nodded in return. Viktor, beside him, pretended to glower. To the right, Ronnie's father among the other Carrutherses and Ronnie, far older than when she'd seen him last. She pressed her comm control and beeped him. He looked up.

"Ronnie—I thought you were stuck on a colony—"

"I am, but I had to make this session. Did my aunt tell you about the problems in colonial administration?"

"Some—I'm glad you made it out." He got out of his seat and came over to crouch beside her.

"Listen, Brun, we didn't even know about your being captured until after you were back. Raffa sends her love. She's my vice-governor, so she had to stay. But I'm hearing rumors that you're leading an Ageist revolt—is that so?"

"Not exactly," Brun said. "Let me explain between sittings, why don't you? Have you heard what Stepan did?"

"No, not yet." Ronnie gave Kell a suspicious glance. "Tell me later?"

"Sure. Lunch?"

"I'm lunching with George and Veronica. You could join us."

"I'll try," Brun said.

Now the Ministers filed in to take their places at the Table of Ministers . . . Brun knew that in the wake of Hobart's assassination and the mutiny, his appointee at the Ministry of Defense had resigned in favor of Irion Solinari who had now returned to the capitol. The head of Colonial Affairs, another Conselline appointee, looked worried and glanced several times towards the Carruthers' table.

Stepan buzzed her and his quiet old voice purred into her ear. "Brun . . . there are more young people here today—and proxies registered for even more. Be sure you speak to their concerns."

"I've just talked to Ronnie Carruthers," she said. "He's here in person."

"Excellent," Stepan said. "I urged his father to ask him back for a Council meeting even before Hobart died."

So that was how Ronnie had made it.

The interim Speaker, Jon-Irene Pearsall, tapped the ceremonial gavel as if he were afraid the head would come off. Several weeks of power had given him no confidence.

"We have several questions before the Council," he said. "A motion to censure the late Lord Thornbuckle's widow for the death of Minister of Foreign Affairs Pedar Orregiemos. A motion to appoint a special investigator to examine the relationship between Pedar Orregiemos' death and the assassination of Hobart Conselline. A motion to appoint a special investigator to determine the cause of the mutiny in the Regular Space Service. A motion to appoint a special investigator to determine the relationship of the Benignity of the Compassionate Hand with the Barraclough Sept. A motion of support for the loyal service of the Regular Space Service . . ." He droned on down a list, most of it motions to investigate, censure, or support.

Brun had already registered her request to speak to certain items on the list. A Conselline representative, one of Hobart's nephews, was up first on item one. He was, she noted, in his mid-thirties, and unrejuved. He read a prepared text in a rapid monotone, with occasional nervous glances at his hearers.

"It is clear that Pedar Orregiemos was killed by Miranda Thornbuckle as part of a widespread plot to bring down the Conselline Sept. This

fiction that he was killed in a fencing accident is just that—fiction—
and if the crime had not been committed on private property far
away from any nonpartisan law enforcement, the murderer would
have been quickly brought to book. Indeed, she has admitted her
guilt by fleeing—which suggests that even the tame militia of Sirialis
weren't satisfied . . ." He went on in this vein for some minutes,
painting a picture of Barraclough scheming to murder Hobart and
Pedar, hinting at other assassination attempts, at a Barraclough
Ageist conspiracy. Finally he ran down.

Brun stood up and waited until the murmurs had died down. She
knew she was about to drop a bombshell and didn't want to waste
any of its concussive power. When the silence had reached a point of
tension she felt in every nerve, she spoke.

"I realize Cerion Conselline would like to believe everything that
goes wrong is our fault," she said. "It would be handy if the
Thornbuckles were really just thorns, and you could be rid of trouble
by plucking us out and tossing us in the fire." Her tone invited a
chuckle from the unaligned, and she got it. "But such easy solutions
have never worked, in the whole history of humankind. However,
I'm not here to discuss human history and psychology . . ." Another
chuckle; this time she spoke over the tail end of it. "Nor am I here to
defend my mother. It's too late for that—" A startled murmur, this
time. Brun went steadily on. "My mother is dead."

"You're lying!" burst out Oskar Morrelline. "She's just run off."

"She and Cecelia de Marktos were traveling to the Guerni
Republic," Brun said. "Alone, in Lady Cecelia's yacht *Pounce*. They
were captured by mutineers on the cruiser *Bonar Tighe*—yes, the one
identified at the beginning of the mutiny—when their yacht came
out of FTL unexpectedly." Now she had their attention again and a
silence heavy with dread. "She and Lady Cecelia were put in the brig
with other loyalist prisoners. Knowing they were doomed anyway,
they all attempted an escape; my mother was with a party that made
their way to the communications equipment and sent off a message
giving the ship's location. Lady Cecelia was with a party engaged in
disabling the ship as much as possible."

"You expect us to believe two rich old ladies could disable a ship?"
Oskar yelled. Pearsall tapped for order, and Oskar glowered at him
and threw himself back in his seat, folding his arms dramatically.

"The loyalist prisoners had the expertise," Brun said. "But my mother and Lady Cecelia made the escape possible. Because they were civilians, and rich ladies, the guards were less careful with them. They managed to disable the guards and unlock the cells."

"How do you know all this?" called another Conselline supporter.

"I was informed yesterday by Grand Admiral Savanche, who gave me permission to inform this assembly. The Regular Space Service will release the story to the news media today. A loyal task force seeking out mutineers found the mutineer ship and destroyed it. Unfortunately, while Lady Cecelia and some of the loyalist prisoners managed to escape in a troop shuttle, my mother died helping others get away. She drew fire from the mutineers to let others escape." Brun drew a long breath. "Fleet," she said, "considers her a hero. I don't ask you all to agree . . . but if you insist on thinking her a murderer, at least she has paid her debt by giving her own life for others."

"Were all the mutineer ships destroyed?" asked a young man from the upper tiers. Brun didn't have to look at her list to know that this was a Kimberly-Dwight, her own age.

"No," Brun said. "We know for a fact that others exist. But the *Bonar Tighe* is thought to have been the flagship of the mutineer fleet."

"How did they disable it?" asked someone else.

"I don't know all the details," Brun said. "But Admiral Savanche said it was one of the most imaginative schemes he'd heard of."

"What commander destroyed it?" asked another.

"I think that will be in today's report," Brun said. "I was most concerned with my mother's fate, as you can imagine. It's—I don't want to be maudlin, but it's been less than a year since my father died." This time she heard murmurs of sympathy as well as the buzz of curiosity. "However, I stand in opposition to a motion to investigate my mother, since she is dead, apparently with credit to herself."

Cerion Conselline huddled with the more senior Consellines, including Oskar, and finally turned back to the Chair. "I withdraw the motion," he said. "In consideration of Sera Meager-Thornbuckle's recent loss. But I will have another motion of investigation later, since all the persons suspected of collusion aren't dead yet. There's still the matter of an Ageist conspiracy." This clumsy threat brought scattered laughter.

"I still think it's a lie," Oskar Morrelline said. "You managed to kill my daughter, plant spies in our facility—"

"Point of order," Brun said. Oskar glowered, but shut up.

"The first motion has been withdrawn by the maker," the Speaker said. "We will proceed to item two. The Minister of Defense will speak to this topic."

Irion Solinari, normally tubby, cheerful and energetic, now looked grim, his full lower lip tucked in. "Ser Conselline and Ser Morrelline have alleged an Ageist conspiracy, my lords and ladies. Unfortunately, what I have to report about the possible contributing factors to this mutiny will sound like a counterconspiracy, and for that reason you might be tempted to dismiss it. I pray you will not." Silence; he sipped from a glass of water, and began with a history of rejuvenation failure in the Regular Space Service.

"We had no trouble with the first ones, the voluntary rejuvenation of senior flag officers. Later, we offered voluntary rejuvenation to the rest of the flag ranks, until we had what we thought were sufficient data to show safety and efficacy. Then we began offering rejuvenation to senior NCOs, our most valuable personnel in actual combat. A few years ago, we began to notice that a few—then more—senior NCOs were suddenly experiencing neurological and cognitive symptoms. As the numbers grew, so did concern about the cause, and after it was discovered that some commercial supplies of rejuvenation drugs were flawed in some way, rejuvenation failure became a live target. Some alert officers noted a correlation between the drug batches and the personnel suffering mental deterioration. Unfortunately, the bulk of Fleet supplies of rejuvenation drugs had come from a single source for the past sixteen years, which meant that if that source was contaminated, all our rejuvenated enlisted personnel were at risk."

"That's a lie!" Oskar burst out.

"Unfortunately, it's true," Solinari said. "A Benignity plot to make all our senior personnel senile would be an effective way of damaging Fleet without firing a shot. We could not, however, be sure that it wasn't just an error of judgment, a cost-cutting decision by someone unqualified to predict the result of that change in technique. Fleet instituted an immediate program of research into rejuvenation fail-ure—naturally we wanted to find a treatment that would prevent the loss of personnel and their own suffering. Ser Thornbuckle approved this plan, and fully understood the risks of losing up to a quarter of Fleet manpower—the most experienced quarter—to rejuv failure."

"Aren't the younger personnel just as qualified?" That was a young voice, from behind her; Brun wasn't sure whose.

"They're qualified, yes. But in war nothing beats combat experience. One reason we embarked on wholesale rejuvenation for our older NCOs is that we've had a period of relative peace—a few outbreaks here and there, but mostly peace—for long enough that most young personnel have never been in combat. We wanted to preserve that experience, to have it when we next needed it."

"Well, I heard that one reason for the mutiny was the lack of opportunity for young people to advance," said someone else.

"I'm coming to that," Solinari said. "They're actually related." He waited, but no one else interrupted. "People in Fleet are like people everywhere," he said. "They don't all agree. There are younger officers and NCOs who believed that rejuvenation froze the promotion scale, and kept them from having a normal career. To some extent this is true. No effective force can be all admirals and master chiefs. So rejuvenation at the top meant fewer slots open for promotion, and longer time in grade at the bottom. If you look at the structure over the past hundred years, promotion slowed markedly in the past ten. Ser Thornbuckle suggested adding a longevity component to pay scales to help make up for this, but the Council has never been eager to spend more money on the military."

"I've always voted for it!" someone yelled.

"When it's for ships," someone else said. "I've heard you talk about military pay, Jas."

"At any rate," Solinari said, ignoring the interruption, "there certainly was a sizeable fraction of younger personnel who were feeling frustrated. Whether a mutiny would have occurred just because of this, we can't know. However, when word began to spread about the failure of enlisted rejuvenations, this led to near panic among the middle and upper enlisted grades who had been rejuved. When Hobart Conselline shut down the research and funding for treatment, this fed the fear that Fleet was deliberately causing rejuv failure to open up the career structure again."

"What was the treatment?" someone asked.

"Immediate rejuvenation with good drugs," Solinari said. "That froze the condition where it was. If caught early enough, the symptoms never developed. But it was expensive, and to ensure good drugs, we went to another source than that from which we'd bought the bad drugs."

"Alleged bad drugs," Oskar said. This time there was a derisive chuckle from most of the chamber; everyone there knew about the problems at Patchcock, at least the recent one: the courts were stuffed with lawsuits.

"Besides concerns about opportunity and failed rejuvenations," Solinari said, "there's a third source of unrest. Any military organization tends to attract some people who seek power in unhealthy ways. We had Admiral Lepescu, who became the focus for those who believed that only the harshest military values mattered. When his policy of using prisoners as human prey in hunts was discovered, we realized that he had followers throughout Fleet. We eliminated those we could identify, but we could not simply condemn everyone who had ever known him."

"Why didn't you find out about him sooner?" asked Ser Carruthers.

"I'd like to say, because he was careful, but probably his superiors were also careless, willing to accept his efficient performance without looking too closely at his methods. I do know that throughout history, his type of personality is one of those which military organizations both harbor and promote to higher rank. At any rate, we think the mutiny began among those who fit several of these critera: frustration at lack of opportunity, concern about the misuse of rejuvenation, and membership in the secret society that Lepescu started. We now have evidence, following the rescue of loyalists from the *Bonar Tighe*, that its captain, Solomon Drizh, was in fact a Lepescu protege."

At this there was a flurry of movement and excited talk among the members. Solinari waited until the room quieted. "We certainly do need to look further into these things, but at the moment, what Fleet needs is your support in putting down the mutiny. This means not only money, but your commitment to the Familias. We know that the mutineers have approached some of you, offering protection or making threats. We know they may try to use your private worlds to hide out or resupply. We need to know that the Grand

Council supports the loyal elements in Fleet, that you won't make any special deals—"

"Well, if you're not protecting us, we have to get help where we can—" said someone from the very top row.

"Traitor!" yelled a young Barraclough; Brun saw Viktor lean toward him, scowling.

"It's just an excuse to ask for more money," said Oskar Morrelline. "The whole thing's a fabrication—"

In moments, the simmering tension of the chamber had boiled over into chaos, members standing and yelling at each other, shaking their fists. The Speaker clearly lacked the presence to bring them to order, and finally abandoned the attempt. Brun, sensing that yelling might soon come to blows, rose and went down the steps to the front. They had hoped no such action would be necessary, but just in case . . .

She noticed that people quieted as she passed their Tables; a few even spoke her name. She ignored them, walking as Miranda would have walked, cool and serene. She knew movement would draw attention, and movement like this—nonthreatening, calm—would compel by its contrast. The noise had lessened considerably by the time she got to the lowest level.

Pearsall was wringing his hands, his face pale. Brun smiled at him, and held out her hand. "May I try, Ser Pearsall?"

"It's—it's hopeless," he said. "You'll have to call in the security to clear the chamber."

"Possibly," Brun said, "but it's worth a try, isn't it? We haven't had to clear the chamber in ninety odd years."

He handed her the gavel and stepped back. Brun flicked on the Speaker's mic and glanced around. Most of the arguers were at least glancing her way now and then to see what was happening, but they weren't ready to pay attention. She reached into the recess under the podium where—as Kevil had told her—a loud-hailer was stowed for emergencies, should the power go out. She picked it up.

"Stop this nonsense." The roar of the loud-hailer silenced them all for a critical moment, as they tried to figure out who held it and what was happening. Brun blinked the lights, and spoke more calmly, but still in the loud-hailer. "We have serious issues to discuss—and I mean discuss, not have screaming tantrums over."

"Who told you—!" began Oskar Morrelline.

"Sit down, Ser Morrelline, and be quiet. If you wish to be recognized, you will request it with your button."

"You—" he glared at her as if he would leap down three tiers and knock her to the ground, but men on either side of him pulled him back to his seat, whispering urgently in his ears.

"Thank you," Brun said. She put down the loud-hailer and set the Speaker's mic to a medium volume. "I see many lights are lit. Please wait your turn; please limit what you have to say to factual information or a brief expression of support or opposition to the topic." She took the lights in order, according to the computer's log.

The first to speak, having pressed their buttons before the uproar, now had trouble remembering what they had wanted to say. Brun waited for them, not rushing them. By the time ten had spoken, the others were all settling down, like a team of restive horses that now felt an experienced hand at the reins. She was careful not to grin, not to let them see the triumph she felt. She went on being calm and cool and perfectly fair until even the Consellines were able to leave off sarcasm and discuss the issues. She had seen her father do this often enough. Boring them into good behavior, he'd called it.

When the debate on Ageists and Rejuvenants heated up again, Brun stepped in.

"This is an important issue. We must come to some new under-standing of how to constitute our government. But right now, at this time, we need to make sure we have a government, and a polity to govern. We have heavily armed warships roaming around inside our borders, any one of which could hold a planet hostage. Suppose one or a group of them decided to take over a colony world? Some colonies do not even have efficient communications access out of their own system. You know more and more of your children have been going to the colonies—do you want to deliver them to slavery?"

"No . . ." came a murmur.

"Most of us here own stock in, if we don't completely own, the trading consortia that move our goods from place to place. What will piracy do to our profits?"

A thoughtful silence.

"What we must do is secure our borders, and rid ourselves of the menace of these mutineer ships. We don't want them defecting to the Benignity or the Bloodhorde—"

"No one would go there—"

"No? Why not? If they are, as Minister Solinari says, part of a cult of strength-through-killing, isn't this just a sophisticated version of the Bloodhorde's beliefs? I can see a mutineer or so running to the Bloodhorde—and then teaching them how to maintain and use the advanced technology of the ships they stole. I can also see the Benignity being extremely upset with us for being so careless."

Another thoughtful silence.

"So—you think we ought to do what?" That was Ronnie's father.

"First give Fleet our support, as Minister Solinari said, to put down the mutiny and secure our borders. When we've done that—which should not take long—then we need to deal with these other issues. We need to reassure our neighbors that we are not planning to encroach on them. We need to find a way to open opportunities to more of our citizens—to the young, now kept from advancement by their elders who have rejuved repeatedly, and to those not in the Great Families—to the many people now shut out from all decision making."

"What? You'd let outsiders into the Grand Council?"

"Not *outsiders*. People who have been in our polity for generations . . . just ignored. But this is for later discussion. Right now, I'm calling a vote on Minister Solinari's request that investigation be deferred, and support be given to the Regular Space Service."

"You can't do that."

"I just did." Brun smiled at Cerion Conselline. "Ser Conselline, we all know that the chamber dissolved into disorder, into name-calling and useless arguments. It was necessary to restore order, and I did that. In doing so, I took over the authority to decide what issues would come up—and right now, I'm calling for a vote. You can criticize me later, but at this moment you will vote or abstain."

Brun stood there, unmoving and silent, as the votes began to trickle in. A flurry of "no" from the main Conselline Seats, a scattering of "yes" from minor houses, then a block of "yes" from the Barracloughs. Another cluster of "no" from several minor families among the Consellines. She'd hoped for a bigger margin; this would be down to the wire. Suddenly she noticed a scurry of movement among the younger Consellines. Votes began to change. She held up her hand. Everyone sat back and watched.

"Excuse me," she said, her eyes on the display, not on the Conselline tables. "I notice votes changing—this is legal, but I want to be sure that the individuals changing their votes do so willingly and not under any duress."

"They're changing your way," Oskar said.

"That's not the point," Brun said. "I'm not here to win; I'm here to see that you all have the opportunity to vote your true convictions. May I have affirmation?"

One of the young Conselline men stood up; Brun nodded. "I'm changing my vote on my own, 'cause I think it's about time we had some young leadership."

Two others rose and without waiting said, "What Jamar said." Brun nodded again, and waited until all the changers had spoken. Cerion and Oskar were white around the mouth but said nothing more.

When all the votes were in, Fleet had its support, with over two thirds of the votes. Brun turned to Solinari. "Ser Minister, we trust you will convey to Fleet our full support."

"Yes, sera." He did not grin, but his eyes twinkled at her.

In the next hours, days, weeks, Brun struggled to convince the Seats of the Great Families of the need to expand the franchise and find a way to organize a society that would be, in the long run, comprised of near-immortal individuals. Fleet's success against the mutineers helped her; as the news came in about the destruction of the mutineer flagship and the other mutineer ships, her prestige grew. When Fleet reported on the fate of Harlis Thornbuckle, other Families who had considered treating separately with the mutineers changed their minds and this also increased her influence.

The young people, those who had not rejuved yet, understood the problems of rejuvenation clearly, though they were less receptive to bringing in non-Family representatives.

"They're rejuvenating too," Brun pointed out, over and over. "They'll live just as long as your parents and grandparents—and they're going to want power. We can't stuff the rejuvenation tiger back into the box. It's out, and it's going to stay out. What we have to do is design a system people can live with, Rejuvenants and those who oppose rejuvenation alike. And right now, if you'll work with me, we have the votes. There are still more unrejuvenated than rejuvenated members."

The young Consellines, eager to profit from rejuvenation, were willing to consider how a long-lived society might work. Some religious groups opposed rejuvenation entirely; Brun listened to their objections and took them back to the pro-rejuvenation faction. "It has to work for everyone," she said again, over and over.

Brun also talked to those Rejuvenants who would meet with her, emphasizing her conviction that multiple rejuvenations gave them special skills and responsibilities as well as privileges. "You can afford to take the very long view," she said. "You can figure out for yourselves how to use that extra time productively, to contribute and not just hoard resources." She began to wonder, after a few of these meetings, if they'd all had bad rejuv drugs somewhere down the line, because most seemed unable to grasp the need to change. They liked the life they had; they could not believe that change might come by force.

"Believe it," Brun said. "When you're outnumbered enough, it doesn't matter what talents and skills you have. I learned that on Our Texas."

It was the first "youth" vote in Council which convinced many of them. Months of hard work lay ahead, but if Fleet could buy them the time, Brun was now sure that they would cooperate in the end.

CHAPTER TWENTY-FOUR

R.S.S. *Vigilance*

Commodore Admiral Minor Livadhi. Arash grimaced at his face in the mirror. He looked well enough—the same tall, trim figure, the same lean face . . . handsome, actually. The same red hair, only lightly silvered at the temples. Decades of service in the Regular Space Service . . . combat experience . . . decorations . . . a fine upstanding officer.

A fine upstanding fool. A fool whose folly was now on his heels, like a hound on the trail of a fox . . . like a hunter after his prey. He shook his head abruptly and glared at himself. Time to quit dithering, to quit making faces in the mirror and do something.

But to lose it all . . . it hurt. The years, the friendships, the trust.

The certainty of his fate if he didn't do something.

It had gone already, gone before he'd realized it. It had gone the moment he went to Jules with his worries about Lepescu, gone irretrievably the first time he'd done Jules a favor that went over the line by so much as a hair.

He contemplated, as he had contemplated before, simply going off on his own. But with Fleet on a war footing, it was even less possible. Commodore Admiral Minor Livadhi, so well known, so distinctive in appearance, could not book a flight off this station without someone reporting it . . . he had to take that convoy out, knowing all the time that the hounds were on his trail, were closing in.

He had kept the contact code all these years, though he had never made contact himself. After the fiasco with the Crown Prince, he had never meant to . . . he had tried to forget. But now, in his need, his memory threw it up on his mind's screen, as clear as the day he first saw it. Perhaps he was in truth what Jules had made him in law.

Or perhaps half his luck would be with him, and there would be no corresponding code on this station. Then he would have to be honorable, have to be the naive prey who does not hear the hounds until too late. He would have to endure the discovery, the disgrace, the ruin of a lifetime's honest service for the sake of a youthful error. In a way, he wanted to be that innocent.

He called up the station's database, looking for the number that he hoped would not be there.

But it was. And as it would have to be, the number's owner was an unexceptionable business anyone might call or visit: Remembrances Gifts and Flowers. He placed the call, and spoke the words that would mean nothing without the knowledge in his head.

Then he had to wait for an answer, his nerves drawn tighter with every passing hour.

"I was afraid she'd faint," Oblo said, holding out his mug for a refill. "Turned white as a sheet, she did."

"You idiot, Oblo," Meharry said. "She maybe hadn't heard before—"

"She hadn't, but I didn't think of that. How's I to know?" His tone of injured innocence sounded real, for once.

"You have a brain," Meharry said shortly. "Wish I'd had time to talk to her."

"What about?"

"Copper Mountain . . . I was wondering if she'd heard more than I have. I wish I could transfer over there. My brother—"

"Your brother is fine, Methlin. You heard that—"

"Mornin' Oblo, Methlin," Petris said. "What's new about your brother?"

"Nothin'," Oblo said. "Methlin just wants to go play big sister."

"Transfer? I doubt they'd let you, right now."

"I know." Methlin bit into a sweet roll as if it were an enemy's neck. "I did sort of ask. Got told no."

"You're not the only one," Petris said. "I heard from the admiral's clerk—Admiral Serrano's, that is—that Commodore Livadhi asked if perhaps Heris's old crew wouldn't like to transfer, seeing as she's so close. Relatively close." He sipped his own mug of coffee.

"Wants to get rid of us, does he?" Oblo asked, scowling.

"I think it was courtesy," Petris said. "He's—sometimes he's almost scrupulously polite. Working at it. The admiral said no, by the way."

"She would," Oblo said.

"Mind yourself," Petris said, grinning. "She's our Heris's aunt, not just a mere admiral—"

"Mustang," Meharry said, grinning back.

"So I am. With everything that implies. So, how are your sections shaping up for this next mission?"

"Better," Meharry said. "It's still not our—not what I'd've liked, all our own people. But the new ones aren't bad, and that first cruise settled 'em."

"Good. We may well see some trouble this time out, from what I hear."

"Me, too," said Oblo, who had sources known only to himself. "I heard some of the mutineers are trying to set up deals with free trader companies, and even the big consortia. Anyone who doesn't sign up gets whacked on their next trip."

"The commodore's not bad," Meharry said thoughtfully, stirring her coffee. "I hear he's got good combat sense. Not up to Heris, of course, but—"

"We don't know that, Methlin," Petris said. "His record's good. And Heris liked him, even when she didn't completely trust him."

"Came to our rescue that one time . . ." Oblo commented.

"Yeah . . . kind of odd he was there, but I don't argue with good luck. Anyway, if it goes as smoothly as last time, we'll be fine, as long as the crew does its job and nothing blindsides us."

"Nothing's going to blindside us with Koutsoudas up in scan," Meharry said.

The convoy proceeded on its way, a string of transport and cargo vessels guarded by *Vigilance* and her gaggle of patrol and escort ships. The original plan, to have each convoy include two cruisers, had foundered on the shortage of cruisers. This made *Rascal's* weapons upgrade particularly valuable, and Livadhi placed her at the tail of the line, where another cruiser would have been. They were held to the speed of the slowest ship, in this case two of the spherical hulls used by the Boros Consortium, loaded with ordnance for the border stations. Esmay's relatively young crew had plenty of practice in adjusting jump point insertions and exits, in interpreting longscan. After the first two jump transitions, she began to feel less like a character playing a part and more like a real captain. Her crew was settling well; she could feel their confidence in her.

Koutsoudas found Methlin Meharry in the enlisted mess and sat down beside her. "Meharry—can I talk to you?"

She gave him one of her looks. "You have a voice, 'Steban. What's up?"

"I don't know, but I'm going to go nuts if I don't tell someone about it."

"Mmm. Is this the best place?"

"Maybe not. Where?"

"You offshift or on?"

"Off."

"Two hours, break room for weapons three. See you." Meharry slapped the table and left without another word. She made her rounds, bumped into Oblo as usual, and suggested that he might want to meet her.

"We need Petris?" he asked.

"Doubt it," Meharry said. "Likely someone's just leaning on the kid about something and he'd like to blow off a bit. You're insurance."

"Got you." They went their separate ways.

Twenty minutes before the two hours, Meharry ambled into the weapons three break room and leaned over the shoulders of the two corporals who were studying a wire model of the main beam supports. "Something needs polishing," she said.

"Sir? What, sir?"

"Find it," Meharry advised. "And polish it very well."

The brighter of the two blinked again and said, "Sir, any idea how long we need to polish it?"

"An hour and a half should do it," Meharry said. They left, and she went to work. In five minutes she had disabled the scan pickup that should have reported everything in the room. Oblo appeared eight minutes later, and checked her clearance before settling into one of the chairs. It creaked under him. A pivot with a mug of something started into the room, saw them, and backed out without a word.

The two of them chatted about inconsequential things until Koutsoudas appeared. He had his own gear bag with him, and produced one of his cylinders.

"You don't trust us?" Oblo said, raising an eyebrow.

"Don't talk to me about trust," Koutsoudas said. Meharry couldn't tell if he was angry or scared or both. Before she could say anything, he rushed on. "This is all slippery stuff, nothing solid. I don't want there to be anything solid. But you need to know."

"Can we have a noun?" Meharry asked in a low drawl. "A subject?"

Koutsoudas glanced at the open hatch as if he expected a killer to step through it. Then back at Meharry. "The bridge crew—is about to lose it."

"Why? We haven't had any action I didn't know about, have we?"

"No. It's—it's Livadhi. The commodore. Something's wrong—he's not like he was."

Meharry felt a sudden lurch in her midsection, followed by a feeling of satisfaction. So. Everyone had told her how wonderful he was, but despite no evidence at all she had never been able to like him. Her instincts were right.

"What's he doing?" she asked, forestalling Oblo with a look.

"It's hard to say. Mostly he's—twitchy. Jumpy. Everything's going fine, but he's wound up tighter than I've ever seen him. I hate—I've known him for years, I was with him before he sent me to Commander Serrano—and I've never seen him like this. I don't feel right telling you, but I don't feel right about whatever's wrong, either."

"What's Captain Burleson say?"

"He's getting tense himself, the way Livadhi's been jumping on everyone. We're afraid to say anything but yes, sir and no, sir on the bridge, and we'd become pretty friendly. You know how it is . . ."

Meharry knew. All her instincts were standing up waving their arms at her. She looked at Oblo. His face showed nothing but his eyes—yes, his instincts too.

"Has he done anything—anything at all—outside what he should? Given any questionable orders?"

"No. I can't believe I'm even thinking he would, but—if he'd been rejuved, I'd be worrying about rejuv failure."

"What about communications?" Oblo asked.

"What do you mean?"

"Has he made any unusual communications? Outside the convoy, or to unusual destinations?"

"I'm not monitoring his communications," Koutsoudas said quickly. Then, "I'll find out. If you think it matters."

"It might."

"You'd better go," Meharry said to Koutsoudas. "We'll talk again."

"All right. I just—I need someone."

"We're with you, 'Steban. We won't let anything bad happen."

After he'd gone, she turned to Oblo. "I was wrong. We do need Petris. If anything's going on, if that bastard's going sour on us—"

"He's not going to lose Heris's ship for her," Oblo said.

Some days later, Koutsoudas passed Meharry a data cube with Livadhi's complete inbound and outbound communications log. When she put it in the cube reader, she found that he'd made notations alongside the entries: this a tightbeam to one or another of the convoy ships, this a tightbeam to a Fleet ansible with destination codes indicating a report to Headquarters. Inbound from a Fleet ansible, origin codes Headquarters. So far so good. Then a civilian origination code . . . his wife, Koutsoudas had noted. Every few days, a message from his wife.

Meharry frowned. Livadhi married? Somehow she'd assumed him to be single. She glanced at the messages; they weren't encrypted, and were about everyday things. His wife was having a new carpet installed; she was sure he'd like it: it was the same color as the old. The price of snailfish fin had gone through the roof; she supposed it was the effect of the mutiny. His uncle the retired admiral had dropped by and talked for an hour about the political situation; he was convinced that if the old king and Admiral Lepecsu had been in charge none of this would have happened. Her sister's youngest child had won a music prize. She thanked him for sending a parting gift from Sector VII Headquarters, but didn't he realize that the shipping charges had tripled the cost? She'd have been just as happy with the usual box of candy from the local confectioners'. The enameled box was pretty, but she didn't understand the message on the paper inside, or was it just something the people in the shop had left in by mistake?

Meharry stopped and reread that message. Livadhi usually sent candy but this time sent a box? Well . . . maybe he'd thought his wife would like a change. Though any woman who would choose exactly the same shade of carpet to replace the old probably wouldn't want a change in gifts, either. And surely Livadhi would know it—though Meharry had, in a long career, seen plenty of marriages founder on the shoals of ignorance. People didn't really know each other better just because they were tied together with a common name. An incomprehensible message inside? Most likely, as his wife mentioned, just a mistake at the shop.

But why send an enameled box that far? Why that box? What was the incomprehensible message?

She glanced down the screen, and found it. Livadhi's wife had included it, just in case it was his message and he cared to translate. A string of numbers and letters. It looked exactly like a jump point address and ansible access code. Koutsoudas' annotation, cautious, said that such a jump point and ansible access code were in the files, but that he couldn't confirm that the writer had meant the string to denote them.

Meharry scrolled on down the log. There—highlighted by Koutsoudas—the convoy had passed through a jump point with the same coordinates as in the message Livadhi's wife had sent . . . and in that system, Livadhi had stripped a message from the ansible, using that code. The message, in clear, said, "Merchandise undeliverable; addressee unknown at that address. Refund waiting at next port of call."

Harmless enough, but the numbers had been inside a box which *was* delivered. What merchandise was undeliverable? Not the box. Something else? Why had Livadhi suddenly bought presents for people at Sector VII HQ and shipped them all over the place? And no civilian should have had a list of the jump points the convoy would pass through, to send a message like this to intercept the convoy. Or have known what the next port of call was, to send a refund ahead.

She read through the rest. Nothing more that didn't fit. Koutsoudas had noted, at the end of the list, that their next port of call would be Mindon Station. Meharry thought about that, retrieved the cube from the cube reader and put it in her pocket, then set off on a purposeful meander to find Oblo. She knew he and Petris had a regular sparring session in the gym.

She found him just as Petris came down the ladder a few meters away. "Joining us, Methlin?" Petris asked.

"You should," Oblo said. "How long's it been since you sparred with me?"

"Can't," Meharry said. "I'm on-shift. Just brought you an entertainment cube—the one you were asking about."

Petris gave her a sharp look. "Not *Bridge to the Moon*?"

"No . . . didn't find that one. This is Michelline-Hernandez's *A Traitor Reveal'd*, with that good looking actor—Simon somebody— playing the general." There was, of course, such an adventure drama. Meharry would not have stooped to anything less complete. She handed Petris the cube, and headed back to work, the lines of the play that were not on that cube echoing in her memory. *It cannot be, that you, my general, have betrayed us.*

"Wouldn't be the first time," Meharry muttered.

By the downjump into the system where Mindon Station's complicated geometry sparkled with the frost of multiple vents, Petris and Oblo had both reviewed the data cube. Now, three days out from the station, they met with Koutsoudas in gym.

"What's going on up there now, 'Steban?" Petris asked.

Koutsoudas looked down. "It's . . . pretty tense. *Rascal* was five minutes late coming out of jump—well within limits, especially since those two Boros ships were three minutes late making insertion and *Rascal* was supposed to keep station behind 'em—and he chewed Captain Suiza out like she'd done something awful."

"How'd she take it?" Oblo asked.

"What could she do? Said yes, sir, no, sir, sorry, sir, in the right places. Didn't make excuses. Then six hours later he calls her up and makes nice. Would she like to go on the courtesy call he's making to the station commander, an' so on. She's polite, gives him her ETA— 'course, *Rascal*'s behind everyone, a good fourteen hours at least before she'd get to Station, and he says never mind, she can be the deep picket, like before." Koutsoudas stopped. Petris waited. "It's not like him, sir. I've never seen him like this. He's always been tough and a bit finicky, yes. But to ream someone out unfairly and then wait six hours to say anything, and then make a dumb mistake like not knowing she'd be that far behind . . ."

"What if it wasn't a mistake?" Meharry asked. "What if he never meant to have her along, and it was just a kind of lame apology?"

"It's not like him," Koutsoudas said. "Look—you know how I felt when he sent me to Commander Serrano. I've been Livadhi's pet scan tech since I finished Basic and ended up on his ship. I didn't want to leave him . . . but I came to recognize Commander Serrano as darn near his equal as a ship commander." He glanced around and said sheepishly, "All right. A better ship commander, but not by much. I know Livadhi—the old Livadhi—the way you people can't. And this is different."

"So what do you expect us to do, 'Steban?"

"Tell me I'm wrong," he said miserably. "Tell me I'm making it up, that there's nothing wrong with him, that he can't possibly be up to anything—"

"'Steban," Meharry said, with unwonted gentleness. "We don't doubt your loyalty. Any of your loyalties. But you have to face the facts you're trying to avoid. If he's changed, if there's something wrong . . . we can't ignore it. You can't ignore it."

"I know that," he said, to the deck. "I just—I just hate it—especially since you didn't know him before."

"I knew him last cruise," Petris said. "He was good enough then. Naturally I think Heris is better, but you're right—not by much. I think he's been a good officer. Is that what you wanted to know?"

"Yes. I had to come to you—I trust you—but I can't—I needed to know you didn't just hate him because he was here instead of her."

"Of course not," Petris said. "Man, I may be Heris Serrano's . . . friend, but I'm still a professional. A good officer is a good officer."

"All right, then. What did you think of the communications log?"

"Damaging," Meharry said, before Petris could.

"Yeah, that's what I thought. I haven't talked to any of the officers, but Sim, one of the commtechs, is worried about it too."

"It could still be innocent," Petris said, playing devil's advocate for the moment. "I mean—suppose he did have—oh, a premonition or something—and decided to send special presents to everyone he knew, and one of them was undeliverable. Maybe the shop figured his wife would pass on the note in the box."

"Without instructions? Just a list of numbers and letters?"

"Well, she did send it on. Maybe things like that had happened before . . ."

"Not on the last cruise," Koutsoudas said. "I asked Sim."

"How's Captain Burleson taking all this?"

"He's tense, too. He's an old Livadhi hand, same as I am, and so is our second and third."

"I wish we had Mackay aboard," Petris said. "He knew us; we knew him . . . we're in a ticklish spot here. The way we're talking, we could be taken up for conspirators—"

"We're not the ones making trouble," Oblo said.

"Yes, we are. By regulation, anyway. In a time of war or mutiny, conversations critical of a commander like this . . . and the last thing this Fleet needs is another mutiny aboard a ship."

"The last thing this Fleet needs is another ship going over to the mutiny," Meharry said.

"Or somewhere else," Koutsoudas said.

"What do you mean?"

"You know . . . I never talked to anyone about why Livadhi wanted me gone. I know he told Commander Serrano I'd gotten in some kind of trouble—"

"So?"

"So . . . I wouldn't have thought of it, 'cept for this. Never meant to mention any of it—"

"'Steban, if you don't spit it out, I'm going to squeeze you dry," Oblo said.

"It was right after I came up with that scan extension, that lets me get a little lead on downjump scan. Suddenly Livadhi had us heading toward the Shaft, just like we were going to use that grav anomaly jump point to skew around it, but then we went into the Shaft instead. Turned out we were going in to rescue Commander Serrano and *Sweet Delight*—"

"What?"

"Yeah, that time you had the prince with you, remember?"

"I remember," Petris said. He glanced at Oblo.

"Well, so after we kicked those Benignity ships—and believe me, we were sweatin' that, attacking them in their own territory—I got to thinking about how Livadhi had known where to look." He took a long breath. "I had a buddy in comm then, and we kicked it around a bit—trying to figure out how he knew, or if it was just luck. Then I said something to Livadhi himself one day, and he rounded on me, told me to be quiet if I valued my freedom. That he'd had secret orders, but no one was supposed to know. And maybe I'd better spend some time away from the ship while he tried to cover up my lapse. I don't know what he told you—"

"He'd heard we'd had bad data from Rotterdam—"

"Nope. We never went near Rotterdam," Koutsoudas said.

"So what you're saying is—"

"I figured it was secret orders, back then. I had nothing else. But now . . ."

"Benignity," said Oblo.

"I hope not," Petris said, but a deep internal flutter told him that his instinct said it was. "What a stinking mess that would be."

"Is," said Oblo again. "Look at it, sir—"

"I am," Petris said. The ramifications unfolded like a flowering bud to his inward eye. "'Steban, when you caught up with us at Naverrn . . . *did* you have orders for that, too?"

"Of course," Koutsoudas said. "The prince aboard—or at least one of the clones."

"Well, that's a relief." Not much, though. Petris ran through the names he knew. Arkady Ginese and Meharry both in Weapons, Oblo and Issigai Guar in Navigation, Koutsoudas in scan, his buddy Sim in communications, himself in Engineering . . . far from enough. Others, who had been in Heris's crew, might trust them, second-hand trust, but how many? If Livadhi were turning traitor, what would he do?

"'Steban, we're going to do nothing now but watch. We still have nothing provable. When he's off the ship, on this courtesy visit, be sure we know."

"Right, sir." Koutsoudas looked more at ease, having transferred his problem to someone in charge. Petris wished again he had someone to hand off this mess to. When Koutsoudas left, Petris turned to Meharry.

"You tell Arkady and start thinking who you trust, and who trusts you. Oblo, you'll talk to Issi, same thing. I'll tackle Padoc. We ought to be able to swap watches around to cover, once we know who's with us." That would buy him time to think.

"I wonder what she'd say," Meharry said. They all knew which *she* that was.

"So do I," Petris said. He had never felt so alone.

"He's gone," Oblo murmured into his comunit. "I'm sittin' first nav, Keller's on the bridge. Burleson went with him."

"Right. Who's on the honor guard?"

"None of us." Oblo read the roster. None of the old Heris crew, only one who had been hers at all.

"All right. Keep us up."

Petris turned away from his comunit. "All right, folks, the admiral's headed for the Station, courtesy call. You know the drill: insystem drive stays hot, we run diagnostics on the FTL. I've got the arrival report to write; you've got my code if you need me."

"Right, sir." Chief Coggins nodded.

Petris beeped Meharry. Neither she nor Ginese was on right now, which made it easier. He hoped.

They met in the Engineering break room. Petris flicked on the workstation, and started his report; Meharry dealt with the scan, though she suspected Oblo could have intercepted it on the bridge.

"Anything new?" he asked over his shoulder.

"Oblo and Sim got a datasuck off the Station communications nexus," Koutsoudas said. "There's a message for Livadhi. They can't read it. It's encrypted."

"Originating?"

"Can't tell for sure. This station automatically strips originating headers."

Arash Livadhi met the Fleet representative—another admiral minor recently promoted—and the station's civilian Stationmaster. The rituals of greeting, of exchanging courtesies, of being served light refreshment, grated on him as never before. The formal handing over of responsibility for the convoy, the necessary several hours of chatting about the news, the likelihood of militia action out here, the recent movement of civilian trade—down 47 percent, with resulting shortages in infant supplies, of all things—nearly drove him crazy. What did he care about infant supplies? People had lived for centuries, he was sure, before someone invented disposable diapers and bottles.

Admiral Minor Ksia invited him to dinner, and Stationmaster Corfoldi urged him to visit the station gardens. . . ."We're very proud of our orchid collection, you'll find it quite unique." Livadhi accepted the invitation—it would have been strange if he had not—and agreed to stretch his legs in the gardens in the meantime.

"And I might just look for something for my wife."

"But, Commodore, it's as I said—with trade off so badly—"

"I'm sure I can find something," Livadhi said. "She likes any little souvenir of a place I've been."

At last he was out of their offices, strolling about a station that was, after all, much less crowded than most. Commander Burleson had gone back to the ship, quite properly. Livadhi considered asking his escort to let him go on alone, but that was irregular, and he could not afford irregularity.

The gardens were gloomy, to his way of thinking, but the orchids in bloom—airy cascades of white hanging down from branches, or weirdly spikey shapes of yellow on the ground beneath—held his attention briefly.

On the far side of the gardens, the shopping arcade was almost empty. Livadhi wandered into Mier's Fine China, and poked aimlessly among the aisles. Behind a counter, a listless clerk watched him as if she knew he had no intention of buying. From there he went into Charlotte's Confectionaries, and bought a kilo box of mixed truffles as a dinner courtesy gift. He needed only a quick glance to realize that every shop had its com number painted on the shop front . . . so he ambled along, in and out of almost every shop, until he spotted the number he wanted. Micasio's, an art gallery. Perfect.

By this time, his escort was, he suspected, both footsore and bored. He turned to them. "I'm going to see if they have any old prints," he said. "My wife's crazy about Sid Grevaire, and sometimes these frontier galleries have old stuff that didn't sell insystem. I'll probably be an hour poking around in there—why don't you get yourselves something to drink, and there's a nice seating area—" He nodded across the walkway, where a cluster of benches and tables gave a good view of the gallery entrance.

"If you're sure, Admiral—we don't mind coming with you."

"I think I can yell that far if I need you," Livadhi said, forcing a grin. "And I have my emergency buzzer, after all."

"Right, sir. Thanks."

He waited until they were safely in place before moving deeper into the gallery, and giving his name to the man behind the counter.

This time the message waiting for him was long and detailed, and he felt a great cold cavern open in his mind and heart. He could not possibly—he could not possibly *not* . . .

Jules, you bastard, he thought. Jules had anticipated even his most urgent concerns, his remaining loyalties. He had removed, as well as words could, the last sticking point, Livadhi's concern for his people.

He rummaged through the print bins, with the owner's help, and emerged 45 minutes later with a wrapped package and a receipt for two Sid Grevaire drawings and a Muly Tyson gouache, unframed. Through dinner with Admiral Minor Ksia, he sustained a lively conversation about trends in modern art. Ksia, as he'd suspected, was an aesthetic nincompoop who completely failed to grasp the challenging theories that underlay Tyson's curious perspectives.

CHAPTER TWENTY-FIVE

Livadhi returned to *Vigilance* in the calm of a decision firmly made.

"Admiral's feeling better," one of the escort detail murmured to Arkady Ginese, by then on the bridge.

"That's good," Arkady said.

"Not so twitchy," the sergeant said.

"Less lip," Arkady said. "I'm on duty." The sergeant shrugged and went off. A few minutes later, the admiral appeared on the bridge. He looked much as usual, though—as the sergeant had said—less tense. That could always be the result of a good wine at dinner. Or not.

"What it comes down to, we can't really do anything without maybe causing more trouble—" Petris ran a hand through his hair.

"More trouble than him taking us over the border?" Meharry asked.

"Can we trust any of the bridge officers?" Petris asked.

"They're not part of it," Oblo said, with utter certainty. "Whatever it is, it's not them. But they trust Livadhi. If he tells them some fairy tale, they'll believe it."

"So—we have to be ready to—what?" Meharry looked ready to pull out a knife and stab someone. She probably was.

"We have to get word to Heris," Petris said. "She'll be able to figure something out." He certainly hadn't been able to.

"We're here and she's there . . . wherever she is. We have to solve this here."

"We *can't* solve this here. Or not entirely." Petris felt that his

712

head was stuffed full of complications, nested into each other, each insoluble without dealing with a hundred others. "'Steban, Oblo, can you get word out to Heris?"

"Without the admiral knowing? Not directly, no. Anything we spike to the ansible, the Station will know about. All we can contact, without causing possible comment, is one of the other convoy ships."

"There's Suiza," Oblo said.

They were all silent a moment, thinking this over.

"If she believes us," Petris said, "she might do it. Relay a message to Heris."

"They'll know she contacted the ansible—" Koutsoudas said.

"Maybe—but she's farther out—she's on outside picket duty."

"It's worth a try," Petris said. "Do it."

Oblo nodded and sauntered off, casual as always.

"How will she know where we've gone?" Meharry asked. "Sure as eggs is eggs, he's going to jump us out of here."

"With Oblo and Issi on nav, we could pass all the nav data to Suiza, and Suiza can follow our course. 'Steban will have to fox the scan data somehow." He looked at Koutsoudas, who nodded.

"I can mask it out. Don't worry." A futile statement. Petris felt he was drowning in worry.

"He can't stay on scan all the time—Livadhi will get suspicious."

"Well . . . two of the junior scan techs are ours, and he trained them. He's crosslinked the tightbeam to the scan desk, and he has two of the communications techs in on it."

"That's too many," Meharry said, a furrow between her brows. "Livadhi's not stupid and a secret quits being a secret after awhile."

"Cover story?" asked Petris. Meharry was good at cover stories; he was too worried to think of anything but decking Livadhi.

"Yeah . . . let me think . . . look, what if there was a test of new stealth and scan gear. Captains aren't told, because . . . I'll think of a reason." She had the half-sleepy look that meant she was concentrating.

"They want it to be a fair test of the equipment," Petris said, suddenly inspired. "Not of a captain's tactical skills. They know good captains could fox the test without meaning to. It's to be reported to Sector HQ upon return only. They put it on small ships first—the stealth stuff—and the big ship's supposed to see if it can see it, and the small ship's supposed to shadow the big one. A few of the technical crew know. I could know, being in engineering. Scan. Comm. That makes sense, sort of."

Esmay Suiza, aboard *Rascal*, would have gnawed her knuckles if that wouldn't have been too obvious to the crew. First Livadhi chewed her out for something that wasn't her fault, and then attempted a clumsy reparation. That didn't seem like the suave, charming commander she'd last seen at Sector VII HQ, but anyone could have a bad day. Then that strange message from Heris Serrano's old crew. She had no idea what was going on, but she had forwarded the message from *Vigilance* to Heris Serrano. Everyone had heard about Commander Serrano's former crew; she didn't know them well, but she had met them, most recently when Livadhi invited the captains of the convoy onto the cruiser for a final toast before departure. She'd wondered how Petris felt about serving under another captain, but that had made her think of Barin, so she pushed the thought aside.

Now she was faced with a command decision. Commodore Admiral Minor Livadhi had ordered her to hold station in this system while he went back for another convoy. Esteban Koutsoudas—himself a legend of technical expertise—had passed on Petris Kenvinnard's request that she follow Livadhi instead, shadow him, and report all navigational information back to Serrano by encrypted ansible flashes.

An admiral's order against a warrant officer's request should have been no contest. Her gut churned. Why was she even considering this? If nothing was going on, if Serrano's friends were just overreacting to some personality quirk of their new commander, she would have no excuse at all for what she was thinking of doing. If no one discovered—but of course it would be discovered, if only afterwards— and then, the court-martial, and the disgrace, and with things as they were at home—she tried to put that out of her mind, or at least on one side.

If she disobeyed orders and nothing was wrong with Livadhi, she'd be court-martialed—that was the worst that could happen. No—she corrected herself. If mutineers came into the system where she wasn't keeping station, that would be another evil come from her decision.

But if Livadhi had lost it—if he'd gone crazy, or—worst case—if Livadhi was a traitor—then if she obeyed his orders, she'd be helping him. If she acted on her own initiative to follow him she might—if he didn't realize she was there—be able to foil whatever plan he had. If he did realize it, *Vigilance* could blow *Rascal* into confetti. Perhaps not easily, but certainly.

Where was the greater danger? Surely, in Livadhi as traitor, loose with a cruiser full of weaponry. And crew, some of whom were definitely loyal. What would happen to them, if Livadhi went over to the mutineers or perhaps the Benignity?

If Heris Serrano had asked her help, she'd have given it without hesitation. Heris Serrano trusted Petris Kenvinnard, Methlin Meharry, Oblo Vissisuan. Esmay tugged mentally at that chain of trust, trying for herself if it was strong enough for the risk they asked. Could she trust what Heris Serrano trusted, just because Heris Serrano trusted it?

She liked Commodore Livadhi. He had been, to this point, a good commander insofar as she had the experience to judge. He had listened respectfully to Captain Timmons' objections to the convoy arrangement, he phrased his orders clearly, they had delivered the convoy safely. Could he be a mutineer or a traitor or crazy?

She wasn't on the ship with him, and had not been for weeks. Things changed. People changed. Had Heris Serrano's friends changed?

Her stomach steadied. Not Oblo. She could imagine Petris, who loved Heris Serrano, making a mistake about Livadhi because he loved Heris, and Livadhi wasn't Heris. Methlin Meharry, concerned about her brother, might overreact. But Oblo, battered and scarred and completely unawed by any circumstance, she could not imagine changing. He might be wrong, but he wouldn't go crazy, and his instinct for trouble, for wrongness, was legendary.

Heris trusted Oblo; Esmay trusted Heris; she would also trust Oblo. She ignored the flaws of formal logic in that emotional syllogism.

Now to convince her own officers that *she* wasn't crazy or traitorous. Would they believe the truth? Or had she better concoct a cover story? Suppose it was a secret exercise, in . . . say . . . stealth technology? She worried at the idea, tugging out its possible fibers, and trying to make a plausible reason why a patrol ship might shadow a cruiser against the orders of an admiral.

"Can you tell where he's taking us?" Petris asked Lieutenant Focalt. They had finally begun talking to bridge officers, trying to prepare them for possible trouble.

"Ultimately, no. He's jumping us in and out of systems with multiple routes . . . someone trying to trace us would quickly have more options than anyone could follow up. Yet we're still in Familias Space; he says he's got secret orders. If it weren't for you, I'd believe him . . ."

Petris could hear the doubt in the man's voice. "If I'm wrong, Lieutenant, I'll 'fess up. But I don't think I am. He made a tightbeam communication to an ansible in the system we just passed, and according to the com watch, it was addressed to one of a list of reportable addresses he'd gotten just before we left Sector HQ."

Focalt swore. "I can't believe he'd be so stupid."

"I think he's desperate," Petris said. "I can't imagine why, either. But we have to be careful."

"I will be," the man said. "I hope our tail's with us."

"You and me both," Petris said.

Esmay could feel the increasing tension in her own crew as they followed *Vigilance* for jump after jump.

"I don't understand," her comm officer said. "Where are they going?"

"We don't know," Esmay said. "But we're finding out."

"It's ridiculous, this course. Where could he be heading?"

Esmay did not tell him what Petris had relayed of his suspicions, though she did encode it for the next tightbeam she sent.

Another jump, this one into an uninhabited system. *Vigilance* had entered at low relative vee, this time, and now decelerated still more. After a couple of hours, during which she'd sent off the new data, Esmay shook her head. "He's been jumping end-on-end or clearing a system within seventy minutes. I wonder what he's waiting for?"

"We are on the border, Captain," said her navigation officer. From the expression on his face, he was reconsidering her original explanation as well as Livadhi's course. "He can reach Benignity space in one jump from here, if that's where he's going."

"We can't just let him cross," Jig Turner said, looking horrified. "That's handing them one of our newest cruisers, and the crew—"

"We don't know for sure that's what he's up to," Esmay said. "Right now he's not doing anything. But that's a possibility."

"Is this what it's been all along, Captain?" the nav officer said. "Did you suspect something?"

"I wouldn't have," Esmay said, "but for Heris Serrano's old crew aboard *Vigilance*. They tightbeamed me that he was acting oddly; they didn't understand, but they were worried."

"Worried enough to risk court-martial—I hope you're right, Captain."

"I hope I'm not," Esmay said. "I'd much rather be wrong, and in trouble, than faced with a traitor admiral in command of a ship like that."

"So what are we going to do?" She noticed the change from "you" to "we." "If he jumps and we follow him over the border—"

"It could start a war. I know that." Esmay turned. "Weapons, tell me what we have that could take *Vigilance*."

"Take a cruiser? That cruiser? And survive a fight? We couldn't, Captain. If they really don't know we're here, we might get some shots up the bustle, just as you did at Xavier. Stern shields have been beefed up since then, though—we might not get through in one salvo. In which case, *Vigilance* would blow us away and go skipping off where she liked."

"Mmm. And slipping in to docking distance and trying to hold if she was running up to a jump would also blow us all. Keep working on it—we're going to stop that ship somehow and I'd prefer to defend my actions in court rather than have one convened on a lot of debris and corpses."

"You could contact him directly . . ."

"I don't think so. If I had another ship to box him with, I'd try it. But he's an admiral minor. Suppose he decided to come back—he could do it as an admiral dragging in a subordinate who had disobeyed orders. And then run another time, with another ship." Esmay shook her head. "No, if he starts running to jump, I'll challenge and fire on him if I have to."

"What if he builds speed by microjumping?"

"We're more agile, and faster," Esmay said. "The problem's not going to be catching him, but how to hold him when we have. I just hope he's not waiting for reinforcements, for some Benignity ship to arrive and give him an escort. We should be able to do enough damage to one ship to prevent its taking off, but two—that will be harder."

The hours passed. Esmay tried to stay calm, tried to think, but felt her nerves drawing tighter with every minute that passed. He could just jump: unlike a civilian ship, *Vigilance* could make a blind jump this far from a jump point and hope to come out in realspace somewhere near its intended destination. Livadhi had to be worrying about pursuit, had to feel, with that commander's instinct, that he was in danger. What if he wasn't waiting for a contact? What if he was waiting a specified number of hours, and might hop out again at any moment?

Her eyes felt gritty with sleeplessness, but she dared not leave the bridge and try to nap. Whenever he did something, she would have to act instantly. What should she do?

Commodore Admiral Minor Livadhi leaned close to the scan desks; Koutsoudas could smell the faint odor of his nervous sweat. "Are you *sure* there's nothing out there?"

"Sir, I'm not finding anything," Koutsoudas said. The scan computers had been told that *Rascal* did not exist; every few hours they kicked up a query, and every few hours he reassured them. Nothing is there, ignore it. He'd just dealt with the query again when Livadhi came on the bridge. He hated direct lying, but evasion didn't bother him.

"I have a feeling," Livadhi said. "You know that itch you get between your shoulders, when you know someone's looking at you?"

"Yes, sir."

"I don't want to fall into any mutineer traps," Livadhi said.

"No, sir. Me, neither. And I don't see any sign of mutineer ships, or any other ships. System's clean, sir."

Livadhi sighed. "You're the best, Koutsoudas; if they were there, you'd know." He paused. "How long have you been on duty?"

"Sir, you said you were worried, so I came on early—I've been coming on at every insertion and downjump, just in case."

"Ah. Good man." Livadhi turned away.

Koutsoudas busied himself with the scan system. Suiza was still there, yes, but if Livadhi was making deals with the Benignity, he didn't want a flotilla of Black Scratch ships jumping in on top of them. He'd experienced that in the Xavier system; once was enough.

The hours passed, and Livadhi did not call for another jump. Instead, he paced back and forth, back and forth. He left the bridge for only moments at a time. Koutsoudas went off for a short nap, but couldn't really sleep. When he came back, he stared at the display, wondering what would happen next. He wished Livadhi would change his mind, be what he'd always thought the man was, a fine Fleet officer, pleasant and competent and thorough.

Then he stiffened. There, far away from the system's mapped jump point, a curious ripple in the scan, as if someone had dropped a very small pebble into the far edge of a pond. He snatched that input for his station.

"Sir!" he said.

"What?" Livadhi stayed across the bridge from him, where he'd been listening to some engineering reports, but Keller, the Exec, came over to look.

"Something coming in, sir, and not at the jump point. At least I think it is; it's too far away. Could be an FTL trace."

"Direction?" Livadhi asked, coming nearer.

"Unclear. It's skipping—it's definitely an FTL trace, someone with a badly tuned drive. Just sort of hitting the surface of normal space and bouncing back out."

"Can you tell anything about mass?"

"Not yet." Koutsoudas watched the screens; the two other scan techs on watch leaned toward him. He growled at them. "Benally, Vince—watch your own screens. There could always be more than one thing going on. I've got this."

Rascal's scan officer, lacking Koutsoudas' personal additions to standard equipment, identified an arriving ship minutes after Koutsoudas did. "Something coming in, Captain," he said.

Esmay looked at the scan and saw the familiar pattern of a badly tuned FTL drive just skip-jumping through. Was it even bound for this system? It didn't come in like she thought Serrano would, a clean downjump.

It could be a Benignity ship, come to lead Livadhi away. She had to do something. "Bring us to red," she said to the bridge. Alarms rang out. Those sitting first at the positions raced to put on p-suits, while their seconds acted. She heard lockers opening, and Chief Humberly held her p-suit ready; she stepped backwards into it. The firsts, suited now, returned to their places and the seconds went to suit up. "Weapons, ready." That would light up *Vigilance*'s scan displays. At least their shields were already active. She turned to her comm officer.

"Get me a tightbeam to *Vigilance*."

Koutsoudas, trying desperately to dissect the fluttery scan signal into something he could identify—he hoped very much it was not a Benignity ship—was shocked when the warning red flashers showed live weapons in close proximity, where scan showed no ship at all.

"What—?!" He and Livadhi said it almost together. Too close for the injumping ship, too close, and no ship icon—Suiza. It had to be Suiza, bringing her weapons live. But why?

"What have you—" began Livadhi, but the Comm officer signalled him.

"Commodore—there's a tightbeam message from R.S.S. *Rascal*, Suiza commanding."

"Suiza!" Livadhi was white to the lips, his red hair in stark contrast to his face. "That stupid—what does she think she's doing?" Then, in a furious hiss to Koutsoudas, "You are relieved—I don't know if you're just exhausted, or a liar, but you let a pissant *lieutenant* crawl up our tail! Get to your quarters; I'll deal with you later." And to the comm officer, "Pipe it to my office."

Koutsoudas, more shaken than he'd ever been, shook his head at the second—luckily one of the old crew—who came to relieve him. "I didn't see it," he said. "I swear I didn't see a thing. It's not there . . . ."

"Go on, 'Steban, you're exhausted. It'll be all right."

Livadhi, on the communications screen in Esmay's bridge, looked thoroughly disgusted and angry.

"Lieutenant Suiza, you are in big trouble. Just what do you mean by disobeying orders and gallivanting around the universe?"

Esmay had thought about what to say that might take suspicion away from the *Vigilance* crew.

"Sir, may I ask if the admiral's bridge crew had detected *Rascal* prior to the tightbeam message?"

"No, you may not ask. Answer my question, dammit!" This was not the suave, pleasant commander she'd met at dinner aboard.

"Sir, the admiral is aware that *Rascal* has been fitted out with a new suite of weapons—"

"Yes, what of it?"

"And a new suite of stealth gear, sir. Which I was told you were not aware of, and which I am under orders—secret orders—to test in a realistic situation. A ship-on-ship pursuit, in fact. So when the admiral left, I executed my other orders, and followed. Since the admiral has not commented before, I presume we were not detected."

"You weren't," Livadhi said, now in a growl. "Not until you brought your weapons live. Care to explain why?"

"Sir, we're out near the border with the Benignity. I'm assuming the admiral is aware of another ship entering the system. On the possibility that it might be hostile, I brought the weapons live, and contacted you so that you would not worry about us when we seemed to jump out of nowhere."

"I didn't know about any such stealth capability," Livadhi said.

"Of course not, sir. It was all highly secret—" So secret it didn't exist; she put that thought rapidly aside.

"And they gave it to a jumped-up captain with a checkered past, an Altiplanan? Somehow I doubt that, Landbride Suiza . . ."

"I'm not the Landbride anymore," Esmay said. "I renounced it officially, before witnesses—I told you that, sir, at the dinner."

"So you did. Still, I could as easily believe you somehow suborned someone in my crew to conceal your presence . . . Suiza, you are meddling in something you do not understand."

"You're right, Admiral," Esmay said. "I don't understand what you're doing, and I am concerned that you are out here alone, on the border—"

"You're not the only one who can have secret orders, Suiza. I'm not here because I decided to go for a joyride. If we end up in a full-scale war because of you—"

"Not because of me, Admiral," Esmay said. She dared not glance aside to see if her scan officer had identified the incoming ship. If she could just keep Livadhi engaged, keep him busy, so he didn't jump *Vigilance* out . . .

"Back off, Suiza. That's an order. Back off, go home, and if I were you I'd keep my mouth shut—" With every word he spoke, she became more convinced that he was, in fact, a traitor.

"No, sir." Esmay took a deep breath. "I don't entirely trust you, sir."

"You flaming idiot! Are you trying to get yourself and your crew killed? You do realize *Vigilance* could blow you apart like tissue paper, don't you?" Out of the corner of her eye she could see a sort of ripple of dismay go through her bridge crew. But she herself felt steadier, now that he'd openly threatened her.

"Sir, I've been yelled at by admirals senior to you—with all due respect, sir, yelling at me isn't going to work. Tell me what you're doing, and why, or I will sit right here watching you until I figure it out for myself."

"No, you won't, because I will run right over you and jump out of here. Dammit, Suiza, haven't you caused enough trouble in this organization? Back off or else do exactly what I tell you." He took a deep breath. "You want to know what I'm doing? I'm under orders to make an illicit jump into Benignity space to pick up a very important defector. I've been told it's of utmost importance. Now that you've stuck your nose in, you can guard my back."

R.S.S. *Indefatigable*, in Copper Mountain system

Heris Serrano was asleep in her cabin when the comm officer buzzed her. "Captain—there's an urgent message, ansible relayed, from a Captain Suiza."

"In code?"

"Yes, sir, in code."

Heris frowned as she shoved her feet into her boots and headed to the bridge and the decryption desk. Esmay Suiza was back in Fleet and a captain? That was good, but now what had happened?

She sat at the desk, inserted her command wand, entered the authorization numbers, and watched the message wriggle into clear.

URGENT URGENT URGENT . . . All right, she'd got that. PETRIS KENVINNARD ABOARD VIGILANCE REPORTS SUSPICIOUS ACTIVITY BY ADMIRAL MINOR LIVADHI. REQUESTS RASCAL RELAY MESSAGES TO YOU AND SHADOW VIGILANCE. WILL REPORT VIA ANSIBLE.

"Captain, there's another from the same source, by a different relay . . . I was just downloading all messages for this ship . . ."

"See how many there are," Heris said. "Forward them all to this desk. We have a situation."

The next message gave a set of navigation coordinates. VIGILANCE TAKING THIS COURSE. WILL FOLLOW AND REPORT.

The third, fourth, and fifth were the same. Heris could almost see the big cruiser trailed by the little patrol, through one jump point after another, zigzagging through Familias Space. What was Livadhi up to? And why didn't he realize Suiza was back there reporting on him?

Petris must have convinced Koutsoudas, she realized.

"Navigation," she called. "I'm going to read off some jump point coordinates—throw me up a visual, and let's see if we can figure out where someone's going." She read the coordinates aloud—she didn't want the bridge crew to know the rest of this yet—and while Nav set up the visual, she wrote out her own quick report to Sector HQ. Whatever Livadhi was up to, she was sure he was not acting under orders.

"Captain, an urgent from HQ was down the queue—"

"Send it." She watched as that message came up clear. ALL SHIPS, ALL SHIPS, REPORT ANY CONTACT WITH CRUISER VIGILANCE OR PATROL RASCAL. THESE SHIPS FAILED TO REPORT ON SCHEDULE. PRESUMED LOCATION 389.24.005. ANY SHIP JUMPING THROUGH THAT POINT, REPORT DEBRIS FIELDS OR OTHER EVIDENCE OF CONFLICT.

Right. Someone had noticed they weren't where they were supposed to be. She encrypted her report, told the comm officer to tightbeam it to the system ansible, and looked up to see the Nav officer's visual up on the main screen.

It looked like a random walk example in a math text. But something about it nagged at her mind.

"What kind of jump points?" she asked.

"All multiples. Nothing under a three. But mostly low-density systems."

Not random at all then, but an attempt to throw off pursuers.

And, except for two jumps early in the sequence, they trended toward the border with the Benignity.

"Damn the man!" Heris said. Heads turned. "Sorry," she said. "We have a situation, a Fleet cruiser possibly trying to abscond to the Benignity. I have just sent a message to Sector HQ, but by the time someone there figures out what to do, it'll be far too late."

"You're going after him?"

"We're going after him. Alone, because we can't strip this system of the other ships. We have evidence that the crew—or some of the crew—may be aware that something's wrong, but they don't know what. In the context of a real mutiny, they're unlikely to start trouble—" Though she could hope Meharry or Oblo would manage to knock Livadhi on the head anyway.

"But—" the navigation officer looked worried. "But, sir, how can we know where to find them? They could be anywhere. And we can't cross the border—that'd start a war."

"There's a tail on them," Heris said. "A very smart junior officer took the initiative and is reporting at every jump point. When we know what point next to the border they're at—"

"But they'll see the tail," someone said. "They have to, they've got scan—"

"Yes, but they've got scan technicians who are loyal. They're covering the tail. What we need to do is get closer to the points they're likely to pick."

"Do you know whose ship it is?" asked the Exec.

Heris nodded. "It's mine—or it was. Admiral Minor Livadhi's on it now. It's my crew who figured out how to get word out."

There was a long moment of silence as they digested this.

"But thanks to the mutiny, and the resulting scrambling of crew, a good part of the crew wasn't on the ship before, and probably hasn't a clue."

"How are you—we—going to stop them if we find them?"

"I'll figure that out when we find them," Heris said. The obvious solution was one she didn't want to contemplate. "First we have to find them."

"Should I put a message to *Rascal* onto the general ansible relay, sir? Do you think they can pick up messages, or are they lying too low?"

"Lying low, I would think, and I don't want to alert Livadhi by sending messages to the shadow we hope he doesn't know he has."

"Right. It must be tough on Captain Suiza."

"Not any tougher than things have been before," Heris said. But she could easily imagine the younger officer's tension . . . she was disobeying orders, she was sneaking along behind a ship that could destroy her if it noticed her . . . she was way out on the end of a very fragile string. Still, Suiza had a habit of making good decisions in emergencies. Keep going, she thought at her. Keep on his tail until I get there.

She did not follow the earlier part of *Vigilance*'s twisting course; she headed straight to the point indicated in the most recent of Suiza's messages. By cranking *Indefatigable* to the limit, she was able to ice through the intervening jump points, and hoped that she would be no more than one jump behind, when she came out and got Suiza's outgoing messsage. Her ship still had that annoying vibrato in its FTL drive, one that would leave its signature scrawled across any system it came to. But that had its uses too—though Koutsoudas wouldn't know it as her ship, he wouldn't miss that it was some ship.

Indefatigable wallowed out of FTL with a last gut-wrenching shimmy, and Heris wished very much she had Koutsoudas here to sort out the wavering bars of probability on the scan. If there was anything in this system, it was likely Livadhi and his tail.

Koutsoudas, watching the downjump transition, barely restrained a triumphant whistle. The others had told him, but he had not quite believed that any of this would work, that Heris Serrano could find them before Livadhi took them over the border into certain captivity and probable death. But the ship's beacon broadcast her identity loud and clear: the R.S.S. *Indefatigable*. Shields up, he was glad to see. Weapons hot—well, they were all running with weapons hot these days. They'd come out of jump a mere ten light-minutes away; the scan clutter cleared quickly. He pressed the button that signalled the others that Heris had arrived.

"Sir," he said to Livadhi. "That's a Fleet ship, a cruiser, *Indefatigable*. She's running like we are, shields up."

"Damn!" Livadhi came up behind him. "How close?"

"Ten light-minutes, sir, on insertion. It was a messy downjump; I'm sure there's something wrong with the FTL drive."

"How long before her scan clears?"

"Well, considering that flutter in the drive, there may be flux refraction for longer than usual. I'd say minimum of three minutes, maybe four, not more than five."

"Can we jump out before she's clear?"

"Not with the course combination, sir."

"Mmm. Why do you think that ship's in this system?"

"Unstable FTL drive," said one of the engineering officers down the row. 'Steban, if you'll 'port those scans over, I can check them, but I'd say that much flutter could yank even a cruiser out of FTL space."

"I'd like to believe that," Livadhi said slowly. "But—tell me, Koutsoudas, do you know who's commanding that ship?"

"I can look it up," Koutsoudas said.

Someone else answered. "Commander Serrano, isn't it? It was Wiston's ship, but she was closer when the mutiny started—"

"I cannot believe," Livadhi said, "that Commander Serrano would permit her ship to have such a badly tuned FTL drive."

"Could have been damaged in combat," the same voice offered.

"I don't think so," Livadhi said, and something in his voice made the hairs on Koutsoudas' arms stand up. "I think Commander Serrano came here for the same reason we did. As to how she knew—"

His gaze swept the bridge. No one said anything. "I'll be in my office," he said. "I expect a message shortly: pipe it there."

CHAPTER TWENTY-SIX

R.S.S. *Rascal*

Esmay Suiza had another of those swooping moments of doubt that had afflicted her off and on with Commodore Livadhi. Could he really be under secret orders, or was his claim as false as hers? Ships did sometimes cross the border on secret errands, both ways. The Benignity did have defectors; she'd met one. And Livadhi's anger seemed so genuine, so straightforward: no tinge of guilt, just the natural annoyance of a commander whose subordinate has screwed up yet again.

Against that, she had only the tightbeam message from Oblo, and her own gut feeling that something was wrong, something false, about Livadhi that had not been wrong before. She was out on a very long, slender limb, far away from anyone who could advise her or help, and the ship coming in might be the enemy.

Her scan officer spoke up. "It's a Fleet ship—a cruiser by the mass—there's the beacon data. *Indefatigable*, Captain."

Esmay felt a rush of relief. Heris Serrano was here; now everything would be all right. She had no idea how Heris would convince Commodore Livadhi not to bolt, if he was planning to bolt, but she was sure the worst was over.

"Lieutenant," Livadhi said, "I'm ordering you to cover our jump. Don't let that traitor follow us—"

"Traitor, sir? My scan tells me that's *Indefatigable*, and Heris Serrano . . ."

"Lieutenant, there's no time—I have to go now, before she

compromises my mission—and you might want to consider how she knew to come here. . . ."

Because I told her stuck in Esmay's throat.

"*Vigilance* is lit," her weapons officer said. "She's targeting us and *Indy.*"

Rascal's screens wouldn't take a direct hit from *Vigilance*, not this close. She could microjump to a safe distance, but then Livadhi could jump out before Serrano was close enough.

Petris, off watch, had just told himself for the fortieth time that he must get some sleep when his com buzzed with the three-one-three signal that meant Koutsoudas had detected Heris's ship. He rolled out of his bunk, and buzzed Oblo and Meharry with the same signal. His clothes, his boots, a dash to the head. His face in the mirror looked strange, a mask of intense concentration. He buzzed Slater and Cornelian. His stomach churned; he gulped a swallow of water, and headed for Drives.

"She's here?" Chief Potter asked.

"Yes. Start getting 'em ready. I don't think he'll be wandering the ship, but try to keep them out of the main corridors."

Down to Troop Deck. Chief Sikes met him at the foot of the ladder. "She made it?"

"Yes. I don't know more than that, but get 'em ready." Troop Deck, he knew, was going to be the hardest to organize. More people, and more of them not in on the secret. If Livadhi did the right thing, and surrendered, they'd be all right, but chances were the fellow wouldn't. He'd try to bargain; he'd try to blackmail Heris with her crew.

And it wouldn't work. He knew the depths of her heart as well as his own: she would not let anyone deliver her ship and her crew—especially her crew—into enemy hands.

She would kill them herself first. They were safe from dishonor, with Heris Serrano after them, but death was a distinct possibility.

A lot depended on where she would aim, and from what distance. Being Heris, she would try to save what lives she could, but Livadhi must not be one of them. And the captain's quarters and offices, like the bridge itself, were deep in the cruiser's body. Heris would have to strike hard in the center, to disable *Vigilance*, or risk losing her and possibly her own ship when Livadhi ordered an attack.

Petris had conferred with the most combat-experienced personnel he dared trust, and they had devised a plan which might—just might—save most of the crew not directly impacted by a weapon. Unfortunately, it required the collusion of at least a hundred of the crew: *Vigilance*'s full array of shuttles (six troop carriers, the admiral's shuttle, the captain's shuttle, the supply shuttle) could hold 541, if they stuffed people in standing up, and hold six hours of life support for that many. But launching shuttles without the captain's knowledge was—and was intended to be—well-nigh impossible.

How long did they have?

Down to Engineering. What was Livadhi thinking? What would he try first? What was Heris thinking? Would she strike first for the heart of the ship, or for the drives? How long would they talk, up there, before something happened?

On the bridge of *Vigilance*, the junior weapons tech had targeted *Rascal*, as ordered. His finger hovered over the launch buttons.

Arkady Ginese glanced at the weapons officer, who looked distinctly unhappy. "Don't do that," he said to his junior. "It's too close. We need to change the options if she stays that close." Then to the officer he said, "We have the solution, sir, but it'll require changing out the fusing options. Permission to contact launch crew?"

"Granted," the officer said. His glance shifted, toward the bridge entrance. "If—I mean, that will take several minutes, won't it?"

"Yes, sir, it will." Arkady had already signalled Meharry, a series of clicks that told her which launch crew to descend on. Now he spoke into his headset. "Launch four, our target is within delay radius, R.S.S. *Rascal*; change out the timing and fusing options for a close-in target—"

Back in his ear came the startled voice of the sergeant in charge of that crew. "What? We're firing on a Fleet ship? That's no mutineer; *Rascal*'s part of our escort—I'm not gonna—"

Meharry's voice then, cutting in. "Arkady. What's going on?"

"Livadhi's told us to target Suiza and Serrano. Pass the word."

"What about the bridge officers?"

"So far they're sticking with him—but it's iffy."

"Idiots." Meharry added the epithet she most preferred for stupid officers, and clicked off.

Arkady glanced again at his officer, then at the bridge officer, who looked equally uncomfortable. His lips moved—he must be talking to Livadhi; the man's face seemed to settle into a mask of sadness. Then he turned and looked at Arkady. "Ginese—Commodore wants to see you in his office. You too, Vissisuan, Koutsoudas. And pipe a call for Meharry, Kenvinnard, Guar . . ." The list included all of Heris Serrano's old crew. Arkady felt cold. Whatever Livadhi was up to, it could not be good. "He wants to ask you some questions about your former commander; he's concerned about her motives . . ."

Not good at all. Arkady got up slowly, under the eye of his supervisor, and dared not look at Oblo or Koutsoudas. Surely Meharry and Petris and the others would have more sense than to come. Surely they would do *something*.

Issi Guar looked at Meharry as his name echoed over the speakers. "Does that sound like good news to you?"

"No. Don't you go. I will. If the bastard's looking for hostages, he doesn't need all of us. Keep working on the plan. Get 'em into the shuttles as soon as you can . . . ."

She headed up the ladders, tapping her tagger so Petris could find her. They met a deck below Command. "He's figured it out," Petris said.

"'Fraid so. Or something. I told Issi not to come. D'you think we can take him?"

"Not if he's got ship's security in there with him, and I imagine he would. Or his own weapons, for that matter." Petris took a breath. "Methlin—go back down and get on one of those shuttles."

She snorted. "I'm not going to be the one to tell our captain that you're dead. And my baby brother will think I'm a wuss."

"I doubt that. And I'm not willing to tell your baby brother that I ran out and let you die."

"This is ridiculous. While we hang around here, he's getting Oblo and Arkady and 'Steban . . ."

"So let's not waste time." She started up the last ladder; Petris grabbed her by the shoulder, and narrowly ducked the blow she aimed at him.

"I can order you," Petris said. Meharry whirled.

"Oh, right. Pull rank. I'm not leavin' my friends in that bastard's hands any more than you are. Now come on."

When they got to Command Deck, they saw Oblo, Arkady, and Esteban sauntering down the passage from the bridge at a pace that could only be considered glacial.

"Now what?" Oblo muttered. "Do we tackle him, or—"

"You get out," Petris said. "I'll go in alone."

"Heris will love that," Oblo said.

"You," Petris said, "go to the bridge and start trouble. We need to be sure that this ship does not fire on any other and doesn't jump. While you're causing trouble, Arkady will take down the weapons. If they aren't lit, Heris is less likely to blow us all away."

"If we can do that, why do you want us to evacuate the ship?" Meharry asked.

"The captain's thumb," Petris said, who had thought of it only on that last dash up the ladder. For a moment they all stared blankly.

Then, "He wouldn't," Meharry said.

"He would if he's feeling trapped enough. Now get out—any minute he'll be out in the passage looking for us."

When they were out of sight, Petris marched smartly up to the hatch of the admiral's command section and announced himself.

Not at all to his surprise, Admiral Livadhi held a very lethal weapon and nothing in his demeanor suggested any reluctance to use it. Moreover, the protective cover of his command console was open, and the large red button of the ship's self-destruct was clearly visible. Around him, the duplicates of the bridge displays gave him access to the same information as bridge crew.

"If you hadn't meddled," Livadhi said, in a conversational tone, "you would have been all right. They'd have repatriated you; they promised me."

"And you believed them." Petris felt no fear for himself; as if a storytape were running in his head, he could see the tiny figures racing through the corridors, then stopping to argue . . . filling the shuttles in the shuttle bay . . . stuffing them . . . and would that even work?

"They've always kept their word to me," Livadhi said. "I wouldn't have done anything that would hurt you—you most of all, Heris's old crew. You're good people—"

"So let us go. Let the crew go."

"I can't do that—I can't fly this ship alone."

"She won't let you take the ship," Petris said. "She'll blow it."

"I hope not," Livadhi said. "I trust not. I'm sure, though, you told the others not to come—"

"Right."

"I could have security bring them in, assuming you haven't suborned ship security, too. I suspect you've done something to interfere with my attacking Serrano and Suiza."

"I believe so, yes."

"Such a waste," Livadhi said. "You realize I can kill everyone—"

Tell him that the crew were even now boarding shuttles to leave? No. Petris waited, as Livadhi—still holding the weapon on him— leaned back in his chair. "You don't want to kill everyone, Admiral," Petris said, trying to believe it.

"No—but I may have no choice." He made a slight gesture with his free hand. "Sit down."

Petris hesitated—sitting down took away any chance of a swift lunge—but every second he could keep Livadhi occupied might save another life. He sat gingerly on the edge of one of the chairs.

Livadhi smiled. "Tell me," Livadhi said, "what was she like?"

"Excuse me?"

"Heris Serrano. You slept with her, I know. What was she like?"

Shock held Petris speechless a moment. "I'm not going to talk about *that*—"

"Why not? We both loved her; you perhaps love her still. She never favored me with the delights of her body, but you—you she raised from enlisted to a commission just for her pleasure—"

"Not just that," Petris said, through clenched teeth.

"Oh, I think so." Livadhi's airy tone, in these circumstances, was obscene. "You're not really command material, you know. Nothing like her. Or me, for that matter."

"I never turned traitor," Petris said. The doubts that so often assailed him when he thought of himself and Heris as a pair—that had interfered, though he tried not to see it, with their love—now rose again to confront him. She was command material, and he—he loved her, but he wasn't her match.

"No, you didn't turn traitor. That's not the point and you know it." Livadhi took a sip from his flask. "You're a good loyal man, Petris Kenvinnard. Competent at your job—but not a commander. If you had been, I wouldn't be here with control of this ship. Heris would have taken me out somehow; in your place, I'd have taken out a traitor admiral. But you dithered. You waited. You missed one opportunity after another."

"I—" He had, he knew, done exactly that. He had waited for Heris to come, for her to make the decisions. But how had Livadhi known? He felt paralyzed by shame.

"And now, because of you, your beloved Heris is going to have to decide between blowing us all away, or letting me escape. You aren't worthy of her, Petris. I was, but she wouldn't have me. She chose you—I suppose she felt sorry for you."

"That's not true!" But was it? He thought back over the course of their love—their acknowledged love—from Sirialis to the present. Surely the depth of his love mattered more than whether he had her gift for command. Their passion—he squeezed his eyes shut a moment, remembering her touch, the feel of her, the scent—

"It is true," Livadhi went on. "But I suppose she wouldn't tell you. I'm sure she did her best not to notice . . ."

Rage blurred his vision. She had not—she had loved him, she'd proven it. If he was less than she in this one way, she had not cared. "You're trying to make me angry," he said in a hoarse voice he hardly recognized as his own. "You want me to do something stupid."

"No," Livadhi said. "I know you're not stupid. But you must realize how it feels to me—how being refused in favor of *you* feels. How long were you hiding your relationship before she ran out on you?"

So much was wrong with that, so many false assumptions, that Petris could not answer them. "We had no relationship before she— before it was proper," he said.

"I'm sure," Livadhi said, amusement sharpening his voice. "Well, perhaps not. But she had her eye on you, I'm sure, from the first. And you, I suppose, worshipped the deck she walked on—" He made it sound disgusting; Petris struggled to control his anger.

"I admired her," he said very precisely, "because she was an outstanding officer."

"I would have said excellent, not outstanding, but a little exaggeration can be expected . . . from lovers . . ." Livadhi cocked his head to one side. "Yes. Definitely a case of hero worship masquerading as sexual passion."

"It is possible to admire the one you love, Admiral, though I don't suppose you've had that experience."

"Oh, certainly. Had she returned my affections, I would have both loved and admired her. But she didn't, you see. We got as far as the hair-rumpling and kissing stage, but then she declined any more of it. Which is why I asked you . . . did she strip as good as I've always thought she would? Was she as good in bed?"

"Better," Petris said. He shouldn't do it, he knew, but he couldn't help it. Something older than military protocol and honor was acting now, and while he might be at this man's mercy, he had one thing Livadhi would never have. "She was mine, and you cannot even imagine how good it was—"

Livadhi's smile widened. "Excellent. Then I think you are indeed the best leverage I could have. She can let me go, or she can watch you die." His free hand came up with another weapon, this one, Petris recognized, loaded with tranquilizer darts.

R.S.S. *Indefatigable*

"What is going on over there?" Heris asked.

"Their targeting's gone, their weapons—they're standing down, Captain." Her weapons officer sounded relieved, and no wonder.

"Is it a trick?" asked Seabolt.

"They do have Koutsoudas," Heris said, "but he's on our side— he's been covering *Rascal*. He's the only one I know who could possibly fox our scan of their arming status."

"Tightbeam from *Rascal*," said her comm officer.

"Put it on," Heris said.

"Captain Suiza here . . . our scans show *Vigilance* is no longer targeting us, and their weapons are down."

"We confirm," Heris said. "Any communication from *Vigilance*?"

"No, sir. Wait—we have something—shuttle bay—"

"Got it," Heris said, watching the change on her own scan screens. "Confirm shuttle bay opening." This was crazy—was Livadhi going to launch an attack on *Rascal* by shuttle?

"Shuttle emerging, *Indy*," Suiza's voice said. "Our scan shows troop shuttle mass—wait—we're getting a signal—"

"Tightbeam? General?" Heris waved at her own comm crew, who shook their heads.

"Tightbeam, sir; I'll relay—"

Over the relayed beam came the voice of Esteban Koutsoudas. "*Rascal*—Captain Suiza—hold your fire. Evacuating the ship. Commodore Livadhi's trying to defect—"

Evacuating the ship—! Heris could hardly breathe for a moment. They couldn't get them all off—unless they could unload and go back. Would there be time?

"Permission to dock shuttle and offload troops?" Suiza asked her, breaking into the relayed message.

"Put out a tube," Heris said. "Tell 'em to go straight out—not wait to swim all the way, if they have p-suits."

A long moment, then Suiza came back on. "Confirm p-suits in this load. Tube's out; ETA four point two minutes."

Heris translated that into real distance; *Rascal* was practically nestled into the cruiser's flank. "You cut that close, Captain Suiza— were you planning to clog an attempt to jump?"

"If I had to," Suiza said. "And it gave me a clear shot."

"Yes . . . I see that. Carry on. When you get those personnel aboard, you should probably let Koutsoudas onto scan. And if there's anyone from my old crew, I'd like to speak to them."

"Yes, sir. Second shuttle emerging—"

Seconds ticked by, her mind hardly needing the chronometer to sense the passage of each one, each meter gained as the shuttles moved toward *Rascal*. One after another . . . the entire complement, like beads on a string. That ship would be most vulnerable when she opened the hatch to let them in—but Suiza had not suggested moving back to a safer distance. Heris reminded herself to be pleased with Suiza later.

R.S.S. *Rascal*

The first shuttle positioned itself close to the end of the transfer tube, and vented its internal pressure on the far side, pushing it gently against the tube. With the shuttle hatch open, the transfer tube with its rope handholds was easily accessible. One of the chiefs reached in and got the spare rope tethers, already secured to one of the tube framing members, and passed it up the length of the shuttle. Everyone took a grip, then those nearest the hatch stepped into freefall, and pulled themselves forward, toward *Rascal*, as the pilot eased the shuttle away again. The others, still inside, were shucked from the hatch by the rope they held.

Koutsoudas was third on the rope, and up the tube; with the first two, he cycled through the lock and into *Rascal*. After *Vigilance* it seemed cramped; he made his way to the bridge faster than he'd expected.

Suiza was watching for him. "Over here," she said, without more than a flip of the hand in return for his salute and request to enter the bridge. "And Commander Serrano wants a report from one of her old crew. Who's aboard?"

"I'm the only one on that shuttle. Issi Guar may be on the next. Arkady, Oblo and Meharry went to the bridge to shut down weapons." He unfastened his p-suit, and pulled a small gray box out of its inner recesses. "Just a second, sir, while I get this going—"

The scan screen blanked, broke into a multicolored hash, and then reformed with far more clarity than before. "There," Koutsoudas said. He glanced back at his new captain. "Captain, there's a real situation over there. The bridge officers are Livadhi's, but they're not in on the treachery—they believe what he's told them. Secret orders, he says, and Serrano's the traitor or she couldn't have trailed him." He tapped one of the controls, and the screen shifted to show a closeup of *Vigilance*'s flank, the open shuttle bay. "They're getting edgy, though, and I'd guess, since the weapons came off, that our people convinced 'em."

"So—do you think they'll arrest Commodore Livadhi?" Suiza asked.

"No, sir—he's got the captain's thumb."

"The self-destruct?"

"Yes, sir. At least, we think he does. He's in the flag office, dual screens an' everything, including the switch."

"But he doesn't want to blow the ship," Suiza said. "He wants to get to the Benignity."

"Which he can't do with you sitting tight like this, and Commander Serrano in a cruiser in easy striking distance. Especially not when he realizes how much of the crew we're gettin' off. We think he'll threaten to blow it, try to get her to let him go."

"She won't," Suiza said with utter certainty. Koutsoudas looked at her. She was a long way from the exhausted, frightened young officer who had saved them at Xavier. She had the same kind of look he associated with Serrano—with Livadhi before he went bad. She turned from him, and told her exec to take care of getting the new arrivals settled out of the way—no easy task on a patrol ship.

The next shuttle bellied up to the transfer tubing, and repeated the unloading maneuver. The first shuttle was easing back into the shuttle bay; the third and fourth were lined up to unload. Koutsoudas wondered how many personnel were waiting . . . how many had been convinced . . . well, there was a way to find out. He tapped into the communications line, and probed for *Vigilance*'s internal communications. Oblo had promised to turn it to full power.

There . . .

"—But this is mutiny!" came the voice of Captain Burleson.

"Yes, sir, and reckless abandonment, that's right." That was Oblo, no doubt about it. In the patient voice he sometimes used with the duller pivots, he went on. "And if we're wrong, then the admiral will do nothing but sit there and talk to Commander Serrano, and when she's convinced we'll all go back and be reamed out. But it's better than ending up a Benignity prisoner, don't you think?"

"He wouldn't—"

"Sir, he has. There's evidence. Thing is, we are not going to get in a fight with loyal Fleet vessels, and we're not going to sit here and let the admiral blow us away. You have a choice, sir, of coming along willingly, or me and Methlin'll carry you."

"He's not going to come," Suiza said. "He's a captain—he'll want to stay."

"The rest of you—come on—" Oblo again, a little breathless. Koutsoudas figured Suiza was right, and they'd had to knock out the stubborn flag captain. "General alert—let's try—"

R.S.S. *Vigilance*

Livadhi still smiled that poisonous smile as he completed the tight-beam to *Indefatigable*. "Commander Serrano . . . it's too bad you came all this way for nothing."

"I wouldn't exactly call it nothing." Heris's voice steadied Petris, but Livadhi's knowing leer still hurt. Petris could feel himself sliding into the tranquilizer's warm dark pool; he wanted to speak, but he couldn't figure out how. "When an admiral and his ship go missing, in time of war, people notice."

"All you're doing," Livadhi said, "is ensuring that hundreds of innocent people die. They would have been safe, but for you. They could be safe still, if you do what I tell you."

"And what is that?"

"Let me go. Pull back, you and Suiza, and let me go. I know what I'm doing."

"I don't think you do, Arash," Heris said.

"They're your people, Heris. People you love. People you hurt once—do you want to kill them now?"

"I'm not killing them, Arash—you're the one who was planning to take them to their deaths."

"They'd have been repatriated," Livadhi said. "Jules promised me—"

"Jules?"

"Never mind. It doesn't matter now. What matters is that your people are at your mercy, Heris. I have Petris right here with me—"

"And you're going to kill him unless I let you go, and then he'll be killed by the Benignity? That won't work, Arash."

Of course it won't work, Petris thought. I could have told you that. Bless the woman; he wished he could tell her he loved her. He relaxed, then, and let the dark pool lap over him.

"You haven't heard me out," Livadhi said. "You always did interrupt. Listen."

R.S.S. *Indefatigable*

"Arash—don't do this," Heris said. She felt useless; she had tried before to persuade traitors not to be traitors, and it hadn't worked then. "You won't get anywhere; you'll only be killed—"

"You can't stop me," he said. "At best, I'll be under suspicion the rest of my life. Why should I do that?"

"Because—" Because they had been friends. He had given her

Koutsoudas when she needed him; he had let her go, with the prince's clones, when he could have blown her away. She didn't try to say that; he knew it already.

"I don't want that life, Heris. I don't want to live that way, with all those meaningful glances."

"So you're going to run off to the enemy, when we need you?"

"You don't need me. You don't even love me—"

"Love you! Is that what this is about?"

"No. Well, not entirely. Now that I'm leaving . . . I'm sorry we never got together. You Serranos are . . . special people." The smirk on his face was infuriating; Heris wanted to wipe it off with a shovel.

"We Serranos are stubborn, arrogant, and rude, Arash. You wouldn't have liked sleeping with me, even if I'd been willing. Now be serious—you always were a good officer. Think. This isn't fair to your crew."

"Life isn't fair, Serrano. You of all people should know that."

"Why not just kill yourself, and let them go?"

"Why would I? Heris . . . look, I wasn't close to Lepescu, and I never went on his stupid hunts. But I knew about them. And that got me sucked in—they had something on me, so I—"

"Arash . . . you blew up two Benignity ships coming to my rescue—you can't seriously mean—"

"Heris, you're such an innocent. Why do you think I was even there, within range to hear you? If you hadn't tried to fight, and that idiot in the Benignity hadn't decided to take you out completely, you'd never have known I was there. You had something the Benignity wanted badly, and the plan was that you'd be boarded, the item removed, and then you'd be towed into a fairly lonesome sector to make your way back if you could."

"You were after . . . the prince? You wanted the prince?"

"Yes, of course. And the clones. The Benignity thought that would give leverage . . . I didn't want you hurt, or that old lady, actually. Her poisoning wasn't a Benignity plan; that's why they killed the poisoner."

"But Arash . . ." It was useless. If he thought he'd have a good life with the Benignity . . . She squeezed her eyes shut. She had been so happy to find out that Petris was on Livadhi's ship—she had trusted Livadhi to care for his crew as she cared for them. And now . . . he was taking them to certain death, one way or the other.

She tried again. "Why not take a shuttle? I'll let you go; you'll be safe—they'll can me, but that's happened before. And your crew"— *my crew*—"will be safe. You can trust me not to fire on you."

"No," Livadhi said. "I need the cruiser and its crew. That's my ticket home."

She could hardly believe, even now, how coldblooded he was. "Come on," she said. "You're an admiral; they'd be glad to have you if you arrived in your underwear."

"No, Heris, they would not." He seemed to be picking his words as if they were berries among thorns. "It is their opinion that I have not, heretofore, justified their investment in me. That is almost their exact phraseology. I must bring the cruiser and its crew—they don't want the crew, but they want to be sure the cruiser isn't booby-trapped."

Away from the audio pickups, someone murmured, "Captain—" and when she glanced aside, held up a board with the number so far evacuated on it. She looked back at Livadhi.

"How about the crew, Livadhi? Did you think how they're going to react, now they know you've sold them over to the Benignity? Can you really keep control of them until you get there? Do you think they'll let the ship go without a fight?"

"Thanks to you and Suiza, probably not. Blast it, Serrano, it's all your fault anyway." Back to that, where he would stick until the end, she realized.

"Is Petris in your cabin with you?" she asked.

"Oh, yes. I couldn't trust him elsewhere," Livadhi said. "Do you want to see him?" And before she could answer, he'd turned the video pickup around. Petris sat slumped in a chair on the other side of the desk. He had a vacant, vague expression, so utterly wrong for that reckless face that Heris could not repress a gasp of dismay.

"A touch of pharmaceutical quietude," Livadhi said; he turned the pickup back to himself and his grin was feral. "He's too dangerous, and besides, I'd had my fun twitting him. He's besotted with you, you know. Though he's not up to your weight."

Her mouth had gone dry; she could not speak. Over half the crew had been taken off, and stuffed like salt fish into *Rascal*'s compartments and passages. The shuttles were even now loading again—this load would have to make the longer traverse to *Indefatigable*, unless they were left dangling on the ropes trailed from *Rascal*'s transfer tube. She knew that if she microjumped closer, Livadhi would press that red button under his thumb. He might anyway.

Petris was dead already. She could see no way of getting him out—Livadhi could push that button before anyone could get into the compartment, even if there had been someone to do it. She raged inwardly at whoever was in Environmental—couldn't they have thought to pump in some narcotic gas? But the flag offices probably had their own separate ventilation system, complete with secured oxygen tanks, for just such possibilities.

All she could do was keep Livadhi talking, as the slow shuttles went and came, ferrying off one meagre load at a time. Maybe—maybe—Petris would be the only innocent to die.

But even as she thought this, Livadhi's gaze turned from her to one of the screens beside him, that she could not see. His eyes widened; he paled. "They're running away! Evacuating! NO! I will not let you win, Serrano."

And his thumb went down.

"I regret to inform you—" The old formula made it possible to say, but not easier. "Commodore Livadhi just blew up *Vigilance*. *Rascal* was much closer than we are; they may have damage. We hope there will be survivors; we are now going to mount a search and rescue effort."

"I ask you all to remain calm, and carry out your duties; when we have word on survivors, you will be informed. For the duration of the rescue, launch bays and medical are cut out of the internal communications net: if you have a medical problem, contact your unit commander, who can contact the bridge."

"Captain, we've got a line back to *Rascal*—"

"—only minor damage, Captain Serrano. But we can't stuff any more in here. I do have a debris plot—"

"Thank you, Captain Suiza. Any sight of those shuttles?" Hardened combat shuttles should be able to survive, if not hit by anything too big. The officers' shuttles, however . . .

"Yes, sir. One at least is whole, but appears to be tumbling out of control. Haven't spotted the others—wait—Koutsoudas says he has 'em."

"We're coming in, but slowly—" Shields up, to avoid damage from debris, much more slowly than she wanted. Please, please let them be alive. More of them. Most of them. All of them, if it's possible, please—

She waited a few minutes on the bridge to deal with any questions from the section commanders, but none came. So, with a last nod at her exec, she went to her office across the passage. There she copied and sealed the scan records, and began her own detailed report for Fleet, as she waited for the first reports on rescue attempts. Petris was dead. Livadhi had "fun" with him—she could imagine what Livadhi had said, how Petris must have felt. And she had come too late, with no miracles, without the chance to tell him what she felt.

The hours crawled by. She acknowledged the first report of success: the tumbling shuttle found, boarded, survivors—most badly injured—stabilized as well as possible. Another shuttle, its hatch open (had it been loading at the moment of destruction?), and all aboard dead. Another, all aboard alive, com mast destroyed, but the pilot had been able to guide it toward *Rascal*.

Her com beeped; she answered, trying to concentrate on item 16(f) in her report, and a voice said, "Captain, do you want lunch in your office, or over here?"

She started to refuse lunch, but experience said eat now or pay later. "Soup and bread," she said, answering the unasked question. "In my office."

"Five minutes, then, Skipper."

The soup tasted flat, and the bread stale. She ate anyway, knowing it was important, alternating two spoonfuls of soup with a bite of bread. He was dead. He was dead forever. He hadn't even been able to hear her, see her, in the moment before he died. All he'd heard had been Livadhi's poisonous words; all he'd seen was Livadhi's arrogant face.

Someone tapped on the door. "Come in," Heris said, glad of anything to break the mood. The door opened, and Methlin Meharry stood there in a rumpled p-suit.

"I'm sorry, Captain," she said. "I couldn't get him out—"

"I know," Heris said. Her eyes filled with tears; she blinked them back. "I know."

"I should've killed that scum-sucking toad the moment I felt that twitch in my gut," Meharry said. "It would've saved us a lot of trouble."

"You did the best you could," Heris said.

"Seemed like it at the time, but now—y'know, if it wasn't for the mutiny—we all worried about starting trouble on the ship, in case we got into combat—"

"It's not your fault," Heris said.

"I know. But dammit, Captain—I know how you felt about him."

"Yes, and I'm going to grieve and cry at the wake . . . but I was lucky to have his love, and that's what I'll remember. I'm not going to let a traitor rob me of that memory, and it's not going to ruin my life." She said it to comfort Meharry, but all at once she felt better herself. It wouldn't last, she knew—the pain would come back, the loss—but that instant's memory of his laughing face in the sunlight, years ago on Sirialis, brought only joy.

CHAPTER TWENTY-SEVEN

Winter rains had finally come to the main Fleet base at Copper Mountain, one front after another dumping snow on the higher elevations and a cold, stinging rain lower down. Q-town glittered in the lights of celebrating bars and restaurants and stores, streets freshly swept by another squall of rain and a bitter wind that rushed people off the street and into shelter.

Inside Diamond Sim's, the main room was crowded with men and women in Fleet uniforms: almost all the tables were full, with a line of people at the bar.

"Just what we need," Oblo said, "a politician horning in on our celebration. By the time our officers get here, we'll all be falling on the floor." Fleet personnel in and around Copper Mountain had chosen this bar for a joint celebration. Crowded as it already was, it would get worse—standing room only by the time they came to the toasts.

"The Speaker isn't just any politician."

"Politicians are politicians," Oblo said. It was not his first mug that stood half empty on the table at his elbow. Methlin Meharry, across from him, shook her head. Her younger brother Gelan sat beside her, newly promoted and decorated for his part in defeating the mutiny. He was still a bit stiff with her shipmates.

At one end of the long bar, a group of civilians clustered around a balding older man in a ridiculous yellow leather jacket like a costume out of a play.

"Like him," Oblo said, gesturing with his mug. "What's he doing here, dressed like that? Is this a costume party, or a proper wake?"

"He saved me," Gelan said, leaning forward. "He's a scientist—and he and the others stole a troop carrier from the mutineers to get the secret stuff from the weapons research lab on Stack Three. They've earned their night out."

"If you say so," Oblo said.

"Who's the redhead?" asked Methlin.

"Ensign Pardalt. She's another one that was on the plane that picked me up, and she was the professor's bodyguard. I heard from the rest of them that she saved his life. Besides that, she put together some kind of signalling device that put the word out about the mutiny."

"*She* did that? Where's she from? What's her specialty?"

"Xavier. Got a Fleet scholarship after that. She's a junior instructor here."

"Waste of talent," Oblo said. "She sounds like another Suiza."

"Prettier," Methlin said.

"Careful," Oblo said, nodding to a young officer a table away. "Young Serrano won't like to hear that."

"Young Serrano won't even notice," Methlin said. "He's far too involved. She's a looker, Ensign Pardalt. And that fat old man knows it."

"He's that kind, then?"

"No . . . I'd say he's using her honey to bait his trap for the people he wants to talk to. Oh, he'll flirt, but my guess is he's thoroughly attached elsewhere."

The outer door opened again, and a new group stood blinking rain out of their eyes. Oblo, facing the door, raised a cheer. "*There* she is! Cap'n—over here!" But there was another cheer, this time bringing the Serrano table to its feet: "Suiza! Suiza!"

Heris Serrano and Esmay Suiza, side by side, came into the room, and behind them was a phalanx of Serrano admirals around a blonde woman in civilian dress and a redhead in uniform.

Oblo gaped. "What?" said Meharry.

"It's—Brun," he said. "Brun Meager-Thornbuckle. She's—it must be she's on the staff, or something . . . and Lady Cecelia."

Methlin turned to look. "By—it is. And—Oblo, look—Heris has her stars!"

"Fff . . . and they didn't ask us to the ceremony."

The Serrano Admiralty, now increased by one, created a wave of silence that flowed from the nearest tables to the far corners, so that the words of the last speaker, an ensign explaining how he'd won a battle, rang far louder than he'd intended: "And then the exec said if I hadn't been there and remembered to shut the ARTI valve, he didn't know what might have happened, but it wouldn't have been good . . ." His voice trailed away as he craned around to see why silence had fallen.

One of the Serrano Admiralty—a tall, hawk-faced man with a scar from cheek to chin, spoke into the silence. "An ARTI valve? How big was the hole in the line?"

The youngster was on his feet, gulping. "A—a—only a pinhole, sir, they found afterwards."

"Well, then, if you hadn't shut it off, you'd have had very high pressure fluid shooting out and slicing things. Like any of your shipmates in the way."

The young man said no more. Admiral Vida Serrano stepped forward. "We ask your courtesy—may we join you?"

"Certainly, sirs." That was Sim, whose hoverchair had the ability to get through spaces difficult for those afoot. "You're most welcome." He cocked his head at Heris. "Are we celebrating a promotion as well?"

"Yes," one of the senior admirals said. "We lost an admiral minor, in Arash Livadhi; we decided we needed another one."

"Congratulations," Sim said.

Heris handed over her credit cube. "The traditional," she said.

"Right, and thank you, Admiral."

When the group moved forward, into the room, Brun lagged behind. She faced the scarred man in the hoverchair squarely. "You told me I had much to learn," she said. "You were right."

"I heard," he said. "I was sorry I'd been so rough with you, seeing what came to you after."

"No . . . you were right at the time, and I needed to hear it. Too bad I didn't learn sooner. Men died because of it." She fished in her bag. "This is a piece of the yacht I was on when I was captured, where my father's men died defending me. Would it—could you possibly— keep it here?"

"I'd be honored," he said. "Do you have their names?"

"Yes—here's a cube that has their names, and pictures, and all for your database. They're worth remembering."

"Everyone is, sera."

"Yes. I know that now."

"I believe you do." His glance, once so challenging, softened. "You're welcome here, sera. You qualify on all counts."

She felt the heat in her face, but met his eyes steadily. "Thank you. I'll do my best to stay qualified."

"I believe you will." He hefted the fragments she'd given him. "Now—go join your friends; it's a pleasure to have you back."

Brun edged between the crowded tables to reach the Serrano crowd, just in time to see Barin and Esmay in a clinch that brought wolf whistles from half the room. A pang struck her: she had never yet loved anyone like that, and she didn't know if she ever would. The fashion-critical side of her mind wanted to carp that Esmay badly needed a new cut again—or something—her hair was still so short there wasn't room for much styling. But she knew that didn't matter to Esmay or Barin or anyone else in the room. Lovers reunited, heroes at the top of their form . . . she glanced at Heris, who was not reunited with her love. But Heris was grinning at them. "What a pair! One sight of each other and you lose all professional decorum."

Esmay turned. "Professional decorum is for ships, sir. This is a bar."

Everyone laughed, including Heris. "Esmay, you're going to suit this family just fine."

"Esmay, I'm so sorry I caused you all that trouble," Vida said. "Old admirals should never be annoyed and then bored; they will get into trouble."

"About the history—"

"That's for historians," Vida said firmly. "Yes, it needs to be studied and known, but there's a time to give up the question of who's to blame, and the quarrels and the shooting, and get on to what we're going to do now. In my view, what we do now is give you and Barin a proper wedding, with a reception where we—your family and ours and as many friends as we can pack together—can all eat and drink and tell stories."

"Hear! Hear!" came shouts from tables who weren't even sure what the issue was, but heard "eat and drink and tell stories" clearly.

At that moment, serving doors opened, and waiters began passing platters of food hand to hand, from the back of the room to the front, until the tables filled with food.

"You didn't mean now!" Esmay said to Vida.

"No—your family isn't here. This is just Heris's promotion party. First she feeds us, then she gets us drunk—"

"If I can," Heris said. "If the credit holds out."

"Consider it a rehearsal," Sabado said, leering at Esmay. "Gives you some idea how it's going to be for your family to host the reception."

"Not a problem," Esmay said, "if you'll come to Altiplano. We're good at feasts, and we have plenty of room."

"You picked a brave one, Barin," Sabado said.

"I know," Barin said. "But that's not the only reason—" Esmay turned red, and the others roared. "But it's *one* reason," he said, above the laughter. In Esmay's ear he said, "They're impossible. They're determined to embarrass us."

"Blushes won't kill me," Esmay said. "I'm not going to run from them."

"Good. Have I told you how proud I am of you—catching Livadhi like that?"

"I didn't do it alone—" Esmay began.

Barin snorted. "Esmaya, don't start that. Of course you didn't go paddling after him bare-naked and alone through interstellar space—"

She giggled, surprising herself.

"But you listened—you understood—you took action."

"I had to."

"Yes. Why I love you. You do the hard things you have to do, always. I can trust you for it."

She hugged him again. "And you—I heard about you, too. I was so worried—"

"I was scared," Barin said. "Then I was too busy to be scared." He wasn't scared or jealous either one, he realized. He glanced over to the bar, caught the professor's eye, and nodded.

Cecelia had not hesitated; whatever the others might think, she had no concern about being unwelcome. She didn't know all the

Serranos, but she knew Oblo and Meharry. She made her way to their table. Oblo heaved himself up, moved the line of people to his right with a glare, then moved his chair and offered it to her. He crouched beside her in the space he'd made.

"Lady Cecelia, ma'am, what are you doing wearing a Fleet uniform with stars on? You can't make me believe they made you an admiral."

"Not . . . exactly." Cecelia grinned. Oblo was going to like this story. "Remember back on Xavier, when that young lieutenant on *Sweet Delight* thought I must be an officer in covert ops?"

"Yes . . ."

"Well, Miranda and I were captured by the mutineers—"

"What?!"

"Are you all right, milady?" Meharry asked.

"I'm fine. Miranda's dead. Let me tell you—"

"'Scuse me, may I join you?" Cecelia looked up to see Chief Jones, with a mug already in hand.

"Of course!" she said. "You can help me tell this—you know Oblo Vissisuan, don't you? And Methlin Meharry?"

"I've heard," Jones said. "Heris Serrano's crew, right? And you survived a takeaway with that Livadhi admiral minor?"

"'Sright," Oblo said. "You helped out Lady Cecelia, did you?"

"She broke us out of the brig," Jones said. "Go on, tell them. That bit's your story."

The whole table was leaning forward, straining to hear, when Cecelia got to the critical part with the mop handles; someone started to laugh and choked it off.

"Then," Jones put in, "these two dragged the dead man back to use his finger on the lock to get us out."

"So how'd you get off the ship?" Meharry asked. "*Bonar Tighe*—where'd they put the brig on that model? Didn't it still have the old combat control center mucking up the design?"

"Right. What we did was break into the damage control lockers and start improvising."

A moment of relative silence at their table, while people retrieved their own memories of what equipment could be found in damage control lockers. Before they could start talking, Jones went on. Cecelia admired her gift for storytelling; she knew just how to set the story up. It sounded better this way, in a roomful of friendly people, with all the noise around them. Jones held them spellbound, all the way to, "And there she was, breaking off sensor petals and tossing them away, chanting *They kill us . . . they kill us not . . .*"

"And then I got tied up in tangleweb," Cecelia said, "and had to be handled like a holiday parcel."

"Yeah, but the uniform," Oblo said. "Not that I'm fussy or anything, you know me, but—" He touched the star on her shoulder. "That's real."

"That's your Heris," Cecelia said. "She needed a . . . er . . . bit more authority than she had. So . . . she suggested it. Jones here coached me."

"She had the command presence already, when she wanted it," Jones said. "All we had to do was get her to quit talking about everything in terms of horses."

"It's my cover," Cecelia said.

"When did they promote her?" Oblo jerked his head towards Heris. "Why didn't she tell us?"

"As for when, about twenty minutes ago, over at the headquarters of the school. As for why no crowd, she knew you were already over here, everyone she cared about, and even for a Serrano getting her star, they can't do it in a bar. She was annoyed."

"That sounds like her," Oblo said. "She knows how it's supposed to be."

Cecelia looked at Methlin Meharry, and the young man beside her . . . "Is that a relative of yours?"

"My baby brother," Meharry said. "Gelan. He was here when it started. He killed Bacarion."

"Who?"

"She'd taken over the prison, the one where they had me and Oblo. If he'd listened to his big sister, he wouldn't have gotten into that mess, but at least he remembered what to do about it."

Gelan turned red. "Methi—"

"Methi," Cecelia said. "Is that your nickname?" She waited for the explosion that seemed to be brewing.

"Even I don't call her that," Oblo said, in a tone of spurious virtue.

"See what you've done?" Methlin thumped her brother on the head. "Troublemaking scamp." But she was grinning, the dangerous glint hiding again in those sleepy green eyes.

Heris leaned over Cecelia suddenly. "Methlin, good—you found your brother. I've heard good things about you, young man. Think you might want to do ship duty again someday?"

"Yes, sir! I'm hoping to be assigned with Lieutenant Serrano, sir."

"Oh." Heris looked startled. "Well, I suppose one Meharry is enough. Oblo, could you find the rest of the *Vigilance* survivors for me? It's time."

"Right, sir." Oblo edged his way past her.

Heris leaned closer. "Cecelia, we have a little tradition for new admirals . . . I hope you'll join in. You are, after all, a new admiral."

"I knew this was going to get me in trouble," Cecelia said.

"Oh, we're in this together," Heris said. "Come on, now—" She offered a hand.

"I'm not senile," Cecelia said, struggling against the ever-thickening crowd. "Just old."

"Good. We have to go outside."

"Why? It's raining, it's cold, it's—"

"Tradition," Heris said. "And here—" She handed over a bag of something heavy and clinking.

"What is this? What's going on?"

"If they'd done my promotion ceremony properly, we wouldn't have to go through this, but they had to rush . . . it's like this. You know—don't interrupt, you do know, because I'm telling you—that after a promotion an officer owes a token to the first enlisted personnel who salutes the new rank."

"Really? It sounds like the owner tipping grooms after—"

"Get your mind off horses, Cece. This is serious."

It was serious if you didn't tip grooms, too. Cecelia looked at the set of Heris's jaw and said no more.

"Shipboard promotions, the newly promoted get a measure of drink chits to give out—same for each of the group being promoted. Dockside, they usually give cash tokens—even if most of the bars won't take 'em and would rather charge a credit cube. Anyway, admirals are supposed to do a bit more. Now I took care of the food part, but we still have to get through the saluting part. These are tokens I had made up, not for this but for another purpose. They'll do. How old are you, anyway?"

"How *old* am I?"

"Yes. See, admirals pay by the year. You have to take and honor as many so-called first salutes as years of your age."

Cecelia thought fast. "On which planet?"

"Be serious. Never cheat your people."

"I don't honestly know. Eighty-something—maybe ninety by now . . . ?"

"Call it ninety. Your arm's going to get tired." Heris stopped and looked back. "You do know how to salute, don't you?"

"No." This was the most ridiculous of the many ridiculous things that had happened since the trim little woman in the purple uniform had appeared on *Sweet Delight* to start over as a yacht captain. "I do not know how to salute. I am, after all, in covert ops."

"Not now, you aren't. You're about to get promoted and retired all in one night. Come on."

Outside, the cold rain had stopped for the moment, leaving the pavements wet. Cecelia balked momentarily at the door. "I don't see why we can't do this inside . . ."

"Because it's a bar," Heris said. "Come on—it won't take long."

"Everybody's inside," Cecelia said. "It will take us hours to find ninety people to salute us." They would be wet and cold and miss the whole party. Surely that wasn't the right idea.

"Come on," Heris said. "Admirals don't loiter in doorways."

Grumbling, Cecelia followed her down the sidewalk. Whatever they designed admirals' uniforms for, it was not staying warm in cold windy rain. "Where are we *going*?"

"Far enough so I can show you how to salute without embarrassing you or the others."

"What others?"

"I can tell you're an admiral, Cecelia, because only an admiral gets to ask that many questions. Now watch." Heris demonstrated. Cecelia tried it, and after a few repetitions, the motion seemed almost familiar. Almost.

"I'll muck it up somehow," she said.

"No, you won't. It's just the same old noblesse oblige with a hand movement."

When they turned back, Cecelia could just make out a double row of figures standing in the cold rain. She shivered, not only from the cold.

"From *Vigilance*," Heris said. "It's their right."

At first it felt awkward, ridiculous, like a travesty . . . Heris was the real admiral, the one to whom salutes should be given. She was just an old lady playing a game, trying to help out but not really what her uniform suggested. But Oblo didn't play games; his salute steadied her. Methlin Meharry would not countenance a travesty, nor lead her brother to do so. Chief Jones was not ridiculous. Koutsoudas . . . others from *Vigilance*, and then the rest of the survivors from the *Bonar Tighe*. Cecelia felt more than rain stinging her face. She didn't deserve this . . . but she had to live up to it.

Her arm was very tired when she handed out the last of the tokens Heris had given her, and they went back inside.

The toasts were just beginning. She could not identify the protocol that determined which toast would come next, but she could tell there was one. She slipped an antox pill under her tongue. At least she wouldn't have to suffer the consequences of what looked to be a very long night. The tables were packed now; so she edged toward the bar, where the man in the yellow jacket still held his place.

Oblo and Meharry moved up beside her and Oblo spoke to her. "How long're we going to have to wait for the politician?"

"Politician?"

"They said we'd have to wait—he wants to make a speech. The Speaker."

Cecelia grinned at him. "We don't have to wait," she said. "The politician's already here."

Oblo looked around. "Who? It's got to be a civilian, right? You're not telling me that fat guy in yellow is the new Speaker! Methlin's brother says he's a scientist—"

"No, *she's* not a scientist," Cecelia said. Oblo glared at her. Meharry grinned.

"Who, then?"

"Look around," Cecelia suggested, nodding toward the tableful of Serranos, where Esmay was snugged up against Barin, and Brun was talking earnestly to Vida.

"Not—her? Brun? That fluffhead?"

"She's not a fluffhead now, Oblo."

"Well . . . I'll . . . be . . ."

Whatever the end of that would have been, it was drowned in a roar of "Speech! Speech!" as a non-Serrano admiral pounded on the bar. Cecelia watched as Vida stood up and waited while the room quieted.

"I have the honor of introducing the Speaker of the Grand Council, who came here from Castle Rock to speak to us."

Brun stood, looked around the packed room, then spoke to someone near her. One Serrano cleared that end of the table for her to stand on, and helped her up. She stood there and let them all look.

"I have a personal reason to thank you," she began, her voice slightly husky; they had to quiet down to hear her. "When I was a young idiot, and got myself into trouble, you came and got me out. Some have argued that it was wrong: that my father should not have asked you to risk yourselves for me. Some have even said it caused the recent mutiny—that it was this misuse of power which drove some of you—some of your former comrades—to break away. But I'm very glad you did it." Her voice invited a chuckle there, and some did.

"The Regular Space Service, since its inception, has been our protection against enemies foreign and domestic. You've had the most difficult of missions, over the centuries, trying to be military and police at the same time, staving off full-scale invasions and handling things like stolen ships and piracy, and you've done it well. Most recently, you've managed to save us from the depredations of your own gone bad. You've had to make hard judgments, you've had to fire on old friends who broke their oath to you. You've done all that well, and your performance is beyond praise.

"Traditionally, the government would authorize a medal for you—and it will—but what is a medal, compared to what you've been through these last few years? We're going to do something else." Brun paused; the silence now was electric.

"You'll have heard rumors about the changes in the Grand Council; I'm here to tell you some facts. The younger members of the Great Families, the Founders, have agreed to cooperate—for how long no one knows—" That brought a chuckle. "That's why I'm Speaker. We're opening the Council to elected representatives of groups other than the Families. We're particularly concerned to open opportunities for young people, to keep rejuvenation technology from being a permanent ceiling under which the rest of us are squashed."

"But you're rich—you can rejuv—" yelled someone from the back of the room.

"No," Brun said. "I have sworn not to and if I break that oath, I will be removed from all power, both in the Grand Council and in my sept. Now—there's a lot more I could say, and I'll be here several days, talking to a lot of you—but this isn't the time for long political speeches. This celebration isn't about me, or the new blood on the Grand Council. This is about you—what you did, and what it cost you. This is the time to say thank you, from everyone you served— thank you from the bottom of our hearts. We can't replace what you lost—we can only offer you our admiration, and our gratitude." She reached down and one of the admirals handed her a glass. "To Fleet!"

She started to climb down; Oblo raised a shout himself. "To Brun!!"

"To Brun!! To the Speaker!! To the Council!!"

After that came one toast after another, until, following one offered by the senior Serrano admiral, an uneasy silence fell. Cecelia could hear the shuffling of feet, the rustle of cloth. She wondered if they were waiting for the civilian guests to make a toast.

Then Heris Serrano held her glass high. "Absent friends," she said. And in a roar she was answered, this time with the names, a cacophony of names, and Cecelia found herself repeating her own list.

As the noise level dropped, first one voice then another began to sing, a haunting tune Cecelia had never heard before.

> *This for the friends we had of old*
> *Friends for a lifetime's love and cheer.*
> *This for the friends who come no more*
> *Who cannot be among us here.*
>
> *We'll not forget, while we're alive,*
> *These hallowed dead, these deeds of fame.*
> *Where they have gone, we will follow soon*
> *Into the darkness and the flame.*

Then we shall rise, our duty done,
Freed from all pain and sorrow here,
We'll leave behind ambition's sting
And keep alive our honor dear.

And they will stand beside us then
All whom we loved and hoped to see
And they shall sing, a glad AMEN
To cheer that final victory.

"My God," the man in the yellow jacket said, loud enough for her to hear. "That's ancient music. Parry's setting of Blake's lyrics. 'Jerusalem'—the battle hymn of the Anglican Masses two centuries or more before humans left Old Earth. But the words . . ." His voice choked, and he shook his head. Cecelia had no idea what he was talking about, and decided he hadn't taken any antox.

After a pause, some of the voices were singing again.

Bring me my bow of burning gold

"That's right," the man said in an undertone.

Bring me my arrows of desire

"That too."

Bring me my ship—O clouds unfold

"It's not a ship, it's a spear . . ."

"Shut *up*, stupid," Cecelia hissed at him. He gave her a startled look over his shoulder, opened his mouth, glanced at Oblo, and turned back to his drink, mercifully silent.

Bring me my chariot of fire.

We shall not cease our faithful watch
Nor shall the sword sleep in our hand
Till we have gone beyond the stars
To join that fair immortal band.

The last voices died away. The man in the yellow jacket turned to her; she saw tears on his face, and felt them on her own.

"Sorry," he said. "It was just—I'd only heard that on recordings. That music was powerful enough there . . . in real life . . . it's overwhelming."

"It doesn't matter," Cecelia said.

"Civilians mostly don't hear it," Oblo said.

Meharry edged up to the man in the yellow jacket and tapped his arm. "My brother, now, he says you're a professor and saved his life."

"Meharry—that young man we pulled out of the raft? I don't think I saved his life—"

"You did put that nasty major to sleep," the young woman said. She grinned at Meharry and Oblo. "I'm Ensign Pardalt; I was there too. I think the professor saved him a lot of trouble, if not his life."

"You're from Xavier, right?" Oblo asked.

"Yes—is that Commander Serrano over there?"

"Admiral Serrano, now. But yes, if you mean the Serrano who fought at Xavier. Lieutenant Suiza's there too."

The younger woman's eyes widened. "Both of them here together? I should—I should go thank them—"

"Come along, then," Meharry said. "I'll take you over there." The professor sighed, then smiled ruefully when Cecelia looked at him.

"It's not even the young and handsome who can compete with me. Alas, I am a useless old windbag—" He sighed again and grinned. "But you, another beauteous redhead—"

"No one says beauteous anymore," Cecelia said. "And I'm not— I'm older than you are."

"Are you sure? I'm over fifty . . ."

"My looks are deceiving," Cecelia said. She couldn't help it; talking to him seemed to make bad dialogue pop out of her mouth.

"Oh, well, then. Since you have stars on your shoulder, I presume you're an admiral, and maybe you can tell me when I can get home to my wife."

"Sorry," Cecelia said. "I'm not in that department. It should be soon, though. I'll be glad to get home, too."

"She's a very bright girl, that Margiu Pardalt," the professor said, gazing after her, "but she's no substitute for a wife. My wife, at least."

A gust of icy wet wind blew in as a group in uniform threw open the doors. Cecelia squinted past the lights; she didn't recognize any of them. But from the sudden tense hush, she knew someone did.

"Who's that?" she asked Oblo.

"Livadhis," Oblo said. "Lots and lots of Livadhis . . ."

"Livadhi—but wasn't that the one who—?"

"Yes." Cecelia could feel Oblo's tension, and she glanced at the tableful of Serrano officers. They, too, had seen the Livadhis. "And what they're doing here—"

"Admiral Serrano," the man in front of the group said. He had, Cecelia noticed, stars on his shoulders. More than any of the others.

"*Which* Admiral Serrano," muttered Oblo, along with something Cecelia refused to admit she'd heard.

All the admirals Serrano stood up, and Cecelia was suddenly reminded of the confrontation scene in a bad historical drama, two rival gangs facing each other down. Sabado Serrano moved, as if to speak, but Heris put out her hand.

"We are sorry for your loss," she said, into the silence.

"You—" that was the senior Livadhi, but his voice choked. He shook his head, then went on. "We came to apologize to you. For what he did."

"I named him," Heris said. "As an absent friend."

Cecelia felt an ache in her chest; it had never occurred to *her* to name a traitor as an absent friend, to grieve for an enemy.

"Is it too late to sing him home?" asked the senior Livadhi.

"It is never too late," Heris said, "to honor the good in a man's life, or grieve his loss." She nodded to the other Serranos and began the song; other voices joined in.

This for the friends we had of old . . .